P9-CEU-262

By Susan Howatch

THE RICH ARE DIFFERENT
CASHELMARA
PENMARRIC

Susan

The Rich

SIMON AND SCHUSTER • NEW YORK

Howatch

Are Different

Published by Simon and Schuster
A Division of Gulf & Western Corporation
Simon & Schuster Building
Rockefeller Center
1230 Avenue of the Americas
New York, New York 10020
Manufactured in the United States of America

Contents

PART ONE

Paul
The Realist

1922

Chapter One

I

I was in London when I first heard of Dinah Slade. She was broke and looking for a millionaire, while I was rich and looking for a mistress. From the start we were deeply compatible.

My presence in London was accidental, since I should have been at least halfway across the Atlantic with my observations on the Genoa Conference, but when it had become obvious in Genoa that on the subject of the American war debt Lloyd George had nothing to say which could conceivably have interested those pedestrian politicians in Washington, I had decided to redeem my visit to Europe by pausing for a vacation in England. I then proceeded to ruin this excellent idea by making a fatal error. Out of a misguided sense of duty to my New York partners I called at our office in Milk Street and to my horror discovered in rather less than ten minutes that I had walked into a disaster of the first magnitude. This denouement could scarcely have been more tedious, for it meant I had to abandon my plans to motor leisurely through rural England, but after suppressing my exasperation I settled down to business with the speed for which I am justly renowned. By the day's end I had extracted our resident partner's resignation; by the end of the week I had a house in Curzon Street, a new Rolls-Royce, an admirable English secretary to assist with my burgeoning correspondence, and a clear idea of how I should put the firm's affairs in order while I waited for a replacement to arrive from New York.

Meanwhile Treasury Secretary Mellon was cabling me for private information on the Genoa Conference, and by hiring yet another secretary to assist Miss Phelps and working until two in the morning for three successive nights I managed to summarize the issues of German reparations, the status of Soviet Russia, the domestic troubles of Lloyd George and the intractability of the French. Hard work deserves a reward. When my report had been consigned to the embassy for express delivery to Washington, my first instinct was to seek the most elegant woman in London and call for oysters and champagne.

It was then that I heard of Dinah Slade.

Just as it had been chance which had delayed me in London, so now it was chance that I ever heard her name. I had two efficient aides-de-camp who protected me from the continual onslaught of beggars and Bolsheviks, and I might never have known of Dinah's efforts to see me if I had not decided to ignore breakfast that morning in order to leave early for the office. Having completed my report I was anxious to attend to the firm's affairs, and as I went to the library, where my aides were inspecting the mail, I was already planning how I could sidestep a commitment to lend five million dollars to prop up a moribund steel plant in south Wales.

The library door was open. As I crossed the hall I heard Peterson exclaim, "It's that girl again!" and saw him pluck a letter from an unwrapped parcel. Peterson always opened my parcels. Having hired him when he had been discharged from the Army as the result of a leg wound suffered at Ypres in 1918, I had found his simple loyalty both frightening and reassuring, but he was without doubt the best bodyguard I had ever had. He was now in charge of all my household security arrangements, but he considered himself personally responsible for my safety and never left the tedious escort duties to a subordinate.

"What girl?" I inquired of him as I strolled into the library and picked up the latest issue of *The Magazine of Wall Street* to reach European shores.

"There's no need for you to concern yourself with this, sir," said my other chief aide, whipping the letter away from Peterson. "I'll take care of it."

As usual O'Reilly's bossiness made me long to contradict him.

"Take care of what?" I demanded, recklessly involving myself in the problem, and glanced a second time at the parcel. Amidst the wrapping paper was a rectangle of carved ivory, and as I lifted this exquisite cover I saw that someone who knew my tastes had sent me a small but unmistakably genuine book of hours.

Medieval manuscripts seldom fail to elicit an enthusiastic response from me. My mouth waters, my pulses race and my mind, seizing the chance to escape from the twentieth century, dives back into the remote past. As I picked up that book of hours I forgot the embittered powers at Genoa, the ravaged countries of Europe, the financial chaos, the half-starved despairing masses whose lives had been irrevocably dislocated by war. The bloody dawn of the twentieth century fell away from me, and I was gazing at the high noon of European civilization when Jean, Duc de Berri, had preferred the arts of intellectual accomplishment to the traditional arts of war.

My fingers caressed the leaves. The illumination was too florid for my taste, but the miniatures were exquisite; the details of dress and the skill in evoking perspective suggested that the artist had been working at the beginning of the Renaissance. I glanced at the Latin text. It referred to an apocryphal incident in the life of the mother of the Virgin, a most unusual detail. Saint Anne rarely has more than a minor role in a book of hours.

My curiosity overwhelmed me. Returning abruptly to the twentieth century, I demanded to know the name of my benefactor.

"Oh, the book's not a gift, sir," said Peterson. "She says it's a loan."

"And who," I said, mentally allocating a suitable sum for the purchase, "is she?"

"A girl called Dinah Slade, Mr. Van Zale," said O'Reilly. "Should you wish for further information, I have a file—"

O'Reilly always had a file. He had a genius for accumulating information on anyone who could possibly interest me, and a tiresome habit of showing off his talent in order to prove how indispensable he was. Unable to resist the urge to deflate him, I interrupted: "Not now. I want to go to Milk Street. Peterson, order the car to the door, will you? You can tell me about Miss Slade on the way to the City, O'Reilly," I added to mollify him as Peterson left the room. After all, he was first-class at his job and it was hardly his fault he had been born without a sense of humor.

We went outside. It was a clear May day, cool but brilliant with sunshine, and I paused to watch a horse-drawn cart rattle down Curzon Street on its way to deliver ale to public houses. Farther down the street, by Shepherd Market, a tramp carrying a board emblazoned with the words "HELP THE UNEMPLOYED" was marching up and down like a man in a padded cell, and suddenly I could smell the odor of the twentieth century even before the fumes of the Rolls-Royce reached my nose.

I sank back with distaste upon the leather upholstery. "Miss Slade," I reminded O'Reilly as I took some papers from the attaché case.

O'Reilly snapped into action. Looking at his carefully combed dark hair and thin, tense, intelligent face I sensed the fanatical desire to serve which had led him to a Jesuit seminary before he had entered my employment, and once more I admired his total commitment to his work. It was really most unreasonable of me not to feel as much affection for him as I usually felt for my protégés—unreasonable, but not unsurprising. O'Reilly knew too much about me. For a moment I remembered his voice saying, "I have some bad news for you about Mr. Da Costa . . ." and then I swung my mind back toward Miss Dinah Slade's book of hours.

"Miss Slade," O'Reilly was saying busily, "is a twenty-one-year-old English girl of good social standing—"

"What the devil does that mean?"

"I don't understand the English class system too well, sir, but I'm told she's what they call 'landed gentry.' Upper-class but no title." O'Reilly cleared his throat. "She was educated at a girls' boarding school in Gloucestershire and at Cambridge University—"

"Was she indeed!"

"—before having to quit last year after her father's death. The father died in debt and there's a wrangle going on over the estate. She's after money, sir, of course," said O'Reilly bored. "There's a political angle, since she's a known socialist sympathizer, but she's not affiliated with any group, Bolshevist or otherwise, so neither Peterson nor I see her as a threat to your safety. I've been sending her letters to Miss Phelps for the 'Charities Refused' file."

"How many letters has she written?"

"This morning's would be the fourth."

"I want to see them. When we reach the office call Miss Phelps and have her send them over," I said, flicking through the papers in my hands and eying the declining figures of the British steel industry for the black months of 1921. Then with a discipline born of long practice I forgot Miss Slade and once again began to consider how Great Britain could most profitably reorganize her capital investment.

II

The office of Da Costa, Van Zale and Company in Milk Street off Cheapside is a stone's throw from the Bank of England and the financial district of Lombard and Threadneedle Streets. We are a new firm in London, less than thirty years old, and unlike New York, where a brash newcomer can blaze his trail into the heart of Wall Street, a newcomer in London must know his place and accept a modest location in the merchant banking community. Yet I liked our office at Six Milk Street. The house itself was part seventeenth-century and must have been erected soon after the Great Fire, but the Victorians with their passion for remodeling had left a Dickensian atmosphere behind them. The interior was heavy with nineteenth-century respectability. Here I felt not like a king in his countinghouse but like a well-brought-up spider in the most civilized of elderly webs. We employed twenty people, who included the usual bookkeepers, statisticians, clerks, typists and office boys, and until the 1921 slump we had made a respectable profit each year.

At half past ten, just after I had sampled some undrinkable coffee and embarked on my correspondence, Dinah Slade's letters arrived. I was roaming around the room as I dictated to my secretaries; I usually dictate to more than one secretary at a time for the simple reason that I have never yet found a secretary who can keep pace with my dictation.

O'Reilly interrupted me. "Miss Slade's letters, Mr. Van Zale." To my secretaries' profound relief I stopped.

Dinah Slade had written in a firm spare hand:

DEAR MR. VAN ZALE,

I am in a highly unusual situation and consider it absolutely imperative that I obtain the advice of a discriminating and sophisticated man such as yourself, so please could you help me by sparing me a few minutes of your time?

Turning to her second letter, I found that the mystery was unveiled further.

DEAR MR. VAN ZALE,

I am writing to you as I know you appreciate the past and have a connoisseur's eye for medieval beauty. I have the most beautiful house in England, small but exquisite like a miniature by Fouquet, and I would like you to see it. You owe it to yourself not to miss such an important esthetic experience.

I looked up. Both secretaries were motionless, pencils poised over their notebooks, a dazed expression in their eyes. It was seldom they had such a respite. Ignoring them, I sat down at my desk and read the third letter.

DEAR MR. VAN ZALE,

Because of an English law which discriminates against females, I am about to lose my home. You should see it before it's lost. If you can't come to Norfolk at least let me see you for a minute in London so that I can paint the house for you in words.

To me the most interesting aspect of this correspondence was not that Miss Slade never asked for money—though this was noteworthy enough in any appeal to me for help. I was intrigued because the letters were obviously part of a carefully planned campaign. Even though they had been mailed on different dates I suspected all the letters had been written on the same day and constructed, like a detective story, to leak information at a calculated pace. Acknowledging my curiosity with reluctance, I embarked on the final letter.

DEAR MR. VAN ZALE,

What a pity you're so zealously protected from the world! But I don't think your secretaries would dare throw away the Mallingham Hours, a book which has been in the hands of my family for over four hundred years. After reading in the *Times* that you recently acquired a medieval manuscript at Christie's I thought you might enjoy the opportunity to examine this perfect example of fifteenth-century art. I must make it clear that it is not for sale, but you may keep it for one week, at the end of which I should be delighted to collect the manuscript in person.

Yours sincerely . . .

The address prefacing all four letters was "Mallingham Hall, Mallingham, Norfolk."

I smiled, and when my letters to Steven Sullivan, my young partner in New York, and Carter Glass were finished I sent for O'Reilly.

"I want to see Miss Slade's file when I return to Curzon Street," I said. "And, O'Reilly . . ."

"Yes, sir?"

"Find out if she's a virgin, would you? I know we're supposed to be seeing the dawn of a new morality, but frankly I'm beginning to doubt if anyone knows that beyond the limits of the West End of London."

"Yes, sir." No man could have sounded more neutral. We looked at each other. I did not quite believe he led the celibate life for which his experience in the seminary had prepared him, but I knew he wanted me to think he did. Toward sexual matters he cultivated an air of supreme indifference which I liked because it meant my private life could never embarrass him, but which also annoyed me because I felt that such a pose was priggish. Until O'Reilly had risen to prominence in my household I had never realized how extraordinarily irritating Sir Galahad must have been to the other knights of the Round Table.

"Will there be anything else, sir?" said this tiresome paragon, and I had to repress the urge to dispatch him in search of the Holy Grail.

It was a long day, but eventually I returned to Curzon Street, glanced at Miss Slade's file which told me no more than I already knew, dictated a few social notes to Miss Phelps, skimmed the evening papers, bathed, shaved, changed and arrived at the theater just as the curtain was rising. The play was execrable, but the leading lady fulfilled all the promise she had shown me at our previous meeting, and after a late supper we retired to her apartment.

I was annoyed when my mind kept straying toward the Mallingham Hours, but not surprised. I had become bored with my leading lady's theatrical gossip and disappointed by her lack of originality, and although I delayed my departure in order to be polite it was a relief to retreat home with Peterson faithfully at my heels. When Peterson was on duty as my bodyguard I seldom spoke to him —the best way to tolerate a surrender of privacy is to ignore the offending presence—but that night as I stepped into the evening air I felt the sinister pressure building behind my eyes and I said quickly,

"You can sit in the back with me, Peterson," as my hand groped in my pocket for my medication. As soon as I had taken a pill I felt better and knew that the symptom had been imaginary, a product of my fear of illness and not of the illness itself. Meanwhile the car was drawing away from the curb, and to distract myself I said rapidly to Peterson's solid comforting bulk beside me, "What do you think that girl Dinah Slade wants?"

"Money and the usual, sir," said Peterson placidly. "Same as all the other broads."

"But no broad's ever sent me a book of hours before— My God, listen to me! Peterson, why is it that when I'm with you I always pick up your detestable slang?"

We laughed. I was relaxing, the pressure behind my eyes fading fast and my fear temporarily conquered. "We'll play tennis tomorrow," I said. "We'll leave the house at seven, motor to Queen's Club and play for an hour or so before I go to the City. . . ." And as I spoke I remembered those far-off days of my secluded childhood when my parents had taken me from doctor to doctor until finally my father had cried out in an agony of guilt, "There's nothing wrong with that boy that a game of tennis can't cure!" Lawn tennis had been a new game in those days, but it had quickly become popular at Newport. I could remember playing with my father as clearly as if it were yesterday, my father and Jason Da Costa—

A curtain came down over my memory. Turning to Peterson, I talked to him about tennis, and I talked until we arrived home five minutes later.

It was one o'clock. After dismissing my valet I was alone at last with the Mallingham Hours, and I retired to bed without a thought of the inevitable insomnia in the hours before dawn.

Time passed tranquilly. I was examining the pictures, imagining myself a craftsman working for three days to illuminate one letter. What could it be like to labor day after day to produce an object of great beauty, a legacy of spirituality as well as aesthetic triumph? My romantic imagination, always at odds with my quest for classicism, overcame me at this point and I visualized myself as a humble monastic scribe, living in creative peace in some remote corner of Europe where money was virtually unknown. Fortunately my common sense reasserted itself before I could continue in this sentimental vein, and I remembered that medieval artists were always anxious to get paid before either they or their patrons were eliminated by a new war, famine or pestilence. . . . The fascination of Europe enveloped me again; I heard its mysterious call, felt it once more stake a claim upon my soul, knew myself hypnotized by that old familiar glamour, and as I fingered my way through the Mallingham Hours from matins to lauds and from lauds to vespers I felt as if I had been given a key to a world which I had always longed to enter but which had remained tantalizingly just beyond my reach.

At two o'clock I put the manuscript aside, and postponing once more the dreaded moment when I would have to try to sleep I began to write to Elizabeth, the woman I had loved for thirty years but had somehow never succeeded in marrying. I felt that Elizabeth would understand how the seductive mirror of Europe had once more caught the sun to blind me with its brilliance, yet when I wrote the words "My dearest Elizabeth" I saw not Europe but her house on Gramercy Park, and then I was back in New York again, back in my own culture among my own people in a world which I had so painfully constructed with my own soiled and bloodied hands.

I got up and began to pace around the room. It was three o'clock before I could bring myself to return to bed and four before I drifted into sleep, but my dreams were so appalling that it was a relief to rise at six to play tennis. By nine o'clock I was already at Milk Street to submerge myself in my work.

Three days passed. O'Reilly submitted a disappointing adendum to his file on Miss Slade and suggested she was merely an ordinary girl from a country backwater who despite her superior education had seen little and done less. Since her father's death the previous autumn she had lived alone at Mallingham Hall and there were no reports of any attentive friends of the opposite sex. At Cheltenham Ladies' College there had been no opportunities for escapades, and at Cambridge she had acquired the reputation for being a bluestocking. Apparently her virtue was not only unquestioned but unassailed, a sad fate for a young lady already twenty-one.

I sighed. I really could not, at my time of life, start toying with virgins. Such a step would involve me in endless complications and was altogether too time-consuming and troublesome. Other middle-aged men might choose to indulge themselves in such senilities, but I was still young enough to find inexperience boring and still sane enough to avoid any risk of trouble in my well-ordered private life.

"Return the Mallingham Hours to Miss Slade, please," I said to Miss Phelps. I had already decided reluctantly not to make Miss Slade an offer for the manuscript, for fear she would interpret my gesture as a sign of interest in her. "The covering letter should read: 'Dear Miss Slade: Thank you for the opportunity you have given me to see this exceptionally fine manuscript, but I would not dream of asking you to come up from Norfolk to collect it. Accordingly I am returning the manuscript to you by special messenger. Wishing you all the best in your endeavors, I remain, et cetera, et cetera.' "

Miss Phelps's small mouth pursed in approval. I felt depressed and wondered glumly how I had managed to surround myself with prudes.

During the next few days I devoted myself conscientiously to hedonism but emerged yawning with a distaste for Epicurean philosophy. I wanted to go home, yet perversely did not want to leave Europe. It rained. I felt fractious. Peterson started to beat me at tennis. I had an overwhelming longing to be entertained, yet seemed to have exhausted every conceivable source of entertainment. I wanted something to happen, I wanted to be diverted, and most of all I wanted to cut myself loose from my worst memories of the past.

On the morning of the fifteenth of May at eleven o'clock Peterson entered my room at the office and waited silently for me to conclude a telephone conversation. It was so unusual for him to seek an audience with me at Milk Street that I ceased jotting down sterling figures in dollars and stared at him. "Yes, Peterson?"

"Excuse me, sir, but there's a young guy outside who says he comes from an outfit called Fortnum and Mason. It seems they're some kind of food joint—"

"Yes, yes, yes." I was getting my decimal points wrong. "One moment, please," I said into the telephone, and added curtly to Peterson, "I've ordered nothing from Fortnum's. Send the man away."

Peterson turned obediently to find O'Reilly blocking the doorway.

"It's Miss Slade again, sir," O'Reilly said with his most insufferable neutral expression. "She's sent you a hamper, and the delivery boy flatly refuses to go until he's delivered the hamper to you personally. I would have sent for the police to remove him but thought I should seek your permission before taking any step which might result in adverse publicity for the firm."

"For God's sake!" It had been a trying morning, Peterson had beaten me again at tennis and I was being interrupted in the middle of an important conversation. "I'm so sorry," I said in my most charming voice to the telephone, "but may I call you back in five minutes? A matter of vital urgency—cable from New York. . . . Thank you so much." I hung up with a crash and prepared to make mincemeat of my aides. "What the devil do you two mean by taking up my time with trivialities?" I blazed. "Your job's to save my time, O'Reilly, not to waste it! And I employ you to make decisions about my safety, Peterson, not to come shilly-shallying in here because you can't make up your mind about some goddamned gift from Fortnum and Mason! Have the boy bring the hamper in! We all know Miss Slade's not an assassin! I only hope she's had the good sense to order me a decent bottle of brandy, although God knows only your asinine behavior could drive me to drink hard liquor at eleven o'clock in the morning!"

They slunk away. I scribbled crossly on my note pad and rear ranged some decimal points. Finally Peterson returned with a young man who was pushing a large wicker hamper on a porter's handcart.

"Mr. Van Zale?" he said nervously in an upper-class English accent. I raised my eyebrows. Despite his overalls this was no ordinary delivery boy. Had unemployment really reached such a pitch that boys fresh from public school were obliged to seek employment as delivery boys? I thought not.

"Bring it in," I said, watching him, "and leave it by the fireplace."

"Yes, sir." The hamper was pulled carefully into position and eased from the handcart.

O'Reilly produced a tip.

"Gosh, thanks a lot!" said the boy disconcerted, and he hung around as if he were unsure what to do next.

A spark of amusement flared within me. "Is there something else you have to do?" I inquired, strolling casually toward him.

"No, sir. At least . . . would you like me to open the hamper for you?"

"Why not? Let's see what Miss Slade's sent me!"

"Sir—" O'Reilly and Peterson were equally horrified, but I silenced them with a wave of my hand.

"If there's a bomb in that hamper," I said pleasantly, "our young friend here will be blown to pieces with us. How long have you known Miss Slade?" I added to the boy.

"Never met her in my life, sir," declared the boy, blushing furiously as he raised the lid. He was quite the worst liar I had ever encountered.

Inside the hamper was a quantity of green paper strands, and nestling in this simulated grass was a jar of caviar and a bottle of Veuve Pommery 1915.

"Delightful!" I exclaimed. "Miss Slade has excellent taste!"

The grass stirred, and as the boy leaped forward to remove the caviar and champagne the strands began to rise with the steadiness of a loaf of bread baking in the oven.

"Watch out!" yelped Peterson, reaching for his pistol.

"Don't shoot!" squeaked the youth, his eyes round with fright as he saw Peterson's holster.

As I lounged amused against the mantel, it was left to O'Reilly to demonstrate his usual efficiency by darting forward to whip away the paper.

"Ouch!" said a voice inside the hamper. "My foot's gone to sleep."

She stood up gingerly, steadying herself by gripping the wicker sides, and peered at me through a strand of hair.

"Are you Paul Van Zale?" she demanded incredulously.

"Yes," I said. "Don't I look the part?" Then unable to resist a smile I added, "Miss Dinah Slade, I presume," and held out my hand to help her from the hamper.

Chapter Two

I

She was neither short nor slender, facts which made her concealment in the hamper the more remarkable. She had some bobbed dark hair, a large nose which needed powdering and a wide mouth which she had colored bright pink. I am old-fashioned enough to dislike paint on women. Her dowdy iron-gray skirt had not risen to midcalf in accordance with the unpleasant dictates of postwar fashion but loitered a couple of inches above the ankle, and her well-worn white blouse had come untucked at the waist. Like many English girls she had a beautiful skin. Her other redeeming feature was her eyes, which were a commonplace shade of brown but so thick-lashed and wide-set that they compensated for her oversized nose and mouth.

She smiled at me and miraculously was no longer plain. As her eyes sparkled I at once sensed her quick adventurous mind, but then she retreated, hiding her nervousness behind a fashionably blasé pose.

"I must look a wreck!" she drawled languidly. "How dare you make me hide in a hamper like that! Mr. Fortnum and Mr. Mason must be turning in their graves!"

"It's lucky you're not already turning in yours, Miss Slade, since Mr. Peterson here was on the point of riddling your hamper with bullets. Congratulations on your survival! May I offer you a glass of your champagne?"

We settled down comfortably. Peterson removed the hamper, O'Reilly disappeared in search of glasses, and Miss Slade, after swiftly patting her hair, tucking back her blouse and crossing her legs to conceal the holes in her stockings, motioned to her henchman.

The boy was evidently older than he looked. He was introduced as "Geoffrey Hurst, my solicitor," and turned out to be a lawyer who had qualified the previous year and was now in practice with his father in Norwich. I was just wondering how to get rid of him when Miss Slade said carelessly, "You can go now, Geoffrey. I'll meet you in the teashop as we arranged. Thanks so much for your help."

The boy clearly thought it would be unwise to leave her in the lion's den. When I saw his mouth turn down stubbornly at the corners I decided to soften the dismissal by offering him a glass of champagne which I knew he would be intelligent enough not to accept. He was a tall fair good-looking young man with a freckled nose and short hair which stood straight up at the crown. I wondered how he had escaped being mentioned in O'Reilly's report.

"An old friend of yours?" I inquired after we had ousted him from the office.

"Very old. His father used to be the Slade family solicitor until my father gave up lawyers for Lent two years ago." She seemed uninterested in Geoffrey Hurst, and already her glance was flickering around the room as she sized up her surroundings. "This place surprises me," she remarked, her blasé pose forgotten. "I thought merchant bankers lived like potentates. Isn't this office a little modest for a gentleman of your standing?"

"I'm afraid I left my harem at home today," I said as the cork popped discreetly out of the bottle. "Now, Miss Slade, before we go any further let me stress that I specialize in long-term capital investment, not short-term loans, and since I deal with the issuing of securities my clients are corporations, not private individuals. If you want a loan I suggest you approach the manager of your local commercial bank in Norwich—or offer your truly remarkable Mallingham Hours for sale at Christie's."

"My dear Mr. Van Zale," said Miss Slade, "I'm not interested in borrowing a couple of sixpences. I want the deuce of a lot of money."

Unable to think of any reply bordering on politeness, I merely handed her a glass of champagne with a smile.

"Thank you so much," said Miss Slade. "Gosh, doesn't that look delicious? Now, Mr. Van Zale, I expect you're wondering about what I propose to offer as my collateral—"

"Believe me, Miss Slade, I've thought of a number of possibilities, all of them alarming. You must understand that I don't normally have the time to talk to people such as yourself, but since I admire originality and find your exploits mildly entertaining, I'll give you . . ."—I pulled out my fobwatch and placed it on the desk—"two minutes, starting from now. Explain yourself."

"With pleasure," said Miss Slade serenely, her knuckles bone-white as she clasped her hands in her lap.

It took her forty-three seconds to outline the family situation which had given rise to her present predicament. Her father had married disastrously three times; on each occasion the wife had borne one child and walked out. Of the three children Miss Slade alone had grown up with her father at Mallingham, but that was only because her mother, the second Mrs. Slade, had died not long after deserting her husband. The children had grown up separated. To Miss Slade her half sister, Chloë, was a stranger who had spent the past twenty years in Yorkshire, and her half brother, Percy, was a mere blurred memory in a christening robe. Before the previous October it would have been hard to imagine how this family could have become further estranged, but then Mr. Harry Slade had committed the grand folly of dying intestate.

According to English law in such circumstances, all real estate went to the "heir," in this case the child Percy, while the personalty (which included the Mallingham Hours—I instantly resolved to buy it at the inevitable sale) had to be divided equally among the three children. Percy's mother, acting on behalf of the child, wanted to sell the house, and Dinah had no legal right to stop her. To complicate the situation, creditors were springing up like weeds and it had become obvious that Slade had died with nothing in the bank.

"So I've not only got to find the money to buy the house from Percy," said Miss Slade, "but I've got to earn the money to keep Mallingham going. The estate can't provide an income for its owner anymore—which is why my stepmother wants to sell it. She thinks it's just a white elephant. It means nothing to her." She started to say more about her stepmother but checked herself when she realized she had entered the second minute I had allotted her.

"So I've got to get a job and since no one is going to pay me the salary I need, I've got to be self-employed. . . ."

She had decided to manufacture cosmetics. She wanted ten thousand pounds. Once she had that she was absolutely certain—"positive, really"—that she could pay me back within five years.

"Cosmetics are becoming socially acceptable now," she said rapidly as the second hand glided on around the dial, "but all the present cosmetics are awful—they smudge and smear and don't smell as attractive as they should. My father's ayah had some marvelous formulae for cosmetics which she brought with her from India, and with certain chemical substitutions I think they could be manufactured easily and inexpensively. I've been experimenting for about six months and I've had some most interesting results. If you were to come to Mallingham and see my laboratory—"

"Miss Slade," I said, wishing I had not waited one minute and fifty-three seconds before aborting this pipe dream, "are you asking me for ten thousand pounds to enable you to play with old wives' recipes at some tumbledown hideyhole in Norfolk?"

"Heavens, no!" she said amazed. "That'll only take five thousand pounds! I need the other five to buy off Percy."

This was certainly a step toward financial reality, but I kept my tone hostile. "Why should I even give you five thousand pounds?"

I saw panic struggle with anger. Anger won. "Why?" she said. "Because you're an American, Mr. Van Zale, and all the world knows the Americans can never resist the chance to make money!"

"*Touché!*" Laughing, I stood up and strolled toward the bottle of champagne on the table. She looked up at me mutely, too scared to be relieved by my change of mood, too suspicious to believe that my amusement was genuine. "And what do you know of Americans, Miss Slade?" I asked her kindly as I refilled her glass. Since she was such an entertaining child, I decided we might as well spend another minute exchanging innocuous pleasantries before I sent her on her way.

"Oh, I know all about Americans!" retorted Miss Slade with spirit. "They wear funny light-colored suits and awful ties and they have big cigars stuck in their mouths and huge hats on their heads and they use strange old-fashioned phrases like 'it behooves' and 'I opine.' They ride horses, own oil wells, talk continuously about money and think that Europe is terribly cute."

"Of course I recognized myself immediately from that description!" I was so entertained that I took a second sip of champagne.

"Now you can understand why I was so surprised when I first saw you! Do you spend most of your time in England?"

"I often wish I did. I spent a year up at Oxford, and whenever I return to England nowadays I feel as if I'm making a pilgrimage—a pilgrimage to the grave of someone who died young," I added wryly, remembering the young man I had been decades ago. And remembering too the poem Catullus had written after making a pilgrimage to his brother's distant grave, I murmured, "'*Multas per gentes et multa per aequora vectus—*'"

"'*Advenio has miseras, frater,*'" said Miss Slade, elliding the last syllable of *advenio* and the single syllable of *has* with a grace born of practice, "'*ad inferias . . .*'"

That was when I knew I was going to see her again. I had been roaming around the room in my usual restless fashion, but now I stopped dead in my tracks to stare at her.

"I do so admire Catullus!" sighed Miss Slade. "So romantic! I love his poems to Lesbia."

"Catullus was a fool," I said, "and his Lesbia was no better than a courtesan. But—"

"Why quote him if you don't like him?"

"—but he was a good poet." I smiled at her. "Well, Miss Slade, I can spare you no more of my time at present, but may I suggest we meet again as soon as possible to discuss your plans further? I'd like to take you out to dinner tonight. Where are you staying?"

"With a friend in Chelsea. Eight, Carisbrooke Row, Flat B. It's just north of Fulham Road."

"I'll call for you at eight."

"Gosh, that would be marvelous! Thanks a lot!" She swallowed the dregs of her champagne and stood up, pink-cheeked and bright-eyed.

"Maybe after dinner," I said, still greatly entertained, "if you're very good, I'll take you home and show you the manuscript I bought the other day at Christie's. It's the Rouen Apocalypse, a most interesting treatment of the Book of Revelation."

"I adore revelations," said Miss Slade, discarding her schoolgirl manner with a flicker of her eyelashes and gazing up at me with great big knowing dark eyes, "and I'd absolutely love to see your manuscript."

She seemed to have an inexhaustible talent for surprising me. Having long since decided that O'Reilly's judgment of her inexperience was valid, I now saw that he had committed one of his rare blunders.

"That girl's no virgin!" I said afterward, delighted to have an opportunity to remind him he was not so infallible as he thought he was, and I began with exquisite pleasure and military precision to plan the details of Miss Slade's seduction.

II

I telephoned Miss Phelps in Curzon Street, told her to cancel my engagements for the evening and asked her to book me a table by the window of the Savoy's restaurant. When I returned home that evening I spent a mere five minutes with Miss Phelps to deal with my domestic correspondence before I retired to my room to attend to my appearance.

"You needn't wait up for me tonight, Dawson," I said to my valet.

I felt sharp and alert. It was delightful to have a diversion at last, and as I returned to the mirror to rearrange my front strand of hair I sang my favorite aria from *Il Trovatore* with verve and wielded my hairbrush with élan. When I was finally satisfied that I could not improve on my appearance I ran briskly downstairs, collected Peterson in the hall and swept outside to my automobile.

We set off for Chelsea, and as I watched from the window I saw the crude marks of the twentieth century staining the London I remembered from my youth. The streets no longer reeked of horse dung but of gasoline fumes; the architectural grace of Nash was no longer so predominant, having been replaced by ugly gray monuments commemorating nineteenth-century imperialism; even the little houses on Park Lane would probably no longer contain ladies holding "evenings" but postwar men and women shouting trivialities at each other through a haze of cigarette smoke, and from the heart of Soho the nightclubs would already be simmering like black caldrons about to burst into flames in some occult kitchen. Virginia tobacco and Dixieland jazz! Was that really all my country could contribute to the cultural life of Europe? But Europe needed a financial, not a cultural, contribution from America, and that at least we could provide.

I thought of Dinah Slade echoing the traditional myth that all Americans were rich, and at once I could hear my first wife Dolly saying furiously, "But you're rich! You've got to be rich! All Americans are rich!"

But I had been poor then. I could remember rushing out of the great bank at One Willow Street in New York when I had been a penniless twenty-one, and there on the corner of Willow and Wall I had come face to face with Jason Da Costa, rich, golden and successful. . . .

I suddenly realized that the car was stationary and that both Peterson and the chauffeur were looking at me expectantly. For five horrible seconds I could remember neither where I was nor whom I had come to see.

"Shall I go in and ask for the lady, sir?" said the chauffeur helpfully.

Without a word I got out of the car and walked up the steps, but before I could ring the bell she had opened the door and eclipsed the past.

"*Salve, venusta Lesbia!*" I exclaimed in tolerable parody of Catullus, and we both laughed. She was wearing a long black coat which concealed her gown, and some glittery rings dangled garishly from her ears. Not only was her mouth painted a deep shade of red but her cheeks were rouged and there was some nasty black stuff on her eyelashes. I wondered why I had decided to take her out to dinner and came to the conclusion I must have been suffering from a premature lapse into senility. Surely only old men could want to take out vulgarly painted little girls.

"I'm afraid I owe you an apology," she said ruefully as we set off in the car to the Savoy. "I was so beastly intellectual this morning."

I looked at her with astonishment. "Miss Slade," I said, "apologize if you wish for daubing yourself with the modern equivalent of blue woad, but there's no need, I assure you, to apologize for capping a quotation of Catullus."

"Well, my father always said men hated that kind of thing—"

"Doesn't that depend on the man? What kind of men have you been meeting?"

"Mostly my father. I think I have an Electra complex," said Miss Slade gloomily, and the remainder of the journey passed very agreeably as she expounded on her imaginary psychological troubles.

It seemed that her father had been an English eccentric of the highest order and had practiced every imaginable social vagary. In between sallies to London to drink himself under the table at the best-known twilight gathering places of the West End, he had stood unsuccessfully for Parliament as a Whig ("A *Whig?*" I said incredulously to Miss Slade; "A Whig," repeated Miss Slade in despair), campaigned for the legalization of prostitution, penetrated suffragette meetings while disguised as a woman and held chamber-music concerts in the nude on the Norfolk barges known as wherries. He had also been known to disrupt matins to register his disapproval of the Church of England. He had written thirty concertos for the flute, mailed sixty-two letters to the *Times* (all unpublished), dabbled in spiritualism, and privately published a book which purported to prove that Shakespeare had been a *nom de plume* for Queen Elizabeth. In addition to these diverse activities he had somehow found the time to indulge in the usual shooting, fishing and sailing which were so popular with the more conventional of the Norfolk gentry, and fancied himself as a "decoy man," a hunter who traps wild duck in nets with the aid of a dog.

"I do understand," I said sympathetically as we reached the Savoy, "that he must have been very tiring to live with, but I don't see why you should imagine you have an Electra complex."

"I loved him," said Miss Slade. "Surely in the circumstances that must mean I was emotionally disturbed?"

"Courageous, I agree, but—"

"You haven't heard the worst of it. I had a most unnatural childhood, Mr. Van Zale."

"What fun it must have been! Come along into the restaurant and tell me all about it."

Well oiled by the best cuisine in London, the saga of eccentricity in a Norfolk backwater unfolded with a truly Gothic splendor. Harry Slade's first wife had been an aristocratic lady in delicate health, and from her chaise-longue she had engaged a governess to attend to her small daughter. "The governess was my mother," said Miss Slade apologetically. "My father fell in love with her, and his wife rushed off with Chloë to get a divorce. It was like a shoddy version of *Jane Eyre* with my father playing a fifth-rate Mr. Rochester. . . ."

The saga continued in baroque style. Her mother had departed when Harry Slade had refused to give up drinking, and Miss Slade had spent two years at her grandparents' Lincolnshire rectory. "My grandparents wanted to keep me after my mother died, but I wanted so much to get back to Mallingham. . . ."

I noted the substitution of Mallingham for her father but made no comment. Presently we had reached Slade's third marriage, to a chorus girl who had insisted that her stepdaughter be sent away to boarding school—"Though I had the last laugh there," said Miss Slade, "because I loved Cheltenham"—and we then proceeded to the saga's gory climax: Harry Slade's alcoholic breakdown, his temporary recovery and his eventual death from cirrhosis of the liver.

"I had to look after him when my stepmother walked out with Percy," said Miss Slade. "I was his keeper. It was frightful. I think I'd have gone mad if I hadn't escaped to Cambridge. And then, of course, he had the nerve to die broke and intestate. Wasn't that the absolute frozen limit?"

"Yes," I said. "He sounds like a fool. But you're no fool, are you, Miss Slade? All that rigmarole about an Electra complex was merely a device to maintain my interest in your admittedly unusual situation. Tell me, why do you avoid talking of your mother?"

She went bright red. "My mother died of tetanus. I don't want to talk about it."

"It's an ill wind, as they say. At least her death allowed you to go back to Mallingham."

She opened her mouth to speak, but no words came. A waiter poured her some more champagne. My own glass was still standing untouched beside my plate of Dover sole.

"Let me see if I've understood your situation," I said amicably. "You despised your father, and your refusal to discuss your mother indicates you've rejected her too. Your half brother wants to deprive you of your home, and your half sister isn't lifting a finger to stop him, so they can hardly be considered your friends, particularly when your home means so much to you. You're destitute and desperate, but whether by skill, judgment or just plain good luck you've thought of an interesting idea for making money. I made a couple of calls this afternoon. Cosmetics today happens to be an interesting field—more interesting than I'd anticipated. It's a pity that a woman is considered a bad business risk."

"But I'm just as well-educated as any man!"

"Forget it, Miss Slade. In the world where you're going to have to earn your living you won't have the chance to scan iambic pentameters."

"Are you trying to tell me you're going to turn me down because I'm a woman?"

I sighed. "Don't waste your emancipated rage on me, my dear, because my mother and sister proved to me early in life that women can be just as able intellectually as any man under the sun. Believe me, if I turn you down it won't be because I think you're a member of an inferior species. It'll be because I know all too well what a handicap your sex would be in the world of commerce, where other men hold less enlightened views than mine."

"People can overcome handicaps," said Miss Slade.

"You might find this handicap too severe. I doubt if you could rise above it."

"Oh yes I could!" she said fiercely.

I stared at her. It was impossible to avoid the conclusion that if she had been a man I would have unhesitatingly added her to my list of protégés. For years I had made a hobby of picking out unlikely people and watching them climb to prominence against long odds.

"How can I prove myself to you?" she said, just as O'Reilly and Steve Sullivan and a dozen others had all said to me in the past. And then she said in a rush, "When *you* were my age did you never once have your back to the wall? And if you did, was there no one who reached out to give you a helping hand?"

My mind spun far out over the curve of memory, and when it returned I saw my own image reflected back at me in her dark earnest eyes. But I knew I had to be careful. This would be a big gamble. I had to be absolutely sure.

"I'll think about it," I said.

"But—"

"I have just one piece of advice to give you: be yourself. I think I've already demonstrated that I'm capable of seeing through any pose you care to strike. Now let's have a little coffee and talk of something else."

She responded so smartly that I gave her an A for adaptability. She said she had read in the paper that I had been in Genoa before I arrived in London, and she asked me to tell her about the Conference. Mentally allotting her another A for effort, I gave her my views on European politics, and then, since those politics were inextricably mixed with economics, I began to talk of the new theories of John Maynard Keynes. Soon we were debating whether the old laws of Adam Smith had reached the stage of disintegration.

"You socialists are in an awkward situation," I said after she had confessed her political inclinations and told me that anyone who had ever been broke must inevitably lean toward socialism. "Until now laissez-faire economics has brought tremendous wealth. You argue that this wealth should be shared—but this implies a belief that the wealth is going to be sustained. In other words you have to support capitalism in order to put your theories into operation—surely an embarrassing situation for anyone veering toward Bolshevist beliefs!"

Miss Slade launched gamely into a distinction between democratic socialism and Communism, and argued that socialism must ally itself with capitalism until the socialists had a majority in Parliament. At that point, within the framework of a democracy, socialism would triumph and capitalism would wither away.

"It's democracy that would wither away," I said, "but that might not necessarily be a tragedy."

"You don't believe in democracy?" She was shocked.

"I believe in Plato. There's only one form of government that's worse than democracy, and that's tyranny."

"I wouldn't have thought an American would pay much attention to Plato's *Republic!* Didn't Socrates advocate that in a state there should be a close connection between ethics and politics?"

I laughed so loudly that people nearby turned to stare at us. Miss Slade suddenly dissolved into giggles. When we had recovered I said smoothly, "May I suggest we adjourn to Curzon Street to view the Rouen Apocalypse?" and pushed back my chair.

"But you haven't paid the bill!"

"Oh, I never handle money—such a vulgar capitalist occupation! Come along, my dear. No, don't feel obliged to finish the champagne."

But of course she had to finish it. I gave her D for recklessness but mitigated it to C. After all, she was very young. What a delectable age twenty-one was! Young women of that age were freed from the awkwardness of adolescence yet were still fluid before the onset of maturity. I decided I was extremely partial to young girls in their early twenties.

When we arrived home I took her to the library and offered her a cigarette from the box on the table.

She looked at me. "I'm sure you don't approve of women smoking."

"My dear, there comes a point when to oppose social change is not only futile but debilitating. Take a cigarette if you want one. I'm sure you'd look charming even if you decided to smoke a Havana cigar."

She still hesitated but finally, remembering my earlier advice, she accepted a cigarette and thanked me when I lit it for her. When she choked on the smoke a second later I had the excuse to sit down beside her and pat her on the back.

My fingers gravitated to her waist. I slid my arm around her, and, removing the cigarette, I extinguished it in the ashtray.

"I'm married, you know," I said as I leaned forward to kiss her.

"How nice! Do you marry often?"

"About once every ten years." I congratulated myself on having extinguished the offensive cigarette before the taste could ruin her mouth. As my hands moved luxuriously over her hips I allowed my kisses to lengthen until I was aware of the most pervasive sense of well-being. It is always so gratifying when events move exactly according to plan.

"We really should take a look at the Rouen Apocalypse," I murmured. "If you can summon the energy to stir from this comfortable couch I suggest we move upstairs."

"Isn't the manuscript here in the library? Oh, I see—it's so valuable you keep it in a safe."

"No, my dear, just under my pillow. This way."

I steered her into the hall. She was by no means drunk, but she was a long way from being sober. As we climbed the stairs she said gravely, "There are two things you should know. First I think marriage is an abominable institution, and second I absolutely believe in the intellectual validity of free love."

"I always knew I approved of higher education for women. Who was your idol when you were up at Cambridge? Marie Stopes?"

"Well, of course I wouldn't expect a Victorian like you to understand. If you disapprove of women using cosmetics you're bound to disapprove of them using contraceptives!"

"My dear, I have many ambitions but the destruction of the human race isn't one of them, and according to Malthus carefree procreation can only lead to a disaster of apocalyptic dimensions." Opening the door of my room, I ushered her inside. "And talking of Apocalypses—"

"Oh, there it is!" exclaimed Miss Slade, and she headed straight for the manuscript, which was lying on the nightstand.

We sat down on the bed together and looked at ten-headed serpents, leering gargoyles and the tortured faces of wicked sinners facing the eternal fires of hell. It took her less than three minutes to become restless, and seconds later I was removing the manuscript from her hands. "The text should really be reviewed in daylight," I murmured. "The script is faint in parts and you don't want to strain your eyes."

"I'm not worried about my eyes," said Miss Slade, "just my—Oh, Great Scott, what a blinking nuisance! Do you have a lavatory near here? I should have gone at the Savoy."

"I think you'll find the plumbing here satisfactory. Through that door over there."

When she was gone I switched on the bedside lamp, turned out the overhead light, shed my clothes, shrugged on a robe and gave my front strand of hair a quick brush. I had just put down my hairbrush when she returned to the room, and, glancing at my watch, I saw that my familiar routine had been accomplished in record time. Apparently Miss Slade was no longer merely maintaining my interest but whipping it into a frenzy. With a detached but sincere admiration I awarded her another A for originality, and then I closed the door on my professional assessment of her and prepared to wipe all our previous conversations from my mind. Miss Slade did not know it, but there was no communicating door between my professional and my private life, and I never allowed my sexual inclinations to distort my business judgment.

To my surprise and pleasure I saw she had washed off all the paint and was looking very fresh and young. "'Be yourself!'" she quoted bravely as I stared at her, and smiled as I drew her approvingly into my arms.

Her smooth unlined skin was erotic in its perfection. I began to undress her.

I was no more than halfway through this leisurely but intensely stimulating pastime when she lost patience (why are the young always so impulsive?), pushed the facings of my robe apart and slid her hands greedily over my body. I deplored her lack of restraint but not for long; her sensuousness drowned all criticism, and within seconds we were lying on the bed. As I paused to look down at her I saw that although her breasts were in shadow the light from the lamp reflected obliquely on the curve of her hips and her full white thighs.

"I presume you practice Marie Stopes's doctrines as well as applaud them," I said, watching her, "because if you don't I have some French letters—"

"Oh God, not another literary discussion!" she groaned, and laughing at her unexpected sophistication I extinguished the light and moved against her in the dark.

My mind relaxed immediately. It was as if the power in some complex electrical system had been dimmed by a hidden master switch, and with my intellectual faculties isolated in this pleasurable state of suspension I was conscious of nothing except my physical ease. My muscles were hard and smooth, my limbs perfectly coordinated, and each gesture I made was fluent yet disciplined. In short, I was in absolute control of myself, of her and of the imminent consummation of our evening together—not a remarkable state of affairs, I admit, but one which, in view of the mess I made of everything seconds later, is at least worthy of a brief mention.

Anyway there I was, supremely overconfident in my effortless competence, and there was she, supremely eager in what appeared to be the light of past experience, and since it seemed by that time that no further pleasure could be obtained by delaying the inevitable, I gathered together my resources, as the Roman war historians might have said, for the ultimate assault.

The next moment I had the rudest shock of my entire sexual experience. In fact, it was such a shock that at first I could not understand what was happening. My brain had long since gone into hibernation, my wits were dulled with the exquisiteness of physical pleasure, and even my instinct for self-preservation was so befuddled that when I first encountered difficulty I simply paused before trying again.

At first I thought it was my fault. Then I knew it was hers. Finally in appalled disbelief I hesitated—and was lost. As my confusion spiraled into horror I lost control over my physical reflexes, floundered around like an ill-starred bull, tried to withdraw and could not, tried to go on and, God help me, succeeded, tried to freeze into a marble statue and, in failing, achieved the ultimate folly of ejaculation. By the time I managed to disentangle myself I was drenched in sweat, my heart was banging like a sledgehammer and I was mentally calling myself every kind of fool under the sun.

It was not one of the better moments of my well-ordered private life. I felt cheated, incredulous and intolerably confused.

At last when I had stopped gasping ignominiously I remembered the girl. She was motionless and so silent that I wondered if she had fainted. Feeling that I was plunging deeper every second into the perversest of nightmares, I yielded to panic and turned on the light. But she was conscious. She screwed up her eyes against the glare, but when she opened them again I saw she was close to tears. I tried to think of something useful to say. "I'm sorry" seemed not only feeble but inappropriate; after all, I had only done what she had obviously wanted me to do. "You little fool" would have sounded unchivalrous. "My God, what a mess!" would have been honest but again was hardly the most courteous of comments for a gentleman to make to a lady he has unintentionally deflowered. I was just thinking irrelevantly what a splendid Victorian word "deflowered" was when she said in a very small voice, "Why are you angry? Was I no good? What did I do wrong? Please tell me so I never make the same mistake again."

"My dear child . . ." It was hard to know where to begin, but I managed to scrape together some semblance of good manners. "You're a most charming and attractive girl," I said truthfully. "I found you delightful. But you did wrong in not telling me you were so inexperienced."

"If I'd told you that, I wouldn't be here," she said with an insight I found disturbing. "My father always said most men think virgins are a bit of a bore."

"Your father," I said, feeling quite unreasonably annoyed, "had no right to burden you with his questionable sexual opinions. Men shouldn't discuss such things with their daughters."

"What do you know about it?" Her resiliency was such that her tears were gone and she was now just as annoyed as I was. "Have you ever had a daughter?"

The silence which followed seemed to last for a long time but was probably no longer than ten seconds. One second to remember Vicky with her fair curls and violet eyes, another to remember her birth and infancy in that squalid apartment . . . The memories flicked on with the jerky reality of a film, my first wife's death, Vicky growing up with my mother, Vicky strolling with me down Fifth Avenue, skating in Central Park, the belle of her coming-out ball, the broken engagement, the recuperation in Europe, the return to New York . . . "I'll give another ball for you, Vicky, to welcome you back!" Glittering chandeliers, Strauss waltzes, the survivors of Mrs. Astor's Four Hundred, the cream of Old New York, and finally Vicky turning to me with starry eyes, Vicky saying radiantly, "Oh, Papa, Mr. Da Costa's so *handsome*. . . ."

The movie film finished, leaving the screen dark. I was in another era on another continent with another woman. "Have you ever had a daughter?" said Dinah Slade.

"Yes," I said. "I had a daughter once. But she died."

"Oh, I'm so sorry. Forgive me—I didn't mean to remind you of unhappy memories—"

"It was a long time ago now. Six years. She died in 1916." I was out of bed, struggling into my robe, touching the manuscript on the nightstand and the curtain by the window in an attempt to reestablish contact with the present. I was in London with an odd little girl who quoted both Catullus and her eccentric father's world-weary clichés in a lethal mixture of pseudosophisticated erudition. Against all the odds she had fooled me neatly and reduced me to the sexual performance of an adolescent. She also wanted to borrow ten thousand pounds. I now had to make up my mind whether she was a total disaster or else the most promising child I had ever been tempted to sponsor, and my mind, fastening thankfully on the problem, crawled back into the present.

"Now, my dear," I said to her briskly as I knotted the cord of my robe and turned to face her, "charming and delightful as you were—and are—I would be failing in my duty to you as your friend if I didn't point out to you how exceedingly foolishly you've behaved tonight. Without wishing to go into crude details, I can assure you that there are less uncomfortable ways to lose your virginity than the one you've just chosen to endure, and besides, although I might possibly not have brought you up here with such alacrity if I'd known you were a virgin, that would have made no difference to our business relationship. Amazing though this may seem to you, I don't award loans on the strength of my clients' sexual prowess, so if you thought you could simply sleep your way into ten thousand pounds you couldn't have been more mistaken. Am I making myself quite clear?"

She nodded mutely. She was looking white and sick.

"Now let me give you some advice which that garrulous old father of yours evidently forgot to mention. Don't play Russian roulette with the risk of pregnancy. Abortions can be most unpleasant. If a man offers to use contraceptives don't toss the offer aside with a flippant remark. It's splendid to be witty but not when your wit could result in considerable trouble and embarrassment. By all means practice free love, but do it, I beg of you, with style and brains instead of vulgarity and ignorance. Again—am I making myself quite clear?"

She hung her head in shame, and I saw her lip tremble before she pressed her mouth into a firm line.

"The last thing your father should have told you," I said dryly, "is to beware of middle-aged married millionaires with few scruples and less reputation. You're a nice little girl, Dinah, and I like you very much, but I'm not entirely a monster and I don't want to hurt you. Have you any idea what you're doing, involving yourself with me like this? Be realistic! Free love is a great sport, but it can be the roughest game in town. Practice with youngsters in your own league before you take on a partner who could treat you as casually as a gourmet consuming half a dozen oysters between courses and tossing the shells over his shoulder into the garbage can."

She did not smile. At last she managed to say in a low voice which shook with anger and fright, "You're brushing me off. You want to get rid of me."

"Don't you want what's good for you?"

No answer.

"I don't think you know what you want," I said abruptly. I had succeeded in manipulating the conversation in such a way that I was now steering her toward the supreme test, but I knew she suspected nothing. She was off guard, and when I sprang the test on her there would be no chance for her to seek refuge in poses. If she stepped into the pit I was busy excavating at her feet, I would reluctantly be obliged to wash my hands of her, but if she avoided it—I would once more be greatly entertained.

"What *is* it you want, Dinah?" I was saying with hostility, and then in a sudden volte-face I sat down on the bed beside her, slipped my arm soothingly around her shoulders and said in my most honeyed voice, "You can tell me—I'll understand! It's not just the money, is it? You want someone who'll look after you, someone who'll replace your father, someone who'll . . . well, all that talk of free love was just a pose, wasn't it? You want to get married. You want some nice kind understanding man to take care of you for ever and ever. You want—"

My arm was pushed rudely away. An urchin's face with tangled hair and huge blazing dark eyes was suddenly inches from mine.

"I want Mallingham!" bawled the child, her plain little features crumpling as she burst into sobs. "I want my home! I want the only thing that never changes, the only thing that's always there, and I'll do anything to get it, anything at all—"

She stopped. I released her immediately and stood up. Terror sprang to her eyes.

"Well, my dear," I said when it became obvious she was incapable of speech, "allow me to congratulate you."

She stared at me blankly.

"I like ambition," I said. "It's the one currency which never depreciates in value."

"You mean . . . No, you can't mean . . ."

"I mean you've passed your final test with flying colors, Miss Slade. You can have your ten thousand pounds. I accept you as my protégée. Welcome to my world."

Chapter Three

I

"Be at my office in Milk Street at ten o'clock tomorrow morning," I said to her after I had escorted her back to Chelsea, and it seemed strange to hear the response of "Yes, Paul," instead of the familiar "Yes, sir."

I did wonder if she would be on time, but of course she was. The clock struck ten, O'Reilly ushered her into my room and I told her to sit down in the client's chair.

"I've arranged for you to have a desk and a typewriter here today," I told her after we had exchanged the usual civilities. "You will write me a detailed report of your plans to launch a cosmetics business. I want to know what kind of cosmetics you intend to sell, how you intend to manufacture them and what kind of marketing techniques you think would be the most successful. I want cost estimates, profit projections and a detailed schedule of the initial capital outlay. You will then write me a short description of Mallingham Hall, listing its acreage, history, the general condition of the house and any unusual features which you think would either enhance or detract from its real-estate value. I shall expect both reports on my desk by six o'clock tonight."

Her eyes were round as saucers, but she spoke up as confidently as if she produced such reports every day. "Yes, Paul."

"I shall of course want to inspect the property, and I suggest we motor down on Saturday morning and lunch at Norwich, where I shall look at the cathedral. I'll call for you at six-thirty sharp. On Friday at eleven you will see a certain Dr. Westfield of Harley Street, who will save you from the dangers of playing the brand of Russian roulette we discussed last night. Kindly keep the appointment and take his advice. Do you have any money?"

"Yes. Three and fourpence three farthings."

I rang the bell. O'Reilly entered.

"O'Reilly, Miss Slade is to have five pounds immediately. Debit her account."

O'Reilly took out his wallet, extracted five one-pound notes, handed them to Dinah and made a notation in a small black book. Dinah went pink and crammed the money awkwardly into her purse.

"Your personal account is not with the bank but with me," I said as O'Reilly left the room. "I shall always tell you if I give you money as a gift, but if I say nothing you may assume it's part of a loan to be repaid at a rate of three percent. I would advise you for your own sake to keep careful accounts and not run up unnecessary bills."

"Yes, Paul."

"It's very important that we establish our business relationship right from the start and that it exists independently of our personal relationship—whatever that relationship may be. I certainly hope we can improve on last night's fiasco, but if this proves impossible you should know that I won't withdraw my financial backing. I keep my business and my pleasure in watertight compartments, and although they may occasionally stand side by side they never mix. As far as business goes I shall treat you exactly as I treat all my other protégés—and how do you suppose I treat my protégés, Miss Slade?"

"Brutally?"

"Sensibly. I don't give second chances. I don't tolerate failure. And I don't give free rides. If you use your brains and work till you drop we can do business. If not you're on your own. Do you have any further questions?"

"No, Paul."

I rang the bell. "O'Reilly, take Miss Slade to her desk and see she has all the stationery she requires. Good day, Miss Slade."

"Good day, Mr. Van Zale," she said subdued, and then just as I was thinking I had put the fear of God into her she winked at me before O'Reilly showed her from the room.

II

The reports were on my desk at six. I read them on the way home to Curzon Street and without comment handed them to O'Reilly to file. The report on her proposed business reflected her ignorance of the world of commerce, but I was more convinced than ever that her ideas were promising. That day I had looked still further into the burgeoning chaos of the cosmetics industry, and it seemed obvious that any smart operator, large or small, stood a chance of extracting gold from such a largely unworked mine. The time was right for a mass market in cosmetics, as right as it was for a mass market in automobiles, radios and phonographs. War paint for women, canned noise and gasoline-powered mechanical horses! "What a century!" I said in disgust to O'Reilly as we went home that night. "'O *tempora! O mores!*'" But O'Reilly, whose memories of the nineteenth century were necessarily dim, merely looked at me politely and refrained from comment. I could well imagine him thinking how tiresome the older generation could be.

Dinah's other report displayed her talents to better advantage. By the time I had finished reading her summary of Mallingham's attributes I was convinced her property was an inspired combination of the Garden of Eden, the Promised Land and all seven wonders of the ancient world. Not even the most dynamic salesman offering a share in the kingdom of heaven could have matched the selling impact of Dinah's purple prose.

"Today's Tuesday, Mr. Van Zale," said Miss Phelps as I paused for my usual session in the library with my domestic correspondence.

"I am aware of that, thank you, Miss Phelps." I was still thinking of Dinah's paean to Mallingham.

"The day you write to your wife, Mr. Van Zale."

"Quite, Miss Phelps. 'My dearest Sylvia . . .'" I dictated two elegant paragraphs, and when Miss Phelps could no longer keep up with me I yawned and picked up the *Times*. The obituary column stared me in the face. Flinging down the paper, I began to prowl around the room.

"Yes, Mr. Van Zale," said Miss Phelps at last.

"'. . . I have every hope that I shall be home in time to celebrate our anniversary, but since my partners seem to be incapable of deciding who should come to England to relieve me at the London office, it is possible—unlikely but possible—that I may be delayed here until July. I know you find it hard to be at ease in Europe, but should you wish to join me for a short time . . .' No, omit that, Miss Phelps. Say: 'Since you dislike Europe and since it's unlikely that I shall be here much longer, I see no point in asking you to join me, although of course if you wish to do so . . .' No, omit that too, Miss Phelps. Omit everything after the word 'July.' Simply say: 'All our old friends here continue to inquire after you and provide daily reminders of our tiresome separation. All my love, darling, as always,' et cetera. No, don't type that last sentence, Miss Phelps, I'll write it by hand."

As I went upstairs to change for dinner I decided I would have to try to explain to Dinah about the relationship I had with Sylvia. She would be much too young to understand, but perhaps if I repeated the information often enough she would eventually believe I had no intention of discarding my wife. I wanted to be fair to Dinah, and I thought it essential that she should have no false illusions about me. Fortunately since Sylvia had no false illusions about me whatsoever I did not have to bother her in the name of honesty with the saga of Dinah Slade. Sylvia was well accustomed to the Dinah Slades of this world and paid no attention to them.

I thought of my mother saying to me ten years ago, "Thank God you've at last managed to marry someone well-bred!" but I cut off the memory before it could lead me further back into the past. I had to be firm with myself. If time could be imagined as a corridor, I had to wall up the passage behind me and look straight to the hallway ahead, but this, as I well knew, was easier said than done. The view ahead contained nothing but dreariness, while at the corridor's end . . . No, that vista was really too depressing. It was no wonder I kept looking back into the past.

Again I dwelt on the concept of time, and again I toyed as I had so often before with the possibility of a fourth dimension. If that dimension existed—if there was no single straight corridor but an infinite number of parallel furrows in the plowed field of eternity—then perhaps I could both escape my past and discover a better future. All I had to do was move from one furrow to another. How attractive it was to think of traveling sideways in time instead of droning onward in that same appalling groove! Yet how did one move from one furrow to another, and what guarantee did one have that the next furrow would be any better? And did a fourth dimension in time really exist beyond the world of semantics?

I found my questions as unanswerable as ever, but at least I could tell myself that the immediate future was not without promise. Dinah Slade was really a splendid diversion to my troubles, and besides, I was becoming exceedingly anxious to see her promised land.

III

"I know America is a classless society," said Dinah as we drove out of London early on Saturday, "but would you consider yourself some kind of aristocrat?"

"America is by no remote stretch of the imagination a classless society," I said, "and, yes, certainly I'm an aristocrat. I realize, of course, that by your standards I'm nothing but an unwashed upstart, but I do have a modest family tree."

My chauffeur was at the wheel of a long immaculate dark-green Lanchester Forty, and Dinah and I were lounging in the back. I was, I considered, admirably dressed for my weekend in the country. It was a little late in the year for tweeds, so I wore a pair of new gray sporting flannels, a soft shirt and an Oxford-blue blazer. My front strand of hair, bewildered by my boater, was clamped sulkily to the top of my head, and my feet reclined in luxury in a pair of shoes which had been delivered the previous morning from Jermyn Street. I had already decided before leaving the house that I looked smart enough to pass for forty.

Beside me Dinah wore her shabby gray skirt, a yellow blouse and a mackintosh which looked as if it had been left over from the War. Apart from the chauffeur we were alone in the car. Peterson, O'Reilly and Dawson, my valet, were following behind with the luggage in the Rolls-Royce.

"I didn't think Americans cared about family trees," said Dinah as we glided through the ugly suburbs of north London toward the meadows of Essex.

"There are many different kinds of Americans. My kind cares."

"But what is your kind? I'm sorry, but after all you *are* a foreigner and I can't seem to attach you to any sort of familiar background."

"How nice to find you're as insular and snobbish as all the best socialists! I was raised among the Anglo-Saxon Protestant hierarchy of the Eastern Seaboard, a sect known as the Yankees and bearing a vague bastard resemblance to the English. They hide their ruthless pragmatism behind a social code which includes such masterly maxims as 'Be loyal always to your class,' and 'Do business with anyone, but go yachting only with gentlemen.' They are clever and industrious and when rich and powerful can be extremely dangerous. They are a small elite minority who run America, and they run it through the great investment banks of Wall Street which control the country's capital."

"Banks like your bank?"

"Banks like my bank. I'm afraid, my dear, that I'm just another Yankee capitalist archvillain hiding behind my venerable Dutch name."

She asked me about my family, so I told her how Cornelius Van Zyl had sailed to America from Scheveningen in 1640 to become a citizen of Nieuw Amsterdam.

"Subsequent Cornelius Van Zales were large landowners in what is now Westchester County," I added, "and intermarried with the British to such an extent that I fear I've inherited nothing Dutch but my name. This explains, of course, my natural inclination to villainy while always pleading for fair play and good sportsmanship, and my natural inclination has been reinforced a hundredfold by having been born a New Yorker."

She wanted me to describe New York, but I merely told her that it was like a European city which one could never quite identify. "How strange it is to think of it now," I said, glancing at the Essex fields, "far out there in the west, roaring along in its separate furrow—"

I stopped. It was then that I first suspected I had begun my journey sideways in time.

The sun shone steadily, and although I still found the air cool Dinah periodically took off her hat and hung out of the window to let the breeze stream through her hair. The Lanchester was running faultlessly, and whenever we passed through a village the inhabitants gaped at its splendor. I wished I could have dispensed with the chauffeur and driven the motorcar myself, but in view of my health that was out of the question.

The countryside was pleasant but not spectacular, and the fields were as neat as fields can be only in land which has been farmed for a millennium. We passed through quaint villages and mellow market towns, unimportant since the end of the Middle Ages when England had turned from Europe to face the New World, and the sight of so many Georgian houses, thatched cottages and Norman churches slowly infiltrated my consciousness until I felt not only the weight of the past but a dislocation in the conventional structure of time.

"Ten miles to Norwich!" exclaimed Dinah as we flashed past a signpost.

Opening the map I saw the ancient roads converging on Norwich like the spokes in an old-fashioned carter's wheel. King's Lynn, Cromer, East Dereham, North Walsham, Great Yarmouth, St. Bungay and Ely—my glance traveled around the rim of the wheel and lingered in the east, where the famous Broads of Norfolk formed two hundred miles of waterways between Norwich and the sea. I had already circled Mallingham in red. It lay southeast of Hickling, between Waxham, Horsey and the Marshes.

"You're very isolated out there," I said to Dinah as she too glanced at the map. I had not been to that part of Norfolk before, although when Sylvia and I had spent two years in England during the War we had occasionally visited friends near the Suffolk border. I had always wanted to go to Norwich, but it's a city off the beaten track and not one of those convenient places which one can visit on the way to somewhere else.

"All of north Norfolk is a backwater," Dinah was saying, echoing my thoughts. "It's the end of the road, and the tides of progress always seem to expire before they reach us. In fact, parts of the Broads are probably much as they were centuries ago—except that in the old days the Broads were larger. There's a most interesting account, written in 1816 . . ." and she began to talk about Broadland history while I tried to imagine a corner of the civilized world lucky enough to escape the twentieth century.

We reached the outskirts of Norwich.

"Where's the cathedral?" I said alarmed, peering up at the mound on which the cathedral should traditionally have stood and seeing only a squat plain castle.

"Halfway down the hill. . . . There! Nice, isn't it?" said Dinah with infuriating British understatement, and she sighed contentedly.

A spire soared behind the massive walls of the close. Gray walls shimmered beyond a cobbled courtyard. Groping for my camera as instinctively as the crassest of American travelers, I leaped out of the car as soon as it had stopped and hurried to the gateway to stare at the medieval architecture.

"Shall I show you around?" offered the native at my side.

Feeling exactly as a lost pin might feel at the sight of a magnet, I led the way swiftly into the cathedral close.

"I say, you're walking fast!" puffed Dinah at my side. Even Peterson had to lengthen his stride to keep at the appropriate distance from me.

I reached the gateway, and the magnet became hypnotic in its intensity. I was no longer a pin but a lemming, and as I crossed the cobbled forecourt my feet seemed barely to touch the ground. I did not understand my massive excitement; it was beyond analysis, but I knew that something of importance was about to happen to me. Reaching the porch I paused beneath the stone carved long ago by nameless craftsmen.

"Paul, wait! Don't leave me behind!"

But my hand was on the iron bolt, and the small rectangle cut in the massive door yielded beneath my touch.

I entered the cathedral. The choir was rehearsing the strange, unorthodox English hymn "Jerusalem," and while the sun streamed through the stained glass far above me I heard the disembodied voices soar in an eerie reflection of William Blake's mystical vision.

I moved forward. The arches towered above my head, the altar shone in the distance, and in a flash the past, the present and the future revolved in a kaleidoscope and I was displaced from my furrow in time.

I felt horribly disoriented. As I shut my eyes Dinah's voice said quickly behind me, "Paul?" and I reached for her hand as if her presence were the one familiar landmark in an alien world.

The choir stopped. I could hear the choirmaster talking faintly. The air of unreality evaporated and I felt better.

"Tell me about it—the cathedral—everything you know," I said, automatically checking my pocket to make sure I had my medication, and she started to talk about the number of years it had taken to build the cathedral and how some of the great pillars were different from the others because the earlier ones had been unfinished. I concentrated on her information and conscientiously noted the features of the chancel, the clerestory, the nave and the choir. We walked around the cloisters, we admired the stonework, and soon I had even recovered enough to smile at my swooningly romantic visions of traveling sideways in time.

Given the chance, my good hard Yankee common sense will always triumph over my sloppy Victorian romanticism.

"Why are you smiling?" said Dinah curiously.

"I must have been remembering my far-off foolish youth when I was a romantic idealist. My God, what's this?"

It was a memorial stone, very old, set in the wall. Below an engraving of a skull ran the morbid rhyme:

All you that do this place pass bye
Remember death for you must dye
As you are now then so was I
And as I am so that you be.
Thomas Gooding here do staye
Wayting for God's judgement daye.

"Can't you just imagine," said Dinah laughing, "what a beastly old killjoy he must have been?"

I turned aside, saw the past, turned back, saw the future, turned aside again and began to stumble away.

"Paul—"

"I've got to get out."

I felt better outside. I stood in the sunshine in the cathedral close, and death seemed a long way away.

"Sorry," I said to Dinah. "I'm not usually so disturbed by medieval morbidity. I must have been to too many funerals lately."

She asked no questions but simply slipped her arm through mine. "Let's go on to Mallingham."

We left the city, and after crossing the river and crawling through the suburbs we emerged once more onto the open road.

I did not speak and Dinah too was quiet. The countryside, pastoral and unremarkable, began to flatten and suddenly I felt the better mood of the cathedral returning, the sense of time being displaced and bent to form a different world. Crossing the bridge at Wroxham, I saw the hubbub of life on the water, yachts and cruisers, dinghies and rowboats, and although Dinah said indifferently, "This is the commercial part of the Broads. Wroxham is a holiday center," the magic had begun again. This time I made no effort to be hardheaded and practical. I turned to embrace my romantic vision of time, and as the road curved through the marshland I saw the sails across the fields although the water was hidden from my eyes. It was as though the boats were traveling on land, and as I stared at this mysterious mirage I sensed a land where the water was king, and waters where the land was encircled to become a hundred private fiefdoms. We streamed through Horning ("*Quite* lost its character since the War," snorted Dinah), and crossed the River Ant at Ludham Bridge, where two windmills, one a skeleton, pointed ghostly fingers to the sky.

We drove on to Potter Heigham.

Somewhere south of Hickling we lost touch with modern times. The reeds swayed on the marshes, the white sails shimmered in distant dikes, and enormous clouds dotted the unending sky.

"More windmills!" I was sitting on the edge of my seat and speaking for the first time in half an hour.

"Drainage mills. They keep the land from flooding."

I stared at the slowly revolving sails of the nearest mill. The sun was still shining. The cattle browsed tranquilly in the fields. Wattle-and-daub cottages basked beneath roofs of an unusually dark thatch.

Beyond Hickling the road ran due north to Palling, Waxham and Horsey, but a mile before we reached the coast we found the weathered signpost which read "To Mallingham and the Marsh."

The lane twisted and turned, ran unexpectedly over two humpbacked bridges and without warning arrived in the heart of the village. The church was even bigger than the church at Ludham, and as we passed by its flint walls I saw the cottages across the green. Some of the walls were whitewashed wattle-and-daub, but there were others built of faced flint with stone quoins. The pub which stood facing the green was called the Eel and Ham.

"Short for Isle de Mallingham," explained Dinah. "The original Saxon settlement was an island when the Normans first arrived here."

The road curved sharply again; as the village disappeared from sight we started to travel along a causeway above the marshes toward a ruined turreted gatehouse set in walls fifteen feet high.

We crossed the last bridge, passed the gatehouse and entered a short driveway bordered by a ragged lawn and some overgrown shrubbery.

I saw the house.

I had read her description and so knew exactly what to expect, but even so I heard myself give an exclamation of amazement. Hardly able to believe that the past could have been so perfectly preserved, I gazed at the traditional medieval house with the hall in the center and the wings, added later, forming the famous H. The walls were flint, some rough, some dressed, with the type of stone quoin I had noticed in the village, and although the windows in the wings were small the windows of the great hall were as long and slender as the windows of a church. I was still marveling that this present hall should date from the thirteenth century when I remembered that the previous hall which had been built on the same site was even older. William the Conqueror's henchman Alan of Richmond had pulled down the Saxon house when he had been granted the Manor of Mallingham in 1067, and had built himself a Norman hall to house his retinue during his visits to East Anglia. Later the entire manor had been described in detail in the *Domesday Book*. In those days there had been two Mallinghams, Mallingham Magna and Mallingham Parva, but Mallingham Parva had disappeared beneath the sea two hundred years ago during the prolonged and continuing erosion of the Norfolk coastline.

Dinah showed me into the great hall, and there I saw the hammer-beamed ceiling and the staircase which had once led to the solar, and the fireplace with the stone carving above the mantel of the coat of arms of Godfrey Slade. This first recorded Slade of Mallingham had built the present hall before riding off to the Crusades. It was thought that he had been the son of a rich Norwich merchant who had aspired to grandeur by buying the hall when the previous owners, the monks of St. Benet's Abbey, had sold the property to meet increased taxation.

"This way," said Dinah, but I was still looking up at the hammer-beamed ceiling, and it was several seconds before I followed her into the far wing where a large chamber had been furnished as a drawing room. A modern architect had built some doors which opened onto a terrace, and as Dinah led the way outside I looked past the Victorian urns decorating the balustrade, down the lawn studded with croquet hoops, to the Edwardian boathouse, the jetty and the shining waters of Mallingham Broad.

The glare of the sun on water hurt my eyes. I closed my lids, and as I stood listening I heard the birds calling to one another in the marshes and the salt sea wind humming through the willows at the water's edge.

Again I felt the past opening up before me, but it was a different past, a past I had never experienced before. In my mind's eye I could see it stretching backward into the mist, layer upon layer, time beyond time, time out of mind, and its vastness was not disturbing but comforting to me.

I opened my eyes and walked down the lawn to the water. The walls of time were very thin, and as I walked I became aware of that endless past merging with my own present, and I knew I had come to the end of my journey sideways in time. A great peace overcame me. Tears blurred my eyes, for I knew I was free at last with the blood washed from my hands, free of the prison I had built for myself in another time and in another world far away across the sea.

The sense of having come home was overpowering. "This is what I've always wanted," my voice said. "This is what I've always been trying to find."

I turned. She was there. We looked at each other for a long moment and then she smiled.

"Welcome to *my* world, Paul," said Dinah Slade.

Chapter Four

I

"What about your entourage?"

"They can wait."

We went upstairs. Her room faced the Broad, and from the window one could see beyond the trees which fringed the water to the Brograve Level and the sandhills of Waxham. After drawing the drapes I turned to find her waiting for me in the fourposter bed.

Awaking later, I went back to the window and lifted the corner of the drape. The sun was still high in the sky although it was early evening, and the birds were still skimming languidly over the mirrored surface of the Broad. Yet the light had changed. The reeds were darker, the water a deeper blue, and far away beyond the sandhills I could imagine a golden sheen beginning to form on the restless waves of the North Sea.

I dressed. The girl was sound asleep, her long lashes motionless against her cheeks. After watching her for a moment I went downstairs to the hall.

O'Reilly was waiting for me. He was sitting neatly in an armchair by the door and reading a guidebook on the Norfolk Broads.

"Is everything in order?"

"Yes, sir. We have our accommodation in the west wing. It's rather primitive by American standards," said O'Reilly fastidiously, "but I'm sure we'll manage. I've arranged for us to take our meals at the village inn. There are no servants here except for one old woman who appears to be deaf, hostile and a mental defective."

"Ah, that must be Mrs. Oakes." I was remembering Dinah's report. Twenty years ago when there had still been money in the family, six in-help, three daily maids, two grooms, two gardeners and a gamekeeper had been employed at Mallingham Hall, but nowadays the head gardener and the housekeeper, Mr. and Mrs. Oakes, had the servants' quarters to themselves. Mrs. Oakes had looked after Dinah when she had returned to Mallingham after her mother's death, and still regarded herself as responsible for running the house. Her husband, who had a Boer War pension, still assumed responsibility for the garden. Neither had been paid since Dinah's father had died. An old marshman who lived in a hut on the edge of the Broad kept out trespassers, guarded the wildlife and fished the waters to prevent overpopulation among trout, bream and tench.

The house was dusty and down-at-heel. Most of the first editions had long since been sold from the library; most of the antique furniture had also gone to pay for Harry Slade's extravagance. The rooms were furnished in a hodgepodge of styles; the walls needed a coat of paint; the evidence of mice was everywhere. I had learned that there was one bathroom, one water closet, no telephone, no electricity and no gas. It was not a large house, a mere five bedrooms in each wing of the medieval H, and the galleried hall was bigger than either wing. The kitchens were primitive, the stables little better than ruins, the greenhouses broken and overgrown. There was no yacht in the boathouse, only a sailing dinghy, and a sole pony occupied the stall next to the Victorian trap. Beyond the stables the fifteen-foot walls enclosed an area of three acres, most of which was grass. I was shown a paddock for the pony, a rectangle which could be marked as a tennis court, and the croquet lawn below the back terrace. Once the Manor of Mallingham had embraced an area of several hundred acres, including the church, the village and all the farms in the neighborhood, but in the past fifty years the farms and cottages had been sold, so that all that now remained of the estate was the house, the garden and the seventy-five acres of water, reeds and marsh which formed Mallingham Broad.

"But I shall make it live again," said Dinah as we dined that evening. "Oh, not in the old way, of course—that's gone forever. I don't expect to be the lady of the manor living on the rents of my tenants. But if—when—I make enough money at my business I'll restore the house and grounds and there'll be a yacht in the boathouse again and a motorcar instead of that dilapidated old pony trap, and servants to look after the house properly, and antiques to replace the ones my father sold. And I'll stock the library with valuable books again, and everything will be as perfect as it was two hundred years ago when William Slade was a member of Parliament and the Slades were a great Norfolk family. Mrs. Oakes, *do* stop looking as though the Day of Judgment were about to dawn! I can't tell you how depressing I find it!"

The old woman had just brought in the summer pudding. "No good was ever a-coming out of foreigners stroaming about these parts, Miss Dinah," she said, taking care not to look in my direction.

"And to think I put on my best English accent!" I said ruefully as she marched out of the room.

"Oh, never mind her—she doesn't even trust anyone from Suffolk."

When we had finished our meal we went for a stroll in the garden. The Broad was golden, flocks of starlings and lapwings flew over the marshes across the pale evening sky, and a bittern was booming far off in the reeds.

"Would you like to see my laboratory?" suggested Dinah.

"About as much as you wanted to see the Rouen Apocalypse."

We paused among the shrubbery. I wondered if Mrs. Oakes was watching in disapproval from some hidden window.

"I actually use the scullery as a laboratory," Dinah explained as she led the way into a greenhouse which had a number of panes missing from the roof. "I need running water for my experiments, but I store the results of my work here so that Mrs. Oakes doesn't throw them away." She moved to a bench which had been cleared of horticultural impedimenta, removed a tarpaulin and revealed a row of bottles confusingly labeled with such instructions as "Percy's cough syrup: one teaspoon every four hours."

Dinah's paternal grandparents had lived in India, and on their return to England they had brought with them the Indian nursemaid who had cared for their infant son. The ayah had remained for twenty years in England before dying of homesickness, and it had been her recipes for cosmetics, conscientiously recorded for posterity by Dinah's grandmother, that had formed the basis of Dinah's experiments.

"The ayah amended the original Indian recipes herself because of the difficulties of getting the ingredients she had used in India," Dinah explained. "Of course she used only natural ingredients and each phial took an eternity to prepare, but the perfumes are so good that I was determined to find the formulae which would create the same scents artificially. I'm going to start with perfumes first, as I told you in my report. The preparations for skin care are all simple variations on a glycerin base, but the secret is to get the texture right and the scent perfect. Here—smell this," she added, thrusting under my nose a bottle labeled "For Back-Ache."

I had expected to be reminded of the exotic East, but instead I thought of an English garden at sunset on a summer evening. "Lavender?" I murmured. "No, too musky. Roses? No, not quite. What is it?"

"A mixture of eighteen scents including nutmeg, magnolia, myrrh and sweet pea. Now try this."

I sniffed. At first the perfume seemed identical. I sniffed again and realized it was sweeter and more cloying. "I don't like that so much," I said.

She was unsurprised. Replacing the bottle, she selected a third. "What about this?"

I put my nose obediently to the rim and was once more back in the English garden. But this time I could see the woods at the edge of the lawn, the leaves on the trees, the moss on the ground. "I like that," I said, sniffing again. "You've caught the scent of flowers, but now it's overlaid with something else."

"Would you say it was a natural scent?"

"Without question."

She smiled. "The only natural ingredients are the herbs, which are cheap and easy to produce. The rest is a chemical compound." She picked up the first bottle. "This is the scent made entirely from natural ingredients, including flowers which are expensive and impossible to obtain all the year round. I couldn't market it as a commercial proposition. This"—she turned to the second bottle—"is the scent which contains nothing but chemicals. The result is similar, but I've never been able to get rid of that cloying sweetness without adding the herbs. They disguise it, though I'm not sure how."

I wanted to make sure I had understood her correctly. "Give me an example."

"Well, for instance, it's easy to make an artificial lemon scent. You use glycerin, chloroform, nitrous ether, aldehyde, acetate of ethyl, butyrate of amyl, alcohol and a couple of other chemicals. But you'll know it's an artificial scent unless you blend it with some natural ingredients. Conversely, many synthetic products often intensify the odors of the natural products, so if you get the right combination your product can be even better than a scent which is made entirely without chemical ingredients."

The idea of man improving on nature always appeals to my basest nineteenth-century instincts. I asked what artificial scents could be used.

"The most important are ionone, for violet perfume, and terpineol, for lilac, and . . ." She talked on knowledgeably, and I learned of essential oils dissolved in alcohol, of pomades and tinctures, of liquid perfume and dry perfume.

"And here's my recipe for Indian sachet powder: three and a half ounces of sandalwood, ten and a half ounces of cinnamon, thirty grams of cloves . . ."

The exotic formulas filled a thick exercise book, but at last we descended from the heights of perfumery to the prosaic instructions for making vanishing cream.

"Four pounds twelve ounces of stearic acid—white triple-pressed . . ."

The list rolled sonorously on. I imagined a million women smoothing their faces with the contents of a million jars of vanishing cream, and soon the landscape surrounding them became dotted with dollars and cents.

"And the chemicals are all easy to obtain," Dinah was saying. "Of course, you have to be careful of adulteration, so your supplier must be quite above suspicion." And she began to explain how one could recognize the adulterates of essential oils.

". . . so they add paraffin or spermaceti to make the mixture congeal readily, because that's characteristic of *true* oil of aniseed," she concluded earnestly. "You do understand, don't you?"

"Absolutely." I mentally allocated another fifty thousand dollars for further expansion and pictured a future public company launched by a flotation designed to seduce even the most cautious investor. It was only when we went indoors and she showed me her packaging designs that I realized how far she had to travel before I could risk making her small business a public enterprise. Glancing at the fanciful gold lettering which curved bewilderingly against a pale-blue background, I forgot my vision of a million-dollar annual turnover and came down to earth with a jolt.

"Very pretty," I said, "but I can't read it. I guess this flowered script is supposed to conjure up an Indian atmosphere."

"Exactly!" said Dinah in triumph. "I'm calling my product Taj Mahal."

I groaned.

"Well, why not?" she demanded angrily.

"My dear, your purchasers among the ill-educated proletariat are never even going to be able to pronounce the name, let alone understand the allusion to India."

"But I'm not catering to the proletariat! I'm catering to all those upper-class women who have until now been inhibited from using cosmetics and who can afford to pay for their new fashion through the nose!"

"Then you're out of touch with the economic facts of 1922. I have no doubt you could make a shilling or two peddling paste to the aristocracy, but if you want to give me a reasonable return for my money you'll cater to the masses. England is ripe for mass production; that's where the money is and that's where I'm putting my capital." I stacked her sketches together and handed them back to her. "Change the coloring. Gold is hard to read, and although I like the blue it's too pale to create a strong impression. I'll bring over a market-research team from New York to decide which colors would create the most sales impact." I began to roam around the room just as I did when I was dictating, and allowed my mind to fasten wholly on the problem. "Scrap the fancy lettering—have firm strong capital letters which everyone can read. Scrap the name Taj Mahal. You want a name which sounds like the virginal heroine of a nineteenth-century novel. Let me see. What were all those Trollope women called? Lily, Belle, Glencora—"

"I am *not* calling my product after some bally awful Victorian heroine!"

"Then let's think of something classical. Why, of course! Diana! That's it! Diana Slade—very pretty and elegant, much more charming than your real name. We'll call the firm Diana Slade Cosmetics, and you can name your perfumes after the different goddesses of antiquity!"

"But what's that got to do with India?" stormed Dinah.

"Absolutely nothing, but who cares so long as the product sells?"

"I care! I care, you beastly, vulgar, money-grubbing American!"

I swung around in surprise but fortunately managed not to laugh. After considering my approach I avoided all apologies and said instead, "Dinah, when I was a young man, a little younger than you are now, I arrived home penniless in New York with a pregnant wife and had to earn my living. I had a bogus Oxford accent, a love of the classics and a passionate distaste for vulgarity. However, it didn't take me long to discover that those dubious virtues were of no use to me when it came to surviving in a town like New York. I learned to survive in a hard school, Dinah. I just hope your course in the art of survival will be easier than mine was."

There was a pause before she said unevenly, "I'm sorry. I was only shocked by how suddenly you changed into a fast-talking, utterly twentieth-century businessman complete with a pronounced American accent."

This time I did laugh. "I warned you I was a New Yorker! You didn't think I made my money by declaiming poetry by Catullus, did you? But maybe I should start quoting again to reassure you that Dr. Jekyll isn't entirely Mr. Hyde. '*Vivamus, mea Lesbia, atque amemus—*' "

" '*—da mi basia mille!*' " responded Dinah promptly, raising her mouth to mine for a kiss, and as I slid my arms around her waist I couldn't help thinking that she really was the most remarkable girl. . . .

II

The next morning after breakfast we went sailing. I had already decided to stay an extra night in Norfolk so that on the following day I could call on the Slade family lawyers in Norwich to discuss the purchase of the estate. There would have to be an independent valuation, but I thought that in view of the dilapidated state of the house and the lack of modern conveniences I should be able to make the purchase cheaply.

By that time London seemed as remote as New York. Deciding

firmly that I would not think of any business for the next twenty-four hours, I hoisted the sail of the little dinghy, and with Dinah at the tiller we set off across Mallingham Broad.

I had never sailed at Newport, because it was felt that the motion might disturb my health, but later when it seemed I had outgrown my illness I learned about yachting during summers spent at Bar Harbor, Maine. Sailing was not my favorite sport but I enjoyed it, and I had never enjoyed it more than I did on that Sunday morning early in June when Dinah's little boat danced over the waters of Mallingham Broad. From the water my perception of the landscape altered. I could see the "Isle de Mallingham," the slight rise in the ground on which the village had been built, and found it easy to imagine the area as part of some ancient inland sea. Unfamiliar birds watched us from the reeds. In the clear water below the prow I glimpsed the flash of small fish and once saw the shadow of a pike lurking in the depths. I was soon longing for a rod, and when I asked Dinah if the fish were fair-sized she laughed and began to talk of trout weighing thirty-five pounds.

At the far side of the Broad the water narrowed into the channel known as Mallingham Dyke, and we had to unlock the padlock of the chain which lay across the water as a warning to trespassers.

"But we have few trespassers," explained Dinah, slipping the key back into her pocket, "because you can only reach Mallingham from Horsey Mere, and Horsey too is a private broad."

We drifted on into the dike. I got out the oars when we were becalmed, but soon a breeze helped us into a second dike, the New Cut, and, picking up the sea wind again, we scudded swiftly south into Horsey Mere.

"That windmill!" I cried above the wind as we tacked back and forth.

"Isn't it grand?"

It took me a moment to realize she was taking me straight to it, and so intrigued was I by the whirling sails that I was nearly decapitated by the swinging boom. By the time I had recovered we were gliding up the little dike and the millman was waiting for us on the staithe.

Heights have always made me uneasy. I declined the millman's offer to show me all the stories of the mill, but I went up the first ladder to peer out at the wild green remoteness of the flats. The clanking sails were making such a noise that it was a relief to return outside and accept Dinah's suggestion that we walk to the sea.

Along the lane I had to stop to see Horsey Church, which was hidden in the woods, and later I stopped again to talk to a yokel gardening in front of one of the flint-walled cottages I so admired. It was he who told me that Horsey and Waxham had been a center for smuggling in times past, when each shipment of contraband had been hidden in the rector's barn while the mill sails were set at a certain angle to warn of the approach of the revenue men. When we finally reached the Brograve Level, those sea fields directly below the long line of the sandhills, we had taken over an hour to walk a mile, but I was enjoying myself as I had not enjoyed myself for months, and beside me Dinah had evidently forgotten the crass commercial streak I had displayed earlier.

A cart track ran through the fields straight to the sandhills. These were dunes, huge mounds of dark sand studded with tufts of sea grass, and the grass rippled in the wind. Beneath the hills the wind dropped, but as we hauled ourselves to the top I could hear the wind mingling with the roar of the sea beyond the summit. It was a stiff climb, and although I wanted to pause for breath I climbed on until I was standing on top of the highest mound and gazing in exhilaration at the dark glowing sea.

The horizon was clear. Waves crashed rhythmically on miles of empty sands, and gulls soared effortlessly above our heads.

I was still gazing across the sea to Holland when Dinah scampered down to the beach and shouted something over her shoulder, but the wind whipped away her words long before I could hear them. My exhilaration overcame me. Kicking off my sand-stuffed shoes, I tore off my socks and cascaded down the dunes to join her. On the beach the sand was hard beneath my toes, and I began to run, the sense of freedom enveloping me until the blood was rushing through my veins.

Dinah was flirting with the waves at the water's edge. "Come on!" she shouted, waggling a naked toe at me.

I sallied boldly into the waves, gasped with shock and backed out. No summer current fresh from Labrador could have been colder than that North Sea in early June, and when I heard Dinah laugh I saw she had kept her feet dry.

"Wretched child!" I hared after her, but she skipped out of reach and raced back into the sandhills.

By the time I caught up with her we were both too breathless to do more than flop down in a small hollow, but the relief of escaping from the wind quickly revived us. My ears stopped tingling. After basking in the unexpected warmth of the sun I sat up, smoothed my front strand of hair and watched the gulls wheeling across the sky.

"I'm trying to think of a suitable quotation from Tennyson," I remarked, "but my poetical memory has apparently been blown away by the wind."

"How fortunate! I always try to avoid Tennyson—so *hopelessly* sentimental and Victorian!"

"I shall give you a volume of his poems at the earliest opportunity." I began to kiss her. We were both warm from our exertions on the beach, so it seemed perfectly natural to start taking off our clothes.

"I suppose in the circumstances I shall have to be careful," I murmured. "The only disadvantage of spontaneity is that one can't make advance preparations."

"My dear Paul, do you think I didn't have this exact hollow in mind when we left the house this morning?"

I gave a shout of delighted laughter, rolled over onto my naked back and pulled her down on top of me.

It grew hotter. The grit clung to our sweating limbs and seeped between our shifting bodies. My throat was dry, and all I could see was the sand, the sea grass and the vast sky blurring into a pattern of reflected light. The sweat blinded me and in one last purposeful gesture I drew together the threads linking the rhythm of our movements and knotted them in an elegant shimmer of power.

Dinah cried out. I held on to her, then rolled away and let the pale northern sun beat feebly on my eyelids. When my mind began to function again a number of thoughts occurred to me, none of them welcome but all shining with common sense. With a grimace I sat up. The wind, dipping into the hollow, made me shiver, and I had to make a great effort to embark on my traditional maneuvers to ensure that this new liaison of mine stayed both civilized and harmless.

"Well, I must confess I find you most attractive both in bed and out of it," I said pleasantly to Dinah as I reached for my shirt. "In fact, I can't recall when I was last so consistently entertained. But you won't make any false assumptions about me, will you? So many women—less intelligent than you, of course—seem to think I indulge in the pastime of falling in love, but in fact I regard that as a time-consuming occupation which I leave with relief to the younger generation. And some women—of course this is a trap you'd never fall into—think I can't wait to leave my wife, but in fact my wife suits me admirably and I have no intention of ever terminating my marriage. In other words, to cut a long warning short, I don't play the role of lovesick swain, I don't run off with mistresses, and I don't dabble with divorce."

There was a pause. She had been listening very solemnly, her arms folded across her breasts, her dark eyes wide and grave. I was just wondering if I had a handkerchief to mop up her inevitable tears when she exclaimed with an admiration which appeared to be genuine, "Oh, I do think that's sensible! If only my father could have organized his life as well as you've obviously organized yours!"

That took the wind out of my sails. I had been ready for her to scream at me that I was a menace to the entire female sex and had been so poised to offer my traditional defense of fair play that I found I now had nothing to say. For one wild moment I wondered if the entire import of my warning had been lost on her, but then she said sunnily, "Well, isn't it nice that you don't have to worry about me wanting to marry you? Not even a millionaire could ever tempt *me* into marriage!" And she started to put on her clothes.

"Quite," I said dryly. All this sounded a little too good to be true. "But don't you want children?" I said, watching her.

"Of course! But you don't have to get married to have children."

I felt myself becoming a shade paler but otherwise maintained my composure admirably. Wondering if there was anyone more dangerous than an intellectual who was emotionally ignorant, I said with a laugh, "You don't have to get married to make a fool of yourself either! It's a free country, Dinah, and you're entitled to believe what you want, but don't, I implore you, try to impose your beliefs on innocent children. But that's your business. So long as you don't make it mine I have no right to criticize you."

"You mentioned your daughter who died. Are there no other children?"

"No."

"Oh. Is that because you don't like children?"

"It's not a subject I care to discuss." I tried not to think of my illness. Standing up, I shoved my fists into my pockets. "But I'll say this: I don't want a child, and if some foolish woman were to present me with one I would refuse to acknowledge it. Pregnancy would be the quickest way to terminate an affair with me, and don't you forget it."

She went white. I suddenly realized that my composure had slipped, my voice had become harsh and my tone brutal. I turned away in shame.

"Let's go home." I reached for her hand and was painfully relieved a second later when I felt it slip into mine. "I shouldn't have talked to you like that," I said. "Forgive me."

"What for? I approve of honesty," said Dinah. "I like to know where I am with people. I believe in honest truthful relationships."

"Why, yes, so do I," I said readily, and then thought with regret of all the truths I would never be able to tell her.

III

O'Reilly arranged for me to see young Geoffrey Hurst's father, the senior partner of Hurst, Rigby and Ashton, at two o'clock the following afternoon, but unfortunately the meeting was not a pleasant one. I was so used to dealing with the steel-cored corporation lawyers of Wall Street that I found myself ill at ease with a lawyer who was a quiet English country gentleman, and Mr. Hurst evidently considered himself so thoroughly *in loco parentis* to Dinah that he was unable to regard me without prejudice. I expressed my interest in the house and we discussed the legal effects of Harry Slade's intestacy, but our conversation was awkward and I decided afterward not to see him again. My lawyer could handle the purchase, O'Reilly could clear up any tiresome detail and Philip Hurst could brood over his disapproval in uninterrupted peace.

There was no other difficulty about the sale, since Dinah's half brother wanted to dispose of the house, and after I had told her with truth that her worries about Mallingham were for the moment at an end we decided to celebrate by spending the next weekend in Paris. I thought I might buy her some clothes, but I regretted the offer immediately, not because I did not want her to be properly dressed by the best couturier, but because I wanted to spend the next weekend at Mallingham. However, since she had given me my best weekend in years it was only fair to offer her a weekend of my own devising in return.

With an effort I tried to focus on the world which lay waiting for me in London, but I was so absorbed by my memories of the weekend that when I arrived back at Curzon Street I felt totally unprepared to pick up the threads of my normal daily life. My lack of preparation was underlined by the sight of Miss Phelps advancing toward me. I had to resist a strong urge to turn tail and run.

"Good evening, Miss Phelps," I said politely, and added without interest, "Has there been anything of importance in the mail?"

"Oh yes, Mr. Van Zale!" said Miss Phelps cozily, and as if determined to drag me back to reality she handed me a letter from my wife.

Chapter Five

I

People thought I did not appreciate my wife but they were wrong. My first wife Dolly had made me so unhappy that I had vowed after her death never again to marry for love. My second marriage, which I had fondly told myself was a marriage of convenience, had turned out to be quite the most inconvenient arrangement I could possibly have made. Indeed my five years spent with Marietta had taught me exactly how uncomfortable a man's life can be when his households are badly run, his social arrangements inefficiently conducted and his monthly bills bizarre in their extravagance. The trouble was, as I realized later, that Marietta had been extraordinarily stupid. I had thought I had made myself clear to her before our marriage, but, as subsequent events had proved, my words had gone in one pretty ear and immediately out of the other.

"Marriage should be a two-way street," I said to her, trying, as I always did, to be fair and honest in establishing a relationship. "You'll get my name and a share of my wealth, prospects and social prestige. I expect to get a well-run household and a showpiece of a wife who never puts a foot wrong." I could see she heard only the word "showpiece" and was imagining it gave her carte blanche to purchase a new wardrobe of clothes every month, so I added to make myself clear, "If you commit adultery I'll divorce you. Showpiece wives should sleep only with their husbands."

"Darling, why should I ever want to sleep with anyone but you?" cooed Marietta, neglecting to tell me that she had long since developed a penchant for fornication.

"I shall divorce you," I said with relief after evidence of her wandering attention had finally been placed in my hands. I would have divorced her long before for extravagance and general uselessness, but unfortunately these were not grounds for divorce in the state of New York.

"If you sleep with other people why shouldn't I?" she screamed.

"Because it wasn't part of our premarital agreement. I said that marriage should be a two-way street—"

"Yes, and for me it was a dead-end alley! What did I get out of it? A husband who works late nearly every night, a grubby little house off Madison and a stingy dress allowance!"

"I've kept you for five excruciatingly expensive years in a style far superior to the one to which you were previously accustomed. I've lived up to every one of my promises—I've shared my wealth with you, my prestige, my name—and what have you given me? Nothing but trouble, aggravation and nonstop vulgarity!"

"Vulgarity!" shrieked Marietta, who always fancied herself a lady.

"Vulgarity!" I shouted back at her. "Even a common whore uses better language than you do!"

"You," hissed Marietta, "should know."

Altogether it was not an experience which made me want to rush into matrimony a third time, and after our disastrous divorce had thrilled every gossipmonger in town I led a bachelor life for a while.

Unfortunately this too had its disadvantages. By this time my success was increasing rapidly, and such were the pressures of my work that I found it impossible to concentrate on domestic matters. I hired people to do the job a wife would have done but it was never satisfactory, and so desperate did I become that I even considered inviting my mother to take command of my household. My mother lived in a house near Madison Square with my daughter Vicky, and for the past ten years she had claimed that my household was quite unsuitable for an innocent young girl.

Much as I had wanted Vicky to live with me, I had had to concede that my mother was right. Obviously while I was a bachelor or married to a woman who not only disliked children but was incapable of setting a stepdaughter a good example, it was best for Vicky to be with my mother, but I continued to dream of a time when Vicky could live with me, and as the years passed after my divorce and my bachelor life became more difficult to manage I reluctantly faced the fact that I had to marry again. To console myself I observed that I could hardly do worse than my first two marriages and that just possibly, if I were sensible, I might do better. By this time I didn't have to marry for my career and I didn't even have to marry anyone beautiful. If I could find a woman who could add up the columns of my household accounts, manage the servants and be kind to my daughter, I resolved I would marry her even if she were fresh from an orphanage and looked like a freak in a circus show.

I cast around among my vast circle of acquaintances and saw only the rich society women with their empty heads and emptier lives, the fortune hunters who wanted only to help me spend my money, and the social climbers who fancied the notion of being the third Mrs. Paul Van Zale. I went to parties and dinners, soirees and balls, and my suitors were continually lying in wait to suffocate me with their eagerness. How do women always know when a man is looking for a wife? I had been a bachelor for four years, yet never was I as oppressed by willing women as I was during that summer of 1911.

I had just given up all hope of finding anyone suitable when the miracle happened. I went to a garden party out on the Island, and while I was talking to three eager females I glanced beyond them across the lawn and saw a woman standing alone, watching me. As soon as my glance met hers she blushed and turned away.

Only a woman of the most sterling virtue ever turned her back on Paul Van Zale. I ran after her, but she had disappeared. I began to question people wildly. At last someone said, "Oh, you must mean Mrs. Woodard. I think I saw her going into the rose garden."

"She has a husband?" It seemed like the last straw.

"I believe she's a widow."

Not even winged Mercury could have sped faster to the rose garden.

She was perfect. I kept thinking there must be some flaw, but there was none. She thought there was, because a doctor had told her she would probably never carry a child longer than three months; after three miscarriages she had been advised not to have another child, and she was sure, she confided to me painfully, that I would want children.

"Definitely not."

"But I should feel I was failing you in some way."

"Never."

We were married. My family adored her. All my friends told me how lucky I was. Vicky promised to live with us after she had returned from her visit to Europe. I was so happy I could hardly believe my good fortune.

It was four years later, when I discovered that the destructive force of my ambition was rebounding on me, that everything had begun to go wrong.

"There must be something I can do for you, Paul!" Sylvia said in despair after Vicky died.

"You can come with me to Europe." I was suffering from a compulsion to escape from New York. "I've decided to be the resident partner in London for a couple of years and pull the London office together."

But Sylvia hated Europe. I could not share my pleasure with her and she could communicate only her misery to me. When we came home in 1919 the shining surface of our marriage had tarnished, and although we settled down harmoniously again in New York we were never as close as we had been earlier.

Three years later when I knew I once more had to escape to

Europe to preserve my sanity, I did not invite Sylvia to come with me.

"I'll be away no more than a month," I said, "and since you dislike Europe I won't take it amiss if you choose to stay in New York."

I saw the relief in her eyes and was surprised when I felt hurt. Afterward I realized that I had expected her to insist on accompanying me, but she did not insist so I went alone.

The night before I left I said to her, "If only I could explain to you about Europe!"

But she answered simply, "Darling, I'm sorry. I know you're annoyed that I can't appreciate Europe intellectually like Elizabeth, but I can't pretend to be an intellectual when I'm not."

I kissed her. "I never wanted an intellectual wife," I said, thinking bitterly that one did not have to be an intellectual to appreciate Europe, and afterward it seemed that in closing her mind against Europe she had closed it too against me.

But I could hardly complain. I had chosen her to be the companion of my hearth, not my soul, and what did it matter if she did not understand me so long as my three households ran smoothly, my social commitments were exquisitely arranged and her name was always absent from any scandal in the popular gossip columns? I had the showpiece wife I had always wanted, and on the whole we got along very well. To want more than that would have been foolish and—worst sin of all—unrealistic. I knew when I was well off, and, telling myself for the hundredth time how fortunate I was to have such a wife, I reluctantly opened the third letter she had written to me at Curzon Street and allowed her words to carry me far away from the peace of Mallingham to the sweating teeming streets of Manhattan.

II

She had had another miscarriage. I was so upset that I could not continue reading the letter and had to ask the butler to bring me a glass of brandy. For reasons connected with my health I drink very little, but unfortunately there are always those rare occasions when I feel willing to risk illness for a shot of hard liquor.

Sylvia had had two miscarriages in the first year of our marriage in addition to the three she had suffered while living with her first husband, but I had thought I had finally succeeded in convincing her that I did not want a child. After many years of dealing with women who wanted to present me with a son and heir I was now word-perfect in my explanation of my aversion to fatherhood, but Sylvia, with that intuition women often possess, seemed to sense that my explanation was a fraud. No matter what I said she remained convinced that I wanted a child as much as she did, and I had now reached the point where I was at a loss to know what to say to her next.

Yet I knew something would have to be said. I lived in dread that by some miracle she would carry a child for the full nine months and give birth to suffering, disillusionment and tragedy. It would be the end of our marriage. I could remember my first wife Dolly shouting at me when our son had died after three days in the world, "You bastard, never telling me such a disgusting thing ran in the family!" But then she herself had died and I had not had to live with her repulsion.

Finishing my brandy, I sat down and grabbed my pen.

My dearest Sylvia,

I am more distressed than you can possibly imagine to hear of your brief visit to the hospital and while, of course, I am sorry you should have been disappointed again I am even sorrier that you apparently cannot believe all I have said to you on the subject of children. At the risk of boring you by repeating myself, may I once again stress three facts: I detest dynasties; I deplore the intellectual poverty of a man who thinks he needs only to reproduce himself in order to ensure his immortality; and I am not Henry the Eighth.

I paused to find more ink and realized, as I discovered Sylvia's letter again, that I had not finished reading it. I sat down and tried to be calm.

Elizabeth heard I was in the hospital [Sylvia had continued, referring to my former mistress] and she sent flowers—so sweet of her. She's very worried about Bruce at the moment. He's become just so red, and she hopes you can have a talk with him when you come back.

This remark was intended to describe not the choleric complexion of Elizabeth's son but his political beliefs. Bruce Clayton, who had once been my favorite protégé, was an associate professor of philosophy at Columbia University in New York and now looked with disapproval on the capitalist practices of Wall Street.

I heard from Mildred the other day—she's hoping to come East this fall with the children but Wade always finds it so difficult to get away from his work at the hospital. Emily and Cornelius are both well, she said, and Cornelius' health is really much improved. . . .

Abandoning the letter again, I scribbled on my memo pad: "Must do something about Mildred's boy." It was a remark I had been scribbling on memo pads ever since my mother had once reminded me that Cornelius, as my only male heir, deserved a little more from me than absent-minded indifference. In truth I was anxious to do something for Cornelius, for I regarded his mother more as a sister than as a niece, but I led a busy life in New York, Cornelius was far away in Ohio, and distance can dampen even the best intentions.

Sylvia continued by replying to points raised by my previous letter and adding that she hoped I would be able to return home soon. "All my love, darling—I miss you very much. . . ."

I crumpled up the letter, smoothed it again, ran my fingers distractedly through my hair and finally found a new bottle of ink. Then I tore up what I had written and wrote pleasantly on a fresh sheet of paper:

My dearest Sylvia,

I was so very sorry to hear of your disappointment and your stay in the hospital. Knowing how much you've always wanted a child, I'm deeply distressed for your sake that yet another attempt at a successful pregnancy has ended in miscarriage. I must now beg you not only for your own sake but for mine as well to take the advice your doctor gave you long before you married me and make no further effort to have children. I assure you I would rather die childless than die knowing I had brought you further suffering and perhaps even premature death, but I'll say no more on this painful subject since my views are well known to you.

My business is progressing satisfactorily at Milk Street, and I now hear by cable from New York that Hal Beecher has agreed to replace me in London. This was my suggestion, and I'm glad it's finally been adopted. Hal has little European experience, but he's a gentleman and I doubt if the English will find him offensive. Certainly he could hardly do worse than our previous resident partner in London.

Because of Hal's inexperience I shall have to stay an extra month after his arrival to ensure that he knows what he's doing, so I greatly fear I shall be unable to be in New York for our anniversary. However, at the present rate of progress I should definitely be home by the end of July.

Postwar London continues to depress me, and my loathing of postwar feminine fashions has reached new heights. I warn you that if ever you bob your hair I shall divorce you on the spot! Fortunately I managed to get away from London this weekend and had a pleasant three days in Norfolk, not the part where the Wetherton-ffrenches live but farther north by the sea above Great Yarmouth. It was beautiful there and very peaceful.

Give my love to Elizabeth and tell her I'll write soon. If she's afraid I might find Bruce embarrassing tell her not to be so silly. I believe in freedom of speech even if he doesn't. Incidentally, what happened to that girl he was supposed to be getting engaged to?

If Mildred's husband can't find the time to come East this fall she should come without him. The man's a bore and why Mildred married him I can't think. My favorite theory is that the tough little farmer she married the first time turned out to be rather more than she bargained for and she decided to play safe the second time around. I'm glad Cornelius' health continues to improve. I must do something about that boy, but what on earth does one do with a silent fourteen-year-old who looks as if the faintest puff of wind would blow him away? My father would no doubt have put a racquet in his hand and hounded him onto the tennis court, so maybe I should follow suit. How history does repeat itself!

Take the very best care of yourself, my dear, until we meet again.

My love as always,

PAUL

I read the letter carefully. I knew the first paragraph sounded cold, but I knew too there was nothing I could do to amend it. I read on. The entire letter seemed to reek of emotional detachment, as if I had been determined to reflect the exact opposite of my feelings. I nearly tore the letter up again, but then telling myself I was imagining the letter to be worse than it was, I stuffed the pages into an envelope and sealed it. I was still troubled by the inadequacy of my response but I was unable to face writing the letter a third time.

I went to bed and dreamed of playing tennis at Newport with Jason Da Costa.

"Fifteen–forty," he called, and suddenly beyond him I could see the sinister disturbances flickering at the far end of my vision while that nightmare elevator, all the more terrifying because it was hallucinatory, was carrying me up and up and up—

"Get out, Elizabeth! Get out, get out, *get out!*" I was in my office thirty years later, but Elizabeth had disappeared and Jason Da Costa was a grinning skeleton sitting in the client's chair.

"All you that do this place pass bye, remember death for you must dye . . ." I was alone in Norwich Cathedral and the Devil was breathing down my neck. I ran up and down the nave but there were no doors. I was walled up alive.

"Dinah!" I shouted. "*Dinah!*"

I awoke. It was dawn. I lay awake for a long time watching the room fill with a pale cold light, and then I began to count the days until I could return to Mallingham.

III

The visit to Paris was a success. I hired a private car on the train which left Victoria on Friday, and when we arrived in Paris the best suite was waiting for us at the Georges Cinq. Visits to the couturier occupied some pleasantly idle hours, but soon we became bored with clothes and set off to the Louvre. Since Dinah had never before been to France, visits to Versailles and Chartres also seemed *de rigueur*, so I borrowed a car and a chauffeur from a banking friend of mine whose American firm had a French office, and on the Sunday we motored into the pastoral country beyond the city. I shall always remember the picnic we had on the way to Chartres. In a grassy field we lounged in Roman style before our repast, and afterward Dinah offered my half-finished champagne to a nearby cow.

When we arrived back in London on Monday she stayed the night with me at Curzon Street so that the next day I could take her to Lincoln's Inn; I intended to instruct my solicitors to form her company, patent her potions and open formal negotiations with Hurst, Rigby and Ashton for the purchase of Mallingham. O'Reilly had received a valuation from a Norwich realtor, and I was thus in a position to bargain for the house on the best possible terms.

In the circumstances it was a surprise when at dinner that evening we had what the English so euphemistically describe as "words."

"I'll tell you what I intend to do about Mallingham," I said after declining my butler's offer of port and dismissing the servants. "I'm going to loan you the purchase price—and the loan will come out of my private account; it'll have nothing to do with the bank per se—and then we can have the house conveyed to you and not to me. I'll keep the deeds as security and you can pay me back with three percent interest over a period of ten years. That won't be difficult for you, because you're going to make a lot of money. Now about the business—"

"But I want *you* to have Mallingham," said Dinah. "I want it to be yours until I can buy it from you outright."

I thought for one greedy moment of being the master of Mallingham, but guessing her plans I made myself put all greediness aside. "That sounds extremely unbusinesslike to me," I said firmly. "Apart from any other consideration I lose my three percent interest, and anyway what's to stop me from turning around and selling the property to someone else?"

"Well, naturally we'd have a gentleman's agreement—"

"Don't make a gentleman's agreement with me, my dear. You'd regret it in no time at all."

"But Paul, I want you to have Mallingham for a while—"

"Yes," I said, "and don't think I can't guess why. You want a guarantee that I'll always come back here. You don't want me to marry you, but you want me to marry Mallingham instead. I'm sorry, Dinah, but I don't like shackles and I detest the idea of Mallingham being used as a ball and chain."

She went bright red. At first I thought she was furious, but a second later I realized she was hurt. Her eyes shone with tears.

"You don't understand," she said. "It's a matter of pride. I want to give you something, and Mallingham is all I have. If you could accept it as a gift—even a temporary gift—I wouldn't feel so like a kept woman, taking your money and sleeping with you in return. How do you think I felt when we ordered those clothes in Paris?"

"But—"

"Oh God, I'm not going to force Mallingham on you if you don't want it! I wish I'd never made the offer!"

I felt ashamed of myself for being so insensitive. "I want it," I said abruptly. "Make no mistake about that." I thought for a moment. At last I said, "No unbusinesslike agreements in writing. The only people they ever benefit are the lawyers. We'll have to have a gentleman's agreement after all, but I warn you, you're playing with fire. I'll do my best to behave like a gentleman, but the trouble with that sort of agreement is that it never allows for any contingencies. Now think carefully. Are you quite sure, absolutely certain, that you want to make me this very generous offer which I'd be only too pleased to accept?"

She smiled at me. "I'm certain."

"Very well. Then I'll buy Mallingham for myself on this private oral understanding with you that you may purchase it at any time at the current market price as established by an independent appraiser. I also undertake not to sell it to anyone else and not to ask for any interest."

"But I thought you said—"

"My dear, either we have a business agreement or we don't. There are no half measures. As far as I'm concerned we now merely have an understanding based on mutual affection, and as far as you're concerned it's the only such understanding you'll ever have with me. Diana Slade Cosmetics is going to be run on strictly professional lines. As soon as I get to New York I'll send out a business manager to give you the best possible start, and perhaps by the new year— Is anything wrong?"

This time there was no mistaking her fury. "This is *my* business!" she burst out. "I refuse to be a mere puppet with a bunch of American businessmen pulling the strings!"

During our previous quarrel over the packaging designs I had felt more entertained than angered by her refusal to acknowledge her ignorance of the world of commerce, but on this occasion I found I was no longer amused. I suspect this was because I was now taking her schemes much more seriously, but I was also annoyed because her arrogance led me to suppose she thought that our intimacy permitted her all manner of infantile behavior in our business relationship. Regretfully I realized I had no choice but to put her very firmly in her place.

"That may not be what you want," I said so sharply that she

jumped, "but that's all that I, as the senior partner of Da Costa, Van Zale and Company of New York and London, am prepared to offer you. If you don't like it, take a walk down Lombard Street and see if any other firm of merchant bankers—or commercial bankers—is prepared to assist a young girl with no money, no experience and no apparent awareness of how exceedingly fortunate she's been so far!"

"Well, I think a banker should at least listen to the wishes of his clients!" she retorted, still defiant, but I heard the uncertainty in her voice and I knew I had shaken her.

I pressed on inexorably, determined to ensure there should be no future misunderstanding of our business relationship. "Dinah," I said, "my business as a banker is not in listening with paternal charity to little orphaned girls in distress. My business lies in raising and channeling capital, not in dabbling in the kind of petty financial aid you require. Have you any idea what I do at Milk Street? No? I thought not. Perhaps I should explain to you so that you can see your affairs in perspective instead of assuming you're my most important client."

"Well, naturally I don't think . . ."

I held up my hand and when she was silent I said rapidly, "I'm a middleman in the financial structure, and in London they refer to my bank as an issuing house. My job is to provide facilities through which savings are directed into long-term investment—a job which serves both the users and the suppliers of capital. Let me give you an example. If I hadn't met you, my interest in the potential of the cosmetics industry would have been aroused only if one of the country's leading industrialists—perhaps Sir Walter Malchin—had come to me and said he was expanding into the cosmetics field and needed extra capital to finance his expansion. I would have examined his industrial structure, investigated the market potential of his proposed products, calculated the risk and evolved the best way of getting him his money—*if* I decided to help him. To raise the capital I would then have to work out the number of securities to issue, when and how to market them, and what kind of securities they ought to be. After that, being in England, I would have insured the issue and distributed it to the brokers for sale to the public. The procedure is different in America, where syndicates are prevalent and the wholesale and retail distribution of securities takes place on a much vaster scale. Now let's go back to you. You're no Sir Walter Malchin. I couldn't possibly issue securities for a paltry little company of no standing. Such money as I provide will in effect be money out of my own pocket, and the only reason I'm involving the bank at all is that you'll have additional status in the commercial world if you can call yourself a client at Six Milk Street. Am I making myself clear? Good.

Now perhaps you can understand why I feel not only that your criticism is impertinent but that I'm entitled to call the tune."

"And I feel that your attitude is unspeakably arrogant!" bawled Dinah, almost in tears at being put in her place so brutally. "And your patronizing contempt not only short-sighted but self-defeating! How dare you talk to me like that! You'd never dare if I were a man!"

It was no use. I could sustain my stern expression no longer. "Is this a prelude to some delightful suffragette panegyric?" I inquired with a smile, but if I thought I was pouring oil on troubled waters I was gravely mistaken.

"And how dare you call me a suffragette!" blazed Dinah, tears forgotten as she gave vent to a rage that seemed entirely out of proportion to my mild remark. "I'm no certifiable political fanatic! I'm a woman who has to work for a living, and I think I should be treated with respect and not regarded patronizingly as a second-rate citizen of the world!"

"I'm perfectly willing to give you my total respect," I said equably, "but you must earn it. It's no good throwing scenes just because I threaten you with an American business manager. While you behave like a child I shall treat you as a child, and I would do so whatever sex you happened to be, male, female or hermaphrodite. Now grow up, wise up and shut up. Shall we go to bed?"

There was a hideous silence. I was just thinking in despair that she would burst into tears and keep us both up all night when she delighted me as usual by doing the unexpected. She giggled. "I do so love American slang!" she said. "Perhaps an American business manager could teach me something after all."

"Allow me to continue your education until he arrives. . . ."

We went to bed. It was the best night we had ever had together. I fell asleep toying with the idea of taking the rest of the week off and motoring to Mallingham directly after our visit to Lincoln's Inn.

The next morning I had to admit that this idea was impossible, but I thought that after Hal Beecher arrived I might be able to escape more frequently from London. I could have a month of long weekends at Mallingham and still be back in New York by the end of July, or perhaps early August. The thought of New York in August made me shudder. August was one of the months we always spent at Bar Harbor, but how much pleasanter it would be to stay at Mallingham! Perhaps if I wrote to Sylvia and said I had decided to take my summer vacation in Europe . . . But then I would really have to ask her to join me. No, there was no alternative. I had to be home by the last week in July, review matters at Willow and Wall and retire as usual to Maine with my wife.

That weekend I returned to Mallingham.

I had to work all day on Saturday, but at seven o'clock I set off north along the Newmarket Road, and by midnight I was back in North Norfolk. I found the candles lit in the dining room, cold roast fowl and home-baked bread on the table, and Dinah, looking vaguely Dickensian in a long black gown, waiting to receive me.

"The champagne is chilling in Mallingham Broad," she said after we had kissed, and we went down to the boathouse to pull up the bottle. On an impulse I suggested a moonlight sail, but since the dinghy threatened to capsize when we made love we returned to the house to complete our reunion.

Later I brought her back to London with me and we went to the theater. We saw the outstanding event of the summer season, a revival of Pinero's *The Second Mrs. Tanqueray,* and discussed Gladys Cooper's performance *ad nauseam;* we saw a new Edna Best comedy, which I disliked; and we spent many happy hours wrangling over the significance of the works of George Bernard Shaw. Tiring at last of such light-weight intellectual activity, we turned to the season's sporting events. I took a thirty-guinea box at Royal Ascot and we saw the fabled horse Gold Myth win both the Gold Vase and the Gold Cup.

However, it was not until the end of June that Dinah's name appeared in the press, for the English gossip columns, few in number, purveyed only innocent items heavily swathed in discretion. We had motored down to Wimbledon where the lawn tennis championships were due to begin on the New Ground, and although rain fell almost continuously the Ground was opened at half-past three when the King himself graciously struck a gong three times in the royal box. Because of the presence of royalty I hardly expected anyone to notice us, but some enterprising journalist recognized me and asked O'Reilly for the name of the lady at my side. Knowing I was never averse to a quick mention in the press, O'Reilly disclosed Dinah's identity.

The next morning he gave me the *Daily Graphic's* report of the events at Wimbledon. Under the subheading "Famous People Among Spectators" it was stated that Mr. Paul C. Van Zale, the well-known American millionaire, had been present at the New Ground with Miss Dinah Slade.

I thought such a discreet little mention could hardly have given offense to anyone, but I had reckoned without the English horror of publicity.

"How vulgar!" exclaimed Dinah, dropping the paper with a shudder. "And dangerous too. Supposing our affair turns into a huge scandal and rebounds against us!"

"I can't think why it should. We conduct ourselves decently in public and behave before the servants. What more do the British expect of their aristocracy?"

The very next day young Geoffrey Hurst traveled from Norwich to London to answer my question.

IV

I was still more occupied at the office than I had anticipated. Hal Beecher had arrived from New York, and although I had at first regarded his arrival as my passport to greater leisure I soon discovered I was more thoroughly chained to the office than ever. Hal was a good fellow and more than willing to become a merchant banker in London instead of an investment banker in New York, but the terminology was not the only difference between the two jobs, and to put it kindly, it is not always easy to teach an old dog new tricks. I was in the middle of putting him through his paces on the morning after Dinah's debut in the *Daily Graphic* when Geoffrey Hurst arrived without an appointment and demanded an audience.

"I'm sure you won't want to see him, sir," said O'Reilly, "but since he's a friend of Miss Slade's I thought I should tell you he's here before I sent him away."

"As usual, O'Reilly, you did the right thing. Tell him to wait." By that time I was almost gasping to have a break from Hal. We had spent over an hour discussing the English laws on disclosure as outlined in the Companies (Consolidation) Act of 1908, and Hal was still marveling at the English taste for regulation. In America we can peddle securities more or less as we like so long as we maintain a vague respect for the loose "blue-sky" laws operating in certain states, but then in America the concept of the freedom of the individual is so inflated that even laws protecting its citizens from investing in fraudulent securities are regarded as infringements on the right of men to throw away their money as they choose.

"I'll see the boy now," I told O'Reilly five minutes later, after Hal had been dispatched with a cup of coffee to browse among the complex clauses of the act.

Geoffrey Hurst swept into the room with the air of a Crusader blazing into battle against the Saracen.

"Sit down, Mr. Hurst," I said, seeing at once how the land lay and not making the mistake of offering him a hand to shake. "I'm delighted to see you again—how kind of you to call! How is your father?"

"Very well, thank you, sir, but I didn't come here to discuss him. I came here to tell you—"

"May I offer you coffee? Or tea?"

"No, thank you, sir. I came here to tell you that your beastly rotten behavior has gone too far and that you have absolutely no right to drag Dinah with you into the columns of the gutter press!"

"I didn't know you read the gutter press, Mr. Hurst, and besides I suspect the *Daily Graphic* might well find such a description slanderous. However, I have no wish to quarrel with you."

"Well, I've every intention of quarreling with you!"

"Oh dear." I regarded him sympathetically. He was such a nice-looking boy and so well brought up. I wondered if he had known he was in love with Dinah before I arrived on the scene, but thought not. He had the anguished air of a man who has discovered a fundamental truth in life too late to do anything about it.

"You've taken advantage of Dinah, you've corrupted her . . ." The predictable tirade continued for some minutes while I listened patiently and allowed my glance to wander over the objects on my desk. I suddenly noticed that my calendar was set at the twenty-eighth, and with a jolt remembered that the twenty-ninth was my wedding anniversary. Seizing a pencil, I hastily scribbled "Cable Sylvia" on my memo pad.

"And how dare you attend to business matters while I'm talking to you!" yelled the boy in a towering rage, and jumping to his feet he tried to sweep the pad off the desk.

I shot out a hand, grabbed his wrist so tightly that he squealed, and shoved him back into his chair.

"Behave yourself, Mr. Hurst," I said shortly. "Your conduct is unbecoming in a gentleman."

Evidently I had selected the appropriate English phrase, for he lapsed at once into a stunned silence. As his shattered expression continued I said without any special emphasis, "Your quarrel is not with me but with Dinah. In my own way I'm trying to look after her. It may not be your way, but that doesn't mean I'm not well-intentioned. I wish to correct you on one detail: I did not seduce Dinah. She seduced me, very deliberately and with her eyes wide open, and if you look back at your personal memories of the incident with the hamper I think your natural honesty will force you to acknowledge I'm speaking the truth. Whether her private conduct is any of your business is not for me to say, although I strongly suspect it is not. You're not her brother or even her cousin, although perhaps you once had some private understanding with her that I know nothing about. If this is true I can only apologize, plead my ignorance and repeat that your quarrel is with her and not with me. If it's not true, then I believe I'm perfectly entitled to Dinah's affections if she chooses to bestow them on me."

"But Dinah doesn't know what she's doing! After all, she's only a girl—"

"Mr. Hurst, you may regard women as mental defectives. I don't. Dinah is twenty-one years old and she knows exactly what she's doing. If she were a man her decision to seek capital to start a business and save her home would be entirely commendable. If she were a man her decision to lose her virginity and embark on a love affair would also be regarded as natural—even healthy. Just because she's a woman should she be expected to give up her home, her potential career and her private life in order to fulfill some illogical masculine concept of how a woman should behave?"

He stared at me. By providing him with a novel idea I had at least succeeded in calming him down. Finally he said with a touching naïveté, "Do you mean you approve of emancipated women?"

"Good God, no, I'm a man! Why should I want to alter a world that suits us all so well?"

He did not hear the irony in my voice. "But you just said—"

"Didn't they teach you in law school to argue a case from both sides?"

He nodded, fascinated. "I always thought Dinah would turn out like her mother," he commented at last. "She always swore she wouldn't, but now I can see she has."

This was the first interesting remark he had made. "Dinah's mother was an emancipated woman?" I said quickly.

"Oh, didn't she tell you? She was a suffragette who got arrested and died in prison. Actually she died of tetanus—her throat was damaged during the forcible feeding and an infection set in."

"Mr. Hurst," I interrupted with my most hospitable smile, "may I offer you a little glass of madeira?"

He drank three glasses of madeira while I gently milked him of information. When I had gathered enough details to make O'Reilly's file on Dinah Slade bulge at the seams, I rose to my feet, smiled regretfully and said that I really did have to return to my work.

"So nice of you to stop by," I murmured, taking his hand and pressing it fondly. "Do give my warmest regards to your father, won't you?"

He said he would. I suspect he did not remember his rage until O'Reilly had escorted him from the building, and I wryly pictured him gnashing his young teeth all the way home to Norwich.

He was a nice boy, but he had a lot to learn.

V

"I'll shoot Geoffrey when I next see him," said Dinah.

"That would be not only tiresome but unoriginal. Why are you so ashamed of your mother? You needn't be ashamed of her with me! I always admired the suffragettes. Such ambition! And such an eye for publicity! They deserved to get what they wanted."

"I despise misplaced idealism! They would have got what they wanted sooner if they hadn't antagonized every man in sight. All this women's-emancipation nonsense makes me ill, it's so trivial. The real issue of the modern world is the struggle between socialism and capitalism, and it would make a lot more sense if women fought for a doctrine which declared that all people should be equal."

"But if you fight for a political doctrine, doesn't it help to have a vote?"

"Oh, you think you're so clever! I'm sorry, but I can't regard my mother as a heroine. I think she wasted her life and died a fool, and if I were religious I'd go down on my knees each night and pray that the same thing wouldn't happen to me. I refuse to discuss my mother, I refuse to discuss emancipation and I absolutely refuse to think it's heroic to throw away one's life without a damned good reason."

I saw at once that her mother's desertion, even though it had been involuntary, had had an effect from which she had still not recovered, and to deflect the conversation toward less painful subjects I said lightly, "Talking of heroic idealism, have you ever read Tennyson's poem 'The Revenge'?"

She was her old self again in a flash. "Paul," she said laughing, "if you mention that wretched Victorian doggerel-peddler to me one more time I shall scream! Yes, I believe I was forced to read it once at school. I detest poems glorifying war."

"Ah, but 'The Revenge' isn't really about war at all. It's about romance and idealism and all the other qualities which the War has made unfashionable. Read it sometime when you're so jaded you have nothing else to do but sneer at the world," I advised her good-humoredly, and remembering my earlier promise I bought her an anthology of Tennyson's poetry with the intention of giving it to her as a parting present. However, I was still not sure when I was going home. Realizing that I would have to stay longer with Hal than I had anticipated, I had written to Sylvia to tell her I would join her in Maine in mid-August but I was seriously thinking of staying in England until early September. A little yachting vacation on the Norfolk Broads was a very tempting prospect.

Meanwhile my weekends at Mallingham were becoming steadily longer, and on the twenty-ninth of July, the day I had originally planned to sail home, I was tacking across Horsey Mere with Dinah once again and thinking how infinitely preferable it was to be in a dinghy on the Norfolk Broads than in a liner on Southampton Water.

We concluded our traditional walk to the sea, took our traditional stroll along the beach and retreated to our traditional hollow. “What a rut we're sinking into!” I said to Dinah as I started to undress her.

I had not made love to her for several days for the usual reasons, and I had not made love to her in broad daylight for almost two weeks. Dinah had unexpectedly developed a preference for drawing the drapes when we retired to her room during the day, and on our previous visit to the sandhills a party of naturalists had inconveniently decided to conduct a bird-watching session within peeking distance of our favorite hollow.

“Remember those awful people on the beach last time?” said Dinah, pulling me close to her.

“Vividly. Aren't you going to take off any more clothes?”

“I'm cold.” She shivered unconvincingly and added as I tried to ignore the complaint, “No, honestly, Paul, I'm freezing! Do you think it's going to rain?”

“You've almost convinced me it's going to snow. Good God, look over there!”

She looked away obediently. I had unhooked her bodice and pulled it away even before she had time to yell in protest, but her yell of protest never came and neither did my next gesture of affection.

There was a long silence.

I looked at her breasts, saw the small but unmistakable changes and knew that our personal relationship was finished. I said abruptly, “You've lied to me, haven't you?” And as the tears streamed silently down her face, I felt myself slipping away from her down the treacherous slope into the past.

Chapter Six

I

"Papa!" cried Vicky. "I'm going to have a baby!"

I was in New York, at the brownstone where she had lived after her marriage.

"Well, Paul," said Dolly as the decades slid backward before my eyes. "It looks like I'm going to have a baby."

I was in my chambers at Oxford, and Dolly wore her parlormaid's uniform beneath her shabby coat. Dolly was blond and pert with an upturned nose which Vicky had not inherited and the violet eyes which Vicky had transformed with her vivacity.

I wanted to stay with Dolly but I could not, for I was sliding backward in time again until my mother said to my father at the house on Nineteenth Street, "Charlotte's having a baby. I suppose all we can do is pray it's not afflicted."

"God damn it, Edith!" shouted my poor father, his guilt making him much too sensitive. "I refuse to tolerate any further snide references from you to the family weakness!"

My father was a stupid man who possessed a certain basic measure of common sense. My mother was a clever woman who thought common sense was admirable but too often the hallmark of a pedestrian intellect. It was popularly supposed by everyone, themselves included, that they had a happy and successful marriage.

"Marriage," said my mother to me after my father's death when we were obliged to sort out his debts and pay off his mistresses, "should not be a single railroad track but a line permitting travel in both directions. Of course your father married me for my fortune—and why not? He needed money and he was not the sort of man who could ever have earned his living in a manner acceptable to someone of his class. But I hardly came away empty-handed from the altar! I got a handsome, charming, well-bred husband, and that's something every innocent girl longs for, especially a girl as plain as I was. Of course, I knew all about the other women, but what else could I have expected? Your father never opened a book and despised culture and he had to have some way of amusing himself in the evenings."

However, I was only fifteen years old when my father died, I had led a sheltered life, and I was deeply shocked. I had often been frightened of my father but I had hero-worshiped him devoutly and longed to be like him. It was many years before I could regard him as dispassionately as my mother did, and during the latter years of my adolescence I recoiled from the thought of his shoddy private life.

Meanwhile my mother had succeeded in her dearest wish and made a classical scholar of me. It was she who hired my tutors—the only stipulation my father ever made regarding my education was that I should be taught to read and write—and when no tutor succeeded in meeting her exacting requirements, she taught me herself, just as she had once taught my sister Charlotte. Charlotte was ten years my senior and good with children; she used to play with me endlessly when I was a toddler, and when she married at eighteen and went away I wept all night into my pillow. In my lonely childhood Charlotte had too often been my sole companion, and when I became an uncle at the age of nine I regret to say I regarded my niece Mildred with all the jealousy of an only child who wakes one morning to find himself obliged to share his parents with an objectionable new infant.

To ease the situation my mother suggested that Charlotte and I write to each other once a week in Greek. Constructing a suitable Greek epistolary style would, she thought, undoubtedly take my mind off my jealousy. Charlotte suggested more humanely that I visit her instead so that I could see she hadn't forgotten me, but my health was poor at the time and it was considered impossible for me to make the long journey from New York to Boston.

I was so disappointed by this decision and so frustrated by my life of absolute seclusion that my parents once more took me to the leading doctors, but all the doctors said there was no hope. The illness ran raggedly through the family, usually passing by the females and affecting two males in three. Few of those afflicted males survived childhood; the illness was severe in infancy and led to complications such as skull fractures which often resulted in death. The Van Zale males who survived infancy either were born healthy like my father or else were never mentioned, like my father's brother or the long-forgotten great-uncle who had spent his days in seclusion.

"I regret to say there is as yet no cure for this most distressing affliction," said the last doctor. "This is unfortunately a cross which the child must become resigned to bear."

My father drew himself up to his full height. I saw his splendidly luxuriant moustaches bristle with antagonism. "You may advocate resignation to my son, sir," he said with all the pigheaded stubbornness for which he was famous, "but I never shall." And turning to me with immense dignity he announced grandly, "I shall cure you, my boy."

Acting on the Victorian principle that a *mens sana* must inevitably repose in every *corpore sano*, he proceeded to devote every moment of his time during the next five years to transforming me into a healthy sportsman. I was dragooned into swimming pools, dragged on twenty-mile hikes and drummed onto the tennis court. My mother objected fiercely; I think it must nearly have terminated their marriage. Charlotte thought he would kill me. The doctors said he was a fool.

But I lived. I was transformed. He won.

How he achieved my transformation must always, I suppose, be a medical mystery, for exercise alone can hardly have been responsible for my improved health. Later I strongly suspected that an element of faith healing was involved. I believed without any doubt that my father could cure me, and combined with my childish faith was my passionate desire to live a normal life. However there was no denying that my health improved enormously, and when I was fourteen and had been well for over nine months my father decided that I could at last meet a contemporary from the outside world. When we retired to Newport that summer he immediately called on our neighbors the Da Costas and asked if the son of the house would join us one morning for tennis.

I was three years younger than Jason Da Costa, but my father had coached me so rigorously that I was already capable of winning a game against boys of seventeen. I would have been more than a match for Jay Da Costa if I had not suffered so acutely from nervousness in his presence, and when I found that his habitual manner was one of condescending arrogance I became obsessed with the fear that he already knew about my illness. My father assured me this was impossible; he had long since boldly informed the world that I suffered from asthma, and any servants who had found out the truth had always been dismissed before they could gossip. Yet my fears continued, and as I lost every match by an ever-widening margin my father's patience with my performance became increasingly threadbare, until at last he bawled out from the sidelines, "For God's sake, Paul, stop behaving like a namby-pamby little idiot!"

In misery I turned back to face Jason Da Costa, and there was my nightmare become reality, the eerie distortions at the far end of my vision.

Afterward I could remember their faces, both ash-white and strained. My father was rigid with tension but Jay was shivering like a dog, his arrogance smashed and his composure destroyed. My father made him promise he would never reveal what he had seen.

I thought I would die of the shame.

"And if you ever break that promise, Jason . . ."

"No, never, Mr. Van Zale, I swear it."

He went away. My father watched him go and wiped the sweat from his forehead. No one ever came to play tennis with me again, and the following year when my father died we had to sell the cottage at Newport.

Ironically that was my last relapse. After that incident with Jay I was well for over thirty years.

A year after my father died my mother decided I should have some masculine company, and as my health had been perfect for many months she took a risk and sent me to Newport to stay with the Clydes. Mrs. Lucius Clyde was her sister, and my cousins the Clyde boys were my own age. To Lucius Clyde himself, the senior partner in the investment banking house of Clyde, Da Costa, my mother awarded the dubious role of substitute father. The Clyde boys thought I was undersized and eccentric, while I thought they were boring illiterate morons. I hated my summer at Newport and I hated it even more when I was once more confronted with my cousins' best friend, Jason Da Costa.

Already Jay was becoming a legend. My cousins regarded him simply as "the best fellow around," my Uncle Lucius regaled me with tales of Jay's brilliance, and in the Da Costa home Jay was surrounded by doting sisters, a worshiping mother and a proud boastful father. By this time he was nineteen years old, handsome, self-assured, clever, perfect and insufferable.

"I kept my promise to your father, Paul," he said as soon as we were alone, "and you needn't be afraid I won't keep it now he's dead." But when he smiled that lazy arrogant smile I remembered so well I saw the cruelty glow in his eyes and knew he planned to eke as much enjoyment as possible out of my fear that he would break his word. He played the game skillfully, making me sweat on countless occasions with his hidden allusions and double entendres, but he never gave the game away. That would have destroyed his fun, and whenever he couldn't be bothered to make me sweat with fear he would regard me with a mixture of absent-minded pity and crushing contempt. I felt deformed in his presence, unspeakably humiliated, and when I returned to New York from Newport I felt that all I ever wanted to do in life was relieve this latter-day Jason of his intolerable golden fleece.

"Revenge," said my mother sternly, "is not Christian, Paul." But she never suggested I spend another summer with the Clydes, and the following year I went not to Newport but to Cape Cod, where my sister Charlotte had a summer retreat. It was there that I fell under the influence of my brother-in-law, an Episcopalian clergyman. No doubt my lingering revulsion with my father's morals coupled with my desire to escape from the harsh world which Jay's behavior represented to me had made me ripe for a religious conversion, and when I was eighteen I told my mother that I wanted to enter the church.

"How nice, dear," said my mother, magnificently suppressing her horror, "but if you're to be a clergyman I insist that you be a well-educated one. I shall ask your Uncle Lucius if he will be generous enough to send you to England so that you can take a degree at Oxford." Of course she knew that once I saw Oxford I would immediately fall in love with the academic life she had always planned for me.

I arrived at Oxford with my idealism and my virginity intact and within six months was deliriously in love with Dolly. We met by chance outside a sweetshop, where she was sobbing pathetically because she had lost the purse containing her week's wages, and since I was a chivalrous young man I offered her a handkerchief for her tears, a cup of tea for her nerves and half a crown to cheer her up. My sole intent was to play the Good Samaritan, not the Wicked Seducer, but when she seemed perfectly willing to be seduced I found I had underestimated my susceptibility to pretty girls. I was nineteen at the time.

I was twenty when she told me she was pregant, and my romantic idealism, despite my lapse from celibacy, was still in full bloom. It never occurred to me not to marry her. I knew, as only a well-brought-up Victorian young man could know, that if one did the right thing all one's troubles would eventually be resolved and besides, I was so infatuated with Dolly that I was quite prepared to give up all for love.

Lucius Clyde cut off my allowance immediately and ordered me home. I had no choice but to go. My mother existed modestly on the small annuity which was all that remained to her after the payment of my father's debts, and I had no money of my own.

When I arrived in New York with my pregnant wife my uncle summoned me not to his house but to his office downtown, and it was then that I first crossed the threshold of the mighty Renaissance-style building on the corner of Willow and Wall.

I saw the starry chandeliers and the high ceilings and the sumptuous furnishings of an exotic alien world, and I forgot the quiet quadrangles of Oxford and the cloistered peace of academic life. I looked down the great hall of the House of Clyde, Da Costa and felt the power shoot through my veins. I was enslaved. I was Saul on the road to Damascus—or De Quincey on his first visit to the opium den. I walked into Lucius Clyde's private chamber with every muscle taut with a sense of mission because for the first time in my life I had absolutely no doubt what I wanted, and what I wanted was to be king of that palace at Willow and Wall.

"You surprise me, young man," said my uncle sarcastically. "You always acted as if banking was far beneath you. However, you're not the fool your father was and if you're willing to soil those patrician hands of yours with a little hard work I daresay we can make something of you. I'll give you a position here—but on one condition. You must divorce your wife. Your marriage is a disaster. No man ever rose to prominence in an eminent Yankee banking house with a parlormaid for a wife, and the sooner you get rid of her the better."

The red rag had been waved to the bull, and the bull at once reacted with predictable madness. "No man tells *me* to divorce my wife!" I said proudly. "I'd give up the whole world rather than break the promises I made at my wedding!"

"Then welcome to penury, and good riddance!" cried Lucius Clyde, and summoning his assistant he said with contempt: "Throw this boy out, will you? Asinine juvenile histrionics are always so damnably tedious."

"I'll be back!" I shouted at him. "And when I come back I'll be sitting in your chair!"

I rushed from the room, ran the full length of the great hall, burst out into the street—and collided with Jason Da Costa. At twenty-four he had already been offered a junior partnership by my uncle, and his success was the talk of Wall Street.

"Why, it's the hero of the tennis court at Newport!" he drawled. "I thought you were loafing around Europe with your nose in a Latin textbook. Oh, no, I forgot—you married a parlormaid! A bit rash, wasn't it? But I suppose with your—shall we say background?—you never thought you'd be capable of fatherhood. May I offer you my congratulations?"

I lashed out at him. He laughed, sidestepping the blow, and ran lightly up the steps into the palace which would someday be his. I stared after him, and in the midst of all my rage and hatred my passing ambition took root within me and set me squarely on the bloody road to revenge.

II

I was penniless.

"But you're rich!" said Dolly frightened. "All Americans are rich, aren't they? You've got to be rich!"

That was when I knew that my money meant more to her than I

did. I had given up all for love only to find that the love was an illusion. So much for my romantic idealism.

I could not get a job. My Uncle Lucius was a vindictive man and he saw to it that not even a second-rank Yankee house would give me a position. My mother flatly refused to receive Dolly, and I was too proud to ask her for a financial aid she could not afford to give me. At last I became sufficiently desperate to venture down the one remaining avenue in the world of banking, but I was convinced before I started that I would be wasting my time.

I went to the Jews. I went to the great Jewish House of Kuhn, Loeb, who refused me outright, I went to Seligman Brothers, who were more polite but equally firm in their rejection, and finally I went to Reischman's.

Although I was unaware of it the patriarch of the house had a bone to pick with Lucius Clyde. Expecting to be summoned into the presence of some minor official, I found instead to my astonishment that I was being ushered into the chamber of the senior partner himself.

"Sit down, Mr. Van Zale," said Jacob Reischman, seventy-three years old and a legend in his time.

He had been born in Hamburg and had come with his three brothers to America when still little more than a boy. They had begun their careers as peddlers, then moved into letters of credit and foreign-exchange commissions. By the time I met him Jacob Reischman had one of the front-rank investment banking houses in New York, a mansion on Fifth Avenue and a complicated dynasty of sons, grandsons, nephews and great-nephews to carry on his illustrious name. His surviving brother was head of the largest merchant bank in Hamburg, and his name was as famous in Europe as it was in America.

"You seem a bright willing young man," said old Mr. Reischman sociably when we had talked for twenty minutes, "but there are a great many bright willing young men in my own family and in the families of my friends. First I must take care of my own, Mr. Van Zale."

"Mr. Reischman," I said, knowing my entire future depended on his employing me, "we may not both be Jews but we're both New Yorkers, and it's as a New Yorker that I come to you to seek my fortune. When you got off the boat from Hamburg all those years ago, was there no New Yorker, Jewish or gentile, who was willing to give you the chance you deserved?"

I watched the faraway memories flicker at the back of his rheumy old eyes, and I was just thinking I could bear the agony of suspense no longer when his face softened as he smiled.

All he said was, "Lucius Clyde has been a fool."

I went to work at Reischman's as an office boy at a salary of five dollars a week, and was the only gentile in the entire establishment. It was popularly supposed that old Mr. Reischman was sinking into his dotage. I was treated with politeness but with a certain intelligent curiosity, as if I were some strange animal acquired from the zoo and given the chance to become a household pet. The other office boys conducted interminable discussions in Yiddish in my presence, and from the way the word *goy* appeared with frequency I knew I was the subject of speculation and possibly scorn. Finally after befriending the senior grandson of the house, a highly educated worldly young man of my own age, I asked him if he would talk to me in Yiddish whenever we met.

"Good God!" exclaimed Young Jacob, much offended. "I don't speak that peasant patois! Who do you think I am? Some unwashed horror from the Lower East Side?"

I apologized hastily, but that night when I returned to our two-room apartment in a Lower East Side tenement I called on the tailor who lived next door and asked him to teach me Yiddish.

I picked it up quickly. I have a certain facility in languages and I already had a working knowledge of German. One morning six weeks later when the office boys were discussing me as usual I turned around and told them in Yiddish exactly what I thought of them.

The news spread all over Reischman's from the top of the house to the bottom in less than half an hour, and for the first time since I had been hired I was summoned to the senior partner's chamber.

"*Chutzpah!*" said old Mr. Reischman, who unlike his grandson had no embarrassment in recalling his humble family background. "I like that!" And my salary was raised by twenty-five cents a week.

It was unfortunate that I was not as successful at home as I was at the office.

Dolly hated living in poverty among the immigrants of the Lower East Side as much as I did, and she was bitterly homesick for England, just as I was bitterly homesick for that other New York uptown. Naturally I could not take her anywhere, and even if we had lived in an acceptable neighborhood we could not have afforded any social life. Pregnancy did not agree with her. I had to borrow money from my brother-in-law to pay the inevitable medical bills. I was cut off from my culture, cut off from my class, cut off from any comfort I had ever known.

The baby came. I had pawned my father's watch to engage a better doctor, but he never arrived and an old Russian woman who claimed to be a midwife was the only person I could find to help. When I could bear Dolly's screams no longer I walked down to the bank and worked through the night. On my return at dawn I found the baby alive, Dolly looking on the point of death and the old woman whining for five dollars.

"A lot of use *you* are!" cried Dolly when she had recovered consciousness. "Running away like that, leaving me in this dump with that old witch—it's a wonder I'm not in my grave! And what have I got to live for, anyway? Two rooms in a nasty dirty foreign city and a spineless husband who can hardly make a ha'penny a week!"

"One of these days—"

"Oh, don't give me that rubbish about getting rich," said Dolly, and she turned her face to the wall.

The baby was small, pale and noisy, but much to my surprise Dolly decided to love it. I had thought she would never love anything which had caused her so much trouble, but evidently I had been assigned the role of troublemaker while the baby had been exonerated from blame.

"And you're not going to choose some nasty American name for her!" announced Dolly. "My baby's going to have nothing but the best, so I'm calling her Victoria after the Queen."

I tried to summon some paternal feeling for the bundle in the shawl, but failed. The trouble was that I was quite unprepared for the baby's survival; I had convinced myself it would meet the same fate as my two brothers who had died in infancy before I was born, and my plans for the future had been built around the assumption that once we were again childless I would somehow borrow the money to send Dolly back to England and arrange for a divorce. For some extraordinary reason she was still the only woman I wanted to sleep with, but by this time I had realized I was being daily humiliated by living with a woman who despised me.

However the baby survived and by some miracle it was healthy. Every time I looked at it I would think how different my life would have been if it did not exist, but every time I looked at it I also knew that there was no longer an easy solution to my problems. I resented the baby's presence in my life, I resented Dolly's absorption in it, I resented the offensive odors which permeated our tiny apartment, the constant crying in the night, the disruption of all domestic peace and orderliness, but I was shackled by my guilt. I was responsible for that scrap of humanity, and I knew that if I sent it away on a ship to Europe I would be forever haunted by pictures of Dolly dying young, my child put into some sordid orphanage and later drifting into inevitable prostitution, debasement and an early death in a workhouse.

There was only one road which offered any hope for the future, so I took it. I worked myself to the bone at Reischman's, and when I finally achieved promotion I did not take my increase in salary home but invested it in the stock market.

Six months later we moved uptown to a better neighborhood, and in a flash Dolly was clinging to my arm and smiling up at me adoringly. She even had the nerve to say she had always known I would make money in the end.

I despised myself for starting to sleep with her again, but she was prettier than ever, I still found it impossible to look at anyone else and making love with my wife was the only pleasure I could afford. I did not trust her, I did not believe one word of her praise and adulation, I detested every vulgar detail of her shallow slipshod personality, but the physical pleasure she gave me was exquisite. I could no more have given it up than I could have refused my evening meal after a hard day at the office.

By the time Vicky was a year old Dolly found she was pregnant a second time. Again the pregnancy did not agree with her, but at least I was now able to engage better medical care and hire a colored girl to look after Vicky so that Dolly could rest as much as possible. I not only believed all would be well with the confinement; I also had no doubt that the baby would be as healthy as Vicky. Perhaps my father too had thought along similar lines after Charlotte was born.

The baby arrived with difficulty and lived three days during which his small body was repeatedly racked with suffering. It was impossible not to feel thankful for his sake when he died. Dolly herself died a week later of kidney failure.

Either one of the tragedies would have rendered me distraught. The two together merely made me numb, aware of little except a vague distress. Vicky was taken away to the New England village where my mother had moved earlier to be nearer Charlotte in Boston. Not one member of my family came to the funerals, though my sister sent a note of sympathy. Not one of my former acquaintances among the aristocracy of the Eastern Seaboard acknowledged my loss. But old Mr. Reischman gave me paid leave from the office, and all my Jewish friends sent flowers, and Young Jacob took me to the cemetery in his own victoria, stood beside me throughout the Episcopalian service at the graveside and even bought me dinner at his favorite chophouse before he drove me home.

Eventually I moved farther uptown and began to live the luxury of a life without ties. I was just congratulating myself on withstanding my losses with the appropriate courage when the shock slammed into me with all the force of a runaway train hitting the platform buffers, and my distress burgeoned into full-scale grief. I could not eat. I could hardly drag myself to work. I had a childish longing to rush to Boston and seek emotional sustenance from my family, but I found I was incapable of performing the simple steps necessary to make the journey. Besides, when I considered the idea more carefully I found I now resented my family more intensely for having refused to receive Dolly. I certainly wanted a reconciliation, but my pride dictated that the first move must come from them.

Meanwhile I decided that I had to overcome my emotional decline unaided, but as anyone who has ever been bereaved knows this was easier resolved than achieved. My worst problem was the guilt which kept sweeping over me; I could not rid myself of the notion that I had led Dolly to her death, and with morbid determination my mind fastened on this hypothesis because I could not endure to think instead of the newborn infant suffering from the disease I myself had transmitted to him.

Finally I found myself unable to bear my misery any longer, and in a paroxysm of grief and guilt I poured out my heart to my current mistress, who happened by a great stroke of fortune to be Elizabeth.

I had not known her long enough to realize she was clever as well as beautiful. We had made love only once and it had not been an unqualified success—she was barely twenty-one, very well-bred and painfully virtuous—but there was an element in her personality which attracted me. I felt comfortable with her. At first I thought this was merely because I appreciated a refined woman after my years with Dolly, but later I realized that I felt so pleasantly at ease because Elizabeth reminded me of the women of my own family.

She had been married for two years to a wealthy leisured gentleman much older than she was who obligingly left her alone in New York while he went on hunting expeditions to the Adirondacks. Since she always spoke of him with affection, I presumed the marriage was not unsuccessful. They had no children, but that was probably because he had so far been too busy chasing bears to concentrate seriously on perpetuating the family name.

". . . so I killed Dolly," I concluded with morbid passion at the end of a muddled monologue.

"No, Paul," said Elizabeth seriously. "That is an arbitrary assumption which is not supported by logic. Kidney disease killed Dolly. Perhaps she would have died of it whether or not she had had a child. Almost certainly she would have died of it if she had had the child while married to someone else. I realize that her death makes you feel guilty, but I don't think you feel guilty because you believe you killed her. I think you feel guilty because you're secretly glad you've been liberated from your marriage—you hate yourself for being glad, but you can't help it. And are you really grieving for Dolly? Are you sure you're not grieving for yourself? You sacrificed everything for her and yet now it must seem that it was all for nothing. No wonder you're upset! It must be intolerable for a man of your intelligence to realize you've made such foolish mistakes, and all in the name of romance, chivalry and idealism!"

"What outrageous things to say!" I cried, vowing never to go to bed with her again, but of course I did, for Elizabeth was the only woman who ever really understood me. I always went back to her, even after she bore her husband's child, even after I married Marietta and even after her husband died and she married Eliot Clayton. Probably I should have married her myself, but we were never both single at the same time, divorce was a messy business and I had already had enough mess in my private life to last me a lifetime. Besides, I had long since resolved that to marry for love could only prove fatal; I knew all about the fires of passion and how one choked to death afterward in the ashes.

"Passion is for liaisons," I said firmly to Elizabeth. "Marriage should be a business arrangement."

"My sentiments exactly," said Elizabeth, and indeed I believe that if I had ever proposed marriage to her she would have turned me down. Both the big-game hunter and her second husband, the Wall Street lawyer, were in their different ways dull steady fellows, and I think in her day-to-day life Elizabeth needed that dependable rock-like predictability which I could never have provided. I was her danger, her intellectual stimulation and her physical adventure; and often it must have seemed to her that a little of me went a very long way.

During the three years which followed Dolly's death I remained estranged from my family. Some months after the funeral my mother had invited me to Boston for Christmas but had spoiled her attempt at a reconciliation by making a snide remark about my apparent lack of interest in Vicky. I was not indifferent to my daughter, but I had been too absorbed in my work and my emotions to think much about her. I knew she was loved and cared for; I knew I did not have to worry about her, and that, as far as my twenty-three-year-old mind was concerned, was sufficient for the moment. Naturally I had resolved to pay more attention to her later when my life was better organized, and meanwhile I bitterly resented my mother's implied accusation that I was shirking my parental responsibilities. I sent a large wax doll to Boston for Vicky, but I myself spent Christmas in New York.

My mother was livid. It took a long time for my sister Charlotte to repair the damage caused by this acrimonious correspondence, but eventually, two days before my third Christmas as a widower, she managed to drag me to my mother's doorstep in Massachusetts.

I was sulky but Charlotte, who had made a special journey to New York, was ruthless. "It's an absolute disgrace, Paul, for you to treat your elderly widowed mother like this. . . . No, I don't care if it *is* all her fault! She's bringing up your child single-handed and you're in her debt. Now just you behave yourself and remember your manners! Don't you think it's time you said 'Thank you,' made allowances for Mama's advancing years and exercised a little Christian charity?"

Evidently it was. I sulked worse than ever, but Charlotte escorted me with the vigilance of a jailer and there was no escape. Late on a dark snowy afternoon we reached my mother's old white house in the little Colonial town ten miles from Boston, and even before we had stepped down from the carriage my mother was opening the door. Beyond her the hall was decked with holly, and as all my childhood memories came out to meet me I was grateful to Charlotte for forcing a truce.

"Well, Paul," said my mother, "have we finally buried the hatchet?"

"What hatchet?" I said, defiant to the last, and then hugged her so hard that I did not at first realize she was hugging me equally hard in return.

When I had finally kissed her on both cheeks I glanced past her and saw the child.

She was small and dainty, like a child in a painting by Velásquez. She had golden ringlets and huge violet eyes, and when she smiled her little face shone with happiness.

"I always knew you'd come someday!" she sang in a clear joyous voice, and running all the way across the hall she flung her little arms around my knees.

III

I gave her everything she wanted not only because I had to make amends for years of neglect but because she made sense of my disastrous time with Dolly. When I looked at her I no longer minded my lost years at Oxford, my lost opportunities with Lucius Clyde and my lost faith in the romantic ideals of my youth. I could only think to myself: I was right; it was worth it all. And in believing that, I found that Vicky had given me back a part of myself which I thought had been lost beyond recall. Naturally I could not then return, even if I had desired it, to the untarnished years of my adolescence for I was no longer the same man as the youth who had fallen in love with Dolly, but my idealism was born again in Vicky, and in loving her I found an expression for that part of my personality which had no place in the cynic's world of Wall Street.

I began my campaign to persuade my mother to return with Vicky to New York. The main obstacle was that I did not want to share a household with my mother, yet could not see how I could avoid my obligation to do so. It took six months of extreme diplomacy before I found out that my mother's views on the subject exactly coincided with mine.

"We would quarrel in no time, Paul," she said sensibly. "I can't pretend I approve of your working at Reischman's; I'm quite sure I would disapprove of most of your friends; and I strongly suspect I would succumb to the temptation to meddle in your private life. I do accept that you're a grown man and entitled to do as you please, and I firmly believe a mother shouldn't interfere in those circumstances, but I know it would be easier to practice what I preach if we didn't live beneath the same roof."

So when my mother returned to Manhattan to buy a little house on East Twenty-first Street I continued to live in my luxurious apartment in Murray Hill, and we remained good friends. I fear that the temptation to criticize me must have severely increased with the years, but my mother exercised an iron will and never breathed one adverse word to me on the subject of my private life until I told her I intended to marry Marietta.

Circumstances forced me to marry Marietta. I would have preferred to remain unmarried, and it was only when my status as a widower became a negotiable asset which it would have been suicidal to ignore that I reluctantly faced the journey to the altar.

The trouble began at Reischman's. Old Jacob had been in semi-retirement since his eightieth birthday, but it was not until he died five years later that his eldest son Max, a cold, ruthless and brilliant despot, seized the reins of power. Even my friend Young Jacob, who was Max's eldest son and most loyal admirer, trembled in his shoes. Within days of the funeral the great overhaul of Reischman's began, the purge was launched and the heads began to roll.

I knew at once I was doomed; Max Reischman had suffered too many social snubs and business slights from people of my kind to want to keep me. But I knew also that I had a strong bargaining position. I was thirty-two years old, loyal to Reischman's, trained by Reischman's and a lucrative source of income to Reischman's; having been promoted as far as I could go without becoming a partner, I did valuable work for the firm and had even brought them clients who might never otherwise have considered going to a Jewish house. Max Reischman might think me no more than a nuisance, but I was determined to show him I could also be a threat to his peace of mind.

I considered my other options but rejected them as unsatisfactory. There was no doubt, for example, that I could now have obtained a job in any Yankee house except Clyde, Da Costa, but thirty-two was an awkward age to change houses, too young to enter a new house as a partner and too old to begin traditionally at the bottom. I would have had to spend years establishing my ability as a banker and my loyalty to my new house, and I might be forty before I achieved the prominence I had at Reischman's. Besides, I did not know how far my years at Reischman's would count against me when I was eventually considered for promotion. I knew I had had a superb training in a first-class house, but the Yankee houses would inevitably be suspicious. I could imagine the partners poking around in my pedigree for some hint of a Semitic name, and when they failed to find one they would assume that my inexplicable choice of house hinted at mental instability. Whichever way they regarded my past career, I lost.

I might have sought a position in another Jewish house, but my chances of a partnership would have been nonexistent. I might have founded my own firm if I had had the necessary capital, but I had always spent freely to recompense myself for past poverty, and as usual there was little money in the bank. However, I liked the idea of having my own firm, and after several sleepless nights of Machiavellian plotting I summoned all my courage and asked for an interview with Max Reischman.

I suggested to him that if he fired me it was in his own best interests to set me up in my own business, since although my clients might not follow me if I founded a new insignificant house, they would undoubtedly follow me from Reischman's to the House of Morgan, the House of Kidder, Peabody or the House of Lee, Higginson.

"Thank you, Mr. Van Zale," said Max Reischman without changing his expression. "I have noted your proposal and will give it due consideration."

I could almost feel the heat of his wrath as I walked to the door.

It took him a week to devise a solution which benefited us both. With a shudder I imagined him pacing his bedroom floor as I had paced mine, and when he sent for me my teeth almost chattered with fright.

"Sit down, Mr. Van Zale," said Max Reischman with his usual impassiveness. "I have been making inquiries on your behalf. Are you familiar with a small house called W. D. Chalmers and Company?"

Chalmers was a conservative little house which had run into prosperity three decades ago and had been declining ever since. The sole surviving partner, William Chalmers, was seventy, a Southerner, but not quite a Southern gentleman; it was rumored that he had made his fortune by profiteering in the Civil War and had never since ventured south of the Mason-Dixon Line for fear of assassination. He had a careful Yankee accent, parsimonious habits and a large house in Brooklyn.

"I've never met Chalmers," I said, "but I've heard of him."

"He's an expert on the cotton industry. I threw a little business his way the other day when someone from the garment district came to us about expansion. It was a small matter, too trivial for Reischman's, but these days Chalmers appreciates whatever he can get. He did a similar favor for my father once when the positions of our firms were reversed." He looked out the window as he allowed me time to digest this information. "Chalmers will take you as a full partner," he continued presently. "He admits he hates the thought of selling his business or merging with another firm, yet he has no sons to succeed him. The firm's ailing but it's basically sound. The old man's ailing too but he can give you what you want."

"I can't bring any money into the firm."

"He says he'll overlook that. I told him you were a brilliant young man who could bring his house back to the prestige it enjoyed thirty years ago, and he believed me."

"Thank you, Mr. Reischman."

"My pleasure, Mr. Van Zale."

He smiled. I smiled. We sat there disliking each other and then he said smoothly, "He's attracted to your name too, of course. For a *novus homo* like Chalmers a patrician name such as Van Zale has a certain irresistible charm."

There was another pause. I waited. At last with perfect timing Max Reischman added casually, "I believe he has a daughter," and all the cynicism of a sophisticated New Yorker was reflected for a second in his chilly blue eyes.

I did wonder if Miss Chalmers was either deformed or a mental defective, and was therefore most relieved to discover she was a vivacious young woman with a figure which would have put an hourglass to shame. I did wonder too why old Chalmers was so frantic to see her settled, but it was only after I was married that I realized he had probably been terrified she would destroy her reputation before she made a good match. Marietta may not have been a deformed imbecile, but she was certainly a promiscuous fool.

However, it took a couple of years for Marietta to become tiresome and meanwhile it seemed that matters had worked out well. Max Reischman had got rid of me without having to set me up in my own firm, and I now controlled a private banking business which, though not yet my own, would certainly be mine in the course of time. I already had a roster of clients. All I had to do was to transform the firm into the most successful second-rank house in town.

To be a second-rank house in New York was not necessarily to be second-rate, for plenty of second-rank houses had stalwart prosperous reputations. The difference between them and the front-rank houses which ruled investment banking lay most noticeably in their clients. Morgan's clients were the leading corporations of America and foreign governments, while Chalmers' clients were more likely to run mail-order businesses or a group of garment factories. However, a second-rank house could be influential, and often the big houses such as Morgan's would use a solid second-rank house as a partner in a deal too inconvenient for them to handle alone. If I could only build up my house's wilted reputation I knew it would be only a matter of time before I could at last cross swords with the House of Clyde, Da Costa at One Willow Street on the corner of Wall.

I worked hard and lived dangerously. I took on any business that came my way and hustled for new ventures with the verve of a flimflam man. I gambled on clients that other houses had turned down, I swung deals no one else would touch and I dived deep into debt as I lived like a millionaire to woo and impress the biggest clients in town. I had a large house off Madison, a brougham, a barouche and an imported 1904 Daimler Landaulette; I had innumerable servants, a gorgeous bejeweled wife, a yacht, a private railroad car and a cottage at Newport; I belonged to fourteen different clubs, gave enormous balls and lavish dinner parties, and made sure my name was constantly before my potential clients in the society columns of the New York newspapers. I dazzled New York, I horrified every banking house by my skill in evading the law that a private banker must not advertise, and I infuriated the snobs who wanted to call me shoddy but could not because of my ancient pedigree.

I also made a great deal of money.

By the time I was forty I was no longer a confidence man fooling New York by pretending I was already successful. I was a millionaire several times over, my creditors had all been paid and I had the sharpest, flashiest, richest second-rank house in New York. The firm was now called P. C. Van Zale and Company, my father-in-law was long since dead and Marietta was my ex-wife. My enemies had given up predicting I was riding for a fall and my friends were hailing me as a genius, but no one dreamed that my greatest ambition was still unfulfilled. In fact, I doubt if anyone thought I now had any ambition other than dressing like a dandy, living like a lord and sleeping with every society woman in town.

However, there was no denying my success, and everyone, even Jason Da Costa, now sought my company.

"Hello, Paul! We always seem to be bumping into each other these days, don't we? How are you?"

I can see him now as he was then, three years past forty but still in his prime. His thick glossy hair still waved in exactly the right places, his florid, arrogant, handsome face was still just as distinguished, and his brown eyes were just as cool, hooded and haughty. He had a trick of letting his eyelids droop lazily as he looked down his long Roman nose. Women found this mannerism irresistible, his opponents found it intimidating and I found it thoroughly ridiculous.

"Paul, there's something I've been wanting to say to you for a long time. I want to apologize for all that verbal hazing I gave you in the past. I'm afraid I was a spoiled insensitive young man and I'd like to think I now have more compassion and humanity. I've always been true to that promise I made to your father, you know. I swore it on my honor as a gentleman and I hope I'm gentleman enough to know that one should always be loyal to one's class."

Normally I would have found this pompous expression of the philosophy of the Eastern-Seaboard oligarchy at least worth a smile, but on this occasion all attempt at humor was impossible. After a pause I said, "I'm well now. I'm cured."

"Well, of course I realized . . ." He droned on for a minute or two about how he had never doubted it. Finally he said, "No hard feelings, Paul?"

"No hard feelings, Jay."

"Fine. I'm glad. Stay in touch, won't you, Paul," he said with his spurious charm and glided away from me among the other bankers at the reception like a big shark cruising among a host of smaller fry.

A month later after we had both participated in a Morgan syndicate, I offered him a place on a list of preferential clients who were certain to make a hundred percent profit if they bought securities in a railroad I was reorganizing. Two months later he returned the favor. Within six months he was inviting me to his house to discuss sharing the load of launching a new copper mine in Utah.

"How kind of you," I said. "Is my uncle involved in this?"

"Well, Mr. Clyde is semi-retired now, but yes, he's interested in this deal."

"Then I insist that you both walk down Willow Street to my office and allow me to be the host at the meeting. I called on Mr. Clyde once and he never returned the courtesy. I think he'll agree it's owing to me."

There was a pause while Jay summed up the situation and decided he had nothing to lose except a useful ally for the copper flotation.

"I'll talk to Mr. Clyde," he said.

My Uncle Lucius protested he had arthritis. I said the deal was off. Jay, much annoyed by my uncle's stubbornness, carted him into my office in a wheelchair.

"Uncle Lucius!" I exclaimed. "How nice!" And I clasped his hand with a warmth which chilled him.

"Suppose I ought to congratulate you, Paul," he muttered into his moustaches.

"Why, no, Uncle Lucius!" I said with my fondest smile. "You

have only yourself to congratulate. It was you who gave me my ambition to be a banker."

Uncle Lucius went purple but said nothing. Jay looked wary. I watched them serenely as sherry and pound cake were served, and reflected how fortuitous it was that my uncle was now a mere sleeping partner while Jay held the reins of power in the firm.

We began to discuss business. After ten minutes Uncle Lucius had recovered from his sulks, and after half an hour he was garrulous. Finally I held up my hand, silenced him and said casually to Jay, "Have that nurse wheel him out, would you? Senile behavior is really so damnably tedious and I think you'll agree that his presence here is quite immaterial to our discussions."

Jay never hesitated. Lucius Clyde was past history and I offered a lucrative future. Like all gifted bankers Jay knew when to cut his losses.

"I realize Paul's being unforgivably rude, Mr. Clyde," I heard him murmur to a sheet-white Uncle Lucius, "but I see little point in arguing with him. For the good of the firm . . ."

After the male nurse had removed the wheelchair Jay and I looked at each other in silence. I knew then that he had my measure, just as I had his, and in the dark sinister depths of the ocean which was Wall Street, shark saluted shark in the teeming bloodied waters.

The bizarrest part of all was that we were the perfect match. Once I thought that success had come early to Jay simply because he had had all the luck and the right connections, but now I saw for myself what I had long since come to suspect: that he was a man whose ability matched my own. Yet our talents differed greatly. Jay had the true financial brain, a skill in dealing with figures and a gift for developing complex mental abstractions which were awesome in their originality. My talent was for gambling, and I gambled with people. I was perfectly capable of working out a merger involving several million dollars, several types of securities, a selling syndicate of a hundred and fifty people, and the profit for all parties down to the last cent, but my success as a banker was primarily because I always knew which corporations should merge and which should not, which people should form the syndicate and which should be omitted, who should deal and who should stay on the sidelines. I knew how to get the most out of my staff too; I set the pace by working harder than anyone else, and I was always unstintingly generous to those who tried to work harder than I did. Jay, who also worked hard, kept himself aloof from his staff and as a result had less influence with them. Part of the trouble was that he had never had to work his way up through the ranks, but he was incurably snobbish and even looked down on Harvard men because they had not been to his beloved Yale. However, with his financial brain and my gambling streak we formed a formidable team.

I have no idea when he first suspected I wanted his palace at One Willow Street. Maybe he always knew but, thinking himself impregnable, enjoyed playing me along, using my talent for his own profit and my obsession for his own amusement. Or maybe he did not at first see the drift of my ambition but knew instinctively that although I made a splendid collaborator I would make a lethal bedfellow. His house was large, but if he ever let my firm merge with his he might awake one morning to find that his house had become too small to hold the two of us in comfort. It was so much wiser to keep me in my house at the other end of Willow Street, so much safer to hold me at arm's length no matter how often our names were joined together in business. Jay was no fool. He had my measure and he knew what was good for him.

I was no fool, either. Jay had something I wanted, but without a mutual exchange of assets I was stuck, and I was just thinking in despair that I would never achieve my ambition of sitting in Lucius Clyde's chair when the deck of cards in my gambler's hands was reshuffled and I saw I had a winning hand.

Vicky came back from Europe.

IV

"Good God!" said Jason Da Costa. "This can't be little Vicky!"

"Oh, Papa, Mr. Da Costa's so *handsome*. . . ."

They had not seen each other for several years, for Vicky had been living with my mother, whose social circle was far removed from my own. Also Jay had been overseas on business when Vicky had made her debut, and since his two sons were younger than she was he did not meet her through them. In the old days he would have seen her each summer at Newport, but since my divorce from Marietta I now retired to Bar Harbor each summer with my mother and daughter. In retrospect it seems odd that Jay had not seen Vicky since she was a child, but at the time it seemed unremarkable. I had not seen his boys for years either, and in fact failed to recognize them when they arrived at the huge ball I gave for Vicky to welcome her back to New York.

It was the late fall of 1912. I was forty-two and had been married to Sylvia for four months. Jay was forty-five and between marriages. Someone had told me that he had developed a fatal weakness for young girls, but I had forgotten; it had hardly seemed important at the time.

Vicky was twenty-one, and since her debut three years before her life had been conducted in the tradition of the most breathless romantic novel. She had fallen in and out of love at least a dozen times and had been pursued by a host of ardent admirers ranging from fortune hunters to rich rakes, from self-important idlers to humble clergymen and from sighing grandfathers to besotted youths. During these trying times I had almost expired with the torments of fatherhood, but eventually Vicky had become engaged to an admirable young man who had just graduated from Harvard Law School and was anxious to begin a career on Wall Street. However, no sooner had I heaved a sigh of relief than disaster had struck: the young man had become deranged over a forty-year-old actress, and the engagement had collapsed. As Vicky sank into a decline and I returned to the torments of fatherhood, my mother had exercised her practical streak with commendable speed and borne Vicky off to Europe immediately after my marriage to Sylvia.

Fortunately the young are very resilient. It took me much longer than Vicky to recover from her broken engagement, and presently my daughter was writing me ecstatic letters about the glories of the Italian lakes. If she had not spoiled her letters by saying she was seriously thinking of entering a convent I might have stopped worrying about her long before she returned, radiant as ever, to New York.

Within two weeks she had fallen in love with Jay, and Jay was mooning around Wall Street in a manner recalling the narrator of Tennyson's poem who had loitered yearningly around Locksley Hall.

My first instinct was to ship Vicky back to Europe. I was actually sitting down with my mother to plot the details of the conspiracy when my mother succumbed to snobbery and aroused all my most contrary instincts.

"For after all," she said, "who are the Da Costas? Everyone knows the first Da Costa was a Portuguese Jew."

It was a fatal error. If she had simply said "a Portuguese merchant" I would have taken no notice, for the first Da Costa had indeed fitted this description. He had reached America soon after the War of Independence, established a small trading post in Boston and prospered in the best American tradition. His descendants had been marrying tirelessly into the best Anglo-Saxon stock ever since and had been practicing Episcopalians for at least a hundred years.

"Jason Da Costa," I said to my mother, "is no more a Portuguese Jew than I'm a Dutch patroon. And even if he worshiped in a synagogue I would consider it a mark in his favor."

"Well, of course, I know you chose to work in a Jewish profession, but—"

"Mama," I said, very angry by this time, "the vast majority of bankers in this country are not Jewish. They're of British stock, Yankees just like you and me, and anyway it was a privilege, not a disgrace, to work in one of the finest investment banking houses in New York. . . ."

And so the well-worn argument continued, my mother insisting that she wished health, wealth and happiness to every Jew in the land—so long as they neither married her granddaughter nor crossed her threshold—and I retorting heatedly that the German Jewish aristocracy of New York did not care about her petty threshold and would have considered a marriage with a gentile to be a mésalliance. My mother and I both knew that the one subject we had to avoid was my loyalty to the Jews, and so when we made the mistake of dragging the subject up we were even more angry with ourselves than with each other.

Finally we both apologized, but the damage was done and I no longer wanted to engage my mother's help in saving Vicky from Jay.

Although my mother had picked a ridiculous objection to the match, there were several good reasons why I did not want Jay and Vicky to marry. The first was that Jay's reputation with women was second only to mine and I was sure his infatuation with her would never last. The second was that Vicky appeared to have fallen in love on the rebound, never a stable state of affairs. And the third was that my desire to have my revenge on Jay for past humiliations remained undiminished.

If he married my daughter I would have to forget, for Vicky's sake, the dreams of revenge which had sustained me when I had been working as an office boy for five dollars a week. On the other hand . . . I considered the other hand. I thought of that great palace at Willow and Wall, I dreamed of a mighty front-rank house called Van Zale's, I pictured myself sitting at last in Lucius Clyde's chair. Even if I had to forgo my revenge I could still satisfy my ambition.

I thought again of Vicky and Jay, and now as I thought of them my first feelings of revulsion toward the match faded away. I told myself sternly that I must be realistic and not indulge in some overemotional Victorian response. I had to draw a line between exercising reasonable care as a father and acting as if I were incapable of letting my daughter go, and to draw the line I had to face the facts. Vicky was obviously going to marry someone, and since she was past twenty it was equally obvious that she was going to marry soon. Since this was so, wouldn't it be better if she married a man of experience instead of some callow youth who hardly knew what he was doing? If she married Jay she would be marrying an eminent man, rich, handsome and brilliant in his field, who would look after her devotedly for two years and possibly three. It would be a good experience for Vicky, and when she emerged from the inevitable divorce she would have sufficient maturity to cope with the fortune hunters and find at last a man who was truly suited to her.

I began to look with increasing favor on the marriage, and although I could still have sent Vicky to Europe I did nothing. I stood by and watched as they became hopelessly entangled with each other, and when Jay approached me at last to seek permission to propose I gave him my blessing without hesitation and even offered him my hand to seal the deal.

V

They were very happy. Vicky seemed to dance through married life with such joy that her feet barely touched the ground, and Jay underwent one of those curious changes of personality which occasionally overtake middle-aged men who fall in love with youthful fervor. The shark had been transformed into a dolphin who did nothing but smile and frolic in the sunniest of waters. I got the merger on the exact terms I wanted, and in the October of 1913 I was sitting at last in my uncle's chair. He died shortly afterward. One of the last things he did was warn Jay against me and tell him he had made a terrible mistake in consenting to the merger.

"Funny old guy!" said Jay affectionately as he showed me the letter.

Frankly Jay was of little use at the bank at that time since his honeymoon mentality made it difficult for him to concentrate on such delights as the financing of a new stretch of tunnel for New York City's subway system, and it was a relief to me when eighteen months after the wedding he took Vicky for a protracted ramble through America. He was supposed to be doing business in a number of major cities, but I knew perfectly well this was just an excuse for a second honeymoon.

What I did not know was that Vicky was upset that she had been married eighteen months without conceiving a child and that the doctor had advised a change of scenery to solve the problem.

As soon as they returned from California Vicky called on me with her good news.

"You've told her the risk, of course," said my mother to me in private, and when she saw my expression she exclaimed, "Merciful heaven, doesn't she know?"

"I couldn't speak of it."

"Charlotte told Mildred!"

"And Mildred took no notice."

"It's just Mildred's good fortune that Emily and Cornelius are both healthy, although I do declare that when I heard Cornelius suffered from asthma . . . But Mildred assures me that that's not a euphemism for something worse."

"Vicky's always been healthy—it never seems to pass through the female."

"Sheer coincidence. The truth is, the Van Zales born over the past three generations have been predominantly males, and so naturally males have been predominantly affected. I've never been able to believe that this dreadful affliction discriminates between the sexes."

"Mama, I'm sorry but I can't tell Vicky. I can't talk about it. It's beyond me."

"Well, naturally you mustn't tell her now—you'd destroy her peace of mind for the next few months. But she should be told afterward, and if you can't tell her I shall. I'm surprised Jay hasn't said anything. He knows your circumstances, and— Dear God, Paul, what is it now?"

"I told Jay it wasn't hereditary."

"Oh, Paul—my dear . . ." She was incapable of reproaching me. She was the one person who knew exactly how much I had suffered in the past, and I knew in turn about that unique and underrated suffering visited on the parents of a chronically sick child.

"It's all over now," I said. "It's exorcized. It's finished. Charlotte's descendants are all healthy and mine will be healthy, too. I've been well without a single relapse for over thirty years."

"I know, dearest . . . a miracle . . . if you only knew how often I've gone down on my knees and thanked God—but there! I can see I'd better start getting down on my knees again and praying for Vicky. You'd better start, too. How long is it since you were in church, Paul?"

Drawing a temporary veil over my agnosticism, I accompanied my mother to church the following Sunday, but in the end our prayers came to nothing. Vicky lost the baby, and the miscarriage was so severe that the doctor recommended a year's delay before she embarked on a second pregnancy.

It seemed hardly the moment to inform Vicky about the family weakness, and my mother herself said she would wait before embarking on such a conversation.

"The whole episode of the miscarriage is Jay's fault from start to finish!" I exploded to Elizabeth. "He should have wiped the blood from his face after he was hit by that scrap of tile which fell from the roof. No wonder Vicky fainted with shock when he walked through the door! It would make any pregnant woman miscarry to see her husband walking around as if he were fresh from some French battlefield."

Elizabeth told me I should calm down before my anger upset Vicky, but Vicky was so upset already that she was barely aware how distraught I was. Jay was distraught too, and when I thought he was being ineffectual and he thought I was being interfering we exchanged sharp words. Finally he took more leave from the office and sailed away with Vicky on his yacht for a two-month winter cruise in the Caribbean.

When they returned and I saw Vicky was radiant again I felt so enormously relieved that I decided to forgive Jay for every ounce of his stupidity.

My forgiveness lasted less than five seconds.

"Wonderful news, Papa—a miracle! I'm going to have another baby right away!"

As soon as Jay and I were alone I said, "I thought the doctor advised—"

"Oh, we saw another doctor in Palm Beach," he said glibly, turning away from me a split second after I had seen the guilt in his eyes. "Vicky's fine."

I was so outraged that it took me several seconds before I could say, "She should have the pregnancy terminated."

"Nonsense. She's doing well and anyway she would never consent to it."

"But—"

"Paul," he said with the brutality I could remember from those faraway summers at Newport, "this is none of your goddamned business. You're not Vicky's husband."

"If I were," I said, "she wouldn't be pregnant now, I can assure you." Then I turned on my heel and left him.

It was the only honest conversation we ever had on the subject, and during the remainder of Vicky's pregnancy we never referred to it again.

She became unwell, always tired, always pale, always struggling with discomfort. I saw the gradual fading of her radiant vitality, and long afterward I remembered that spring and summer of 1916 when I called daily at Jason Da Costa's home and watched my daughter die.

The baby was born soon after noon in mid-September. Jay had not come to the office but had called to tell me the baby was on its way.

"You'll let me know as soon as—"

"Sure."

I heard nothing. Naturally I could not work, so telling my staff I was not to be disturbed I sat alone in the office to wait for the telephone call which never came.

At three o'clock my secretary announced that Elizabeth had come to see me. I remember thinking without emotion how extraordinarily understanding it was of Sylvia to send Elizabeth to break the news. I said politely that I would see her and she was ushered into my office.

She told me. My rage was so violent that I never noticed the sinister pain building behind my eyes, and I was still spewing out abuse when suddenly I looked past Elizabeth and saw the terrifying distortion at the far end of my vision. Comprehension burst upon me, but it was too late and there was nothing I could do. Thirty years of perfect health dissolved in far less than thirty seconds, and in those last few moments I was back once more among all the horrifying memories of my childhood and the roof of hell was grinding shut above my head.

Later I found that Elizabeth was holding me in her arms, and when I saw the pity in her eyes I knew I could never sleep with her again.

She took me home. I felt deaf, dumb and blind with pain, unable to perform even the simplest tasks.

At the funeral four days later I saw Jay for the first time since Vicky's death. The baby, who was later to die in infancy, was still alive so there was no double funeral. No doubt that was just as well. I had not expected to be shocked by Jay's appearance, but when I saw his eyes, bloodshot with drinking, and his hands, trembling whenever he unclenched his fists, even I was appalled. He cried throughout the service. He kept rubbing his knuckles against his eyes like a little boy, and his sons had to pass him a succession of handkerchiefs.

My eyes were dry. I had obtained some medication for my illness—there was a new drug called phenobarbital which had been produced in 1912—and I had drugged myself into a stupor. All I wanted to do was sleep.

After the funeral I shut myself in my home and refused to see anyone. No one thought this odd, since Vicky's death was certainly enough to send me into seclusion, and it was only my mother who guessed I was suffering from more than my bereavement. After a week she insisted on seeing me. She was an old woman by that time and had not long to live, but as usual her mind was sharp and clear.

"This isn't like you, Paul," she said. "You always turn to your work when you're upset and do a dozen things at once to take your mind off your troubles. Why are you shutting yourself up here as if you're afraid to go out?"

I told her. Caught between my grief and my shattered self-confidence, my drugged composure crumbled and I broke down.

My mother said three words: "Remember your father," and suddenly I heard him declare to the specialist as we were leaving the consulting room, "There's nothing wrong with this boy that a good game of tennis won't cure!" I knew then what I had to do.

I summoned my young partner Steven Sullivan. I trounced him in straight sets on the tennis court. Then scraping up a nerve I hardly knew I still possessed, I stopped cowering at home and walked the six miles downtown through the crowded streets to the bank.

I felt better after that. I even did a little work before my chauffeur drove me home, and the next day when Jay too returned to the office I felt strong enough to face him.

Our rooms were side by side on the ground floor at the back of the building. Originally there had been one enormous room like a double drawing room, but thick folding doors had been inserted into the archway by Lucius Clyde when he had become joint senior partner with Jay's father, and Jay had restored the doors when his firm had merged with mine.

When he heard me arrive that morning he knocked before slowly pushing back the doors and stepping into my half of the room.

"Sorry we couldn't talk at the funeral," he said, groping for words. "I guess we were both too upset."

"Yes."

He closed the doors and we were incarcerated with our suffocating grief and intolerable memories. My hand went instinctively to my pocket for my medication.

"Don't be too hard on me, Paul," he said in a low voice. "I realize you blame me, but—"

"No." I wanted only to terminate the interview and abort the tension which threatened me.

"—but oh God, I'll never get over this, never—"

I mentally gave him a year to recover. One cannot replace a daughter, but one can always replace a wife.

"Yet grief can draw two people together, can't it? I know we've never been truly close, but perhaps now . . ."

"Yes," I said. "Of course."

"I hope we can become better friends—for her sake. . . ." His mawkishness was unforgivable. He even thrust out his hand in a rush of emotion and I, seeing no alternative, took it in mine. The hand he offered was large and thick-fingered, the back of it dotted with black hair. As I pictured it resting on Vicky's white skin I wanted to vomit.

"No hard feelings, Paul?"

"No hard feelings, Jay," I said, and thought, I'll ruin you, I'll crucify you, I'll tear you apart until you wish you'd never set eyes on my daughter. . . .

He left the room, and finding the nearest basin I began to wash the hand he had held. I washed it over and over again, but by that time I hardly knew what I was doing, for I was back once more in my cherished past with Vicky and she was exclaiming with all her spell-binding radiance, "Wonderful news, Papa! I'm going to have a baby . . ."

Chapter Seven

I

"You're going to have a baby," I said to Dinah Slade.

As the past merged with the present the drawing room in New York dissolved into the sandhills above the Brograve Level, and the young woman with the violet eyes blurred into a plain girl with tear-stained cheeks. I rubbed my hand across my eyes as if I feared that the transition of time was an illusion, but it was real. I could hear the thudding of the waves on the dark sands, and when I looked up the gulls were wheeling in the clouded sky. A gust of wind made the grass flick like a lash against my arm. Shivering, I reached for my shirt.

"Don't be cross, Paul," wept the girl. "I'll never ask you for anything, I swear it. I know it's all my fault because I didn't tell you I was a virgin—"

I leaped to my feet. "Don't try to pretend this is the accidental result of one isolated occasion!"

"But Paul—"

"I've had enough of your lies! You've been lying to me at least once a month in order to pretend there was nothing wrong with you, and you've been lying to me by insisting you always used the device the doctor gave you to protect yourself. This was no accident! You planned this from the beginning because you're stupid enough to believe that by having an illegitimate child you'll have a guaranteed source of affection. My God, what a fool I've been!"

I grabbed my blazer and walked away from her down the dunes. Suddenly I became aware of the dull ache building behind my eyes, but when I stopped to search for my medication I could not find it. I panicked, then forced myself to remain calm. I must have dropped the phial in the hollow when I shed my jacket. Should I go back or should I go on and hope for the best? Fear swept over me. My glance raked the flat fields of the Level and saw nowhere to hide if I felt ill. I realized I was pacing up and down so I made myself stand still, but I continued to rub my eyes and the back of my neck with short sharp compulsive movements of my hand.

"Paul!"

I spun round. She was stumbling down the sandhills with my medication in her hand. "You dropped something—"

I grabbed the phial, swallowed three pills and rammed the phial into my blazer pocket.

"I have to be alone," I said. The pills took half an hour to work, and anything might happen while I waited. Also they were no guarantee against a recurrence of my illness; they merely lengthened the odds. "Wait for me by the mill, please."

"I'll wait here if you like."

"My God, can't you do as you're told?" I blazed, frightened to death by this time, and saw her flinch before she turned away.

Retreating to the sandhills, I flung myself down out of sight in the tall grass and immediately felt better. By the time my medication started to work I was wishing I had not taken such a heavy dose, for the tension had already left me and the pain had faded from behind my eyes.

I was so sleepy from the drug that I could hardly drag myself back to Horsey Mill, but I managed it and found Dinah waiting miserably by the staithe. We traveled back to Mallingham in silence, and on our arrival I went to bed and slept for three hours.

When I awoke I felt ill, but that was the aftermath of the pills. I drank some water, washed my face and decided I was capable of rational thought. After pausing long enough to marshal my well-worn arguments I went downstairs to confront her in the library.

She had sought escape from reality in a mystery novel. As she uncurled herself from the window seat she dropped the shawl she was clutching like a small child and regarded me fearfully.

"I apologize for my abrupt behavior," I said with as much civility as I could muster. "I realize I was very rude, but I had had a considerable shock. Now, my dear, let's try to discuss this news rationally without getting too upset. You do realize, of course, that it's quite impossible for you to have this child?"

Half an hour passed most unpleasantly. I spoke fluently, I employed a forensic skill which any leading trial lawyer might have envied, I deployed both low cunning and high intrigue, I flattered, pleaded, bullied and cajoled.

I got nowhere.

The trouble was, as I was slowly forced to admit, that Dinah did not react like a normal woman who found herself pregnant out of wedlock. It was no use stressing that a wedding ring would not be forthcoming, because Dinah had no interest in wedding rings. Neither was it any use stressing that my lawyers had more than enough muscle to kill an affiliation order stone dead with dire results for the mother's reputation; Dinah had no interest in legal action and said at once she had no intention of suing me. When I told her I could arrange an abortion with the maximum of secrecy, she merely looked at me in amazement and said, "No, thank you."

Wearily I turned to the moral arguments. She was having a child for all the wrong reasons. It was sheer selfishness to have a child out of wedlock. A child deserved two parents, not one.

"Better to have one loving parent than two who don't give a fig," said Dinah.

"What about the stigma of illegitimacy?"

"Oh Paul, how Victorian!"

I was suddenly very angry. "You just don't know what you're doing!" I exclaimed, jettisoning my role of calm, wise, supremely rational counsel. "You have no right to do this!"

"Oh yes I have!" she shot back at me. "It's my body and I can do what I like with it—I don't need anyone's permission to have a baby! Anyway, you always told me you'd refuse to accept responsibility for an illegitimate child, so why are you now trying to interfere? You forswore all your rights! Now leave me alone and stop trying to dictate to me!"

I was dumfounded. I felt like a knight who had ridden into battle with a shining new lance to meet an opponent who not only seized the precious lance but proceeded to add insult to injury by flagellating him with it. In shock I floundered around amidst half a dozen arguments, rejected them all and ended by staring at her in infuriated silence.

"This is the end of our affair," I said at last.

"I don't care!" she cried, but her lip trembled.

I saw my chance and took it. It was a dirty chance, like hitting a man below the belt, but by that time I was so desperate I could hardly afford to be chivalrous.

"It's also the end of our business relationship," I said shortly. "I don't accept pregnant women for clients."

She rushed up to me, her eyes glittering, her face crimson with rage, and before I realized what was happening she had slapped me hard on each cheek.

"You bastard!" she screamed at me. "You swore to me that whatever happened between us in private our business relationship would be unaffected! How dare you make such promises when you had no intention of keeping them!"

She rushed out of the room without giving me a chance to reply, but I dashed after her. My face was still tingling with the marks of her hands and I was conscious of the most extraordinary mixture of emotions jostling for front place in my mind. To say I felt confused would hardly begin to convey my rage, guilt, mortification, affronted pride, battered honesty and dire suspicion that she had been justified in hitting me.

We raced up to her bedroom. She tried to slam the door in my face, but I shoved my way in and caught her as she tripped and fell.

"Dinah—"

"You brute, get out of my house!"

"It's mine," I said. "Remember?"

"Oh, you—you—you—"

Words failed her. I started to make love to her on the threadbare Indian carpet.

"Paul, don't . . . please . . . I love you so much. . . . If you're going to go away, for God's sake go now and don't put me through any more—"

"No one's putting you through anything. You're setting out along the road to disaster all by yourself and it seems there's nothing I can do to stop you."

We made love. After we had crawled onto the bed to recover she said in a small voice, "Do you accept my decision, then?"

"No," I said. "I deplore it. But I'm beginning to accept the fact that I can't alter it."

"If you could give me just one good reason why I shouldn't have the baby . . ." Her voice trailed away.

There was a long silence. I realized this was my last chance, but all I could say was, "I've stated my reasons at length. My daughter—"

"It must have been terrible for you that she died in childbirth, but Paul, I don't have Vicky's medical history and I'm strong as an ox!"

I was silent. The seconds ticked by. We were very close, she lying on her side and propped up on her elbow, I sprawled against the pillows.

"What is it, Paul? Is there something else? Something you haven't told me?"

I thought of the pity in Elizabeth's eyes and felt cold. At last I said slowly, "When I married Sylvia I promised her that any child I had would be hers. I never promised her fidelity, but I did promise her that and I like to think that when I make a promise I keep it."

"But if she can't have children, doesn't that revoke your promise?"

"I don't want children."

"If that's true, why did you ever trust me to practice birth control when I told you frankly I saw nothing wrong in having an illegitimate child?"

Silence fell again. With shock I realized that my throat was aching with useless emotion, and I at once stood up and walked away.

I went down the passage to the bedroom where my valet and I both pretended I slept each night, and sat on the edge of the bed.

Later Dinah came to sit beside me and slip her arm through mine.

"You do want it, don't you, Paul?"

"I can't concede that," I said, not looking at her, "but I do concede that I'm fully responsible for what's happened. For my wife's sake I can't acknowledge the child officially, but if you wish I'll send you money for his support."

"There's no need for that if you support my efforts to start my business."

"You know I will. I'm sorry I threatened you like that; it was unworthy of me. As I've already said, I like to keep my promises."

She kissed me lightly on the cheek. "Promise me you'll come back to Mallingham, Paul. I know you'll have to return to New York eventually, but promise me that when you go you won't forget all about me."

"To forget would be a mental impossibility!"

We kissed with increasing passion for some minutes. At last I made myself say, "I'm glad you still realize that I'll someday have to go back to New York."

"Someday. Yes."

"I'll never leave my wife, Dinah."

"I accept that."

I immediately wanted to leave my wife and never return to New York again. After allowing myself a smile at the contrariness of human nature, I seriously wondered for the first time where my seductive journey sideways in time was leading me.

That night I lay awake considering my position. It seemed that I had two possible courses of action: either I could cut off the affair immediately and return to America before matters got any further out of hand or I could go on, indulging myself to the hilt on the assumption that any fiery love affair was bound to burn itself out within six months. On the whole I favored the second option. To leave now would be exceedingly painful for both of us and might even result in the prolongation of a relationship which would otherwise have died a natural death, but if I went on we would have our pleasure, achieve the appropriate degree of satiation and part peacefully, still the best of friends. I tried to estimate when we would reach the point of satiation. September? We would have known each other three months by that time, and I seldom wished to extend an affair longer than that. However, Dinah was an exceptional girl. I extended the affair till October. Apart from natural satiation the baby would be muting our relationship by that time, for she would be uninterested in intercourse and I would be uninterested in her figure. I have never been one of those men who find pregnant women irresistibly erotic.

The next morning I said to her, "I want to spend the rest of my stay in England at Mallingham. I'm going to turn Milk Street over lock, stock and barrel to Hal Beecher, cut myself off from society and take the long vacation I've been promising myself for years. Can you put up with me till the end of September?"

"Monster!" said Dinah, hugging me. "And to think that only yesterday I was wondering how I put up with you at all!"

"I suppose I should offer to take you on a grand tour of Greece and Italy, but—"

"Quite unnecessary," said Dinah happily, "I'd much rather stay at Mallingham and build my nest. Anyway the political situation in Greece looks awful. If the British Army is going to fight the Turks there I for one want to be as far from Greece as possible."

So it was settled. I instructed O'Reilly to get rid of the Curzon Street house, pay off Miss Phelps and sell the Rolls-Royce; I decided to keep the Lanchester Forty. Then after a final meeting with Hal at Milk Street I abandoned him to his fate and cabled New York to let them know I was going on vacation. I even sent a separate cable to Steve Sullivan to say no one was to communicate with me on any business matter unless there was a disaster equal to the financial panic of 1907.

After that all I had to do was write to my wife.

I tore up six drafts before I wrote:

My dearest Sylvia:

I have taken this sudden decision to have a long vacation in England because I believe it will ultimately be the best for both of us. I apologize in advance for the embarrassment my continuing absence will undoubtedly cause you, but must ask you to trust me to do what is right. I miss you and think of you often, but this vacation is something I have to do.

All my love,
Paul

I paused, fidgeting with my pen, and then added:

P.S. If anyone should ask you if I have permanently emigrated to England you can tell them I have given you my word that I shall return.

I looked down at my promise, resplendent in black and white. For one long moment I hesitated, but then I slipped the folded paper into an envelope, sealed the flap and sent the letter on its way across the ocean.

II

I remember the strong cool sunshine of an English August, and the fine soft English rain which cloaked the Broads in mist. I remember the light of long evenings and the windmill sails turning slowly against huge golden skies and the brown dots of cattle grazing on the windswept farmland. I remember the miles of lonely sandhills and the oak woods bleached by salt floods and the lost ancient churches drowsing in a wild forgotten landscape. I remember that summer of all summers, the parting of still waters beneath the prow of our yacht, the cry of the redshank, the boom of the bittern, the flash of trout in bright waters, the gleam of wild geese and the thunder of wild fowl on the wing. I remember rising at dawn and seeing the light changing on the dark meres and secret waterways, watching the movements of the bullrushes and reedmace, the swaying of the marsh grasses as the birds began to stir. And at night the mists would swirl up from the marshes and drift through the dikes and Dinah would talk of the eynds, the water ghosts of the far-off days when the mystery of that land had been unpenetrated for centuries by the outside world.

I remember the jostling crowds at Wroxham and Horning, the roar of the motorboats, the screams of the raucous vacationers, the soiled waters, the litter in the reeds. I remember going under the low bridge at Potter Heigham and having half the village yelling navigational advice. And I remember sailing through the throngs of small boats up Breydon Water to the modern sprawl of a town which had once been a quiet fishing village, Great Yarmouth by the sea.

But best of all I remember escaping from those parts of Broadland which the twentieth century had discovered. I remember the hidden private broads like Mallingham far from the blare of the phonographs and the offensive young flappers and lounge-lizards in their London clothes. I remember all the isolated splendor of the Brograve Level, and I remember the gleaming fastnesses of reed and swamp, the timelessness of undiscovered villages and the walled magnificence of Mallingham Hall.

"It'll be better still in October," Dinah said to me. "The holiday crowds go back to London and Birmingham, the pleasure cruisers are moored for the winter and Broadland goes back to the marshmen again. The eel nets are set across the rivers, and the long guns for duck shooting are taken down from their thongs on the farmhouse walls and the woodcock come down from Scandinavia and the wind starts to blow across the North Sea. Oh, and you should see the reed beds! The golds and the reds and the rusts—it's all so beautiful, so unmarked, so unspoiled, and when the wind starts to blow, the cattle gallop in exultation and the wild geese fly in from the coast at dusk and all the while the eels are running to the sea. . . ."

I stayed on into October.

At the beginning of August I had bought a twenty-two-foot yacht. It had a plain little cabin where we could sleep, cook and eat, and for the remainder of that magic summer we divided our time between relaxing at Mallingham and embarking on long unhurried expeditions by water to comb the Broads from end to end. Peterson worried about my safety and wanted with admirable loyalty but total lack of romantic imagination to follow us in a motorboat, but I refused to allow it. Dinah and I spent our voyages alone together and lived with a simplicity I had forgotten could exist, while my employees were left to vegetate at Mallingham Hall. I knew they were all miserable, but it was so impossible for me to share their homesickness for the city lights that I found it hard to sympathize with them. My valet Dawson tried to conceal his boredom as he tended my clothes with scrupulous care, Peterson read every novel Edgar Wallace had ever written, and O'Reilly, whose sole tasks were to telephone Milk Street once a day from Norwich and buy anything that I might require, amused himself by rereading the plays of Ibsen. Despite his Irish name O'Reilly was half Swedish and had long been drawn to Nordic literature.

Naturally all of them thought I was eccentric, but theirs, as Tennyson wrote of the Light Brigade, was not to reason why. I was indulgent with them, but although they were polite in return I occasionally caught their looks of despair whenever they thought my back was turned

I finally gave Dinah not only the Mallingham Hours (recently purchased at the inevitable sale) but also the volume of Tennyson which I had bought her as a farewell gift. However, since I had again canceled my passage to New York I was able to enjoy the task of selecting a dedication for the flyleaf. At first I thought I would quote a couple of romantic lines from *Oenone,* but then I remembered I had decided to buy her the book after we had discussed the idealism of *The Revenge.* Finding the poem, I read again about the heroism of Sir Richard Grenville, who with his little English ship "The Revenge" had fought fifty-three Spanish galleons singlehanded, and by the time I reached Sir Richard's final exhortation to his men I was awash with all the emotions which the War had made so unfashionable.

Seizing my pen, I found the lines which seemed to mark the highwater mark of the poem's romantic idealism and copied the words which Tennyson had put into Sir Richard's mouth:

"Sink me the ship, Master Gunner! Sink her—split her in twain!
Fall into the hands of God, not into the hands of Spain!"

I sighed with nostalgic pleasure, and having completed the couplet I wrote underneath: "From a realist who aspires to be a romantic to a romantic who aspires to be a realist—or should it be vice versa? In profoundly grateful memory of the summer of '22. Paul."

"Dreadful Victorian sentimentality!" said Dinah with a shudder, but she refused to be parted from the book. She even took it to bed with her and would read the most flesh-crawling episodes of *Maud* aloud to me by candlelight. "Tennyson will always remind me of you," she said when I managed to wrest the book from her hands.

I knew it upset her that I could never bring myself to refer to the child, so I made a special effort and said with a smile, "I give you full permission to call our daughter after Tennyson's most enigmatic *femme fatale!*"

"Maud?"

"Who else?"

"Supposing it's a boy!"

But I dared not think of that. The only way I could face thinking about the child was to imagine it as a little replica of Vicky, pink and white, flawlessly healthy.

"Paul, if it's a boy I want to call him Alan—after the first recorded owner of Mallingham, William the Conqueror's henchman, Alan of Richmond. Do you approve?"

I nodded. It was too hard to speak. Presently she herself changed the subject and I was able to close my mind against the memory of Vicky's infant brother suffering long ago in that second apartment I had shared with Dolly.

The days drifted past. Sometimes I thought they would go on drifting by indefinitely, but at last in early November we came back from a day's duck shooting to find that our world had been invaded and our peace destroyed.

We had moored the punt and left old Tom Stokeby the marshman to tend to the ducks and the guns. It was a gray day and the wind was blowing across the marshes from the sea. We were halfway across the lawn to the house when Dinah glanced up onto the terrace and stopped dead.

I stopped too, and following her glance I saw that O'Reilly had stepped out to meet us. Directly behind him was my partner in London Hal Beecher, and at once I saw the end of my cherished furrow in time. Taking Dinah's hand in mine, I walked on with her up to the terrace.

"Paul, do forgive me for intruding like this. Good afternoon, Miss Slade."

"Good afternoon, Mr. Beecher," said Dinah.

I said nothing. We all went inside.

Dinah said in a rush, "Perhaps some tea . . . I'll go and talk to Mrs. Oakes."

O'Reilly and Hal had a race to see who could open the door for her. Hal won. The door opened and closed. Dinah's footsteps retreated into the distance, and suddenly the stench of New York was so strong that I wanted to run after her.

"Yes?" I said politely to Hal.

There was an awkward pause before Hal said in a low voice, "It's Stewart and Greg Da Costa. I'm afraid Jay's boys are after your blood, Paul." And as I held out my hand without a word he gave me the cable which had arrived that morning from my partner Steven Sullivan in New York.

III

"We'll make you pay," young Gregory Da Costa had said to me at his father's funeral earlier that year.

I had not wanted to go to the funeral, but I had had no choice. It would have looked suspicious if I had stayed away, but no murderer could have felt more haunted by his crime than I had felt when I had stepped into the church that afternoon, and no retribution could have been more terrible to me than the specter of my shattered health. It was odd to think that Jay's death had taken me completely by surprise. It had made me realize how imperfectly I had known him. My one persistent thought throughout the funeral had been how greatly upset Vicky would have been if she had lived, but if Vicky had lived I would never have meddled in the affairs of Mr. Roberto Salzedo of the Mortgage Bank of the Andes.

It was after Vicky's death that Sylvia and I had spent our two years in Europe. I had felt unable to work alongside Jay any longer, and the War gave me the necessary excuse to take over the firm's affairs in London. Capital was badly needed in England, and our house was heavily involved in war loans.

I returned to America in 1919.

He had remarried by that time, of course—another young girl like Vicky, but not so pretty. He was cordial to me and I was cordial to him, but I found it hard to estimate the thoughts which were passing through his head and I doubt if he had any idea of the kind of thoughts which were passing through mine.

I was infinitely patient because I knew I could afford no mistakes. One cannot move against a man like Jason Da Costa without risking one's neck, and I did not want to erect the scaffold only to find the noose slipping over my own head.

It took me another two years to assemble my materials for the scaffold, but in 1921 I at last had the chance to start building it. Huge selling syndicates were then the fashion in investment banking, and the pace of business had increased to such an extent that large flotations would sometimes be launched and disposed of within twenty-four hours. The burden on the members of the originating syndicate was therefore much heavier, for since there was no time for the selling syndicate to inquire into the caliber of the flotation, they had to trust that the originating syndicate had made the proper investigations and that the securities offered for distribution were a sound investment. Naturally, all the front-rank houses could be expected to conduct proper investigations into their clients' affairs, but mistakes were inevitably made and in such cases the selling syndicates stood to lose face with their customers; no one likes to be confronted with an irate customer who has lost his money.

However, there was little that the selling syndicates could do to protect themselves. If they refused to be included in the next syndicate, the originating house would not offer them syndicate participation again and business would be lost. As a rule they chose to participate, but as their world became increasingly dangerous, so correspondingly did it become more vital for the investment banking houses which formed the originating syndicates to be of unimpeachable integrity. An investment banker had always lived by his reputation, but now more than ever before we found that too many errors or the merest whiff of fraud could finish a banker overnight.

In 1921 Da Costa, Van Zale and Company were principally engaged in pumping capital into Europe, but we also maintained some profitable South American business, and that spring I had a visit from Mr. Roberto Salzedo, a client I had helped twice before and was willing to help a third time if the circumstances merited it. Salzedo was one of those men who are so cosmopolitan that one never thinks of them as having any nationality at all; it came as a great surprise to me when I later discovered he was a secret but rabid nationalist of the hilly little republic where he had been born. He had been brought up in Argentina in a German section of Buenos Aires, had been educated expensively in Switzerland and had spent the past ten years living in New York in between frequent business sorties to South America. He looked vaguely Scandinavian and spoke excellent American English with an unidentifiable foreign accent. In any event he was an able man with considerable experience in international banking, and in those days when American banks were panting to jump on the bandwagon of foreign expansion, particularly in South America, men like Salzedo were highly prized by their employers.

Salzedo's employer was the Mortgage Bank of the Andes, a huge concern which seemed to have blossomed forth from nowhere and which in 1925 was to be wound up ignominiously, a victim of the overextension in foreign markets which was the natural consequence of so much mindless expansion. However, in 1921 it was at its zenith. It had been incorporated under the laws of the state of Connecticut in August of 1916 with an authorized capital of five million dollars, and had sixteen foreign offices scattered throughout South and Central America, and one domestic branch, in New York.

Salzedo, who operated out of New York, had responsibility for the South American branches, and on the two previous occasions on which we had done business together I had helped him set up branches in Lima and Valparaiso. The flotations had sold well; the American public was a little bored with Europe, and although South American investment always seemed to have a dubious flavor there was something reassuring about investing in a bank. When Salzedo came to see me to seek a loan for further expansion I could see no reason why I should refuse him, particularly since his new branch was to be in the hilly little republic where he had spent his early years. When expanding in foreign countries it always helps to have a native's-eye view of the terrain, and in fact if he had not received a certain telephone call as we were sitting in my office discussing the final terms I might never have discovered he had become so embroiled in local politics that he had every intention of embezzling my new loan in the cause of patriotism.

When he took the call his first words were, "Oh, it's you!" And then to my extreme surprise he began to speak not in Spanish, which I as a North American might well have understood, but in Yiddish. Of course he had no idea I had trained in a Jewish house.

Many words have been wasted in speculating whether Salzedo was Jewish, but the question is really irrelevant. Salzedo claimed that he was not, that he and his brother had merely picked up the dialect in the German section of Buenos Aires, and personally I saw no reason to disbelieve him. I doubted if I were the only gentile in the world with a working knowledge of Yiddish. Anyway, Jewish or not, he must have considered himself a patriot who was not working for his personal gain, and I am sure there are many people in South America who still regard him as a hero and not, as the American public later judged him, a villain of the first degree.

What he said in Yiddish was innocuous. He simply criticized his brother fiercely for interrupting him at a critical point in the meeting and swore that everything was going according to plan. If he had spoken in English or in Spanish I would hardly have thought twice about the conversation, but the fact that he spoke a language he was sure I could not understand aroused my suspicions immediately. Alternatively if he had merely explained afterward that he was Jewish I would also have accepted his choice of language as natural, but Salzedo had to deny he was Jewish, and so in alarm I reopened my investigations not only into his South American banking operations but also into his private life.

Putting O'Reilly to work in the strictest secrecy I discovered that

Salzedo had committed himself to financing a revolution with the loan which I was willing to grant to his bank in the form of a six-and-a-half-percent gold bond issue. O'Reilly, always miraculously adept at digging up dirt, had excelled himself. I gave him a bonus to express my admiration, doubled it to ensure he kept his mouth shut, and sat back to decide what to do next.

I had no illusions about the dangers of the course I wanted to take, and for one long moment I hesitated on the brink. It was only when I remembered Vicky that I no longer cared how great the risks were.

It was the gamble of my gambler's life. I staked my entire career, my immense reputation and the future of my house to gamble for the ruin of Jason Da Costa.

"I'm afraid I won't be able to manage the final details of the loan myself," I told Salzedo. "I'm going out of town next week, but my partner Jason Da Costa will complete the arrangements with you."

Later Jay asked me as a matter of routine about the investigation. "Everything's fine," I said. "I'll send you all the reports."

But I did not. I kept back the secret file from O'Reilly about Salzedo's political activities and submitted only the Mortgage Bank of the Andes' spectacular South American balance sheets and Salzedo's enthusiastic scheme for expansion in a hilly little republic which had had the same stable dictatorship for twenty years. Then with the fatal die cast I crossed my Rubicon and took Sylvia on a vacation to Bermuda.

At One Willow Street Jay signed the purchase contract with Salzedo and granted a participation on the original terms to Reischman's. On the same day they started organizing a banking syndicate, and while this was being arranged letters were sent to numerous dealers to ask them to join a selling syndicate. Within twenty-four hours after the original syndicate had bought the bonds the one organized to sell had disposed of the issue.

Salzedo pocketed the money, abandoned the New York branch of his bank and returned in triumph to his revolutionary friends in South America to overthrow the government, but unfortunately for him people other than myself had discovered his grandiose plans. The revolution failed. The government shot Salzedo, annexed as much of his capital as it could find and denounced both the American government and the Mortgage Bank of the Andes, while far out in the American hinterland an enraged army of investors demanded a full-scale inquiry to establish why their hard-earned money had been used to finance a South American revolution.

The Mortgage Bank of the Andes, frantic with fright, claimed that since Salzedo had had virtual autonomy in the bank's South American affairs, it had been our responsibility, not theirs, to unmask him in our necessary investigations. That put the ball squarely in our court, and Wall Street began to hum.

Returning from Bermuda, I took O'Reilly's secret report, headed it "For Da Costa: Private and Confidential," and mailed it to the *New York Times*. I reminded O'Reilly that I could circulate an untrue but plausible story about why he had left his Jesuit seminary, and advised him that it was in his own best interests not to leave my employment without a reference. When I promised him a thousand dollars every time he had to tell his story the way I wanted it told, our agreement became not only sealed but indestructible. O'Reilly may not have been the most amusing protégé I had ever had, but he was certainly the most venal.

O'Reilly claimed that when I had transferred the Salzedo file he had routed his special report to Jay through the interoffice mail. He denied having shown me the report before I left for Bermuda because he claimed it had been incomplete at the time.

Naturally the report made a splash in the *New York Times*, and there began to be talk of fraud and collusion. In Washington the President had awakened to the fact that there might possibly be some truth in the rumor that a firm of New York investment bankers had knowingly attempted to finance a revolution in South America, and Congress, which had been trying to keep the lid on a possible scandal, now gave up the attempt and started muttering about a Senate inquiry. Questions from various sources of law enforcement mounted daily, the press was in full cry and the public was howling for retribution.

Jay denied everything, but his standing was destroyed among his fellow bankers and with the dealers his integrity had been reduced to dust. The single fact that he was suspected of collaborating with Salzedo in defiance of O'Reilly's report was enough; an investment banker must be above suspicion, and although no one, not even the grand jury, could prove that Jay had privately gained from the loan the firm had made Salzedo, the rumor continued to reverberate through Wall Street until by 1922 it was obvious that for the good of the house, the Street and the profession he would have to resign.

But he clung to his power and his innocence. "I'll never resign!" he said fiercely at our final partners' meeting. "It's not a crime to make a mistake, and I never saw that report!"

Nobody said anything. The others were too embarrassed and angry by that stage and I did not want to overplay my hand, but Jay called me out. Rounding on me in fury he shouted, "How much did you pay O'Reilly to lie?" And then pandemonium broke loose as the blood began to flow behind the exquisite facade of our palace at Willow and Wall.

The other partners tried to stop us. Everyone was shouting, but

Jay outshouted them all. As Charley Blair and Lewis Carson dragged him back and Steve Sullivan pinned me to my chair, Jay yelled at me, "You sonofabitch! You goddamned crazy—"

I knew what he was going to say the second before he said it. My secret was to be dragged out of the closet at last, my most private humiliation was to be aired in public, and soon there would be no one in all New York who did not know that I, Paul Cornelius Van Zale, was an—

"*—epileptic!*" shouted Jason Da Costa.

I was mute. There was no escape. I tried to move but was paralyzed. I could barely breathe.

"This guy's crazy, he's sick. He's getting his revenge on me because he thinks I killed his daughter. He's got no business to be walking around the streets—he should be locked up in an asylum along with all the other insane hallucinating—"

He used the word again. I felt myself flinch, but although I prayed for someone to interrupt him no one spoke, and when I forced myself to glance around the table I saw only their blank faces, frozen with shock, and the faint fatal flicker of repulsion.

". . . and they wouldn't let him out when he was a child! They kept him locked up, but later they let him out occasionally—yes, it's true! I saw him have a fit once—we were playing tennis and he fell to the ground and thrashed about and foamed at the—"

"You shut your goddamned mouth!" But it was not I who spoke but Steve Sullivan, the most loyal of all my protégés, the younger brother I never had. I was still beyond speech, immobilized by the huge sodden weight of my shame, but Steve went for Jay like a boxer bursting from his corner, and it took not only Charley and Lewis but also Clay and Hal to tear him away.

"Get out of here!" roared Steve to Jay. "You've ruined yourself, but I'm damned if you're going to drag us all down with you!"

"Steve's right," said Charley suddenly, and Lewis intoned, "For the good of the firm . . ."

Jay protested, but they silenced him. They came at last to my defense. I think it was because I said nothing. They thought I was behaving like a model Christian gentleman by turning the other cheek to my enemy, and they mistook my dumb humiliation for a dazzling display of dignity.

Afterward it was Charley Blair who said to me kindly and with great tact, "I guess none of us knew you'd ever suffered from epilepsy, Paul, but you can be sure that every one of us will hold that information in confidence. How long have you been well now?"

"Since I was fourteen."

"So of course you think of yourself as cured?"

"Of course."

I managed to get home and shut myself up in the library before I had my next seizure. No one saw. No one knew. Afterward I was bruised on my left ribs, and a muscle in my shoulder was torn, but I said nothing, took more medication and forced myself to accompany Sylvia to the opera. I felt very unwell and very frightened, but I did my best to behave normally and Sylvia merely thought I was tired. It was somewhere in the second act that O'Reilly tiptoed into our box to inform me that Jay had blown his brains out.

I had never thought he would kill himself. I had envisioned an obscure humiliated retreat to Florida but not that blood-spattered self-inflicted end in the heart of Manhattan. I had not understood him when he swore he would never resign.

His suicide created a sensation in the press, but soon we saw that instead of increasing the scandal it had ended it. It was as if he had after all assumed the responsibility for the Salzedo affair, so that the rest of us were exonerated from blame. We knew then that the firm would live. All my partners stood behind me because they knew their survival depended on mine, and beyond the walls of One Willow Street the profession closed its ranks to protect us from the world as we nursed ourselves painfully back to health. I remember the secret handshakes, the public expressions of confidence, the tough words in private and the honeyed smiles for the press, but at last the nightmare was receding and I knew not only that I had won my gamble with Salzedo but that I had achieved everything I had ever wanted in those far-off days when Lucius Clyde had banished me into the penury of the Lower East Side.

More days passed. I was a big man on Wall Street now. I rode in my Rolls-Royce to my palace at Willow and Wall, and I lunched with Lamont of Morgan's, and the President himself would call me for advice from the White House. I had my mansion on Fifth Avenue and my cottage at Bar Harbor and my estate in Palm Beach; I had my showpiece wife and my loyal ex-mistress and all the women I could possibly want; and I had my wealth and my glamour and my fame.

By March I knew I could endure my world no longer, but I knew too that I would have to be careful how I escaped. It would never do if people suspected I was running away. I would have to find a cast-iron excuse for leaving New York and I would have to find it at once before my health collapsed completely and all America started to talk about my seizures.

That was when I made a telephone call to the Treasury Secretary and won the prestigious role of observer at the Genoa Conference, but I was deceiving myself when I thought an escape to Europe would automatically mean an escape from the gold-barred cage in which I had imprisoned myself. I found I had taken my prison with me, gold bars and all, and I had remained in my prison until Dinah led me to freedom.

Yet now that freedom was coming to an end. Hal Beecher was the jailer sent to bring the escaped convict back to the prison yard, and from across the Atlantic the summons was raking me home.

"Jay's boys are after your blood, Paul," Hal said, and as soon as he spoke I knew I could not turn my back on the position I had hacked out for myself at One Willow Street. If I gave up now it would mean that my past suffering had been for nothing. It would mean I had sold my daughter and killed her husband yet still won nothing but ruin and disgrace.

I had to go on. The prison gates swung wide before me, but it was I myself who stepped inside and threw away the key.

I looked at Hal. I looked at O'Reilly, and suddenly I saw myself as the world must have seen me in recent months, a middle-aged man making a fool of himself with a girl young enough to be his daughter and ignoring his work to moon around some rural waterways in a nickel-and-dime sailboat. No wonder Stewart and Greg Da Costa thought I had grown soft and vulnerable! My resolve hardened, my will toughened and all my old instincts for survival reasserted themselves.

"We leave at once for New York," I said curtly to O'Reilly, and had the satisfaction of seeing his jaw sag before I strode from the room.

IV

In the hall the hammer-beamed ceiling soared above me. I had to stop. It was quiet in the house, and at last, unable to bear the weight of the silence, I ran upstairs to her room.

She was sitting motionless on the edge of the bed, and when I saw her shoulders hunched as if to ward off some attack I saw what I had subconsciously realized all along, that I had made the wrong decision when I decided to stay with her. If we had parted at the end of July the farewell would have been painful but endurable; I would have returned to New York, hired her a business manager and arranged that she should be thoroughly occupied with her business. Now she had nothing and it was hard to imagine her coping with a business until after the baby was born. How could I ever have believed that the affair would burn itself out and leave us free to part in peace? The affair was not extinguished but exacerbated, our emotional desire had become an addiction and the pangs of withdrawal would without doubt put us both through hell. I felt sorry for myself, I felt even sorrier for her, and all the time I was cursing myself for having mishandled the episode of Dinah Slade from its lively original beginning to its sticky, drab, appallingly conventional end.

"You're going, aren't you," she said.

"Yes, I must. I'm sorry."

"Well, you always said you'd have to go one day. How soon will you have to leave?"

"I'm leaving now, Dinah. As soon as Dawson has packed my clothes."

"Oh."

I sat down beside her. Neither of us spoke. After a long time she began to cry.

I started kissing her. After a while I heard myself say, "Come with me to America."

"Oh, yes!" she said without thinking, and then fearfully, "Oh, no . . ." As she glanced around at the walls of the room I almost saw her backing away into the security of the womb which Mallingham represented to her. "I want to," she said muddled, "but I can't . . . not yet. . . . I don't think I could bear to be alone and pregnant in some foreign city, and here at least I have my home . . . friends . . . Mrs. Oakes . . ."

"I understand."

"But I could come later!" she said in a rush. "When I'm not pregnant—yes, that's it! I could bring the baby to America to see you."

I pressed her against my breast again so that whatever expression crossed my face was invisible to her.

"Paul . . ."

"Yes?"

"If I did come to America . . . when I come . . . I couldn't share you with your wife. That would be against all my principles, but there's no difficulty, is there? I mean, if it's just a marriage of convenience—if she really is only a glorified social-secretary-cum-housekeeper . . ." She paused.

"I can't help thinking," I said, almost too distraught to know what I was saying, "that this is an extraordinarily inappropriate time to discuss my marital affairs." And I started kissing her again.

When O'Reilly came tapping at the door I was in the worst imaginable state, half dressed, sexually exhausted, emotionally annihilated and hardly fit to travel three yards, let alone three thousand miles.

"Go away!" I bawled at O'Reilly like a small child.

He did go away, but I knew that on the other side of the Atlantic the Da Costa brothers would not. Crawling off the bed, I reached for my clothes.

"We must talk of practical matters," I said hazily as I groped for my shirt. I hardly knew what I was saying. "When you write to me at One Willow Street, mark the envelope with my initials and not with any words like 'Private and Confidential.' Then the letter will be sure to reach me. Don't worry about money—I'll arrange something with Hal. Now about Mallingham—"

She at once sat up and pushed away her tears. "Don't try and convey it to me out of guilt or pity, Paul," she interrupted strongly, "or I shall start to feel like a paid-off mistress. The task of buying Mallingham back from you will be an incentive for me. Don't try and deprive me of it."

"Very well, but I'm not carting all those legal documents back to America—the abstract of title alone would sink the ship. I'll take the actual deed of conveyance and you can keep the rest under your pillow. Are you really sure you don't want me to transfer the ownership to you? It'll be some time before you make any money, and I don't expect you to work until the baby's born."

"Oh? I'm to lie on a chaise-longue all day, I suppose! Really, Paul, how Victorian!"

Quite unable to continue dressing, I abandoned my clothes and sank down weakly upon the bed.

"Oh, Paul, don't go—please. Stay here—don't go away." All her strength had vanished, and her face was once more awash with tears.

"Oh God," I said. "Oh Christ. Oh hell." This outburst was most unlike me, as I consider it grossly uncivilized to reel off a string of even the milder expletives in the presence of a woman.

"Oh, how could I—please, please forgive me!" wept Dinah, mistaking my despair for exasperation. "I was so absolutely determined to be brave and gay and unsentimental—"

"Were you? How sickening! I don't think I could have stood that," I said frankly, and by some miracle all grief was erased as we laughed together again.

When I had finished dressing she said, dry-eyed but incoherent, "What can I say? There must be something, must be, but I can't think—everything's hurting so much . . . no words . . ."

"How about '*Ave atque vale*'?"

She shuddered. "So final!"

"For Catullus, but not for us." I leaned over the bed to give her a last kiss. "Take care of yourself. Forgive me. We'll meet again."

The next thing I knew I was stumbling down the hallway. At the head of the stairs I paused to listen, but there was no crying, only the silence of desolation, and I groped my way downstairs into the hall.

They were all there, watching me.

"Well, come on!" I shouted, in such a haze of misery that I could hardly speak. "What the devil are we all hanging around for?" And leaving them gaping at the ruins of my urbanity, I pushed past them outside to the motorcar.

V

The ship sailed from Southampton the next day. I stayed in my suite, ordered a series of light meals which I could not eat and started drinking scotch. Since an undistorted mind has always seemed to me the greatest possible blessing, I hated to resort to such a measure, but I found that the effects of hard liquor were more acceptable than the foggy aftermath of my medication. I missed Dinah unbearably, of course; but my state of mind was more complicated than mere bereavement. I felt disoriented again, as if I were adrift in a vacuum, and my confusion was heightened because the farther we sailed from England the more convinced I became that I had made the mistake of a lifetime. I should have stayed at Mallingham. I had been happy, my health perfect, my mind at peace. I belonged in Europe, so why was I now leaving it behind? I felt hopelessly out of tune with America, as if it housed a culture I could not begin to understand, and when I compared Europe, with its beauty, history and eternal fascination, to the cheap glamour and abrasive vitality of my native land I could no longer understand what I was doing, heading westward into a succession of monotonous sunsets.

The ship was due to dock on the afternoon of November the tenth, and with a fatalistic, almost morbid curiosity I struggled out on deck to watch my two worlds collide.

We were going through the Narrows as I stepped outside and gripped the rail. It was a beautiful afternoon, crisp and cold, and the waters of the Inner Bay were a clear ice-blue. They were there still, all the famous landmarks, the Whitehall Building, the Adams Express Company, the twofold mass of Equitable Life, the Singer Building like a giant lighthouse with its cupola, and most magnificent of all, the Woolworth Building, shining white and subtly spiritual in its resemblance to a modern cathedral. For a second I closed my eyes as if I could not believe that nothing had changed, and when I looked again I was aware only of the extraordinary originality of the view. I saw a hundred boats and a thousand spires; I saw the shining towers of my town glinting wickedly in the sunlight like a row of predatory teeth; I looked into the jaws of New York City.

It was then that the miracle happened. Perhaps I had always known it would. I was traveling sideways in time again, slipping effortlessly back into the furrow where I truly belonged, and when I looked again at that city it was beautiful to me, its soaring towers ciphers of a world where nothing was beyond man's reach, its gilded spires symbolic of all that man could achieve. My pulse quickened, and my pulse was the pulse of New York, quick, terse and vibrant with vitality. My two worlds collided, spun apart as I watched, and now it was Europe which was ugly to me, Europe which was corrupt, ripe with decay, bound to memories which could never be reborn, turned inward on itself as it sank back into its wartorn, decadent past. As the illusion of romance fell from my eyes and I once more reached out to grasp reality, I knew I was no longer a refugee in a culture where I would remain forever alien, no longer an immigrant racked by ambivalence as I floundered between two worlds, no longer a traveler seduced by a dream which would have robbed him blind of all ambition.

I was a New Yorker who had come home to New York.

The ship's horn blasted in my ears, and as I watched the tugs chugging toward us my confusion evaporated and my mind became brilliantly clear. Long-delayed decisions streamed through my consciousness. Deal with the Da Costa brothers. Shake all my partners out of their doze. Whip the office into shape. Dazzle everyone who thought I was either senile or dead by throwing a ball of extravagant proportions. Do something about Mildred's boy. Talk to Elizabeth about Bruce's Bolshevist leanings. Buy Sylvia a belated anniversary present at Tiffany's. Hire a man who would set Dinah up in business . . .

I sighed yet again as I thought of Dinah. Of course I would see her again someday. And Mallingham. It was unthinkable that I might not see Mallingham again.

The tugs were pushing us toward the pier, and as I leaned over the rail to watch them puffing with exertion New York towered above me and I was drawn back into its mighty shadow.

The truth was that Europe was bad for me and it would be a disaster if I saw Mallingham again. And the really brutal truth was that I would be not only a fool to prolong my emotional relationship with Dinah but selfish as well. I knew that nothing could come of such a relationship. What right did I have to keep her dangling, sustained by her loyalty to me, until I chose to resume our affair in New York? The affair could drag on for years and she, not I, would be the loser. It would be different if she were an older woman sophisticated enough to regard the affair with mere casual enjoyment, but she was very young, she had admitted she was in love with me, and I could offer her nothing but an extended diet of pain, anger and humiliation. If I really cared for Dinah—and I knew I did care very deeply—would it not be kinder to cut her loose from me by telling her as soon as possible that our affair could not be resumed? She would still suffer, but in the long run she would suffer less. Of course it would be very pleasant for me to have Dinah available whenever I wanted her in the future, but after six months of altering her life beyond recognition I decided it was time I thought of someone other than myself.

The ship docked. The line handlers were busy fastening the cables, and when I heard the hum of the city I knew I was home.

I thought of the child. It would probably die, but if it lived . . . That was hard. I gripped the rail tightly. Perhaps Dinah would marry when she discovered how difficult it was to be an unmarried mother, and perhaps if it were very lucky the child might have that nice boy Geoffrey Hurst for a father. It seemed the best I could hope for.

Perhaps someday I might . . . I tried to cut off the thought, but it was difficult. I remembered how Vicky had looked at the age of four when I had been reunited with her, and the ship's rail blurred before my eyes.

"The captain says we can be first off the ship, sir," said O'Reilly's voice behind me.

I walked off the ship into the chaos of the customs hall, but naturally I did not have to wait. Dawson would be taking care of the bags.

I took a deep breath. My decisions had been made. Now all I had to do was implement them. Squaring my shoulders, I flicked the dust from my cuffs, straightened my tie and then, wearing my most charming smile to conceal my monumental guilt, I walked down the customs hall to confront my wife.

PART TWO

Sylvia
The Romantic

1922–1925

Chapter One

I

The Cunard liner *Aquitania* reached New York on Friday afternoon, and I was at Pier 54 on the North River to meet Paul when he emerged from the customs hall and smiled right into my eyes, just as he always did when he had something to hide. He looked remarkably well, very lean and tanned, and as he swept off his hat to wave it at me I saw that his scanty brown hair was much fairer, as if he had spent long summer days beneath an alien sun. He was immaculately dressed, and knowing that every stitch of his clothing would have been made in England I thought how ironic it was that he would never have been mistaken for an Englishman. The English have a casual understated way of being well-dressed. Paul was much too smart, much too well-groomed.

I saw all the heads turning as he walked toward us, and from a distance of fifty feet I felt the familiar pull of his magnetism. He had a way of walking that suggested he could cross a marble floor in hobnailed boots without making a sound, and such was his athlete's elegance that it was easy to believe he was as tall as the six feet he always claimed to be. He was as sensitive about that missing inch and a half as he was about his thinning hair, and although some people thought him vain I knew that his sensitivity merely arose from his hatred of imperfection.

He had a high forehead, deep humorous lines about his straight mouth, and brilliant dark eyes.

"Sylvia! You look wonderful!" I had expected him to speak with the English accent he sometimes affected, but he did not. His voice wrapped itself effortlessly around the conventional words and infused them with immense warmth and sincerity. "How are you?"

I had carefully prepared a series of noncommittal opening responses but now found myself speechless. I was so ashamed. As his hands clasped mine my face turned upward automatically and in a flash he had kissed me on the lips. At once the press swarmed forward in delight and somehow I produced a smile for the cameras, but although I leaned on Paul's arm for support he had already glanced away from me to acknowledge the presence of his favorite partner.

"Steve!"

"Welcome back, Paul!"

They shook hands. I stood alone, hoping he would not linger to talk to the press, but when the reporters showered him with questions he naturally stopped to answer them. Paul was a master of creating a smooth public personality for the newspapers.

"Mr. Van Zale, is it true you plan to retire permanently to Europe?"

"At my age? Why, I've barely embarked on my career!"

"Can you tell us what's going to happen to the market?"

"It will fluctuate."

Everyone laughed. A dozen plebeian faces gazed at him with affectionate admiration, spellbound by his patrician elegance.

"And Mr. Van Zale, how does it feel to be—"

"To be back? Gentlemen, you know what a New Yorker I am! What could be better than being back in the greatest city on earth" —his arm slid smoothly around my waist again—"with the most beautiful woman in the world? And now, if you'll excuse me, I haven't seen my wife in months and I'm naturally anxious to make up for lost time."

The reporters tittered sycophantically and cast admiring glances in my direction while the photographers indulged in a final orgy of picture taking.

"This way, my dear," said Paul.

As soon as we reached the car he said to Steve Sullivan, "Pretend you're going to the office. You don't want to look as if you're intruding on my reunion with my wife."

"Sure." Steve disappeared just as Wilson, our senior chauffeur, stepped forward, beaming from ear to ear.

"Good day, sir. Welcome back to New York!"

"Thank you, Wilson! It's wonderful to be back!" He really did sound as if he meant it.

I felt confused, not knowing any longer what to believe. I still had not said a word but now I had to find something to say, for we were alone in the back of the automobile and Paul's bodyguard Bob Peterson had closed the glass partition to give us privacy.

"You look awfully well, Paul."

"I feel marvelous!"

I could not quite look at his face, and I was aware that he was looking out of the window as if he could not quite look at mine. Suddenly I had a moment of complete despair. I had spent hours during the past months trying to decide how I could cope with this revival of his old love affair with Europe, but now that I was face to face with the problem I felt as helpless as I had felt in 1917 when we started our two-year stay in London. The girl, Dinah Slade, did not concern me; he would have had no trouble discarding her as he discarded all the other women who attracted him, but Europe . . . One can fight another woman, but how can one fight an entire civilization? In theory I admired Europe, but in practice I had found it unbearable. I shuddered as I remembered that oppressive grandeur, the crushing sense of times past, the strangeness, the sense of being cut off from all familiar customs, standards and ideas. I had hated being a foreigner and I had longed for my home. But Paul had felt just as much at ease in Europe as in New York, and possessed an astonishing gift for achieving a dual nationality. His secret, as I had discovered so painfully when I was with him in England, was that he had a dual personality. The American Paul, who had resurfaced on our return to New York in 1919, was the Paul I had married, while the English Paul was the foreigner who would always remain a stranger to me.

I wondered if he had ever given me more than a passing thought during those lost months near the Norfolk coast that summer, but I doubted it. When Paul was mesmerized by Europe all memory of his American life faded into the distant background, and his waking hours became dominated by medieval art and architecture, classical ruins and museums, historic libraries and monuments. No mistress could have been more demanding than the all-embracing silken net of Europe's interminable past.

He had decided what to say to break the silence. I felt his hand slip winningly into mine. "Well," he said in a cheerful voice, "I lost my head and my heart, but thank God not my homing instinct! I can't tell you how good it feels to be home. Ah, I see the Fifth Avenue traffic is as appalling as ever! Is it true they're going to bring in those traffic towers by Christmas? That should make a difference if anyone takes any notice of them. . . . Now how many stores have crept farther uptown in my absence, and which restaurants have disappeared? Tiffany's is still there—and Lord and Taylor. . . ." We moved uptown through the Thirties into the Forties. "Delmonico's still on its last legs, I see! And Sherry's . . . De Pinna . . . St. Patrick's—gothic as ever! . . . The Plaza . . . the park . . ." He sighed over the landmarks as if they were long-lost friends, and summoning the courage to look at him directly, I saw that his eyes were sparkling and his smile was radiant. "I love it all!" he exclaimed laughing as he turned to me, and I thought, Yes, you love places, cultures, civilizations, but not people. I have never once heard him say "I love you" either to me or to anyone else.

Our glances met at last, and suddenly I saw beyond his exuberance to his concern and anxiety. The English Paul with his crushing indifference had vanished and I was once more in the presence of the American Paul who was so proud of his marriage and who so intensely wanted all to be well between us.

"Paul . . ." Tears sprang to my eyes.

"Ah Sylvia, don't be sad!" he exclaimed impulsively, and when he tilted my face to his I was a slave to his quicksilver moods again, overpowered by his vitality and his charm. "If you knew how glad I am that I decided to come home . . ."

He never finished his sentence and I never gave him the chance to do so. He drew me to him, I slipped my arms around his neck, and as he began to shower me with kisses the tears streamed down my face to wash away the last traces of my pride.

II

We lived in a fifty-room house which faced the park on Fifth Avenue. It was built in the classical style, with pillars, porticos and long symmetrical windows, and certainly looked stylish although, as my housekeeper was always telling me, it was not an easy house to run. Paul had had it built after we were married, and when I remarked vaguely that it was a pity townhouse gardens always had to be so small, he bought the house next door, demolished it and had the grounds suitably landscaped for me. He even had a tennis court made, as well as an indoor swimming pool. I did enjoy the garden, but when we first moved into the house I was more absorbed in choosing which rooms would be set aside for the nursery.

Those days seemed long ago now.

My responsibility as Paul's wife was to supervise his domestic affairs, organize his social calendar, represent him on various charitable committees, and see that he was never troubled by details which would unnecessarily consume his time. It was a demanding position but I enjoyed it, and if I had merely been Paul's employee I could have handled my duties tranquilly. The trouble was that being Paul's wife was far more difficult than being Paul's employee.

Paul's shining virtue was his honesty. He did not live as other people lived and his standards were hardly those of the conventional world, but he had his own code of honor and he stuck to it through thick and thin. Before he embarked on either marriage or an affair he always told the woman exactly what he expected of her and what she could expect of him, and if he ever made a promise to her he kept it. He never promised anyone fidelity, a calm life or peace of mind, and yet in his own way he could be both loyal and trustworthy. I knew that so long as I did my job well he would never discard me to run off with someone else; I knew he was genuinely proud of me and always praised me to his friends; and I knew I occupied a special place in his life. Knowing these things did not make my difficulties disappear, but it did make them easier to endure. I accepted the fact that his work came first and that the bank consumed enormous amounts of his time. I accepted the fact that for a man who barely drank or smoked women were an inevitable vice, and I accepted too that for Paul a casual liaison was of no more importance than a hard set of tennis or a fast swim in the pool. He lived with tremendous pressures, and it was vital that he could relax whenever he wanted in whatever way he pleased. Yet acceptance was hard. There were so many evenings I spent alone, but I loved Paul and I knew it was futile to try to change him. I had to accept him as he was.

Once long ago when we were first married I had thought I could change him. I was only twenty-five then, and although I had been married before I was still naïve. I had thought that if I loved him enough he would never look at anyone else, and even later when I was disillusioned I still thought I could put matters right in the simplest of ways.

I can still remember the appalled expression in his eyes when I had told him I was pregnant.

"But you told me you couldn't carry a child!" he said accusingly as if I had been guilty of some gross deception, and when one look at my expression told him how insensitive his response had been, he began to talk rapidly about his horror of childbirth. His first wife had died from some postpartum complication and he had blamed himself terribly; for months after her death he had been plagued with guilt and when he eventually recovered from the tragedy he had decided he wanted no part in any future pregnancy.

It was not until I miscarried again that he tried to tell me he did not like children. It was quite impossible to believe him. He idolized his daughter Vicky, and it took no modern psychiatrist to interpret the role Paul's ambitious young protégés played in his life. However, I did believe that for some reason he was afraid of fathering another child, and I became determined to find out what that reason was.

Summoning all my courage, I called on my mother-in-law, an aristocratic, erudite and forceful old lady who by some miracle had always approved of me, and asked her outright if she knew of a reason for Paul's fear.

"I can tell you nothing," she said, neither hostile nor sympathetic but merely neutral. "You must ask Paul."

Paul's sister Charlotte was dead by then, but the next time I saw her daughter Mildred I made further inquiries.

"My dear, I'm just Paul's niece!" said Mildred. "What would I know about anything like that?"

I had an absurd impulse to discuss the problem with Elizabeth

Clayton, the woman who had been Paul's mistress on and off for more than twenty years, but of course that was impossible. It was not until Paul's daughter Vicky died that Elizabeth and I became close friends.

I was very fond of Vicky. She did not resemble Paul in looks, but whenever I was with her I was reminded of him constantly. She had that same zest, that same quick mind, that same source of ready humor, but where Paul was hard she was sensitive, generous and sweet-natured; she had all Paul's warmth without the layer of steel underneath. Paul spoiled her abominably, but somehow it never mattered. She had the humor to see the absurdity of the pedestal on which he wanted to place her, and the innate good sense not to think of herself as a fairy-tale princess who could have everything she wished. Paul's mother had brought her up, and this stroke of fortune undoubtedly saved her from becoming unbearable. Old Mrs. Van Zale was the sort of woman who stood no nonsense from anyone, and Vicky was a glowing example of a sensible, balanced upbringing.

I can vividly recall the panic which swept over me when I realized someone would have to break the news of her death to Paul.

It was not Vicky's husband who telephoned me with the news but Stewart, Jay's elder son by his first marriage, and as soon as the call had finished I rushed to Paul's mother. But shock and grief made her cold. When I cried in despair that I did not know how to tell Paul she merely said, "It's your duty," and after that there was nothing I could do but leave her to grieve alone. I was crying when I left her house. The tragedy of Vicky's death seemed far more than I could cope with, and finally I became so desperate that I turned to the only other person in New York who could help me, Elizabeth Clayton at her house on Gramercy Park.

"I know it's shameful, Elizabeth, I know I'm being weak, but . . ."

"I'll tell him," said Elizabeth.

I never found out what happened between them because neither of them ever spoke of the meeting, but I always remembered how Elizabeth had come to my rescue and Elizabeth always remembered how I had paid her the ultimate compliment of asking her to take my place at Paul's side. The incident created a strange bond between us, and not long afterward when Paul himself promised me that the affair was finished my natural awkwardness with Elizabeth dissolved and we began to meet occasionally for lunch. I was worried about Paul's health at the time, and it was a relief to have someone to confide in.

"He has this awful fear of fainting," I said. "I think it must be some legacy from his childhood asthma, although I don't like to ask him about it."

"No, never discuss his delicate childhood with him, Sylvia. He hates to be reminded of it. As for his present health, I shouldn't worry too much about it—he'll recover soon enough once he gets to Europe."

How right she was! But then Elizabeth always did seem to understand Paul much better than I did, and I could not help but think it strange that he had never married her. She was only a year younger than he was, and very grand in a quiet dignified intellectual way which had deeply intimidated me when we had first met. I was not her social inferior, for both my parents had come from families well known along the Eastern Seaboard and our wealth had sprung from land, not from a vulgar enterprise such as mining or railroad expansion, yet Elizabeth always made me feel as gauche as a girl whose father had made a fortune out of hatpins. Nor was I uninterested in culture. I had always enjoyed my novels and my evenings at the theater, but whenever Paul and Elizabeth drifted into a discussion of some fine point in French literature I would feel as idiotic as any retarded servant girl fresh from some charitable institution.

This was my fault, not Elizabeth's. I was being too sensitive, for like Paul's mother Elizabeth had always approved of me, and even in the awkward early days of our acquaintance she had made it clear that she wished me well.

When Paul's health deteriorated again after Jay Da Costa's suicide it seemed only natural that I should once more turn to Elizabeth for advice.

"I know it's right that he should make another visit to Europe," I said, "but should I go with him or not? You know how I feel about Europe, Elizabeth! Of course I want to be with Paul, but maybe I should try not to be so selfish and let him go alone. I don't want to spoil his trip, and maybe if I went along he wouldn't be able to relax because he'd be afraid I wasn't enjoying myself. What do you think?"

"Let him go by himself," said Elizabeth. "I think he needs to be alone to sort himself out. The Salzedo affair coupled with Jay's suicide has been a severe drain on him."

I accepted the advice of the oracle thankfully and for at least three months congratulated myself that I had made the right decision. Paul became involved with European politics at the Genoa Conference, he reorganized the office of Da Costa, Van Zale in London and he wrote spirited happy letters home to say how much he was enjoying himself. He even had this new mistress, a young English girl called Dinah Slade. Later I saw a photograph of her in the rotogravure section of the *Sunday Times*. I was surprised she was so plain, but when I heard she owned some ancient manor house in

Norfolk I immediately understood Paul's interest in her. Paul had a weakness for ancient manor houses. I could imagine him poking around Mallingham Hall with great enjoyment, and of course the fact that the lady of the manor was hospitable would have been an additional attraction to him.

When the affair showed no signs of wilting I did begin to wonder if I had been right in taking Elizabeth's advice, but by then there was nothing I could do but wait for the inevitable end. I was certainly surprised he stayed so long with Miss Slade, but I knew Paul too well to be seriously alarmed. I wondered whether she thought—as I had thought before her—that she could change him, and if I had not long since trained myself to feel no emotion on the subject of Paul's women I might even have pitied her when in November he left her so abruptly to come home.

But I did not pity her. I was too busy being grateful that Paul always kept his word to a woman, no matter how brutal that word might be. I knew he would have said to Dinah Slade, "I can never marry you," just as he had written to me in July, "I give you my word that I shall return," and now I saw that his honesty was unchanged. I had trusted him to keep his word; he had not failed me, and now all that mattered was that we were together again to resume the partnership which meant more to me than all the conventional marriages in the world.

III

We had no time alone together at first. Steve Sullivan arrived at the house soon after we had stepped into the hall, and Paul immediately took him to the library. It was futile for me to speculate on the nature of the crisis which absorbed them. Paul never discussed his work with me and I had long since realized that the world of his bank at Number One Willow Street was a world I could neither enter nor share with him.

Later they left the house for a partners' meeting downtown, and Paul said he did not know what time he would be back. "Don't delay dinner for me."

"As you wish. Don't work too hard, darling."

At least, I thought as I watched him go, he looked fit enough to cope with his work. I remembered how haggard he had been after Jay's death, and shuddered. That had been a terrible time for Paul. Jay had somehow managed to involve the firm in a major scandal. I never fully understood the details of the Salzedo affair, but a regular loan had been used to finance a South American revolution, with the result that everyone, from the White House to the poorest American investor, had called for an explanation. I did not believe Jay had deliberately aligned himself with revolutionaries, but it was obvious he had been negligent and would have to resign. The fact that he had preferred suicide to resignation was the first hint I had that the balance of his mind had been disturbed by the disaster, and when I heard he had accused Paul of engineering the whole episode to disgrace him I knew he had taken leave of his senses. Paul never demeaned himself by repeating this accusation, but Jay's sons had behaved outrageously at the funeral and had bandied the slander around as if it were gospel truth. Stewart and Greg Da Costa had always been wild. Jay had been too busy to spend as much time with them as a father should, and a succession of stepmothers, all barely older than they were, had hardly helped the situation.

If Dinah Slade had helped Paul forget Jay's suicide I was going to be the last person to deplore her lengthy presence in his life. Finishing my dinner, I glanced at my watch and wondered when he would be coming home from Willow Street.

It was eleven o'clock when I heard the automobile draw into the courtyard, and pulling aside the drapes of my boudoir, I looked down as the Rolls-Royce halted by the steps. Paul sprang out with alacrity even before Wilson could open the door for him, but Peterson was slower and O'Reilly lagged behind in obvious weariness. When Paul was fit he exhausted all the people who worked for him.

Leaving the window I put my book aside, turned out the boudoir lights and retreated to the bedroom to brush my hair. I was still toying with the brush five minutes later when I heard Paul enter his room next door and start talking to his valet. I listened, my fingers curled tightly around the brush's handle. Wardrobe doors opened and closed. Finally the valet left. There was a silence.

Remembering that I had barely begun to give my hair its traditional hundred strokes, I brushed so furiously that the hair crackled, but before I could count to ten Paul had opened the communicating door and was strolling across the threshold. He was wearing his favorite bathrobe—his "dressing gown," as he sometimes called it in the English fashion—and reeked of such casual elegance that I felt both too formal in my Parisian peignoir and too disheveled with my hair still flying from the brush. I suddenly realized I was immensely nervous, and desire, resentment, anger and love were all twisted together in my mind in a heavy emotional knot.

"I thought you'd gone off to Europe again," I said lightly, patting and smoothing my hair into place.

"I've no doubt you did. It's been a hard day."

For me as well as for you, I thought, but managed not to say the words aloud. "I do understand," I said instead to my hairbrush, "that there must have been so much to catch up with at the office."

He sighed. He was lounging gracefully against the mantel of the fireplace, and as I glanced at him in the mirror I saw him straighten the Dresden ornaments. "Do you think I wouldn't rather have spent the time with you? However,"—his glance met mine in the mirror and he gave me his brilliant smile—"tomorrow I shall make amends. Can you meet me for lunch? I'll book our favorite table at the Ritz-Carlton in belated celebration of our anniversary and afterward we'll go to Tiffany's to choose our presents."

"That would be nice," I said levelly. It was an event I had dreamed of during the months of our separation and I could not understand why I now felt so angry. I felt I was being unreasonable, and I was just willing myself to smile at him as he deserved when he abandoned the fireplace to move closer to me.

"Sylvia . . ." He took a strand of my hair, and as he curled it around his finger I felt that the gesture was symbolic of our relationship. My body became rigid with tension.

"Do you want to be alone?" he said at last.

Oh, how I wanted him! As I shook my head violently I tried without success to sort out my confused feelings, but fortunately he understood me better than I understood myself. As my eyes filled with tears he drew a chair close to the vanity stool where I was sitting and prepared to take infinite trouble to set matters right.

Ironically this small evidence that he cared was enough to make me feel better, and even before he began to speak I had conquered the desire to cry.

"My dearest, I hope I'm not so insensitive as to suppose I can come home five months late after you've been obliged to tolerate God knows what kind of gossip and expect you to fall willingly into bed with me with no questions asked, no reproaches given and no explanations either sought or received. . . ."

He was giving me back a little dignity, allowing me to recover my self-respect. I fought against feeling grateful to him and lost. He was saying what I wanted to hear, and he was saying it with the charm which had overpowered braver, stronger, angrier women than I. I allowed myself one last resentful thought: How clever he is! And then my resentment became admiration and my anger mellowed into amusement at his ingenuity. I felt quite recovered now, strong enough to grasp the dignity he was offering me and scoop up my self-respect. As I turned clear-eyed to face him he said with all the honesty I loved, "Ask what you want—say whatever you like. After all these months you should at least be entitled to freedom of speech."

All I had wanted was his acknowledgment that I had a right to be angry, and now that I had it I had little interest in asking the routine questions. However, since my new dignity obviously did not allow me to let him escape unscathed I did my best to assume the role of inquisitor.

"Why did you stop writing in August after you went to Norfolk?" I said at last.

"Because I was ashamed," he said without a second's hesitation. "Do you think I didn't feel guilty about indulging myself with a lengthy European vacation when I should have been on my way back to America to join you at Bar Harbor?"

I fidgeted with my hairbrush. "What finally brought you back?"

A less honest man would have said, "You." But Paul said, "I would have come back anyway, as you know, but my actual decision to return when I did was prompted by a business difficulty in New York. That was why I had to spend all my time away from you this evening. There was a matter which required my immediate attention."

"I suppose I guessed that when Steve insisted on coming with me to meet your ship." I fidgeted with the hairbrush again.

"Go on," he said.

I did not know what to say. It was no use asking him why he had stayed so long in England. His obsession with Europe was a matter best not discussed, since I could not understand it and he was incapable of giving me a rational explanation. Groping for a safer subject, I remembered Dinah Slade with relief.

"This girl," I said, "the girl you met there. It's over?"

"Of course."

It was the answer I had expected and I felt sure he was telling the truth. I had filled up a few more seconds, but I was tired of my role of inquisitor and was about to tell him I had no further questions when he said unexpectedly, "I was attracted to her for what she represented to me. You know what a sentimental fool I am about Europe."

I stared at him. At last my voice said, "She represented Europe to you?"

He saw his error. I had never seen Paul make such a slip before, and part of me watched with detached interest as he bent all the power of his personality on redeeming it.

"Well . . ." He shrugged, smiled, made a careless gesture with his hands. "Forgive my poor choice of words, but it's been a long day. What I meant was that the world she lived in had enormous appeal for me. She had this old manor house—the hall was really a perfect example of medieval architecture complete with hammer-beamed ceiling . . . Well, I won't bore you with the details. I'd like to go back there someday, but I doubt if I shall—in fact, I doubt if I'll go back to Europe for some time. I have too much to do in New York, and besides, America does have certain attractions which

Europe can't offer." He smiled at me. His hand smoothed my hair and drifted to my shoulders, but I did not lean against him.

"Sylvia, there's something I want to say."

"Yes?" I turned to him at once, my heart beating more quickly.

His voice was low, little more than a whisper. "I was so sorry last June . . . your miscarriage . . ."

"Oh, Paul!" In my agitation I rose to my feet. I was disappointed that he had not told me he loved me, but at the same time I was moved by this unexpected reference to the baby. In the second after he spoke I told myself that I was a fool to be disappointed because he had not told me a truth he was incapable of expressing in words, and that I should be grateful he was not angry about my third attempt to give him a child he had sworn he did not want.

"I expect you thought I didn't care, but I did feel for you so very much. I'm sorry I could only write you that cold empty letter." He too had risen to his feet, and when I saw that his distress was genuine I moved unquestioningly into his arms.

We kissed. He held me very tightly and at last I heard him say, "You of all women deserve a child. There's no justice in this world, is there? None at all."

Although the subject was a sad one I felt illogically happy that we should be so close.

"'God moves in a mysterious way,'" I quoted lightly, trying to steer the conversation away from past unhappiness by making him smile, no matter how wryly, at my deliberate choice of cliché.

I was successful. "Why, Sylvia!" he said amused. "How Victorian!" And then the expression of amusement faded from his face and his eyes became darker as if mirroring some intense inner pain.

"Paul . . ."

"It's nothing."

"But—"

"Don't say anything else. I need you, Sylvia," he said, reaching for me blindly. "I want you very much, more than I've ever wanted you. Help me."

I did not answer him in words. I simply drew his mouth against mine until finally, all anger forgotten and all passion fired, I shut my mind against the past and we went to bed.

Chapter Two

I

When I awoke the next morning I stretched out my hand to touch him, but he had gone. It was already half-past seven and he would have left the bed an hour ago to swim in the pool before dressing for breakfast. In the hope of catching a glimpse of him before he left for the office I rang for my maid and had just put the finishing touches to my appearance when he swept into the room to look for me.

"Oh Paul, I was going downstairs to join you for breakfast! Am I too late?"

"Yes, but never mind, we'll make up for it at lunchtime." He kissed me and I clung to him. My maid eased herself tactfully from the room. "You look wonderful!" he exclaimed, kissing me again. "The sort of vision every man should see first thing in the morning. Can I be very brutal and discuss domestic affairs with you before you've had your first cup of coffee? I can only spare ten minutes, so you won't be deprived for long."

"Of course! I'll just get my notes."

"I'll be in the library."

When I reached the library he was pacing up and down as he waited for me, and I had barely closed the door before he launched into instructions for a dinner party for thirty, his favorite number.

". . . and then I think it's time we had another ball—can we fit it in before everyone runs off to Florida? Find out the best date and get the invitation list drawn up—not less than three hundred but no more than four hundred, and I'd like to approve the list as soon as possible. . . ."

I scribbled frantically in my notebook. There was no time to look at the clock, but I heard it strike the half hour.

". . . And now tell me what's happening in New York."

"Well, Lord and Lady Louis Mountbatten will be the guests of Brigadier General and Mrs. Cornelius Vanderbilt before returning to England—their names are appearing in connection with a new supper club which is being inaugurated by Count and Countess

Zichy. . . ." I skimmed over other important social events, dances at the Plaza, Sherry's and the Colony Club, a thé-dansant at the Ritz-Carlton, a musicale at the Rockefellers'. "There are a series of lecture-musicales being given at various private houses, and I'm on the committee with Mrs. Winthrop Chandler, Mrs. Otto Kahn, Mrs.—"

"What's the Kahn lecture to be?"

"Significant periods in the history of choral music. I've volunteered the use of our house, of course, Paul, and suggested a guest speaker on bel canto."

He approved. Our conversation gravitated naturally to the opera. "I've seen the list of new boxholders—fewer changes than usual in the Golden Horseshoe this year, and since none of the prominent families who own parterre boxes are in mourning this season, there are fewer absentees." I talked about *Boris Godounov* and a production of *Der Rosenkavalier*. "Oh, and, Paul, the talk of the town is that *Hamlet* opens on the sixteenth with John Barrymore in the lead."

"Get tickets at once." He glanced at his watch. Time was running short. "How are the charities?"

"The December ball at the Ritz-Carlton is being given to raise funds for Grosvenor House . . ." I skimmed feverishly through the charities and listed the appeals while he said "Accept" and "Refuse" whenever I paused for breath. "Then there's Christmas," I added rapidly. "The question of the servants' bonus."

"Draft a proposal and show it to me later."

"And Mrs. Wilson's in the hospital. I've sent flowers, of course, but the bill—"

"Pay it."

Another minute had ticked away.

"Yes—oh Paul, what about Mildred? She's invited us to Cincinnati for Thanksgiving."

"Out of the question, but write and invite them all here instead. I must do something about that boy of hers." He was moving toward the door. My ten-minute audience was about to expire. "Twelve-thirty at the Ritz-Carlton," he said, smiling at me over his shoulder as he moved into the hall.

"I'll be there." I hurried after him. Peterson was waiting as always, and Mason the butler held Paul's coat and hat.

"Goodbye, darling!" I gasped, and just had time to snatch a kiss before he disappeared outside and left me breathless with exhaustion in his turbulent, exhilarating wake.

II

He was five minutes late for lunch. "But I had to stop," he said, "to buy you this." It was a corsage of orchids, pale and graceful.

I had been waiting in the lobby for him, but now we set off through the Palm Room and up the short flight of stairs into the main restaurant, which had long been a favorite of ours. It was a delightful room decorated in white and robin's-egg blue and adorned with girandole mirrors reproduced from the eighteenth century. In the corner by the Georgian windows our special table was surrounded by banks of flowers which provided both romance and privacy—the latter an essential ingredient, since I soon realized we were about to break the law.

"And where's that lemon soda you promised me?" exclaimed Paul to the headwaiter as soon as we were seated.

A tray of hothouse lilies was raised to reveal a bottle of vintage French champagne.

"Paul!" I protested halfheartedly as all the waiters smiled, but Paul only said, "The Eighteenth Amendment is the enemy of all fine restaurants—look how it's wrecked Delmonico's," and after that I felt it was my duty if not my legal right to drink champagne.

"To us, my dear!"

"To us . . ."

We had dressed crab, roast duck and Florida strawberries. For Paul, who liked the English custom of concluding a meal on a savory note, there was some Camembert, but I merely contented myself with a cup of fresh-ground coffee.

Afterward we both thanked the headwaiter and then leaving O'Reilly to attend to the delicate task of handing out the tips, we walked into the sunshine of Madison and Forty-sixth Street and took the Rolls south to Thirty-seventh and crosstown to Fifth Avenue.

Inevitably O'Reilly had informed the press of our impending visit to Tiffany's, and as the cameras clicked, the representatives of the *Tribune*, the *World* and—most celebrated of all in its reporting of society news—the *Herald* converged upon us, followed closely by reporters from the *Post*, the *Mail*, the *Globe* and the *Sun*.

"A little late this year, aren't you, Mr. Van Zale?" inquired a large overrouged lady whose skirts rose embarrassingly toward her knees.

"What is time," said Paul, "when one's in love?"

They lapped that up greedily, said it was "just lovely" and asked if they could quote him.

"Why not quote Tennyson?" said Paul. He was quite shameless. "He says it so much better than I do."

"Pardon me?"

"'Love took up the glass of Time, and turn'd it in his glowing hands; every moment, lightly shaken, ran itself in golden sands.'"

"Well, isn't that nice! You're a lucky lady, Mrs. Van Zale. Are you glad he's home?"

I simply laughed because the question was so ridiculous. The cameras clicked again as Paul led me into the store, and no sooner had we crossed the threshold than the chief floorwalker came gliding up to us.

"Good afternoon, sir . . . madam . . ." More pleasantries were exchanged.

"Well, my dearest," said Paul, "what would you like?"

I had one of those helpless moments which often assail me when I walk into a store such as Tiffany's.

"Perhaps one of the fancy gold pins," I began, but he waved that aside.

"You had a brooch last year. This time you must have something special! After all—ten years! I've never been married ten years to anyone before."

"Might I suggest diamonds, sir?" breathed the floorwalker.

"An excellent suggestion," said Paul. "Let's look at diamond rings."

He bought me one of the most exquisite rings I had ever seen, a large central yellow diamond surrounded by small white diamonds, all set in a plain circle of gold. He wanted to have the band engraved with the date of our anniversary, but I said that was unnecessary. I did not want to be reminded of the day I had been alone in New York, and the ring alone would recall memories of our reunion.

"Now what can I possibly buy you?" I said in despair. "And please, please don't say cufflinks!"

Paul laughed. The floorwalker began to murmur discreet suggestions and I continued to pray for inspiration.

I finally chose a watch. I had no idea how many watches he already had, but he always enjoyed wearing a new one. It was a plain gold fob watch with Roman numerals, a touch which appealed to his fondness for the classical.

Not a penny changed hands, of course. I doubt if Paul had more than a nickel in his pocket, for he hated to carry money. Later in the month when the bill came I would give it unopened to Paul, who would write a check drawn on one of the accounts in which I had no share. I never knew how much our anniversary presents cost. It was a tradition between us.

"I guess you have to go back to the office now," I said as we emerged from Tiffany's with Peterson trailing in our wake.

"No, I think I'll walk down to Gramercy Park and see Elizabeth."

I was shocked by the pang of jealousy which shot through me. It was a long time now since I had had any real excuse for being jealous of Elizabeth, and again I remembered Paul saying to me with curt finality sometime after Vicky's death, "It's over. I promise you I shall never sleep with Elizabeth again."

I knew that as usual he had kept his promise. Elizabeth's changed attitude toward me proved that, and our friendship, dating from that time, had never faltered.

"It'll just be for an hour or so," said Paul, watching me. "Then I'll come home."

"An hour doesn't seem long when you haven't seen each other since March," I said, pulling myself together abruptly. After all, I could afford to be generous. "Stay longer if you wish. And darling, thank you—for everything."

He kissed me warmly and walked off downtown with Peterson while I traveled home alone in the Rolls.

He returned at six, asked for a plain omelette and said he would really have to go back to the office. I had a cup of coffee with him in the dining room while he ate the omelette and talked about his visit to Elizabeth. At seven he ordered the car to the door.

"Don't wait up for me, will you?" he said in the hall. "I may be very late. There's a large amount of reading I must do in order to find out what's been going on in my absence."

I told him I understood. After he had gone I fingered my diamond ring as if to remind myself conscientiously how much time he had spent with me that day, and then, determined to regard my solitary evening as an ideal chance to catch up with my correspondence, I retired to my boudoir to write to Paul's niece Mildred in Ohio.

III

I liked Mildred. She was the only child of Paul's only sister Charlotte who had died of pleurisy soon after my marriage. I had never known Charlotte well; she had been ten years Paul's senior, twenty-seven years older than I, and although she had been as gracious to me as Paul's mother I had never imagined our becoming close friends. But Mildred was different. Since her mother had married young, Mildred was only nine years younger than Paul, and this small gap in their ages made Paul regard her more as a sister than as a niece. She was large, good-looking, good-humored, and endowed with a great sense of melodrama, a gift she had exercised to the full when she met an Ohio farmer on a train, fell in love violently and resolved to marry him. What her chaperone was doing while all this was going on I have no idea, but I was quite sure any chaperone would have been as powerless as everyone else to deflect Mildred from her chosen course. The family finally yielded to Mildred's iron will when exhaustive inquiries revealed that her farmer was not only hard-working and religious by Eastern-Seaboard standards but by Midwestern standards was prosperous and well-to-do. Mildred married her farmer, bore him a daughter and a son and as far as anyone could tell lived happily ever after. Naturally no one ever visited her, but once a year Mildred made the pilgrimage back East and stayed one month with her parents. Her husband did not accompany her, and although the family never failed to inquire after his health solicitously they remained relieved that he had the good sense to stay at home. It was generally agreed that Mildred had managed a déclassé marriage with skill and good taste.

When her farmer died shortly after their seventh wedding anniversary, Mildred plunged herself into deepest mourning, declared she would remain a widow for the rest of her life and then remarried with a speed that shattered even those who knew her well. Fortunately her second husband Wade Blackett was acceptable to the family. He was a younger son of a prominent St. Louis family, and by the time he met Mildred he was a successful surgeon in Cincinnati. After their marriage they moved to Velletria, one of the most exclusive of the Cincinnati suburbs, and when Wade formally adopted Mildred's two children Mildred's story seemed to resemble the happy endings of the romantic novels she read in such profusion. This time the family's verdict was that after a disastrous start Mildred had done better than anyone had dared hope.

The children were pretty but painfully shy. Mildred was loquacious, and no doubt in her household it was hard to get a word in edgeways. Emily had good health and like all the Van Zale women was gifted scholastically, but Cornelius was delicate, suffering from asthma, and showed no great interest in his lessons. I always felt sorry for him. He was such a dear little boy, with his golden curls and huge solemn gray eyes—or at least he was when I had married Paul in 1912. Cornelius was now fourteen, but neither Paul nor I had seen him since our return from Europe in 1919. Cincinnati is an awkward place to visit from New York and Paul was always so busy. We kept inviting the Blacketts to visit New York, but Wade was too busy with his surgeon's schedule and whenever he did get time off he felt it his duty to visit his widowed mother in St. Louis.

When it seemed that Paul would not be returning from Europe before the end of November, Mildred had invited me to Cincinnati for Thanksgiving, and now it was at least a pleasure to tell her he was back in New York even though I had to decline her invitation. Following Paul's instructions I invited her instead to New York, and although I expected to receive a reply in the mail Mildred as usual preferred the drama of a long-distance telephone call. The telephone service had greatly improved—the other day I had even been connected to Philadelphia in sixty seconds—but unlike Mildred I felt that such electronic communication was cold and I much preferred to put pen to paper.

Apparently it was quite impossible for the Blacketts to leave Cincinnati.

"Some frightful operation, my dear—the day before Thanksgiving —*so* thoughtless and uncivilized." Mildred, whose accent was pure Beacon Hill, always talked like an extract from Queen Victoria's diaries. "Sylvia, when on earth *are* we going to see you and Paul again—it's been such *eons!*"

"Isn't it difficult, Mildred! Perhaps in the new year? Paul's very anxious to see Cornelius."

There was a pause.

"Mildred?"

"Yes, I'm still here. Darling, how sweet of Paul! I hope he's not laboring under some dreadful family obligation because of Cornelius being his only nephew. Of course Cornelius would love to see Paul too, but his health still isn't what it should be, the poor pet, and I really don't think he's up to that ghastly journey to New York at present. Maybe next year."

When I reported this conversation to Paul he commented wryly, "Mildred's using the wrong approach. If she wants me to lose interest in her boy she shouldn't try and keep me from seeing him."

"But Paul," I said astonished, "why would Mildred want to keep Cornelius from you?"

"Do you think it's an accident that we haven't seen the Blacketts for years?"

"But we're always exchanging invitations—and Mildred's devoted to you, Paul!"

"Of course she is, but any mother is going to protect her innocent little boy from a rich wicked uncle in the richest wickedest city on earth."

"Oh, for goodness' sake!" I exclaimed, half amused, half exasperated. "What on earth does Mildred think you intend to do with him?"

"Leave him my money, of course. All those millions! I can just imagine Mildred going down on her knees at church every Sunday and praying for deliverance!"

I suddenly realized not only that he was serious but that he was probably right. Mildred was an Episcopalian minister's daughter who had no doubt been brought up to hold the traditional Christian views on great wealth, and on her mother's side she was a Van Zale, aristocratic enough to condemn rapidly accumulated riches as "shoddy." Paul had made his money, not inherited it, and Mildred, who might possibly have found "old money" acceptable, could well have felt overpowered by the stench of this new fortune. After considering all this I said curiously to Paul, "But do you intend to make Cornelius your heir?" Paul had so many protégés, and I often thought it was easier to imagine him leaving his money to someone like Bruce Clayton than to an unknown youth who happened to be his only male heir. "Old money" of course would have stayed in the family, but I had the feeling that Paul would consider that the newness of his money gave him the license to dispose of it exactly as he pleased.

"I'm undecided about a future will at present," Paul was saying. "My present will divides the money among a number of people, a sensible but unadventurous solution. Money is power. To divide money may make some people happier, but it dissipates the power so that what I may give with one hand I in fact take away with the other. In terms of power it would be much more interesting to leave the whole lot to one person, but you can be quite sure I'd never leave well over fifty million dollars to anyone unless I thought they could handle it. Mildred underestimates me, you see. I don't want to ruin her boy. I've spent a lot of time and effort making my money and I have no intention of dumping it on someone who would immediately snap like a twig beneath the burden. Whether Cornelius is in fact a frail twig or a chunk of solid mahogany I have no idea, but I'd like to find out—if Mildred ever gives me the opportunity, and I must say this is beginning to seem increasingly unlikely."

The day after this conversation I had lunch with Elizabeth, and out of curiosity I told her about Mildred's dilemma. We were lunching at the Claytons' tall rambling house which overlooked Gramercy Park, and after we had finished our spinach soufflé and fruit salad we retired upstairs to the drawing room for coffee. As the butler brought in the tray I settled myself on the couch and glanced vaguely past the paintings and the tapestries to the bare trees of the park beyond the long windows.

"My sympathies," said Elizabeth, "are entirely with Mildred."

Elizabeth was tall and her clothes were always perfectly plain, perfectly tailored and perfectly suited to her figure, which in middle age was classically statuesque. Her dark-gray hair was swept straight back from her handsome face into a heavy bun at the nape of her neck. She had beautiful gray-blue eyes, a firm attractive voice and an oddly shy smile which did not match her air of total self-confidence.

"You mean you think Mildred should continue to keep Cornelius from Paul?" I said surprised. "But Paul is so good with young people! You should know that even better than I do, Elizabeth, since your son was a Van Zale protégé!"

"That's exactly why I wouldn't wish such a fate on Cornelius. However, I don't want to go raking up the past. Coffee?"

I accepted coffee in astonishment and tried to restrain my desire to rake up the past as vigorously as possible. It was true Paul had seen little of Bruce Clayton in recent years, but I had always assumed Bruce still remained his favorite among his protégés. "Was there some trouble between Bruce and Paul, Elizabeth?" I couldn't help saying. "I never knew."

"Oh, it was all long ago, Sylvia, at least ten years, and I should hope we've all got over it, but all the same I can't help sympathizing with Mildred now. I've always identified myself very much with Mildred, you know. In some ways our situations are similar: I've been married twice, my second husband adopted my son from the first marriage, and Paul has always played a large part in our lives. Too large in mine, I'm afraid. At least Mildred doesn't have to cope with Cornelius thinking himself Paul's son. Milk and sugar?"

I made some feeble gesture toward the milk jug. I was astounded not only because Elizabeth had deliberately chosen to introduce a most intimate aspect of her affair with Paul—we had long since tacitly agreed never to discuss our relationships with him in detail—but because although Bruce Clayton's paternity was a favorite topic among the gossips of New York society I had never thought Elizabeth would refer to it either to me or to anyone else.

"Of course Paul isn't Bruce's father," said Elizabeth off-handedly, as if it were amazing to think there could be any doubt on the subject. "At least biologically he's not, but then there's so much more to being a father than merely begetting a child, isn't there? Bruce can't remember his own father and although Eliot is kind he has no real gift for children. Paul filled a void in Bruce's life and this gave him a special position in our family—a position which he abandoned with unforgivable brutality when Bruce was seventeen. Poor Bruce was completely crushed—in fact, I often think he's never got over the rejection—and I myself was so angry with Paul that . . . well, we remained close for another four years, as you know, but it was never the same. Forgive me for not going into detail, but really it's too painful to discuss even now."

"Of course. I shouldn't have asked you about it, Elizabeth. I'm sorry."

"I seem to remember it was I who brought up the subject—oh yes, we were talking of Mildred, and I was approving her decision to insulate Cornelius as far as possible. I don't think Paul means to hurt people, but when one is as detached emotionally as he is one tends to make any relationship an annihilating experience."

I knew now how wise we had always been never to discuss our relationships with Paul in detail. With our cardinal rule broken, we were no longer two civilized women who could afford to be friendly but two rivals in a competition which could never end.

"I think that's unfair to Paul," I said sharply. "Of course he's capable of being close to people. Look how he adored Vicky."

"Yes, he did adore her, didn't he? But he traded her to Jason Da Costa in exchange for half that bank at Willow and Wall."

"Elizabeth!" I could no longer control my anger, and as I rose to my feet I felt the color rush to my cheeks. I blush easily and never more easily than when I am both angry and shocked.

"I'm sorry." She rose to her feet equally swiftly and stood before me, her hands twisting together in her distress. "That was unforgivable of me. I shouldn't have started talking about the way Paul treated Bruce. It always upsets me. Of course Paul adored Vicky, of course he did—"

"And anyway," I said in a rush, "Jay and Vicky were in love. It had nothing to do with the merger. That was just incidental, and besides, you're talking as if Paul had complete control in deciding whom Vicky married—" I stopped, remembering stories Paul himself had told me of how he had terminated various unsuitable romances by dispatching Vicky to Europe. "Well," I said, "I guess he did have a certain amount of control, but since he and Jay were such special friends I'm sure he had no ulterior motive in encouraging the match."

"Sylvia, Paul and Jay's relationship was certainly special, but do you honestly think it was ever genuinely friendly?"

I said nothing.

"They were clever men who had a use for each other on Wall Street," said Elizabeth, "but they were rivals before they were allies, and they were enemies long before they were friends."

It occurred to me that this description could well have applied to her own relationship with me. I finished my coffee and stood up awkwardly. "Well, I mustn't keep you any longer, Elizabeth. It was a lovely lunch."

She made no effort to detain me, but in the hall I knew she was anxious for us to remain friends when she said, "I love your ring. Is it new?"

"Yes—thank you. It was a belated anniversary present from Paul."

"Ten years, isn't it? Congratulations, Sylvia!"

Since there was no doubting her sincerity it was easy for me to say a warm word of thanks, but all the way home I remembered her bitterness and tried to imagine the disaster which had upset Paul's friendship with Bruce. However, by the time I arrived home I had realized that all speculation was futile. Elizabeth had already said as much as she was ever going to say on the subject, while Paul never talked of the past.

IV

I was very busy during the weeks which followed Paul's return, and somehow managed to survive Thanksgiving and Christmas without feeling too blue. Christmas was the worst holiday. The toys in the store windows, the children thronging Fifth Avenue, the ubiquitous image of Santa Claus—I would dread seeing them all. The baby from my first pregnancy with Paul would have been eight by now, the second baby would have been eighteen months younger and the third would have been newborn. A baby for Christmas! I could not help crying as Christmas passed in emptiness, but I cried in private and was self-possessed in front of Paul. I had never reconciled myself to my childlessness. Part of the trouble was that no one had been able to tell me with certainty why I could not carry a child longer than three months, and because uncertainty existed I still secretly hoped for success. One specialist had suggested that a muscular weakness of the uterus was causing the trouble; another had theorized about a hidden genetic defect which made each fetus imperfect enough to trigger a spontaneous abortion; but whatever the difficulty, it was not Paul's fault. I had endured three miscarriages during my first marriage, although I did not start making the rounds of the specialists until I was married to Paul.

I felt better in the new year. I was frantically organizing the last details of our first ball in three years, and almost before the society columnists could hail it as the event of the season I was swept up in our annual migration to Florida. Paul liked to spend February swimming and playing tennis at his Palm Beach estate, and the house had to be opened, certain servants transferred and arrangements made for Paul's three private railroad cars to embark on the long journey south. The very thought of coordinating the movements of luggage and servants on such an extensive scale was enough to make me feel exhausted, and when we finally arrived in Florida I had to have a day to rest before we embarked on our social life among the Palm Beach set. Logically the move to Florida for a month should have been less exhausting than the move to Maine for the summer, but Maine was more informal, we needed fewer servants since the cottage at Bar Harbor had no more than twenty-five rooms, and Maine is an easy journey compared with the trek to Palm Beach.

Paul's house occupied a superb position by the sea and was built in the style of a Spanish castle, with half a dozen patios linking the thirty-seven rooms and the sunroom auditorium. There was also a ballroom which hung out over the sea so that when one was dancing one felt as if one were on board ship, but in fact we seldom held dances in Florida, and Paul preferred to limit his activities to swimming, tennis and dinner parties. Occasionally he played bridge, but that bored him because he usually found the other participants too slow, and anyway people did not like it when he won too often. He refused point-blank to go to any of the cocktail parties which were becoming fashionable, although he could occasionally be coaxed away from dinner to an after-dinner party. However, one such party was his limit and we were always in bed by midnight; probably the younger members of the Palm Beach set thought we were hopelessly staid. To my surprise he never gambled, always protesting facetiously that he had enough gambling on Wall Street and that he came to Palm Beach for a vacation. Those were before the days when one poker chip was reputed to cost ten thousand dollars in Palm Beach circles, but the stakes were notoriously high and gambling was popular among the local millionaires.

By the end of our fourth week in Florida Paul always became bored, and that year was no exception. He returned to New York ahead of me while I stayed on to close the house, but when I arrived home I wished I had stayed away longer. I found myself knee deep in correspondence, my housekeeper's accounts did not balance and the steward told me our best bootlegger had gone to jail. The servants always go to pieces at the end of the long New York winter, particularly if they are left unattended, so I could not be too severe with them, but after I had straightened out the housekeeper's poor arithmetic, dismissed a light-fingered footman, asked O'Reilly to find a new bootlegger and sent the latest foolish housemaid to the usual institution for unwed mothers I began to think how nice it would be to live simply with Paul in a little country cottage with only a hired girl to look after us. I even thought longingly of quiet evenings free of dinner parties and soirees, but came to the conclusion I would miss the glittering lights of Broadway. The production of *Hamlet* had led to a Shakespeare revival, and although I had never enjoyed reading his plays with my governess long ago I was always enthralled by a live performance on the boards.

It was in early April that Paul suddenly decided to see Cornelius. The decision to force Mildred's hand came quite out of the blue and as far as I could see for no reason. One day he was saying with his usual lack of enthusiasm, "I must do something about Mildred's boy," and the next he was saying, "I'm going to have a showdown with Mildred about this!" and was reaching for the telephone.

But Mildred had her excuses ready. Cornelius' health had improved; he was about to attend school for the first time and would be fully occupied until the end of the semester. Then after the Fourth of July the entire family was heading for Canada for Wade's first long vacation in years.

"When are you due back from Canada?" said Paul. "The end of August? Very well, you can send Cornelius to New York directly afterward and he can spend a week with us before his school starts again."

They argued, but Paul won. Perhaps Mildred had always known she was fighting a losing battle. For a moment I wondered what Cornelius thought of the situation, but I suspected that no one would have asked his opinion. Perhaps he did not want to come. Indeed by this time I myself was wondering if Paul's pulverizing orbit was the best place for a delicate sheltered boy, and when I remembered Bruce Clayton I could only hope that Cornelius would be more fortunate in his career as a Van Zale protégé. It even occurred to me that he might be better off altogether if he failed to qualify as a protégé and was allowed to withdraw quietly to Ohio.

The entire situation troubled me increasingly as the summer passed, and the suddenness of Paul's interest in Cornelius troubled me most of all because I felt sure there was a reason for it yet I could not guess what that reason was. "I don't want a son," Paul had said to me over and over again, but he behaved all that summer as if it were of vital importance to him to discover the perfect substitute for the son he had never had, and as the time of Cornelius' visit drew closer I no longer knew whether I wanted Cornelius to succeed or fail. I only wanted neither of them to be hurt.

It seemed like an impossible dream.

Chapter Three

I

The train from Cincinnati was on time, and as the doors opened I strained my eyes for a glimpse of Cornelius. Passengers streamed past. I was just thinking he must have missed the train when I saw him walking toward me.

Although I had not seen him for some years I had no trouble recognizing him, for his hair was still golden and his features had not greatly changed. He was small for his age but neat and compact. As I watched, someone bumped into him but his expression never altered. He merely adjusted the coat on his arm and walked on down the platform.

"Cornelius!" I raised my hand to attract his attention and when he saw me he smiled. It was a shy smile, very trusting. He looked angelic. If hearts could melt, mine would have dissolved instantly.

"Hello, Aunt Sylvia." His voice had finished breaking, and the educated accent of the Midwest was pleasant to the ear. "Thanks for coming to meet me."

I asked him about the journey and inquired after his family while Abrahams, the junior chauffeur, claimed the baggage and took it outside to the Cadillac.

"Paul was so sorry he couldn't meet you," I said to Cornelius as we left the terminal and began our journey home, "but he had some important conferences downtown. However, he should be home by six—he said he'd make a special effort to get home early."

"Yes." He was staring out of the window at New York City, and the light, slanting on the classically molded bones of his face, gave his black-lashed gray eyes a starry look. I suddenly realized with surprise that he had inherited the fine straight Van Zale mouth which looked so odd on the women of the family and so very attractive on the men. For a moment I envied Mildred her beautiful son, and then in a painful effort to divert myself I pondered on the appropriateness of the word "beautiful." That was surely the wrong word to use, since in an adolescent boy it implied effeminacy, yet it was impossible for me to connect effeminacy with that familiar Van Zale mouth.

I toyed with other adjectives. "Good-looking" implied someone rugged like Steve Sullivan, and Cornelius with his slight build hardly reminded me of Steve. Perhaps "handsome" was a better word, though to me that implied a maturity which a fifteen-year-old boy hardly possessed. The dubious word "beautiful" returned reluctantly to my mind, and as I gazed at Cornelius' curling golden hair, his fair unblemished skin and his exquisitely chiseled features I could understand why Mildred was so anxious to protect him from the corruption which Paul's New York world represented to her.

When we arrived home I showed him to his room and left him to settle down. I had expected him to be shy with me and so I was surprised at lunch when he talked easily about his home and school. It occurred to me that his mother's absence made it easier for him to behave with confidence. Mildred could be very overpowering.

After lunch he said he wanted to go out for a walk and I tactfully left him to amuse himself for the remainder of the afternoon.

Shortly before Paul was due home I found Cornelius loitering by the library and suggested we go up to the drawing room. "Would you like anything to drink?" I added. "Paul always has tomato juice and I always have sherry, but do have whatever you like."

"Tomato juice would be just fine. How do you manage to have sherry, Aunt Sylvia?" he said with puzzled innocence, and wondering in alarm if he would report my answer to Mildred, an enthusiastic supporter of the Eighteenth Amendment, I avoided all mention of the lax New York attitude to Prohibition and said Paul obtained the sherry through influential foreign clients.

Mason had just brought our drinks when far away I heard the sound of voices and knew Paul had returned.

Opposite me on the couch Cornelius sat bolt upright and assumed a studiedly neutral expression.

"Paul's so looking forward to seeing you!" I said encouragingly, aware that I was just as nervous as he was, but I believe he barely heard me. His eyes, dark with concentration, were focused on the door which Paul flung open a second later.

"Well!" Paul paused on the threshold. Both Cornelius and I rose to our feet as obediently as puppets in the hands of their manipulator, and for a moment the scene was a tableau taut with indefinable undercurrents of emotion. Then Paul smiled, said to me, "Good evening, my dear!" and gave me a kiss before turning to his great-nephew.

"Hello," he said easily. "You've grown. How are you?"

Cornelius tried to speak but could not. As I watched in an agony of embarrassment he began to blush.

"What's the matter?" said Paul with a brutality which made me want to retreat to some quiet corner and shrivel up in despair. "Did your mother never give you the chance to learn to talk?"

"Yes, sir," said Cornelius, absolutely wooden.

They shook hands, and the family resemblance, slender and elusive, danced fleetingly before my eyes. To my relief the butler chose that moment to arrive with Paul's tomato juice.

"Thank you, Mason," said Paul. "Sit down, Cornelius. Now . . ."

The most dreadful ten minutes followed. Under ruthless cross-examination Cornelius revealed that he had hated his first semester at school so much that Mildred had decided to keep him at home again and a new tutor had been hired.

"That's a bit feeble, isn't it?" said his inquisitor. "Why don't you make more effort to stick it out?"

"It seemed a waste of time, sir. Did you ever go to school?"

Surely, I thought, he knew that Paul too had suffered from asthma and had been kept at home! But then I saw that Cornelius had found the weak spot in Paul's attack and was exposing it as politely as he knew how.

The amusement flared in Paul's eyes. "No," he said. "I never went to school." There was a pause before he added, "Tell me more about it. What sort of things did they try to teach you?"

More agonizing minutes followed during which Cornelius was shown to be painfully ignorant in the fields of literature, history and the classics.

"My God, what a barbarian!" exclaimed Paul. "It's plain to see *you* come from beyond the Allegheny Mountains! Don't you have any interest in culture at all? What do you do with your spare time?"

"My spare time, sir?" said the unfortunate boy, looking inexplicably more nervous than ever.

"Do you swim? Play tennis?"

"The doctor doesn't permit . . ."

"Then what do you do? Sit and look at the wall all day?"

Cornelius stole a glance at me and blushed again. By this time I was suffering such agonies for him that it was a relief to seize the chance to escape.

"If you'd rather be alone with Paul—" I began, but Paul interrupted me.

"No, stay where you are, Sylvia, and don't pretend you're not just as intrigued as I am by this reticence! Now, Cornelius—my God, that's a terrible name for an adolescent boy to endure! I'm going to shorten it to Neil. Now, Neil, speak up! We're waiting! What do you do in your spare time?"

"I—I bet on the horses, sir."

"You *what!*"

"Oh sir, please don't tell Mama! It's not real money anyway—I only bet on paper."

Paul started to laugh. Cornelius looked as if he wanted to crawl under the couch and die. I was in such a state of anguish and astonishment that I merely gaped at both of them.

"Go on!" said Paul, still highly amused. "Tell me more! Do you go to the racetrack?"

"Oh no, sir, Mama wouldn't permit that. But once a week I get the train into Cincinnati and I buy a sports magazine and a racing paper. I follow other sports too, not just the horses, and I make bets on football teams in winter and baseball in summer. I've got a system—it's worked out in charts, with all the odds calculated. It really helps to pass the time."

"And what does your mother think you're doing while you're locked in your room being a secret gambler?"

"She thinks I'm reading the classics. But there's a very good book I found in the library which gives the plots of all the world's greatest novels—"

"Quite. How much money have you won on paper so far this year?"

"Two hundred and seventy-three dollars, thirty-nine cents."

"Good God!" To my enormous relief I saw that Paul was more entertained than ever. "And you enjoy it, of course?" he added casually as an afterthought.

"Oh yes, sir, it's exciting—in fact, it's really the only excitement I get. Cincinnati's a fine city, but it's kind of dull back there in Velletria," said Cornelius, glancing wistfully out the window at New York, and when he looked back at his great-uncle I saw their glances meet and lock in one long moment of absolute recognition.

II

Cornelius arrived on a Friday, and on Saturday morning Paul took him downtown to show him the bank before leaving him to do some sightseeing. It was years since Cornelius had been in New York, and on previous visits he had had no chance to wander around on his own. Before we all went to the theater that evening to see *The Devil's Disciple* he told me he had gone to the top of the tower of Metropolitan Life and had been very impressed with the electric elevators to the forty-fourth floor.

"And what did you think of the view?" I said, remembering that only the Woolworth Building offered a comparable view of the city.

"Pretty good," said Cornelius, but I could tell that the highlight of his visit had been the journey up and down in the elevator.

"Pretty interesting," was his comment on *The Devil's Disciple,* but he proved quite unable to discuss it afterward with Paul.

On Sunday we went to church at St. George's on Stuyvesant Square, where Paul's mother had always worshiped, and afterward we paid a brief visit to the graveyard of Trinity, where there was an ancient Van Zale tomb.

"Kind of quaint," said Cornelius politely. "I guess in those days New York must have been almost a one-horse town."

"Just like Velletria!" said Paul laughing, apparently undisturbed by Cornelius' lack of interest in the past, and later that afternoon he took him to tea with Elizabeth.

"And what would you most like to do while you're in New York, Cornelius?" said Elizabeth, no doubt hoping for a response indicating interest in a museum or an art gallery.

"See Jack Dempsey fight Firpo on the fourteenth," said Cornelius promptly, "but unfortunately that's the day I'm due to leave town."

"Stay on if you wish," said Paul. "I'll get you a ticket. Who's going to win?"

"Dempsey, sir. I think he'll knock Firpo out—probably in an early round."

"Let's have a bet," said Paul while Elizabeth looked on with incredulous disapproval. "I'll bet you five dollars Firpo will survive at least five rounds."

"I'll bet you ten he won't," said Cornelius, and he was right. Dempsey won in the second round.

"Well, Neil," said Paul as he parted with ten dollars, "you'd better not tell your mother I've encouraged your gambling or she'll never let you come here again." And the next day when it was time for Cornelius to return home he said, "Make good use of your new tutor, start taking some proper exercise and try to open a book occasionally. When you're a little less of a barbarian you can pay me another visit."

"Oh, Paul!" I said, weak with relief as the train steamed out of the station. "Thank God you were pleased with him!"

Paul said nothing.

"I thought he was delightful," I said as we walked back to the car. "He was so polite and well mannered—and self-assured too when he got over his shyness. I think he's going to be very attractive in a few years' time. He really does have the sweetest smile."

Paul was still silent.

"What do you think?" I said, unable to resist pressing him for an opinion.

"I think he's a very odd little boy," said Paul. "I shall wait with interest to see if he develops a passion for Latin and Greek."

My heart sank. "But in view of Cornelius' natural inclinations, isn't that a little unlikely?"

"The odds, as Cornelius himself would say, are certainly unfavorable. That's why if he does develop a zest for the classics I shall know that his ambition knows no bounds."

He said no more, and during the weeks that followed he never spoke of Cornelius unless I myself raised the subject—which I have to confess I often did. I felt bereft when Cornelius had gone, and with shame I realized how much I had been enjoying myself by pretending he was my son. It was only then that I wondered if in assuming Paul to have been intent on finding a substitute son that summer I had in fact only been assigning my feelings to him, and the dull nagging ache of my childlessness became a sharper, less bearable pain.

"I'm afraid I didn't care for him at all," said Elizabeth when I inevitably mentioned Cornelius to her. "Perhaps I was disappointed that he was so unlike Paul. I thought he was cold and withdrawn."

"I expect he was shy of you, Elizabeth!" I protested. "You're very imposing, you know, particularly to someone of his age."

"Perhaps," conceded Elizabeth graciously. "Anyway, I'm glad he won your heart even if he didn't win mine."

I suspected Elizabeth was too involved with her own son at that time to pay much attention to Cornelius. Bruce Clayton had just got engaged and planned to marry in the spring. At twenty-eight he was an associate professor of philosophy at Columbia University, and since his lectures brought him into contact with all manner of modern ideas Elizabeth had been terrified he would commit himself to some student "jazz-baby" with Marxist leanings. When he finally announced his intention of marrying a respectable girl from a well-known family, I knew at once that no one would greet the news with more enthusiasm than his mother.

"A Rochfort of Greenwich!" commented Paul ironically. "Trust Bruce to find a blue-blooded wife—these Marxists never practice what they preach!" But he was full of approval when we invited the couple to dinner. Grace was five years younger than Bruce, and I feared Paul might not like her bobbed hair and generous use of makeup, but when she proved herself both intelligent and well-read he was impressed. She had majored in French at Vassar and had just completed a traditional grand tour of Europe, but she was by no means wedded to tradition. Indeed, her main thesis, which she was only too ready to expound to us after dinnner, was that women should be educated to the hilt so that they could be released from their bondage to men.

"But all women are different, Grace," I said reasonably. "A lot of women don't wish to be highly educated or given the chance to be self-supporting."

"But surely, since it's a question of freedom or slavery—"

"Shouldn't it always be a question of women doing what they're best suited to do, whatever that may be? I'm not well-educated and I don't work for a living, but I certainly don't consider myself enslaved."

"I should tell you, Grace," interposed Paul, "that Sylvia works harder than many women who have a salaried position. She's no lily of the field."

"Of course not," said Grace Rochfort, trying not to look too pitying.

"I do so resent people who insist on inflicting their opinions on everyone else!" I exclaimed to Paul in our room after the guests had gone. "I'm not against emancipation—I quite understand that some women want to lead totally independent lives. But why must such women so often assume there's only one road to heaven? Sometimes I think girls like Grace Rochfort are just as repressive as the traditional Victorian paterfamilias who kept all his women at home under lock and key!"

Paul laughed. "You took Grace too seriously. Wasn't it obvious that her dedication to emancipation is only skin deep? She's getting married. She intends to be dependent on her husband. Probably by the time she's forty she'll be thoroughly conservative and opposed even to votes for women, but meanwhile she's young enough to enjoy supporting modern social trends. What do you suppose emancipation really means to Grace Rochfort? Smoking incessantly in public, drinking appalling cocktails and pretending to be blasé about other people's disordered private lives!"

"Hm." I pondered over what he had said. Presently I put down my hairbrush, slipped out of my peignoir and moved toward the bed. "I guess very few women are truly emancipated," I said. "Do you know anyone who is? I don't think I do."

Memory flickered in his eyes. I looked away at once, but when he realized I had seen his expression he said vaguely, "I have a client who's launched her own cosmetics business. She's doing quite well, I believe."

"Like Elizabeth Arden? How exciting! Does she have a salon?"

"In London, not New York."

"But is the product available here?" I said with genuine interest as I slipped into bed beside him. "What's the name of your client's company?"

"It's not available here," he said, reaching across me to snap off the light on my side of the bed, and the next moment his mouth closed on mine to terminate the conversation.

I thought no more about Paul's mysterious female client. Obviously he had had a passing affair with her, and since he never discussed either his mistresses or his clients with me he had a double reason for not expounding further on the subject. But I was interested in cosmetics, particularly those which were discreet and tasteful, and when one day in the new year I met the wife of a British diplomat at a Lord and Taylor fashion show I could not help but notice that her lipstick was just the shade I wanted but had never been able to find. At the table where a group of us had coffee after the show, my interest increased when I noticed that the lipstick barely marked her cup.

"Excuse me," I said, overcome with curiosity, "but may I be very inquisitive and ask where you bought your lipstick? It looks like just the kind I want."

"Isn't it nice! I'm glad you like it, but I'm afraid I won't be able to help you because I bought it in London. Do they have Diana Slade cosmetics over here?"

For a split second I was back in that lonely summer of 1922. "Is that D-I-N-A-H?" I said.

"No, D-I-A-N-A."

I wondered if it could be a different woman, but the coincidence was just too great. I began to consider Dinah Slade not merely as a discarded mistress but as a successful client. No wonder Paul had stayed with her so long! Protégée and mistress—what a stimulating combination, especially when the roles were combined in the person of a young girl who could offer him a medieval mansion and a set of postwar morals.

By the time I arrived home I was in the most unreasonable panic, but the more I told myself I was being ridiculous the more panic-stricken I became. I thought he would have severed all his links with Miss Slade when he left England, but now I saw that it was more likely that the two of them were still in touch.

Eventually I pulled myself together, dressed with care for the evening and drank two glasses of sherry too fast as I waited for Paul to come home.

Of course it took him no more than five minutes to find out what was wrong.

"I was just so startled!" I said, trying not to talk too rapidly. "I think it was the idea of your having a protégée—with an extra *e*—for a change! She must be awfully clever. How exciting that she's making a success of it!"

"She's been lucky," he said abruptly. "She didn't do a single thing I told her and I hear she's turned Hal Beecher's hair snow white. Still, she's Hal's problem, not mine."

"Oh, you mean you're not in touch with her?"

"No. Well, occasionally she writes a line to brag about her sales figures. That's all." He drank some tomato juice and seemed about to change the subject, but he could not resist saying, "It was good lipstick, was it?"

"Marvelous! I wish I could get hold of some!"

"I dislike lipstick on women," said Paul.

I felt much better once I knew he was not in regular correspondence with Miss Slade, and I did not think of her for some months after that conversation in January 1924. I was too busy with the migration to Florida, and at the end of February I sailed with Paul from Fort Lauderdale on a visit to South America. Paul had business in Caracas and we did not get back to New York until mid-April. As usual on my return I was engulfed in domestic problems, and I had hardly straightened out my correspondence when the bill from Tiffany's arrived.

I had bought some additional dinner plates there before we departed for Florida, and my first reaction when I saw the Tiffany envelope was that I was still being billed for them. I know the rich are supposed to be chronically tardy about paying bills, but I was brought up to believe this was ill-bred as well as inconsiderate behavior, and I paid my bills promptly.

I sighed, reached for my paper knife and slit the envelope.

At first I thought Tiffany's had gone mad.

"One silver christening mug," I read with astonishment, "engraved: 'A.S. March 27, 1923'. . ."

Various thoughts flashed dizzily through my mind. "A.S." Anthony Sullivan? But Steve and Caroline's little boy had been born directly after Christmas in 1922. And anyway I had sent him a silver rattle. Which baby had been born in March just over a year ago and had recently been christened? No baby I knew, and I definitely had not bought a silver mug at Tiffany's on . . . I checked the date. April the fifteenth. That was the day after our return from South America. In bewilderment my glance swept on down the page.

". . . plus registered postage to England as per the address below . . ."

I reached the bottom of the bill.

"Master Alan Slade, Mallingham Hall, Mallingham, Norfolk, England."

After a long while I realized that my hand was shaking, so I put down the bill. As I sat motionless in the still room I could hear the rain hurling itself futilely against the windowpane.

Putting the bill back into the envelope, I tried to find some sticky tape to hold the slit envelope together but then realized I had no idea why I wanted to reseal the envelope. Perhaps I had thought I could avoid the implications of the bill if I pretended I had never read it. What cowardice! Reality was dangerous only when one refused to face it. Taking a deep breath, I drew out the bill again and reexamined the information it contained.

"One silver christening mug . . ." Imagine Miss Slade having her illegitimate child christened! It seemed a hypocritical gesture, but the English considered christenings a social tradition which had little to do with religion.

"Master Alan Slade . . ."

I liked the name Alan but there were other names I liked better. My son would have been called Michael.

I swallowed with difficulty. Reality was proving too harsh for me after all and I told myself there had to be some explanation other than the one I could not face—obviously the baby had nothing to do with Paul, but perhaps Miss Slade had asked him to be godfather and he had felt obliged to send a handsome present.

Born at the end of March. Conceived . . . And again I remembered the hideous summer of 1922 when I had been alone in New York and Paul had been in England.

I groped for composure, for reassurance, for a peace of mind which I knew was already destroyed. The baby could not possibly be Paul's, because he had promised me before we were married that if he ever had any other children they would be mine as well as his. Paul never broke such a promise, never, it was unthinkable, for after all if he started breaking his word like that, who knew what other promises he might cast by the wayside?

I felt as if the foundations of my life had been uprooted by some monstrous plow, and although I searched for something recognizable in that distorted new world I saw only the bill from Tiffany's, the slit envelope and beyond them the rain hammering against the pane.

"I don't want a son. . . . I'm no longer in touch with Miss Slade. . . . It's over. . . ."

How he had lied! And I had believed him, every word, all of it.

My fear was gone. I was immensely angry, so angry that for some minutes I merely sat trembling in my chair, but I never cried and gradually I became more composed. I waited a full half hour to make sure I had myself totally in control, and then I rang the bell and summoned the Cadillac to the door.

Chapter Four

I

"Willow Street and Wall," I said to the junior chauffeur.

"The bank, ma'am?" said Abrahams incredulously.

"The bank."

I had been to One Willow Street to celebrate the merger of Van Zale's with Clyde, Da Costa in 1913, but I had never been there again. The bank was a world I could never enter, a masculine preserve from which women were automatically excluded, and Paul had always made it clear to me that my place was at his home on Fifth Avenue and not at his office on Willow and Wall.

When the chauffeur opened the door I climbed out awkwardly, my limbs stiff with tension, and paused in the rain while the doorman dashed out with an umbrella. He had recognized not me but Paul's monogram painted on the side of the Cadillac.

"This way, ma'am."

I followed him up six marble steps to the pillared doorway. The great doors, steel-studded and silver-embossed, stood open, but the inner doors beyond the vestibule were closed. Long ago before I had visited One Willow Street I had imagined "the bank" to be much like an ordinary commercial bank, with a host of ordinary customers who cashed checks, made deposits and asked for loans. I had pictured a solid little building with the name over the doorway and a pleasant friendly atmosphere within. But no name marred the splendid façade of One Willow Street; if people did not know that the premises represented the great House of Da Costa, Van Zale and Company, the bank most certainly had no wish to know them. Neither did one walk in off the street and open an account. One had to be invited to be a client, and if one was granted such an honor one had to keep at least a hundred thousand dollars on deposit. The clients of Da Costa, Van Zale could only regard it as a small price to pay for the privilege of doing business at Willow and Wall.

The doorman touched a bell concealed in a pillar as he opened the inner doors for me, and I walked into the cold bleak marble lobby. I stopped. Before me was a line of columns, and beyond them I could see the hushed splendor and mesmerizing opulence of the great hall.

A clerk hurried to meet me. He was white-haired and wore a wing collar and spoke in a voice slightly above a whisper. "May I help you, madam?"

"I'm Mrs. Van Zale. I would like to see my husband, please."

He looked at me incredulously over the top of his spectacles. My self-confidence faltered. I blushed.

"Please be seated over here, ma'am, and I shall ascertain if Mr. Van Zale is in the building."

He never asked if I had an appointment. Wives did not make appointments with their husbands during business hours, and good wives never upset tradition by appearing without warning at the bank in response to some eccentric feminine whim.

Without a word I sat down and tried to recall the anger which had carried me downtown in such style, but now I was only terrified of interrupting Paul in his work. I waited, trying to cling to my composure. It was immensely quiet. I could not even hear the rustle of papers in the great hall nearby. I was just succumbing to panic and wondering if I could tiptoe away before the clerk returned, when the inner doors of the vestibule swung open and Steven Sullivan strode into the lobby.

I tried to hide by shrinking farther into my chair, but he saw me and stopped short in surprise.

"Sylvia! Land's sakes, what are you doing here?"

"Well, I—I—"

"Who kept you waiting? That little dried biscuit with the wing collar? Just wait till I see him— Ah, here he is! Fullerton, do you know who this lady is? What do you mean by keeping her out here as if she was a two-bit grafter chasing the cheapest loan in town? My God, if you'd tried that on my wife she'd have disemboweled you, wing collar and all!"

"I beg pardon, ma'am," said the little man flustered to me. "I meant no incivility. I thought Mr. Van Zale had gone out to Reischman's, but it seems he came in through the back entrance. He's in conference now, sir," he added hastily to Steve.

"Forget it. I'll take care of Mrs. Van Zale. This way, Sylvia."

I followed him obediently into the great hall. In the old days before the merger the partners had sat at mahogany desks isolated like islands in the vast sea-green carpet, but now that the bank was bigger lesser luminaries had taken over the hall. The partners had comfortable rooms upstairs, and only the senior partner's room, a large chamber on the ground floor at the back of the building, had remained unchanged by the reorganization.

"You mustn't mind Fullerton," Steve was saying to me. "He's

such a period piece he still refers to the bank as Clyde, Da Costa, and even now that we're officially P. C. Van Zale and Company you can bet the most he'll ever manage is to call it Da Costa, Van Zale. You've been here before, haven't you?"

"A long time ago." I followed him down the aisle. The chandeliers, fully lit despite the hour of day, glowed on the moldings of the high ceiling and illuminated the oil paintings on the walls. The paintings were of past partners, some lean and melancholic, some rosy-cheeked and benign, some hatchet-faced and inscrutable, but although I looked for Jay's face I could not find it and later I realized Lucius Clyde's portrait too was missing.

At last we reached the pair of doors which opened into the back lobby. A superb staircase curved without apparent support to the floor above, and as we emerged from the great hall Paul's chief assistant, Terence O'Reilly, appeared on the upstairs landing.

He could hardly believe his eyes when he saw me. An expression of consternation crossed his face as he hurried downstairs.

"Mrs. Van Zale! Is something wrong?"

"Is he in his office?" said Steve before I could reply.

"No, he's in the second-floor conference room with Mr. Carson, Mr. Blair, half Morgan's and all Reischman's. I'm afraid the meeting will last till lunchtime."

"Go and tell him his wife's here, will you?"

"Well, I don't know if I should interrupt—"

"Come on, Terence, this is his wife, remember? Of course he must be told she's here!"

They stared at each other crossly. They were both in their midthirties, both Paul's protégés, and both had Irish surnames, but there the resemblance ended. Steve, who was the youngest of Paul's six partners, was well over six feet tall, with such a muscular physique that whenever I saw him swimming with Paul in our pool I had to make a conscious effort not to stare. He was undeniably a good-looking man, but I must have been one of the few women in New York who found him resistible, for I thought his charm was abrasive, his wit vulgar and his physique coarse. However, his position as Paul's protégé had always fascinated me. Most people would have looked at him and seen only his brawn, but twenty years ago Paul had looked at him and seen only his brains. He was certainly the only investment banker I knew who might have been mistaken for a football quarterback.

Glancing from Steve to Terence O'Reilly, the ex-Jesuit who had left his seminary, quarreled with his family and arrived in New York with twenty dollars and Paul's address, I was aware of a great contrast. O'Reilly was slim, not tall, and had some well-combed dark hair which was never out of place, a stiff erect bearing and one of those voices which seem to belong to no particular region or class, although once after a glass of champagne at Christmas he had betrayed the trace of a Boston accent. Paul had put him through Harvard and had employed him ever since his graduation—in fact, it was hard for me to imagine how Paul would have managed without O'Reilly, whose job in some ways resembled mine. I managed Paul's domestic life, and O'Reilly managed Paul's business life, while each of us controlled large staffs. Since we were both available to Paul twenty-four hours a day seven days a week, it could even be said that we worked the same hours, and although those hours suited me admirably I could not help but think they constituted a very unnatural life for a young man.

Presumably O'Reilly disagreed with me, although it was hard to guess what went on in his mind. Seemingly incapable of small talk, he was so reserved that I found him unwilling to discuss any matter which did not relate to his job. It had been a surprise to discover he had known Bruce Clayton socially since their days at Harvard. It was not simply that I could not imagine when O'Reilly ever got time for a social life, but I could never imagine him having any inclination to be sociable. He was several years older than Bruce, but since he had gone late to Harvard they had graduated together in the class of '17.

O'Reilly had a suite set aside for him at our house on Fifth Avenue, and once when he and Paul had been away on a business trip I had taken a quick look at his room. It had been both immaculate and impersonal, devoid of bric-a-brac, the bookshelf containing only American novels like *Babbitt* which were so popular that they gave no real clue to his literary taste. Afterward I had despised myself for pandering to such curiosity and had told myself crossly that it was all O'Reilly's fault for being such an enigma. An enigma he had remained too, and certainly I knew no more about him now, as I stood facing him in the back lobby of the bank, than I knew when he had joined Paul's staff in 1917.

"Please don't worry, Mr. O'Reilly," I heard myself say embarrassed. "I don't want you to get into trouble by interrupting my husband in an important conference."

"Don't take any notice of him," said Steve Sullivan. "He's always like this. He loves to be pernickety. Go on, Terence. The sooner you go the less chance there is of my carrying you bodily up to the conference room and throwing you across the threshold."

"That's just fine, Steve," said O'Reilly unperturbed. "I don't mind interrupting Mr. Van Zale so long as you accept full responsibility. Mrs. Van Zale, would you care to wait in your husband's office, please?"

The office consisted of two rooms linked by a broad archway. The room we entered was where Paul worked, while the far room was furnished as a drawing room. It was even used as a drawing room too; every afternoon at four o'clock various carefully selected people withdrew from their labors and gathered there for a fifteen-minute break. To be invited to drink tea with the senior partner was considered an immense privilege. Wedgwood china was used, English biscuits were circulated and if anyone was so crass as to smoke he was immediately asked to leave.

"I can't offer you any ladies' magazines to read while you wait," said Steve, who had followed me into the room. "But there's always the *New York Times.*"

"Oh, please don't worry about me anymore, Steve—I don't want to keep you from your work! Thanks so much for rescuing me in the front lobby."

"Any time!" He gave me his wide smile and I told myself I was unreasonable not to like him more than I did. Underneath his flashy manners he could be very kind.

When I was alone I wandered restlessly to the window. In the middle of the patio beyond stood a fountain which had been imported from Europe, and nearby, rising in gnarled splendor against the fifteen-foot back wall, was an ancient magnolia tree. The wall was surmounted with spikes, broken glass, wire and burglar alarms, for it separated the bank from Willow Alley and the outside world. Set into the wall was a door, reinforced with steel, its triple locks glistening in the rain. This back entrance of the bank was seldom used—only the partners had the necessary keys—but Paul occasionally found it convenient to slip in and out of the building unobserved. The patio was inset into the building so that it was surrounded by the bank on three sides, while the high wall completed the quadrangle.

For a time I watched the birds singing by the fountain, but when I became too nervous to stand still I began to wander around, looking distractedly at the books, the furniture and the objets d'art. Paul's desk was uncluttered. There were no photographs. The bookcases which rose from floor to ceiling on either side of the Adam fireplace contained works ranging from bankers' reference books to untranslated editions of Homer and Virgil, and on the Chippendale table by the window a vase of uncertain age and great beauty also bore silent witness to Paul's devotion to classical civilization. On the walls hung some rare prints of Old New York together with a framed deed recording a grant of land to Cornelius Van Zyl of Nieuw Amsterdam, and one of Rembrandt's more cheerful self-portraits hung above the fireplace. I was just staring blankly at the brilliant use of the oils when the door opened again.

I spun round, but it was only O'Reilly.

"I'm sorry, Mrs. Van Zale, but your husband sent me to tell you that he'll be engaged for a further half hour. May I have some coffee brought to you while you wait?"

My anger returned with a force which took my breath away. I forgot my nervousness, forgot my fears, forgot everything except that I had been humiliated quite enough for one day and was determined not to tolerate my humiliation for one second longer.

"Mr. O'Reilly," I said strongly, "you will please return to my husband and say I must see him at once. It's very urgent."

O'Reilly's straight back curved sulkily, but although he opened his mouth to argue with me he thought better of it. In despair he departed in silence.

Two minutes later, just as all my fright had rolled back to obliterate my brave anger, the door of the office was flung open and Paul swept into the room.

II

I stood up. We looked at each other. His face was taut with an emotion which might have been concern but which I suspected was rage.

"Yes?" he said.

I suddenly found I was as speechless as Cornelius had been when Paul started to interrogate him. In misery I groped in my purse, found the Tiffany bill and held it out to him with a shaking hand.

He unfolded the paper. His glance flicked over the words and the figures. Not a muscle of his face moved. At last he said abruptly, "This is an error."

"An error?" I had to sit down. "You mean—"

"I paid cash with the express intention of circumventing the usual monthly bill. I'll have O'Reilly call them to set matters right. I'm sorry if you've been embarrassed."

"Embarrassed!" I stared at him. My eyes were hot and my throat was aching, but my voice was clear and outraged. "Did you say 'embarrassed'?"

He was silenced. He looked away, checked the door to make sure it was shut and ran his fingers through his front strand of hair. It was the first indication that he was upset, for Paul was fastidious about his appearance and once he had arranged his hair he took care not to disturb it with a thoughtless gesture.

"Maybe you'd better have a drink," he said, moving rapidly to the bookcase which concealed the liquor cabinet.

"I don't want a drink, Paul. I want an explanation."

He ran his hand through his hair again and abandoned the liquor cabinet. "Let's go into the other room."

We sat down on the couch. A china clock ticked rapidly beneath a large mirror. Paul looked out of the window at the rain, he looked at the clock, the carpet and the Wedgwood tea service in its display cabinet, and finally he looked at me.

"The christening mug has no more significance than the silver rattle we sent Steve's son," he said. "It was just a gift. My affair with Miss Slade is finished and her child has nothing to do with me."

"But he's yours, isn't he?"

There was a silence.

"I'm not acknowledging him," said Paul.

"But—"

"I told Miss Slade that from the start. I made myself absolutely clear. I—"

"You broke your promise to me, Paul!" My voice was suddenly harsh and trembling.

"My God, do you think I did it deliberately?" He got up and began to pace up and down the room. "It was an accident," he said rapidly, "a terrible accident. I underestimated both Miss Slade's psychological need for a child and her indifference to a society which deplores unmarried mothers. I know you must think it's extraordinary that I should have got myself into such a mess, but Miss Slade was so clever, you see, such a smart, intelligent girl, and I just couldn't believe she'd be such a blind selfish little fool. By the time I found out she was irrational on the subject, it was too late. Of course I tried to persuade her to change her mind—I used every argument I could think of—but one can't reason with someone who's irrational. When I repeated that I couldn't acknowledge the child she wasn't fazed at all—she merely said she accepted my decision. We had a protracted quarrel on the whole subject of the child. I was distraught."

"So distraught you then decided to retire to Norfolk for three months to be alone with her!"

He stopped dead in front of the fireplace. "Sylvia . . ." He sank down beside me on the couch again. "That's past. I ended my affair with Miss Slade. I came home to you. That promise at least I didn't break."

"But the baby—your own child—how can you consider your involvement with Miss Slade finished when—"

"Ah come, Sylvia, let's not be romantic and sentimental about this!" He was on his feet again. I could almost hear the air crackle with the tension which emanated from him. "Let's be practical and realistic! I had two choices where the child was concerned: I could either acknowledge him or not acknowledge him. I considered the circumstances and when I realized it would be disastrous for everyone concerned if I acknowledged him, I came to the decision which thousands of people make every year when for various reasons they put their children up for adoption. I decided to sever my connection with him and play no part in his life."

"But—"

"Very well, supposing I had acknowledged him—supposing I had! I had already broken my promise to you on the subject of children—do you imagine I wanted to compound my shoddy behavior by holding my broken promise up for public inspection? Do you think I could possibly do such a thing to you? Do you think you mean so little to me that I'd ride roughshod over all your most private grief?"

"Oh, Paul, I—"

"And what about the child? He's going to have enough problems growing up as the bastard son of the notorious Dinah Slade. Do I want to multiply his problems by having him grow up the bastard son of the notorious Paul Van Zale? And what good would my money and my fame do him? All that child is going to want is the chance to grow up in humble obscurity without his parents' reputations hanging around his neck like twin millstones. Do you think I want him to accuse me later of ruining his life by selfishly laying claim to him as soon as he entered the world? Wouldn't it be better if he grew up not knowing me? Then at least someday he might realize that I did the unselfish thing, the right thing, the only decent thing by letting him go."

I could not speak.

"I suppose you doubt my sincerity," he said, misinterpreting my silence. "You don't think I've really made up my mind to have no connection with the child. Well, why do you think last year I made such an effort to take an interest in that odd little boy of Mildred's? I thought if only I could have a son here I wouldn't care—"

He stopped. In his distress he had said too much. In the silence which followed I knew we were both thinking of those innumerable times he had told me he did not want a child. At last he said, "I feel so angry. I had totally accepted the fact that I had no children—I genuinely meant it when I told you not to distress yourself on my account if you couldn't have a child. But when the baby was born—and lived—I was disturbed. I couldn't help myself. Of course I'll get over it—in fact, I've got over it already. I've made my decision, I know it's the right one and I intend to live with it. I absolutely refuse to let Miss Slade's behavior alter our lives."

I managed to say, "Did you never think of marrying her?"

"Good God, no, it wouldn't have lasted six months! Miss Slade could never cope with being my wife. She's very young, you know, and still has a lot of growing up to do."

"I just thought that perhaps—"

"No."

"—the mother of your child—"

"It makes no difference. It's extremely important to be clear-headed about this and not be carried away by a tide of sentimentality. If I were in fact obsessed with the desire for a child I'd be in England with Miss Slade, but I'm not; I'm in America with you because I know you're the best wife I could possibly have and I want to share my life with you, child or no child. Now listen to me, Sylvia. I can never apologize sufficiently to you for my mistake with Miss Slade, but that's all it was: a mistake which we now have to accept and put behind us. I know it's hard; I know it's painful, but we must try and forget Miss Slade and think of ourselves. We have a successful, satisfying marriage and I intend to do all I can to ensure it remains so, but I need your help, Sylvia. Please—it's vitally important. We've got to close the door on this incident. Please promise me you'll try."

"I will if . . . if you can give me your word that everything really is over between you and Miss Slade."

"I give you my word."

He took my hands and held them tightly in his. I felt his tension run through my body like an electric current, and when he released me I was limp.

"I'm afraid I really have to go back to my meeting," he said after he had kissed me. "Will you forgive me if I leave you now? I'll be home early this evening. Cancel our engagements—we'll have a quiet dinner together."

I nodded. Stooping, he gave me another brief kiss, touched my bowed shoulders gently and was gone.

After a moment I returned to the other room but felt so faint I had to sit down. I had just sunk into the chair by the desk when O'Reilly reappeared.

"Can I escort you to your car, Mrs. Van Zale?" I heard him say from a long way away.

I went on sitting by the desk. Dimly I was aware of him closing the door and drawing closer to me.

"Are you all right, Mrs. Van Zale?"

"Perhaps a glass of water . . ."

He went immediately to the bookcase and touched the spring which made the middle shelves swing outward to reveal the bar. There was a small sink built into the wall next to the liquor cabinet. O'Reilly took a glass, reached for the tap and paused.

"Would you like me to add a shot of brandy to the water, Mrs. Van Zale? Brandy often helps if you feel temporarily unwell."

"All right. Yes. Thank you." I did not have the strength to argue with him. I started to grope in my purse but I did not know what I was looking for, and it was only when the tears streamed down my face that I realized I was hunting unsuccessfully for a handkerchief.

A shadow fell across me. A handkerchief was pressed into my hand and a glass was placed on the desk beside me. The brandy was neat. I had started crying before he could add the water.

I was horribly embarrassed by my tears. If he had been a servant I would have been simply annoyed by my lack of self-control, and if he had been a friend I would merely have apologized, but O'Reilly was neither servant nor friend and because our behavior with each other had always been so excruciatingly formal I now felt as if he were seeing me naked. After hiding my face in the handkerchief in a vain effort to stem my tears I abandoned all attempt at concealment and reached for the brandy.

To my surprise he seemed to understand the depths of my embarrassment, for he turned away from me tactfully and looked out the window.

I sipped the brandy and became calmer. This time when I tried to dry my tears I was successful, but glancing in the little mirror I kept in my purse I saw to my dismay that my eyes were red and swollen. I was just reaching for the brandy again when he said quietly without turning around, "Your husband gave me the bill."

The brandy slopped in my glass.

"I'll raise hell at Tiffany's," he said, running his finger around the rim of the ancient vase. "I'll get the clerk who made the error fired."

After a mouthful of brandy I said levelly, "What good would that do now?"

"It's the principle of the thing. Why should you have to go through this just because some clerk made a wrong entry in a billing system?"

"I would have found out later in some way, I expect. I can't blame the clerk."

"Well, I know who I blame," he said, flicking a speck of dust from the surface of the table. "I blame that little nuisance Dinah Slade. The smartest thing Mr. Van Zale ever did was to tell *her* goodbye."

"Mr. O'Reilly . . ."

As he swung around to face me I noticed that his eyes were not blue, as I had always imagined they were, but green.

"You don't have to concern yourself with that girl, Mrs. Van Zale," he interrupted with such strength that I quite forgot that his habitual manner was one of wooden neutrality. "She's made every mistake she can possibly make with Mr. Van Zale, and now he just wants to wash his hands of her. I often used to think of you when I was with them at Mallingham. I used to wonder why Mr. Van Zale ever looked twice at a plain, silly, immature little girl like Dinah Slade when all the time he could have been with you, always so beautiful, so elegant, so charming—" He stopped.

I stared at him openmouthed. The pass was familiar enough, for after nearly twelve years of marriage I was more than accustomed to dealing with men who assumed I had no more use for fidelity than my husband had, but I was so stunned that the pass was coming from O'Reilly, who I had long since decided was uninterested in women, that I was caught off guard. O'Reilly's reserve, his self-control and his position as Paul's most trusted assistant all combined to make me wonder if I had imagined his speech. I stole a horrified glance at my brandy as if I had just discovered that it contained a hallucinatory drug, and then told myself O'Reilly was simply trying to make me feel better by giving me some kindhearted compliments.

"Thank you," I said weakly. "How very nice of you to go out of your way to cheer me up, but I feel much better now and I don't think I should outstay my welcome here a second longer. Please don't bother to escort me to the door."

"I'll see you uptown."

"No, I . . . Thank you, but I'd prefer to travel alone."

He opened the door for me. I did not look at him as I left the room, but I was very much aware of his presence as he insisted on escorting me outside to the Cadillac. He even held the doorman's umbrella for me himself as we stepped out into the rain.

"Mr. O'Reilly, I'm really most grateful to you for being so kind, but I'm sure you'll understand if I say I'd prefer we treated this conversation as if it had never happened."

"I'd prefer it too," he said easily. "If Mr. Van Zale ever knew I'd discussed Dinah Slade with you he'd break me in half. Goodbye, Mrs. Van Zale. Are you sure you don't want me to see you home?"

"Quite sure, thank you. Goodbye, Mr. O'Reilly."

As the chauffeur drove away I looked over my shoulder and saw O'Reilly still standing on the sidewalk in the rain. For a second I thought he had recaptured his wooden neutrality, and I was just thinking in relief that I need worry no further about him when I saw that his green eyes were shining in his quiet set face.

Chapter Five

I

I was disturbed by O'Reilly's behavior, but there were several reasons why I paid no further attention to it at that time. First, I thought that O'Reilly cared too much about his job to risk certain dismissal by making his veiled pass more direct; second, I myself was too absorbed by the painful fact of Alan Slade's existence to dwell on O'Reilly's unstinted admiration, and finally, I was diverted from both O'Reilly and Alan Slade by a crisis which blew up on the eve of Bruce Clayton's wedding.

The wedding was due to take place on the first Saturday in May, a few days after my journey downtown to the bank. It had been a difficult week. Paul had done his best to ease the situation by offering to take me away for a long weekend, but all I wanted was to be alone while I sorted out my feelings and recovered my equilibrium. Finally I said to him, "I think it would be best if we just went on as usual—at least for the time being." So we had postponed our long weekend and I had tried to immerse myself in my daily activities. But my mind kept wandering. I thought of Alan Slade and how lovely babies were when they were fourteen months old, and all the time at the back of my mind was the nagging thought: How could a man like Paul possibly have made such a mistake? Yet I had believed him when he insisted he had not broken his promise to me deliberately.

I returned to my doctor to ask if there had been any new medical advance which might help me, but he again advised against another pregnancy. I was in despair when I left his office. In fact, I was so depressed that it took me a day to remember there were other doctors in New York, and I had just decided it was time to make the rounds of the specialists again when Bruce telephoned to ask if he could see Paul.

We had some people coming to dinner that evening, but Bruce was willing to call later. I wondered in alarm if there could have been some last-minute hitch in the wedding arrangements. Grace's parents had planned a large wedding, and both Bruce and Grace had expressed annoyance that the event had burgeoned into the society affair for which Mrs. Rochfort had yearned since the day Grace entered the world.

Our guests had gone by the time Bruce arrived, and I was about to go up to bed when he was announced.

He was a tall dark-haired young man with heavy-rimmed glasses which hid the fine eyes he had inherited from Elizabeth and which gave him a vague air of distinction. New York society was always maliciously disappointed that he did not look like Paul, but I had always thought there was a strong resemblance in their natures. It was one of the reasons why I wondered if Elizabeth was as sure of her son's paternity as she appeared to be. A passionate devotion to classical civilization had originally drawn him toward the field of philosophy in which he now earned his living, and in pursuing these intellectual leanings he was sensitive, idealistic and just a little too serious. "Exactly like Elizabeth when she was young," Paul had often said to me, but I had pieced together enough of Paul's past to know that such a description might well have applied to him also years ago.

"Hello, Bruce!" said Paul. "Not celebrating your last night as a bachelor?"

"I escaped all that half an hour ago, thank God. I can imagine nothing more barbaric than being hung over at one's own wedding."

"Well," I said tactfully, "if you'll excuse me . . ."

I left them alone, but later after I had dismissed my maid I did not go to bed but sat brushing my hair absent-mindedly. I was trying to decide which specialist I should consult next, but when I realized I was thinking far too much about the unbearable burden of my childlessness I tried to turn my thoughts elsewhere. Would I ever have the nerve to get my hair bobbed? I tried to imagine myself with a modern style, but I knew Paul would be sure to hate it. He liked a woman to have long hair.

I wondered if Dinah Slade's hair was long, but judging from the hat she had worn in the newspaper photograph I guessed this was unlikely. Of course, when one was very young one could look attractive in even the most outlandish modern fashions . . .

Must stop thinking about Dinah Slade.

I tried to imagine what Bruce was discussing with Paul. It was odd how hard it was for me to believe they were unrelated, but that was probably because if I had been Elizabeth I would somehow have contrived to have Paul's child. But had Elizabeth ever loved Paul as I loved him? Surely she was much too dignified to succumb to the headiest of passions, but perhaps that was why Paul had always felt so safe with her and why their friendship still survived even though they were no longer lovers. I tried to imagine Elizabeth in bed but could not. Surely she would think the entire act was nothing but an inexcusable breach of good taste. . . .

Must stop thinking of Paul in bed with other women.

He had been surrounded with women when I had first seen him. How long ago that seemed, almost as long ago as the days of my first marriage! I had been married for only two years before Frederick died of typhoid during a diplomatic mission to Mexico, and in retrospect it seemed we had hardly known each other at all. I had been given a sheltered upbringing by my grandmother in Philadelphia after my parents had died in a railroad accident, and Frederick had received an equally sheltered upbringing in the care of his elderly uncle, a Hudson Valley recluse. We had loved each other in a pleasantly romantic way, but "the darker side of marriage," as my mother's married sister was pleased to describe it to me on the night before my wedding, had remained not dark but certainly obscure. I had been glad to give myself to Frederick, glad to make him happy and glad when each mysteriously pointless episode came to a rapid conclusion, so when Frederick died I did not pine for lost pleasures as other women might have done, but slipped uncomplainingly into the quiet life deemed suitable for a young widow in those far-off days before the War.

Then one day, three years after Frederick's death, some friends I was visiting on Long Island gave a garden party and I met Paul Van Zale.

I knew his reputation. Anyone who was anyone on the Eastern Seaboard had heard of Paul Van Zale, his meteoric rise to riches, his spectacular divorce and his unending stream of women. When I first saw him he was talking to two of the famous beauties of the day, while a third was offering him a glass of champagne. He stretched out his hand to accept it, glanced carelessly past his companions and saw me. One look at those dark eyes was enough to remind me instantly of "the darker side of marriage," and blushing in dismay at my uncontrollable imagination, I turned tail and fled.

I was much too unsophisticated to know that this immediately made me irresistible to him, and I was much too ignorant of his circumstances to know he was tired of his bachelor life and wished to remarry. He knew exactly the kind of wife he wanted—he even had the most important attributes numbered and could tick them off on his fingers—and although I did not know whether I could satisfy his requirements I soon knew I would rather die trying than live the rest of my life without him. I admit I was clay in Paul's hands, but I might not have been if he had treated me with a style which matched his reputation. However, nobody could have been more of a gentleman than Paul was when he first began to call on me, and no young woman could have dreamed of a more romantic and chivalrous suitor. Even later when he described his concept of marriage to me in such painfully unconventional detail I could not quite believe he would be unfaithful to me after we were married—or even during those winter months of our courtship.

We became engaged in April 1912 and agreed to marry in June. I was afraid society would think we were being hasty, but my secret dread was that Paul would change his mind if we waited too long, so I did not argue about the wedding date. Besides, by that time I could hardly wait to be his wife, and Paul, as I soon discovered, was not prepared to wait at all.

"My yacht's in the water now," he said in May, "and the weather's nice. Let's go away for the weekend."

I told him I would prefer to wait until we were married.

"After this weekend I won't ask you again until our wedding night."

"But—"

"Supposing you hate going to bed with me."

"I can't imagine—"

"I'm forty-two years old, I'll probably live at least another twenty years and naturally I'll want to make love to you as often as possible. Three hundred and sixty-five days times twenty is seven thousand three hundred—and that's not even counting leap years! I agree we should deduct six months for total physical exhaustion, but even so do you really want to commit yourself to going to bed with a man over seven thousand times without knowing exactly what you're committing yourself to?"

We laughed. I tried to be worldly and sophisticated instead of old-fashioned and straitlaced, and to be honest I did not have to try very hard. I was too much in love with him, and in my own mind I had already committed myself to him for the rest of my life.

I went away on the yacht for the weekend.

It was a revelation to me. I had never thought I would ever stoop to a love affair, even with a man who had promised to marry me, and having stooped I was quite prepared to be crushed by guilt, but the guilt never came.

"I know I should be feeling wicked and immoral," I said to Paul as we leaned on the deck rail and watched the sunset, "but I only feel happier than I've ever felt in my life. What sort of a creature does that make me?"

"Human," said Paul, and immediately suggested we continue our affair when we left the yacht.

"Oh, but supposing I start a baby! That awful word 'premature' in the birth announcement and everyone counting up how many months we'd been married . . ."

"Good God," said Paul, "don't you really trust me to look after you properly?"

So ignorant was I about birth control that I had not realized how much care he had already been taking on board the yacht. "And besides," said Paul, taking the opportunity to remind us both of a truth I preferred not to think about, "since your doctor has given you certain advice about the dangers of further miscarriages I'd be criminally negligent if I made love to you with no thought of the consequences."

When I returned from my honeymoon I found another doctor and persuaded Paul to let me undertake the task of avoiding conception. I managed to convince us both that my subsequent pregnancy was accidental, but the second time he was openly skeptical, and after that he took control of the situation for some years. It was not until 1921 that I won permission from him to use a new device which was supposed to be the last word in reliability for women who wished to avoid having children, but inevitably in 1922 I found I had once more managed to conceive.

After our reconciliation later that year we had been obliged to discuss the problem again. It was very difficult for both of us even to mention the subject, let alone discuss it unemotionally, so it was hardly surprising that in his anxiety not to hurt me and in my anxiety not to anger him, we achieved only the most facile communication.

"Perhaps I should take care of matters again," he had said awkwardly.

"But that's so tedious for you."

"You mustn't think that."

"But I understand the doctor's device better now."

"But that's tedious for *you.*"

"No."

"Well, if you think you can manage—"

"Yes."

"—without accidents—"

"Yes," I said, but I knew that the only reason why I wanted to persist with the responsibility was because I could not bear to think I would never again have a chance of becoming pregnant.

Paul never had accidents.

"It was an accident, a terrible accident. . . ."

I thought of that clear pragmatic mind, so uncluttered by passion that it was capable of analyzing every detail of a romantic relationship and taking the necessary efficient decisions to guard against trouble. If Dinah Slade's pregnancy was indeed an accident, something had gone very wrong not only with Paul's obsession for self-protection but with that cool uncluttered analytical mind.

"I don't believe in romantic love," he had said to me long ago. "It's really just another form of mental derangement, destroying logic and leading to irrational behavior."

After talks with Elizabeth I realized that his experiences with his first wife were responsible for this attitude, and since there was no altering the past I resolved to live with it as best I could. There was no point in getting upset because Paul felt himself unable to say the magic words "I love you." I knew that in his own way he loved me very much, and that had to be sufficient. Besides, as I left my twenties behind and became more experienced in the ways of the world it occurred to me that the husbands who chanted the ritual "I love you" to their wives every day of their married lives were all too often the ones who ran off with other women. Better silence than insincerity, I told myself, and I fell back with relief on the old cliché "Actions speak louder than words."

Actions. "One silver christening mug . . ."

Must stop thinking about that, must, must, must. . . .

I was still staring at my reflection in the mirror with troubled eyes when a sound next door made me jump. Paul had slammed the door of his dressing room and was dismissing his valet. The next moment the communicating door was flung open with a bang and I rose automatically to my feet, the hairbrush still in my hand.

Despite the violence of his entry he looked more exhausted than angry, and I saw at once that he was deeply upset.

"Paul, whatever's happened? Did you—"

"Yes, I had the most godawful row with Bruce." He shed his jacket, kicked off his shoes and slumped onto the bed. "Sylvia, you know how fond I am of that boy. It's true we've seen little of each other in recent years, but I didn't realize until tonight that he's never got over that time when . . . Well, there was a scene years ago. I've never talked to you about it because I wanted to believe the whole matter was closed. It was only when he told me tonight that he didn't want me to be at his wedding tomorrow that I saw the issue was very much alive."

"But why on earth shouldn't he want you at his wedding?" I exclaimed astonished.

"He said he had had enough of New York society thinking I was his father and that he was determined to demonstrate the truth once and for all by excluding me from an important family occasion."

"But surely wouldn't that create even more gossip? Oh Paul, he must have had too much to drink!"

"No, he was reasonably sober. He didn't call me a selfish capitalist son of a bitch until I told him it was nonsense to say I'd ruined his mother's life."

"Paul! I just can't believe Bruce would—"

"I regret to say I was then fool enough to embark on an anti-Marxist polemic, and we had one of those ridiculous quarrels over politics which ended when he lost his temper and tried to hit me. Fortunately my reflexes are good and he missed, but when I saw he obviously wanted to try again I went to the door and shouted for Peterson. You can imagine how I felt having to call my bodyguard to protect me from a man who for the first seventeen years of his life always treated me with as much affection and respect as a boy would treat his father."

He got up from the bed, reached inside his discarded jacket and pulled out his gold pillbox. Watching him I said slowly, "What happened when Bruce was seventeen?"

"This scene I mentioned earlier. To cut a long and very painful story short, he came down to the office to discuss a certain matter with me and during the course of the discussion he revealed he believed himself to be my son. Naturally I was appalled. I couldn't believe that Elizabeth—*Elizabeth*, of all people!—had been less than honest with him about such a fundamental fact of his life. I myself had always been honest with him, and when he became old enough to ask questions about my relationship with his mother I was glad he was able to come to me without embarrassment. Certainly I made every effort to repay his confidence by trying to explain the situation as adequately as one can ever explain such things to an adolescent boy who knows nothing of life, but since he never asked me outright if I was his father, I never came right out and said, 'You're not my son.' I simply assumed he had his facts straight, and it wasn't until he said to me that day at the office, 'You're my father and therefore you should do this, that and the other,' that it occurred to me that Elizabeth could have misled him."

"Paul, are you absolutely one hundred percent sure . . . ?"

"My dear, he was conceived while Elizabeth and her first husband were spending a summer in Europe. I was three thousand miles away, and unless Elizabeth underwent a twelve-month pregnancy there's no possibility whatsoever that I'm Bruce's father."

There was a pause. He moved toward the communicating door but then changed his mind and slumped down once more on the bed. "I told Bruce that," he said. "I felt it was essential that he should know the truth, but Elizabeth was furious with me and that led to another row. She said that although she had never directly lied to Bruce she had made no effort to disillusion him, because she thought it was best for him to believe I was his father."

"I expect she liked pretending to herself that you were."

"But my God, how could she do such a thing to that boy? When I think of all the times she and I used to agree on the intellectual necessity of truth and honesty!"

"One can't always live life intellectually, Paul."

"But Elizabeth and I did! Over the years we evolved this mutually satisfactory relationship which incorporated all the principles which we held to be intellectually valid. I'm afraid you just don't understand."

"I understand that Elizabeth wanted her son to be your son. I understand that she must have loved you, otherwise she wouldn't have cared about that. I understand that if you love someone you want to be with them, and that it's easier to be with them in marriage than in an adulterous liaison."

"You're seeing everything from the typical woman's point of view. Elizabeth wasn't a typical woman. If you could stop looking at the situation so romantically—"

"Romantically! Paul, I'm talking realistically! I'm talking about the way things really are, not the way they are in some intellectual theory which has no relation to reality whatsoever!"

"I was always realistic!" cried Paul, suddenly becoming more overwrought than I had seen him since Jay's death. "It was Elizabeth who lost touch with reality, lying to Bruce like that! She blamed me for the way Bruce and I became estranged, but it wasn't my fault, it was hers! If she hadn't lied, I wouldn't have had to tell him the truth, and I hated having to tell him, hated having to hurt him, hated the whole damned interview—"

"Oh, darling, don't upset yourself so!"

"—but I had to tell him, didn't I? What choice did I have? How could I have let him go on believing a lie like that? I had to tell him!"

"Yes," I said, "you did. It was just sad such a confrontation had to happen, that's all. Isn't it a terrible irony that in any—" I fumbled for the tactful word—"unusual relationship it's always the children who seem to suffer most?"

"I wouldn't have hurt Bruce for the world." He dragged himself to his feet. "God, I'm tired! I'd better go to bed."

"Stay here with me."

"No, I must be alone, I feel so disturbed. I mean," he added clumsily, as if the effort of arranging words in a sentence was too much for him, "I don't want to disturb you and I'm sure that no matter how tired I am I shall find it impossible to sleep."

I did not press my request since it was obvious he wanted solitude, but when he had gone I lay awake for a long time while I wondered if I could somehow assume the role of peacemaker. Obviously there could be no quick reconciliation between Bruce and Paul, but perhaps later I could attempt to pour oil on the troubled waters. It would be a challenge for my diplomatic talents, it would make Paul deeply grateful to me, and it would certainly take my mind off all thought of Dinah Slade.

II

It was October when I spoke to Bruce. He and Grace had spent the summer months in Europe before returning to New York for the start of the academic year, and Paul and I had gone up to Bar Harbor as usual after the Fourth of July. I had paid secret visits to four more doctors who specialized in female medical problems, but although they had all been discouraging I had heard there was a doctor on the West Coast who had had success in helping women through difficult pregnancies, and I thought that when I was next visiting some cousins in San Francisco I would make an appointment to see him.

Meanwhile there was no opportunity to visit the West Coast. When I returned from Bar Harbor it was late September, my New York social calendar was already full and it was hard enough finding a free afternoon when I could see Bruce.

We eventually agreed to meet in the Tea Room at the Plaza, and three days later beneath the glass dome I began my attempt at peacemaking. The palms drooped elegantly in the muted indoor light, and the small orchestra was playing Viennese tunes as the waiter arrived with our tea.

"Of course it's about that row you had with Paul before the wedding," I said after we had spent an awkward five minutes exchanging pleasantries.

He sighed, ran his fingers through his thick hair and took off his glasses to polish them with a grubby handkerchief. He was dressed casually in a tweed suit with an unpleasant red-spotted necktie. There was a smudge of ink on one of his cuffs. He looked erudite, distracted and vaguely bohemian.

"Sylvia, I don't see how we can possibly have a profitable conversation on the subject. If you're aiming at a dramatic reconciliation complete with tears of joy on both sides and a pounding piano accompaniment in the best tradition of motion-picture melodrama, you're just wasting your time."

"What about a quick cocktail on Christmas Eve? No tears, no pounding piano, no fuss. I'll invite about a dozen other people and we'll have the traditional eggnog."

"I'm afraid you don't understand. Paul and I are finished. I spent twelve years trying to pretend for my mother's sake that we were still friends, but when my wedding came I realized I couldn't go on with such a farce just to please my mother. Was Paul really so upset? He surely couldn't have been surprised. He must have been well aware that we haven't had an honest conversation with each other since I was seventeen."

"Yes, Paul told me what happened when you were seventeen."

"He did?" He flushed. "I bet he didn't tell you the whole story."

He looked away from me as the orchestra began to play *Tales from the Vienna Woods,* and when he said nothing more I felt obliged to add, "He told me there had been a very unhappy scene."

"We quarreled." Unexpectedly he looked me straight in the eyes. "It was about you."

"Me?" I stared at him. "I don't understand."

"When I was seventeen it was 1912, Sylvia. The April of 1912."

"When Paul and I became engaged."

"Exactly. I went down to Willow Street—it was before the merger, so he was still at Nineteen Willow in his old office—and I told him to break off the engagement with you and marry my mother."

After a moment I took a sip of tea. "Go on."

"Is this going to upset you? I have no quarrel with you now, Sylvia—"

"Go on, Bruce."

"Well . . ." He took a tea cake and shredded it with quick nervous movements of his hands. Across the room *Tales from the Vienna Woods* swept into a lush new coda. "My mother had been hoping to marry Paul for several months. She told me so—she was quite frank about it. She said she knew he'd decided to remarry, and she was convinced that he'd eventually come to the conclusion that she was the only woman who could possibly be an adequate wife to him. But when I asked her why she didn't immediately seek a divorce from Eliot and make Paul aware of what she wanted, she said no, she couldn't do that, because that would put her in the same category as all the women who chased him, and her entire success with Paul had always lain in the fact that she had never put any kind of pressure on him. Well, you know what happened. She knew about you, of course, but she never thought he'd marry you. She said you were too young and unsophisticated, and that Paul needed a mature woman, not an inexperienced girl. Paul was visiting our house, you know, all that winter he was seeing you, and—I'm sorry, I guess I shouldn't have said that."

"Dear Bruce, don't let's get bogged down in embarrassment. I'm perfectly well aware he continued his affair with your mother both before and after he married me. What did Elizabeth do when she heard he was engaged to me? Was there some frightful scene between her and Paul?"

"Oh God, no! My mother had too much pride for that. She congratulated him and said she hoped he would be very happy. Then she went to her room and cried all night. Eliot, thank God, was away somewhere, but I was down from Groton for the Easter recess, and after I'd heard my mother cry all night I couldn't bear to think of her suffering anymore, so I went downtown to see Paul. Of course it was a complete failure. He just told me I was too young to understand his relationship with my mother, and then I ruined everything by dragging in the paternity issue to try to persuade him to listen to me. What a mistake! The entire issue of his marriage was forgotten and we had to exhaust ourselves establishing just who on earth I was. However, when he had finally finished demonstrating that I wasn't his responsibility and that he didn't give a straw about my mother, he went on board his yacht with you and sailed off into the sunset. Happy ending!"

"I can see Paul must have hopelessly mishandled his interview with you, Bruce," I said steadily, "but he sincerely felt he had to be honest with you. I'm sure you'll admit what a passion he has for honesty."

"Honesty? Paul Van Zale? My God, he's the biggest liar in town! All that trash about what a unique relationship he had with my mother—all that garbage about how he was so fond of me! He treated my mother like a whore and our home like a brothel and me like some amusing little lapdog who could be trained to perform clever tricks. He didn't care about me! When I got in his way and made a boring scene I was just a nuisance to be flicked out of the way. Year after year he pretended to be a father to me, and then suddenly it's 'No, we're not related, I'm sorry, can I get you a cab uptown?' I no longer amused him, so I was discarded—and the same thing happened to my mother. For years she listened to him saying she was the most important woman in his life, and then suddenly it's 'Oh, I don't think I want to sleep with you anymore. Goodbye, see you again sometime.'"

"I always wondered why their affair ended so suddenly." I was trying to deflect him from his pain by altering the focus of the conversation. I was disturbed to see how distressed he had become; his face was white, there was sweat on his forehead, and his hands had abandoned the ruined tea cake and were locked together in a tight agonized clasp.

"It had something to do with Vicky's death," he said at once. "It all dated from that time when she broke the news to him. My mother would never speak of it afterward except to say she had come to know Paul so well that the affair could no longer be sustained."

I was baffled. "What on earth could she have meant by that?"

"I think she found out what a liar he was," said Bruce. "I think she discovered that although Paul pretended to be bosom friends with Jason Da Costa he hated his guts and planned to ruin him. In the shock of Vicky's death Paul could easily have admitted that."

"But it's not true! Are you saying that Paul hated Jay even before Vicky died?"

"When my mother first knew Paul," said Bruce, "when she was twenty-one and he was twenty-two, he told her that the one man on earth he was going to get even with eventually was a young banker down on Wall Street called Jason Da Costa. Later she thought he'd got over all that, particularly when he encouraged Jay to marry Vicky, but—"

"You surely don't think . . ."

"I think it just took Paul twenty-five years to rig the Salzedo affair and get the revenge he'd always wanted."

"Bruce, that's the most terrible slander!" I tried to rise to my feet but was riveted to my chair. "How can you possibly believe such a thing?"

"I know the Da Costa brothers."

"Ah, that explains it! They'd say anything against Paul!"

"Can you blame them? Quite apart from what he did to their father, he's succeeded in forcing them out of the country. They were being investigated for tax evasion. Paul fixed that because they were trying to make trouble for him by reopening the investigation into the Salzedo affair—they unearthed some secretary who said she saw the confidential report on Paul's desk, and of course Paul always swore he never saw that report from Terence O'Reilly. Anyway, Paul came back from Europe at the end of 1922 in order to put an end to the trouble. He bribed the secretary in order to prove she was venal and her evidence worthless, and then he told the I.R.S. to hustle Stewart and Greg out of town."

"Paul couldn't possibly do that!" I exclaimed, but I knew he could. I tried to keep my voice steady. "Not even the President could do such a thing!"

"Sylvia, there's nothing that husband of yours can't do. He's so darned rich and so darned powerful he can buy himself whatever he wants, and if he can't buy it he can extort it. Those people in government all owe him favors. All he ever has to do is pick up the phone and exert a little pressure."

I fell back on the defense which had always reassured me whenever I had felt ambivalent about Paul's power. "But Paul is an honorable man. The investment bankers rely absolutely on their integrity. All the bankers said that to Untermyer during the Pujo investigation."

Bruce shrugged aside the ancient testimonies of 1912. "I can't speak for all investment bankers—I can only speak for Paul, and all I know is that there's no law that can touch him, and his very existence makes a mockery of American democracy. Why do you think I became attracted to Communism? It was because I came to resent not only Paul's private life but his public life as well. I think it's a crime that men like Paul Van Zale can make half a million dollars by a couple of handshakes on Wall Street while people are starving in the rural South or toiling in the industrial sweatshops of the North!"

"I don't want to argue with you about politics, Bruce. I just want to argue with you about the Da Costa brothers. If the tax evasion was a trumped-up charge, why didn't they stay in this country to fight it?"

"The choice was between footing a huge legal bill—and maybe going to jail—and retiring to a beautiful ranch in Mexico with a guaranteed annual income. Greg and Stewart aren't rich—Jay left most of his estate to that fifth wife of his—and they're not particularly smart. I've no doubt they probably did get into a fiscal mess with the money they inherited from Jay before they blew it all in the market, and in the circumstances a life south of the border could have had certain attractions."

"But how on earth do you know Paul bought them the ranch in Mexico?"

"Greg told me."

"I don't believe Greg Da Costa!" I was pulling on my gloves, or trying to. My hands were shaking.

"Sylvia . . . Look, I'm sorry. I didn't mean to upset you, I really didn't. But your husband's a dangerous man, and if you don't know that then I can see he's been lying to you as efficiently as he's been lying to everyone else. How well do you really know Paul, Sylvia? Do you know him well enough to realize you're much too good for him?"

"Bruce—"

"Don't let him treat you as he treated my mother, Sylvia. Don't let him take and take and take until one morning you wake up and find there's nothing left."

I had finally managed to get my gloves on, but although I looked around feverishly for the waiter I could not remember what he looked like. The desire to escape from the opulent prewar atmosphere and the Strauss waltzes was overwhelming.

It was Bruce who discovered the waiter and insisted on paying the bill.

"I expect you're now wishing you'd never suggested this meeting," he said as he escorted me outside. "I'm sorry."

"Are you?" I kept my voice calm and pleasant. "Well, if you're really sorry, you'll stop by with Grace on Christmas Eve for a cup of eggnog."

He swallowed awkwardly. "Well, I . . . All right. What time?"

"Six-thirty. And please be civil to Paul. I shan't expect you to stay more than ten minutes, so you can say you're on your way to another Christmas Eve party."

"May I ask whom I'm doing this for? I can't believe Paul truly cares whether we're estranged."

"You're doing it for me. It's the price I'm asking you to pay for repeating all those wicked rumors the Da Costa brothers have been inventing ever since Jay died. And you're doing it for Paul. He does care, Bruce—and I can say that because I know him better than you do. And you're doing it for your mother, because I happen to know she's upset that you and Paul are estranged. And lastly you're doing it for yourself, because I don't think you'll ever be at peace with yourself until you're at peace with Paul."

"Are you trying to tell me I'm neurotic?"

"I don't understand all these fashionable modern words. I think you're unhappy about Paul and I'd like to give you both the chance to sort things out. That's all."

"It'll never happen, Sylvia."

"Six-thirty on Christmas Eve, Bruce. Don't forget," I said, and left him abruptly on the steps of the hotel.

III

Paul was out that evening, but although I meant to write some letters I did nothing. I went to bed early and when midnight struck I was still thinking about Bruce. Two of his many disturbing disclosures ran persistently through my mind. The first was that the Da Costa brothers had been responsible for bringing Paul back from Europe in 1922, and the second was that Elizabeth, calm, dignified, self-controlled Elizabeth, had cried all night when she had heard of my engagement to Paul. It was hard to know which disclosure troubled me most, but the two together were certainly enough to ensure insomnia.

I lay awake till dawn.

I had never taken the Da Costa brothers' hysterical accusations seriously, but Bruce's claim that Paul had come home because they had made trouble for him had the unpleasant ring of truth. It would have taken a crisis of that dimension to drag Paul back from Europe, I could see that now, but if I believed Bruce's story I would also have to believe Paul had something to hide.

It took me some time to devise an explanation which still allowed me to believe in Paul's innocence, but I managed it in the end. Guilty or innocent, Paul would have had to suppress any whiff of scandal because the bank could never have afforded a resurrection of the Salzedo affair. Any preposterous lie could thus make life awkward for Paul, and the Da Costa brothers, bent on trouble as usual, would have had no scruple in exploiting the situation for their own ends. A ranch in Mexico would certainly have been worth a lie or two to them.

In the end, I thought to myself at two in the morning, and in the absence of proof, one was thrown back on the personalities of the people involved. The Da Costa brothers were notoriously unreliable, with bad reputations. It was far easier for me to believe they had dabbled in lies and extortion than to believe that Paul had arranged the Salzedo affair to ruin their father.

I discounted Bruce's nonsense that Paul had always hated Jay, because I could see no reason why such bitter hatred should have existed. They had seen little of each other in their early years, and if there had been some dramatic clash—over a woman, perhaps—someone would surely have been only too willing to tell me about it. I conceded that they might have disliked each other when young and that on Paul's side the dislike had been tempered with jealousy, since Jay had won success so early in life, but I did not see why this early antipathy should preclude a later friendship. People change, and besides, Paul himself had often said that he and Jay were uniquely well-suited as business partners.

On the other hand, I thought as a faraway clock struck three, there was no doubt that when Jay died Paul's feelings were tortuous in the extreme. I began to wonder if anyone would ever unravel the full story of Paul's relationship with Jason Da Costa, and then just as I was debating with myself how much Elizabeth could possibly know, I remembered O'Reilly.

O'Reilly was the only person still alive who knew beyond a shadow of doubt whether Paul had arranged the Salzedo scandal, because the scandal could not have been arranged without O'Reilly's connivance. I thought of him for a long time, but could see no possible way of asking him for the truth without creating a flammable situation. O'Reilly and I had ostensibly returned to our formal relationship, but I had the uneasy feeling that once he was certain I would not report him to Paul he would think nothing of making a heavier advance.

Brushing the worrying thought of O'Reilly aside, I was at once confronted with Elizabeth again. How she must have resented me at first! I felt shattered when I remembered how courteous she had always been to me, and when I wondered how long it had taken her to come to terms with Paul's decision my thoughts inevitably turned to the beginning of our friendship—when she had stopped sleeping with Paul.

Bruce had not solved this mystery, only made it more unfathomable. What could possibly have happened when Elizabeth had broken the news of Vicky's death? Even if I had believed Bruce's theory that Paul had immediately revealed a long-standing hatred of Jay, I could not for the life of me see why this should result in the instant termination of a twenty-five-year-old love affair. It seemed more plausible that Paul had made some very emotional scene which had afterward embarrassed him so much that he could never see Elizabeth without being reminded of it. Yet that didn't sound like Paul either. I myself had seen him prostrate with grief after Vicky's death, but he had shown no sign whatever of being hysterical.

"How well do you really know Paul, Sylvia?" Bruce had asked me hours earlier, and as dawn broke over Central Park the next day I could only answer: well enough to know that I love him whatever he's done. But I could no longer tell myself that his past could not affect our present, and as the days passed and the unsolved mysteries seemed to grow larger, I began intuitively to be afraid of a future when they might overwhelm us all.

IV

I was surprised when Bruce duly appeared at our house on Christmas Eve. I had not told Paul I had invited the Claytons because I had doubted they would come, and when Bruce walked into the room I wondered if he could remain unmoved by the spontaneous expression of joy which swept across Paul's face. They shook hands and then I kept Grace busy with the other guests while Paul and Bruce talked in a corner. To my delight the Claytons stayed a full half hour, and when Bruce said goodbye to me I told him how grateful I was that he had made the effort to keep his promise.

It was only when he said in a low voice, "I'd rather you didn't ask me again," that I knew the entire episode had been a failure.

Paul never guessed. "Bruce said he'd come downtown and have lunch with me!" he exclaimed pleased, and seemed to have no doubt that Bruce would keep his promise. It was not until we were in Florida two months later that I said to him casually, "Did you ever have that lunch with Bruce?" And he answered without looking at me, "Not yet."

After that we did not speak of Bruce for some time.

It was the spring of 1925. Paul was enviously watching Dillon, Read, another front-rank Yankee house, pull off a dazzling banking triumph. After purchasing the Dodge Brothers Automobile Company for one hundred and forty-six million dollars, they formed a banking syndicate—which Van Zale's rushed to join—to pass out to the public the securities of the new Dodge Company. The two issues of bonds, preferred and common stock, were all oversubscribed, and the profits of the banking syndicate soared into the millions.

"It's nice the stock market is so popular now," I said to Paul, privately glad that this Dodge coup had taken his mind off some adverse publicity he had suffered the previous year. The Internal Revenue Service had made its records public for the first time and revealed that he had legitimately paid only fifty thousand dollars in income tax, a disproportionately small portion of his earnings. However, I thought this disclosure proved Paul did not have the influence over the I.R.S. that Bruce had attributed to him, and the more I thought about it the more convinced I became that Bruce had exaggerated Paul's power.

Our social life was as busy as ever, and although I was always meaning to catch up with the latest Galsworthy novel I never seemed to have the time to open a book. We saw a dreadful play by Eugene O'Neill (I did try to keep up with Paul's intellectual tastes, but sometimes it really was impossible), attended a disappointing production of Shaw's *Caesar and Cleopatra* and endured an interminable evening of *Siegfried* at the Met. We were also at Carnegie Hall when Igor Stravinsky made his American debut, but afterward to my relief Paul declared he had no patience with modern music. I often wished we could go to a motion-picture theater, for some of the modern films were supposed to be so enjoyable, but Paul thought motion pictures were a debased art form and would have nothing to do with them. I always felt so left out when my friends would sigh over Rudolph Valentino or revile Pola Negri in *East of Suez*.

There were the usual weddings and christenings, with each glimpse of little bridesmaids or infants in long robes reminding me of the baby I wanted so much to have, but I had calmed down considerably since the episode of the Tiffany bill and knew it would be a mistake to rush into another pregnancy without sufficient forethought. When someone told me that the illustrious West Coast doctor had proved to be a quack I had despaired of finding a doctor who would promise me a nine-month pregnancy, but then it occurred to me that since only a dishonest doctor would guarantee to perform miracles, I would be wiser to remain in the care of my doctor, who knew my medical history so well. The real problem, I now saw, was not finding a doctor but coping with Paul's morbid fear of childbirth, a legacy bequeathed to him by his first wife and reinforced by Vicky's tragic death.

Carefully I worked out a plan of action. It would be best for me to conceive in the very happiest circumstances so that the event would mean something special to him. Our summer vacation at Bar Harbor sprang at once to mind; the unpretentious surroundings of the cottage always drew us closer together, and directly after our vacation that year I knew he was planning a business trip to Chicago and the West. That meant that if I became pregnant and miscarried he would never know about it. I would have to disclose a visit to the hospital, but I could always say I had had to attend to some minor feminine complaint.

And if I kept the baby . . . I hardly dared consider such a miracle, but I was sure that once all danger to my health was past Paul could not help but be pleased with the news.

Meanwhile I had my charity work to fill the void that the empty nursery created in my life, and in May, a year after Bruce's wedding, I was just returning from a committee meeting to raise funds for the Orphan Asylum Society when O'Reilly cornered me in the hall.

"Is my husband here as well?" I said surprised, for it was still early in the afternoon.

"No, I just came uptown to retrieve some papers. Mrs. Van Zale, before I go back to Willow Street could I have a word with you for a moment, please?"

I thought he wanted to discuss a domestic matter. The recent supply of gin had been most unsatisfactory and Paul always liked to have the best liquor to offer his guests.

"Is it about the bootlegger?" I asked, still thinking of the children in their orphanage at Hastings-on-Hudson as I followed him into the library. "Did you find a new one?"

"Not yet," said O'Reilly closing the door purposefully behind me. "I'm still looking. Are you still interested in Dinah Slade?"

Chapter Six

I

To hear the name Dinah Slade was unpleasant enough. To hear the name spoken by O'Reilly in an atmosphere chilling in its familiarity was a nightmare. But there was no escape. He was blocking the door.

"He's writing to her," he said. "Personal letters, not just letters about her business, and she writes back. The way they're going he'll send for her before long, and then once she's in New York—"

"Mr. O'Reilly," I said in my calmest, firmest voice, "the subject of Miss Slade is not one I care to discuss with you either now or at any other time." I felt sick. My heart was thumping painfully and the strength seemed to be vanishing from my legs. Moving closer to the door—and to O'Reilly—I said levelly, "Excuse me, please. I wish to leave."

"Don't you want to see the letters?" he said, not moving an inch. "I could arrange—"

My self-control deserted me. In fury I lashed out at him, but he caught my wrist before the blow reached his face and gave my arm such a tug that I tumbled against him. In shock I tried to speak, but he forestalled me. His arms tightened around my waist, my breasts were pushed hard against him, and his hot dry tense mouth closed on mine.

I jerked back my head to escape, but his tongue was already sliding past my lips. I went limp. It was not just because it was useless to fight anyone so intent on having what he wanted. It was because it was my only way of disassociating myself from such violence. I felt unspeakably humiliated, and in a second tears were scorching my cheeks. At once his kisses stopped, but he did not release me and when I could see through my tears to his hard set face I saw it naked for the first time, not closed to all emotion but wide open and passionately alive.

"I love you," he said.

"Oh, I . . ." But speech was quite beyond me. I still made no attempt to struggle, but for different reasons.

He started to kiss away my tears.

"I've loved you for a long time . . . always, really . . . but I knew I'd have to wait until you became disillusioned with him, and he was so clever, never putting a foot wrong, but oh God, it's been hard to endure, knowing how he treated you, seeing him with all the other women, I—" He stopped as if it was too painful for him to say more. His fingers pushed themselves into my hair in hard quick distracted movements. At last he said, "I couldn't give you a life in a Fifth Avenue mansion, but I have a lot of money saved and we certainly wouldn't starve. And I could give you everything he could never give you—I'd never look at another woman, never."

He started kissing me again. Hardly knowing what I was doing, I touched his dark hair. My fingers were shaking. I closed my eyes as if to blot out the sight of a world turned upside down, but all I heard was him begging me in his tense urgent voice, "Let her have him. They're two of a kind, and someday he's going to leave you flat to go off with her for good. But you don't have to wait for that to happen, Sylvia. Let me take you away from here as soon as possible and you'll never regret it, I swear it."

"I—"

"Shhh." He was caressing my hair again, and the thick uncoiling strands were sliding through his fingers. I was immensely aware of his physical excitement and immensely shocked to find that it was contagious.

I groped to reassemble the fragments of my defenses. "Paul would never leave me. He's always promised—"

"There's no promise he wouldn't break if it suits him."

I thought of Alan Slade.

"He'd never bring her here—with the child—"

"There's nothing he wouldn't do."

I thought of him brutally disillusioning Bruce.

"You don't know Paul as I do."

"And you don't know him as *I* do," he said. "Which of us knows him best?"

"If you hate him so much, how can you bear to—"

"Remain in his service? Because there's a lot of money in it for me and I wanted to save up enough to afford to take you away."

I immediately thought of blackmail. Appalling thoughts about the Salzedo affair flashed into my mind, but I could not face them. My courage failed me. I could not cope. "But to work with him every day," I stammered, "to live beneath his roof—"

"Your roof. That's all I cared about."

"How could Paul never have guessed?" There was something sinister about the fact that Paul, who was so astute, had been deceived for so long.

"He thinks I'm only interested in celibacy."

"But if he should find out . . ."

He laughed unexpectedly, and this eased the tension between us. He had been holding me tightly but now he released me, stepped back a pace and fumbled for a cigarette. "If he finds out," he said amused, "he'd have a fit. Literally, maybe." He paused, the cigarette case still unopened in his hands. Then he added softly, "He's an epileptic, isn't he?"

"What! An *epileptic?*" The suggestion was so ridiculous that even I finally had to laugh. "Of course he's not! Whoever told you that?"

"The Da Costa brothers."

"Oh, my God, is there nothing they won't say about Paul? How despicable they are!" I cried, and the next moment all my emotions of the past five minutes clashed together.

I burst into tears.

Abandoning his cigarette case, he at once took me in his arms again and began to stroke my hair. When he had finished apologizing he said curiously, "You know nothing about it?"

"I know it's not true!" I dashed away my tears. "Lately I've been wondering about the Da Costa brothers' slanders, but that statement at least is an outright lie! Why, you must know that perfectly well yourself—you see almost more of Paul than I do! Have you ever known him to have an epileptic seizure?"

"No, I never have."

I felt quite illogically relieved. "Well, then—"

"He behaves pretty oddly sometimes, doesn't he? Those times when he won't go out. . . . That drug phenobarbital."

"That's all a legacy from his childhood asthma. It runs in the family—why, Cornelius suffers from it! Do the Da Costa brothers say Cornelius is an epileptic too?" I broke away from him, too angry to be still any longer, and the abrupt movement loosened my hair completely so that it cascaded down my back. Raising my hands, I groped helplessly for the pins.

"I'm sorry," he said again, following me to the mirror where I was attempting to recoil my hair. "I didn't mean to upset you. I've always known that where your husband's concerned I must concentrate on hard facts if I'm ever to get anywhere with you, so it was stupid of me to raise the issue of his health. Let me stick to his correspondence with Dinah Slade. The letters show beyond any doubt that—"

"I don't want to see them. I've always accepted his infidelities, and because I've accepted them they can never humiliate me. But if I now start behaving like the traditional jealous wife I'm quite sure I shall be traditionally humiliated, and that's why I absolutely refuse to read or discuss his correspondence with another woman."

He was silent. I saw his eyes watching me in the mirror, and my hair felt so heavy that I could no longer hold it up. As it slipped through my hands he bent his head to kiss me on the neck.

"You have the most beautiful hair I've ever seen."

I tried to push him away but he only drew me closer to him. Again I was fearfully aware of the disastrous physical excitement generated by his fanaticism.

"Be with me now. Please."

"No, I—"

"We could go to my room."

"Absolutely impossible!"

"All I'm trying to prove is that I won't disappoint you."

That was just it. I was terrified of giving in to him. It had never even occurred to me before that any man but Paul could arouse such a response in me.

"I have to think," I said unsteadily. "I must have time. Please, Terence. Let me go now."

"You can't go like this," he said, kissing my loose hair, but he stepped back and made no further effort to touch me while I put my hair up. When I had finished he said, "I shall be out of town with him on business next week until the end of the month. Perhaps in June we can discuss all this again."

"July," I said. "Bar Harbor." I would be safe in Maine because Paul and I were so close there.

"That doesn't offer me much opportunity," he said, guessing my thoughts.

"I'm sure you'll make the best of what opportunity you can find."

"Sylvia—"

"I can't talk any more, Terence, I just can't," I blurted out, my tongue tripping awkwardly over the simple words, and before he could destroy my remaining defenses I rushed upstairs to my room.

II

My mind was in such turmoil that it was at least an hour before I grasped the fact that I was on the brink of an infatuation which threatened to distort, perhaps destroy my grip on reality. I did not love Terence. That was impossible, since I still knew next to nothing about him, and to tell myself that I could easily fall in love with him when I knew him better was to traffic in dangerous illusions. The truth was that Terence was no different from all the other men who had in the past tried to persuade me that infidelity could be amusing. The only reason why I had become so confused was that I happened by chance to find him physically attractive. In my labors to recapture my sanity I paused to marvel that I should now find Terence O'Reilly attractive. Then remembering that fanaticism I shivered, though whether because I thought such single-mindedness sinister or erotic I hardly knew.

I struggled on. Naturally there was no question of my giving in to him. I did have sympathy for wives who unsatisfied by their husbands sought passion elsewhere, but I could hardly put myself in that category. Paul satisfied me. I loved him. We had, as he himself had said not so long ago, a successful marriage, and if I were to risk ruining it by a pointless lapse with another man I could rightly tell myself I was insane.

All the same . . . just what *was* Paul doing with Dinah Slade?

My calm rational common sense lurched and broke down. I thought of loving someone who never looked at other women, someone who could say "I love you" without difficulty, someone who was strong and sympathetic without being remote and detached.

Eventually, noticing the time, I changed for dinner, and by taking that trivial action I was able to regain my grasp on reality and think practically again. It was no good moaning about Paul's infidelity. I had made up my mind long ago to accept him as he was, and although the Dinah Slade affair was thoroughly distasteful to me it would be stupid to lose my nerve over it and go to pieces. Obviously I had to find out what was going on, and since it was in Terence's best interests to lie it would be a mistake to accept his information about the Dinah Slade correspondence as gospel truth. In fact the more I thought about it the more unlikely it seemed that Paul would break yet another important promise by reviving if only by letter his moribund affair with Miss Slade.

"You look tired," said Paul when he came home that evening. "Is something wrong?"

"Oh, Paul!" As soon as I saw him Terence became insignificant and I could dismiss all thought of Dinah Slade. He kissed me, held me close and sat down with me on the couch as Mason brought in our drinks. "It's nothing," I said. "I've just felt blue all day. I don't know why."

"Well, there must be some reason!"

"Perhaps it was because I saw Caroline Sullivan today at one of my committee meetings and she showed me some new photographs of Tony—he's such a cute little boy now, and suddenly I remembered that he'd been born just before Dinah Slade's child . . ." I saw him look away and knew he was angry, for this was a subject we had both studiously avoided since the incident of the Tiffany bill. I had to summon all my courage to go on. ". . . and I wondered if you ever heard from Miss Slade nowadays. Doesn't she ever send you any photographs of her little boy? I would if I were her."

"You're not her." He drank half his tomato juice and picked up a magazine which lay on the table.

"You mean she never writes?"

He tossed aside the magazine, yawned and fidgeted impatiently with his glass. "We exchange classical quizzes occasionally. It's an amusing pastime, quite harmless. She started it by sending some photographs with no covering letter, just a few lines of Latin, Catullus' description of a baby—quite clever. I capped the quote and sent her another one to identify, and soon the game developed into a regular quiz. As a matter of fact I received a letter today which I want to show to Elizabeth—there's a question I can't answer, and I think Elizabeth might have some ideas. You can read the letter if you like," he added as if the conversation were of no importance to him, and pulled a sheet of paper out of his pocket.

I looked at the folded notepaper but did not take it. "I see," I said, thinking I spoke neutrally, but some element in my voice must have upset him for he exclaimed irritably, "Why are we discussing this, anyway? Do you object to this completely trivial correspondence? If you do I'll stop writing, but I really can't see why—"

"It's all right. But are you sure you should seek help from Elizabeth? That sounds like cheating to me!" I said lightly, and as I spoke I was thinking of Dinah Slade, smart, determined, *ambitious* Miss Slade far away in England, and I knew she wanted him back.

I also knew that Terence, gambling on the fact that I would refuse to read the letters, had exaggerated their importance in order to turn me against Paul. So much for Terence O'Reilly.

I was very angry, but at least I knew where I stood. Paul was mine and he was going to stay mine, and not even the most unscrupulous young woman on earth was going to take him away from me.

Anger made me passionate. Sensing that I was angry about the correspondence but not realizing my anger was directed only at Miss Slade, he stayed in his room when we went to bed that night, but I went to him and slid naked between the sheets and presently we began to make love. Usually I preferred to be in darkness or twilight, but I told him to turn on the lamp and later we left the bed and went to the long mirror. By that time I was too intent on seeking an emotional release to be plagued by reserve. The smallest details seemed extraordinarily exciting, the sweat on Paul's back, the reflection of the light on his muscles, his hot steamy breath on my body, and most exciting of all was to see his suave mannered detachment dissolve beneath the barbarism of physical intimacy.

He kept saying how beautiful I was, as if he could not quite believe it, and when we went back to the bed he kissed every part of my body until I wanted him so much that I drew him back into me. He rolled over, pulling me with him, and I felt the excitement rush forward beyond my control. I cried out, but he did not let me go, only held me closer until we were still. When he moved at last I saw his body glisten in the light again. My thighs were wet.

Later he said with a laugh, "After thirteen years you're still capable of surprising me!"

"And shocking you?"

"Yes, it was delicious," he said, still smiling, and although he started to stroke my breasts I decided that this time it was my turn to initiate the kisses. I was surprised by the speed of his response. I had hardly expected him to make love to me a second time directly after such an exhausting experience, but evidently he was in one of his dazzling moods when all exhaustion was a mere irritation to be swept aside and his energy blazed from him with an electrical intensity. I have no idea what time it was when we finally fell asleep. Paul's valet tried to wake him at six-thirty but abandoned the attempt. As he left the room I was aware of him turning off the lights we had left on.

At eight Paul reached for my hand. "I shall be thinking erotic thoughts about you all day at the office!" he murmured. "Lewis, Charley and Steve will be discussing business and I shall say 'breasts' when I mean debentures and 'thighs' when I mean common stock." He kissed me. I felt his body move under my hand. "My God, if I don't leave this bed now I'll never get to the office!"

When he tried to sit up I pulled him back beside me and we kissed again.

"I love you, Paul."

"My darling, how extraordinarily seductive you are! Have you been paying secret visits to the picture theater to study the notorious lady—whose name I forget—who purports to be something called a vamp?"

"It's you who must have been paying secret visits if you know about Theda Bara!"

"Is there anyone alive today who doesn't gloat over such actresses? Really, one of the most irritating aspects of the nineteen-twenties is that everyone behaves as if sex has only just been discovered!" He got out of bed and as he looked around for his robe his naked body twisted and turned gracefully in the shafts of sunlight. He looked much younger than his years.

We had breakfast together in my room, but as he was late he did not stay long.

"My perfect wife!" he said smiling as he kissed me goodbye, and I knew that Dinah Slade's memory meant nothing to him then just as the memory of Terence O'Reilly now meant nothing to me.

"Goodbye, darling," I said, returning his kiss, and as I watched him go I wondered in almost unbearable excitement if I had once more managed to conceive.

III

I had not. At first I was bitterly disappointed, but then I remembered my earlier resolution to wait until we were in Maine and I made up my mind to be patient. Patience was far from easy, though, and those last few weeks in New York might well have seemed interminable if both Paul and I had not received an unexpected diversion.

Cornelius reentered our lives.

I had not seen him since his visit to New York in 1923, although Paul had called on Mildred when he had been in the Midwest on business the previous summer. I had often suggested, even pleaded with Paul that we should invite Cornelius to visit us again, but Paul always insisted that the next move must come from Cornelius.

"But I don't understand!" I had exclaimed in despair, thinking Cornelius would be too shy to invite himself to stay, but Paul had only answered placidly, "Cornelius understands—or if he doesn't I'm not interested in seeing him."

We had waited. Nothing had happened. Paul had even begun to look annoyed whenever Cornelius' name was mentioned, but at last in early June his confidence was rewarded.

"A letter from Cornelius!" he said, smiling broadly at me across the breakfast table, and tossed the sheet of notepaper in my direction.

I picked up the letter. It was in Latin.

"Paul!" I said staggered, and when he laughed I laughed too. It was plain to see he was in excellent spirits. "What does he say?"

"He says he's been working hard at his Latin and Greek ever since he left New York. He's been studying Gibbon's *Decline and Fall of the Roman Empire,* and he asks if it's necessary to read beyond Attila the Hun's death on his wedding night."

"And is it?" I said, still dazed by this unlikely transformation of Cornelius into a classical scholar.

"No, but it's certainly essential that he learn the difference between a gerund and a gerundive. Write to him immediately, Sylvia, and invite him to Bar Harbor for the summer."

No one could have been more delighted than I was by this revival of Paul's interest in his great-nephew, but I was anxious when I discovered that the purpose of the invitation to Maine seemed to be to make Cornelius' summer as arduous as possible. Before I could protest, a tutor had been hired from Harvard, the tennis coach had been engaged from the club and Paul was casting around for three other young men of seventeen who would give Cornelius competition and companionship.

"Remember his delicate health, Paul," I said nervously. "Make sure there's plenty of rest and relaxation in the schedule."

"My dear, Cornelius is bored to tears with rest and relaxation—why do you suppose he wrote me that letter? He wants to live a tough busy life for a change, and I don't intend to disappoint him."

"But how will you ever find three other boys to endure it with him?"

"Easily. Boys of seventeen can stand anything except boredom—they like a challenge. The main problem will lie in choosing the right boys from among the crowd who'll volunteer for the ride."

I was still doubtful, but he was soon proved right. When he passed the word around among his friends he was swamped with applications from their offspring, but Paul was ruthless in selecting his protégés and only two boys met his exacting requirements.

"I'll take young Jake Reischman," he announced, for all the world as if he were concluding a shopping spree at some big store. "I don't suppose Cornelius has ever met a Jew before, and I've always had my eye on that boy of Jacob's—he's much the most promising of the new Reischman generation. And I'll take that boy Kevin Daly whose father's making such a fool of himself in politics at the moment. I liked the way Kevin compared the British presence in Ireland to the Roman presence in Europe and even quoted that Tacitus cliché about the Pax Romana. Now, let me see. Whom can I choose to complete the quartet?"

I suggested several names, but Paul merely said, "Insufficient intelligence" or "No ambition." I had already told my housekeeper at Bar Harbor that only three boys would be staying with us that summer when Paul unexpectedly discovered his fourth new protégé.

The discovery took place on the night of our arrival when we were taking a stroll in the gardens after dinner. In the old days it had been considered unhealthy to build near the water, and so the cottages like ours which dated from the nineteenth century were separated from the water by as much garden as possible. On the terrace below the house Paul had his swimming pool and tennis court, and farther down the sloping hillside were terraced lawns surrounded by shrubs and ornamented only by weathered garden furniture. These rustic chairs were typical of Bar Harbor, as informal as the Indian-made wicker baskets which were traditionally kept for calling cards, and as unsophisticated as the popular Bar Harbor hobby of "rocking," the search for rocks along the seashore. Even Paul abandoned his city tastes at Bar Harbor and indulged in sailing, walking on Mount Desert and picnicking among the landmarks of Ocean Drive.

It was sunset when we left the house. I hardly expected to find any of the gardeners still working, but on the second lawn below the house a young man in overalls was busily clipping a hedge.

"Hello, Sam!" I called.

He was the son of the head gardener who looked after the cottage in our absence and whose wife served as my housekeeper during the summer months. The Kellers were German immigrants. When we had first employed them Sam had been called Hans-Dieter, but in 1917 he had abandoned the name in response to anti-German sentiment at school and had rechristened himself Sam after the popular cowboy hero in a boys' magazine. Paul had been entertained by this determination to be American. I could remember him saying to the Kellers, "Your son has *chutzpah!*" But the Kellers were Prussian Lutherans, not German Jews, and the compliment had been lost on them.

"Good evening, Mrs. Van Zale," said young Sam Keller, straightening his back with a smile. "Good evening, sir. Welcome back to Bar Harbor!"

He had always had excellent manners. He was not a good-looking boy, but he was tall and broad-shouldered with a friendly smile.

I saw the acquisitive look flare in Paul's eyes.

"Since when has your father been making you do all his work for him?"

"Since school let out, sir. This is by way of being a summer job. I'm mowing lawns at another cottage too. There's always a lot of work to do when the visitors come back to Bar Harbor, and most of the estates use extra help."

"Making money, are you? What are you going to do with it?"

"I'm saving for college, sir. I'm going to put myself through law school."

"All lawyers are crooked!" said Paul, teasing him.

"Gee, do you think so, sir? Wouldn't that be against the law of averages?"

They laughed, and when Paul asked more questions I almost saw the silken net being thrown around Sam Keller to draw him out of his humble background into a harsher, headier world.

"But how on earth will he get on with the others?" I said distracted to Paul. "Think of Jake Reischman—a Fifth Avenue aristocrat! And Cornelius, with his maternal ancestry going back to the Dutch patroons! Why, even Kevin is a millionaire's son! How is Sam going to manage?"

"Excellently, I should think, since he's got more self-assurance than the other three put together. Worry if you wish about Cornelius, who's unaccustomed to mixing with boys his own age, but don't worry about Sam Keller."

But I worried about all of them and was convinced Paul had chosen a most ill-assorted quartet. I should have known better. Sam moved from the caretaker's cottage by the gates into one of the guest rooms as if he had been mingling with Bar Harbor's summer society all his life, and presently even Jake Reischman was asking for ketchup with his ground beef; Cornelius' agonized shyness melted away, and soon even Kevin Daly's ugly prep-school accent had mellowed into an imitation of Cornelius' Midwestern inflections. All four boys ate enormously, and after their mornings spent in classical study with their tutor they would swarm into the dining room, pick every dish clean and race outside like a bunch of puppies liberated from a traveling basket. At two-thirty the tennis coach would arrive for an hour, but after his departure they would linger on the tennis court as they slammed the ball to and fro amidst shouts of laughter.

The days passed. The sun shone. All the boys became browner, and Cornelius and Jake became more blond. Cornelius was having no trouble with his health and I knew this pleased Paul, who was finding his new protégés very entertaining. After dinner he would draw them into debates, and whenever I stayed to listen I noticed how he guided their conversations and encouraged them to express themselves. I saw him watching them, sensed him keeping relentless score of their errors, but he never betrayed which boy he favored above the others, although naturally they all vied for his attention. Time and again I would see their eager young faces turned to his, and when I recognized the hero worship in their eyes I could not help but wonder if Paul was right to manipulate their lives for his amusement. It was as if he had enslaved them by the power of his personality so that forever afterward they would remain in his thrall. Seventeen is a very impressionable age.

There were times when Paul was absent. To my relief he left Terence behind in New York when he joined me at Bar Harbor, but at the end of July after a quick trip to New York he brought Terence back with him to Maine.

I was plunged into panic. I spent a sleepless night trying to plan what I should say to him, but when he cornered me the next day I still had not made up my mind how to defuse the situation. Terence's fanaticism now only frightened me, and I was terrified that if I mishandled the inevitable confrontation he would abandon his iron self-control and make some disastrous mistake which would cost him his job and endanger my marriage.

"Can we talk?" he said, slipping into my little sitting room that afternoon when Paul was out playing tennis with the boys.

"It's a little awkward . . ."

"Wait, I'll close the windows." Helplessly I watched as he shut out the sounds from the tennis court and turned to face me. "I've been thinking about you all the time since we last spoke. I've got to talk to you."

"Yes, I've been thinking, too. Terence, I—"

"He's going down to Boston next week for a session at Kidder, Peabody, but let me invent an excuse to stay behind for an extra day. I can arrange that, I think. Then when all those kids are tucked up in bed I can come to your room."

"No." His physical attraction was touching me again and I felt more frightened than ever. For some reason, perhaps because I had been so much involved with Paul's recent recruits, Terence suddenly seemed to me to be the quintessential Van Zale protégé, tough, ruthless and brutally ambitious, and when I thought of those four boys who were now being so strongly influenced by Paul I trembled for them.

"Sylvia, don't get upset." He kissed me quickly before I could draw away. "There's no need. If you could only face reality by accepting me you'd find it a lot less painful than these romantic illusions you've been clinging to all these years."

My chin tilted up. My hands pushed hard against his chest. I was afraid no longer.

"Terence," I said, "if you think I'm just a fragile flower drenched in romantic illusions and thoroughly out of touch with the cold hard facts of life, you couldn't be more mistaken. No such woman could stay married more than one month to Paul Van Zale! You're the one who's clinging to your romantic illusions by believing I have to be swept off to some fairy-tale paradise where we can live happily ever after. Now shall we both try and face reality together? I find you very attractive—*very* attractive, as you well know. But I'm not in love with you, I'm not going to bed with you, and I'm staying with Paul."

"If you could give me just one sane logical reason—"

"I'm going to have his child."

I couldn't have shocked him more. There was a stunned bitter silence as his face closed, emptying itself of expression until he was once more just O'Reilly, Paul's most trusted assistant, but then the effort was too much for him and the anger blazed into his eyes.

"So in the end you found you couldn't resist the compulsion to compete with Dinah Slade!"

"This has nothing to do with Dinah Slade!" I said furiously. "And how dare you bring up her name again after you lied to me about her correspondence with Paul!"

"I didn't lie!"

"You implied they were exchanging love letters and all the time it was just a harmless exchange of classical quizzes!"

"My God, is that what he told you? And you believed him?"

"Get out!" I cried in a trembling voice. "Leave me alone! I never want to speak to you again like this!"

He went white. Immediately I was racked with regret, and although I already knew I had mishandled the interview I was unable to stop myself from making matters worse by showing compassion. "Terence, I'm sorry. Forgive me—I didn't mean to hurt your feelings."

"If you think I'm going to give up you couldn't be more mistaken."

"Oh, but—"

"Don't worry. I'll leave you alone while you're pregnant. I hope you stay in good health."

The full enormity of my lie suddenly caught up with me and I was speechless.

"Excuse me, please," he said, brushing my hand from his arm. "I won't embarrass you further by prolonging the conversation."

The door slammed. He was gone. I had bought myself a little time but had achieved nothing else, and sinking down on the sofa I saw to my despair that the situation was worse than ever. Terence remained determined to have what he wanted, all my doubts about the Dinah Slade correspondence had been reawakened, and I still, despite repeated efforts, showed no sign of conceiving Paul's child.

Chapter Seven

I

I would have spent more time worrying about Terence if I had not already been so worried about Paul. By the end of July I was certain he was working too hard; often he would begin his dictation to his secretaries as he finished dressing, and every few days he would be dashing up and down the Eastern Seaboard in response to telephone calls from New York. I was accustomed to his dabbling in business while he was on vacation, but that summer his work claimed him to an unprecedented degree, and even when he was supposed to be relaxing at Bar Harbor he would be too busy supervising his protégés to rest for long. Although the weather became very hot he insisted on playing tennis every afternoon, and when he retired indoors he seemed incapable of sitting down for more than two minutes. During his debates with the boys he would pace up and down the room, and later in the middle of the night I was often aware of him leaving the bed to ease the boredom of insomnia. I fully expected him to be too exhausted to pay me much attention at night, but the more tense he became the more he sought relaxation in our physical relationship. I became uneasy. I was glad to have so many chances to conceive the baby, but the mechanical repetition seemed to inhibit true communication between us, and I began to think we would be much closer if we simply sat down and talked about the matters which were troubling him.

But I knew he would never discuss his work with me.

One afternoon when Paul was out sailing with the boys my housekeeper told me there was yet another urgent personal telephone call for him. Terence was away in New York on some mission, his deputy Herbert Mayers had the afternoon off, and the stenographers were not allowed to handle Paul's private calls.

"Whoever it is, tell them to leave their name and say my husband will return their call later," I said, but Mrs. Keller came back to say the caller had asked for me.

"Who is it?"

"A Mr. Stewart Da Costa, ma'am."

The shock was so unpleasant that it took me a moment to recover myself. "I'm not at home to either Mr. Stewart or Mr. Gregory Da Costa, Mrs. Keller," I said evenly. "They'll have to call again."

Outside I wandered restlessly through the garden. It was another hour before Paul returned and I was able to tell him of the call.

"Stewart Da Costa? How dare he call me here!" His dark eyes blazed in his white face. "I'll leave for New York right away."

"Oh, but Paul . . ." It was several hundred miles to New York, and the exhausting journey involved many hours in a train.

Of course he ignored all my efforts to detain him.

He was away four days, and when he returned his rage was gone, replaced by a feverish cheerfulness.

"Those boys of Jay's are no damned good," he said carelessly as if he realized I was longing for a reassuring explanation, "and now that they've run through the money Jay left them they expect the bank to foot their bills. What insolence! I told them it was time they stood on their own feet and stopped sponging on everyone in sight." And he hurried off to play tennis with the boys before dinner.

He dreamed of tennis that night. When I awoke he was twisting in the bed beside me and saying, "Fifteen–forty, but I can win. Two more points to deuce. It's all right, Papa, I'm going to win, I'm going to— Oh no, not that, it can't be, all those years, get out, Elizabeth, get out, get out, *get out!*"

"Paul!" I flung my arms around him as he sat bolt upright in bed. "Darling, it was a dream, only a dream."

He was shivering. I found the light. His forehead shone with sweat.

"It was nothing," he said. "I dreamt I was playing tennis at Newport with Jay. All over now, all past. Nothing at all. . . . I'm sorry I disturbed you."

"Shall I turn out the light?"

"Yes, for God's sake let's get some rest," he said impatiently. But unable to sleep he left the bed twenty minutes later and did not return that night.

Terence arrived back from New York the following evening, but I did not see him until breakfast the next day when he entered the dining room with the morning mail. The boys were already closeted with their tutor. Paul and I were having coffee by ourselves.

"Good morning, sir. Good morning, Mrs. Van Zale." He carefully did not look at me as he handed the mail to Paul.

"Good morning, Mr. O'Reilly," I said, hurriedly reaching for another slice of toast.

"Letter for you, Sylvia," said Paul, pushing an envelope across the table to me.

I glanced at it as the footman refilled my cup of coffee. The address was typed. I noticed that the stamp seemed to have escaped the machines at the post office, but before an explanation could occur to me I was breaking the seal and drawing out the letter.

The notepaper was white, unembossed and expensive. Underneath the address, "14, Hengist Mansions, South Kensington," someone had written in a clear firm hand:

My dear Paul,

Of course I'd like to see you again! But we workers of the world—unlike you investment bankers and other people of ill-repute—have to earn our living and have neither the time nor the money to go jaunting from continent to continent (and please don't insult us both by offering to pay my fare). Yes, of course I remember the wonderful times we had together at Mallingham, and no, I don't believe you when you say you think of me every day. I find it hard to imagine you gazing yearningly across the Atlantic like some utterly celibate, utterly boring lovesick Victorian swain, and anyway if you really mean what you say (and we both know you don't) why don't you issue me a frank, straightforward, honest-to-God invitation to New York instead of sending letter after letter full of coy hints and dismal "wish-you-were-here" refrains . . .

The letter dropped to the floor. My sense of balance seemed to be deserting me. Instinctively I groped for the edge of the table to steady myself.

"Sylvia!" Paul's voice was sharp with alarm. I heard his chair scrape backward, but when I opened my eyes I felt dizzier than ever. I managed to take several deep breaths, but when I saw he was stooping to retrieve the letter an iron weight seemed to descend on my lungs.

"Sir," I heard Terence say urgently, "shall I call a doctor? In view of Mrs. Van Zale's condition—"

Sheer fright effected a miraculous cure. "No!" I screamed at Terence with such force that Paul dropped the letter with a start upon the table. When the letter fell face upward I knew we were all headed straight for disaster.

Paul dismissed the servants.

As the door closed on the last footman Terence tried to explain away his intimate knowledge of my health. "Mrs. Van Zale suffered a similar spell before I went away, sir," he said levelly, "and that's how I happened to know about her pregnancy."

Paul looked at me. I could not speak. He looked at the letter. I could not move. Out of the corner of my eye I saw that Terence's face was no longer white but gray.

Paul read the letter without expression, reached for the envelope and noted the unmarked American stamp. "Since when have you been accustomed to forwarding Miss Slade's letters to my wife, O'Reilly?" he asked pleasantly.

"Sir, I must absolutely deny—"

"You're responsible for handling Miss Slade's letters. I've never seen this one before. Obviously you picked it up in New York this week and decided, for reasons best known to yourself, to present it to my wife after pretending it had come through the mail."

"Sir—"

"We'll discuss this fully later. Now leave us, please. I want to talk to my wife."

Terence left the room without a word.

There was a pause before Paul said: "Shall I call a doctor?"

I shook my head.

"Are you pregnant?"

I shook my head again.

He sighed, slipped the letter into his pocket and gently made me sit down in my chair. "Then what on earth's going on?" he said mildly as he drew up another chair for himself. "No, don't tell me—I could hear the throb of passion in O'Reilly's voice when he suggested calling a doctor. Very well, let's discuss this sensibly without becoming upset. O'Reilly, incredible though it seems, has overcome his Jesuit background to such an extent that he's fallen violently in love with you. You, in a valiant effort to dampen his grand passion, told him you were pregnant. O'Reilly, in a mixture of fury, disappointment and God knows what else, sent you this letter, which I regret to say doesn't show Miss Slade in the best of lights—"

"Nor you," I said, and ran stumbling from the room.

He followed me. I had barely reached our bedroom when he flung open the door.

"Sylvia—"

"Terence told me you'd send for her someday and I didn't believe him. I didn't believe you were capable of inviting her to New York to humiliate me . . . with her child . . . all the gossip . . ." My voice faltered, but I controlled it. "You told me your private correspondence with Miss Slade was inconsequential and I believed you. Yet now I see you've been writing her the most intimate letters—apparently for some time—and hinting if not actually demanding that she should come here."

"I wasn't serious. I've never invited her."

"I don't believe you! I can't believe you anymore!"

He stood motionless. His fists were clenched at his sides, and as his debonair mask was discarded the tension made his face stark and hard. He said roughly, "I notice you call O'Reilly by his first name. Have you slept with him?"

"No," I said, and began to cry. "I wish I had slept with him!" I sobbed. "I wish I had!"

He was silent. At first I thought he was too full of contempt to speak, but when I dashed away my tears I saw instead that he was deeply shocked. He stared at me, still without speaking, and then backing away he disappeared into his dressing room. But he did not close the door. I could hear him pacing up and down, and when I closed my eyes I could imagine every muscle of his body braced against his tension while his quick mind twisted and turned endlessly for a solution.

At last he paused, and as I rose unsteadily from the bed he walked back into the room. He had gone no more than a pace past the dressing-room threshold when he stopped. He was looking at me, then past me. I glanced over my shoulder, but there was nothing there.

He said confused, "Oh, I have to be alone, I—" And then his voice was cut off as he twisted his head to one side.

"Paul!"

I ran but could not reach him in time. He took a step forward, and although there was nothing which could have caught his foot he seemed to trip on the highly polished wooden floor. His left leg turned inward, his right leg was flung off balance. For one horrible second he was still, frozen in that eerie posture, and then without further warning he crashed to the ground like a corpse.

II

My first instinct was to panic. I thought of stroke and heart attack, but before I could rush from the room, rouse all the servants and scream for a doctor, Paul had a convulsion which flung him over onto his back.

I remembered the Da Costa brothers. It was then I knew that their lies had been truths, and that the truths by which I had lived had all been false.

I was paralyzed with the shock. Paul was still, and that too confused me because in my ignorance I had thought epileptic convulsions were always continuous. His limbs twitched. I shied away, but a second later, realizing how frightened I was, I made a considerable effort to clamp down on my fear. Paul couldn't hurt me. The only person he could hurt was himself.

I groped in my memory, tried to recall what ought to be done. Something between the teeth . . . Stumbling to a drawer, I found two handkerchiefs, wound them together and forced myself to kneel down beside him just as the saliva, frothy and unnatural, began to spill sideways from his mouth. I found I could not part his teeth;

he was rigid, and I was just sitting back on my heels in despair when his back arched and he flung himself over so violently that his face banged against the floor.

I gasped. My hands were clenched so hard they hurt, and I had to make another great effort to keep calm. Surely I had read somewhere once that such attacks always looked much worse than they were? Anyway I had to stop Paul from hurting himself unnecessarily, that was quite obvious. I moved a nearby chair well out of his way and nerved myself to loosen his tie and unbutton his shirt. When he remained motionless I tried to slip the handkerchiefs between his teeth again, and this time I was successful.

Relief streamed through me, and it was only then, when I had done all I could, that I began to imagine how he would feel when he recovered consciousness. Suddenly I thought: Elizabeth! And when I guessed at last what must have happened after Vicky's death I felt ill with fear.

I glanced wildly at the clock by the bed. How long had he been unconscious? It seemed as if I had been kneeling beside him for at least half an hour, but it was probably no longer than three minutes. How long did such attacks last? How long did I have to decide what I should say? I seemed to be incapable of rational thought. More saliva was spilling out of Paul's mouth, and hardly knowing what I was doing I fetched a washcloth from the bathroom and wiped his face clean. His eyes flicked open, giving me a shock, but they saw nothing. He was still unconscious.

His eyes closed again, but he seemed to be breathing better and his skin gradually lost its frightening bluish sheen. I knew my time was running out, but the more I searched in panic for the right words, the more speechless I became. It was no good pretending I had not seen the attack, because he would remember I was in the room, and it was no good telling myself that Paul wouldn't care that I now knew he was an epileptic; anyone who had gone to such great lengths to conceal his illness would undoubtedly have very strong feelings about being found out. I was dealing with a burden Paul evidently felt unable to share with anyone, least of all with those closest to him, and when I tried to imagine the size of that burden I knew it could crush my marriage in seconds, just as it had annihilated his long love affair with Elizabeth.

He moved. The handkerchiefs fell from his mouth as his muscles relaxed, and aware of the movement he turned his head to stare at the crumpled linen.

In the end I said only the simplest words. I told him that it was all right and that we were alone in our bedroom.

"What bedroom?"

"The bedroom at the cottage. Bar Harbor."

He sat up. His eyes, dark with confusion, glanced briefly around the room.

"I'll get you a glass of water," I said.

When I returned he had not moved, and I suddenly noticed that his trousers were stained and that water was seeping onto the floor. I had been so busy watching his face for some sign of consciousness that I had noticed nothing else.

"Would you like to be alone for a minute?" I said. "I can go and sit on the window seat at the top of the stairs, and when you want me you can just open the door and call."

He nodded. His face, devoid of all vivacity, was so blank that he did not look like himself at all but like someone I barely knew. The pain was beginning to show in his eyes.

I left the room and waited a long time. It was very difficult not to go back, tap on the door and ask if he was all right, but I knew I had to wait until he was ready for me. It was over an hour before he opened the door and looked down the hallway to the stairs.

"Oh God," he said, "are you still there? You shouldn't have waited all this time. I've been asleep."

"That's all right." I stood up, smoothed my skirt and walked toward him. For a moment he watched me before he turned to disappear into the bedroom. "Do you feel better now?" I said as I followed him inside.

"Of course. You weren't foolish enough to send for a doctor, were you?"

"No."

The room was immaculate. He had cleaned everything up, changed his suit and covered the cut on his cheekbone with a strip of plaster.

"Well, now," he said, "where were we? I think we were talking about O'Reilly."

Despite his normal tone of voice he was so disturbed that it was difficult to look at him without flinching.

"We don't have to talk about that now, Paul," I said steadily. "O'Reilly's not important at present and neither is Miss Slade. We're the ones who are important, you and I. I know you must hate my knowing, but you needn't. I understand everything much better now. I'm only sorry I didn't know from the beginning, because if I had I wouldn't have made you endure all those awkward discussions about having children."

"You would never have married me."

He spoke as if there could be no doubt whatever about it, and although I at once repudiated the statement as strongly as possible I saw he could not believe me. I was appalled. I had never before thought much about the difficulties of epileptics, but now I realized with shock that their sufferings extended far beyond their seizures.

At that point his air of nonchalance, which must have cost him so much to assume, dissolved distressingly before my eyes.

"Oh my God," he said, sinking down on the bed and giving way to utter despair. "If Jay could see me now!"

"This was at the bottom of your whole relationship with Jay, wasn't it?"

"He knew," he said, squeezing his hands together until the knuckles shone white, and those two simple syllables at once suggested unimaginable horror and shame. "It gave him power over me. He put me through hell and enjoyed it. After that I could never rest until my power equaled his . . . and surpassed it." He stopped.

"Everything Stewart and Greg said was true, wasn't it?"

"Yes. It was all true, all the unspeakable things. And even my worst nightmares are coming to life. This is the second attack I've had in a month, Sylvia."

"How often does it happen?"

"I was well for over thirty years. Then after Vicky's death it came back. It was just once, but always afterward I was afraid . . . Then after Jay died there was another seizure, but Europe . . . I was well there and for some time afterward. But this is the third attack I've had during the past year. The other two times I managed to be alone."

"Is there much warning?"

"Directly before the attack I have half a dozen seconds, but there's nothing I can do to stop it. However, long before the aura I can usually tell when I'm in danger and then I do everything I can to head off an attack. I've been very near an attack at least a dozen times since Jay died, but mostly the attacks have never happened—sometimes I think I merely imagine I'm close to one because I'm so afraid of it happening. It's difficult to tell." He rubbed his eyes nervously with his hand as if to erase the memory. "You can't imagine what it's like. You're always wondering when it's going to happen again, wondering where you'll be, who'll see you, who'll find out, who'll talk, who'll laugh, who'll sneer behind your back and say you're insane. But my form of the illness has nothing to do with insanity—"

"Yes, I understand."

"—and that's what makes it all the more unendurable, to have a quick, sharp, clear mind and yet be unable to stop it from exploding, careering out of control—"

"Yes."

"Those seconds of hallucinations, that terrible moment when you know you're going to disintegrate, and in such a disgusting, repulsive, *uncivilized* manner—I've only to think of it and I feel unspeakably debased. I've never been able to tell anyone, never. Occasionally someone like Jay has found out, but—"

"And Elizabeth?"

"Yes. She was revolted. I could see. She was always so fastidious."

"But surely—"

"Oh yes, she tried to hide it but I felt so humiliated, like some sort of animal." He broke off again. "I can't talk about it anymore."

"I have only one more question: What can I do to help you avoid these attacks?"

He gave me a thin smile. "You already do all you can. Sex helps." He winced as if the blunt words offended him, but when he spoke again I realized he was only afraid they had offended me. "I mean that the times when we make love are very important."

"Yes." I wanted to communicate to him that he could be as blunt as he wished so long as he told me the truth. "I understand—or at least I think I do. Anything which helps you relax is important."

"Every case is different. What helps me may be of no use to others." He started to talk about his father's triumph in transforming him into a sportsman. "I always assumed that my physical fitness was responsible for my remission," he said, "but perhaps that was merely a coincidence. However, it certainly seemed to help when I was a boy, and later when I was a man and discovered women . . ." He gave his thin tired smile again. "If I were in the mood to make jokes I could say I found sex the best sport of all. But it hardly seems the right moment for jokes, does it?" He stood up and began to roam around the room. I longed to beg him to sit down, but I knew that would annoy him. Presently he said, "I have to rest. You'd better cancel all our engagements for the next week, and whatever happens I'll stay here and not allow myself to be dragged back to New York."

I was greatly relieved. "Are you sure you shouldn't see a doctor?"

He looked bitter. "There's nothing they can do. They know so little." As I watched he started to clench and unclench his fists in his agitation. "I'll be all right. I've cured myself before and I'll cure myself again. I just need a little time, that's all."

We were silent for some time, but at last he sat down beside me on the bed and put his arm around my shoulders. "I suppose it's useless to hope this won't make a difference to us."

"It'll make a great difference, yes. Now I shall find it so much easier to accept your infidelities. It'll even make it easier for me to understand your attachment to Miss Slade. You were ill after Jay's death and she helped you get better."

His arm tightened around me. After a pause he said in a low voice, "I don't know why I became drawn into such a foolish correspondence with her—no, that's not true. I do know. Whenever I become exhausted with my New York life I think of her more often. She's part of a romantic illusion—escaping to Europe, recapturing my lost youth, all those abominable middle-aged fantasies. I despise them, I don't believe in them, yet occasionally I can't resist indulging myself with them. But I'm still a realist, Sylvia. You're my reality, New York is my reality, and I know that even when I'm writing silly letters to Dinah Slade."

"Does she know about your illness?"

"Good God, no!" His arm slipped from my shoulders. He began to twist his hands together but I covered them with mine.

"Don't, Paul. Everything's going to be all right."

"Of course. But what the devil am I going to do with O'Reilly? I can't possibly fire him. He knows too much about me." And at last I heard the full story of the Salzedo affair.

He talked for an hour. For a long time I managed to conceal my distress but when he said, "And O'Reilly knows I lied to the grand jury," I gave an exclamation of despair.

"I'm a fool to be telling you all this," he said at once. "I can see this is shocking you far more than my illness."

"Yes," I said, "but if you at last feel you can talk to me about it, that must be for the best. Paul, I've always felt able to cope with our marriage so long as I thought you were being honest with me. I could stand the truth; it was the lies which were undermining my feeling for you. I wanted to turn to Terence because I felt you'd duped me and made nonsense of the trust I had in you."

"I'll have to get him out of the house," he said, wringing his hands again. "I'll promote him. There's nothing else I can do." He turned to look at me. His face was white with strain and his dark eyes were feverish. "You'll stand by me?"

"Yes. If we can be honest with each other."

"But my illness . . ."

"What difference can that possibly make to me? You're still Paul."

He looked at me as if he would like to believe what I said but dared not for fear he had misunderstood. Knowing instinctively I must show no trace of a pity he would only find humiliating, I leaned forward and kissed him passionately on the mouth.

His response was painful in its fervor. I saw he had finally allowed himself to believe I might love him despite his illness, and although every instinct I possessed urged him not to make love to me when he was still in a state of exhaustion, I said nothing. If he thought I was rejecting him our relationship would never recover.

I did everything I could, but when his failure became intolerable to him he rolled away from me without a word and began to dress. His face was very still. He did not look at me, and after saying he was going for a walk before lunch he left the room without a backward glance.

I was alone. I had the terrible feeling I had lost him forever, just as Elizabeth had lost him nine years before, and, burying my face in the pillows, I sobbed until I lay limp with exhaustion. Our troubles seemed endless. The desolation stretched ahead of me as far as the eye could see.

III

He stayed well while we remained at Bar Harbor, but when we returned to New York he had another seizure. Again we were alone together, discussing household matters before his departure to the office, but the recurrence after such a brief remission terrified him and he became obsessed with the fear of collapsing in public. That was when he went back to the doctors. He saw the most famous specialists and was tested for a multitude of illnesses, but the doctors diagnosed only the epilepsy and there was nothing they could do. He was told to live quietly, avoid the pressures of the business world and take only moderate exercise so as not to overtax his strength. He was also exhorted to take his medication regularly, but Paul hated the drug he was prescribed and said it deadened his wits, rendered any exercise an effort and made him feel unwell. He had never taken the drug regularly before for any prolonged length of time.

"But you should at least try to do what the doctors say!" I pleaded with him, but he said it had been his father, not the doctors, who had cured him long ago. With great courage he abandoned his pills and began a rigorous routine of exercise. I saw his mind focus on his health in a mighty effort to subjugate his physical weakness, and soon, contrary to the doctors' expectations, he began to improve. He returned to the office, he permitted me to arrange a few social engagements, and in late October he tried to make love to me for the first time since that disastrous morning at Bar Harbor.

The second failure was very difficult for us both. At Bar Harbor he had said later that day, "When I'm better everything will be well," and because this statement had seemed both obvious and sensible I had recovered quickly from my despair. But the second failure, occurring when he was physically fit and rested, shattered me almost as much as it shattered him. We tried to discuss it but could not. He found he had nothing to say, and I have never been one of those outspoken women like Caroline Sullivan who can discuss such matters as easily as they discuss the weather.

The rift between us widened. I was just wondering if I had ever felt so unhappy when Paul had his next seizure.

He was swimming in the pool, and had it not been for Peterson's strength and speed in pulling him from the water he might well have drowned.

Terence had long since been promoted, but his replacement Herbert Mayers rushed to my room to tell me the news.

"No one must know about this. It's not to be discussed," I said strongly when I reached the pool, and Peterson, white-faced, said, "Yes, ma'am," while Mayers added without expression, "Of course, Mrs. Van Zale."

I tried to deny to myself that it would be only a matter of time before the rumor was spreading over New York.

"Why don't we go away for a while?" I suggested to Paul. "Have the captain sail the yacht down to Florida, and then we can join the ship at Fort Lauderdale. It's not the rainy season in the Bahamas, is it?"

"Nobody goes to the Bahamas at this time of year," he said desperately. "Everyone will say I'm having a nervous breakdown if I go away so soon after that long absence from the office in September. I refuse to run away from New York now."

But he did. We spent November idly cruising in the Bahamas, and again he began to improve although we had separate cabins and he never once suggested we sleep together. When we stopped at Nassau he spent three evenings ashore on his own, but I did not mind that and only hoped that the unknown women who spent time with him managed to restore his confidence. Yet when we left Nassau he did not approach me. The sun shone, the exquisite cays shimmered in the sparkling sea but they were remote from us. I felt as if we were seeing them through barred windows, and eventually, realizing there was no alternative, we returned with reluctance to New York.

In early December, on his first day back at the office and in full view of all his partners, he had the worst seizure of all and was rushed to the hospital.

When I arrived I found his two greatest friends among his partners, Steve Sullivan and Charley Blair, waiting in the lobby.

"Sylvia, we're so sorry . . . thought we ought to discuss what we're going to say . . . the press . . ."

"High blood pressure," I said. "He fainted and now has to undergo treatment."

"Sylvia's right," said Steve, and I left them debating together while I went up to Paul's room.

He had drawn the curtains and was not resting in bed as he should have been, but sitting on the edge. His right arm was in a sling and there was a dressing on his head. His feet were bare. He wore only the hospital gown, thin, white and cold.

He looked at me but did not speak. Closing the door, I gave him a kiss and sat down beside him on the bed.

"Is your arm broken?"

"Fractured."

"What did the doctors say?"

" 'Take drugs, lock yourself up and throw away the key.' " When he swallowed awkwardly I saw that his eyes were bright with tears and I got up at once to look out of the window. He would never have forgiven himself if I had seen him break down.

At last I said, "There must be something we can do. I can't accept that there's nothing."

"There's nothing you can do. But if I could—" He broke off.

There was a silence, but I thought of all he had told me about his illness, how he had kept it at bay for so many years with such complete success, and I knew what he had wanted to say.

I said tentatively, "Those evenings in Nassau . . ."

"It was no good. I've got so little self-esteem left. That kind of expedition wiped it out altogether."

I thought for a moment. My mouth was dry and my nails were digging into the palms of my hands. "It would make a difference, wouldn't it," I said slowly, "if you could see someone you liked, someone who admired you, someone who knew nothing about all this."

He did not answer, only leaned forward and stared at the floor. I sat down beside him again but before I could speak he said haltingly, "If I can get over this I know we can be together again. But you yourself can't help me get over it."

"Then we must find someone who can."

The silence seemed to go on and on. In a bizarre moment of fancy I felt as if every step I had ever taken in my marriage had led up to this point, and that now my entire future depended on what I said next. For a second I panicked. I thought I would never be able to decide what to do, but then my mind cleared, just as one's mind so often does in moments of extreme crisis, and the solution seemed obvious. Either I loved him enough to do anything to make him well or I didn't love him at all. It was as simple as that.

I said firmly, "Send for her."

He raised his head. As he turned to look at me I saw the expression in his eyes.

"It's all right," I said quickly. "There's no need to answer. There's nothing you have to say."

"Oh yes there is," he said, and taking my hands in his he said with all the passion I had waited thirteen years to hear, "I love you."

PART THREE

Dinah Losing

1926

Chapter One

I

The brute sent for me in 1925, just before Christmas. God, how angry I was! I damned nearly tore up the letter and jumped on it, but I made the mistake of reading it again and before I had even finished the first paragraph I felt myself weakening beneath the onslaught of his charm.

"Monster!" I said aloud, grabbing a cigarette to steady my nerves, and my poor secretary who chose that moment to walk into the room sniveled threateningly. "Oh, for God's sake, Miss Jenkins, I wasn't talking to you! Fetch me some more tea, would you, please?"

"Yes, Miss Slade." She fled. Next door on my left Harriet was saying in dulcet tones, "Oh yes, Lady Uppingham, we would be delighted. . . . Yes, we have acted as cosmetic consultants to a number of brides lately. . . ." while next door on my right Cedric was screaming into the telephone, "Who the ruddy hell do you think we are? Peddlers of paste to ruddy Woolworth's?"

I was hunting for a match. I wished I had never started to smoke. The telephone rang again and beyond the open door of my office Mavis intoned through her nose, "Diana Slade Cosmetics—may I help you?"

I found a match, lit the cigarette and remembered I had been wanting to go to the lavatory for half an hour. I was just sneaking purposefully through the doorway when Cedric rang off with a crash, shot out of his office and blocked my path.

"Honestly, Dinah, those bloody people from Gorringe's!"

"Goodbye, Lady Uppingham!" crooned Harriet behind us.

"Miss Slade!" called Mavis from the reception desk. "Mr. Hurst on the phone for you!"

"Oh, Lord. Coming, Mavis! Hold on, Cedric! Harriet, I hope you told that old trout that we have to have carte blanche with the facial."

"Darling, the carte is absolutely blanche and I've doubled the price of the wax treatment! Cedric, did you talk to Gorringe's?"

"Miss Slade . . ."

"All right, Mavis." I sped back into my office, saw Paul's letter still sitting on my desk and felt more in need of the lavatory than ever. I yanked the telephone towards me. "Yes?"

"You're throo-oo," sang Mavis.

"Dinah? Geoffrey here. Look, I'm up in London unexpectedly. Can you meet me for dinner tonight?"

"Lovely, Geoffrey. Eight o'clock?"

"I'll pick you up at the flat."

"I'll be ready. Thanks. Excuse me if I dash now, but . . ." I extricated myself, grabbed Paul's letter and raced to the cloakroom. There in the peaceful gloom of my favorite end cubicle I had the chance to read the letter again without interruptions.

When I emerged I looked at myself in the glass above the basin. I was white with some emotion which I wanted to believe was still anger but which I strongly suspected was now a mixture of excitement and fright.

"'Once more into the breach, dear friends!'" I quoted to my reflection, and wished I did not have such an urge to add, "'*Ave Caesar, te morituri salutant!*'" I could not remember Tiberius Caesar's exact reply to the gladiators' assertion that they were about to die, but thought he had given some cynical retort such as "Or not, as the case may be," whereupon the gladiators had taken great offense. Doubtless they had derived a morbid pleasure from their situation, just as I was now deriving a morbid pleasure from mine. I laughed in an attempt to be debonair. After three years of innumerable cold business letters and studiedly unemotional personal correspondence, Paul was graciously allowing me another bite of the legendary apple of temptation. Well, if that was what he wanted, that was what he was going to get, but one day, I thought fiercely, one day Mr. Paul Cornelius Van Zale was going to discover that he had got one hell of a lot more than he had bargained for.

II

I loved him. I had never loved any man before and had never loved any man since. By the December of 1925 I was secretly afraid I would never love any man again.

I was secretly afraid of so many things that it always amazed me when people occasionally remarked how bold I was. Of course they seldom meant it as a compliment, but there are nevertheless times when it is an advantage to be considered a tigress instead of a quivering jellyfish. If people believe you're brave you may not only half believe them but even draw a spurious courage from their delusion.

The list of my fears stretched endlessly into the furthest reaches of my mind. They were all there, the big fears, the little fears, the real and the imaginary, the boundless and the groundless. I used to examine them minutely with loving care on my sleepless nights. I was afraid of being alone and unloved, although this fear had lessened considerably since Alan was born. I was afraid of dying. I was afraid of being poor. I was afraid of my business failing with the result that I would lose Mallingham, and losing Mallingham was my most racking fear of all. I could not conceive of a world without my home, the one place in a hostile world where I could retreat and feel secure. I felt I would have no stability without Mallingham, and I was mortally afraid of instability and its attendant demons of alienation and madness. My worst nightmare was of dying destitute in a lunatic asylum and being buried not at Mallingham but in some pauper's grave where I would be quite unable to rest in peace.

It will be obvious from this catalogue of neuroses that it was as well I had to work to save Mallingham, for if I had been wealthy enough to be a lady of leisure with all the time I needed to indulge my fears I would soon have become as eccentric as my father.

The irony of my situation was that I had always yearned to be ordinary. I believe this is a common desire among children from eccentric families, and certainly when I was obliged to put my father to bed after one of his chamber-music orgies I longed to return to my grandparents' Lincolnshire vicarage, where I had once spent two quiet, well-regulated, blissfully conventional years. After my father's third divorce I did go through a brief phase of vowing never to get married, but in fact I longed for a husband, children and the trappings of a respectable married life.

It was not until I was up at Girton and contemptuously labeled "bluestocking" by young men who barely knew me that I realized sadly that I might be too well educated to receive a marriage proposal. It seemed men were prepared to overlook feminine intelligence only if the woman was beautiful, and since I was fat and plain I saw no alternative but to abandon my dreams of a romantic white wedding, a tall dark handsome hero of a bridegroom and a leisurely honeymoon spent cruising the Greek Isles in a private yacht. Sinking myself in my studies, I became the bluestocking that everyone had already decided I was, and pretended with a nobility as false as it was nauseating that I was "above" a sybaritic life. I had actually convinced myself I was happy in this role when my father died, but in the harsh events which followed I found I could no longer afford to cut myself off from men and wander around in an intellectual haze. I had to go down on my knees and crawl to those men for whatever help I could get.

I was told that Mallingham would have to be sold, and when I protested that I would work my fingers to the bone to buy it and keep it, I was told it was not suitable for a young girl to live alone and unchaperoned in a big house, not suitable for a young girl of my class to go into any form of business, and most definitely not suitable for a young girl of my station in life to be anything except a wife and mother or, if I were less fortunate, a spinster teaching in some old maid's school.

These masculine rulings were presented to me in the great hall at Mallingham after my father's funeral. Philip Hurst, Geoffrey's father, was there with his partner, and there were solicitors representing my half sister and half brother. The vicar was standing by the fireplace with his hands folded, and the local doctor who had attended my father during his last illness stood beside him.

When they had finished I stood up. For the first time in all my encounters with the opposite sex my anger was stronger than my fear.

"You *bloody* men!" I shouted, and saw them flinch at my language. "How dare you speak to me as if I were a lunatic in need of a keeper! How dare you speak to me as if I had no pride or self-respect! And how dare you say things to me that you'd never dare say to any man!"

They gaped at me. I despised them. "You listen to me!" I said furiously. "I'm going to keep my home! I'm going to make the money! And I'm going to make you all look damned fools if it's the last thing I ever do!"

One of them laughed. I shall always remember that. It gave me the courage to go on.

"Don't talk to me of losing everything I have!" I cried. "I'm not interested in losing! The word 'losing' doesn't form part of my vocabulary! I'm only interested in winning!"

"But, my dear . . ." Philip Hurst made a helpless gesture with his hands, and because I knew he was the only one in the room who cared what happened to me I did not interrupt him as he fumbled for his words. "You'd need a millionaire to help you out of this mess."

"Then I shall find one," I said, and walked out of the room.

An hour later I bicycled to the nearest telephone and asked my friend Harriet, who worked on the "Personalities of the Week" page of *The Illustrated London News,* if there were any foreign millionaires in London at the time. I thought a foreigner, being more ignorant of the social structure than a native millionaire, might be more lenient towards my eccentric ambition.

"And it's got to be someone who might like to help a girl in distress," I concluded to Harriet.

"Well, there's Paul Van Zale. He's an American banker."

"Good. He'll do."

"But Di, his reputation's awful!"

"So much the better!" I said, and began to hatch my plans.

Since it was clear by this time that I had no hope of living a respectable conventional life, I saw no point in hoping for a respectable conventional relationship with any member of the opposite sex. I knew I would have to sleep with Paul Van Zale, but for Mallingham I was prepared to sacrifice my virginity; it hardly seemed worth hanging on to it for a wedding night which would never take place. Besides, I have to admit that by that time (I was twenty-one) I was curious to discover whether copulation was as fascinating as everyone seemed to think it was. I was no longer religious, so I was determined to have no moral qualms; I knew enough about Freudian theory to tell myself it was unhealthy to be prudish; and I was certainly desperate enough to sleep with a complete stranger. My one worry was whether Paul Van Zale would be desperate enough to sleep with me, but I reassured myself by remembering my father's dictum that middle-aged men always found young girls attractive.

The more I thought about Paul Van Zale, the more determined I became to detest him. As I was wheeled into his office in a food hamper I even thought, Wretched man, forcing me to endure all this! I had never seen a photograph of him, but I was convinced he would be short, fat and bald. Even the thought of his American accent made me shudder.

But then the lid of the hamper was flung open. I struggled to my feet, looked across the room and saw him.

That was when my miracle happened, and my miracle was not that Mallingham was saved but that I found someone to love at last, and in loving Paul I overcame my deep-rooted fear of men and for the first time in my life was able to enjoy being female.

III

He left me. I'd known he would. From the beginning he had been honest, never making promises he had no intention of keeping, but his honesty only made him the more irresistible to me. After my disillusionment with men I saw clearly how my father had always lied to his wives, and after I had realized that no man would ever want to marry me I consoled myself by deciding marriage was nothing but a sham. I knew what happened to people who promised to love each other for ever and ever, and I told myself I wanted no part in such romantic twaddle. If Paul had been less than honest with me I could never have trusted him, but his dread of romance with its accompanying delusions not only matched mine but surpassed it. His dread was genuine, whereas mine was merely a pose I struck to preserve my self-esteem, yet when romance came it was I who was realistic enough to accept it, while he, the self-styled realist, was the one who retreated into fantasy by refusing to believe our lives had been altered.

The first time I noticed his occasional inability to face the facts was when he let me become pregnant. I had made no secret about wanting a baby, and since I was unable to live a conventional existence it must surely have been obvious to him that I had no choice but to have the baby out of wedlock. In the circumstances I would have thought that even the stupidest man would have guessed I wanted part of him to remain behind when he eventually had to leave, but I was wrong. He never guessed. I still thought his shock and anger on learning the news were quite uncalled for, but because by that time I was terrified of him leaving me I made renewed efforts to be the model mistress so that he would have no further cause for complaint.

I could well remember what kind of feminine behavior my father had found intolerable. He had not liked inquisitive women who had pried into his past, he had detested jealous women who had intruded upon his present, and he had loathed clinging women who had tried to chain themselves to his future. So I never asked Paul too closely about his background, and always tried to convey the impression that he was free to leave whenever he wished.

But he stayed, and as he stayed my expectations changed. Thinking myself to be fundamentally unattractive I had at first expected nothing from him beyond a little affection, yet slowly as his affection increased and I came to realize that in his eyes I was very far from being unattractive, I could not help but wonder if he might be able to love me a little as well. Our long holiday together on the Norfolk Broads that autumn was as memorable as any honeymoon, and although I still knew he would one day return to America I had become convinced that our separation would be only temporary. That was why, when he finally had to leave, I was able to scrape together the courage to let him go without too many humiliating tears.

He promised to write to me but did not. I was a part of his life, yet he tried to pretend to himself I had never existed. I was set aside together with his passion for European civilization and his romantic vision of traveling sideways in time, and in this rejection of his true nature I saw that his pride in his honesty was misplaced and his so-called realism was a fraud.

Or so it seemed to me as I waited daily for the letters which never came.

It would be too boring to chronicle the sleepless nights, the endless tears, the black despair, the suicidal inclinations, the impotent rage and the frustrated passion which overwhelmed me at this point. Those days do me no credit and I prefer not to dwell on them, but I do remember thinking that there was nothing more demeaning than building one's life around the daily visit of the postman. I felt as if Paul had given me self-respect only to tear it to shreds afterwards, and as those tortured days passed and the baby stirred more vigorously within me I saw myself as the world saw me, a stupid naïve young woman who had been discarded by an elderly roué, a girl who had "got into trouble" in the best tradition of the Victorian kitchen-maid while society applauded this just retribution for her sins.

The picture repulsed me, and amidst all my despair I felt the first faint stirrings of defiance.

Early in the new year Paul's London partner Hal Beecher wrote to say that the American business manager and market-research specialist had arrived in London to launch Diana Slade Cosmetics. Did I wish to confer with them? They would be delighted to meet me, but naturally they would quite understand if I preferred to remain in seclusion.

Reading between the courteous lines, I saw that Mr. Beecher was kindly giving me the chance to be no more than the nominal head of my business while Paul's money allowed me to cower at Mallingham, as anonymous as the most pathetic of discarded mistresses.

I was face to face with my future, but as I looked out over Mallingham Broad with Hal Beecher's letter in my shaking hand I knew there could be no turning aside. Either I abandoned all self-respect and sank into ignominious obscurity or else I went out into the world to fight to the last ditch.

On January the tenth, 1923, when I was nearly seven months pregnant, I packed a suitcase, ordered Mr. Oakes to drive me to the station in the pony trap, and caught the train to London.

IV

Paul did write to me then. He apologized for not having written before, explained that he had been very busy and expressed the hope that I was well. Having disposed of the necessary platitudes, he proceeded to inform me in the smoothest and most ruefully charming of styles that while he hoped we would always maintain a cordial business relationship he was afraid our personal relationship would have to end; he had reached this decision for my sake because he felt he could not offer me what I wanted and therefore felt obliged to set me free to find someone more suitable. There was no need for me to worry about money—or about working myself to the bone in the world of commerce. Hal Beecher would send me all the money I needed to live quietly at Mallingham and enjoy motherhood to the full.

When I had finished reading the lavish compliments and fond farewells in the last paragraph I permitted myself the smallest of cynical smiles and wrote back:

MY DEAR PAUL,

How sweet of you to write such a divine letter! I think you're absolutely right about ending our personal relationship and it's wonderful of you to be so sensible and self-sacrificing for my sake. But darling, I'm just the tiniest bit distressed about the logic behind all your chivalrous offers of financial help. Are you really implying that it's better to be a kept woman than an emancipated one? "O tempora!" as Cicero would have said, "O mores!" Still, at least you weren't misguided enough to offer me Mallingham as a gift before I've had the chance to repay you with interest. Lots of love, darling—I'd write more but I'm too busy working myself to the bone in the world of commerce.

DINAH

There was no reply to this letter, but at least he never said to me as everyone else did, "You can't do this!" Perhaps he was the only person who knew I was quite capable of launching a business when I was seven months pregnant.

Hofstadt and Baker, the two Americans who were supposed to give me my commercial start in life, quickly decided that I was a dangerous lunatic, and although Hal Beecher did not share these views there was no doubt my behavior sent him into a flap. To do him credit he was extremely worried about my status as a fallen woman. He was a respectable American gentleman of fifty-five, and my plight struck all manner of responsive chords in his decent puritan bosom. When he found out I was staying in Chelsea with Harriet, he commented unhappily that Chelsea was too avant-garde and offered me a room in his house in Mayfair.

"I'm sure my wife would be delighted . . ."

I was sure his wife would be horrified. No woman in her right mind would welcome a girl who had just finished an affair with a man of her husband's generation. "Thank you, Hal, but it's really not necessary." I reassured him by revealing that Harriet was Lady Harriet, the daughter of a marquess. Americans are always so impressed by titles.

No sooner had I succeeded in soothing Hal Beecher than both Hursts, father and son, stormed up to London to carry me back to Norfolk, and by the time I had convinced them of the futility of their mission it was a relief to escape to Harriet's little flat, drink some strong tea and put my feet up. I was an uncomfortable shape by that time and I tired more easily than usual.

Harriet had been a year ahead of me at Cambridge, so she had obtained her degree in history before my father's death had concluded my varsity education. Unknown to Hal Beecher she was the rebel of her aristocratic family, and having turned her back on the idiocy of a debutante season she had decided to earn her living. Her family had been shocked, but Harriet had had no regrets. She was employed, she had her own home, and independence, as all young men have known for centuries, is very sweet.

Harriet was thin and rangy, with a long bony face, dark bobbed hair and tawny eyes which Robin, the pale poet who lived in the flat below, called "twilight pools of infinite wisdom." Robin was a very bad poet and lived on a war pension; he had been invalided home from the front in 1917, suffered a nervous breakdown and escaped from his country home to drown his shell-shock in Chelsea. The friend who lived with him, a tough little Cockney and football fanatic, was called Cedric.

In the flat above us lived Dulcie, an unmarried mother who had a nine-month-old daughter; Joan, who worked as a cigarette girl in a nightclub; and Joan's lover, a ragtime musician called Eddie. Dulcie had an allowance, and although she would never divulge its source we suspected that a certain M.P. was responsible. Joan and Eddie had taken her in after they had found her crying on a bench in Kensington Gardens, and soon she was looking after their flat and cooking their meals for them. I thought they were a splendid advertisement for a *ménage à trois*, but Cedric prophesied darkly that it would never last.

I liked Cedric. He took me to the flicks once or twice—a move which made Robin cross, but since he despised the cinema he had no excuse to be annoyed. I was also interested in Cedric because he was a salesman for a cosmetics company called Persepolis.

He lost his job just before Alan was born. Returning home one afternoon from Hal's office in Milk Street, I had just stepped into the hall of the house when Cedric flung open the door of his flat, grabbed me by the arm and marched me straight into his sitting room.

"Oh Gawd, Dinah, I'm desperate—Persepolis is on the skids, they're guillotining all the staff and my head's just rolled into the ruddy basket! Christ, what am I going to do? Nobody can get a job nowadays, men with large families can't even get a job, and I've got no real education and, oh Christ, we'll never be able to live on that ruddy Robin's pension, not with him drinking like a fish the way he does. Dinah, can you . . . ?"

"I can," I said. "Be my sales director. The Americans are looking for one, but I'd thought of offering you the job for some time."

"Oh my Gawd!" He tried to hug me, but my stomach got in the way. Finally he compromised by shaking my hand and demanding, "Who says women shouldn't be in business?"

"Hofstadt and Baker will when they hear I've appointed a sales director without consulting them."

I was right. The Americans said I was ignorant, that the important post should be filled by someone well-educated, that they would cable New York to arrange for my removal from power.

"Go ahead," I said, guessing correctly that Paul would refer the matter back to Hal.

There were further heated scenes. By this time my employment of Cedric was only one of the long list of mistakes the Americans attributed to me, and at last they announced outraged that if I persisted in ignoring their advice I would be bankrupt within a year.

"That won't concern you," I said politely, "since you won't be working for me. I'll arrange for Mr. Beecher to give you the necessary severance pay and you can leave for America at your earliest convenience."

They asked incredulously if I was giving them notice. I confirmed that I was.

"But you can't do that!" they chorused in horror.

"I'm terribly sorry," I said, "but I rather think I can."

As soon as they had roared out of the room on their way to Milk Street I telephoned Hal.

"They've got to go," I said to him. "They're useless. London isn't New York, and England isn't America, yet they persist in applying the wrong set of rules to the wrong set of circumstances. Hal, I've never asked you for anything before, but I'm asking you now. Back me up. I know I'm right. Trust me. Please."

He trusted me. The salaries were terminated, the Americans departed in fury, and before I had had the chance to recover from my first board-room battle, Alan entered the world.

V

Harriet and Cedric came with me to the hospital, but after that I was on my own. I was nervous yet immensely excited, and suddenly as all my business struggles faded into insignificance I could think only of Paul three thousand miles away in New York. During the hours of labor I said his name aloud as if he could hear me, and when the word fell emptily into the silence the tears streamed down my cheeks. All my bitterness towards him dissolved. I no longer cared how badly he had treated me, and as the pain of labor deepened I drew strength from my memories of that splendid summer until I knew not only that I still loved him but that I was going to move heaven and earth to get him back.

That was when I recovered from the overwhelming blow of his rejection. That was when I realized that although he himself had made the mistake of thinking our affair was over I did not have to compound his error by accepting it. It no longer mattered what Paul thought. That was irrelevant. I knew he belonged with me at Mallingham, and when Alan was placed in my arms all my hatred of losing surged through me and I vowed to pour my whole soul into winning what I wanted most.

"I'm going to get Paul back," I said to Harriet as I walked out of the hospital with his son ten days later. And when she exclaimed in horror, "But you can't possibly do that!" I laughed till the tears came into my eyes and said, "Oh yes I can!"

VI

I took a lease on a large old-fashioned flat in South Kensington and invited Dulcie and her baby to move in with me. Joan and Eddie had just separated, the lease on their flat had expired, and Dulcie was in need of a home and people to look after just as I was in need of a housekeeper and nursemaid. We both missed Cedric, Robin and Harriet, but I thought it was time I left the raffishness of Chelsea, and soon Harriet too moved to a better area as we increased our efforts to woo the cream of society to our Mayfair salon.

Once I had decided that my product must first appeal to the aristocracy I had realized that I must launch my venture by opening a salon. Paul had talked glibly of mass production, but in fact there were already on the market for the working classes various lotions and pastes ranging from hair tonic to bust-food cream as well as the cheap scents which one would expect from companies who seldom charged more than a few pence for their wares. I wanted to make a large amount of money rapidly, and I saw no quick profit in selling lavender water at twopence a bottle. Moreover, after buying a bottle of skin tonic from a competitor and having the contents analyzed I discovered that the so-called magic properties of this aid to beauty consisted only of water, grain alcohol, boric acid and perfume. The ingredients may have been cunningly balanced, but the cost of the materials could hardly have been more than threepence a bottle. The product was retailing for nine shillings.

"There's a moral in that story," I said to Harriet, and we calculated that even after the costs of labor, distribution, expensive packaging and advertising we would still be able to net a margin of more than twenty-five percent on each bottle sold at wholesale.

"The moral," agreed Harriet, confirming my earlier theories, "is not to chase a mass market who only have pennies to spare for cosmetics, but to woo the select few who think pennies are only for tipping page boys."

After calling on numerous estate agents I found suitable business premises in the heart of Mayfair. The ground floor was then converted into a salon, while the upper floors remained as offices, and after protracted arguments about the salon's décor we settled on a style which managed to be reminiscent of both Versailles and a Toulouse-Lautrec bordello. Our speciality was gold mirrors. We also had plenty of pink, a color I abhor, but as Cedric said, "It's feminine, dear," and I had to admit that the dusty-pink velvet upholstery gave an added voluptuousness to the gilt furniture and to the gilt-framed reproductions of the paintings of Rubens at his most sensuous. The carpet, I regret to say, was baby blue. The only redeeming feature was that the color reminded me of Cambridge. In this profusion of nursery pastels our clients were manicured and massaged and had their hair dressed, their chins strapped and their faces painted by three expert beauty consultants whom we captured at great expense from Oxford Street, Bond Street and—this last was a great triumph—Paris. The Parisian had been personal maid to Harriet's mother for some years, and when the marchioness died that Christmas Harriet ensnared the maid, whose talent for hairdressing had long been a by-word in the family.

These experts had the burden of putting our theories into practice, and we came to rely heavily on their advice. At first our major emphasis was on shampoo and hair tonic, with soap and bath salts in three different perfumes, but soon the emphasis was directed to skin tonic and skin food, particularly our skin cream, which I had insisted should be featherlight and as greaseless as possible. I had to work long hours to find the right texture, but in general the preparations were easy to make. The challenge lay in ensuring they smelled not only unique but irresistible.

I had to borrow more money from Hal in order to make the advertising splash I knew our salon deserved, but I was determined not to skimp on a single detail. In addition to all the paid advertisements in the magazines, Harriet's friends on *The Illustrated London News* gave us an enthusiastic paragraph on the "World of Women" page, and Harriet herself used all her aristocratic connections to lure our clients through our baby-blue Georgian front door. The salon was launched. It swayed, tottered but stayed afloat, and when within six months it was sailing triumphantly on the crest of the waves Cedric and I packed a large suitcase with our wares and set out to conquer the provinces. I had thought we should start the search to find wholesale outlets in the West End, but Cedric had enough experience of the cosmetics business to know that we would have to produce evidence of provincial conquests before Harrods would grant us an audience.

My life became busier than ever. I was concerned with all aspects of the business, and my waking hours were occupied with problems which ranged from matters of taste, such as whether to advertise eye makeup, to matters of production, such as whether I could afford to expand the laboratory facilities and engage a first-class chemist to perfect my lipstick formula. Lipstick was in many ways the easiest product to manufacture. The basic formula was simple, and fashion decreed only three shades, light, medium and dark, but it was a messy product and I longed to eliminate a woman's chance of a smudgy disaster.

I finally decided I could afford a specialist when my perfumes started to make money. I had devised the idea that fashionable women should change their perfume when they changed their clothes, and as my clients changed clothes three or four times a day this naturally led to increased perfume sales. I advocated Hera for the tailored suit, Artemis for the afternoon frock, and Aphrodite for the evening gown, and soon we had abandoned our limited laboratory facilities by the river in Pimlico and I was buying a small warehouse which could be converted into a factory. By the end of 1925 I no longer had to beg for a loan, and amidst the clamor of the sales conferences and the advertising meetings, the marketing and the research, the warehouse and the salon, the staff and the clients, I dimly realized I not only was making ends meet but was launched firmly on my road to independence.

By this time I had written many letters to Paul and had received many in return, but the correspondence had been initiated only after much hard work and frustration. When Alan had been born in the March of 1923, I had written again to Paul. Having told myself that I was now not merely his discarded mistress but the mother of his only child, I had thought it would be easy to write with confidence, but it had taken me three days before I achieved a pleasant neutral style which ran no risk of alarming him.

My dear Paul,

Alan came punctually on the twenty-seventh of March and weighed seven pounds one ounce. Since you and I both have brown eyes I thought there had been some mistake when this blue-eyed baby was offered to me for inspection, but apparently his eyes will turn brown later and the doctor assured me that it was most unlikely that I had produced a genetic freak. My housekeeper is looking after him at present while I work, but before she collapses with exhaustion I am going to offer Mrs. Oakes's daughter Mary the post of full-time nanny. This will be a promotion for Mary, as she has only been a nursemaid up till now—although God knows being employed by the notorious Dinah Slade can hardly rank in respectability with her present post among the aristocracy of Suffolk! However, enough of domestic trivia. I won't refer to the business, since that subject is best left to our official correspondence, but if Hofstadt and Baker continue to whine that I'm an incompetent woman unhinged by pregnancy I assure you that I intend to make them look even stupider than they look already. When I find the time to dust the lens of my camera I'll take some photographs of Alan and send them to you. He's pink, bald and interesting.

Yours,
D.

Of course I had already taken two rolls of film, but I did not want to inundate Paul with a tidal wave of maternal bliss. My father had always said how dreary he found women who gushed endlessly about the joys of motherhood, and I wanted to intrigue Paul, not to bore him.

His reply to my letter was pleasant but polite, as if my news had rendered him uncharacteristically at a loss for the appropriate charming phrase. He said he was extremely glad to hear that I was well, and he added in a quaint Victorian fashion that he did hope the experience of childbirth had not been too severe an ordeal. He was glad to hear Alan was thriving. After that remark he seemed unsure what to say next, but he did comment that it would be "nice" to see a photograph at some later date. He concluded the letter: "Affectionately, PAUL."

I did send some photographs, two at a time in a steady stream, but received only the briefest of acknowledgments. However, when I informed Paul with icy courtesy that Alan's christening was imminent I received a registered parcel containing a silver christening mug. There was no card enclosed, no message of any kind.

"You *bloody* American!" I shouted, hurling the mug at the wall in a rage, but afterwards I remembered how Paul had insisted he could never acknowledge Alan and I saw that the mug was a gesture in my favor.

Calming down, I selected the best of my latest batch of photographs, enlarged it and posted it to New York with a note which read:

Torquatus volo parvulus
Matris e gremio suae
Porrigens teneras manus
Dulce rideat ad patrem
Semihiante labello.

By return of post came a note quoting the second verse of Catullus' poem in praise of a baby. I smiled. Presently I sent more pictures, more scraps of Latin and an occasional epigram in Greek, and in a bright, breezy, studiedly unemotional correspondence we discussed the role of the chorus in Greek drama, the structure of the Theban plays, the true meaning of *Lysistrata,* the Socratic concept of democracy, and the homosexuality of Alexander the Great. Tiring of the Greeks, we then discussed the influence of Cato on Marcus Junius Brutus, the virtues of Sulla (I claimed he had none), the mystical properties of Lucretius' *De Rerum Natura,* Virgil's views on beekeeping, the philosophy of Marcus Aurelius and the sexual inclinations of Gaius Julius Caesar (I suggested that the famous incident in Bithynia had been an isolated incident magnified by his enemies until it had assumed mythical dimensions). Eventually we devised quizzes to test each other's knowledge; they were great fun and brushed up my classical skills enormously.

He would ask politely after Alan, and sometimes he would make some awkward comment on the photographs. He truly seemed to have no idea what to say on the subject of his son, and in his reticence I sensed some Protean conflict clouding his clear incisive mind. However, I was determined to be patient because I knew that once he had accepted that I still had a part to play in his life I would be well on the way to winning him back.

Meanwhile I was well on the way to winning a reputation for my products in London. Harrods at first turned us down, but Marshall's and Gorringe's agreed to give us a try, and it was when they rapidly sold out of stock that Harrods reversed their decision. With my salon expanding, my staff increasing and my cosmetics on sale in Knightsbridge, I visited Paris to cull new ideas and even toyed with the idea of a salon across the Channel, but Hal told me I should shore up the success I had won in London before I looked for fresh worlds to conquer.

It was a relief to take his advice. I was probably much more exhausted than I realized, for the strain of working seven days a week with few breaks for nearly three years was considerable. At home I lived quietly. Every spare moment I had was spent with Alan, and although I longed for Mallingham I seldom saw it. At first I tried to go there every other weekend, but the pressures of work made this impossible and I became more confined to London. This in turn precluded the hermitlike existence for which I yearned whenever I escaped from the office, for Harriet gave numerous dinners and luncheons to cultivate our clientele and I reluctantly found I had to attend. At first I thought I could escape by pleading that my past private life rendered me socially unacceptable, but to my surprise Harriet promised I would be lionized. She was right. Apparently my refusal to fade away into obscurity just like any other decent unmarried mother had enthralled the gossips who had been following my career, and now my phoenixlike resurgence from the ashes of my love affair had transformed me into a *femme fatale.*

No one could have been more amazed than I was. I still thought of myself as too well-educated to appeal to anyone except Paul, and so it came as a shock to discover men of all ages brazenly displaying their ambition to step into Paul's shoes. In vain I explained that I did not belong in the demimonde, but when I started talking about self-respect and claimed that promiscuity was psychologically untenable, my pursuers all laughed in delight and said how original I was. I became exhausted fighting off these Lotharios, but there was no doubt that their admiration, spurious though it was, was good for my self-esteem. I did become more confident socially, but since all my admirers seemed vastly inferior to Paul I was never tempted to embark on another affair. Anyway, I had no time. One can do only so much, and being a mother and running a business took all the energy I had.

Alan grew. He became the most beautiful baby in the world. He sat up, smiled, screamed imperiously. Soon he crawled. At eleven months he was staggering beside me as he clutched my fingers in his hot little hand, and when he began to talk he became not only the most beautiful baby in the world but the cleverest. My camera clicked constantly, and far away across the Atlantic Ocean at the offices of P. C. Van Zale and Company, Paul received a continuing record of his son's progress.

Paul's interest became less guarded. His letters became not only more frequent but more relaxed. Gradually even his references to Alan became less strained, and shortly after Alan's second birthday he began to write vaguely about how amusing it would be if we could meet again in New York. I retorted: "Isn't it time you made a pilgrimage to England again?"—for I knew that the leading investment bankers made such visits annually. But all Paul said was: "If I went to Europe again I fear I'd never come back!" and I knew then that if I could only coax him across the Atlantic I would win my arduous waiting game.

I wrote how beautiful Mallingham looked in the spring and described every inch of the house lovingly for him. It was no use. He persisted in saying how much I would enjoy New York, until my patience, worn thin after two and a half years of diplomacy, finally snapped. "If you really want me to visit New York," I wrote in exasperation, "why don't you issue me a frank, straightforward, honest-to-God invitation instead of sending letter after letter full of coy hints and dismal 'wish-you-were-here' refrains?"

There was a silence. I waited for his reply but received only a formal acknowledgment from his chief assistant, O'Reilly, saying that Paul had been unwell with some minor ailment and would attend later to his private correspondence. I waited. Then I wrote three times asking if he felt better. There was still no reply. I was just thinking in despair that he was either dead or repelled by my unwise display of impatience when I received his irresistible invitation to visit him in America.

I should have realized that this powerful example of epistolary seduction was as mysterious as his long silence, but I was too sick with relief to analyze Paul's motives. I did allow myself the luxury of indignant rage ("How dare he think I'd drop everything the moment he crooks his little finger!"), but then all I could do was long for him with such a passion that I hardly knew how to stop myself from rushing aboard the first ship to New York.

VII

I arrived in New York on Saturday, the seventeenth of April, 1926, after a windy transatlantic voyage, and leaving Alan and his nanny Mary Oakes in their cabin, I staggered up on deck to inspect Paul's city.

The weather was misty. I moved feverishly from port to starboard but could see nothing.

"Where is it?" I asked a passing sailor anxiously as I clung to the rail.

"Don't worry, miss, it's there—we've never lost it yet!" came the reassuring reply, and as I turned away from him the sun shone fitfully somewhere above us, the mist parted and I saw a series of towers, gossamer-thin and ethereal, etched delicately against the pastel morning sky.

I was astonished. I had imagined the tall buildings of New York to be solid, ugly and vulgar, and when I could summon none of my anticipated feelings of repulsion towards the city which had lured Paul from Mallingham, I felt curiously defenseless. It was my first warning that all was not as it seemed to be, and to smother my confusion I retreated below to find Alan.

I felt weaker and weaker at the thought of Paul. In Alan's cabin I caught sight of myself in the looking glass, and my heart sank. How plain I was! How fat! Six days of gourmet cuisine on the high seas had produced regrettable results. Supposing Paul took one look at me and decided that all passion was lost beyond recall! I sweated at the prospect of such humiliation and felt so enervated that I could hardly drag myself back on deck.

"Where's my daddy?" asked Alan. He was barely three years old, but he spoke clearly, enunciating each syllable like an adult. His dark eyes were bright with excitement, the wind ruffled his fine fair hair, and his little hand was locked tightly in mine.

"We're not quite there yet. Look at all the tall buildings!"

"Um. . . . Mummy, it's cold out here. I want to go inside again."

I took him back to Mary, but when they set off for a walk around the public rooms I returned to my cabin. Dissatisfied with my makeup, I washed it off and began to apply it afresh, but my hands were shaking so much that my special nonsmudge deep-garnet lipstick wandered disastrously over my upper lip. I poked around among my foundation creams, chose the wrong one, wiped it off, slapped another one on and upset the powder. My nose looked too big. I stared at it and in my distraction applied too much perfume. The cabin began to reek in a way which conjured up fevered images of Nell Gwyn selling cloves in a Chinese restaurant. In an effort to ward off utter despair I said to my reflection in the glass, "I'm going to win. I'm going to get him back. Back to Mallingham. Back to me." And, struck by the resemblance of my mutterings to Coué's famous incantation "Every day in every way I am getting better and better," I laughed and felt braver.

By the time the ship docked I was on deck again, but although I peered down onto the quay the ship was so high that the people below were unrecognizable. Eventually the baggage was unloaded and we were permitted to leave, but once we were ashore all the passengers became enmeshed in the formalities of the customs inspection. Our baggage had to be found, opened and submitted to prying hands. Forms had to be stamped. Questions had to be answered. I felt sick and started to chew my nails. Alan became bored and announced he had to go to the potty.

"You'll just have to wait, love," said Mary sympathetically.

"But I don't want to wait!"

Hell on earth, I decided, was undoubtedly being imprisoned in the customs hall of a foreign port with a three-year-old who wanted to go to the lavatory.

Our last bag was cleared. "Help you, ma'am?" offered a huge man who I dimly realized was a porter.

"Oh, please, please, yes," I said wildly, and we all set off for the distant barrier beyond which throngs of people were waiting to meet the passengers.

I strained my eyes for a glimpse of Paul but there was no sign of him. The swine! He had decided not to meet me after all. Oh, how dared he do this to me, how dared he!

"Where do you want to go, ma'am?"

I had no idea where to wait or even if I should wait at all. Despite the chilly weather I was sweating, and I was sure my makeup was already wrecked. There was a hole in my stocking. The crowd swirled around us. The noise was appalling.

"Make up your mind, lady!"

No sooner had he finished speaking than there was a diversion. Someone shouted, "Make way, there!" and someone else gave my surly porter a five-dollar bill. He almost swooned—I saw him rocking on his feet—and barely recovered in time to hear the curt order "Take the bags to the Rolls-Royce outside."

"Yes, *sir!*"

I looked at the stranger giving the orders. His face was unknown to me, but when I looked past him I saw Paul's bodyguard.

"Peterson!" I gasped, but as I rushed towards him he stepped aside and suddenly, magically, I was face to face again with the man I wanted—and the man I was determined to have no matter what obstacles might stand in my way.

Chapter Two

I

He looked much older. I was shocked to see how much he had aged. At fifty-two, when I had first met him, he had looked no more than forty; now, four years later, he looked the wrong side of sixty. His graying brown hair was sparser than ever, his face was thinner and the deepened lines about his eyes and mouth made him look haggard as if he had long been struggling beneath an intolerable burden.

Then he smiled. He had eyes which because of his fair complexion seemed darker than they really were, and when he smiled they blazed as if powered by some mysterious source of electricity. His mobile features, expressive enough to reflect a dozen lightning changes of mood, mirrored this flash of electrical excitement and charged up the power of his dazzling smile to a hypnotic intensity.

The years fell away. So did all my past fits of rage and resentment. In a moment of weakness I wanted to burst into tears, cling to him in an orgy of passion and, like a heroine abducted by Valentino, beg him to do whatever he wanted with me.

Surely no man had the right to reduce a woman to such groveling self-abasement! As I groped for common sense I wondered how I could ever have forgotten how attractive he was.

"Dinah!" exclaimed the brute in his light flexible utterly charming voice. "You look wonderful!"

"Oh, Paul!" How I despised myself! I could only gulp and gaze at him adoringly. In panic I tried to think of an intelligent remark. "It's been a long time!" I gasped inanely. "Heavens, what a long time it's been!"

"It sure has," he said, and when he used that raw American phrase I knew that he too was temporarily incapable of urbanity.

He had just drawn me to him for a kiss when Alan said behind us in a clear cross little voice, "Mummy, I want to go to the potty."

I laughed, Paul laughed and miraculously we both relaxed. "Alan darling—" I stooped over him with Paul's hand still in mine—"this is your daddy."

"Does he know where the potty is?"

"What admirable single-mindedness!" said Paul, stooping awkwardly to pat Alan's head. "Mayers, show Master Slade and his nurse to the nearest ladies' room, please, and then take them outside to the car. . . . This way, my dear."

He remarked how blond Alan's hair was. I said that it became even fairer in the summer. We marveled at this prosaic piece of information and he asked me if I had enjoyed the voyage. I chattered feverishly about the *Berengaria* and told him how wonderful the food had been. While this dreadful conversation was progressing we edged our way through the crowds and emerged into a dingy cobbled street which reminded me of Cruickshank's sketches of Dickensian London. Around me American accents rendered my mother tongue as incomprehensible as a foreign language, and when I looked past the grimy nineteenth-century tenements at the hard blue sky I was aware of the strangeness, the alien light and the power of a mighty civilization glittering with barbarism.

"Dinah, may I suggest you and Alan and I travel in the Rolls with Peterson while Mayers accompanies the nurse and baggage in the Cadillac. Didn't you bring a maid?"

"Don't be funny, Paul! It's as much as I can do to afford a housekeeper, a nanny and a daily."

Alan scrambled eagerly into the Rolls-Royce and sniffed the upholstery like a puppy. "Nice smell!" he said approvingly as I scrambled in after him. He turned to Paul and hesitated before hissing to me in a stage whisper, "What's his name?"

"Darling, I told you he was—"

"Yes, I know he's a daddy but what do I call him?"

"'Papa' would be nice," said Paul as the chauffeur closed the door.

"Oh, Paul!" I said. "How Victorian!"

Our glances met. He laughed. "Yes," he said, "nothing's changed."

"Oh Mummy, look!" cried Alan excited. "The man who's driving the motorcar looks just like my golliwog!"

"Good heavens, darling, you mustn't say that!"

"Why not? What's wrong? I love my golliwog! Papa, how can I become black like that man driving your car?"

Paul embarked on the story of the leopard who could not change his spots, and the Rolls, leaving the docks, moved into a wide straight boulevard.

"This is West Fourteenth Street," Paul added when the Kipling lesson had been concluded. "When we reach the intersection with Fifth Avenue we'll turn north and start to ride uptown."

I had been reading about New York. "Fourteenth Street was smart at one time, wasn't it?"

"Yes, but the center of New York has been moving steadily uptown for decades. In my young day lower Fifth Avenue was purely a residential street and the mainstream of commerce was along Sixth Avenue and Broadway, but now Fifty-seventh Street is the new 'boulevard of trade,' as they call it, and the residential area has moved north into an area which was once a slum. I can still remember the shanties on the very spot where I now have my home. . . ." And he went on talking about New York while I gazed at the buildings and Alan embarked on a new sniffing examination of the upholstery.

The time came to turn north, and as the Rolls swung into Fifth Avenue I saw the famous street stretching uphill as far as the eye could see.

"Look behind you," said Paul, "and you'll see the arch of Washington Square."

I was soon trying to look in every direction at once. We passed the towering triangle of the Flatiron Building, the trees of Madison Square, the dome of Metropolitan Life, the huge department stores in the Thirties, the stone lions outside the library on Forty-second Street, and finally came to a halt in heavy traffic outside St. Patrick's Cathedral. I leaned forward, craning my neck to peer at the Gothic spires, and as I heard the screaming horns and roaring engines around us the past of Europe blended with the cacophony of that American present and I was gripped with the most vibrant excitement and anticipation.

"I love it!" I said to Paul.

His eyes sparkled. "Welcome once again to my world, Miss Slade!" he said laughing, and added, flinging out his hand in a showman's gesture, "And welcome to the Plaza."

A baroque building soared above a magnificent fountain, and beyond the open space of the square I saw the trees of Central Park and the mansions of the rich marching north up Fifth Avenue.

"Heavens above," I said weakly, "am I going to stay here?"

"Well, the hotel's very convenient and I think you'll find it comfortable."

"Oh, I'm sure we shall manage very nicely!" I had forgotten his predilection for grand hotels. Adjusting my hat, I did my best to emerge graciously from the Rolls-Royce and glide up the steps into the foyer.

"It's a palace, isn't it?" said Alan impressed. "Mummy, is this like a fairy tale?"

It was. We were welcomed by people who bowed from the waist and spoke in hushed voices. A gilded lift conveyed us noiselessly to an upper floor, and we were escorted into a gargantuan suite which faced the park. Every room was filled with flowers; I had never seen so many orchids gathered together outside a conservatory, and when

Paul slipped one of the orchids into my buttonhole I was so dazed by my surroundings that I hardly had the strength to thank him. I was still trying to recover when two waiters rolled in a trolley bearing a bucket of ice and a jar of caviar, while Mayers produced a bottle of champagne from a bag.

"We'll let it chill for a few minutes," said Paul as Mayers retired.

This time speech was quite beyond me. I gazed at the red velvet curtains which stretched from floor to ceiling, the golden carpet, the gilt fixtures, the Louis Quinze (could it possibly be genuine?) furniture. There was even a marble fireplace fashioned by some disciple of Robert Adam. Next door in the larger of the two bedrooms Alan cried, "Mummy, look!" and when I wandered over the threshold I found him clutching the largest toy bear I had ever seen. A round-eyed Mary Oakes had already collapsed on a striped satin chaise-longue.

"Look, Mummy! Look, Mary! Look how big he is!"

"What a lovely teddy, darling, but what do you say to Papa? Remember your P's and Q's."

The bed could have accommodated four people with ease, and beyond the far doorway was a marble bathroom bedecked with mirrors. Backing away into the sitting room, I heard Alan thank Paul for his present.

"You like it? Good. Ah, there you are, Dinah! I've got a present for you as well."

He handed me a box. It was dark blue, three inches square, and the lid was embossed with the words "TIFFANY & CO." Opening the lid, I found a pair of earrings.

"I hope green's still your favorite color," said Paul.

I stared at the emeralds.

"Remember your P's and Q's, Mummy!" piped Alan.

"Little monster!" Smiling at him, I kissed the top of his head before turning to Paul. "Thank you, darling—for everything. What a wonderful welcome! I feel quite overcome. What can I possibly say?"

"Say nothing!" he advised, with an erotic alternative effortlessly implied in his extraordinary smile, and bent his head in a flash to kiss me on the lips.

As soon as my mouth was free I burst out laughing. "You exasperating man!" I exclaimed. "Keeping me on tenterhooks for three years and then sweeping me off my feet despite all my determination to remain rooted sensibly to the ground! Why am I so incredibly glad to see you again? I must be demented."

"Have a little champagne, my dear, and let's forget the past three years. May I offer you some caviar?"

Half an hour later he inquired if I still found him exasperating.

"I can think of no other word to do you justice!"

"Then I can see I shall have to take time to expand your vocabulary. Obviously you'd like the chance now to settle down, but I thought this evening we might have dinner together. I'll call for you at—shall we say six-thirty?"

We said six-thirty. He left, patting Alan on the head again after shaking hands with the enormous bear, and I sank down on the sofa. In fact I was in such a state of exhaustion that it was not until I took off my emerald earrings half an hour later that it occurred to me to wonder what Paul was trying to buy.

II

Paul knew I was sensitive about receiving his money. He had given me presents in the past but nothing which had matched the extravagance of those earrings, and although he had offered to return Mallingham to me as a gift I had always insisted that I must buy back my home with my own hard-earned money. It was true that I had wanted him to own Mallingham temporarily in order to strengthen the bond between us, but my main reason in forcing the ownership upon him had been that I had wanted security. I had been hedging my bets. If I had ended up a bankrupt my creditors could never have taken Mallingham so long as the title remained vested in Paul, and if the worst did come to the worst I knew Paul would always help me continue to live in my home. I hated the thought of being a kept woman, but I hated the thought of losing Mallingham even more.

However, since I was making ends meet and Mallingham was in no danger, I could afford to be sensitive about taking Paul's money. For some time I fingered the earrings reluctantly, but then telling myself I was becoming neurotic in my fear of being "kept," I thrust them into my jewel box and took Alan and Mary for a walk in the park. Although I reasoned that Paul owed me hospitality in return for the months he had spent as my guest at Mallingham, I was even beginning to feel uncomfortable about my paid Plaza suite, and when I started shying away at the sight of the orchids I knew I needed some fresh air.

"It's a jolly odd sort of park, isn't it?" I said to Mary later as we paused at one end of a small lake.

"Oh, it's ever so foreign, Miss Dinah, all them nasty black rocks and no flowers and hardly any grass to speak of. My dad would weep if he could see that grass."

We savored our homesickness together. Mary was nineteen, plump and rosy-cheeked. I hoped fervently she wouldn't fall in love with an

American, because Mrs. Oakes would never have forgiven me for inflicting her with a foreign son-in-law.

I was unsure how long we would stay in New York. Paul and I had never discussed the exact duration of my visit, but I had told my friends I would need two months to complete my investigation of the American cosmetics industry with a view to opening a salon in New York. "For after all," I had said glibly when all my friends had deplored my decision to return to Paul, "one might as well combine business with pleasure." Two months would take me until the middle of June, a sensible time to embark for home, since the weather would be becoming unpleasantly hot and Paul would be making his plans for his annual sojourn in Bar Harbor, and in two months I should certainly be able to judge whether there was any future in continuing our affair. If there was none then that, of course, would be that. No matter how much I hated the idea of defeat it would be suicidal to turn a blind eye to reality. But if some future existed I was confident I could lure him back with me to Mallingham. All I had to do was to be calm, detached and sensible as I followed my plan of action without the smallest deviation in strategy.

Unfortunately anyone less calm, detached and sensible than I, as I prepared for my first night with Paul in three and a half years, would have been impossible to imagine. I was trembling with anticipation yet quivering with dread, one moment dreaming of moonlight, roses and whispered "I love you's" and the next sweating in horror at the thought of stifled yawns, awkward platitudes and the hideous epilogue "I'll telephone you sometime." Filing my nails in a frenzy, I told myself that both the romantic dream and the nauseous nightmare were equally unrealistic. He had never once stifled a yawn when making love to me—and he had never once said "I love you" either—so it was most unlikely he would start now. Probably we would make each other laugh and rip a sheet or two and afterwards say how much we had missed each other.

Yet I could not help wondering if he had missed me at all. I realized that after he had returned from England he had at once found someone else; it was the only plausible explanation for his long silence and his attempt to end our personal relationship, but although the thought of that was distasteful I no longer minded it. Obviously there could be no other woman in his life at present or he would never have sent for me. For the hundredth time I speculated fruitlessly about his true feelings. If Paul had actually said to me, "I love you," I would probably have disbelieved him, yet I knew he had loved me at Mallingham and although I could admit that the love had faded I preferred to think it was dormant rather than dead.

I hoped I was avoiding the sin of wishful thinking.

The thought of sin cheered me up and the next moment I was

quivering again, not with fright but with lust. It was odd to think that in Victorian days lust had been considered an exclusively male vice. I reflected on the ghastly heroines of Tennyson with their pure alabaster brows, and wondered what they would have thought of a nude male. After thanking God I hadn't lived seventy years ago I spent some time daydreaming of myself with a pure alabaster brow and some disembodied male organ, and then with reluctance I tore myself away from my stimulating thoughts to choose a dress for the evening.

Thanks to the gourmet cuisine of the *Berengaria* I could hardly squeeze myself into an evening dress which would match my earrings, but where there's a will there's a way. The dress had narrow shoulder straps and dropped straight from the bust to the hips in a bead-encrusted green tube, while at the hips the satin hung in draped folds to form a dipped hemline somewhere around the knees. Unfortunately my hips destroyed the elegant tubelike effect by bulging at the exact point at which the beads ended, but I told myself that since Paul had never cared for the masculinity of postwar women's fashions he would be glad to see that my hips were still much in evidence. Wriggling into my slave bangle, I grabbed my ostrich-feather fan, pursed my lips into a Clara Bow bee-sting and did a little Charleston in front of the looking glass.

By the time Paul arrived I was again standing before the glass as I admired my brand-new flesh-colored rayon stockings.

"My God," said Paul, "what's that peculiar stuff on your legs? And why are you wearing a bracelet above the elbow?"

"Oh, I'll take everything off—"

"So soon? Even the Romans waited till after the stuffed dormice!"

"But if you think I look awful—"

"My dear, you look riveting! I hope I'm not so old that I can't resign myself to modern feminine fashions. Peterson, you're the expert on repulsive American slang—could Miss Slade be described as a jazz-baby?"

Peterson laughed. He was not in the least dour, as bodyguards are popularly supposed to be, and I had never once felt embarrassed by his presence when Paul and I spent our long summer together in 1922.

"What happened to O'Reilly?" I asked idly, remembering Paul's other employee who had accompanied him on all his visits to Mallingham. We had said good night to Alan and were walking outside to the Rolls-Royce.

"He was promoted," said Paul in exactly the same tone of voice as if he had said, "He died," and began to talk about the restaurant where we were to have dinner.

"It's across town on Park Avenue," he was saying, "and it's called the Restaurant Marguery. In my opinion it's even better than its namesake in Paris, but we'll see what you think of it."

By that time I would have been enthralled by a workers' café, but the Marguery would no doubt have satisfied the most discriminating of epicures. The decoration was formal, with gray paneled walls in the style of Louis Seize; evidently the French kings were popular among the interior decorators of New York. The pale-green furniture was decked with rose-and-ivory brocade, and the lighting came from sparkling chains and pendants of crystal reminding me of a series of elaborate fountains. There were secluded nooks for dinners *á deux*. Ours was decorated with pink and white carnations, and beneath a napkin another illegal bottle of the best French champagne reclined in a silver bucket.

"Whatever happened to Prohibition?" I could not resist asking as the champagne was uncorked. "Isn't it against the law to drink like this?"

"Welcome to Mayor Jimmy Walker's New York, Dinah, where even the law is for sale to anyone who can afford it! Now what would you like to eat? The filet de sole Marguery is the speciality of the house. . . ."

I decided that ancient Rome was not dead after all but reincarnated in the Western Hemisphere.

"No, I think eighteenth-century England would be a closer parallel," said Paul, and as he talked, littering his explanation with philosophical, historical and literary references, I felt my mind sharpening against his until it seemed to expand with exhilaration.

Some time later we were deep in a discussion about obscenity in literature, but it was only after I had lost the thread of my masterly argument three times that I suddenly realized he had been drinking water while I had consumed almost the entire bottle of champagne.

"Paul, you villain, you've got me drunk!"

"That's so that I can now ruthlessly cross-examine you on how you've spent the last three years!"

"You know exactly how I've spent the last three years! I was the one who always wrote. Remember? *I* never indulged in long rude baffling silences!"

"My dear, Americans forgot the art of letter-writing as soon as the telephone became popular, but when it becomes possible to phone London from New York I promise I'll make amends to you." He finished his coffee, and when he replaced his cup I saw to my astonishment that his hand was shaking. "Shall we go?"

"Back to the hotel?" I said confused as he thrust his hands out of sight beneath the table.

"No, I have a *pied-à-terre* near here by the river. I thought we could drink some brandy while I point out the famous landmarks to you."

"How divine! I'd love that," I said, baffled by the discrepancy between his casual invitation and his unmistakable signs of tension.

"Dinah," he said as soon as we were in the car, "I'm really sorry about those letters."

"Which letters?"

"The ones I didn't write. Are you angry?"

With astonishment I realized he was beside himself with nervousness because he thought I was nursing some dark satanic grudge. It seemed so funny to think of Paul—of all people—being even remotely ill-at-ease in a woman's presence that I laughed out loud. It's remarkable how the least humorous facts can seem amusing after one has consumed nearly a full bottle of champagne.

"Well, Paul," I said frankly, "I *was* absolutely livid with you, but after I decided to accept your invitation to New York I also decided to let bygones be bygones. And of course as soon as I saw you again I immediately forgot there had been any bygones at all."

He gave me a worried little smile. "So everything's forgiven?"

"For God's sake, Paul, what's the matter with you? Don't pretend you don't know how beastly attractive you are, because I loathe false modesty."

"You didn't think I'd changed?"

"Well, when I first saw you I did think you looked as though you needed a holiday. Have you been working too hard?"

"I regret to say I have. It was foolish of me. You got O'Reilly's letter last summer telling you that I was ill?"

"Paul, I wrote three times to ask if you were better!"

He looked confused. "I'm sorry. Mayers was dealing with my personal correspondence by that time and O'Reilly must have forgotten to tell him your letters had to be acknowledged."

"But were you very ill? What was the matter?"

"It was nothing, just exhaustion forcing me to rest for a couple of months, but I'm better now." He smiled and gave me a kiss. "As soon as I saw you," he teased, "I sloughed off my nineteenth-century chains and felt twenty years younger!"

I kissed him back.

"Sutton Place, sir," said the chauffeur after the car had been stationary for over a minute.

"Thank you, Wilson," said Paul, springing out of the car with all his old alacrity. "Peterson, you'd better come up with us. It's probably quite unnecessary, but I'd hate to be assassinated by some Bolshevik at this particular moment, because it would be so very tiresome for Miss Slade."

We entered the gleaming foyer of a tall block of flats and I was led reluctantly into a lift with an amazing array of numbers on the panel.

"I have the penthouse here," explained Paul as the lift attendant closed the doors. "It's on the twenty-eighth floor and the views are really very fine."

"Oh yes?" I said, trying not to think of twenty-eight floors receding beneath me. As soon as the lift stopped I rushed out before it could plummet to the ground.

Peterson stepped past me to unlock the door, and when he moved inside, switching on the lights, I followed him across the threshold.

"Paul!" I had seen the view. "My God, what a sight!" I exclaimed as Peterson finished his inspection and left us alone in the flat.

Later I discovered that the building stood on the extreme east side of the city and that the windows of the living room faced both south down the East River and west into midtown Manhattan. The skyscrapers stood facing one another like an army of monsters poised for conflict, and their glowing windows and floodlit spires gave the sky an unearthly glow. Despite the darkness I felt I could still clearly see the radiant steel and shining glass of those miracles of construction, and as I stood by the window it seemed to me that I saw a country barely touched by the disillusionment which the War had brought to Europe, a world still gripped by the nineteenth-century delusion that all scientific achievement led to progress while all progress led to the improvement of mankind. For the first time I understood why America had entered the War so reluctantly and retreated afterwards into isolation. America lived in a different world, a world of shining optimism, boundless achievement and unblemished hopes. The tortured failures and writhings of Europe would have seemed not only boring but irrelevant; I was reminded of a rich man who will not leave his castle because he is both embarrassed and annoyed by the crude spectacle of the poor man suffering at his gate.

"I suppose America will never be invaded or occupied," I said slowly. "It'll never suffer as the European countries have suffered."

"No country is impregnable from disaster," said Paul, "and not all disasters come complete with bombs and bayonets. Think of Roman Britain. The trouble didn't begin when the Saxons decided it was an amusing place to visit. The trouble began when something went wrong with the economy and the cities became unmanageable."

"But what could possibly go wrong with the American economy?" I said astonished.

"There's a lot wrong with it already."

"But the stock market! I thought—"

"That's our rich golden façade," he interrupted, making a gesture which included the brilliant city lights with the market, "and at present few people care to look beyond it. But the boom only applies to certain sections of the market. Agriculture's depressed. The government is essentially impotent and growth is unstable. Do you remember Tennyson's Kraken?"

"The monster that no one knew about? The one who awoke and rose out of the depths?"

"How gratifying that your knowledge of Tennyson has improved!" He paused to take some glasses out of a cabinet. "Tennyson's Kraken's sleeping peacefully on Wall Street," he said presently. "He's an economic version of Frankenstein's monster, designed by the investment bankers for a public in love with a roulette wheel, and someday he's going to wake up and breathe fire in all directions. . . . Why, how like Cassandra I sound! I must stop at once. Do you want to take a look around? The bedroom has a fine view to the north and east."

The bedroom looked as if it had been designed by Casanova with help from an Arabian sheik. Hidden lighting illuminated the most incongruous feature of the room, an eighteenth-century ceiling inset with exquisite miniatures of cherubs.

"My God, Paul!" I called amazed. "This looks just like an Angelica Kauffmann ceiling!"

"It is," he said, appearing in the doorway with the brandy glasses. "There was a house called Cullom Park for sale in 1919, just before I left Europe, and when no one bought it I arranged for this particular ceiling to be shipped over here before the house could be demolished. Why are you laughing?"

"Because it was such a typically American thing to do and I never think of you as being typically American!"

"I fail to see your point. The ceiling was very fine. I saved it. I see nothing humorous in the situation," he said shortly, and walked out.

My heart thudded with fright. "Paul . . ."

"If you don't like it we'll go somewhere else," he said, drinking his brandy rapidly.

"I do like it! I was laughing in admiration—admiration for your American resourcefulness!"

"No, it would be better if we went somewhere else. This is the wrong atmosphere. I should never have brought you here."

I protested further, but when he insisted on going I followed him in silence to the lift.

We waited in the hall by the shaft, but I could think of nothing to say. I was too conscious of his tension, and in terror I saw the evening turned sour, our reunion ruined, our affair cut off before it could be renewed. I made frantic efforts to guess what was going on in Paul's mind but soon decided I would have had a better chance of understanding a series of Etruscan hieroglyphics.

The lift came. I had to think of a solution before we reached the ground floor and he made some excuse to abandon the evening. The doors of the lift closed. I looked wildly around for inspiration, and when my glance came to rest on Paul I saw the deep lines about his mouth and remembered that he had been ill.

Memory returned with the force of a punch between the eyes. I saw my father hobbling back into my stepmother's room too soon after a debilitating attack of gout and growling in frustration the next morning, "Damn it, it's no fun being fifty-five!" For at least half an hour I had been obliged to listen to a boring dissertation on the recurring problems of middle-aged men, and I was still trying to remember how my father had cured himself (his cures had become increasingly bizarre) when the lift reached the ground floor.

"Well," said Paul stiffly, "we may as well return to the Plaza."

I saw the memory floating past and pounced on it. My father had locked himself up with his current mistress in the belfry of Mallingham Church and had made love among the bells. Obviously the remedy was to be thoroughly original with a touch of the spiritual.

"Oh, Paul!" I said, trying to sound disappointed yet soothing. "The night's so—so—" Could I really say "so young"? I could and did. Desperation will occasionally drive me to excessive lengths. "Don't let's go to the Plaza just yet!" I said winningly. "After all, there's plenty of time later for all that sort of thing, and just now there's only one place in all New York that I really want to see. I know it sounds absurd but could we motor down to Wall Street to see the bank? I've been looking forward for years to seeing where you make your millions and dictate the economy, and I don't think I can control my curiosity a single hour longer. Oh Paul, do let's go! It's not impossible, is it? Surely nothing's impossible in New York!"

He swung to face me. I saw the stillness in his eyes before he gave me his special smile.

"I'd be the last person ever to tell *you*," he said laughing, "that something's impossible!" And walking over to the car where the chauffeur was dozing and Peterson was smoking a cigarette, he told both men they were dismissed for the evening.

They stared at him openmouthed.

"But sir," stammered Peterson, "if you're going for a walk—"

"I'm not going to walk. I'm going to drive."

The chauffeur's head jerked up. Peterson blanched. "But sir! Sir, I'll drive you if you want Wilson to go home—"

"Do you want me to fire you, Peterson?"

"No, sir, but—"

"Then do as I say and go home."

The two men backed away in silence as we scrambled into the car.

"The hell with them!" said Paul as he pushed the starter on the floor with his foot and the engine roared exuberantly into life. "The hell with everyone! All right, Dinah, close your eyes and say your prayers—we're off to Willow and Wall!"

I clutched my seat as the car shot forward. "Paul, have you ever driven a car before?"

"I drove all the time before the War—when motoring was a true adventure! I lost interest later when automobiles became so predictable."

Howling to the left, the car plunged down another of New York's wide straight boulevards before careering to the right into a side street.

"We'll go down Lexington and across Twenty-third to Broadway," said Paul as we shot underneath two overhead railways. "Scared?"

"No, no. Does this car fly or am I merely imagining you're trying to take off into the air?"

He roared with laughter as the car screeched into Lexington Avenue and at least three different taxis blared their horns.

We seemed to find Broadway more by luck than by judgment, but after that we had an uneventful run down to the bottom of the island. When I realized we had left the midtown traffic and were entering a business district which was deserted at night I even stopped cowering in my seat and began to enjoy the journey. I was just gazing at the surprisingly rural sight of a large graveyard surrounding an old church when Paul swung the car to the left and we plunged into the deep shadows of a narrow winding street.

"That was Trinity Church representing God," he said, "and here's Wall Street representing Mammon. Since this is New York you'll have no trouble guessing which is the better patronized. Now"—he slowed the pace of the car—"there's the Stock Exchange, and that Greek structure over there is the Sub-Treasury—"

"What's that very grand white palace on the corner down there?"

"One Willow Street. How flattering that you should have totally ignored the House of Morgan, which we've just passed! Now let me see—how does one stop this car? Perhaps if I turn off the engine I'll be able to find the brake."

I screamed, but he was teasing me and we halted exactly in front of the flight of steps which led up to the pillared entrance. A night watchman met us at the outer doors.

"How many floors of this building belong to the bank?" I whispered as I tiptoed into an oval hall where marble pillars rose to meet some remote shadowed ceiling.

"All of them, naturally. On the top floor we have the telephone operators, the mail room, the partners' dining room and the kitchens. On the fourth floor we have the tax experts, the economists and the advertising department, and below them on the third you can find the railroad section, all foreign operations and the municipal department. The partners' private offices, the conference room and the library are on the second floor, and on the first—the ground floor, as you would say in England—are the syndicate operations and the senior partner's office, also the senior clerks and securities analysts, who since the merger have taken over the great hall. And talking of the great hall, come over here and watch as I turn on the lights."

I stood between two pillars as the switches clicked, and as if by magic the Renaissance sprang to life before my eyes. I was in a palace, on the brink of a vast brilliant chamber. Huge clusters of lights blazed above us. Long slim windows soared above oak-paneled walls. The dim oils of somber portraits reminded me again of a long gallery in some postmedieval mansion. Beyond the waist-high wooden wall which rose in front of us, a number of mahogany desks slumbered like heraldic animals on either side of a wide aisle.

I stared at the scene for a long time before I became aware that Paul was watching me. I looked at him. My thoughts were too primitive to be expressed in words, but I knew he could see into my mind and effortlessly decipher what he saw.

He smiled.

Still without speaking we moved down the long aisle, and beyond the doors at the far end we entered another hall, where a staircase with wrought-iron banisters curved to the floors above.

A moment later I found myself in a double chamber of graceful proportions. One room was furnished as a library, while the other, which I could only dimly see beyond the archway which divided the chamber, appeared to be a reception room of some kind. The word "drawing room," conjuring up images of twittering Victorian ladies, would have been inappropriate, even banal, in such surroundings.

We still said nothing.

I stared at his Attic vase, his Rembrandt, his leatherbound first editions and his flawless collection of eighteenth-century English furniture. The only anomaly in the room was the carpet. It was thick, lush and modern. It was also the color of American money.

Instinctively I knelt to touch it, and as I ran my fingers deep into the rich pile I heard Paul turn the key in the door.

The quality of our silence changed. I felt the electrical excitement spiraling between us and knew we were locked into some irreversible pattern of wealth and power.

Turning abruptly, he removed one of the prints from the wall, opened the safe behind it and pulled out a wad of money. When he fanned the notes apart, as a gambler might show a winning hand of cards, I saw they were all crisp new one-hundred-dollar bills.

"The finishing touch to our décor!" he said.

I started to laugh. He laughed too, and suddenly his hand shot upwards and the bills rained down on us like confetti.

"Oh, Paul, Paul . . ." I could laugh no longer. I was already diving deep into the rising waters of our eroticism, and the next moment when he was beside me on that soft sinuous carpet I felt his mouth closing powerfully on mine.

Chapter Three

I

"My mirror image," he said. "My other self."

"Just like one of those unpleasant doppelgänger legends. Schiller, wasn't it?"

"Heine." He smiled, kissed me and eased his body from mine. I was in a satiated stupor and had lost all count of time. Probably I was very drunk.

"God, I've missed you!" he said as I pulled him back on top of me with my last remaining strength. Hundred-dollar bills were clinging to his damp back and entwined in my tangled hair.

"What was it about me you missed most?"

"I missed the way you made me laugh."

"Oh, Paul!" I bawled, suddenly overwhelmed by postcoital *tristesse*, and burst into tears.

"You poor little girl, I should never have written—I should have cut myself off from you entirely and let you marry that nice boy Geoffrey Hurst."

"Don't talk bilge, Paul. You're all I want."

"No, we've missed each other in time, Dinah. You're too young to cut the umbilical cord which ties you to Mallingham and I'm too old to begin again in another world."

"Rubbish! Here we are, together again just as we were in 1922, except that on this occasion I'm the one who's traveled sideways in time! Anyway, how can you say we've missed each other in time when we have Alan? You're being quite illogical, Paul, you really are."

He offered no further argument and gave me his brilliant smile as he started to kiss me. For a while I hoped he would make love to me again, but at last he rolled away, reached for his shirt and offered me some more brandy.

"If I have a drop more to drink you'll have to carry me out of here!" I wondered vaguely if his recent nervous exhaustion had made him so pessimistic, but instinct told me that the subject of his illness was best avoided. If he really had been suffering from impotence the last thing he needed was to be reminded of it. "Paul," I said, turning to a subject which I hoped would be happier, "talking of Alan . . ."

He was buttoning his shirt. "Yes?" he said politely as I paused. He did not look up.

"For God's sake, Paul!" I burst out. "Why can't you talk about him? We've spent a whole evening together and you've hardly mentioned his name!"

This time he did look up, and when I saw the guilt in his eyes I was so startled that I gasped. "What is it?" I said frightened. "What's the matter?"

He groped for words. That too was as uncharacteristic as his pessimism earlier. "I'm sorry," he said at last. "I didn't mean to hurt you. Alan's a fine little boy and I'm very pleased. I . . . have often thought of him during the past three years . . . and wanted to see him. I'm afraid I've never been greatly at ease with small children, but just because I'm not demonstrative you mustn't think I don't care."

I relaxed. "Of course! I should have realized you're not used to children. I understand."

"I'm better with adolescents. I have four young protégés at the moment. . . ." And as we dressed he talked of the boys he had gathered to his house in Bar Harbor the previous summer and how he planned to reunite them there in July.

"Cornelius is the little one with asthma, isn't he?" I said, remembering Paul talking at Mallingham of his great-nephew. "The one you were always saying you'd have to do something about. Is he still a delicate child?"

Paul laughed. It was a great relief to see him recover his urbanity. "My dear, Cornelius is an eighteen-year-old young man with the face of an angel and a vampire's trick of going straight for the jugular vein. You and Cornelius!" he added, laughing again as he linked me with this unappetizing character in a way which I could only find offensive. "Such ambition!"

"Thank you," I said coldly, "but I'm not interested in jugular veins."

"No, just in the concepts represented by this bank. My dear, it's useless to deny it—I looked at your face when you first saw the great hall and I knew exactly what you were thinking! I stood in your shoes once and thought the same thoughts. Why are you so upset? Surely you're much too intelligent to be jealous of Cornelius!"

"Much too intelligent," I said tartly. "But I can't help thinking you ought to have more sons, Paul—and daughters too—instead of all these peculiar protégés. We ought to found a dynasty! I often dream of being a little old lady surrounded by hordes of descendants at Mallingham, although who would have thought that I, of all people, would have such Victorian ideas on procreation!"

"Anyone who knew how starved you'd always been of a normal family life. Did you have your Dutch cap checked after Alan was born?"

There was a silence. I felt as if someone had thrown a bucket of cold water in my face. In the end I did not answer but smoothed the beads on my dress with shaking fingers.

"Forgive me," he said at last. "I know you were joking, but I suspect you were also half serious and I think this is a subject on which we should be quite certain we understand one another. I don't want any more children and I don't want a repeat of the 'accident' which conceived Alan."

"Then why don't *you* assume the responsibility for birth control?" I blazed. "God, men are so bloody selfish sometimes!"

"I—"

"Oh, all right, all right, all right! Good heavens, Paul, what sort of a fool do you take me for? I know damned well Alan's conception nearly ended our affair. Do you think that after three years of waiting and three thousand miles of travel I'm going to ruin everything by making the same mistake a second time? Yes, I did have the bloody thing refitted and yes, I jolly well am wearing it this very minute, and now please talk of something else before I slap you in the face. What goes on in my body is my affair and I don't see why I should discuss it either with you or with anyone else."

He ran his hand through his hair in a distracted gesture and looked so miserable that I took pity on him.

"Paul, I'm sorry!"

"No, it's all my fault. Any talk about having children upsets me. I can't help it. Maybe someday I'll be able to explain to you—"

"Well, I think I understand. You did tell me once you'd promised Sylvia that any other children you had would be hers."

A great stillness descended upon his face. His eyes were so dark that they seemed black. Then: "We won't talk of Sylvia," he said, and turned away abruptly towards the door.

I felt as if the floor had moved beneath my feet. I even looked stupidly at the carpet, but of course it was I who had moved, not the floor. I had leaned backwards against the edge of the desk, and as the silence lengthened I irrationally began to count the scattered bills.

"I'd better take you home," he said. "It's late."

I found my tongue. "Hadn't we better pick up all this money?"

"My dear, I've no intention of groveling around on the floor collecting bills! I'll send Mayers down early tomorrow to clean up after us. Stop being so bourgeois!"

I laughed, linked my arm through his and walked with him

through the great hall to the foyer. I was still thinking of Sylvia and feeling sick. I wished I had drunk less.

In the car he said he would find another place where we could meet, and when I asked if Mary, Alan and I could move into an apartment available on a short lease he suggested we might try an apartment hotel which could provide the amenities of hotel service with the informality of a private flat.

"That sounds much more suitable," I agreed with relief. "Then Alan can have lemonade whenever he pleases and Mary can cook his boiled egg just the way he likes it and I won't have to worry about his toys being strewn all over the sitting room. I do love the Plaza, but . . ."

"I'll keep your present suite so that we can meet there."

The journey uptown seemed endless. I tried to imagine what Sylvia was like. Perhaps she was not middle-aged and well-corseted but young for her years, her face cunningly lifted, her body rigorously exercised, her clothes the most fashionable that money could buy. I had pictured her in perfect country tweeds with a cashmere jersey and a faultless string of pearls before I realized that the woman I was visualizing was English.

But Sylvia Van Zale wasn't English and I was a stranger in her world.

Unable to picture her, I could only tell myself that Paul had a wife whom he respected too much to discuss with his mistress, and this unwelcome knowledge disturbed me as greatly as if I had missed a trick in a vital card game. At Mallingham it had never occurred to me that his reticence about his wife could have sprung from reasons other than indifference, but now I knew I had been mistaken. Indifference and the most meticulous respect hardly go hand in hand.

I was still searching my memories of 1922 for clues when we arrived at the Plaza.

"Will you come up?" I said in a low voice after the length of his farewell kiss had pushed all thought of Sylvia from my mind.

"Tomorrow, not tonight. I'll call you," he said, but when he pressed my hand impulsively against his body I knew he was tempted. He laughed, releasing me. "It was a marvelous evening!" he exclaimed, his eyes sparkling, and suddenly it was as if we were at Mallingham again and he belonged only to me. "You're a wonderful girl, Dinah!" he said, as he had said so often in the past, and while the uniformed commissionaire observed us blandly from the entrance we kissed for another five minutes before Paul let me go.

I watched his car disappear and at once I became aware of the cold night air, the lateness of the hour and my own isolation. With a shiver I ran into the hotel, but long after I had gone to bed I lay awake thinking of him driving home up Fifth Avenue to the wife he refused to discuss.

II

Later I made a renewed effort to be sensible. There was no reason why Paul should not be fond of Sylvia. They had been married for many years and she no doubt worked hard at the challenging job of being Mrs. Paul Van Zale, a pillar of New York society. He could not love her or he would hardly have sent for me, and there was no reason why I should regard her as a threat just because he was gentleman enough to accord her some well-deserved respect. I was obviously being irrational and ought to be ashamed of myself.

I slept.

At half-past five Alan began to bounce on my bed, but I was too deep in sleep to do more than groan. Finally he snuggled under the covers and fidgeted for ten minutes, but when that too bored him he pattered away to torment Mary. I told myself I should increase Mary's wages, and sank thankfully into an oblivion which lasted until ten o'clock when the telephone rang.

Frowning to beat back the pain which hammered through my head, I reached feebly towards the bedside table. My mouth felt as dry as scorched leather.

"Hullo?" I croaked.

"Miss Slade?" It was not Paul. The shock made me forget my headache and sit bolt upright in bed.

"Yes," I said, knowing I had heard that quiet voice before yet unable to identify it. "Who's this?"

"Welcome to New York, Miss Slade," said the stranger, and as his polished manners struck a chord in my memory I knew who he was. "This is Terence O'Reilly."

I was astonished. During my summer with Paul I had become so accustomed to his two ubiquitous aides-de-camp that I could still remember every feature of their faces, but although I had often chatted to the friendly bodyguard Peterson, I had barely spoken a dozen words to O'Reilly. At first I had thought their positions were of equal importance, and it was only later that I had come to realize that O'Reilly's title of personal assistant was a euphemism. I had never managed to discover the full extent of his duties. Since all Americans except Paul had seemed alike to me, it had also taken me some time to realize that O'Reilly was in a different social class from Peterson, better educated, better spoken and better dressed. In spite of his Irish name he was the exact opposite of the "stage Irishman" which the English find so comical and the Irish so insulting. He was one of those wintry people, cold, silent and rigorously conscientious, the sort of man who in a previous age would have enjoyed toiling in isolation in some chilly northern monastery.

"Mr. O'Reilly!" I was so astonished that I hardly knew what to say. "What a surprise!" I said lamely at last.

"I've no doubt it is. Miss Slade, Mr. Van Zale will be in Boston for two days next week and I was wondering if you'd care to have dinner with me while he's away. I have some information which will be of interest to you."

I wished my head were clearer. "What kind of information?" I said warily.

"For reasons of my own I'm on your side, Miss Slade, and I thought that as you know no one else in America you might welcome a little support and sympathy. I assure you there's nothing sinister about my offer of dinner, although for reasons which I'll explain when we meet I'd rather you said nothing about it to Mr. Van Zale. Can I call for you at seven o'clock next Thursday?"

My curiosity overcame my doubts. "All right," I said. "That would be very nice. Thank you."

It was only half an hour later after my second cup of coffee that I started to wonder what on earth was going on.

III

He was about Paul's height but without Paul's grace of movement. He had some dark hair, thinning at the crown but thick in front, and a pair of eyes which were a peculiarly glacial shade of green. It was difficult to guess his age, but I assumed he was in his midthirties. Like many Americans he had wonderful teeth, very white and even, and when he smiled the taut muscles of his face relaxed enough to make him look attractive. I was just wondering why I had never previously thought him attractive when I realized I had never before seen him smile.

Even off duty he was flawlessly efficient. As soon as we stepped out of the Plaza a taxi was waiting and his voice was saying firmly to the driver, "The Village, please, Thompson and Bleecker." He held open the door for me, and the next moment the taxi was bouncing down Fifth Avenue past the shop windows which by that time were as familiar to me as old friends.

It was to be my last night at the Plaza. Alan, Mary and I were due to move into a two-bedroom suite in an apartment hotel a block away, and we were all looking forward to the independence afforded by the tiny kitchen. A disadvantage was that the apartment was on the tenth floor, but since it was the only disadvantage I resolved I would have to overcome my fear of lifts. I did wish the Americans had curbed their mania for tall buildings when they had been running wild in Manhattan.

"How are you getting on in New York, Miss Slade?"

"Very well, thank you. Mr. Mayers has found us this nice flat. . . ."

It was almost a week since I had arrived in New York. I missed the English newspapers and the English voices on the wireless and the ritual of afternoon tea. I missed the twisting London streets and the placid parks and the Georgian elegance of Mayfair. Most of all I missed the skies of Norfolk, the long vistas over water and reeds to the whirling windmills, flint walls and ragged lawns of my home.

"And how do you like New York, Miss Slade?"

"Oh, I love it! I love the Metropolitan Museum and the Woolworth Building and the ready-to-wear department at Bergdorf Goodman and all those gorgeous ice-cream sundaes at Schrafft's and Alice Foote MacDougall's coffeehouse and the Cascades on the roof of the Biltmore and the endless avenues and the elevated railways and the Broadway lights. It's all so new and exciting! I'm trying to persuade Paul to take me to a cab-joint, but he won't."

"I should think not! There are different kinds of speakeasies, you know, and besides, someone in Mr. Van Zale's position doesn't have to go to a speakeasy to get liquor. He can buy the privilege of having it wherever he wants. . . . Have you been down to Greenwich Village yet? You haven't? Well, I thought we'd dine at Mori's and go on afterward to Barney's, which is the biggest and smartest nightclub in town—they're both in the Village and off Mr. Van Zale's usual track. He likes the midtown restaurants and is old enough to believe the Village has become unpleasantly decadent."

I had seen Paul every day, although sometimes he had been too rushed to pause for more than a few minutes. But he had taken me to the theater to see *Pomeroy's Past*—a very relevant comedy about a girl who had a child out of wedlock—and the following week he had promised to take me to a much praised revival of *Iolanthe* at the Plymouth. The Metropolitan Opera had closed for the summer, but he could hardly have taken me there without causing widespread comment and anyway I did not share his passion for opera. I was more interested in learning to dance the newest tango, but Paul abhorred all modern dancing and continued to react to the word "Charleston" as if it were merely a town in South Carolina. However I soon forgot these nineteenth-century foibles of his whenever we shared intimate dinners at our Plaza suite, and afterwards in bed I was soon able to recognize the man I had loved at Mallingham.

Nothing else mattered except that.

"And how do you find Mr. Van Zale?" asked Terence O'Reilly pleasantly as we reached Washington Square.

"Fascinating as ever—the brute!" I said, making him laugh, and I suddenly realized I had never heard O'Reilly laugh before either. It did occur to me to wonder why he was making such a typically efficient effort to be a charming escort, but I was enjoying myself by that time and could no longer bother to be suspicious.

We reached Mori's, which stood at the foot of an old-fashioned little street, and walked in past the columned façade to a dignified interior. The plain walls, lightened by an occasional grilled opening, formed an atmosphere which the menu confirmed was Italian.

O'Reilly ordered soda water, and when it arrived with a bucket of ice he produced a hip flask. "Scotch?" he offered as I watched round-eyed.

I repressed the memory of my father intoning that no decent woman would be seen dead drinking whisky. When in Rome it would be shortsighted not to do as the Romans did, particularly since there appeared to be nothing else to drink.

"Jolly nice," I said. "Thanks."

"I'm afraid it doesn't come from Scotland, but it's quite drinkable. I was going to mix some martinis, but I wasn't sure that you'd like them. They're strong stuff."

At first I thought the whisky was revolting, but by the time I had finished it I discovered to my surprise that I was anxious for another. We looked at the menus, ordered a first course of pasta followed by lobster in a spicy Italian sauce, and chatted sociably about current affairs. We had just decided that there would be a general strike in England but probably not a revolution when our first course arrived and I realized I was feeling exceptionally mellow and content.

"All right, Mr. O'Reilly," I said, sinking my fork into the fettucine, "open your Pandora's box. Why are you so anxious to encourage my affair with Paul?"

"Because I think you're the only woman who can persuade him to leave his wife."

"But what's that got to do with you?"

"I want his wife."

Fettucine slithered off my fork and sprawled across my plate. "Good God!" I said. "Does he know?"

"Sure he knows. That's why I was promoted out of his house."

"But why on earth should he continue to employ you?"

"I'm indispensable," said O'Reilly placidly.

"But, Mr. O'Reilly—"

"You'd better call me Terence since we've turned out to be fellow conspirators."

"—Terence, what does she feel about you?"

"She'd like me well enough if he wasn't around."

"You mean she's infatuated with him?"

"He's got her just where he wants her."

"Where's that?" I said nervously, but he laughed.

"No, he doesn't want her there. Not anymore."

"What makes you so sure?"

"Because my successor in the Van Zale household, Bart Mayers, tells me everything I need to know."

I felt as if some huge weight had been lifted from my mind, and in the enormity of my relief I gobbled down the rest of my whisky-and-soda. Terence promptly poured me another.

"Relax, Dinah," he said easily. "You've got a winning hand. He's ripe for an early retirement to Europe, and if you remind him of Mallingham skillfully enough he'll quit on New York before the summer's through. Has he mentioned to you that he's been ill?"

"Yes, he said he'd been suffering from exhaustion."

"Exactly. That was all it was. Now you may hear all kinds of rumors about his illness, but pay no attention to them. The real truth of the matter is that he can't do as much as he used to do, and that's why I think he'll be tempted to take an early retirement."

"Of course. Yes, I see. Heavens, that's marvelous news—better than I'd hoped!"

"I thought you'd be pleased. Now whatever you do don't mention his illness to him, will you? He hates being reminded he had a nervous breakdown. He's sensitive about it."

"Oh, I do understand! Poor Paul. . . . What's Sylvia like?"

"You don't really want to hear me tell you she's the most wonderful woman in the world, do you?" he said with irony. "If I could discuss Sylvia with detachment I wouldn't be here now, suggesting we keep in touch and offering to be friends."

Since I knew almost nothing about this new friend of mine I felt obliged to ask him some questions about himself, and within minutes I was hearing about his downtrodden mother, his tyrannical obnoxious father and half a dozen other equally detestable relatives. I learned about the Boston Irish and summers spent on a farm with Swedish cousins in Minnesota and everyone being "trapped in their ethnic heritage" and nobody understanding "real life." I heard how he had run away from home at sixteen and found "real life" so awful that it was a relief afterwards to enter a seminary and study for the priesthood.

"That wasn't what real life was all about either," he added, "but after that I met Mr. Van Zale and then I knew what kind of life was real to me."

"But wasn't it very unreal being Paul's flunky?"

"I might have started out as a flunky, but I sure as hell haven't ended up as one. When I eventually marry Sylvia and quit Van Zale's I think I'll apply for the job of chief of police in some dictatorship. God knows I've got all the necessary experience."

"And seriously?"

"Seriously I'd like to try ranching. Owning several thousand acres in Texas can't be so very different from being boss of some small state in Europe."

"I think you're mad as a hatter," I said frankly, "but I suppose in your own way you're no more ambitious than I am." And I began to tell him about my business.

By the time we emerged from the restaurant he had forgotten his promise to take me to the most glamorous nightclub in New York and was suggesting we have a drink at his apartment down the road.

"Sweet of you," I said, remembering the London Lotharios and giving him a long hard look. "Don't think I don't sympathize with your situation—you'd be even madder than a hatter if you'd spent all these years yearning for Sylvia in celibate frustration—but it's as much as I can do to cope with Paul and I don't see how I could possibly take on you as well. What was the name of that nightclub you mentioned earlier?"

"Barney's." He sighed, looked around for a taxi and then linked his arm through mine. "Let's walk. It's not far."

We wove our way north to West Third Street while he told me about Barney's—"just like a transplanted bit of uptown, not bizarre at all, just bright and smart and imaginative"—and I asked questions about the entertainment we could expect to find there. Terence said Barney's offered everything the heart desired. It sounded like a cross between the Savoy Grill and the west pier at Brighton.

However I never saw the inside of Barney's, for as we reached the entrance half a dozen people in full evening dress and various stages of drunkenness reeled out, almost sweeping us into the gutter. Fortunately Terence scooped me out of the way before I could be mown down, but I was still fuming at such an animal display of behavior when one of the men bellowed, "Jesus, it's Terence O'Reilly! Whoa there, Terence! Who's the gorgeous gal?"

"Christ!" muttered Terence.

A very tall man had detached himself from the revelers and was bounding over to us. He had a large amount of curly brown hair, the build of a heavyweight boxer and a small white scar on one cheekbone. I wondered enthralled if he was a bootlegger.

"So you do have a private life after all, Terence!" exclaimed the stranger, looking me up and down as if I were meat on a butcher's slab. "I always thought you did! Does the little lady have a name?"

I detest men who leer at me as if I had no clothes on. "Not as far as you're concerned," I retorted coldly. "Terence, shall we go?"

"Oh my, she's English! Honey, I just love that cute little English accent! Say that all over again, Lady Buckingham-Palace!"

"Terence," I said, thoroughly enraged by this time, "who *is* this awful man?"

Terence, whose expression could only be described as confused, decided to make the best of a very bad job. "Dinah Slade—Steven Sullivan," he said at top speed. "Steven Sullivan—Dinah Slade. Let's go, Dinah. So long, Steve."

"Jesus Christ!" said Steven Sullivan. "Are you that English girl friend of Paul's?"

"Good God!" I said. "You surely can't be Paul's favorite partner!"

We gazed at each other in horror and then both saw the funny side of the situation at exactly the same moment. He roared with laughter and so did I.

"We'd really better go, Dinah," said Terence, making a second effort to draw me away.

"Not so fast!" drawled Steven Sullivan. The lascivious expression had faded from his very blue eyes, but he still looked greatly amused. "What are you doing out on the town with Paul's girl?"

"I met Dinah by chance on Fifth Avenue today," said Terence so smoothly that I did not at first realize he was lying, "and when I remembered that Mr. Van Zale was out of town I asked her to have a drink with me tonight. She's only recently arrived in New York and I'm one of the few people she knows."

"All alone in New York?" said Steven Sullivan. "Well, we can't have that! Terence, you're coming out to our house next Saturday, aren't you? Give Miss Slade a ride in your car!" He turned, sloughing off his aura of drunkenness as easily as I might have shrugged off my new knitted coat from Best's, and gave me a wide winning smile. "We're having a little party for about three hundred people out on Long Island," he said easily. "Come and join in the fun and make some new friends! Hell, I'll even introduce you to my wife! Oh, and bring your little boy. My son Tony's about the same age and we can put up an extra bed in the nursery."

"That's very kind of you." I felt bemused by such extravagant hospitality, but the prospect of meeting more people was appealing. "Thank you. Will Paul be there? Oh, no, I forgot. He won't be in town this weekend."

"Yeah, he and Sylvia are going off somewhere together. All right, I'm coming!" he called to his friends, and added cheerfully to me over his shoulder, "See you Saturday!"

He was gone. I was left feeling numb and cold. A second later I realized that the quantity of whisky I had consumed at dinner was threatening to make me embarrassingly ill.

"Terence, I'm sorry but I've just got to go home." How I managed to avoid vomiting I have no idea, but he helped me by finding a taxi without arguing.

As we reached the Plaza he said, "Remember that I told Steve our meeting was accidental. It's better that way, I think. You'd better tell the same story to Mr. Van Zale."

"Yes," I said. "Before he goes off with his wife for the weekend."

"Hell, Dinah, Steve just put that clumsily because he'd had too much to drink. The Van Zales are only going to visit some old friends in Connecticut. It's no second honeymoon."

"It's not exactly a business trip to Philadelphia either!"

"Who said it was?"

"Paul!" I blurted out, wanting to burst into tears, and retreated to the Plaza for another sleepless night.

Chapter Four

I

"Are you still going down to Philadelphia this weekend?" I said to Paul when he telephoned me the next morning. I had just finished telling him about my supposedly accidental meeting with Terence and my genuinely accidental encounter with Steven Sullivan.

"No, the Philadelphia visit has been postponed," he said easily, "but I have to go to see some friends in Connecticut instead. It's a nuisance and I'm hoping it'll be canceled. What did you think of Steve?"

"I mistook him for a white slaver, but when he found out who I was he invited me out to Long Island to meet his wife. I even thought I'd go. It would be fun to meet more people." I was feeling better after his casual dismissal of the coming weekend, and had already decided I had once again been worrying over nothing.

"Well, I'd like you to meet more people, of course," he said, "but to be honest I'd prefer it if you didn't make a habit of seeing O'Reilly. I had some trouble with him awhile back and our relationship's become strained. What on earth did you find to talk to him about?"

"Religion. Oh, I do so enjoy lapsed Catholics! But don't worry, darling, he's not really my sort of person. However—" But before I could tell Paul that Terence was giving me a lift to the Sullivan house the next day he was interrupted by a call coming through for him on another line and we had to conclude our conversation in a hurry.

When he telephoned me again some hours later he was again in a hurry, but he arranged to have dinner with me after the weekend. I said I hoped he would enjoy his visit to Connecticut. He said he supposed he would once he got there, and after an affectionate goodbye we went our separate ways.

In an effort to avoid a second successive sleepless night I tried to think not of Paul but of Steven Sullivan with his free and easy manners and his hot bold blue eyes.

Terence telephoned the next morning at ten. "Dinah, something's gone wrong with my car, but some friends of mine are giving us a ride out to Great Neck, where the Sullivans live. Can we call for you at six?"

"Yes, of course—thanks!" I said brightly, and immediately began to wish I weren't going. I told myself it was a disgraceful attack of nerves, but as the morning went on and I became more depressed I realized I was thinking not of the ordeal of meeting unknown people but of Paul going away for the weekend with someone who had been described as the most wonderful woman in the world. I at once became determined to go to the party. It would be too demeaning to sit at home wondering if he could possibly be sleeping for eight hours entirely by himself.

Sensing my uneasiness, Alan became increasingly obstreperous. "I want to come too!" he wailed when I told him I had to go out that evening, and I remembered how Steven Sullivan had extended the invitation to include him. However, I had already decided that although American children might be invited to adult parties and be permitted to run wild at all hours of the night, my child was going to be bathed, kissed and tucked up in bed by six o'clock at the latest.

"I'm sorry, Alan," I said firmly, "but it's a grown-up party."

"I want to come!" he howled, and lay on the floor as he kicked his little legs at the ceiling and enjoyed his tantrum. My head began to ache. I supposed I ought to spank him, but it was too much effort and I felt incapable of coping afterwards with his heartbroken sobs. Finally Mary appeared, said severely, "Naughty boy!" and bore him off to eat ice cream.

By the time Terence telephoned from the foyer to announce his arrival I felt exhausted before the evening had begun.

"Who are your friends?" I asked, glancing through the glass doors to the young couple sitting in a smart green Studebaker.

"Bruce and Grace Clayton."

"Bruce Clayton! Elizabeth's son?"

He smiled wryly. "They don't know who you are—I just told them you're someone I met in England and that you're in New York on vacation. Elizabeth Clayton probably knows all about you, but Bruce and Grace never read the society columns and Bruce never discusses Mr. Van Zale with his mother."

The Claytons were a good-looking couple. Grace wore cobweb-sheer silk stockings which must have cost a fortune, but her dinner frock, though knee-length and waistless, needed a fringe to make it truly fashionable and I did not think her evening wrap in metal brocade was as smart as my silver-embroidered wrap in black crepe with the chiffon and lace inserts. However, she had an enviably slim figure and her fair hair curled without the aid of a permanent wave, so no doubt she looked more striking than I did. Her husband, who emerged from the car to shake hands with me, was tall and distinguished. His dark hair was prematurely gray at the temples, and although he wore glasses I saw he had intelligent light eyes.

"Miss Slade, how are you?" They both spoke with plain expensive American accents, each vowel flat as a pancake, each consonant mercilessly articulated and all hint of an ill-bred drawl studiously avoided. Even though I was a foreigner I was aware of being in the presence of some native aristocracy. Yet they were not aloof; unlike their English counterparts they were immediately friendly and informal. Surnames were soon discarded, and by the time we were crossing into Queens Grace was asking me if I were interested in women's rights. When I said I wasn't (inwardly shuddering as I always did at the thought of my mother's death) she looked disappointed, but it never occurred to her to ask me if I had a job. After discovering that I was unmarried and had come to New York to visit a friend, she obviously decided I was hopelessly frivolous, a society girl who had come to America instead of India to search for a husband.

"And who's your friend here in New York, Dinah?" asked Bruce kindly at last.

"Paul Van Zale."

They both swiveled to look at me. The car nearly careered off the road.

"For God's sake!" exclaimed Terence as Bruce grabbed the wheel.

"Sorry—stupid of me." He was too stunned to say more.

"Land's sakes!" said Grace, boggling at me. "How did you meet Paul?"

"I'm his client. He financed my business."

When Grace recovered she bombarded me with questions, but throughout our conversation I was immensely aware of her husband's silence.

"And just wait till I tell Caroline!" exclaimed Grace. "Have you met our hostess, Caroline Sullivan? She's much older than us but really modern in her outlook." And she went on talking about modern women as she described the girls who had been to college with her at Vassar. When I revealed that I too had been to a university I could see she regarded our friendship as irrevocably cemented.

We reached the town of Great Neck and drove out along the road where the palaces of the rich faced Long Island Sound and the distant shore of Connecticut. Thinking of Paul again I told myself Sylvia was just a nice old trout who reminded Terence of his downtrodden mother.

"Ah, here we are at last!" exclaimed Grace as the car passed some wrought-iron gates and swept up a long drive.

The Sullivan mansion was set in five elaborately landscaped acres and bore a small but telling resemblance to the Taj Mahal.

"I always forget how vulgar it is," murmured Bruce, breaking his long silence. "Every time I come here I'm surprised."

"Oh, darling, you're not going to plunge yourself into Chekhovian gloom already, are you? I know how you hate this sort of party, but I absolutely promised Caroline—"

"I know, I know."

"Have a couple of martinis, Bruce," said Terence, "and you'll soon be enjoying the vulgarity."

"I detest drinking to excess!"

"You drank enough vodka last weekend with that crazy Russian Krasnov!"

"That was different. I wanted him to feel we were brothers, although I confess I don't really agree with his views on Trotsky."

"Oh, don't let's talk about politics now—I couldn't bear it!" begged Grace. "My, look how many other people are already here, and I thought we'd be among the first to arrive! Oh, there's Caroline."

We had been escorted into a ballroom which led onto a vast terrace. A band was already playing energetically, but it was too early for people to consider dancing and most of the guests had wandered outside to the marble fountains and manicured lawns. Numerous Negro servants, all in livery, were circulating with silver trays of hors d'oeuvres and silver pitchers of cocktails. The chandeliers glittered wickedly as if beckoning decadence to emerge from the shadows.

A very smart woman with sleek short black hair, a tanned face and scarlet lips jangled briskly towards us.

"Bruce—Grace—Terence—darlings, *wonderful* to see you!" she cried as the band swung into a spicy version of "Tea for Two." She kissed Grace fleetingly and then eased Terence aside to look me in the eye. "Miss Slade! I'm Caroline Sullivan. How are you? Did you bring your little boy?"

Behind me I heard Grace gasp. "I'm afraid not, Mrs. Sullivan," I said pleasantly. "It was so kind of your husband to invite him, but he tires easily and I thought it would be best if he stayed at home with his nanny."

"Well, he must come out some other time to play with Scott and Tony! I'm sure they'd just love to make a new friend and— Well, hello there! Wilma darling, *lovely* of you to come! Excuse me, Miss Slade . . . ."

"Drink, Dinah?" murmured Terence.

"Thanks." I turned to accept a sea-green cocktail.

"How old is your little boy?" asked Grace in a voice which suggested she was on the verge of expiring with curiosity.

"Three."

"You did say— I'm sorry, I must have misunderstood you. I thought you said . . ."

I had long since become accustomed to coping with other people's embarrassment. I smiled reassuringly at her. "No, I'm not married," I said. "I don't believe in marriage, but that's just my own personal philosophy which I wouldn't dream of imposing on other people, so I hope you won't find it intimidating."

"Why, no, of course not. But . . ." From the glint in her eye I could see she was about to raise the subject of emancipated women again, and it was a relief when Terence offered to introduce me to some people he knew.

"Dinah Slade!"

I spun round. It was Steven Sullivan.

"You look great!" he drawled, looking me up and down with his hot blue eyes. "Come down to Willow and Wall sometime and let me negotiate your next loan!"

"Not while you look at me as if I'm a cow in a cattle market!" I retorted. "Have you any idea how offensive it is to be treated like a lump of meat?"

"Some meat!" he said laughing. "Some cow!"

"Oh!" I would have thrown my cocktail at him, but at that moment his wife called sternly, "Steven!" and he padded away to attend to some other guests.

"Don't pay too much attention to Steve," said Terence soothingly. "He acts that way with every woman he meets. He means to be complimentary."

I looked skeptical, but Terence, refusing to take my complaint seriously, embarked on the task of introducing me to as many people as possible, and soon I had forgotten Steve Sullivan. Inevitably I became separated from Terence, and I was just thinking in panic that I could remember no one's name when a kind stranger claimed me, introduced himself and provided yet another example of American friendliness. English people may well scoff, "But Americans are so superficial!" but all I can say is that if I had to be on my own at a large party I would be only too glad to discover that the other guests exuded easygoing courtesy and New World charm.

The Americans loved my accent, demanded to know all kinds of extraordinary facts about England ("What do the royal family eat for breakfast?" "Has London changed since Dickens' day?") and asked proudly what I thought of their magnificent country. Had I read about the Teapot Dome Scandal? What did I think of President Coolidge? Would the League of Nations work? I began to feel like the Delphic Oracle and had great fun giving the ambiguous replies demanded by classical tradition. It was such a relief to go to a party and not hear someone whispering behind my back, "She's Harry Slade's daughter, you know," while someone else muttered darkly, "All that Norfolk inbreeding . . ." Here no one was the least interested in my antecedents and everyone accepted me, for better or for worse, exactly as I was.

I drank another cocktail (a pink one this time), nibbled some hors d'oeuvres and was glad I had come.

Dusk fell. The floodlighting was switched on and the Americans complained how cold it was although to me it seemed just another spring evening, perhaps a little warmer than it would have been in Norfolk. The center of the party began to shift as people drifted across the garden towards the house, and it was while I too was wandering across the lawn that I saw Terence standing by the biggest of the marble fountains below the terrace.

He did not see me. He was talking to a woman I did not know, and as I drew closer I wondered who she was, for she was beautiful. She wore a sheer floating gown in one of the new Paris shades with the fashionable gossamer-thin fringe, and her dark unshingled hair, worn up in an Edwardian style, gave her a mysterious air of timelessness. Yet the obsolete style suited her, emphasizing her delicate features and her long slender neck. Her skin was so fair that I looked at her hair a second time, and suddenly I realized it was not brown but auburn, rich and glowing in the dim evening light.

I turned to my companion of the moment. He was a young bond salesman who lived in Manhattan.

"Craig, who's that woman over there with Terence O'Reilly?"

He glanced towards the fountain and looked surprised. "Gee, I thought someone said she and her husband were out of town this weekend! That's Mrs. Paul Van Zale, the banker's wife."

I stood quite still. Someone laughed behind me, a bat swooped overhead and a servant flitted past with a tray of empty glasses. Far away in the ballroom I could hear the wail of the saxophone as the musician's careered headlong into the Charleston.

"Dinah? Something wrong?"

"No, nothing. Craig, would you mind fetching me another drink? Thanks so much."

Having got rid of him, I backed away into the shadow of a marble nymph and sank down on the edge of the plinth. I felt insignificant, defenseless, ugly.

When I eventually nerved myself to look at the fountain again Terence had gone but she was still there. Some friends of hers paused beside her and she smiled, murmuring a few words. Her smile was warm and natural, and as she stood there on the fringes of that noisy modern party in front of that rich vulgar house her lack of artificiality was as dazzling as her simple effortless elegance.

Tears sprang to my eyes. I went on staring, the lump in my throat swelling until I could hardly breathe, until at last it occurred to me to wonder why she was lingering by the fountain when everyone else was moving indoors.

I backed away quickly, but not quickly enough to escape seeing what happened next.

Paul ran up the steps of the far lawn at the side of the house. He moved gracefully, just as he always did, and when she saw him her face lit up and her lips formed the first letter of his name.

He smiled at her. I had never thought I would see him give that special smile to any woman but me. When he reached her he slid his arm around her waist and said something which made her lean against him fractionally as she looked up into his eyes.

She was radiant.

Tears spilled down my cheeks. Unable to watch any longer, I turned away and ran as fast as I could across the lawns to the distant waters of the Sound.

II

The beach was narrow, and the Sound, reflecting the afterglow of the sky, glistened with copper lights. Halting at last I leaned against one of the trees which fringed the sandy shore, but when I was unable to stop my tears I stumbled down to the beach, sank onto the sand and wept without restraint. I was just wondering dimly if I would ever be able to stop crying when a voice said shocked, "Dinah!" and a man's hand, firm and gentle, restrained me as I tried to struggle to my feet.

Bruce Clayton squatted beside me. "Is there anything I can do?"

"Take me home!" I sobbed, my pride in ruins, and clung beseechingly to his sleeve.

"Certainly. I'd be glad of the excuse to leave." We were silent while he passed me a handkerchief and I tried to mop myself up. At last he said, "You didn't know Paul and Sylvia would be here?"

"Did anyone? They were supposed to be in Connecticut!"

"Paul canceled that this morning, apparently. I was talking to Sylvia just now."

"But they were going last night!"

"No, he took Sylvia out last night. We were dining at Voisin's with friends of my mother's, and later the Van Zales came in— I'm sorry, you don't want to hear this, do you?"

"Oh yes I do!" I said fiercely, dashing away the last of my tears. "Go on. Why was the Connecticut visit canceled?"

"Sylvia said Paul felt too exuberant for a quiet weekend in the country. He thought it would be more fun to turn up at the Sullivan party and take everyone by surprise. Didn't you tell him you were coming here? No, don't bother to answer that. Have another handkerchief."

"It's silly, but I can't stop crying."

It was another five minutes before I was dry-eyed again.

"I'm so terribly sorry, Bruce."

"So am I! What's a nice girl like you doing mixed up with a bastard like Paul Van Zale?"

"Don't you like him? But he's so fond of you! He often talked about you when he was in England."

Bruce took off his glasses and stared at them. "Come on, I'll take you home."

Halfway back to the house I remembered Terence and Grace. "How will they get back?"

"There are plenty of people who can give them a ride. Terence won't mind, and Grace and I agreed long ago that I could feel free to walk out of a party like this any time I liked. She won't be surprised."

He led me to the green Studebaker parked among the crowd of other cars in the drive, and leaving me in the front seat he returned to the house to find his wife. Ten minutes later we were on our way to Manhattan.

After several miles of silence he said, "I'm going to stop for gas," and we swung off the road into the forecourt of a petrol station. As we waited he remarked to me neutrally, "I guess you hope to marry Paul."

"I don't really care about that so long as he comes back to Mallingham with me and doesn't belong to anyone else."

"Dinah, Paul doesn't practice monogamy. He's incapable of it."

"That's not true! He was faithful to me in England. Of course I knew he found someone else as soon as he got back to America, but . . ." The shock of discovery overwhelmed me again, and I squeezed my eyes shut to ward off the pain. "I never imagined—never dreamed . . . Oh, God his *wife!* To think he really loved her all the time and I never knew! But why, why, why did he send for me? I don't understand, nothing makes sense, what the hell's he doing sleeping with both of us?"

"My God," said Bruce, "you're very young."

"You don't understand!"

"I'm afraid I do. My mother was Paul's mistress on and off for over twenty years."

"But I'm different! I'm special!"

"So was my mother! She was beautiful, intelligent, well-educated, steeped in a knowledge of the classics—"

"Stop it!" I screamed at him.

"Pardon me, sir," said the freckle-faced petrol-pump attendant, "but that'll be a dollar twenty-five."

Bruce gave him a couple of bills. "I'm sorry," he said to me. "I didn't mean to upset you. I'm sure Paul does think you're special if he invited you to come all the way from Europe to share his convalescence. You know about his illness, I guess?"

"Of course." I gathered together the shreds of my dignity. "If Paul thinks I'm going to share him with someone else he's made a very big mistake," I said. "I have my pride and I have my self-respect, and I'm not sacrificing it for anyone, not even him."

"Then you *will* be different," he said smiling at me. "Then you *will* be special."

I did not answer. I was staring towards the distant lights of Manhattan while I planned exactly what I was going to say to Paul.

III

I lay awake half the night planning brilliant dialogue and finally fell into an exhausted sleep sometime after four. At seven o'clock precisely the telephone rang at my bedside.

I was deep in unconsciousness and could hardly open my eyes. "Yes?" I whispered into the mouthpiece.

"Dinah, it's Paul. I'm downstairs in the lobby. I'm coming up," he said, and hung up before I could gasp.

I felt as if someone had walloped me over the head with a sledgehammer. I got up, blundered against a chair, caught sight of my face in the mirror and began to scrabble frantically for my makeup. My hair had a stringy uncombed appearance, and my nightdress, torn at the shoulder, looked as if it had been rescued from a jumble sale. My mind felt blank, bleak and beaten.

The doorbell rang.

"Oh, God," I said. I grabbed my best negligée and reached for my powder puff. There was barely time to take the shine off my nose before the doorbell rang again.

"The bell's ringing, Mummy!" called Alan.

"Yes, darling." I could not cope at all. Flaying my hair with the brush, I tried to remember the brilliant dialogue I had invented the night before. Naturally I could not remember a word.

"Can I open the door?"

"Yes, darling."

"It's Papa, Mummy!"

I dropped the hairbrush, glanced in the glass and saw Paul in the doorway.

"I wanted to talk to you."

"Yes," I said, knees shaking.

He smiled gently at Alan. "Can you help Mary get breakfast or are you too little?"

"No, I'm big! I often help get breakfast!" boasted Alan, and pattered away proudly to the kitchen.

Paul locked the bedroom door. "Steve told me you were at the party," he said. "Caroline told me Bruce had taken you home. Mayers found a young bond salesman called Craig Harper who recalled pointing out my wife to you while she was waiting for me by the fountain."

I was pulverized. I opened my mouth to stammer, "Paul, I'm really not capable of scenes like this at seven o'clock in the morning," and then I realized that this was exactly why he had chosen to call at such an appalling hour.

I stared at him. He was immaculate, his black suit perfectly tailored, his shirt snow white, his tie dark and discreet, and as I saw him watching me with expert intentness I felt the first flicker of a slow scorching rage.

I found my voice. "Your wife's beautiful," I said. "I was delighted to have the opportunity to see her. Is that what you wanted me to say?"

"I suspected you might have been upset, and I thought perhaps I should explain—"

"Why you lied when you said you were going to Connecticut on Friday night when in fact you'd planned a dinner *à deux* at Voisin's with your wife? Oh, come, Paul! Let's be sophisticated about this! You wanted to take your wife out to dinner—well, why not? After all, she *is* your wife! And since you awoke the next morning feeling too 'exuberant' to bury yourself in Connecticut—goodness me, *what* a night that must have been!—why shouldn't you have decided to take Sylvia to your best friend's party? After all, she *is* your wife! I don't deny I was a little surprised to discover she's twenty years younger than you and no doubt the belle of every ball she attends, but then life's full of little surprises, isn't it, and I really couldn't have expected you to give me a detailed description of her. Of course, it would have been interesting to know you still slept with her and that she obviously adores you, but I can't complain, can I, Paul? That wouldn't be playing the game at all!"

He said nothing. His dark eyes were expressionless.

"You and your games!" I said with a laugh. "What fun we have with them, don't we? Oh yes, I adore your games, Paul, but there's just one snag you may have overlooked: *I don't like your bloody rules!*"

There was another silence. At last he said in a low voice, "The situation isn't as you think it is."

"Don't try and tell me you're not sleeping with her, Paul, because I simply shan't believe you."

His face hardened. "I never promised you fidelity."

"Oh yes you damned well did!" I shouted at him. "You implied it when you asked me to come here! You knew me—you knew I wouldn't come to New York just to be your tart who could amuse you whenever you became bored with your perfect wife! You know I'm not that kind of woman, Paul, so how dare you now treat me as if I had no pride, no self-respect and no damned shred of common sense!"

"I'd better come back later," he said shortly, turning to unlock the door. "It's obvious that you're now incapable of listening to explanations."

I was at once terrified of him leaving. "Paul . . ." I gasped before I could stop myself, and as if on cue he spun to face me.

"Listen, Dinah," he said in a quick urgent voice, "you must—please—make some effort to understand. When I was ill Sylvia stood by me, and I just *cannot* ignore her or abandon her now as you might wish—it's impossible. Try and be patient. You know how important you are to me."

"As important as a bottle of medicine which gets thrown away as soon as the patient recovers!"

He went sheet-white.

I was too angry to care. "My dear Paul," I said acidly, "you may think I'm hopelessly naïve, but before we met I spent some time living with a man your age and I'm not so ignorant about the problems of middle-aged men as you might think. My father was always recalling his favorite girl friend whenever he ran into temporary difficulties with his wife."

I had partially redeemed my mistake by not mentioning the disastrous word "impotence," but I fully expected some explosion of wrath. It never came. In fact when I nerved myself to look at him again I saw to my astonishment that he was neither furious nor humiliated but curiously relieved. Finally he even laughed.

"My dear," he said amused with all his old urbanity, "I think you're on dangerous ground if you start to compare me with your father! Take it as a compliment that when I really needed a woman the first person I turned to was you."

"But—"

"I'm glad you realize how important you are to me. Now I know this is a difficult situation, but I know too that you're intelligent enough to see beyond the present awkwardness to the long-term pattern of the future." He had moved slowly towards me until we were only inches apart, and as he started speaking again he took me in his arms. "I'm extremely sorry you were upset last night. As you know, I wouldn't have upset you for the world." He paused to kiss me. His hands slipped between the facings of my negligée. "All I ask is for you to be patient."

I found my tongue. "You're asking me to share you with Sylvia," I said, "but I can't do that. I'm sorry, but I can't."

"If you care for me—"

"I love you more than anyone else in the world, but there's no future in a three-sided love affair."

He could have had an easy victory then. All he had to do was say "I love you" and my resolve would have crumbled like rotten wood, but instead he said abruptly as he turned away from me, "Your trouble is that you really love no one but yourself."

"That makes two of us!" I shouted in rage and terror as he strode to the door.

As the door was wrenched open Alan, who had been pressing against the panels, fell headlong into the room and began to cry.

"Alan, I'm sorry!"

"Poor darling!"

We helped him to his feet, kissed him better and made an unnecessary fuss of him. Alan loved it. He clung to Paul's hand and sobbed emotionally against my bosom until finally, wrinkling his nose at the smell of bacon, he ran off to see if breakfast was ready.

"You'll forgive me if I leave you now," said Paul politely, "but I see no point in continuing our discussion."

I stared at the ground. My whole will was bent on the task of remaining silent, and I hardly knew how to stop myself begging him to stay.

He left. The door closed. His footsteps receded into the distance and I heard the whine of the lift as it responded to his summons.

I dashed out into the hall.

"Paul!"

But the doors of the lift had already closed and he was gone without a backward glance.

IV

At eleven o'clock, unable to endure my misery a moment longer, I telephoned Terence O'Reilly. Alan and Mary had gone out for their Sunday-morning walk so I was alone in the apartment. I was still in my negligée. After the iciness of Paul's withdrawal I had been too numb with shock to either eat, dress or cry.

"Something wrong?" said Terence sharply when he heard my voice.

"Everything. You were mistaken. He's sleeping with her again."

There was a silence. Finally he said, "I don't believe it."

"He admitted it to me. He won't leave her."

"He actually said that?"

"Well . . ."

"Wait a moment. We can't talk about this over the phone. Let me come over."

"Oh Terence, I'm not even dressed!"

"All right. You come down to me whenever you're ready. You've got my address, haven't you? I'll have a drink waiting for you and we can talk this over."

I almost wept at the thought of seeing someone sympathetic. Thanking him, I rang off and went to have a bath.

I did feel better once I was dressed. Alan and Mary were still out, so I left a note for them before taking a taxi to Terence's flat.

The townhouse in which he lived stood on a pretty tree-lined street west of Washington Square, and his spartan flat occupied the whole of the top floor. The modern furniture was cool and expensive, like a model room in an exhibition, and the living room was not only spotlessly clean but immaculately tidy. His pictures were ruthless modern abstracts and there were no photographs, no bric-a-brac, no clues to the past.

"Let me introduce you to the genuine American martini cocktail," he said, offering me a glass of pale liquid. "I think you'll find it soothing."

I also found it made me garrulous, and after only one sip I was pouring out every detail of the disaster. He listened without interrupting and when I had finished he offered me a cigarette without comment.

"Terence, for God's sake say something!"

"Finish your drink and I'll fix you another. He did imply, didn't he, that the future was going to be different?"

"That was just to soften me up." I felt miraculously placid, able to voice painful truths without feeling any pain. "I say, this is a jolly nice drink, isn't it!"

He refilled my glass.

"I think I understand the situation now," I murmured, still marveling at my composure. "He loves me best, I'm sure of that, but he's shackled to her because she's one of those women who build their entire existence around their husbands with the result that they have no lives of their own. If he left her she'd just wither away, like a Victorian heroine, and he'd blame me when he inevitably ended up feeling guilty and miserable."

"Trash. She'd survive. And once he'd left her she'd go to bed with me and like it."

"Well, I concede you may know Sylvia better than I do, but I know Paul. He's not going to leave her. He's a Victorian and not only true to his double standard but morally bound by it. He's devised this incredibly old-fashioned game in which he's allowed to have any number of mistresses so long as he never breaks the cast-iron rule which demands he stays married to his wife, and if you think he would ever break that rule you don't understand what being a Victorian's all about. Paul may be immoral by conventional standards, but he's not amoral. He has a rigid moral code and he's never going to embrace the twentieth century by deviating from it. You won't find Paul trying to maneuver a quick divorce! You won't find Paul walking out on a perfect wife! And you certainly won't find Paul risking a trip to England and falling in love with Mallingham again!"

I stopped. We stared at each other. His green eyes were dark with some emotion which I could not identify but found deeply disturbing.

The doorbell rang.

"Oh!" I was so startled that the liquid jumped in my glass. "Who's that? Are you expecting someone?"

"Not a soul. Relax and stay right where you are." He moved out into the hall to open the front door.

"'Lo, Terence!" said Bruce Clayton's voice. "Excuse me for stopping by unannounced, but I've got someone here who wants to see you again. We've just had brunch at the Brevoort and we thought we'd stroll across Washington Square to see if you were home."

"Well, I'm sure you're both welcome— Christ! What are *you* doing back in town?"

"Just paying my annual call on Mr. Paul Cornelius Van Zale." A tall dark man wandered casually past Terence into the living room. He had a hard jaw, heavy-lidded eyes and a flat, battered, vaguely sinister face. When he saw me he stopped, raised a thick eyebrow and allowed the lids to droop lazily over his yellowish brown eyes. "Why, hello there!" he drawled sociably. "We haven't met, have we? My name's Greg Da Costa."

"Dinah!" exclaimed Bruce before I could register any emotion whatsoever. "What are you doing here?"

"Weeping on Terence's shoulder," I said. "I've just had the most awful row with Paul." It occurred to me that I was dangerously lightheaded. With growing suspicion I looked down at my martini.

"Paul who?" said Greg Da Costa.

"As far as we're all concerned there's only one Paul," said Bruce. "This is Dinah Slade, Greg. She's in New York as Paul's guest."

"You mean this is the latest victim? Welcome to the club, sweetheart!"

"I'm nobody's victim," I said abruptly. "Terence, I think I'd better go now."

Terence looked as though he agreed with me, but before he could speak Da Costa said with a surfeit of well-oiled charm, "Hell, don't run away—what's the rush? I can tell you all kinds of things about your pal Paul!"

Terence stepped instantly between us. "Dinah's too modern to enjoy past history, Greg. How's Stew? Don't tell me you came to New York without your brother!"

Da Costa's face seemed more battered than ever. "Stew's dead."

"*Dead?* My God! How the hell did it happen?"

"He took a slug at one of those private detectives Van Zale has keeping watch over us, and the goddamned dick drew a gun and cracked him over the head with it. They got him to a hospital, but his skull was smashed and he never came out of the coma. That's why I'm here. I figured Van Zale owed me compensation and I hit town yesterday evening so that I can see him in person tomorrow."

"It was planned, obviously," said Bruce tensely to Terence. "The man provoked Stewart into attacking him—probably on Paul's orders."

"That's nonsense!" I cried horrified. "Bruce, how could you even think such a thing!"

"Have a martini, Bruce," said Terence, "and wise up. You're showing about as much delicacy as an elephant on eggshells. Dinah, if you want to go I'll come downstairs and find you a cab."

"I'm with Bruce on this," said Da Costa. "Someone should tell this little girl the facts of life. Say, talking of Van Zale, Bruce tells me he's been sick as hell lately and you guys in the entourage are having a tough time keeping the facts under wraps—"

"Dinah," said Terence, "I'm sure you have no interest in hearing the latest gaudy rumors about how your friend's suffering from everything from acne to cancer of the brain. Let's go."

"He's stringing you along, sweetheart!" called Da Costa after me as we escaped downstairs. "What's the big game, Terence?"

We emerged into the street.

"What on earth—" I began incredulously but he cut me off.

"I'm sorry about that, Dinah." He sounded genuinely distracted. "I don't know how much Mr. Van Zale's told you about the Salzedo affair, but—"

"Oh, that! Yes, I know Jason Da Costa blew his brains out and his sons went around afterwards making mad accusations against Paul. Obviously nothing's changed! But Terence, I wasn't going to ask about Greg Da Costa. I was going to ask what on earth someone so nice as Bruce is doing in his company."

"Yes, Bruce is a nice guy." He sighed and added with reluctance: "I'm afraid the truth is that he's irrational on the subject of Mr. Van Zale. He always has been, ever since I first met him at Harvard, but lately for some reason the irrationality's become more marked. I tend to humor him on the subject because I've realized he can't help himself. He's all mixed up about his mother."

"Oh, God!" I felt too exhausted to grapple with Freudian theory, but fortunately at that moment a taxi came around the corner.

"Will you be all right?" said Terence, flagging down the car. "Sorry our conference got wrecked like that. I'll call you later and we can fix another."

"I think we'd already said all there was to say."

"You can't mean you're going to give up and go home!"

"It's either that or ditch my self-respect. Oh, what does it matter to you anyway! Whether I go or stay he'll never leave her."

I was in such a morose mood by that time that I forgot to thank him for the martinis, and after I had been borne bumpily uptown by a surly driver my mood had hardly improved. Trailing into the apartment hotel, I was in such a haze of gloom that I did not at first hear the desk clerk calling my name.

"Letter for you, Miss Slade!" he called a second time.

I was thinking of Paul and wondering if I could live like a nun until he was able to swear he no longer slept with Sylvia. But no, that would never work because he would never weaken; I had no choice but to slink home without him, although perhaps I could salvage some pride by staying to the end of my allotted time in New York in order to produce the cosmetics survey I had promised my friends. But no, that would save my face but probably not my sanity, and I simply had to leave while I still had the mental strength to turn my back on him.

Feeling utterly devoid of all strength, I opened the envelope and dragged out the message inside.

"My dearest Lesbia," Paul had written, recalling all our past classical correspondence. "I've taken Alan and Miss Oakes to our Plaza suite for lunch to make amends for interrupting their breakfast this morning. Will you please join us? Repentantly, Catullus."

"Oh, God," I said as my knees threatened to buckle. I wished I had refused the second martini. "Oh, Lord."

"Oh, and these are for you, too, Miss Slade," smirked the desk clerk, and from beneath the counter he produced a sheaf of red roses.

"Oh, no!" To my despair I saw there was a card. Knowing my only hope was to tear it up unread, I ripped it open without hesitation.

"*Da mi basia mille . . .*"

I was quite unable to cope with all the numerous kisses the poet had demanded from his Lesbia, and stumbling into my flat, I shoved the roses into water and collapsed on the sofa. I did try tearing up the card, but it made no difference. By that time my longing had become unbearable, and after saying "Oh *hell!*" very loudly three times, I changed into a crepe-de-chine frock, set my Milan hat at its jauntiest angle and with a sinking heart set off to the Plaza.

V

They were all sitting around a table in the suite, and Alan and Paul were swapping nursery rhymes. Alan, covered in chocolate from ear to ear, was sitting on Paul's knee, while Mary was sitting pink-cheeked and upright in front of an empty glass of champagne. The fourth member of the party, the bodyguard Peterson, was lifting the bottle of champagne out of the ice bucket to offer her a refill. Mary liked Peterson. I saw them eye each other approvingly as Alan piped, " 'Georgie Porgie Pudding and Pie, kissed the girls and made them cry!' "

"Detestable Georgie Porgie!" I said. "Brute, monster and sadist!"

" 'There was a little girl,' " said Paul unperturbed, " 'who had a little curl, right in the middle of her forehead. When she was good she was very, very good, but when she was bad—' "

" '—she was *horrid!*' " squeaked Alan triumphantly.

Peterson rose to his feet. "Miss Oakes, can I take you and Master Alan for a stroll in the park?"

Mary went pinker than ever and said she was sure that was very kind of him. Alan was detached from Paul, mopped with a napkin and led away chanting "Boys and Girls Come Out to Play."

The door closed. Paul's eyes began to sparkle. "From Catullus to nursery rhymes!" he said laughing. "What a long way we've come in four years!"

I managed to say, "I'm going back to England, Paul."

"My dear, of course you are! And what right have I to dissuade you? After all, you're not my wife! I can't give you orders or expect you to accede meekly to my wishes. But before you rush back to England let's at least drink a little champagne together and toast your departure in style."

"I'm not going to bed with you, you know."

"Of course not." He flicked some crumbs away elegantly with his napkin, stood up and slipped his arms around my waist.

"I don't care how many red roses you send. I don't care how many reams of Catullus you quote. So long as you're living with another woman I can have nothing more to do with you. It's a matter of principle."

"I absolutely believe in matters of principle," said Paul, guiding me gently towards the bedroom.

"If you think I'm just another feeble female incapable of saying no to you . . ."

"A wilted Victorian heroine? Not quite your style, my dear!"

"Well, dash it, Paul, what do you expect of me?" I shouted frenziedly as he closed the bedroom door and started to unbutton my frock. "I'm jolly well not going to let you have your beastly cake and eat it! Why should you live with us both at once?"

"I don't want to live with you both at once."

"Then just what *do* you want?"

"I want to see Mallingham again someday," he said, drawing us down together onto the bed. "I want to see the sun shining on the deserted beach at Waxham and to feel the wind blowing over the reeds of Horsey Mere and to sail across Mallingham Broad to the most perfect house on earth."

Tears streamed down my face.

"Ah, Dinah!" he exclaimed with all his most passionate and romantic enthusiasm. "Can't you understand how often I dream of going back? Sylvia must come first with me now, just as you came first in 1922, but when the opportunity comes to me again do you really think I could ever turn my back on another chance to travel sideways in time?"

"But, Paul, you're simply not facing reality—it'll never work out and we'll all be the losers!"

"This is the only reality I care about right now," he said, pulling me to him.

"But I'm losing, losing, losing . . ."

"No," he said. "You've won, Dinah. You've won." And then as his flesh slid smoothly against mine I forgot all my compromised principles in the ecstasy of my Pyrrhic victory.

Chapter Five

I

Sometime at the end of the afternoon I said to Paul, "I shall still go home at the end of June, you know," and when he answered, "I know you'll have to go someday and I accept that," I wondered if he meant what he said any more than I did. We may have believed intellectually in what we said but emotionally we believed something else. The sane logical side of my mind told me that he had promised nothing, yet despite this I was wholeheartedly convinced he would return to Mallingham for an extended visit. The specter of Sylvia receded. The sane logical side of my mind still told me he would never leave her, but now I no longer listened, because I was once more convinced that when he returned to Mallingham he would never be able to tear himself away. Like Paul I had lost touch with reality, and just as he believed in all honesty that he could repay his debt to Sylvia while still being fair to me, so I told myself once again that Sylvia was of no significance, a woman who as little more than an unpaid social secretary could not hope to hold Paul for much longer.

April slipped into May. In England the shadow of a general strike towered on the horizon, and my friends were writing me long memos about the firm's plans to cope once the disruption began. The crisis seemed immensely distant, particularly since the American newspapers were obsessed only with the gory details of the Hall-Mills murder case and the trivial antics of Mr. Browning and his fifteen-year-old bride, Peaches. In fact sometimes I even wondered if the continent of Europe still existed, for few Americans bothered to peer across the Atlantic Ocean. Their myopic gaze reached no further than Wall Street, and in the shadowed streets of lower Manhattan every public utterance from the bankers assumed the divine force of an oracle.

Paul was very busy. When I encouraged him to talk about his work I heard about the rising star of the investment trusts, of fifty-million-dollar bond issues floated by a casual stroke of the pen, of a voracious public gobbling up anything from debentures to common stock, of the "spread," the "gravy," the "bucket shops" and the "pools."

"I made a million dollars today," Paul once remarked. "Half a million in commission on two separate deals. My clients are happy, the investing public's happy and I'm happy—what a wonderful invention capitalism is!" And when I reminded him of America's Kraken he only laughed and said, "*Après moi le déluge!*"

Later he offered me money to play the market, and unable to resist the temptation I accepted it. He told me what to buy, I did as I was told, and within a month I had doubled my money and paid him back.

In my spare moments I spent much time on Fifth Avenue investigating my competitors. Using a pseudonym, I patronized the salons of Elizabeth Arden and Helena Rubinstein and was proud to discover that Diana Slade of Mayfair could match them in opulent surroundings. Cedric would have got on well with Miss Arden, whose premises shimmered with pastel colors, but I preferred Madame Rubinstein's dramatic dark-blue walls. Since the two tycoons copied each other in as cutthroat a fashion as possible, I found little difference in their products, but I bought every jar and bottle I could find and sent them off to England to be analyzed.

Eying the mass market I also discovered that huge corporations such as Pond's and Colgate were trying to compete for the small but lucrative market belonging to Arden and Rubinstein, and I made notes on their techniques to break the monopoly. Pond's advertising was especially effective, a series of endorsements by leading social figures, with the advertisements taking a full page in all the leading women's magazines. "How unfortunate that this technique is unavailable to us in England!" I wrote wryly to Harriet. "Can you imagine Lady Uppingham's face if we asked her to endorse our lipstick in the press?" Yet not all the American marketing tricks were unsuitable for English use, and soon I had collected a file of slick advertisements and slicker packaging designs.

When Paul offered me the services of one of the Van Zale research analysts I discovered that American women were spending an estimated six million dollars a day on beauty products, and that even in the mass market, calculated at ninety-seven percent of the female population, the average woman spent one hundred and fifty dollars a year on cosmetics. An indiscreet masseuse at the Elizabeth Arden salon told me that the Arden clients, drawn from the remaining three percent, thought nothing of spending a hundred and fifty dollars a week to ensure their beauty. With my mind in a whirl at the thought of all this money cascading from feminine handbags in search of the ideal cosmetics, I could hardly restrain myself from opening a New York salon, but Paul, like Hal Beecher, advised me to spend more time conquering the British market.

Unless Paul was away on business I saw him at least three times a week. Usually we preferred to dine in the privacy of our Plaza suite, but sometimes we would go to the theater and pause afterwards at Montmartre, a restaurant at Broadway and Fifty-second Street where the supper dishes were delicious and the music was soothing. I knew it was useless expecting him to take me to nightclubs, but I was surprised when he shied away too from the cinema. He said the flickering screen reminded him of various visual disturbances he had suffered in the past, and although I told him that modern films were much easier on the eyes he still refused to be tempted.

As if to compensate me for our old-fashioned evenings he began to see me at weekends. We motored up the Hudson Valley and picnicked by the river; we sailed in his yacht along the Connecticut shore; we crossed to New Jersey by private launch and walked along the winding paths beneath the Palisades. As the weather became warmer he talked of finding a retreat so that Alan could enjoy a summer by the sea, and at the end of May he announced that he had arranged for me to have the guest cottage on Steven Sullivan's estate at Great Neck.

"It'll be fun for Alan to play with the Sullivan boys," he said, "and he'll probably enjoy himself more there than he does in the city."

So we moved to the little house above the beach on Long Island Sound, and three times a week I went to the city to meet Paul at the Plaza.

England had staggered through eleven days of a general strike without dissolving into revolution, but that crisis seemed further away than ever and now I, like the rest of America, preferred to read only about the disappearance of Aimée Semple McPherson and the sensuous upward swing of the stock market. Although I continued to respond conscientiously to my friends' communiqués from London, their problems had become unreal to me, and at last I began to understand the psychological state Paul had sought to describe when he had talked of traveling sideways in time.

"It's like being dead," I said to Paul. "England's going on as usual, but I'm not there. I can only peer across from my parallel furrow of time and try to see what's happening."

Being by the sea heightened the sense of illusion. I would wake in the morning, gaze at the waters of the Sound bathed in that fierce foreign light and imagine myself in a dream. It was only when I overheard the gardeners discussing the stock market that I was aware of the steady drumbeat of reality, and then in my mind's eye I saw not the clouds scudding across the Broadland of Norfolk but the sun beating steamily on the canyons of Willow and Wall.

When the Sullivans made efforts to draw me into their set Paul subtly sought to prevent them, for reasons which he never explained but which I assumed arose from his desire to ensure that Sylvia and I never met. I raised no objection. I certainly wanted no repeat of that disastrous evening when I had seen Sylvia, and accordingly I found that my social life revolved not around the Sullivans but around the Claytons in their apartment on the Upper West Side of Manhattan. Whenever I was due to meet Paul in the evening I would have lunch with Grace; if I met Paul for lunch I usually stayed on in Manhattan to spend the evening with the Claytons. Having made a pact not to talk about Paul, Bruce and I soon found there was no friction between us, and although Grace could be tiresome on the subject of emancipation she was so interesting on French literature that I found it easy to overlook her one blind spot. I enjoyed meeting the professors, students, artists and bohemians who filtered continuously through the Claytons' apartment. The conversation was stimulating, the atmosphere relaxed, and Bruce's intellectual rhetoric brought back all my happiest memories of Cambridge, when I had worn myself out debating the doctrines of Nietzsche and Marx with my intensely earnest fellow bluestockings.

Somehow it was more fun discussing them with Bruce. Most intellectuals who fall into the trap of political idealism can usually be made to look idiotic, but Bruce combined an awe-inspiring intellectual range with considerable oratorical skill. His views might be both extreme and unpractical, but it was exceedingly difficult to make them look ridiculous. His main theme was that capitalism should be abolished—a theme which should have seemed utterly absurd in New York at that time, but somehow when Bruce said that the big roulette wheel of Wall Street was a social evil and that the bankers who oiled that wheel were a menace to society, all my doubts about the morality of capitalism were awakened from hibernation.

By the time I met him Bruce already regarded himself as the lone voice crying in the wilderness against the evils of capitalism, and the more the wealth gushed into Wall Street that summer the more strident his lone voice became. In early May he founded a society called the Citizens for Militant Socialism, and on Sundays they would make speeches in Union Square to the sardonic crowds who came to listen.

"I do wish Bruce wouldn't dabble with that sort of society," Grace confided to me anxiously in June. "It does so attract the lunatic element, and yet Bruce refuses to admit that. What do you think I ought to do? Think how awful it would be if he got arrested! How on earth would I break the news to Elizabeth?"

"I don't see any harm in them meeting here once a week and saying 'Hail Lenin' to one another, but I do think Bruce should get rid of that awful man Krasnov. It's not just that I think he's schizophrenic. I don't even think he's a Trotskyite. He's more like a disciple of Stalin."

"But he's the only genuine Russian we've got!" said Grace distractedly, and bewailed the fact that all the Russian emigrés in New York seemed to be royalists.

"How's Bruce's society going—the Citizens for Militant Socialism?" asked Paul, taking me by surprise one Saturday afternoon as we sunbathed on the Sullivans' private beach. "Are you a member?"

"God, no! It's far too eccentric for me, thank you very much! How did you find out about it?"

"I employ people whose business it is to find out such things. So you think Bruce has become eccentric?"

"Well, I know Grace is worried about him."

"That's a pity," said Paul shortly. "I thought he'd quieten down once Greg Da Costa had returned to Mexico."

I had told Paul of my meeting with Greg Da Costa, but he had already known about it. He had Da Costa watched and the detective had seen me leave Terence's apartment.

"Da Costa made quite an impression on me," I said after a moment. "I don't think I'd expected him to be quite such a . . . what's the American word which describes him?"

"I know how I'd describe him," said Paul. "I'd say he was a peculiarly depressing example of how an aristocratic American family can hit rock bottom in one generation. A rotter, as you English would say so succinctly."

"I hated the way he talked as though you owed him a living. Paul, he isn't blackmailing you, is he? I know you said you felt obliged to help the Da Costa brothers financially because they had once been Vicky's stepsons and you were so upset about Jay's suicide, but—"

"I should have known better than to be so sentimental. Let that be a lesson to you, my dear! If you ever meet a sponger like Da Costa, clamp down on your charitable instincts and never show him the color of your money!" He paused, still smiling, but when I only shivered he added abruptly, "Don't worry about Greg. I know very well how he feels about me, but he's the least of my problems. You won't find Greg Da Costa seriously meddling with the goose that lays the golden egg."

Alan was staggering up the beach towards us with his bucket full of water.

"And Bruce Clayton?" said my voice in a rush.

"All talk and no action, like all the best intellectuals. My only fear about Bruce is that he'll do something politically stupid and ruin his very promising academic career. Ah, here comes Miss Oakes with the lemonade. Let's leave her in charge of Alan for a few minutes, Dinah, and take a stroll along the shore. There's something I want to discuss with you."

I paused for some lemonade, but when my glass was empty I slipped my hand into his and we set off along the sand. The waves of the Sound thudded peacefully on the deserted beach. The afternoon was hot and hazy.

"It's about my will," said Paul suddenly. "I've just given my lawyer instructions to revise it."

"Oh, Lord!" I said nervously. "What does that mean?"

He laughed. "Relax—I solemnly promise not to leave you a cent! But I want to settle a small sum on Alan, Dinah, not enough to spoil him but enough to make him aware that I . . ." He paused for the right phrase but could not find it. Finally he continued, "However, I don't want to make this settlement in my will. I have this strong conviction that Alan would be better off growing up in anonymity, and my will is sure to be well-publicized. I'd rather settle the money on him while I'm still alive."

"Yes, I can see that would be better. Thank you, Paul."

"You're not going to tell me I can't do it?"

"I wouldn't dare! No, Paul, you know why I can't accept your money, but I can think of no justification for saying Alan can't accept it either. Besides, it'll be good for Alan to know . . ." This time I was the one who couldn't find the appropriate phrase.

"That I didn't completely repudiate him. Exactly. Very well, now before we wallow in sentimentality and lose sight of my will, may I raise the delicate and controversial issue of the ownership of Mallingham Hall?"

"You may not," I said. "We'll discuss it further when we next walk across the Brograve Level on our way to the sea."

"So Mallingham is still the carrot!" he said laughing. "And I'm still the proverbial donkey! But Dinah, be serious for a moment. In 1922 I added a codicil to my will to say that Mallingham should return to you when I died. Am I to incorporate this codicil into my new will or can we arrange a conveyance while you're in New York?"

"Paul, I meant what I said!" I exclaimed annoyed. "We'll discuss it when you return to Mallingham."

His mouth hardened. We were master and protégée again. "You're being both foolish and unbusinesslike. Supposing I signed a will which made no mention of Mallingham and then promptly dropped dead. What would you do?"

"Buy it back from your estate, of course, at a fair market price, just as I've always planned. I don't see your difficulty, Paul."

He stopped dead on the sand. A breeze ruffled his scanty hair, and behind him the little white sails of a hundred boats bobbed on the dark-blue waters of the Sound.

"I think I should tell you," he said slowly, "that the bulk of my estate will go to Cornelius."

To my amazement I was at once overwhelmed with jealousy on Alan's behalf. It was not because I wanted Alan to have Paul's fortune; I was intellectually opposed to inherited wealth on a colossal scale and had studied enough history to know that such wealth could be disastrous for the beneficiary. I was jealous because Paul was able to regard someone other than Alan as his son and heir.

He understood at once. "Dinah, it's because I care for Alan that I'm doing this."

"I know." I pulled myself together. "I suppose I was just surprised. You hardly ever mention Cornelius."

"He's a good boy in many ways," he said, but although I waited for him to continue he was silent.

"Yet you think he'll make trouble for me if I have to buy back Mallingham," I persisted. "Why?"

"He's devoted to my wife. He's also taken immense trouble to maneuver himself into a position where I can regard him as a son, and knowing the scope of Cornelius' ambition I'd say it's not a position he'd be willing to share."

I looked back at Alan. A number of vistas, all of them unpleasant, opened up briefly in my mind before dissolving into darkness. I felt cold.

"How dismal Cornelius sounds!" I said with a laugh. "I hope we never meet!"

"In that case you won't leave Mallingham in a legal limbo."

"All right. Leave it out of the will. I'll buy it back."

"Good. Now you're thinking more like a Van Zale protégé. When?"

"I'll cable Geoffrey on Monday and ask him to arrange for the property to be appraised by two different firms. I must offer you a fair market price. Oh but Paul, I do wish you could see Mallingham again before you sell it to me!"

He looked across the water. "I could be there in October," he said, "when fall comes to the Broads. I can still see those reeds flame-red and the wild geese migrating—"

"Oh, Paul, it would be wonderful! We could take the yacht again and cruise down to Yarmouth. Everything would be just as it was before . . . except that I wouldn't be pregnant. Of course I wouldn't be pregnant. But . . ."

He said nothing.

"Perhaps . . ."

He looked back at Alan.

"I give you my absolute solemn promise that I wouldn't . . . without your consent. But Paul . . ."

He turned back to face me.

"It would be nice, wouldn't it?" I whispered. "It would be nice."

"Yes," he said. "It would be nice."

I slid my arms around his neck and kissed him on the mouth. It was only when our lips parted that I saw his eyes were bright with tears.

"It's all a dream," he said. "We're living on dreams, Dinah."

"Well, why shouldn't they come true?" I demanded fiercely. "Why shouldn't they?"

He was silent, drawing me close to him again. For a while we watched the boats on the Sound before we heard Alan calling and saw him running across the beach to join us. He ran as fast as he could, his little feet pounding on the sand, his fair hair flying, his dark eyes bright in his small suntanned face.

"Tony and Scott have come to play!" he shouted, and as I glanced towards the house I saw the two Sullivan boys racing down the path to the beach while Steve paused to watch us from the shadow of the trees.

II

Paul had to return to the city that evening, and immediately after he had left I telephoned Grace.

"My, how excited you sound!" she said affectionately as she recognized my voice.

"Grace, marvelous news—I just had to ring you and tell you all about it! Do you have a minute or are you in a rush? Well, listen—I really think I'm getting somewhere with Paul at last. . . . Yes, honestly! He's more or less promised to come to Mallingham this autumn, and Grace—this is the best news of all—he actually said it would be nice if I had another baby! Oh Grace, isn't that absolutely *terrific?*"

"Well, gee . . . yes, that's great, Dinah, but . . . well, do you think that's wise? I mean—"

"Oh God, Grace, don't shower me with platitudes about illegitimate children because I shan't listen to a word! Anyway I think Paul will marry me. He's too much of a Victorian to approve of having children out of wedlock."

"Oh, my stars!" said Grace, casting aside her doubts and beginning to enjoy herself. "My mother-in-law will just die if you succeed in marrying Paul! Just think—she tried for twenty-five years and never made it, while you carry him off after one torrid summer in New York! Oh, how am I ever going to stop myself from saying something to her this evening when Bruce and I go down to Gramercy Park for dinner—how am I going to resist it! If your name comes up and Elizabeth makes one of her snide remarks I just know I'll let the cat out of the bag."

"Poor old Elizabeth," I said fondly. I really did feel sorry for her. "Well, have a good time, Grace, and ring me up tomorrow to tell me what happened when you let out the cat."

She telephoned at eleven-thirty that night. "Di, did I wake you?"

"Yes, but I don't care! Tell me everything! Did she have a fit when you let out the cat?"

"No, my dear—quite the reverse! That's why I just couldn't wait till morning to call you. After I let the cat out Elizabeth just looked at me for a long moment, and then just guess what she said!"

" 'That girl is a disgrace to womanhood'?" I suggested gamely.

"No, no, no—you're hopelessly wrong! She said, 'Maybe I should invite Miss Slade to tea. I think it's time she and I had a talk together.' Now, what on earth do you make of *that?*"

III

The note from Elizabeth arrived on Tuesday morning after Paul had departed for Maine. It was July by that time, but of course I had not returned to England. I had now postponed my departure until the beginning of August and Paul had promised to come down to New York every week, ostensibly to attend to business but also to spend nights with me at the Plaza. It was getting unpleasantly hot in Manhattan and when I saw that Elizabeth was writing to me from her Gramercy Park address I was surprised, for I knew she and her husband had a summer home at East Hampton where they retired when the New York summer became unbearable.

She had written in black ink on thick white paper:

Dear Miss Slade,

My son has taken scrupulous care to ensure that we have never met, but I suspect you may share my opinion that his desire to protect us both is unnecessary as well as misguided. Why should we not meet? Beyond my natural curiosity I also have a genuine interest in meeting a friend of my son and daughter-in-law, and so I should be delighted if you would visit me this Thursday at four o'clock. If you have no means of transport, let me know and I shall send my chauffeur to Great Neck to collect you.

Sincerely,

Elizabeth Clayton

P.S. Please bring Alan and his nurse.

Paul and I had agreed not to communicate by telephone when he was at Bar Harbor, and since he had already left by the time Elizabeth's note arrived I had no chance to tell him of the invitation. I could have written to him, but I did not. Instead I looked forward to regaling him with the story of my visit when he returned to Manhattan.

Gramercy Park was a beautiful square framed by sumptuous houses. It was exactly four o'clock when her chauffeur deposited us at the door of her home.

We were admitted by an elderly maid whose uniform crackled with starch, and an English butler led us to an upstairs drawing room. The atmosphere was heavily prewar, almost pre-twentieth century, and as we moved at a funeral pace up the staircase I shuddered at the gloomy still-life paintings which peppered the olive-green flocked wallpaper.

"Miss Slade, madam," intoned the butler, opening the handsome double doors.

We entered a large light room which faced the square at one end and a long narrow walled garden at the other. The carpet was Persian, the porcelain in the cabinets was Chinese, the paintings were English. I was just gazing incredulously at a Turner when a woman's calm authoritative voice said, "Miss Slade—so nice of you to come! How do you do."

She was a tall woman who had probably once been slender. Even now she was not stout but merely heavy in that unobtrusive fashion common among the middle-aged. She was conservatively dressed in dark blue, and her hair, drawn off her face and coiled in a heavy knot, was gray. Her eyes were gray too, and beneath her regal nose her mouth was strong and firm. So completely did she seem to personify the virtues of a Roman matron of the early Republic that I did not at first remember she had been consistently unfaithful to two husbands during her many years of married life.

"It was so nice of you to ask us, Mrs. Clayton."

We shook hands. Her glance, politely welcoming, flicked over me in two seconds, ignored Mary and rested briefly on Alan. "Hello!" she said to him, but before he had had time to hide himself shyly behind Mary's skirts she had turned to gesture to the sofa. "Do sit down. I've asked for tea to be served in the garden—the weather's so much cooler today and I know children prefer to play outside. When Jackson has everything ready we'll go downstairs. By the way, how do you find our New York weather? Rather trying, no doubt, in comparison with an English summer."

We discussed first the weather, then New York. She was perfectly at ease, as if all awkwardness of manner were unknown to her, and by the time we moved downstairs I had already discarded my preconceived notions. Whoever Elizabeth Clayton was, she was not a pathetic old woman.

I felt a twinge of uneasiness but suppressed it.

She did try to talk to Alan again, but when he remained too shy to sustain a conversation she wisely left him alone. "Bruce was shy at that age too," she said. "I remember it well."

As if embarrassed by this comparison Alan squeezed his doughnut until the jam spurted out, and asked if he could get down.

"Not until you've finished, darling."

He immediately wriggled off his chair and, still clutching the doughnut, skipped off to the far end of the garden.

"Alan!" I exclaimed annoyed as Mary dashed after him, but Elizabeth said, "It doesn't matter—he's been very good. Tell me, is it my imagination or does he really look a little like Paul?"

"There is a small resemblance, I think."

"Heredity's always so interesting, isn't it. More tea?" She reached for the silver teapot. A fly buzzed lazily over the cakes. The sun shone. The little garden was warm and drowsy. "Paul took after his father in looks," murmured Elizabeth, filling my cup. "The Van Zales were a handsome family, but unfortunately poor Charlotte, Paul's sister, took after his mother and was very plain. But they were remarkable women intellectually. No doubt that explains why Paul, unlike most men, is very much at ease with strong clever women. It must have been intimidating to him when he was younger—of course that was why his first marriage was to a girl who was his social and intellectual inferior—but once he had proved to himself that he was stronger and cleverer than his mother and sister, his interest in stupid women declined. More cake, Miss Slade?"

I resisted the cake but not the bait of her reminiscences which she was dangling before me so invitingly. "You knew his first wife?" I said, trying not to sound too vulgar in my curiosity.

"Oh no, no—she was quite unpresentable and he could never take her anywhere. Besides, my association with Paul only began after her death. While she was alive he was quite besotted with her even though I suspect she gave him a very difficult time. Sexual attraction is really such a curious phenomenon, isn't it, Miss Slade?" she added casually, pouring herself another cup of tea.

The word "sexual," used so unexpectedly by that extremely dignified woman in that overpoweringly Victorian setting, was so erotic that I actually blushed. "Er—yes," I said floundering. "Yes, I suppose it is. Quite."

"Although he would never admit it I suspect there was a strong element of that nature in his relationship with his second wife Marietta, whom he ostensibly married for convenience. However, he was quite in control of the situation on that occasion, and although the marriage was as disastrous as his first it was by no means as painful to him. After he got rid of her we had some happy years together; Eliot was traveling a great deal and I was often alone. Of course there was no question of divorce. Things were so different before the War, and I didn't want Bruce to suffer from any stigma which might have resulted from my socially unacceptable conduct. Besides, I think both Paul and I knew that we were too alike to make each other happy in marriage. Paul needs someone who can absorb his faults instead of reflecting them back at him like a mirror. However, there was no question that a man in his position had to remarry, and after his previous disasters you can imagine what a relief it was for us all when he finally found the right person to be his wife."

There was a silence. I suddenly realized I was clutching my cup of tea so hard my fingers ached.

"You haven't met Sylvia, have you, Miss Slade?"

"No."

"Oh, she's charming! Much the best wife Paul's ever had, as everyone always says! And Paul's as devoted to her as she is to him. Perhaps you don't quite realize, Miss Slade," said Elizabeth Clayton in the kindest and most considerate of voices, "how very happy they are together—and how well-suited."

"I—"

"Oh, but I do understand! It's *quite* natural that you've misunderstood the situation! As I was implying earlier, passion does so distort one's judgment and affect one's perceptions. But my passion's all been spent, Miss Slade, and I can see your situation with a detachment which you cannot possibly hope to attain."

"Mrs. Clayton," I said strongly, rallying at last from this blistering assault, "you may presume to know Sylvia's feelings towards Paul, but since we're strangers you can't conceivably presume to know mine. Besides, isn't the main issue not our feelings but Paul's? And surely isn't it his business, not yours, whom he finally decides to live with?"

"I'm afraid you're mistaken, Miss Slade," said Elizabeth politely, "but then you're very young and allowances should be made for your immaturity. The real issue doesn't revolve around Paul's feelings. He never could afford the luxury of high romance in his personal life, and he certainly can't afford it now. The real issue revolves around who has the most to offer him—and what can you offer him, Miss Slade? I understand you're not interested in marriage."

"Well, if Paul wants to marry me to satisfy some Victorian corner of his conscience, that's his affair, but I love him too much to care whether he marries me or not. When he was at Mallingham with me in 1922 we had this totally honest, totally monogamous, wholly worthwhile relationship—"

"Did you?" said Elizabeth Clayton. "Are you sure?"

"Of course I'm sure!" I said incensed, and wanting only to shock her out of her composure, I added passionately, "And if you really want to know, I'd much rather have that than marriage!"

"Why, yes," said Elizabeth, quite unshocked and more composed than ever, "I expect you would. Marriage involves such a heavy commitment, doesn't it, and so many promises."

"Hypocritical dishonest promises! How can one possibly promise to love someone for ever and ever—"

"For richer, for poorer," said Elizabeth, "in sickness and in health."

"Well, I mean, it's simply not practical, is it? Everyone knows love can die! After all, if we're to be honest—"

"Ah yes, Miss Slade," said Elizabeth, "let's by all means be honest. Let's call a spade a spade. The scope of the relationship you share now with Paul falls very far short of the vows he once exchanged with Sylvia, doesn't it?"

"Well, I—I didn't mean—that wasn't what I—"

"Be honest, Miss Slade! If Paul became so sick that he could no longer live a normal life, you wouldn't stay with him, would you?"

"Yes, I would! Of course I would!"

"But I thought you just implied that love can die in that sort of circumstance?"

"Yes, but— Mrs. Clayton, don't you think this discussion has wandered a little far from the point?"

"In view of his illness?" said Elizabeth surprised. "I should have thought that in the circumstances our conversation could hardly have been more pertinent."

It was so peaceful in the garden. Far away Alan was chattering to Mary, but I could not hear what he said. I wanted to look Elizabeth straight in the eye but it was too difficult, so I looked instead at the hazy sky, the parched trees and the scorched coarse grass of the lawn.

"Of course, since you're so honest with each other, he would have told you all about the illness which runs in his family."

I could not speak.

"The cruelest part of the whole business," said Elizabeth, sipping her tea, "is that he should have relapsed after more than thirty years of perfect health. I know he was very ill as a child, but he did recover and lead a normal life. It was only after Vicky died . . . But of course he would have told you all about that."

"Of course," I whispered. "Of course."

"During this past year his deterioration was really most severe. Thank God you were able to help him back to health, Miss Slade! It really gave Paul a new lease on life, didn't it, when Sylvia suggested he bring you over from England."

At first I thought I must have misheard her. Again I was beyond speech, and as I stared at her dumbly the shadowy figure of Sylvia seemed to move forward into the light.

"Oh, you didn't know?" said Elizabeth surprised. "Yes, it was Sylvia who sent for you—I can't really claim any credit, because I only gave her moral support. It was, as you can imagine, a very difficult decision for her to make, but she was the only one who could make it because Paul, loving her as he does, would never have sent for you without her consent. But you see, she was desperate. Paul was so ill, and nothing the doctors did seemed to work. I also got the impression—although naturally Sylvia is too well-bred to discuss private marital matters with anyone but her husband—that there were certain difficulties which Paul thought could only be resolved by someone such as yourself. . . . What a powerful attraction you and Paul have for each other, haven't you, Miss Slade! Sylvia's been concerned, I know, but I've always told her not to worry. I know Paul. He's no fool. He's well aware that his illness is going to return eventually, and he's well aware that Sylvia is the one women who'll always stand by him. It's so sad that the illness is incurable. In fact, there's no denying it really is the most tragic fate," mused Elizabeth Clayton, looking down the garden towards Alan, "to inherit epilepsy."

We sat in silence for twenty seconds. Twenty seconds is a long silence where there has been a steady flow of conversation for more than an hour.

At the end of the garden Alan left the flower bed and rushed up to me. "Mummy, there's a huge great butterfly down there!"

I looked at him, my beautiful little boy with his dark eyes shining in his small bright face, and the sickness started to churn in my stomach.

Elizabeth said, "Is he still there, Alan? Can you show him to me?" When she stood up, taking his hand in hers and leading him across the lawn, Alan forgot his shyness. I heard him chattering to her, but I never heard her reply because by that time I was indoors. Meeting the butler I asked for the cloakroom, and two minutes later I was being violently sick in a dark little room behind the stairs.

Chapter Six

I

At first I could only remember the small incidents: Bob Peterson's horrified expression when Paul had said, "I'll drive," Paul's distaste for the flickering screen of the cinema which reminded him of some vague unexplained visual disturbances, Bruce Clayton's confident assumption "You know all about his illness, I guess," Grace's doubtful comment "Is that wise?" when I had talked of having another child. I remembered that epileptics were supposed to avoid alcohol—and I saw Paul's countless untouched glasses of champagne. I remembered Paul saying, "*Mens sana in corpore sano!*"—and I saw him swinging his tennis racquet on the grass court at Mallingham.

Then the larger mysteries, all unsolved, began to billow back into my mind: Paul's insistence that he wanted no children when it was obvious he felt the lack of children keenly, Terence O'Reilly's determination to reassure me about Paul's illness so that I would not ruin his plans to use me, Paul encouraging my inclination to avoid the Sullivan set and associate with people who either did not know him or who, like Bruce, would refuse to discuss him with me.

When there were no more incidents to resurrect I could shield myself no longer. I was face to face with Sylvia at last and forced to acknowledge how profoundly I had been deceived.

I had thought I understood their relationship, but I had understood nothing. In my arrogance I had continued to think of her as a weak limited woman who had no identity beyond her married name and no existence except a life lived vicariously through her husband's triumphs. But Sylvia had her own identity—I could see it taking shape before my eyes—and the identity had an independent will of its own. The woman who had manipulated my visit to America had been not weak but strong; I tried to imagine the inner resources needed for such a gesture but could not, for it was *I* who was limited, not she; *I* was the one trapped in Paul's identity, abandoning my work in London to be at his beck and call in New York, imprisoned by my glib platitudes about free love and honest relationships.

I had been deceived by others but first and foremost I had deceived myself, and in turning a blind eye to Paul's evasiveness I had indulged myself in a relationship which was as much a fraudulent sham as the institution of marriage that I had long pretended to despise.

"Take me to the Plaza," I said to Elizabeth's chauffeur as we left Gramercy Park, and I added to Mary, "I want to stay the night in town but I'll catch the train home tomorrow morning."

As soon as I reached Paul's suite I raided the cache of drink but found that Mayers had forgotten to replenish the supplies. After drinking half of the lone bottle of champagne I picked up the telephone with a steady hand.

"Grace?" I said a minute later. "Why did you never tell me Paul was an epileptic?"

"My God, Dinah, didn't you know? I always assumed—"

"But you never once mentioned it!"

"Well, of course not! How could I? I mean, it's just not the sort of thing one mentions, is it? After all, you were the one having an affair with him—I thought that if you wanted to discuss it you should be the one to bring up the subject."

"Yes," I said. "Of course. That was the tactful thing to do. That's all right, Grace. It doesn't matter."

I rang off before she could ask more questions, drank another glass of champagne as if it were lemonade and then, summoning all my courage, placed a call to Paul's house at Bar Harbor.

The butler told me Paul was playing tennis with his young protégés whom he had reunited for the summer, but as I was about to ring off he told me to wait. Paul had just walked into the hall.

"Dinah? How are you?"

For some reason the sound of his voice made me feel faint.

"Dinah? Hello—are you there?"

"Yes." I swallowed with difficulty. "Paul, first let me apologize for breaking our agreement and phoning you like this."

"Never mind, you picked a good time to call. Is something wrong?"

"No, just the usual monthly bore, but I don't think I shall feel very sexy this weekend. I was going to suggest you postpone your visit to Manhattan until next week. Is that going to create difficulties for you?"

"Not at all. However, some cousins of Sylvia's are arriving from San Francisco on Wednesday for a brief stay in New York before they sail to Europe, so I'll have to be back in Manhattan by Tuesday at the latest. Why don't we meet on Tuesday evening?"

"That would be lovely. Thanks, Paul. Sorry about the weekend."

He said he would be looking forward to Tuesday evening. Before we said goodbye he sent his love to Alan.

Finishing the bottle of champagne, I paddled my way drunkenly through the telephone directory and phoned Thomas Cook, the travel agents, to inquire about a passage to England.

II

The next morning I went to the New York Public Library on Forty-second Street and read about epilepsy. I discovered that it was a diverse disease, that not all forms of epilepsy were hereditary, that the stigma attached to it was in most cases unjustified and arose through superstition and ignorance. I read that research was being conducted to find a drug which would eliminate seizures so that epileptics might lead normal lives; some doctors suspected that the hereditary form of the disease was caused by a recurring chemical imbalance in the brain, while others speculated that where the epilepsy seemed to be related to stress the brain might be the inherited weak point in the body through which mental stress was manifested in physical illness. There were instances of remissions; these were being studied with interest. I read of petit mal and grand mal and auras. I read of convulsions, blackouts and hallucinations. I read that for epilepsy there was as yet no known cure.

With a shudder I caught the train to Great Neck. Four days later on Tuesday evening I was back at the Plaza to meet Paul.

He arrived late but brought a bouquet of carnations and a box of my favorite chocolates.

"How are you?" he said, kissing me.

"I'm all right."

He looked tanned, fit and youthful. Throughout dinner I was comparing his appearance with that of the haggard aging man who had welcomed me to New York that April.

We dined at the Marguery on Park Avenue, just as we had dined on my first evening in New York, and we had our same private corner with the same chairs cushioned in rose-and-ivory brocade. We chose the sole Marguery too, and again I marveled at those softly sparkling chains of light which reminded me of fountains frozen in some mysterious hiatus of time.

"Why did you particularly want to dine here tonight?" asked Paul when our fish was finished, and glancing at his glass of champagne I saw it was empty. That was when the evening took a different course from that evening in April, and I knew he had sensed my tension and was responding to it.

"I think perhaps I wanted to go backwards in time."

"There's no going back."

"No."

"There's something wrong, isn't there?"

"Yes, I'm afraid there is. I've decided I must go back to England, Paul. I'm awfully sorry, but Harriet and Cedric seem to be fighting worse than ever, and—"

He stopped me with a gesture. "Let's go back to the Plaza. We can talk better there."

"I'd rather talk about it here, Paul."

He smiled at me so brilliantly that I could not quite identify the emotion at the back of his eyes.

"So the Plaza has become as inhibiting as my forgotten penthouse with the Angelica Kauffmann ceiling! Tell me, have you set the date for your return?"

"Yes, I have. I'm leaving tomorrow. The *Mauretania* sails at five in the afternoon."

He was motionless for no more than three seconds before he shrugged his shoulders and gave me yet another careless brilliant smile. "You haven't left me much time to talk you out of it!"

"I know. Paul, I'm terribly sorry to leave like this, but I feel a rapid departure would really be less painful."

"Yes. Are you packed?"

"I've been packing since Friday and this morning I borrowed the Sullivans' car and chauffeur to take the trunks to the pier."

"What happened on Thursday?"

I stared at him. Something in my expression must have betrayed me, for he reached automatically for the bottle of champagne to refill his glass. But the bottle was empty, buried nose first in the bucket of ice.

With a gesture of annoyance he glanced around for the waiter but then changed his mind and put his napkin aside.

"Well, if this evening is to be a repeat of our first," he remarked with all his most effortless urbanity, "let's end as we began—in style at Willow and Wall!"

I knew I could not refuse. Panic pricked the nape of my neck as we left the restaurant.

This time neither Peterson nor the chauffeur was dismissed and we traveled downtown in silence, Paul and I sitting six inches apart on the back seat. I wanted to take his hand in mine, talk to him, cry, but I did nothing, said nothing and my eyes were tearless.

At the bank we left Peterson in the entrance hall with the night watchman and walked through the glittering main chamber to Paul's office.

"Brandy, my dear?"

"Thanks. I wish I had the willpower to say no. I seem to have been drinking rather a lot lately."

Evidently he had more willpower than I did, or perhaps he was merely afraid to drink more. Opening the bar concealed in the bookcase, he poured one glass of brandy and put the bottle away.

I had to sit down. There was a large chair on the other side of the desk, and I sank into it slowly as if I were falling in slow motion from a great height.

He sat down opposite me and we regarded each other, banker and client, across the desk which separated us.

Suddenly I said, "I love you, Paul," and burst into tears.

He reached to take my hand. When I could speak again I said unsteadily, "Paul, I don't want to leave you, I really don't."

"I don't want you to go." He was stroking the back of my hand with his index finger. "Stay until the fall and then we can go back to Mallingham together."

I began to cry again, and when he saw I could not answer he said with great kindness, "Very well, let's get to the bottom of this. God knows, I'm a businessman and I should hope I can always recognize an ultimatum when it's staring me in the face! You've declared your intention of returning to England. Very well, that puts the ball squarely in my court. I now have to make you an offer to induce you to stay."

"Oh, no—no, it's not like that—"

"But of course it is—and of course I'll make you an offer! I don't want you to go any more than you do, and in fact it's very important to me that you stay. Well, what would you like? Name your terms! I'm quite prepared to give you anything you want, so I can't imagine there'll be any difficulty."

"Paul, what I want you can't give me."

I shall never know how I said those words. They were torn out of the most private reaches of my mind, and afterwards I felt in excruciating pain as if a limb had been hacked from my body.

"Ah!" he said at once with relief. "At last I'm beginning to understand! How slow I've been—and I always knew how much you wanted more children! Very well, if you think I'm a suitable candidate to help you with your dynastic schemes—"

He stopped.

I was mute.

Our private world came at last to an end.

For ten terrible seconds I saw him grow old before my eyes, and then he rose awkwardly to his feet, fumbled to open the bar and slopped brandy into a tumbler. I watched him drink it, watched him refill his glass.

Finally he was able to say, "All right, let's discuss this calmly. I do understand the difficulty, but I'm sure there must be a solution. We have such a unique relationship. I can't believe—" He stopped. His calmness disintegrated. In a low voice he said rapidly, "I feel so well when I'm with you. You give me such confidence. Even now I don't mind your knowing. I always wondered if I'd mind, but now I can see it doesn't make any difference, I just know I'll stay well as long as you're with me, I'm convinced of it. So you see you really mustn't leave. If you leave I shall start slipping into that open grave again, and I can't bear to think of it, can't face it. It's not death itself I mind but the gradual disintegration, the diminishing of my world by the steady loss of everything that's important to me. I would have to abandon my work first, then my social activities, my friends—God, can't you understand? It's the *living* death that terrifies me. I dwell upon death a lot, often late at night when I can't sleep, and all I can think is: when it comes, let it be quick! Let it be absolute! And then I remember my father, dying young at the height of his powers, and I envy him." He stopped talking. The brandy glass was empty again. He was waiting for me to speak.

But I did not know how to reply. In the end, wanting to show sympathy, I said falteringly, "You're physically fit now, Paul. I think you exaggerate your dependence on me—your fears are all in your mind. Perhaps—perhaps a good psychiatrist . . ."

He got up and walked away into the other half of the double room. It was unlit, and when he sank down on the sofa I could not see his expression. Leaning forward, he covered his face with his hands.

I was terrified. I knew I had made matters worse and now I did not dare go to him for fear of what new distress I might uncover. I felt paralyzed by guilt, and having been cruelly made aware of my inadequacy, he made no further appeal to me for help.

At last he stood up, moving stiffly as he stepped back into the light. The weight of his pain brushed past me. I was nearly annihilated by it.

"I'll take you back to the Plaza," he said.

"Paul, I must say this—it's not your illness itself. I mean, I'm not frightened of it or anything stupid like that—heavens, how could I be with my classical education? Epilepsy, the mark of the gods! Paul, what I'm trying to say is that my decision to leave isn't primarily concerned with your illness."

"We'll leave now. This way, please."

"You see, it was because you lied to me—never trusted me. I was manipulated and deceived—"

He swung to face me. We had left his office and were standing at the far end of the great hall. His eyes were black and bitter. "What do you mean?"

"Well, it wasn't you who sent for me, was it? It was *she* who sent for me, and when I found that out—"

"Who told you?"

"Elizabeth," I said faintly, and saw him bow his head in acceptance of some massive and terrible defeat.

I followed him to the car. I was trembling from head to toe, and he was beyond speech. At the end of our silent journey I blurted out, "Will I see you again before I go?"

"Of course," he said politely. "I hope I'm not so discourteous that I'm incapable of coming down to the ship tomorrow to wish you a safe voyage. Besides, I must say goodbye to Alan."

I started to cry again as the car halted outside the hotel.

"Good night, Dinah," he said, and stared out of the window as I crawled from the car.

The next thing I knew I was upstairs in the suite and hunting for something to drink. For a time I was too occupied with my sobs to think or see clearly, but eventually I did realize that the suite was dry. Mayers had still not restocked the bedroom cupboard.

"Oh, God!" I wept, as distraught as any alcoholic, and wasted five minutes futilely cursing Prohibition. I thought of a speakeasy and quailed. I considered bribing a waiter and flinched. Finally I telephoned Grace Clayton.

It was Bruce who answered.

"Oh Bruce, it's Dinah!"

"Yes?" That was a cool reception. Amidst all my distress I remembered his growing eccentricity and rebelled against it.

"Is Grace there?" I said coldly.

"No, she had to go up to Greenwich. Her mother's not well."

"Oh." I felt desperate. "Bruce, could I come over and cadge a drink? I feel just like jumping off the Brooklyn Bridge."

"Well, frankly it's not very convenient. I'm having a very important meeting of the C.M.S.—tomorrow's our Wall Street parade. Can you go and get a drink somewhere else?"

I hung up on him in a fury, wasted some more time cursing his Citizens for Militant Socialism, and dialed Terence O'Reilly's number in Greenwich Village. I had seen nothing of Terence for some weeks. After I had conspicuously compromised my principles by sharing Paul with Sylvia he had no doubt decided I could be of no further use to him in his attempts to detach Sylvia from her husband. As I waited for him to answer the telephone I wondered if he would be as rude to me as Bruce but decided I was too distraught to care.

"Terence? Oh Terence, it's Dinah Slade. Listen, I'm in desperate need of a good strong drink. I promise I won't stay longer than five minutes, but—"

"Come right on over," he said, "and I'll fix you the biggest martini in town."

I gasped with relief, grabbed my handbag and fled downtown to his flat.

III

"Problems?" said Terence, dropping a sliver of lemon into a glass the size of a goldfish bowl. He was casually dressed in a thin blue shirt and off-white slacks. It was hot in his neat apartment although a fan labored valiantly by the window.

"Unspeakable problems, yes." I collapsed on the sofa and guzzled the martini. "You're looking very smug!" I commented sourly as I paused for air. "In fact, you remind me of a cat—it must be the green eyes. Where's your bowl of cream?"

He laughed. I was aware of his excitement, as if he had a delicious secret and was savoring it ounce by ounce in some intensely private corner. "Go easy with that drink!" he warned. "If you're not careful you could well find yourself dead drunk in five minutes! What's been going on?"

"I can't explain, it's too complicated, but I ended up at the Plaza with nothing to drink and I phoned the Claytons but Grace was away and that *idiotic* Bruce was in the middle of a meeting—"

"Ah yes, the C.M.S.! They're due to parade up Wall Street tomorrow with the usual anticapitalist jeers and sneers. The Van Zale clerks have been drawing lots for the best positions by the front windows. It's not often we have that kind of excitement on the Street."

"Well, I used to like Bruce very much," I said, "but I think he's gone absolutely mad and I feel jolly sorry for Grace. He's not going to try and blow up Van Zale's, is he? That would be the last straw!"

"A repeat of the 1920 rumpus when some lunatic tried to blow up the House of Morgan? Not a chance! Bruce may be eccentric but he's nonviolent. He's even forbidden his followers to carry guns. If you want my opinion the entire parade is going to be a complete waste of time, but— Is anything the matter?"

"Heavens, I think I'm going to be sick. Where's the—"

"This way." He steered me adroitly into the bathroom and abandoned me at the basin.

I tried to be sick but failed. I had had enough of the martini to feel like death but not enough to embark on the road to recovery. After five minutes I staggered out.

"I'll get you some medicine," said Terence when he saw my face. "Go into the bedroom and lie down."

"You won't jump on me?"

"No, I like my women a little soberer than you are."

I heard him opening the medicine cabinet in the bathroom. "Here," he said, offering me a glass of effervescing liquid, "drink this."

"Thanks. Goodness, I'm sorry—how awful of me. I do feel low. I never used to get blotto like this in London."

"It's Prohibition," said Terence sympathetically. "People drink twice as much as they normally do when they have to make an effort to get the drink." He opened the bedroom door for me and I closed it firmly in case he had any idea of following me inside. There was an unmistakable sexual edge to his simmering excitement; I had the uneasy feeling that the smug cat with his bowl of cream could be transformed all too swiftly into a tomcat on the prowl.

I did drink some of the medicine, but when my head started to spin I lay down on the bed. The medicine felt as if it might work. I drank some more. Ten minutes later, overcome by the desire to extricate myself from Terence's bedroom, I pressed my right hand down upon the book which sat on the bedside table and levered myself to my feet. The room promptly revolved, and when I clawed at the table to steady myself the book shot off onto the floor. Presently I crawled to the rescue. The book's spine was broken. The pages had fallen open at Terence's place, which was marked by a letter, and as I was reaching for the book I saw the Mexican stamps on the envelope.

I remembered that Greg Da Costa had a ranch in Mexico.

I did not normally read other people's letters, but this one tempted me because I could think of no good reason why a Van Zale employee should be in private correspondence with a man who had a huge grudge against Paul.

Perhaps the letter had come from someone else. I took a peek into the envelope and deciphered the word "Greg." That settled it. Abandoning any attempt to behave like a lady, I read the letter from end to end.

"Come down whenever you want," Greg Da Costa had written in a large curiously uneducated handwriting, "but my advice is don't wait too long. Hope all goes well with the parade down Wall Street. Workers of the world, unite! Christ, how my poor father would have laughed, God rest his blue-blooded, Eastern-Seaboard soul! Cable me if there's any hitch. Good luck, Greg."

I read the letter three times and became more disturbed with each reading. What interest could Greg Da Costa possibly have in a parade which Terence had told me would be a complete waste of time? What was the "hitch" he feared and why was Terence to cable him? And why was Terence being advised to flee to Mexico at the earliest opportunity?

Yet the letter betrayed nothing, and there was no phrase which was incapable of a trivial explanation. Terence could be cultivating Greg to keep an eye on his activities. It would be consistent with his position as Paul's chief of police. If the marchers planned some noisy demonstration of their political beliefs on the doorstep of Van Zale's, Greg could well be gleeful in anticipation of Paul's embarrassment, and the "hitch" might refer to the possibility of Bruce's being arrested. Even the invitation to Mexico, when seen in the context of Greg's illiterate handwriting, might possibly have no connection with the subject of the parade which followed it. Greg could even have been referring to some change in the climate when he had advised Terence not to delay his visit too long.

I told myself repeatedly that there was no melodramatic explanation, but when I read the letter a fourth time I was conscious not of its ambiguities but of the air of conspiracy which permeated it. It was only after I had replaced the letter that I saw the book's title. It was *The Great Gatsby,* Fitzgerald's story of a man who had created a new world for himself in order to win a rich man's wife.

"Dinah, are you feeling better? Can I come in?"

My heart banged against my ribs. I stood up hastily. "Yes, I'm much better now, Terence."

Somehow I escaped without seeming as if I were rushing headlong from his apartment, and as soon as I reached the Plaza I telephoned Paul's house.

"I'm sorry, madam," said the butler, "but Mr. Van Zale has given the strictest orders that he is not to be disturbed."

"But he'll talk to *me!* Miss Slade—S-L-A-D-E."

"I'm sorry, madam—"

"It's urgent!" I shouted at him. "It's a matter of life and death!"

"One moment, madam, I shall ascertain if Mrs. Van Zale is at home to talk to you."

"No!" I screamed, but he had gone.

I clutched the phone and stared wildly around the room. My first instinct was to ring off, but I did not; I had to know if she decided to take the call. My second reaction was to hang up as soon as she had said hello, but that idea too I rejected; I had to know what she intended to say. My third reaction was to plan a speech. Jane Austen would have phrased it delightfully. "Pray don't be offended, Mrs. Van Zale! I must apologize for offending your sensibilities in this distressing manner, but . . ." No, that was really too nineteenth-century, and Sylvia and I were twentieth-century women.

I thought of Schiller, glibly writing in *Mary Stuart* of a confrontation between two historical characters who in fact had never met. At least I had been spared a face-to-face meeting! But then as the line clicked I realized with dread that any face-to-face meeting would have been preferable to a faceless confrontation by means of that cold cruel modern instrument, the telephone.

"Miss Slade?"

I tried to clear my throat. Nothing happened.

"The butler said it was very urgent, but Paul was insistent before he retired that he wasn't to be disturbed. If there's some message . . ." She paused politely.

I saw her again before the marble fountain, no longer languishing in fragility but standing where I had once fooled myself I could stand, unbowed, unbeaten, winning.

"Miss Slade?"

"Yes," I said. It was so difficult to speak. I had to make a great effort to recall Greg Da Costa's letter. "He—he mustn't go to Wall Street tomorrow. The parade . . ."

"Yes, he knows about that."

"But there's something beyond the march—some plan. They're all in it—" I stopped myself from mentioning Terence's name. I did not know how she felt towards him, and I could not risk her dismissing my suspicions because she refused to believe he could be involved. "Greg Da Costa's implicated," I said unsteadily at last.

"Da Costa?" I heard the fear in her voice.

My strength was almost exhausted. "Tell him not to go," I whispered. "Persuade him to stay at home."

There was a pause before she said, "Yes, I will. Thank you for calling, Miss Slade."

We waited. Neither of us could hang up, yet neither of us knew what to say. I was just thinking in panic that the conversation could only be ended awkwardly when she said in a quiet pleasant voice, "I hear you're going home tomorrow, Miss Slade. May I wish you bon voyage?" And while I remained unable to reply I heard the soft final click as she replaced the receiver.

IV

It was hot and getting hotter. The New York summer seemed to consist of a series of crescendos, each culminating in a meteorological explosion; the temperature would increase, starting in the upper seventies, moving day by day through the eighties and finally soaring into the nineties. At that point a colossal thunderstorm would settle over Manhattan for some hours to bring the temperature down twenty degrees, but within a day or two the cycle would begin again. Ten days before, a violent storm had followed a record temperature of ninety-four degrees and now the heat was increasing again, eighty-four for the past two days and ninety forecast for the morrow. I thought the storm would break that night. In the early hours of the morning when I was too hot to sleep I leaned out of the window and waited for the thunder to bang blindly against the cliffs of the Palisades, but the storm never came, dawn broke swelteringly over the East River and by breakfast the mercury had already soared past eighty in its race to the nineties.

Mary and Alan were not due to arrive until the afternoon so my morning was free, but when I went out, walking east to buy a cup of coffee in a drugstore on Lexington Avenue, the fierce heat bludgeoned me into dizziness and I looked for a taxi to take me home.

Home made me think of Mallingham. I stood on the corner of a crosstown street, and while I waited for a cab I longed for Mallingham, for the cool fresh breeze from the sandhills of Waxham, for the singing reeds of Horsey Mere, for the damp ancient mysterious walls of my house. For a second I was there; I could touch the grass, caress the polished flint of the walls, smell the rosemary and thyme in the herb garden. But then a car hooted as I stepped unthinkingly into the road, brakes screeched, a driver bawled obscenities, and I was back in the sweltering chasms of Manhattan, trapped in a fierce prison of concrete and glass.

I had a great urge to talk to Paul, but I knew it would be futile. I had destroyed the fragile bond created by my ignorance of his illness and could offer him no bond to take its place. I wanted to restore the bond but did not know how to renew it; I was too ignorant, too young, and in his pride he had withdrawn from me just as in my painful confusion I had instinctively withdrawn from him. Sheltering from the heat in another drugstore, I tried in vain to see a solution to our estrangement, but all I saw was Paul's bitter face and all I heard was his bleak judgment: "We've missed each other in time."

In grief I wished he were younger, and in a moment of useless rage I saw again his vision of the plowed field of eternity, and knew that the gap which separated his furrow from mine had ultimately proved unbridgeable.

I rubbed my eyes. I was outside in the street again, and behind me a train roared along Third Avenue's elevated railway. I started to move west, crossing avenue after avenue, and as the heat beat down upon me it seemed I was already moving sideways in time, crossing furrow after furrow to crawl back in relief to the world where I belonged.

It was noon when I reached the Plaza. My makeup had been ruined long before and my clothes were soaked with sweat. I had just dressed again after a shower and was drinking my third glass of water when the telephone rang.

Thinking it was Paul, I rushed with a sob to the bedroom.

"Hullo?" I whispered into the mouthpiece.

"Dinah."

I did not recognize the caller's voice. "Who's this?" I said confused.

"Steve Sullivan."

I still did not recognize his voice. A horrible premonition crawled through me and I had to sit down on the edge of the bed.

"I'm downstairs," he said. "In the lobby."

I could not speak. The room began to go dark before my eyes.

"I have to talk to you," said the man. "Can I—" He stopped as if he knew I would be unable to answer the question. "I'm coming up," he said, and rang off.

I went on holding the phone and listening to the empty line. At last the operator said, "Hello, can I help you?" and I replaced the receiver.

I waited, still sitting on the edge of the bed, and a long time seemed to pass.

When the soft knock came I could think only how odd it was that of all the people I knew in New York it should be Steve who was with me at the end. I remembered him reeling out of Barney's, posturing before me at his party, angering me with his irrepressible sexual appraisals whenever we had met.

I opened the door.

His blunt features were blurred with shock. His blue eyes were bloodshot. His wide straight arrogant shoulders were bowed with grief.

"I had to come," he said, his lips hardly able to form the words. "I had to see you." And as he groped to take my hands in his I saw that his suit was streaked with blood.

PART FOUR

Steve
The Sportsman

1926–1929

Chapter One

I

"He was assassinated," I said.

She burst into tears. She cried and cried. I had to remind myself that this was slick smart hardboiled Dinah Slade, adventuress, troublemaker and gold-digger de luxe.

"I loved him!" she sobbed. "I did, I did! Oh, I want him back, he's got to come back, I can't believe he's dead!"

"Believe it, honey." I sat her down on the couch and started opening closets. "Where's the liquor in this place?"

"There isn't any," she said, sobbing louder than ever.

"For Christ's sake!" Calling my bootlegger, I told him to send his boy over at once with a bottle of rye. Then I dug out my hip flask and filled a couple of tooth mugs to the brim.

She became calmer and I became number. When the rye arrived we started speaking to each other again.

"I knew it was going to happen," she whispered. "I even telephoned *her* last night—"

"I know. That's why I'm here. Drink up, honey, and let's exchange a little information before I put you on the ship to England. I have to know exactly what you've been up to."

"And I have to know exactly how he died." She was rock-steady now, her voice cold.

"Maybe later."

"No. Now."

I shrugged, opened the bottle of rye and topped up the tooth mugs. "All right," I said abruptly, "this is the way it was. . . ."

II

But I didn't tell her the way it was. I wasn't going to give her the satisfaction of knowing she'd reduced Paul to rubble and I wasn't going to mention a conspiracy when I knew she was a close friend of the Claytons. Maybe she'd thought Paul had left her a fortune in his new will and had seen the chance of grabbing the money before he got wind of her plan to give him the gate. Since the world had gone crazy I felt I could believe anything, and anyway any woman who could twist Paul Van Zale around her finger so successfully had to be treated with maximum suspicion.

I set down the bottle of rye. "He called me this morning," I said. "I was staying in the city. He invited me over for a swim and we had breakfast together. . . ."

My voice recited the facts, but my memory saw beyond them to a scene I could never have described to her. I was in the pool, the famous indoor Van Zale pool with the gilded skylights and the miniature palm trees and the gallons of heated water glinting beneath the central chandelier. Paul and I had had a race and I had beaten him by half a length. That was when I knew he had to be sick, and the next moment he proved it by starting to talk like a maniac.

He said his world was falling apart, that his life was finished and that he had no future. Somehow I got him out of the pool and into the changing room. I could hardly believe that this was Paul, smooth, efficient, well-organized Paul Van Zale who arranged his personal life with the fluency of a fast pool operator jacking up the price of shares on the ticker. Then he revealed the final horror. He was out of his middle-aged mind over this expensive little jazz-baby with the plump hips, the classical education and the keep-your-hands-off-me-you-brute English manners.

He poured out the whole story. I was so appalled I just stood there like one of those dumb Greek statues he used to like so much. It was only when he said he was going to throw up everything and run after her that I gasped for air, found my voice and ripped into him for all I was worth.

"You're crazy!" I shouted. "Insane! This goddamned little girl runs three thousand miles when Elizabeth Clayton mentions the word 'epilepsy'—she doesn't want to know you, Paul!"

"She'd been deceived—she was hurt and shocked—but if I were to go after her . . ."

He was white. His hands were shaking. I wondered if he was going to be ill, but I knew I'd be doing him no favor if I softened my attack. I had to dam up this craziness and bludgeon him back to his senses.

"So go after her!" I yelled. "But what about Sylvia? What are you going to tell her? What are you going to say? What do you think it'll do to her? *What about Sylvia, Paul?*"

He broke down. He sat stark naked on the bench in the changing room, put his hands over his eyes like a little kid and shuddered with sobs. I'd never been more shocked in all my life.

"You poor bastard." I draped a towel around him awkwardly and lit him a cigarette. "Here, have a smoke."

He took a puff and choked. He wasn't used to cigarettes. "I love Sylvia," he said.

"Of course you do," I said, "and she's the right wife for you, as you've been busy telling me for God knows how many years. Now listen, Paul. You're going to get over this. Remember your smart sane sensible advice to me and all your other people on the subject of women."

"All that trash I talked!" he said, the cigarette shaking in his fingers. "All that shit!"

I was glad to hear him use an obscenity. It meant he was toughening up.

"Let's get dressed," I said. "You'll feel better when you've had some breakfast."

"I can't eat."

"Crap. Stop behaving like a half-baked poet. You've got to eat or you'll be ill."

I shoved him into his clothes, pulled on my own and marched him off to eat in the huge dining room which was littered with dark sideboards and yards of velvet drapes and the Sargent portrait of his daughter Vicky smiling down at the Tudor banqueting table. I had half a melon, three eggs sunny side up, bacon, sausage, rolls and coffee. He had a slice of unbuttered toast and a cup of tea, but halfway through the slice he said, "Sorry I made such an exhibition of myself," and I knew he was on the mend.

He had just put some butter on the remaining half of his toast when Sylvia came in and ruined everything.

"Oh, Paul—excuse me, Steve—why is Wilson waiting outside with the car? You promised me you wouldn't go to the office this morning!"

"I've changed my mind."

"Oh, but—" She broke off, harassed. She was one of those women who look like an illustration out of some old-fashioned storybook for ladies, all pastel colors and pure thoughts and washed-out delicate features. I liked her; she was a nice lady, but she rang no bedroom bells on my particular switchboard. My wife Caroline used to make great capital out of the fact that Sylvia was the one woman Paul would never discuss with me, but in my opinion the reason for that was obvious: there was nothing to discuss. In bed she would be placid and passive, dull and dutiful, and as I considered this picture with a yawn I found it easier to understand why Paul had dabbled with a red-hot, smart-aleck little go-getter like Dinah Slade.

"Paul, you promised!"

"My dear, there's no need to get hysterical over an anonymous phone call! Steve, reassure Sylvia I'm in no danger of assassination, would you?" He was upset again, his fingers drumming on the table, his eyes glancing at the clock as if he longed to escape. I saw at once that he felt so damned guilty in her presence that he hardly knew how to remain in the room, and I tried to cut off the conversation as swiftly as possible.

"Forget it, Sylvia. The police know all about the parade, and Bob Peterson and I'll be with Paul."

"But—" The wretched woman was going to persist. I jumped to my feet. "Come on, Paul!" I said. "Time to go!"

"Paul . . ." She clung to him. "Please don't go."

For the first time since she had entered the room he looked at her directly. I saw his face soften.

"I want to," he said.

"But you don't have to!"

"It's what I want."

They stood together for a moment and then she draped her arms around his neck. Rolling my eyes despairingly at the ceiling, I walked out into the hall.

I thought he'd give in to her, but he didn't. He crawled wearily after me into the car, and as we set off down Fifth Avenue he pulled a letter out of his pocket and started turning it over and over in his hands. I glanced down at the envelope and saw the single word "DINAH" printed on it. I could have groaned out loud.

"I wrote this last night when I couldn't sleep," he said. "I thought I'd give it to her when I saw her off. Her ship sails this afternoon."

"Uh . . . yeah. Paul, don't you think it would be smarter if—"

"Maybe I should keep it for a few days," he said uncertainly. "I wrote it when I was very upset."

I wanted to tell him to tear it up but was afraid he would immediately rush to give it to her.

"That's a sensible decision," I said. "Lock it up for a couple of weeks and then see if you still want to mail it."

There was a silence. Together we looked down at her name, and against all my better judgment I was fascinated. No woman ever told Paul Van Zale goodbye, and suddenly I had a hint of her glamour, although just what that glamour was I was damned if I could decide.

The car purred on downtown. Somewhere south of Canal Street Paul said, "What a wonderful summer it was!"

"Hell, it's not even over yet," I said, conscious of the sweat beneath my collar. The air was so humid that a sheet of blotting paper would have fallen apart, and the temperature had to be well on the way to ninety.

"Oh, I didn't mean this summer," he said. "I meant the summer of '22. My summer at Mallingham."

"Hm." I couldn't make up my mind whether it was best to let him be maudlin or whether I should clamp down on the sentimentality right away. The car swung off Broadway unexpectedly into the network of streets north of Wall and I remembered we were heading for the bank's back entrance in Willow Alley.

The alley was teeming with police, and when the car stopped outside the door set in the high spike-topped wall Bob Peterson jumped out with Paul's keys. The triple locks clicked, the door swung wide, Peterson and the police took a final glance around the rooftops for any sign of a sniper, and I got out of the car.

"All clear, sir," said Peterson to Paul.

Paul stood in that grimy sweltering little alley. It was almost as if he was waiting for the sniper who wasn't there.

"Let's go, Paul," I said, touching his arm.

We went through the door in the wall and crossed the patio to the garden doors of his office. Bart Mayers was already holding them open for us and we walked through into the library. The other half of the double room, the drawing room, was closed off to keep the library cooler.

"How are the Citizens for Militant Socialism, Mayers?" said Paul to his personal assistant as his chief secretary, Miss Schulz, entered with the coffee pot.

"Lively, sir," said Mayers, who was a nice kid not long out of Yale. He was supposed to be bright but he was always forgetting to do things, and I suspected that the only reason he had lasted so long in the job was because Paul had found his fresh-faced innocence such a pleasant change from Terence O'Reilly. "They paraded down Wall Street as scheduled and now they're milling around on the corner of Willow with their banners."

"Mr. Clayton hasn't been arrested, I hope? Good. All right, Mayers, that's all for now."

After Paul arrived at his office he followed a set routine. He would spend ten minutes drinking coffee while he inspected his mail, and then he would summon his assistants and deal with as much business as possible before the partners' meeting at nine-thirty.

"God, it's hot!" I muttered again, trying to summon the energy to tackle the stairs to my office.

"If it's as hot as yesterday we'll have to send everyone home early. Yes, what is it, O'Reilly?"

"Excuse me, sir," said Paul's fixer, pussyfooting into the room, "but one of the marchers has just hurled a brick through the front window and Bruce Clayton's so upset that he wants to see you in person to apologize. Shall I send him in?"

"Of course! I'm never too busy to see Bruce."

"I'll get hold of Peterson," I said at once. Peterson was always dismissed as soon as Paul had arrived at the office. "In the circumstances you shouldn't see Bruce alone, Paul."

"Oh for God's sake, stay yourself if you're so worried about me! Anyway, you may as well stay because I want to go over that memorandum for the Goldman, Sachs meeting at eleven. Pull up a chair."

O'Reilly was stock still by the door. "Pardon me, sir, but before you discuss the memorandum I wonder if I could just get Steve's approval on the latest brochures for the investment trust. They have to be at the printers' by ten."

"Yes, yes, yes!" Paul found Terence O'Reilly just as irritating as I did. "All right, let's keep the printers happy, but come back right away, would you, Steve? We've got to go over that memo."

"Sure, Paul." I looked back at him as I left the room, but he didn't look up. He had taken the letter to Dinah Slade from his pocket again and was turning it over and over in his hands as if he still couldn't decide what to do with it.

"Come on, Steve," said Terence O'Reilly, laying some long thin fingers determinedly on my arm.

I shook him off, strode ahead of him across the back lobby and bumped into Bruce Clayton coming the other way. He muttered something to me. Not bothering to hide my distaste, I grunted an acknowledgment. He was looking pale, but those intellectuals with their high white foreheads and soft delicate hands never look as if they get any exercise.

"Mr. Van Zale will see you, Bruce," said O'Reilly, and he added to the guard who was sticking to Bruce like glue, "You can wait out here."

"Has he been searched?" I demanded.

"Don't be ridiculous, Steve. Bruce wouldn't carry a gun if you paid him. Do you want coffee in my office?"

"No. What's this big deal about the brochures anyway?" I said annoyed. O'Reilly was officially in charge of advertising and public relations, but that was just a front. Unofficially he was still in charge of the public relations which had to be kept private. Paul never dealt directly with gangsters, but inevitably in big business there were times when we had to pick our way along their little primrose paths.

"Well, you're the one who's been making the big deal about the brochures," said O'Reilly, "and we all know the investment trust's your baby. You'd be the first to complain if the stuff went to the printers without your approval."

We went into his office, which was just by the stairs on the third floor. I flung myself down in a chair.

"That's odd," he said. "Where did I put that file?"

I was just about to tell him that I didn't have all day to waste watching him play hunt-the-file when all hell broke loose below us. The drowsy silence was split by a storm of gunfire, and a second later Miss Schulz started to scream.

III

The blood was everywhere, soaking the carpet, drenching the desk, spattering the white marble fireplace. I knelt by his body and the blood was staining my clothes, smearing my hands, even seeping under my fingernails as I searched for the heartbeat. The room seemed to swim in blood and the blood became a red mist which thickened before my eyes.

Bruce Clayton was shivering against the wall.

"You sonofabitch!" I shouted, out of my mind with shock and pain, and rushed forward to beat him to pulp.

I never reached him. I fell over a second body and crashed into another pool of blood. Over by the wall Bruce Clayton started to retch. Outside, Paul's secretary was screaming again. People were moving like stricken shadows in the doorway. Someone said, "Oh, my God . . ." Someone else vomited. Someone kept saying, "Call the police! Call the police!" and the guard who had been waiting for Bruce waved a revolver impotently. As I struggled to my feet I saw Bob Peterson, dumb with the agony of his failure, kneeling beside Paul's body.

The cops came crashing in.

Nobody could figure out what had happened. Bruce Clayton was dragged backward and forward. Someone passed around some brandy. Some unknown time later I found myself in the other half of the double room with my five surviving partners, two police lieutenants, one precinct captain and Bruce. The folding doors had been closed to blot out the blood. It was hotter than high noon in Death Valley.

"I'm innocent," said Bruce Clayton, teeth chattering. "I want to call my lawyer."

"But who the hell's the second corpse in there?"

"A man called Krasnov."

"But who shot who?"

"Don't answer that, Bruce," said my partner Charley Blair.

The police let Bruce call his lawyer. By that time the press were howling on the doorstep, and after a rapid partners' conference Lewis Carson, whose Hollywood profile always photographed well, was dispatched to make some kind of statement. The other tasks were less easily assigned, but within minutes Charley had agreed to calm down the employees, Clay Linden had volunteered to be the liaison man with the police, and Martin Cookson and old Walter Maynard had offered to handle the important incoming calls from the famous names of Wall Street.

I got the dog's job of breaking the news to Sylvia.

I balked but was overruled. I had been the partner closest to Paul and one of his earliest protégés. As far as my other partners were concerned I was as good as one of the family.

I went uptown.

I tried to think clearly but could get no further than the basic assumption that Paul had been shot by the Bolshevik, who had in turn been shot by Bruce. What Bruce, who supposedly abhorred violence, was doing toting a gun only his lawyer now knew for sure. And how Krasnov had managed to get into the building was a mystery which I suspected was already scaring the pants off us all. Paul killed by a lone assassin was just another sensational news item. Paul killed by a crazy Bolshevik who had got into the building with inside help was an investment banking house's kiss of death. I knew, just as we all knew, that Van Zale's couldn't survive another scandal like the Salzedo affair.

I was on Paul's doorstep before I realized what a state I was in, with brandy on my breath and blood on my clothes. I still had no idea what I was going to say to Sylvia and could only pray she wouldn't have hysterics. I didn't even have a clean handkerchief to offer her.

The butler let me in, and one look at his face told me some punk of a journalist had already broadcast the news from the rooftops. He said the rumor had reached the house ten minutes before and Sylvia had just spoken to Charley Blair to confirm the story.

I waited. She came. She was very still and tearless. I was the one who cried.

She was really nice about it. She was such a lady, I'd always liked Sylvia. I knew she wouldn't tell anyone, knew she'd never mention it again. It made me feel close to her.

"Oh, Steve," she said when I tried to apologize, "can't you see how glad I am that there was at least someone who genuinely cared for Paul?"

After a while we mentioned Bruce.

"He'll get off," I said. "The Claytons can buy the best lawyers in town. He'll claim he shot the Red in self-defense."

"And did he, Steve?"

We looked at each other. "Well, if it wasn't self-defense," I said, "he was firing to avenge Paul's murder."

"There's another possibility," she said.

"No," I said, shaking my head. "Definitely not. No other possibility. None."

"If Bruce killed the man to silence him—if there was a conspiracy—"

"No, Sylvia. That just can't be. Out of the question."

"But she said they were all in it—"

"She? Who, in God's name?"

"Oh, Steve, I told Paul the call was anonymous because I didn't want to mention her name, but—"

"Jesus Christ," I said, "not Dinah Slade . . ."

IV

". . . So I didn't mention Terence's name to Sylvia," said Dinah Slade abruptly, "and I didn't mention the letter linking him to Bruce's parade. The only name I dropped was Greg Da Costa's."

I walked to the window of her Plaza suite. She had drawn the shades to keep out the sun, but the opulent décor still looked as overheated as melting frosting on a birthday cake. For a while I stood motionless, the shade drawn aside as I looked across the park.

"Did you know that Terence was in love with Sylvia?" said Dinah at last.

"Sure. Paul told me. It seemed kind of a joke at the time."

"A joke?" She looked at me incredulously.

"Yeah—that Sir Galahad had become Sir Lancelot. Terence was never interested in girls."

She laughed in my face. "He just made his passes more discreetly than you do, that's all!"

I was amazed. "You mean he made a pass at you?"

"Of course he did! What did you think?"

"Jesus! Did you accept?"

"No, you unspeakable man, I didn't. Give me some more of that awful whisky, please. . . . Thanks. I suppose it's impossible for someone like you to believe that I was absolutely faithful to Paul."

"Honey, I don't care whether you lived like a nun or laid every guy in town. I'm just interested in this goddamned Terence O'Reilly. Now let's go over it all again."

We went over it all again, the unholy trinity of Clayton, O'Reilly and Da Costa, the innocent letter with its odor of conspiracy, the strong likelihood that O'Reilly had believed Dinah when she told him Paul would never leave his wife.

"Well, that gives Terence a motive," I agreed, "and Bruce is too nuts to need one, but I can't see Greg Da Costa, who has to rank as the world's best sponger, kissing a lush annuity goodbye. That doesn't add up at all."

"But with or without Da Costa there must have been a conspiracy."

That was the last thing I wanted to hear anyone saying out loud. I gave her a quick hard look. I no longer believed she was involved in any plot to kill Paul. Her grief had seemed genuine, and her manner, once she had recovered, had seemed open and honest. But this was a tough girl, and I knew I would never feel completely at ease about her until she had proved to me beyond any shadow of a doubt that she had a strong motive for keeping Paul alive. Whichever way you looked you couldn't escape the fact that she had been having intellectual jam sessions with Bruce Clayton whenever she hadn't been getting drunk with Terence O'Reilly.

"You don't like that word 'conspiracy,' do you?" she said, watching me. "And don't think I can't guess why. If a high-level employee like O'Reilly organized Paul's murder the scandal would be very damaging to the bank. If a conspiracy exists you'll sweep it under the rug and Paul's murderers will escape scot free."

"Not while I'm at Willow and Wall." I sat down beside her. "But you're right about the rug. I'm going to ask you not to talk to the police."

"Not to talk to the police!" She was horrified. I had forgotten she was English. No suggestion could have shocked her more.

"Honey . . ." I groped for the words to bridge our cultures. "This is Jimmy Walker's New York, not King George's London. This is where it's every man for himself and the devil takes those who make one dumb decision. Now here are the facts: Bruce Clayton can buy his way out of trouble. Greg Da Costa has already got himself stashed in Mexico. Terence O'Reilly's smart enough to outwit what passes for law in this town. The police can't get these men. All they can do is muddy the bank's name until we all end up panhandling on the Bowery—and that'll mean victory for the murderers. If the bank's ruined they'll have got what they wanted."

"But—"

"I'll get them," I said. "It'll take about five years, but I'll get every damned one of them. Paul was the older brother I never had and he believed in me when everyone else thought I was nothing but a high-class juvenile delinquent. I'll see his murderers into hell even if I have to tap the big dog on the shoulder to let them in. What was that dog called?" I added, absent-mindedly refilling my tooth mug.

"Cerberus."

Of course she couldn't resist the chance to show off her classical education, but when I saw how her reply had disturbed her I realized she had reminded herself of Paul.

She glanced around the room and shuddered violently. "If only I were at home," she whispered. "If only I were at—" She stopped.

She couldn't have looked more horrified if she'd met old Cerberus face to face.

"For Christ's sake!" Half the rye in my tooth mug slopped onto the carpet. "What's the matter?"

"Steve, did Paul sign that new will he was making?"

"Yes, he did. Why?"

"Oh my God," she said faintly and passed right out.

It turned out she had the best motive in the world for keeping Paul alive. Having owned her beloved Mallingham since 1922, Paul had agreed to convey it to her, and Dinah had been negotiating a fair market price to offer him. Because the conveyance had been imminent they had agreed that all mention of the property should be omitted from the new will.

"So the house goes to Cornelius!" I said. "Well, he'll sell, won't he? What's the big deal?"

But for some reason she seemed to regard Paul's little great-nephew as a cross between Frankenstein's monster and Jack the Ripper.

"That little pansy?" I scoffed. "Forget it! He's just a kid still wet behind the ears. I'll fix him."

"Would you?" She looked as though she could pass out again with relief.

"Honey, trust me. I have the Van Zale lawyer in my hip pocket. I'll find the deed to Mallingham—it's just the deed conveying the place to Paul, you say? You've got all the other stuff? Great—and once I find it you'll get the transfer of title before you can sing all the verses of 'Yes, We Have No Bananas.' However,"—I wasn't one to let a golden opportunity pass by—"let's make it a real business deal. You keep your mouth shut about the conspiracy and I'll see that Cornelius never knows he's the owner of Mallingham."

I thought she might be insulted by this display of muscle but she was so worried about Cornelius that she swallowed the deal whole.

"Great," I said. "We're in business, honey—I wonder why I keep calling you 'honey.'" I was trying to screw the cap back on my hip flask, which I had just refilled. The cap kept missing the top and sliding down my wrist. I paused to summon all my powers of concentration.

"You're the sort of man who doesn't see women as individuals," she said nastily, knocking back the rye in her tooth mug. "You probably never call a woman by her own name."

"Wrong," I said. "I call my wife Cal." The cap finally made it onto the hip flask. I stood up, fumbled in my pockets and produced a key. "I want you to get out of here and wait in my apartment until it's time to go down to the ship," I said. "I don't want anyone asking you awkward questions. Where are Mary and Alan?"

"They should be arriving any moment. Where's your apartment?"

"I'll write down the address. I'd wait to take you all there myself, but I've got to get back to the bank."

I gave her the address. It was dark in the suite's small hallway and as we were both swaying with liquor I'll never be sure who brushed who first, but I held her for a long moment and she clung to me. It was quiet. We didn't kiss.

At last she said in a small voice, "I'm sorry I was always so nasty to you."

I laughed. "I hardly encouraged you to be nice!"

"You're not as I thought you were."

"It's hard to see people properly," I said, "when there's a big shadow blocking the light."

We were silent. It was a good ten seconds before I opened the door into the corridor.

"Will I ever see you again?" she said in a smaller voice than ever, and I knew that the shock was hitting her again, making her feel frightened and alone.

"Why, sure!" I said, taking the hand she offered me and kissing her on the cheek. "I'll come riding over the horizon someday on my white horse to bring back your deed to Mallingham!"

I saw the courage flow back into her as she laughed. I saw the tilt of her chin and the zest in her eyes and the curve of her warm wide mouth. I saw the spark which had set fire to Paul.

"I'll roll out the red carpet!" she said. "And I'll open a magnum of champagne!"

"That's the best deal I've heard yet!" I was still holding her hand. I gave it one last squeeze. "Take care of yourself, Dinah. Stay in touch. So long."

"Goodbye, Steve," she said as I walked off down the corridor, and as I turned the corner to the elevators she called after me softly, "Thanks for remembering my name."

Chapter Two

I

Avoiding the front entrance of the bank, I talked my way past the cops and opened the Willow Alley door with my set of partners' keys. The bodies had been removed from Paul's office. Two maintenance men were busy taking up the ruined carpet, and in the back lobby I had to stop to wipe the sweat from my forehead before I toiled upstairs to the second floor.

I reached Charley Blair's office. The door closed as I was yanked inside. The six surviving partners of P. C. Van Zale and Company were at last alone to let their back hair down and have hysterics.

"Jesus Christ," said Clay Linden, "what a catastrophe."

Nobody bothered to deny it.

"How did poor Sylvia take the news, Steve?" Charley Blair was visibly upset.

"How do you think?" I collapsed into the nearest chair. "What the hell's been going on here while I've been spreading the bad news uptown?"

"I've been talking to the police commissioner," said Lewis Carson, "and the district attorney. I even talked to the mayor." Lewis was such a snob that he managed to make Jimmy Walker sound like a creature from another planet.

Eventually I learned that the police were still busy downstairs interrogating employees in the great hall, that the Street's army of baying press hounds had now been augmented by crowds of sightseeing ghouls, and that the market had declined three points. The leading bankers had all called to express their horror and sympathy.

"What did you tell them?" I said.

"What could I possibly tell them?" said Martin Cookson, who had fielded most of the calls. "I said the assassin was a stray Bolshevist maniac who had been killed immediately afterward."

We all looked at one another.

"God, is there any coffee?" I said. "My head feels like the inside of an alki-cooker."

Charley rang the bell for his secretary.

Sagging back in my chair, I gazed vacantly around the room. Charley's office was large and comfortable, like a room in one of the famous clubs uptown. There were leather armchairs around a woodburning fireplace, a solid mahogany desk in front of solid mahogany bookshelves, and nineteenth-century English fox-hunting prints on the austerely papered walls. Charley was large and comfortable, like his office, and had silver hair above a round friendly sociable face. He and Lewis were both in their midfifties, but Lewis was everything Charley was not, stuffy, humorless and aloof. Jason Da Costa had been notorious for selecting partners who looked like caricatures of the Eastern Seaboard Yankee aristocracy. Even old Walter Maynard, whom Jay had inherited from Lucius Clyde, had the same blue eyes, the same distinguished features and the same elegant shade of silver hair.

Paul's men were different. Paul had believed in youth, so we were much younger than Jay's men, and Paul had also taken a perverse pleasure in picking men who looked as if they never went near a bank except to cash a check. Clay looked like a salesman, the slick expensive California type with gleaming hair and sharp modern clothes and a mind like a cash register. Martin, with his thinning hair and owlish spectacles, looked like a small-town college professor, the kind that would hardly know the difference between a nickel and a medieval groat. And I looked like a Marine fresh from bawling out recruits in boot camp—or so my wife used to tell me in her less complimentary moments.

I was the youngest, but I had the seniority among Paul's men. I had worked for Paul since the age of eighteen, while Clay and Martin had not entered the firm until after the merger with Clyde, Da Costa. I had also been Paul's favorite, and as soon as he had made me a junior partner and taken me to Europe with him in 1917 I had known he was grooming me to be his successor. However, no one could have foreseen his dying when his contemporaries Charley and Lewis were still in their prime, and I couldn't quite see how I was going to muscle past the two of them immediately to grab the senior partner's chair. I'd have to lie low for a while as I figured out how to shuffle my cards into a winning hand.

The coffee arrived, interrupting my thoughts.

Charley was engaged in an elaborate reconstruction of events, I discovered as I plugged myself into the conversation again.

". . . so anyway," he was saying, "the parade became more violent than poor Bruce intended and he even had to take a gun away from one of his supporters, who was brandishing it at a policeman. At that moment another maniac tossed a brick through the front window and Bruce at once decided to apologize to Paul. Just as he was in the middle of his apology this anarchist Krasnov, who had been hiding in the closed-off half of Paul's office, burst through the folding doors and started firing. Bruce, who purely by chance had this gun he'd removed earlier from his supporter—"

"You don't really believe all this, do you, Charley?" said Clay like a salesman sneering at a rival's inferior product. "We're New Yorkers, not little old ladies from Dubuque."

I made a split-second decision. We all obviously suspected a conspiracy. We were all, equally obviously, scared silly by our suspicions. Therefore the partner who took the lead in unraveling the conspiracy, neutralizing it and sweeping it under the rug was going to come out on top. I had information from Sylvia and Dinah which no one else had. To share that information, I now saw clearly, would be to throw away the aces from my winning hand.

"Don't be dumb, Clay," I said. "So long as there's some kind of yarn for the police to swallow, what does it matter what we believe? The six of us know Bruce was nuts enough to have set this up, but once you start talking about a conspiracy instead of a stray anarchist we're in trouble."

"Steve's right," said Charley. "As far as this bank's concerned, 'conspiracy' has to be the most obscene word in the English language."

"Most distasteful," said Lewis grandly.

"Quite unthinkable," muttered old Walter into his moustaches.

The old guard had spoken, but the new guard were beginning to unscramble their brains.

"That's all very well," said Martin, "but—"

"You're all nuts," said Clay. "If anyone's going to believe this myth that the Russian acted alone, we've got to explain how he got into the building. So what the hell are we going to say? That he coasted across the sky on a brace of reindeer and let himself down the chimney?"

"And anyhow," said Martin, polishing his spectacles furiously and looking more like an academic than ever, "just how did this guy get in? Even if we admit between ourselves that he was in league with Bruce, there's no way Bruce could have slipped Krasnov into the building. There has to be another person involved. There has to be a conspiracy."

The dam broke. Everyone roared with rage and fright. I was just wondering furiously if I dared keep the information about O'Reilly to myself any longer when there was a knock at the door.

"Yes?" called Charley, scarlet-faced and perspiring heavily.

The door opened. We all stared.

"Excuse me, gentlemen," said Terence O'Reilly, "but I've come to confess."

II

My first reaction was that he was crazy as a coon dog. My second, when I realized he hadn't come to confess at all, was that he was clever as a cobra—and just about as harmless. I should have realized as soon as I saw the way the plot was shaping up that the conspirators, who were as anxious as we were to transform Krasnov into a lone assassin, would have to provide an explanation for his undeniable presence in the building.

"I was responsible for a breach of security which has ended in tragedy," said O'Reilly, "and I wish to tender my resignation."

We watched him in silence. Even Clay had locked up his California manners in the presence of an outsider and presented a conventional Connecticut Yankee front. Martin replaced his spectacles. Old Walter looked shocked. Lewis wore his stuffiest expression. I was still boggling. It was left to Charley to say mildly as he wiped the sweat from his forehead with a sodden handkerchief, "There's no need to be so melodramatic, O'Reilly. We've had enough melodrama for today. Come in and close the door. Is it my imagination, fellows," he added to his partners, "or is it really about a hundred and ten in the shade?"

That defused O'Reilly nicely. We sat around in our leather armchairs discussing the weather like a bunch of pseudo-English gentlemen while O'Reilly was left standing by the door. At last when we had finally made it clear to O'Reilly that he was a first-generation Irish-American in the presence of a bunch of Yankee aristocrats, Charley said with all the nice-guy charm for which he was famous, "I'm sorry, O'Reilly. Bring up a chair and sit down. You look exhausted. Now what's all this about a breach of security?"

O'Reilly was the one who was sweating now, but he kept both his dignity and his nerve.

"Thank you, Mr. Blair, but I'd prefer to stand," he said. "I wanted to explain that I knew this man Krasnov. Every weekend this summer Bruce and Grace Clayton have held open house for various intellectuals and political extremists, and since I was a friend of the Claytons, Mr. Van Zale suggested it might be wise if I stayed in close touch with them to keep an eye on what was going on. I reported to Mr. Van Zale on the society Citizens for Militant Socialism. Krasnov was a member. I thought he was unstable, but Bruce so abhorred violence that I decided the C.M.S. presented no serious threat to Mr. Van Zale's safety."

"An inspired judgment!" drawled Clay. "Just what the hell are you leading up to?"

O'Reilly flicked the sweat from his forehead and plowed on. I could tell what rough going it was because I was sitting behind him and could see his hands clenching and unclenching behind his back.

"Krasnov came to see me yesterday afternoon," he said. "It was late—about a quarter of six. He asked for me at the front entrance and they sent an office boy up to my room. I went down. My first reaction was to get him out of the building, but he said he had some information about the parade, so I took him up to my office. It then turned out he had no information but just wanted me to get him a job. Bruce had evidently exaggerated the importance of my position at Van Zale's. When I said it was impossible for me to get a job in the bank for a known Bolshevik, he tried to tell me he was no longer a Communist, but of course I didn't believe a word of it. The man was obviously unbalanced. I got him out of my office at last and took him downstairs to the back lobby. Then I opened the doors into the great hall, said, 'That's the way out,' and left him. I was expecting an important call from Chicago at six and I wanted to get back to my desk. I realize now I should never have left him, but—"

"Disgraceful!" thundered Lewis and Walter together.

"Jesus Christ!" snorted Clay.

"Wait a minute," said Martin. "The doorman in the front lobby must have recorded Krasnov's entry into the building. Why did no one realize he hadn't left?"

"They did." O'Reilly's hands tightened behind his back again. "The doorman went off duty at six. At six-twenty, when I finished my call from Chicago, the night watchman sent someone up to check if Krasnov was still with me and I said he'd gone. It seemed obvious to me that Krasnov had left when everyone was leaving the building at six and hadn't bothered to sign himself out. I never thought twice about it at the time."

"Well, it's easy to see now what happened," said Charley heavily. "Krasnov hid himself somewhere—perhaps in that broom closet by the stairs—and later when the coast was clear he slipped into the drawing-room half of Paul's office. I understand a map of the ground floor was found in his pocket. He would have had to hide again when the night watchman made his rounds, but there's a coat closet in that far room and it would have been easy to lie low there."

There was a pause. O'Reilly had certainly come up with a story supporting the lone-assassin theory, and now if luck was running his way the Van Zale partners would gobble up his story in a frenzy of relief and prepare to convince the world there had been no conspiracy. Unfortunately luck wasn't running all his way. I knew that Dinah and Paul had been in Paul's office the previous night, and neither of them had noticed a stray anarchist soft-shoeing around looking for something to do.

I clamped my mouth shut. Let the other partners believe him. Let them spread the word and save the bank. The bank had to come first. But when the danger was past I'd turn that conspiracy inside out and emerge top dog at Van Zale's.

I was just congratulating myself on my iron self-control when O'Reilly said outrageously in a meek little voice, "I'll carry the memory of this mistake to my grave, I swear it, gentlemen. Mr. Van Zale was like a father to me."

I leaped to my feet. "You sonofabitch!" I shouted at him as they all jumped out of their skins with shock. "Get the hell out of here before I knock the shit out of you!"

Of course everyone thought I had lost control because he hadn't bothered to see Krasnov off the premises. None of them suspected him. He had been one of Paul's people, a favored protégé. No one knew, as I knew, that he had wanted Paul's wife.

"Easy, Steve," said Martin, grabbing my arm.

"Get out," said Clay to Terence.

"Yes, leave us, O'Reilly," said Charley.

The ranks were closing. Someone opened the door. O'Reilly was put out, like a cat who had forgotten his housetraining and made a mess. The door closed again. Charley poured me another cup of coffee. Lewis patted my shoulder with stagey sympathy. Clay offered me a cigarette.

"Sorry about that, fellows," I said when I had my stiff upper lip firmly back in place. "I know we all hate scenes. The truth is, I never could stand that guy Terence O'Reilly."

Someone made an Irish joke to cheer me up. We all exchanged thin Anglo-Saxon smiles. At last Lewis said in relief, "Well, at least we now have enough evidence to convince the public that Krasnov acted alone."

I began to fear for my self-control again. I got up at once. "Will you all excuse me for a moment?" I said. "I feel pretty beaten up and I'm going to have to lie down."

Everyone made sympathetic noises and I staggered along the corridor, shut myself in my room and reached automatically for my hip flask.

After a while I began to think more clearly. After a longer while I felt bothered. Something wasn't adding up. Somewhere along the line I'd missed a connection.

I marshaled my thoughts as carefully as a snake charmer collecting friends from the snake pit. I was almost one hundred percent certain O'Reilly's story was a lie, but why was a lie needed? How in hell *had* Krasnov got into the building?

I considered O'Reilly's story again, just to make sure I didn't believe it, and the more I considered it the more implausible it became.

The truth was there was no way O'Reilly could have guaranteed that Krasnov would remain undiscovered if he had stayed in the building overnight. The night watchman might well have called a guard to search the building when he found there was no evidence Krasnov had checked out. Krasnov might have skipped nimbly from closet to closet, but every time he moved he would be taking a risk. The night watchman or the guard made regular rounds. The cleaning women arrived soon after midnight and rattled around for a time. And someone might have been working unusually late or—like Paul and Dinah—visiting after hours. As a story explaining Krasnov's presence in the building O'Reilly's rigmarole was just about plausible, but as a plan of action guaranteeing that the assassin was in the right place at the right time it was riddled with the possibility of failure.

I pretended I was O'Reilly evolving the perfect plan for getting Krasnov into the building, but I didn't have to pretend hard, because of course there was only one way. I don't know why I spent so long beating around the bush pretending I couldn't think of it. Fear of facing the truth, probably.

I swiveled in my chair and looked out the window. My room was directly above Paul's office, and when I looked out I could see across the patio to the door in the wall, the bank's back entrance into Willow Alley. There was no access to the building from the roof. The front was guarded night and day. The top of the high back wall was spiked and glassed and wired with the most elaborate alarms. The door, with its locks which would have driven even the best safecracker to suicide, was the only way Krasnov could have entered One Willow Street.

I was O'Reilly again, pussyfooting around setting the scene. The night watchman on his first round would have turned on the burglar alarms covering the doors which opened from Paul's office into the patio, but O'Reilly, pretending to work late, would have run down later to switch them off. No problem. Afterward O'Reilly would have gone home, briefed Krasnov for the last time and given him the keys of the Willow Alley door plus the key of the patio doors. Krasnov would have delayed entering the building for as long as possible but would probably have walked in while it was still dark and stashed himself in the drawing-room closet. Still no problem.

But one problem was insurmountable. O'Reilly could never have had access to those keys. Only the partners were allowed to use the Willow Alley entrance and enter the building through Paul's office, and only the partners had the keys which opened the door in the wall.

I told myself O'Reilly must have had a set of keys himself when he was Paul's personal assistant. There could be no other explanation. But I had to find out for sure. I had to know.

"Get Terence O'Reilly down here," I said to my secretary. "I want to talk to him."

III

He tippy-toed reluctantly into the room and paused about one inch past the threshold. "You wanted to see me, Steve?"

"Yeah. Sorry I lost my temper just now. Take a seat. Drink?"

"No, thanks." He sat stiffly on the extreme edge of the client's chair. His polish was worn and chipped, like crockery which has seen better days. His hard bright light eyes were dull with exhaustion. His mouth drooped sullenly.

"Before you quit and wander off into the blue," I said, "I'd like to fix a time when I can go over your files with you. I don't expect that kid Herbert Mayers knows much, does he?"

He hadn't expected to discuss business. I saw him struggle to focus his thoughts. "Bart understands the filing system. He knows where everything is. Of course, there's some hush stuff he doesn't know about, but I can fill you in on that."

"Does Mayers know the safe combinations?"

"Sure. You forget he's had my old job for over a year."

"Does he have all the keys—all the keys I would expect you to have on your office key ring?"

"All except the keys for my own file cabinets, but I'll turn those in to you before I leave."

"Swell. By the way, do you have the keys to the Willow Alley entrance? I think I must have left mine out on the Island last weekend and it's goddamned inconvenient trying to crash through all those ghouls at the front entrance."

"No, I never had any partners' privileges," he said bitterly without stopping to think. "You should know that better than anyone, Steve."

I wanted nothing better than to move at top speed away from the subject of the Willow Alley keys. Trying not to think of the implications of his denial, I said mildly, "What's the big grudge?"

"Well, we're the same age, aren't we? And we're both Van Zale protégés. I know you're a smart guy, but I'm no fool, either. Don't you think we both should have ended up partners?"

I was genuinely surprised. "It's not my fault if Paul thought your brain was better suited to administration than to finance."

"Oh, I could have done just as well as you!" he spat at me, suddenly coming apart at the seams. "But just because your father ran through two million dollars of old money while my father was an immigrant who ran a hardware store—"

"Oh, Christ!"

"And just because my family were Catholics from Connaught while your family were Protestants from Ulster—"

"We came from County Cork!" I yelled, although no one knew where the first Sullivan had come from before he turned up fighting the British in the Hudson Valley. However I'd read somewhere once that Sullivan is a common name in the Irish southwest.

The crazy slanging match went on and on. I'd had no idea O'Reilly had such a chip on his shoulder about being a first-generation Irish-American Catholic. Later I realized he was probably still smarting from the way he had been treated in Charley's office when all the partners had pulled out their Yankee stops to put him in his place, but at the time I didn't bother to analyze why he was so furious, because I was too busy welcoming the chance to let off steam. In the light of my private knowledge about the assassination I was having a hard time restraining myself from beating O'Reilly to bloody pulp, and his ethnic drivel, heavily laced with religious idiocies, was just the excuse I needed to lose my temper and roar obscenities at him.

We never came to blows because we were too hot. We just sat gasping in our chairs until he muttered, "Fuck you!" and staggered out.

Ten minutes later when I had cooled off, I remembered he had denied ever having had a set of keys for the Willow Alley door. I believed him too. His resentment in being refused such a partner's privilege was all too obviously genuine.

But somehow he had got hold of a set of keys. The whole phony explanation about Krasnov hiding overnight in the building was to cover up the fact that someone had produced the keys for the Willow Alley door.

Paul had had his keys with him that morning; Peterson had used them to let us into the building. My own keys had never left my possession.

That left my five surviving partners, Charley, Lewis, Walter, Clay and Martin.

I backed away in panic. That was the kind of disaster I'd never be able to keep under wraps. It would kill the bank, kill us all. If a partner was involved we were doomed.

Finishing the rye in my hip flask, I put my head in my hands and in despair tried to figure out a way we could survive.

IV

My stomach finally rebelled against all the liquor I'd fed it, but after I was through with the men's room I took some salts and felt I could cope again. My panic was gone. My mind was clear, so clear that it was easy for me to sit back in my chair and knock all my crazy suspicions squarely on the head.

The truth was that shock and grief had temporarily sent me over the edge. Krasnov must have been stashed overnight in the bank after all. Of course that was a big risk to take, but life's full of little risks if you're bent on assassination, and it was just the assassins' good luck that nothing fouled up their scheme. The idea of a partner being involved was so ludicrous that I actually laughed, and when my laughter sounded forced I reminded myself of a fact which as far as I could see was undeniable: none of the partners had had a motive. It was true that Charley, Lewis and I all coveted the senior partner's chair, but we were hardly going to knock Paul off in order to get it; this might be Jimmy Walker's New York but it wasn't the Wild West, and investment bankers just didn't do that kind of thing. Also it was no use thinking that Jay's men—Charley, Lewis and old Walter—might have plotted to kill Paul in belated revenge for Jay's death, because the point about these three was that they had always got along better with Paul than with Jay. That was why they had stayed in the firm. Anyway, respectable investment bankers didn't go around murdering for revenge like a bunch of Chicago hoods.

I picked over a couple of other motives. It was true we all stood to gain financially from Paul's death because his fifty-percent share of the profits would now be redistributed when we re-formed the partnership, but we were all rich men already. You didn't become a Van Zale partner and then find you were wondering where the next penny was coming from, so it was no use theorizing that Paul had been killed for his money.

The only other motive I could dream up involved some unknown eternal triangle, but even that seemed farfetched. Paul had seduced countless wives, but he was always careful that the husband was either complaisant or indifferent, and as a matter of common sense he tended to avoid running after the wives of his partners. I won't say he didn't do it. I knew he had slept with Lewis' wife a couple of times, but that was only because the wife had almost raped him, and Lewis had wanted a divorce at the time anyway. I couldn't seriously imagine Lewis feeling murderous on account of that incident, and even assuming he did I found it even harder to imagine him sitting down with that gangster Greg Da Costa, that carpetbagger Terence O'Reilly and that Bolshevik Bruce Clayton to hash out an assassination scheme. Lewis, the archcapitalist, was just too much of a snob to associate with such people.

I glanced at my watch. It was three o'clock, I had had no lunch and I knew my partners would be needing my help, but before I left the room I glanced at the outdoor thermometer that stood in eternal shade on the window ledge which faced north. The mercury was glued at ninety-seven degrees.

Sometime that evening I dragged myself back to my apartment in the East Sixties. I felt limp, blank and about a hundred years old.

"Steven!" cried my wife, scooping me into the apartment and flinging her arms around me purposefully. "You poor lamb, you must be so upset, what a dreadful thing to happen, why the hell didn't you return my calls? No, don't say a word, I quite understand, come on in and sit down, you poor poor darling, I'll fix you a drink."

I slumped on the couch. I liked it when Caroline made a big fuss over me. It didn't happen often.

"I got here this afternoon and found Dinah encamped. You know, Steven, I think we got that girl wrong. I think she really cared for Paul, it wasn't just the money and the glamour. She was in such a state I took her down to the ship myself to make sure she got the right one, and she was really quite warm when she thanked me, I almost forgot she was English. That little boy's so cute—quite like Paul too, I only hope he doesn't start having epileptic fits. Now, you poor lamb, drink this up and tell me the *whole* story. Is it really true Bruce Clayton went berserk with a hatchet and ran through the main hall carving everyone up?"

"Oh my God," I said in disgust, and roused myself to give her a heavily censored version of the facts.

"Steven," said Caroline sternly when I'd finished, "are you being entirely truthful with me?"

"Hell, yes!" I suddenly didn't want to talk anymore. I just wanted to switch off my mind and forget. Caroline's thigh looked up at me invitingly beneath the skimpy folds of her frock.

"Oh no!" she said at once as I slid a hand upward from her knee. "Not until you've told me the whole story!"

"God damn it, Cal, give a guy a break, can't you?"

"Can't we ever conduct a conversation which doesn't end with you suggesting I lie on my back with my legs apart and my mouth shut?"

I groaned. "Jesus, why did I ever marry a woman like you?"

"Paul told you to," she said. "Remember?" She stroked the back of my neck efficiently. "And damn it, it was good advice. . . . Steve,

I'm terribly sorry about Paul, I really am—I know how you must feel. Was it a conspiracy?"

"Nope."

"Are you going to be senior partner?"

"Yep."

"Darling!" cried Caroline before I could add the words, "But not yet." And she began to roll down her stockings.

Thanks to her tank-sized martini, the *coup de grace* after a day's drinking, I was damned-near impotent, but Caroline had great technical competence and we did achieve some kind of coupling before I passed out.

There was a storm that night, and the next day was cooler. However, it was still hell at the office and by midafternoon I was already longing for my first drink of the evening. I had made up my mind not to drink at the office that day, but when my secretary told me that Paul's great-nephew was asking for an audience I automatically reached for my hip flask.

"Christ, I can't mess around at present with a little boy just out of diapers! Pass the kid on to one of the other partners, for God's sake," I ordered irritably, and thought I had rid myself of Cornelius, but ten minutes later there was a knock on my door and old Walter peeked in.

"Sorry to interrupt you, Steve—"

I had been about to call the undertakers about the funeral, but I hung up with a crash.

"—but I've just been talking to young Cornelius and he's really most anxious to speak to you."

"Show him in," I growled. The day was obviously going to get worse before it could get better. I tried not to grind my teeth.

Walter withdrew. The door opened wider, then closed very softly. I had been pretending to read a letter, but at last I had no choice but to drop it and take a look at Master Cornelius Blackett from Cincinnati, Ohio.

"Good afternoon, Mr. Sullivan," he said.

He was slim, slight and narrow, with some sharp little features, dusty-gold curls and a pair of gray eyes which would have looked well with mascara. However, there was nothing effeminate about his clothes. He was conservatively dressed in black. His manner, punctuated by a meticulous Ohio accent, was both civil and charmless.

"Hello, Neil," I said. Out of respect for Paul's memory I mustered a smile and gestured to the client's chair. "Have a seat."

He sat down. We faced each other. He waited for me to speak, but when he realized I wasn't about to commiserate with someone who had hardly known Paul and had just walked into umpteen million dollars he said respectfully, "I hear Mr. Blair is to be the new senior partner, but you're the partner who really counts, aren't you, sir?"

This was very gratifying. I hadn't expected him to be so smart. "You could say that, I guess," I said benignly. "How can I help you, sonny?"

"Well, sir," he said, meek as a bishop in gaiters and pretty as a daisy chain, "I just wanted to assure you I have no intention of withdrawing Paul's capital from the firm."

There was a silence. I forgot the police, the press, the funeral. I even forgot the power struggles that morning at the partners' meeting before Charley had been elected senior partner.

"I believe the amount is twenty million dollars," said little Cornelius Blackett from Cincinnati, Ohio.

"Yeah," I said, getting my breath back. "Something like that."

"I guess it would suit you better if it stayed in the firm."

My lips were dry. I quickly slid my tongue around them. "Yeah. Well, yes. Uh, let me explain . . ."

"I realize the firm's in an unstable state right now and it wouldn't help if there was a massive withdrawal of capital."

"Uh . . . exactly. Right. That's it." I wished the other partners were listening in. We had all been so busy arguing about the redistribution of profits that it had never occurred to us to worry about a capital withdrawal. I guess we had all assumed an eighteen-year-old nonentity would just do as he was told.

"Of course we'll make a suitable financial arrangement with you," I said smoothly, deciding it was time to rev up the Sullivan charm. "You won't be out of pocket, I promise you."

"Thank you, sir," said the kid without batting his long curling eyelashes, "but I'm not pressed for cash. I was thinking in terms of a place in the firm."

"You were?" I said, amazed. He looked like the sort of youth who would be incapable of doing anything except writing bad poetry in a garret. "Well, that's nice!" I said, remembering the twenty million dollars and swallowing my amazement in a single gulp. "You'll go to Yale first, of course, and then have a year in Europe."

"No, sir, what I have to learn is right here at One Willow Street, and I'd like to begin my training immediately after the funeral."

Well, it was obvious he wouldn't last six months, but I knew I had to humor him.

"That's wonderful!" I said, smiling so broadly my face ached. "Congratulations and welcome!"

"Thank you, sir. Incidentally, I have a friend whom I'd like to bring with me into the firm. His name's Sam Keller."

I remembered Paul talking about his latest protégés. "Is he one of the kids who have been spending the summers with you at Bar Harbor? Keller—wouldn't that be the caretaker's boy? Well, I don't know whether socially he'd be able to make the transition . . ."

"Paul chose him, sir."

It was odd to hear the kid calling him Paul. Disrespectful and too familiar. I didn't like it.

"Well . . ." It was becoming harder to remember the twenty million dollars. I had to make a great effort. "I'm sure that can be arranged, Neil."

"Pardon me, sir, but I prefer to be called Cornelius. 'Neil' was Paul's special name for me, and only my Bar Harbor friends use it. Oh, and talking of names, Paul wanted me to take his name when he died—so there'll still be a Van Zale at Van Zale's," he added unnecessarily, flashing me a tight triumphant little smile.

"That's nice!" I said, instantly resolving to give him the toughest training any would-be investment banker ever had, but I wasn't worried. With fifty million dollars at his fingertips in addition to his twenty million in the firm, he'd soon discover there were more amusing ways of occupying his time, and besides, he was just too much of a pretty-boy to take seriously.

"If he had balls it'd be different," I explained later to Caroline. "God knows what Paul could have seen in him."

"People used to make similar remarks about you," Caroline reminded me tartly. "'God, what's Paul doing with that lout who looks like a bouncer?' I can hear them saying it now."

"I may not look like an investment banker," I shot back at her, "but at least no one could ever have thought *I* had no balls! Hell, Cal, that kid couldn't even be a pallbearer at the funeral. He'd be ground to dust as soon as he tried to shoulder the coffin!"

"Talking of the funeral," said Caroline, "have you—"

"No, I haven't."

"Well, go and lock yourself in the library and don't come out till you've done it."

I sighed. I had to get some words about Paul down on paper, and the time was coming when I could put it off no longer. Not only was the funeral looming large on the horizon, a test of endurance for anyone who'd been close to Paul, but Sylvia had gone and asked me —me of all people!—to give Paul the eulogy he deserved.

V

I'm not much of a one for speeches. It's one thing to sit back at a partners' meeting and chat for half an hour about the financial state of a big corporation, and quite another to stand up before a packed church and talk of one's dead friend.

I tried to get out of it. "Perhaps Charley—or Lewis," I urged Sylvia. Lewis was such an expert eulogizer that he had almost reached the stage of patenting the entire performance and retiring to live on the profits.

"I don't want someone who just liked Paul," said Sylvia. "I want someone who cared."

She was implacable. I gave in.

"And for God's sake don't be too maudlin," advised Caroline as I settled down to prepare the speech. I sharpened six pencils and sat in front of a blank pad of paper. I even wrote at the top of the page: "Paul Cornelius Van Zale: 1870-1926."

I wrote no more, but for hours I looked at those words and thought of him.

I remembered how we had met. I was eighteen years old, I'd just been tossed out of military academy and everyone had agreed I was unmanageable—no big news, since my brothers and I had been unmanageable for as long as anyone could remember. Part of the trouble was that our father died young—I was only nine at the time—and there's no doubt three boys get into bad habits when there's no father around to knock them into shape. I remember my father well. He was good-natured and generous, always the life and soul of every party, but if we put too big a strain on his good nature we soon regretted it. I can still remember not being able to sit down for two days after I'd put an egg in each of his riding boots.

There was plenty of money in the family but my father, being generous, spent pretty freely so that when he died there wasn't too much left in the bank. All in all, it was probably a good thing when my mother remarried quickly. My mother was a lovely lady, better connected than my father, although I never once heard her make any derogatory remark about our Irish name, and she was slim and always looked very cool and read expensive fashion magazines whenever she wasn't getting dressed up to go out. They don't make ladies like that anymore; nowadays nobody knows how to be idle with grace and beauty and style. She was the kind of woman who should have had daughters instead of three rowdy sons, but after Matt and Luke were born she had no more children, not even when she remarried.

My stepfather was a nice guy, generous and good-natured like my father but without my father's tough streak. Of course, being a stepfather's a hard job, I realize that. He wanted us to like him, so he turned a blind eye to our escapades until we were walking all over him. We liked him well enough, but we didn't respect him and we never knew how well off we were in his care until he died and Uncle took charge.

My expulsion from military academy coincided with Luke and

Matt's simultaneous expulsion from school, but my mother was too distraught by my stepfather's death to cope with us, so she was relieved when my father's younger brother, the sober industrious president of Sullivan Steel Foundries, arrived to sort us out.

Uncle took one look at us and decided we were steel bars who had to be welded very firmly into some kind of conventional shape. Luke and Matt were sent to different schools, both institutions run by Methodists, and I was given a one-way ticket to New York to earn my living. I was also given an introductory letter to a distant family connection, the son of my maternal grandmother's second cousin, Mr. Paul Cornelius Van Zale.

I'll never forget the interview he gave me. It was an interrogation. I started out bullish and brazen and ended up contradicting myself, stammering and damned near weeping with humiliation. When I was finally reduced to a white-faced, sick-to-the-stomach, trembling young kid humbly silent in his presence, he said shortly, "You're a bright boy. It's possible I can do something for you, but I shall expect absolute obedience, total loyalty and more hard work than you can at present imagine. If you can't face that . . ."

I said I could. By that time I was in such a state I would have said anything, but he must have known that after years without discipline I would find the rewards of hard work addictively sweet. I grasped the chance he gave me, but although he always took a sharp interest in my progress we were never close friends until he took me with him to Europe after his daughter Vicky died. The seventeen-year gap in our ages began to close. He taught me how to play tennis. We swam and sailed together. I have no doubt all his intellectual friends had a hard time figuring out why he enjoyed my company, but the very reason why Paul and I got along so well was because we were so different. Anyway, I think Paul often got bored with his intellectual friends and the effort of being so exquisitely civilized. When he was out with me he could just be one of the boys. He'd had a stuffy sort of upbringing from that old battle-ax of a mother of his, and in later life he found it a real luxury to bum around with someone like me and say "shit" or "fuck" without anyone having the vapors.

That was a side of Paul his women never saw.

I often wondered what Paul really thought of women. He had more success with them than any other man I knew, and I couldn't for the life of me figure out why. He wasn't tall. He wasn't broad-shouldered or spectacularly well-muscled. He didn't have much hair, although curiously women never seemed to notice that. Maybe that was because he was capable of spending ten minutes in front of a mirror while he arranged his front strand as cunningly as possible. He had cheerful dark eyes, a gap between his two front teeth, and deep hard lines around his tough straight mouth. Some people thought he had an English accent, but they were always the people who had never been to England. He spoke very fast and could outtalk anyone under the sun—a fact which could help explain why women so often ended up in bed with him—and of course he was charming to women, I'm not denying that. But the charm was like a light switch which could be flicked on and off. Until I saw him fall apart under the pressures of his affair with Dinah Slade I had always wondered if he was capable of a truly spontaneous relationship with a woman.

His wealth alone would have made him a target for the gossipmongers. His wealth combined with his spectacular success with women was enough to drive them crazy with curiosity, disbelief and just plain jealousy. No rumor was so wild that it couldn't be tacked onto Paul Van Zale and passed off as gospel truth, and one member of a certain uptown club even asked me once if Paul was bisexual. Yet when I repeated this story to Paul in a fever of indignation, Paul just laughed. No rumor could faze him. As far as he was concerned all publicity was good publicity in his ceaseless efforts to get around the law that a private banker must never advertise.

"But supposing people believe that kind of stuff!" I said horrified.

"How can they," he said placidly, "when it's so patently untrue?"

And indeed he was so damned busy making a fortune and laying every woman in sight that he hardly had the time to step out with his own sex. I think the rumor began because there was a gap between what Paul said and what he actually did. It was one of his nineteenth-century characteristics. He was quite capable of arguing in some intellectual discussion that the laws against homosexuals should be reformed and that it was irrelevant how people expressed themselves sexually, but in practice he made damned sure that all his close friends chased nothing but skirts. The most any queen could ever have expected from him was a cool handshake over a business deal.

He gave me some severe lectures about skirt-chasing when I was young, but when I still managed to marry the wrong girl he helped me get the divorce and introduced me to Caroline. Caroline and I had always got along pretty well. We'd been married fourteen years so we had to be doing something right, and the only serious bone of contention between us was children. I wanted more and she was content with our two boys. However, as she herself said, if I'd had to spend nine months being pregnant, maybe my views would have coincided with hers. Caroline's pet project was the dissemination of birth-control literature to the poor, and she was always chasing around organizing groups of emancipated females who agreed with her that birth control was the only defense women had against a lifetime of oppression by lusty males. At first this had annoyed me but now I'd got used to it. Modern women were really kind of cute, and anyway every woman should have a hobby to keep her occupied.

Our two boys were the greatest little fellows in the world and well worth all the tussles and spats Caroline and I used to have. Scott was six years old and already very spunky with a baseball bat, while Tony was three and could rip up the nursery in less time than it took to recite his favorite nursery rhyme. We had waited a long time to have children because Caroline hadn't been able to face it, and she had given in only when our marriage was within an ace of running onto the rocks. Scott was planned, but Tony was an accident—and Caroline, in between her speeches about birth control, never let me forget it. However, underneath all this tough talk she was devoted to both kids and always made sure they had nothing but the best. Even their nurse had once worked for European royalty.

Caroline was thirty-six, three years younger than I was, and looked smart as paint. She had black hair, black eyes, a sleek streamlined figure which always gave me a thrill whenever I prised it loose from those godawful boyish-form corsets, and legs which made one want to praise God that women's hemlines had finally risen to the knee. She was no fool either. She read *Vanity Fair,* so she knew exactly what Frank Crowninshield's intellectuals were saying, she played a steely game of bridge and she could arrange a dinner party for sixty people without turning a hair. She kept my domestic life ruthlessly well-organized and had no patience with slackers.

"Well, Steven!" she said sternly, sweeping into my study at midnight to find me still sitting in front of my blank notepad. "Time to start rehearsals! Where's the eulogy?"

"It's still an unwritten masterpiece. Fix me a drink, Cal."

"Oh, darling, you *can't* get drunk tonight and be hung over tomorrow at the funeral!"

"Oh, yeah?"

After I had crawled into my black suit next morning I took some salts for my stomach, added a slug of gin to my orange juice to wake me up, and set off for the funeral still with no idea what I was going to say.

The service was to be held at St. George's on Stuyvesant Square, with a private interment later at the family mausoleum in Westchester.

Everyone was there, all Wall Street and half Washington, the big names, the famous firms, the men who, like Paul, were legends in their time. The twin aristocracies of New York, Jewish and Yankee, for once met and mingled, for Paul had spanned the two worlds in his long unorthodox career. Jacob Reischman—always "Young Jacob" to Paul even though he was now in his midfifties—said, "I remember when he was very young and first came to our House." But someone younger said, "I can't remember when I first met him, because it seemed he was always there."

"And with us still," said someone else, and suddenly I knew that for once this was no empty platitude but the truth. For there was another contingent at the funeral, a group unrecognized by the press and unknown by the sightseeing crowds, a club only dimly acknowledged by Wall Street but just as exclusive as any club uptown.

Paul's protégés had come to pay their final respects.

We all knew one another. I kept seeing them as the crowds swirled and parted like patterns in a kaleidoscope. Martin, Clay and I were the oldest and most successful, but there were others descending in age and achievement all the way to little Cornelius Blackett and his three eighteen-year-old friends.

Paul was dead but his people lived on, and I was just about to wallow in maudlin sentiment when I came face to face with the truth.

I saw Bruce Clayton. I never thought he'd have the nerve to come. He'd been formally arrested for Krasnov's murder but had later been released and everyone knew the charges had been dropped. He was with his mother, who was heavily veiled. I was just thinking I had never seen anyone as pale as Bruce when I noticed his wife walking beside him.

He saw me, flinched, and turned away.

Rage burst through me. I stared, still standing stock still, and as the kaleidoscope of people shifted again I saw Terence O'Reilly. Of course it would have looked odd if he had stayed away.

The shock of seeing the two of them in such rapid succession stripped the sentimentality from my eyes. Paul hadn't been killed by strangers. He had been killed by two of his own people who had used the brains and ambition he had admired so much to plot a murder successful enough to outwit the law.

The full horror of his murder wiped my brain clean of muddle and grief. Facts like that were capable of only one resolution. Paul might have been killed by his people, but he was also going to be avenged by them, and as I took a look into the blurred future I knew that the power of his personality would continue to manipulate us all from the darkness on the far side of the grave.

"I know what I'm going to say," I said to Caroline.

"Oh, God, Steven, are you sure?"

The streets of the square were choked with cars. The sidewalks were overflowing with people, and the photographers preceded us every step of the way into the church.

It was an old church, grave and cool. The organ was already playing and twenty minutes later the doors were closed.

I can't remember the service. I only remember walking up to the lectern and facing the packed congregation. I looked out over the sea of faces, and when the silence was so deep I could hear it I said in my strongest voice to Paul's murderers:

"He's still alive!"

VI

I stopped speaking. Some journalist wrote later that I had spoken for eight minutes. I felt as if I had been speaking for eight hours. When I stopped, the silence was not only audible but thundering in my ears. I groped my way down from the lectern, and as the organ began to play the English hymn "Jerusalem" I felt Sylvia's hand seek mine.

I hadn't heard that hymn since I was in England. It was a damned odd hymn and I'd always wondered what the hell it meant, but now as the voices of the choir soared to the rafters I knew I was in the presence of some idealistic vision, all the more romantic for being incomprehensible, and I saw again the hidden side of Paul, the side he had tried to conceal even from those closest to him. Listening to that hymn which he himself had chosen, I felt as if some line had opened up between us, and my thoughts streamed out to meet him. I was watching some distant point above the altar. I neither moved nor spoke, but in my head I was talking to Paul, apologizing for not taking immediate action against his murderers, telling him I was putting the bank first, just as he would have wished.

Sylvia was crying. I put an arm around her and drew her to me.

The service ended. Eventually a few people started to move. The sun shone through one of the windows. After a while I found I was standing in the aisle while people clustered around to shake my hand.

My partners looked wiped out. Even Lewis' Hollywood profile seemed dented, and Charley Blair was unable to speak as he wrung my hand. Clay was like a ghost, Martin was endlessly polishing his misted glasses, and Walter was like an old, old man who has lived too long and seen too much.

I had to break away from them to attend to Sylvia. After days of unnatural calm she had at last broken down completely.

"Leave this to me, Steven," said Caroline competently, but Sylvia had already turned to Paul's niece Mildred and there was nothing Caroline could do.

We fought our way outside. It was a battle every inch of the way to our car and when we finally crawled inside we were on the verge of collapse. Halfway uptown to the Van Zale mansion Caroline was able to say, "Steven, I didn't know you had it in you. I've never been so proud of anyone in all my life."

We held hands tightly. All I could say was, "That hymn 'Jerusalem.'"

"Darling, don't remind me. I feel on the verge of complete and utter disintegration. God only knows how Sylvia must feel—I expect she'll have to be hospitalized."

There was to be a small reception at Paul's house for the family, the partners and their wives, and within minutes of our arrival we were feeling better. In his minutely detailed instructions for the funeral Paul, smart to the last, had ordered the very best champagne to be served to his mourners.

"Remember you didn't have any breakfast," warned Caroline as I knocked back my first glass in a single gulp and tapped the nearest footman for a refill. "You'd better eat something."

I grabbed half a dozen canapés and tried to step on the urge to get very drunk very fast.

Sylvia had just reappeared with Mildred. I went over to her.

"Yes, I'm better now, thank you, Steve," she said evenly. She looked almost transparent with exhaustion, and her eyes were swollen with weeping. "It was just that when you said 'He's still alive' I realized for the first time that he was dead. So ironic! Silly of me. It was such a wonderful speech, Steve, perfect, I always knew you were the one who should do it." She started to cry again and presently Mildred led her away.

I was still staring unhappily after them when I heard a polite cough and found Cornelius, still as a statue, at my elbow.

"Mr. Sullivan, may I present Sam Keller?"

I saw the tall dark youth who had been sitting next to Cornelius in church. He had shaggy short hair, friendly brown eyes and an adolescent air of not knowing quite what to do with his arms and legs.

"Hello," I said kindly. "Cornelius was talking about you the other day."

"Mr. Sullivan—how are you." He accepted the hand I offered. He had a strong firm masculine clasp.

I glanced from him to Cornelius and wondered if I could make one plus one equal one, but when I looked back at Sam Keller my instinct was to like him. Despite his adolescent movements his manner was unusually self-assured for the son of working-class immigrants. He had an easy smile, an alert expression and the damnedest Down-East accent I had heard in some time.

I would have asked the boy some questions, but at that moment Charley called me away to ask about Sylvia, and when I left the room to make inquiries I met Mildred Blackett in the hall. She told me that Sylvia had asked to be alone.

"Of course I knew beforehand it would all be too much for her," said Mildred. "Those *frightful* crowds outside the church, those *vulgar* journalists, that *inexpressibly* moving service . . ."

Mildred was a large handsome woman in her midforties who liked to flash her dark eyes imperiously and heave her full bosom at the first sight of emotion on the horizon.

". . . And by the way, Steven, there's something I simply must discuss with you." She put a bejeweled hand firmly on my wrist and propelled me into a quiet corner of the hall. Offhand I couldn't think of a single other woman who could have swept me off like that. Mildred was a very powerful lady. "Wade and I," she said, referring to her husband, "are *desperately* worried about Cornelius, Steven. Of course inheriting all that *dreadful* money was the very last thing I wanted for him. I know it's hardly the time to say one word against dearest Paul, but *really*, Steven! What a thing to do. *And no guardian! No trustee!* All that money *outright!* Naturally Paul didn't expect to die when Cornelius was only eighteen, but surely he should have provided for every eventuality!"

"It does seem kind of unfortunate," I agreed sympathetically.

"Unfortunate!" Mildred abandoned her stage whisper, drew herself up to her full height and regarded me over the top of her heaving bosom. "It's disastrous! And now Cornelius is talking of casting aside his education and coming to live here in this perfectly *ghastly* house, all on his own, only eighteen years old, in this—this *Babylon* of a city! Of course, Cornelius has had a good solid moral upbringing, but nevertheless . . ."

Nevertheless he was just at an age when he would enjoy celebrating his liberation from the maternal apron strings. I did feel sorry for Mildred, whom I liked, but I didn't see how I could help her.

". . . so Wade and I thought that if you could have a *word* with Cornelius— oh, Emily! I was wondering what had happened to you, dear. Steven, you remember my daughter Emily, don't you?"

There was such a strong resemblance between Emily and Cornelius that they could have passed for twins. His features looked better on her, though. Now I found those dusty-gold curls pretty, the sharp little nose and chin delicately attractive, the gray eyes starry and stunning. Twenty-year-old virgins aren't exactly in my ball park, but Emily was a cute little thing and I could tell right away she was nice-natured.

"We met about five years ago, didn't we?" I said, smiling at her. "But you've changed, Miss Emily! You had pigtails when I last saw you."

"It was ten years ago, actually," said Emily, blushing as I took her hand. "Vicky's funeral."

"It's too bad we never meet except at funerals! What are you doing with yourself nowadays? I guess school must be no more than a distant memory by this time."

"Well, not exactly, Mr. Sullivan. I'm at college and majoring in classical studies."

Those Van Zale women were amazing! I had a vivid memory of Paul making a wisecrack in Latin and old Mrs. Van Zale capping the joke in Greek.

"Congratulations!" I said amused. "I think it's great for a woman to study when she doesn't need to."

"I don't quite understand." She looked anxious.

"Well, you're so pretty you could just sit on your high-school diploma and wait until your husband comes along!"

"Oh, I . . . well, thank you, I . . ." She blushed again and stammered to a halt. I grinned at her encouragingly. It always amuses me to see a brainy girl covered with confusion.

"Who's that blonde you were flirting with in the hall?" demanded Caroline later.

"Emily Blackett. Didn't you notice the likeness to Cornelius? By the way, did you see Cornelius' boy friend?"

"Shhh! Here comes Mildred."

When we dragged ourselves home I was so exhausted I slept for sixteen hours, but next morning I felt as if I had just passed some monumental milestone. My partners believed Krasnov had acted only with the aid of Bruce Clayton. Everyone else, including the press and the law, had swallowed the story that Krasnov had acted alone. All I had to do now was to shore up the bank's position, and then once I was sure the storm had blown over I'd go after those assassins and send them one by one down to hell to be fried.

Chapter Three

I

I had them watched, but they never met. Greg Da Costa ran through his remaining money as effortlessly as a barracuda rippling through tropical waters but then dumfounded me by marrying an heiress and winding up in California. The heiress must have been the dumbest of dumb broads, but that was Greg's lucky break. I gave him no more than five years to dispose of his new fortune, but my brothers, who had idled around with Greg during faraway summers at Newport, said I was being optimistic.

Bruce Clayton might have escaped trial, but Columbia University didn't like one of their young professors knocking people off, so they fired him. After six months spent having a nervous breakdown in one of those plush sanitariums upstate he was packed off on a world cruise, and when he returned he tried teaching for a time in a private boarding school up in Canada. That didn't work out, and in the spring of 1928 he and Grace rented a cottage by the sea at Montauk, Long Island, so that Bruce could write a book. I never found out what the book was about, but the operative who kept an eye on him for me reported that he led a secluded law-abiding life.

Terence O'Reilly disappeared. He was too quick for me, and although my operative began surveillance less than twenty-four hours after the funeral he found only a deserted apartment, closed bank accounts and a neighbor who thought O'Reilly might have gone on vacation to Atlantic City.

Since I knew that O'Reilly would eventually surface to claim his bride, I wasn't unduly worried by his disappearance, but I was certainly puzzled when the best operatives failed to trace him. It wasn't just that I couldn't figure out where he was. I couldn't see how he was supporting himself. Once he had a new job and a permanent address my operatives should have been able to turn him up, but when they had no success I had to conclude he was unemployed. Probably he had plenty of money saved, but I knew he'd want that to feather a nest for Sylvia. It was puzzling. I half wondered if he'd changed his name, but that would have been the act of a man who had something to hide and O'Reilly would want to act innocent. He'd have a lot of explaining to do to Sylvia if he resurfaced with a new name.

I made a strong effort to find O'Reilly, not just to satisfy my own curiosity but because by chance we needed him in connection with the bank. Bart Mayers was killed in an automobile accident only ten days after the assassination, with the result that all attempts to sort out Paul's papers were severely hampered, and O'Reilly's encyclopedic knowledge of the private files would have been more than useful to us.

Eventually everything was sorted out, but two major personal files remained unaccounted for. One was the file containing all Paul's correspondence with Vicky, and the other was his entire private correspondence with Dinah Slade.

Six months after the funeral I wrote to tell Dinah that the Mallingham deed had never surfaced and asked her what she wanted to do about it. As far as Paul's estate was concerned Mallingham didn't exist. I said that if she wanted to forward all the documents she had retained I'd take the matter of the missing conveyance up with the Van Zale lawyers, but my personal recommendation was that she should wait another six months. I found it hard to believe the deed would stay lost indefinitely, and once it did turn up I could still fix the transfer of title to her with a minimum of fuss.

Dinah wrote back to say she'd wait. More time slipped away. She was as busy with her business as I was with mine, and our correspondence was irregular, but I always read the reports Hal Beecher mailed from our Milk Street office and was glad to see that Diana Slade Cosmetics was making a mint and expanding fast. I could just imagine Dinah putting on hot-shot airs to all her clients while old Hal secretly pulled the strings and told her what to do.

Meanwhile I'd finished pulling all the available strings to conceal the conspiracy, but I'd had one particularly nasty moment before the police closed the assassination file. It turned out that two days before the assassination Krasnov had paid ten thousand dollars in used bills into his bank account. Since the police were acting on the theory that Krasnov had acted alone, it was of vital importance that the amount should be explained away before they thought it was blood money from anyone connected with Van Zale's.

Fortunately I had a friend in Washington who owed me a favor, and he promised he'd shut the police off by saying the money had come from a foreign government and was already the target of a top-secret investigation. I took the opportunity to check whether this might even be true, but my friend said Bruce Clayton's society had received no foreign funding and Krasnov had not been affiliated with any secret Bolshevik group operating in the States.

I spent some uncomfortable nights thinking about that ten thousand dollars but came to the conclusion O'Reilly must have put up the money. Bruce would surely just have told Krasnov he should commit the murder for the cause without expecting financial reward, although my partners, who still had no idea O'Reilly had a motive for murder, had no difficulty in assuming Bruce had donated the cash. None of us wanted to think much about it anyway. It was so much more comfortable to look the other way whenever the conspiracy began to raise its ugly head, and once the police let the matter drop I for one was certainly relieved to turn back to the soaring numbers on the ticker and tell myself it was a great time in the history of the world to be an investment banker.

My special project, our investment trust Van Zale Participations, was launched in the fall of 1926 and took off with all the glory of a rocket heading for the stars. The project was also special to me because I was at last able to provide properly for my brothers. Matt became the trust's figurehead president, and Luke's small brokerage house got all the trust's business.

By that time we were all in love with the idea of investment trusts. This kind of trust issued shares to its subscribers and then invested the money in the shares of other corporations. In the early twenties investment trusts had been rare, but after 1926 an avalanche of them hit Wall Street because the market was swinging upward so hard that new ways had to be designed to cope with the huge flow of capital coming from the investment-hungry public. To enable themselves to expand in the market, the commercial banks promoted the affiliate company, and the investment banks championed the investment trust.

They took little extra manpower, hardly any space—some firms used a corner of the office, but at least we had the decency to rent a suite farther down Willow Street—and a few good connections to inspire confidence. Naturally Van Zale's connections were first-class, and there was never much doubt that once we started milking the cow we'd skim off one hell of a lot of cream. After Van Zale Participations had been incorporated (we incorporated in Delaware for the usual tax reasons) we issued only common stock, a million shares in all. The bank, P. C. Van Zale and Company, took a hundred thousand shares at 100 and sold the rest to the public at 104 with a resulting profit of around three million dollars. Some cream! However, that was just the hors d'oeuvres of the financial feast. The capital was then organized and invested in a number of big enterprises—electrical goods, insurance companies and so on. These all paid superb dividends, and so successful were we that we were soon approached by another investment trust run by a strong second-rank house. In the resulting merger we came out on top, retaining the name Van Zale Participations and increasing the corporation's assets to double the amount we started with.

It was a great game, the investors were happy as larks and we bankers went laughing all the way down Wall Street. The market boomed. Capital kept streaming in, and soon everyone was playing pyramiding, creating paper corporations which the public could gobble up and investing the proceeds not in commodities anymore but in other paper corporations created specifically to issue shares for the greedy public.

Occasionally I did lie awake at night wondering about it all, but I came to the conclusion that we were providing a public service. There was nothing the public wanted more than to slug the Wall Street gambling machine by buying into the big bull market, and anyway all the best firms were falling over themselves to be helpful. Even the great House of Morgan eventually got in on the act when it launched its mighty holding company the United Corporation, and we all knew they were kicking themselves for not jumping on the bandwagon sooner.

I was just proud that I'd got Van Zale's in on the ground floor.

On paper all the partners of P. C. Van Zale and Company officered Van Zale Participations, but in practice I was the one who managed the business, showing Matt where to sign his name and telling Luke where to invest the money. This worked out well for me because Van Zale Participations had made a big noise on the Street, and soon I was regarded as a wizard by the financial community.

The other partners were pleased for the firm's sake, but except for Charley Blair, who was too much of a nice guy to be jealous, I could tell they were getting restive. Lewis got very cool behind his patrician profile, and old Walter called me "racy." In apology he confessed he didn't really approve of modern banking practices, although he did have the grace to admit he was behind the times. With any luck he'd retire soon, but I was fond of old Walter and it was nice to have him around as a sentimental keepsake of times past.

Martin and Clay too had come to resemble something the iceman had left behind, although Martin was at least polite enough to pretend he disapproved of my activities for academic reasons. As soon as I heard him say "theoretically" I knew I was in for some dreary talk. "Theoretically," Martin would say, "the investment trust now serves no financial purpose. We're no longer investing in industry but in bits of paper which have no real worth. Theoretically this can't last."

I wanted to tell him to go stuff himself with ticker tape. Behind his back I contented myself with referring to him as Cassandra.

Clay was as bored as I was by Martin's pessimism, and he was certainly more honest about his jealousy. He didn't like the investment trust because he didn't have a big enough share of it, and since he was always trying to muscle in on my territory we had some godawful fights in the partners' meetings. In the end Reischman's invited us to join them in launching a new public-utility holding corporation and I managed to channel Clay into this new venture and out of my hair. Since we were playing a secondary role in the scheme I didn't have to worry about his getting too successful, because I knew Reischman's would win all the credit when the cream was skimmed.

There were still only six New York partners, with one partner in London. We had talked of finding two new partners—even three when business reached a record-breaking pace—but since we could never agree on a man who might have worked with us on a partnership basis we merely hired extra assistants and talked vaguely of offering them partnerships later if they turned out well. Later we found we couldn't agree on whether they were partnership material. In fact, we found it hard to agree on anything, and Charley's main function as the head of the firm was to pour oil on the constantly heaving waters. It made us realize how much we all missed Paul. He had taken our diverse personalities and welded them into a cohesive whole. Without him it was a continuous struggle for unity, although as the months passed we did become more stable. The prosperity helped. It's easier to get along with people when you have a hypnotizing financial interest in staying together, and besides we were too damned busy to afford time out for a civil war. After we had finally agreed on the redistribution of the profits, we had maintained the status quo, reviewing the partnership every six months, but since the longer we waited the more difficult it became to make any alterations, we all preferred the status quo to the inevitable bloodbath of change.

I should have said there were seven New York partners, but no one really counted Cornelius. We had felt obliged to give the kid a nominal partnership out of respect for the capital he had allowed to remain in the firm, and although he did come to the partners' meetings in order to gain experience he always had the good sense to keep his mouth shut. In fact, he and Sam weren't doing too badly. I was surprised. I still didn't care for Cornelius, but I couldn't help liking Sam Keller. He was a nice down-to-earth all-American boy, and what he was doing tangled up with a little pansy like Cornelius I had no idea. However, some kids take longer than others to outgrow that kind of thing, and I was sure he'd get himself straightened out eventually.

For Mildred's sake I did my best to point out to Cornelius what a rocky road he'd chosen for himself, but I wasn't surprised when he took no notice. I decided to let the matter rest. If Mildred was right he'd have a hell of a good time while he destroyed himself, and if she was wrong she'd live to be proud of him. Anyway, as time passed I began to think Mildred had been worrying unnecessarily. Cornelius may have been sharing a bedroom with his boy friend, but they lived quietly at Paul's house on Fifth Avenue and when they did condescend to entertain the partners their dinner parties were as wholesome as apple pie—and just about as conventional and boring.

"And never a queen in sight!" I commented with interest to Caroline. "Except for Cornelius, of course."

"Maybe they're innocent!" speculated Caroline in an orgy of lewd curiosity. "Two little babes on the edge of the Central Park woods!" And when I ridiculed that idea she said slowly, as if she were looking at the scene from a new angle, "You know, Steven, I've come to the conclusion Cornelius is really rather cute. I should think those gorgeous eyes of his could get quite a bedroom expression in them if he put his mind to it, and his smile is just darling."

"Cal!" There were no words to express my horror at her appalling taste, and when she saw my expression she laughed and said she'd rather have my balls than Cornelius' bedroom eyes any day.

My marriage had miraculously taken on a new lease of life. Caroline had always taken a strong interest in my career, and as my success with Van Zale Participations increased, her admiration overflowed into the bedroom. Caroline's interest in sex could plummet from one hundred to zero in no time flat, but now to my delight I found that zero never showed up on the wheel of sexual fortune, while the one-hundred slot reappeared with dazzling frequency. In the spring of 1928 I even dared to ask her if she had changed her mind about having another baby, but that was pushing my luck too far. I didn't bring up the subject again, but I was sad. Scott and Tony were both in school by this time, and it would have been nice to have had another little tot in diapers rollicking around the nursery floor. I didn't see much of the boys during the week because I worked such long hours that I stayed in town, but every Saturday at noon I'd be off to Long Island to take them on outings and expeditions.

I led a busy life but not busy enough to forget Paul's murderers, and by the spring of 1928 I had maneuvered myself into a striking position. I was going to take Greg Da Costa first. He was available, unlike O'Reilly, who appeared to have fallen off the face of the earth. Of course, Greg's role in the conspiracy had been essentially passive, but Dinah Slade had proved he'd had prior knowledge of the assassination, and that was good enough for me.

Through my brother Matt, who had a fatal gift for meeting people who would have felt at home with the Borgias, I had become acquainted with a Mr. Federico Diaconi who was raising money for a chain of hotels in California. With Greg Da Costa in the forefront of my mind, I had condescended to help Mr. Diaconi in his heroic efforts to raise money legally in order to sink into a respectable retirement, and now he and I both knew he had to help me. Greg Da Costa was always chasing a fast buck. It didn't take him long to accept Mr. Diaconi's kind offer of employment, and the next thing I heard he was running one of the hotels. I never did find out if the word "hotel" was a synonym for a high-class whorehouse, but I wouldn't have put pimping past Greg and he was the kind of guy who always knew where the nearest poker game was. Since his income was probably coming from several sources, licit and illicit, Mr. Diaconi suggested tactfully that one of his accountants could "handle" Greg's financial affairs.

Knowing Greg, I figured it wouldn't be long before he decided that he needed the taxes on his legal money more than the federal government did, and at a word from Mr. Diaconi I could tip off the Internal Revenue Service. That would put Greg in a tight spot. Of course he would turn to Mr. Diaconi for help, and Mr. Diaconi would play him along gently until Greg, maddened by the scent of easy money, would try a spot of blackmail connected with the hotel's illicit activities.

After that I knew I could confidently leave everything to Mr. Diaconi. Gangland rubouts were as common as Lindy-worshipers nowadays, and the only difference between L.A. and Chicago was that Al Capone preferred the Midwest to the West Coast.

With Greg Da Costa dead, I could inform Bruce Clayton that since Greg had made a full confession the game was up. Bruce might choose to call my bluff, but with his past mental history I doubted it. He'd take his own way out, particularly if I told him I'd wait to give him the chance to do the right thing, and he wasn't the sort of guy who'd have any trouble figuring out what the right thing was.

That left Terence O'Reilly, and he'd be the hardest of all to take but I'd manage it somehow as soon as he surfaced again. O'Reilly's disappearance was now really bothering me. It was twenty-one months since the assassination and he still hadn't come tippy-toeing into town to claim his bride. I made up my mind that after the second anniversary of Paul's death I was going to launch another full-scale search for him.

It was a Sunday at the end of April when all my plans went up in smoke. I was helping the boys rebuild their tree house, which had been damaged by winter storms, and just as I was nailing down the roof Caroline arrived at the beach.

"Steven."

One glance at her face told me it was important. "What's wrong?"

"I just had a call from Sylvia Van Zale. She says Bruce Clayton drowned this morning off the beach at Montauk."

II

It was supposed to have been an accident. Obviously he did his best to spare his family, but you don't go swimming in April in the Labrador Current unless you're the toughest of athletes, and Bruce was never known as an outdoor sportsman.

I knew I'd have no rest until I found out if he'd left a suicide note for his family.

I drove into town. It wasn't my intention to harass the bereaved, but I felt I had no choice. At the house on Gramercy Park Eliot Clayton told me Elizabeth wasn't receiving visitors and more or less asked me to get the hell out. Having always thought him a cuckolded nonentity, I was considerably surprised by his tough stance, but after he'd told me flatly there was no suicide note because there had been no suicide I had no alternative but to retire defeated to my apartment.

I called Sylvia, but she knew no more than she'd already told Caroline, and I was just wondering how I could get the truth without persecuting the surviving relatives when the day after the funeral Elizabeth herself asked me to call on her.

III

I had always admired Elizabeth Clayton. I liked her manner, which was graciously intelligent, and I stood in awe of her regally handsome looks. Caroline always dismissed her by demanding to know how Paul could possibly have found her sexy, but I always thought Elizabeth was much sexier than Sylvia. Elizabeth gave a man the impression that she understood him absolutely and that while making no demands she would always be available if ever he needed her help. This intuitive sympathy, coupled with a total absence of possessiveness, was far more alluring than a dozen pairs of perfect thighs, and I could well understand why Paul had fallen for her in a big way. Good thighs are a dime a dozen, but Elizabeth's personality was unique.

I had been jolted by her appearance at the funeral, and now I was jolted again. Her face was haggard, her eyes shadowed, her hair white. She looked nearer seventy than sixty.

She gave me the note. I didn't have to ask her for it. She just unlocked a drawer inside her bureau, took out an envelope and gave it to me.

"Read this," she said. "I want you to read it." Her voice was calm, but her hand shook as she pressed it to her forehead.

"If you're quite sure . . ."

"Yes." She turned away and walked to the other end of the room. She was silent, but presently I realized she was crying.

I unfolded the letter. My heart was banging away like Jack Dempsey revving up for a knockout. At first I couldn't focus on the small disorganized handwriting. I had to steady myself and try again.

The first paragraph was spent apologizing for his suicide and ended: ". . . but I can no longer live with my guilt."

In the second paragraph he admitted that he had plotted Paul's murder and had shot Krasnov to silence him.

The third paragraph began: "For months I deceived myself that the action would be justifiable on both moral and ideological grounds, but as soon as he was dead I could only remember how good he was to me, how much he contributed to my growing up, and how happy the three of us used to be together. . . ."

At that point I lost my place, and it took me a good ten seconds to find it again. I had anticipated the truth but not such suffering. I was hating him and thinking "The poor crazy sonofabitch" at one and the same agonizing moment.

At last I managed to read on: "When I came out of the sanitarium I knew I owed it to Grace and to you to put my terrible remorse behind me, but whenever I met the elder of my two fellow-conspirators and saw that he was not only unrepentant but profiting richly from his crime . . ."

The bottom dropped out of the world.

Unable to believe the sentence, I read it again. O'Reilly was my age, but Greg Da Costa was a contemporary of my brothers, who were five years my junior. That meant that Bruce had to be referring to O'Reilly, but I had had Bruce watched since Paul's funeral and I knew for a fact not only that O'Reilly had disappeared but that he and Bruce had never met. I also knew that where O'Reilly was concerned there were two possibilities: either he had retreated to some remote corner of the world or else he was dead, and a guy like Terence O'Reilly doesn't go kicking the bucket when he has a girl like Sylvia to look forward to at last. I was prepared to bet he was alive and scheming in a smartly feathered nest overseas.

I thought of O'Reilly putting his feet up in some alien Eden, apparently untroubled by the need to earn a living.

I thought of the ten thousand dollars in Krasnov's bank account.

I thought of Paul's fifty-percent share of the profits being split among his surviving partners.

I thought of the keys to the Willow Alley door.

Elizabeth took one look at my face and rang for brandy.

I was in such a state I couldn't even dig out my hip flask. I just sat on the couch with the letter in my hands, and eventually I remembered I hadn't finished reading it. I went back to that terrible paragraph but kept getting stuck, just like a phonograph needle trapped in a groove. The butler was placing brandy before me by the time I managed to complete the sentence: ". . . whenever I met the elder of my two fellow-conspirators and saw that he was not only unrepentant but profiting richly from his crime I knew my guilt would never let me rest. Forgive me, Mother, but . . ."

There was more, but I couldn't cope with it. Putting down the letter, I swallowed my brandy, wiped the sweat from my forehead and tried to think what I could say.

After a long silence Elizabeth took the letter and locked it away again in the bureau drawer. Her hands were steady now and her eyes were tearless.

"I never believed the Russian acted alone," she said. "I always knew Bruce was guilty, but I knew too that he couldn't have planned such a thing by himself. The murder was so . . ." She paused for the right word and found more than one. "Calculated. Cold-blooded. Bruce wasn't like that. I don't know how long it was before I thought of Terence O'Reilly. During that summer, the summer of '26 when Dinah Slade was in New York, Sylvia confided so many things to me—poor Sylvia, she was so desperate and I was the only one she could turn to. She told me how O'Reilly had approached her, and later when I remembered her story I knew it was O'Reilly who had planned the assassination. I wanted to talk to you then, but I couldn't. I couldn't talk to anyone, even Eliot. All I wanted was to protect Bruce."

"I understand."

We were silent again. She was sitting opposite me. The empty brandy glass stood on the table between us.

"I thought there was just one other conspirator besides Bruce," she said. "I never dreamed there were two. I never imagined that there could be someone here in New York—someone Bruce saw regularly—someone unrepentant and profiting richly from his crime. . . . Steve—" She stopped.

We looked at each other. I knew she knew, but I knew too that I didn't have to worry. It was very quiet in the room.

"Eliot's firm does such a lot of business with Van Zale's," she said. "You know how often we entertain the Van Zale partners."

"Yes. And Bruce and Grace were so often at your dinner parties." I got up abruptly and went to the window. When I turned at last she was right behind me. "Elizabeth, has anyone else seen that letter?"

"No. Not even Eliot. No one else is ever going to see it. When I feel strong enough I shall burn it." Her eyes shone with tears again. "Everyone knows I've paid a high price for my personal life," she said, "but I want you to be the only one who knows it's bankrupted me."

I took her hand in mine and held it.

After a moment she said unevenly, "You'll . . . take care of it, won't you?"

"Yes."

"Privately?"

"Of course."

"I don't want anyone calling my son a murderer," she said. "I don't want anyone knowing. They wouldn't understand how he was used—how other people played on his emotions . . . other people . . . unrepentant . . . profiting richly . . ."

"I'll crucify them."

I left. Outside, the sun was shining brightly and the birds were chirping in Gramercy Park.

I walked uptown.

Two hours later in my apartment I tossed an empty bottle of bourbon into the trashcan, lit a cigarette and called my brothers.

IV

My brothers came bounding up to my apartment and immediately headed for the liquor cabinet. They were twins who just missed being identical, but all three of us were alike enough for people to guess we were brothers.

"You're the top copy," Paul had said brutally when he had turned down my request that my brothers should work at Van Zale's, "and your brothers are the two blurred carbons."

It was a cruel description, but although I hated to admit it I knew later that Paul had been right not to accept Luke and Matt as protégés. Those boys would never have made investment bankers. Luke didn't have the eye for financial detail, Matt didn't have the brains and neither of them liked to work hard. However, I'd always felt deeply responsible for my brothers. Since my stepfather had wanted his role to be friendly and not paternal, I was really the only father those boys had ever known, and from the moment my father died I'd known they were my responsibility. I'd done my best, but it's not easy to assume the role of father when you're only nine years old, and as I've already said, I had problems of my own.

Luke was the smart one. He had a presentable wife who had put up with him for ten years, a respectable job as a partner in the flashy little brokerage firm of Tanner, Tate and Sullivan, two cute kids, a

Packard and an Oldsmobile and a house in Westchester that he could at last afford. It was over a year now since he had asked me to foot his mortgage bills for him. He wore clean-cut well-pressed clothes and conservative neckties and read the *New York Times* on the train each morning on the way to work.

Matt, who had been married three times and was now hamming it up with a fifty-year-old actress, was the one who needed looking after. Before I made him the figurehead president of Van Zale Participations he had been officially peddling bonds, but unofficially he had made money by following various pools and selling out before the operator pulled the plug. The art of boosting nondescript stock on the ticker so that fortunes were made for the group which formed a pool was an art which Matt had lyrically compared to a composer penning a symphony score. The stock would rise as the pool bought in, rise again as interest developed in it, drop slightly to reassure the public it was bona fide, continue to rise and fall evenly over a carefully calculated period of time and then rise for the last time. The pool bought and bought, the public, lured on by the pot of gold at the end of the rainbow, charged in and drove the price up through the roof, the pool sold out, scooping the maximum profit, and the public was left holding the bag as the stock was abandoned to slide down to its genuine value. As Matt himself said, "It sure beats poker any day," but the pool operators were a sharp crowd and I lived in fear he'd get mixed up in something he couldn't handle. It was a great relief to me that I'd finally got him settled in a job where I could keep an eye on him.

"Sit down, boys," I said after they had poured out the scotch, "and see if you can help me for a change. I want some information from Greg Da Costa."

V

I had to be careful what I told them. Having swallowed the public version of the assassination, they believed Krasnov had acted alone, and for Elizabeth's sake I still wanted to keep Bruce's name out of the story. Naturally I couldn't mention either the suicide note or its hair-raising implications, yet in order to enlist my brothers' help I had to let them know that there was a large amount of money knocking around as the result of a conspiracy which only Greg Da Costa could unravel. In the end I fell back on the theory quashed by my friend in Washington—that Krasnov had been backed by a foreign government.

"Find out what the real story is, would you, boys?" I said casually.

"I want to know where Greg's money comes from and what he knows about Paul's murder."

They looked at me trustfully. I sighed. Sometimes I couldn't help wishing they were just a little quicker on the uptake.

"Hell, fellows," I said, "think of those summers at Newport when you and the Da Costa brothers smoked cigars behind the greenhouse, swigged port on the sly and tried to figure out how to unlace a whalebone corset. If you go out to California on business Greg's going to weep with nostalgia as soon as you walk through the doors of his hotel."

"What business?" said Matt.

"Oh, I see!" said Luke, but he didn't.

I plowed on. "You're the president of Van Zale Participations," I said to Matt, "and, Luke, you're the broker who handles the trust's investments. Tell Greg you've heard he's hit the jackpot and offer to double his money. Then take him out to dinner, feed him the best hooch in town and—since you're talking about money—find out just where his wonderful fortune came from."

They chewed that over. Matt was thrilled by the cloak-and-dagger aura of the mission. Luke was cool.

"I don't like Los Angeles," he said, "and Greg Da Costa's the kind of guy I'd prefer not to be seen with nowadays."

"You've got to go, Luke," I said, and as our glances met I saw he knew why. I didn't trust Matt to handle the job alone.

Luke looked glum. He was the smart twin, the respectable twin, but when I held up the hoop he knew he had no choice but to jump through it. "All right, Steve," he said grudgingly, falling into line, and two days later he and Matt left for L.A.

VI

The call came when I had just returned to my office after a partners' meeting.

"Steve?" said Luke. "It's us. Jesus Christ, you won't believe the beans that have been spilled."

I felt so sick I could hardly speak. "No names on the phone, please. Where are you calling from?"

"Chicago. No problem, Steve. Greg was stewed as week-old prunes and won't remember a damn thing, but I thought we ought to get out of L.A. and head east on the first available train."

"Swell. I'll meet you at the station. What time do you hit town?"

He told me. I was there. I stuffed them into a cab, whipped them up to the apartment, slammed the door and reached for the scotch.

"All right, boys, let's have it."

"Paul was knocked off by Bruce Clayton and Terence O'Reilly!" they chorused.

I just stood there holding the bottle of scotch. "And?" I said blankly.

"Christ, Steve," said Luke, "isn't that enough? Listen, this is the way it was—"

"Greg came to New York in the summer of '26 after Stew got killed," interrupted Matt, bursting to hog the limelight, "and Bruce Clayton—if you can believe it—asked him for a loan."

"That just proves there's nothing so dumb as a highflown intellectual," said Luke dryly, "but Greg was living well in Mexico at the time, and apparently Bruce thought he was making a mint ranching. Bruce said he knew some crazy Russian who would knock off Paul for ten thousand bucks and was Greg interested in putting up the money and paying back Jay's suicide with interest."

"Of course, as we all know," said Matt, "if Greg had to choose between avenging his father and a steady income he'd choose the income, but he suddenly had this bright idea about how he could have his cake and eat it."

"He said he couldn't spare the cash," said Luke, "but he cheered them on from the sidelines. Then after Paul was dead he turned around and blackmailed the hell out of both Bruce and Terence."

"Say, Steve," said Matt, "are you going to go on nursing that bottle or do we have any hope of getting a drink?"

I fixed the drinks. I was still feeling weak at the knees. "How did Greg know where to find O'Reilly?"

"O'Reilly kept in touch. You can bet *he* didn't trust Greg to keep his mouth shut. O'Reilly's no dumb intellectual. Of course, if he planned to disappear for good it wouldn't matter how much Greg talked, but apparently he plans to come back to New York for a while. Greg thought there was some broad involved, though he didn't know who it was."

"But where the hell is O'Reilly, for God's sake?"

"Argentina," said Matt placidly. "He's bought a huge ranch and he's acting like he's king of the pampas."

"You were right about the money, Steve," added Luke. "There's one hell of a lot of it floating around. That's some bill the Russians are footing for Paul's murder! Quite apart from O'Reilly, Greg's living so high on the hog that he even has two chauffeurs. It was true that the broad he married had money of her own, but Greg soon showed her how to spend it. Wherever his money's coming from now, it doesn't come from her."

I said very carefully in my best casual voice, "Did Greg tell you in words of one syllable just where all this fairy-tale loot was coming from?"

"Sure. Terence O'Reilly. He gets a check every month."

"O'Reilly must be in direct contact with the Russians," said Luke. "Cigarette, Steve?"

I smoked a cigarette to the butt while the boys marveled at their discoveries. When the cigarette was finished I congratulated them on their detective work, confessed I didn't know what I would have done without them and told them that if they breathed one word about the existence of a conspiracy I'd toss them out of Van Zale Participations and never speak to either of them again.

They swore earnestly that there was no need for me to worry. "Because we know what it would do to the bank, Steve," said Luke, "if word got around that a high-grade employee like O'Reilly had been involved."

It was nice to know that at least one of the boys wasn't always slow on the uptake. I patted him on the back and gave him another drink. Eventually they wanted to know what I was going to do next.

"Well, if O'Reilly's king of the pampas," I said dryly, "I think it's about time he paid America a state visit." And the very next day I called with reluctance on Sylvia Van Zale.

VII

By that time, May 1928, New York was whipping through its brief spring toward yet another torrid moneymaking summer. People had stopped talking about Lindbergh's flight to Paris, and the Street was once again the universal topic of conversation. There was only one Street in America now and everyone knew it began across from Trinity Church and glittered down past Morgan's to the corner of Willow and Wall. The ticker tape was blazing its mighty message of unlimited riches, and in response to our servants' pleas we had a ticker installed in our kitchen on Long Island. There were tickers everywhere now, in the clubs, in the hotels, in the restaurants, even on board transatlantic liners—for Wall Street was the promised land, and the milk and honey would flow for anyone who had a couple of nickels to spare.

My chauffeur, ferrying me uptown with a client, would leave the dividing panel ajar so that his long ears could pick up the hottest market tips. Even the housemaids could read the mesmerizing symbols of the great bull market, and at the elegant dinner parties and the debutantes' thé-dansants, the swell nightclubs and the lowest speakeasies, people spoke in hushed tones of the gods who made all financial miracles possible, the magnificent, bighearted, lovable investment bankers who floated issue after issue of mouth-watering pieces of paper, the chips for the greatest gambling machine of all time.

We were celebrities. Following Paul's example I tried to keep on close terms with the press, but eventually I had to call a halt to the interviews. I just didn't have the time. The press interviewed Caroline instead and photographed our Long Island home. Charley Blair's new yacht was front-page news in the tabloids, and Lewis' Hollywood profile reappeared with monotonous regularity whenever he went to Washington to confer with the Treasury Secretary. Martin gave a guest lecture at Columbia. Clay was interviewed on the radio. Ward McAllister's traditional society of Old New York finally blended with the Café Society chronicled by Maury Paul when the Yankee aristocrats achieved the glamour of upstart film stars, but as I was driven uptown in my snow-white Rolls-Royce to meet Sylvia I couldn't help wondering what our doting public would think if they knew that a handful of their heroes were up to their aristocratic necks in extortion, conspiracy and homicide.

Paul had left the Fifth Avenue mansion to Cornelius, but Sylvia had received the homes in Maine and Florida. She had sold them. She had wanted only to live quietly, and after making pilgrimages to both Bar Harbor and Palm Beach as if to say goodbye to her past memories she had bought a townhouse on Fifty-fourth Street between Madison and Park. She hadn't wanted the mansion on Fifth Avenue—no doubt Paul had been aware of that when he made his will—and it wasn't until I was invited to her new home that I realized how she must have disliked the grandeur of those homes she'd shared with Paul. Her little brownstone was simple and cozy. There were no antiques, nothing which would remind her of Fifth Avenue. In the morning room there were some nice books like the Edith Wharton novels, a couple of watercolors of San Francisco and a small photograph of Paul which somehow managed to dominate the room. I looked at him while the butler went off to announce my arrival and discovered that no matter where I stood the eyes in the photograph watched me. Once in Europe Paul had dragged me through an art gallery and I'd seen paintings like that. It was the damndest trick I ever saw on canvas.

When Sylvia entered the room I gasped, because she'd had her hair cut. It was the first indication I had that she was recovering from her loss, for Paul had never let her bob or shingle her hair.

She blushed like a schoolgirl. "Do I look awful?" she said nervously. "I only had it done yesterday."

"You look wonderful!" I said, and meant it. The new style made her look years younger. No one could have guessed that she was now the wrong side of forty, and suddenly I felt sick. She looked like a woman who either had a lover or was expecting one to arrive any day from Argentina.

"Sylvia," I said after the maid had brought in coffee, "you must have wondered why I asked to see you like this during business hours."

She at once became tense. "I knew you were signaling that it was something important." She finished pouring the coffee and set down the pot with care. "Is it about Bruce?" she said fearfully. "Was it suicide after all?"

I said nothing. At last she realized I had made a pact with Elizabeth, and she tried again. "Was Dinah Slade right?" she said in a rush.

"Yes and no. It's turned out that Greg Da Costa was no more than a bystander. But there was definitely a certain other person involved."

She got up very suddenly, moved to the fireplace and then stopped as if she couldn't remember why she was on her feet. As I watched I saw her twisting her wedding band round and round on her finger.

"It's no one I know, is it?" she said, not looking at me, and when I didn't reply she collapsed onto the couch. "But it can't be—it just can't be. I've been telling myself over and over again . . ."

"Have you heard from him, Sylvia?"

"Two weeks ago. He wrote to me for my birthday. It was the first I'd heard of him since Paul's funeral. I thought—" She stopped.

"That he'd forgotten you?"

"That he'd finally taken no for an answer." She kept smoothing her skirt over her knees. She looked so pretty with her short hair. "It was a long silence," she said. "I didn't mind. I was glad. I didn't want to hear from him again. But when he wrote . . . He said nothing had changed, nothing would ever change, he said he'd come into some money and had bought this ranch in Argentina—he even sent me some pictures of it. He said he wanted to come to New York to see me but he wouldn't come unless I was willing—ready—recovered . . ." Her voice trailed away.

"And are you?"

"I don't know," she said, twisting her wedding ring, but I looked at her new hair style and thought I could see the truth better than she could. "I just don't know. I've been thinking and thinking about him, wondering how it would be to get away from New York and start afresh. In some ways I think it would be the best thing for me, yet I don't know whether I've got the strength to make such a break with the past. Probably if he came here he'd give me the strength." Her eyes were dark with memory and I knew then that O'Reilly had some special sexual message for her that I'd never be able to read. But the next moment she was saying with a shudder, "He was so fanatical. I always knew there was nothing he wouldn't do to get what he wanted."

There was a long silence before I could bring myself to say, "Sylvia, I want him back in New York and you're the only person who can help me."

"Are you sure—quite sure . . . beyond any reasonable doubt . . . ?"

"It's not just Greg Da Costa's uncorroborated story. I've been in touch with the manager of Greg's bank in L.A. Every month Greg gets a check drawn on a Swiss bank account and signed by Terence O'Reilly. And there's Dinah Slade's evidence too, Sylvia. Before she called you that night she'd just read a letter from Greg implying knowledge of the conspiracy, and the letter was written to O'Reilly. Finally, there are the facts that not even O'Reilly himself disputes. He had infiltrated Bruce's society, he knew Krasnov—and that means he just had to know what was going on, because I've never met anyone smarter at digging up dirt than Terence O'Reilly. Hell, he even exposed Salzedo! Exposing a lunatic like Krasnov would be child's play in comparison. Anyway, if you add all those facts to the knowledge that he had the strongest possible motive for wishing Paul dead, there's only one conclusion to be drawn."

I thought she might shy away from such a verdict, but her reaction was strong and immediate.

"Then that's that," she said flatly. "I'll get him here for you."

"Sylvia, I sure hate to use you like this."

"No," she said more strongly than ever, "don't apologize. If he had a hand in killing Paul I want him brought to justice."

"It'll be a vigilante justice," I said, watching her. "You realize that."

"Just do whatever has to be done." Her face was bleak. Even the shine seemed to have gone from her pretty hair. "I won't talk about it and I won't ask any questions."

We stood up. Her hand was cold as I took it in mine and drew her to me for a kiss. Paul's eyes watched us from the photograph frame.

"Let me know when the next letter comes from Argentina, Sylvia," I said, and then leaving the house I traveled rapidly downtown to the bank.

VIII

He never answered her letter. He just packed his bags, jumped on a ship to Florida and caught the train north from Fort Lauderdale. He reached New York on the sixteenth of July, five days before the second anniversary of Paul's death, and checked into the St. Regis, a stone's throw from Sylvia's brownstone.

I was in Philadelphia and had just returned to my hotel after a long business meeting when the phone rang.

"Steve, this is Cornelius."

I was surprised. I couldn't think of a single reason why Cornelius should need to phone me. "Yeah?" I said. "Some problem at the office?"

"No, I'm speaking from Sylvia's house. Terence O'Reilly turned up on her doorstep today. Being upset, she called the bank and when she heard you were out of town she asked for me." Cornelius' prim Midwestern accent was as neutral as a tract of virgin snow.

"Let me talk to her," I said abruptly.

Cornelius transferred the receiver without a word. Sylvia's voice said breathlessly, "Steve?"

"Sylvia, how much have you told that kid?"

"But that's the amazing thing, Steve! He seemed to know it already! As soon as I mentioned Terence's name—"

"Let's not go into details on the phone. Are you all right?"

"Yes. No. Well, I mean I was shattered to see him without warning, but fortunately he understood and said he'd give me twenty-four hours to adjust to the idea of his being in town. He said he'd telephone later from the St. Regis."

"Fine. I'll come back to New York right away to take care of everything. Now let me speak to Cornelius again, please."

"Steve?" said Cornelius presently.

"We'd better talk, hadn't we."

"I'd appreciate that," said Cornelius, still chillingly neutral.

"One o'clock tomorrow at the Colony."

"I'll be there."

We hung up. I stared into space for ten empty seconds, and then I unscrewed the cap on my hip flask and poured myself the stiffest scotch in town.

IX

I returned to New York, calmed Sylvia down, snatched a few hours' sleep, hired private detectives to watch O'Reilly, put in an appearance at two board meetings, interviewed a client who wanted twenty million dollars, glanced over the statistical analysis of a proposed merger between two utility companies, called Matt to check he wasn't trying to run a bucket shop out of the office of Van Zale Participations, and raced uptown for lunch.

I was ten minutes late and Cornelius was waiting for me. Naturally he would have arrived on time. As I was shown to the table he stood up, for he was always scrupulously deferential to me. In fact no junior partner could have shown more respect for his elders and betters than young Master Cornelius Van Zale of Van Zale's.

I ordered ginger ale.

"Scotch?" I offered him as I produced my hip flask.

"Thank you," said Cornelius, "but I never drink liquor at midday."

I grabbed the bread basket, pounced on the largest roll and bit it as hard as I could. Cornelius daintily nibbled a breadstick. As soon as the waiter arrived with my ginger ale I snatched a couple of menus from the maître d' and said we'd order right away.

"I'll have the pâté," I added, "followed by a filet mignon, medium rare, with creamed potatoes and a salad. French dressing."

"I'll have a hamburger," said Cornelius without opening the menu. "Well done. No potatoes."

Ernest, the maître d' who ruled over that dimly lighted, high-ceilinged palace of a restaurant like a high priest over a temple, blanched but somehow got the order down. One of the nice things about having fifty million dollars is that you can order a hamburger in a joint like the Colony without being flung out into the street.

I took a long pull at my drink, lit a cigarette and made a great business of shaking out the match. When there was nothing else left to do I said shortly, "All right, let's have it. Talk."

Cornelius went right on nibbling his breadstick. A minor waiter filled our water glasses. When we were alone again Cornelius said respectfully, "Well, I have to congratulate you, Steve. You did a brilliant job."

I stared at him. He gazed back. His starry gray eyes were effortlessly innocent.

"You must have bribed every cop in town."

I shifted uneasily in my chair. "You realized—"

"Why, sure. I'm not dumb. I knew from the start that the conspiracy reached beyond Clayton and Krasnov, and I knew exactly why you had to cover it up. Say, it was real smart of you to lure O'Reilly back to town, although I'm sorry you had to use Sylvia. What do you plan to do next?"

I shifted again in my chair and took another long pull at my drink. "What made you suspect O'Reilly?" I said at last. "None of the other partners do, because they figure he had no motive for wanting Paul dead."

"They should have seen the way he used to look at Sylvia during that first summer I spent at Bar Harbor."

There was a silence. The kid finished his breadstick and wiped his little paws on his snow-white napkin. My uneasiness increased.

"How come you kept so quiet about all this?" I said.

"I figured the last thing you needed was noise. However, I must admit I did plan on approaching you on the second anniversary of Paul's death and asking you if I could help fix O'Reilly. Incidentally—just out of interest—did you suggest to Bruce Clayton that he should commit suicide?"

"I did not." I pulled myself together, struggled out of the trance he'd put me in and prepared to whip him into line. "Now, listen to me, Cornelius . . ." I began and launched into a speech about the dire consequences for the bank if the conspiracy became public knowledge.

"Yes, Steve," said Cornelius, looking at me with dutiful gray eyes.

By the time our main course had arrived I was feeling more relaxed. ". . . So you can rely on me to tidy matters up satisfactorily," I concluded with relief.

"Yes." He signaled the maître d', who immediately swerved to our table. "Ketchup, please."

Ernest shuddered and withdrew.

When the ketchup arrived Cornelius annointed his hamburger, closed the bun and sank his teeth into it.

"Right," I said affably, carving up my steak. "Any other questions?"

"Uh-huh," said Cornelius. "Who's the guilty partner?"

I put down my knife and fork and reached for the scotch. My stomach felt as if it had been kicked at close range. "Guilty who?" I said feebly.

"Partner. Come on, Steve. Let's quit waltzing around and get down to brass tacks. According to Sylvia, O'Reilly just happened coincidentally to walk into enough money to buy up a large slice of Argentina, but we don't really believe that, Steve, do we? Expecting us to believe that would be like expecting us to believe in Santa Claus, and anyway if you go right back to the assassination it's obvious O'Reilly had to use the Willow Alley exit—with help from a partner willing to lend his keys. The problem was not how to get Krasnov into the building, but how to convince Krasnov he had a chance of getting out."

"But . . ." I opened and closed my mouth twice, but nothing came out.

"Face facts," said the kid agreeably, pouring some more blood-colored sauce onto his plate and dipping a chunk of bun in it. "Krasnov wasn't one of these assassins who kill for glory and don't mind dying in the attempt. He had ten thousand dollars waiting for him in his bank account. He would never have agreed to kill Paul unless they fixed him up with a plausible escape route, and since he couldn't walk out of the front door, fly out of a window or disappear up the chimney in a puff of smoke, he had to use the back entrance. So they let him in that way to prove he could get out that way. They had to. He wouldn't have gone near the building without the Willow Alley keys in his pocket. Of course they knew he'd be rubbed out, but Krasnov had to believe he'd leave the building alive."

"Yeah. Sure." I cleared my throat. I wondered what kind of expression was on my face. "Well, all right, but O'Reilly could have had copies made of those keys."

"How? By picking a partner's pocket?"

"Well, when he was Paul's personal assistant—"

"That was just when he didn't need any duplicates. He had access to Paul's keys. Anyway, why would he have wanted a spare set back then? He knew damned well he wasn't allowed to use that entrance unless he was with Paul."

"I still think—"

"You can explain the Willow Alley keys away till you're blue in the face, Steve, but you can't explain why O'Reilly's living like a millionaire."

I tried to float my foreign-government fairy tale. Cornelius sank it in seconds.

"Oh please, Steve, I really am too old to believe in Santa Claus!"

"How about the stock market? You believe in that, don't you?"

"If O'Reilly had made a big killing on the market your operatives would have heard of it and traced him. I presume you did have operatives looking for him."

I played my trump card. "None of us partners had a motive for killing Paul."

"You mean one of us did but we can't prove yet what it was. I'd guess it was financial."

"But we were all rich!"

"Are you sure?"

We stared at each other. Cornelius' sharp little face had a white pinched look. Suddenly he shivered. "It was an obscene conspiracy," he said in a low voice, "and it's still going on. How are you going to end it?"

I hesitated but knew I had no choice but to take him into my confidence. He knew too much to be fobbed off. "I'm going to start by bribing O'Reilly to give us the name," I said slowly. "Paul always said O'Reilly was the most venal of his protégés."

"And then?"

"Then Sylvia tells him she'll follow him to Argentina as soon as she's sold her house and wound up her New York life. O'Reilly goes back to Argentina to lay out the red carpet. I'm expecting our clients the Argentinian government to pay us their usual visit next month, and when I negotiate with them I'll make damned sure there's an unwritten condition on our next loan."

Cornelius nodded. As far as I could see he was neither shocked nor surprised, merely approving. "May I make a suggestion?" he said politely. "When you find out from O'Reilly who this guilty partner is, you should record the entire conversation. Otherwise the partner can always deny it, O'Reilly will be back in Argentina and you won't be able to prove a damned thing."

I was skeptical. "How the hell am I going to do that? Suggest to O'Reilly that we rendezvous in a recording studio?"

"We can use an ordinary room."

"We?" I said, fearing the worst.

"You, me and Sam. Sam'll fix it. He knows all about that kind of thing."

"Now, don't get me wrong," I said sweating. "I like Sam. He's a good kid. But—"

"Look, Steve," said Cornelius, "you want to crucify this partner, don't you? Well, if you're planning a crucifixion, for God's sake make sure you nail the guilty party good and hard to the cross."

I looked at his tight tough little face. His eyes were arctic gray. Suddenly I laughed. "So you've got balls after all!" I said amused, and as he blushed, betraying both his youth and Mildred's upbringing, I laughed again. "All right, sonny," I said, crossing the Rubicon at last. "We'll talk it over with Sam as soon as we get back to the office."

I should have known as I watched the blood oozing out of my perfect steak that I was playing with matches around a box of dynamite.

Chapter Four

I

"Terence?" I said, the phone fit to melt in my hand. "Steve Sullivan. Welcome back to town."

He stood the shock well. "Steve? No kidding!" he said warily after a taut pause. "How are you doing? This is a surprise!"

"I've got bigger surprises in store. I'd like to meet you tonight at ten o'clock to discuss them. I'll leave the Willow Alley door unlocked for you and we can have a nice long private reminiscence in Paul's office about the summer of '26."

He thought about it. I could almost hear that cool competent brain ticking over like some complicated power meter. Finally he said, "I don't like rehashing the past."

"Knowing your past," I said, "that doesn't surprise me. Be there, Terence, or I spell out to Sylvia in words of one syllable exactly how you murdered her husband. Bruce Clayton left one hell of a suicide note." And cutting off the appalled silence at the other end of the wire, I hung up.

II

At eight o'clock, when the other partners had left and only a few clerks were left catching up on the day's paperwork, I opened the garden doors of the office which now belonged to Charley Blair and crossed the patio to unlock the Willow Alley entrance. The black Cadillac was already parked outside, but there was no chauffeur. Cornelius himself was at the wheel. He and Sam Keller were smoking cigarettes in suspenseful silence.

"All right, boys," I said. "Bring on the props."

Cornelius had told me that Sam, whose hobby was recording amateur jam sessions, had friends at the RCA studios, so I had expected the worst—enough equipment to fill a concert hall, a microphone as big as a melon and enough cable to run all the way down Wall Street to Trinity Church. So it was a pleasant surprise to discover that the props consisted of a smart wooden cabinet, an item with dials and knobs mounted on a panel and two small square boxes with a couple of cute little microphones attached. Even the inevitable cable looked as if it might just fade away into the background.

I was impressed. "Where did you get this junk?"

"Jake Reischman lent it to me," said Sam. "He brought it back last summer from Europe. Apparently there's a guy in Germany called Stille who's putting out this invention, the Vox Diktiermaschine, for use in offices. You dictate letters into them or record conferences and telephone conversations. Jake says that the Reischman bank in Hamburg has several of them and they're real useful. The big advantage is that they go on recording much longer than any other system—even longer than the new system they've developed for making 'talkies.'"

We toted the stuff inside and I watched fascinated as Sam set up the equipment. In fact, I was so interested I almost forgot why we needed the machine.

"How does it work?"

"It's a system of magnetic recording on steel wire," said Sam enthusiastically. "The sound is recorded on a steel wire passed between a pair of magnetic poles which have coils of wire wound round them to form an electromagnet, and the electrical impulses which are set up—"

"How easily does it go wrong?" I said, getting nervous again.

"Well, the wire can break and the motor speed can go haywire, but don't worry, Steve, I've thought about this very carefully. Neil and I will be in the coat closet with the cabinet and this control panel—it'll be a squeeze, but we can make it. Then I can operate not only the recorder but the mixer which balances the level of the speech from the microphones. There's no problem about the cable, because we can run it out of the closet under the folding doors and around the edge of the library under the carpet. The only real risk lies with the microphones. I've substituted these RCA condenser mikes for the original Vox mikes because of the superior frequency response, but—"

"Let's have it in good plain English, Sam. Where are you putting these microphones?"

"One can go in the fireplace behind the grill of the fire-screen," said Sam. "There's no problem about that, because the screen will conceal both the mike and the preamplifier—that's the little box—and the cord can run under the rug as soon as it leaves the grate. But the other mike'll just have to go on the desk."

"Wonderful!" I said sarcastically. "And what do I tell O'Reilly when he marvels at my new paperweight?"

"Well, this is the way I figure it, Steve. The little preamplifier can be concealed in a drawer of the desk. We'll have to drill a hole in the side of the desk next to the wall so that the cord can run out, but it won't take me a minute to fix that. Now, the mike itself can stand right by the lamp at the edge of the desk so that the cord will fall directly between the desk and the wall to the carpet. The odds are that O'Reilly won't notice the cord and if he does he'll assume it's the cord from the lamp. Then we can cover the mike with a loosely arranged handkerchief. I know it'll look shady to us, but I'm gambling on the fact that a handkerchief is so ordinary that O'Reilly won't look at it twice."

"And don't forget, Steve," added Cornelius, with his trick of cutting through the details to the heart of the matter, "it'll never have occurred to O'Reilly that we might try and record the conversation."

"I almost wish it hadn't occurred to you. Are you sure it's really necessary to have two mikes, Sam?"

"I'm playing safe, Steve. One might do the trick, but I couldn't guarantee it. With two we've got less chance of failure."

I resigned myself to the inevitable. "All right, go ahead," I said, and turning to the bar concealed in the bookcase I added, "Drink, kids?"

Cornelius said he never drank after dinner. Sam said he'd wait until he had everything arranged.

"If you're not drinking," I said to Cornelius as I added a sling of the poison that passed for vermouth to my glass of gin, "you can go and hide that Cadillac. It's about as unnoticeable out there as an acre of jungle in the Sahara."

Cornelius got rid of the Cadillac. Sam connected the microphones. I downed my martini. After that we had to see if we could make the machine work, so Cornelius and I struggled to maintain a conversation while Sam crouched in the closet and twiddled the dials.

"Keep going!" called Sam as Cornelius and I ran out of small talk for the fifth time.

"'At Flores in the Azores Sir Richard Grenville lay,'" recited Cornelius, and he paused to say to me, "Tennyson. *The Revenge.* One of Paul's favorite poems." He continued the recital. It was one hell of a long poem, but at least it saved us the trouble of talking to each other. "'. . . and he said: "Sink me the ship, Master Gunner! Sink her—split her in twain! Fall into the hands of God, not into the hands of Spain!"'"

"Great!" yelled Sam. "I've got it! All right, guys, you can relax."

It was nine-thirty. I fixed myself another martini. "We won't close the double doors into the other half of the room," I said, prowling around with my glass in my hand, "or O'Reilly's going to get nervous wondering what's behind them. I only hope to God he doesn't demand to search the premises."

"It's up to you to put him at his ease, isn't it?" said Cornelius nastily.

"Can I have that drink now, please?" said Sam. "Thanks. Gee, I'm nervous! Steve, I wouldn't be in your shoes for all the oil in Texas! Supposing he tries to kill you?"

"Thanks for reminding me, sonny," I said and produced a gun from my briefcase. The little kids boggled at it as if it were a naked lady. Flicking off the safety catch, I laid the gun down carefully in the middle of the desk. "That's just to stop O'Reilly from getting ideas," I explained, "but he's not going to do anything stupid until he's heard what I have to say."

"Is it yours?" asked Sam in awe.

"No. My brother Matt took it off a drunk in a speak a month ago when the drunk tried to pistol-whip him for winking at his wife."

We sat in silence looking at the gun. Finally I told them to take up their positions.

"Steve," said Cornelius in a small voice, "is there any gin left?"

I reopened the bar, poured him a double, showed it the vermouth bottle and handed him the glass.

He downed the drink in two minutes and disappeared after Sam into the coat closet in the other half of the room.

Putting away the glasses, I hid all but one of the dirty ashtrays and fidgeted with the communicating doors.

"I'm going to turn on a small light in here," I said, moving into the drawing room. "I think it'll give O'Reilly extra reassurance that nothing's hidden in this half of the room."

They thought that was a good idea. I pottered around some more before sinking into the chair behind the desk which had belonged to Paul. The gun was still glinting in the light as I finished my martini, and everywhere was very quiet.

I was just wondering whether to fix myself another drink when I heard the tap on the garden doors.

Walking woodenly to the window, I pulled aside the drape. He was there. For one long moment we looked at each other through the darkened glass, and then I unlocked the doors to let him in.

III

"All right," he said. "Where is it?"

For one bad moment I thought he meant the recording equipment.

"Where's what?"

"The suicide note."

I recovered myself in a flash. "That's in a safe in the vaults. You didn't seriously think I'd give you the chance to tear it up, did you? For God's sake, Terence, sit down and stop acting like a cat on hot coals. I called you here to do a deal, not wipe you off the map. Drink?"

"No." He hesitated but finally sat opposite me on the edge of the client's chair. His skin was stretched tightly over his cheekbones. He had lost a little more hair on top of his head, but otherwise he looked the same. His eyes were as bright and hard as jade on ice.

"Let me start by saying," I said, "that Greg Da Costa's spilled the beans. He never could handle his liquor. He admitted Bruce had asked him to put up the blood money."

"That idiotic bastard with his crazy society and crazier schemes! I could have told him he'd be laying his bank account on the line if ever he was fool enough to tangle with Greg Da Costa!"

"Then why didn't you?"

"He'd already done it by the time I got wind of the lunatic scheme he was dreaming up. God, Bruce Clayton was the most unpractical academic that ever lived with his head in the clouds! I saw right away that if he was ever to get what he wanted I'd have to stage-manage the entire operation."

"I kind of figured you took over."

"What choice did I have? Anyway, it was a great opportunity. What I liked best about the scheme was that no matter how many of you partners figured out what had happened you wouldn't be able to do a damn thing, because you knew that if you did you'd ruin the bank. All I had to do was provide a story for the police to swallow and then I knew I could leave it to you to cover my tracks. Steve, I do wish you'd put that gun away. You know damned well you wouldn't dare shoot me any more than I'd dare shoot you. Anyway, I want to hear about this deal you have in mind. You realize, I hope, that you haven't got a shred of evidence against me except the uncorroborated word of Greg Da Costa, a man who'd say anything for money?"

"You're forgetting Bruce's suicide note."

"You're lying about that note, Steve! It's a bluff! Bruce was a gentleman. He was Groton and Harvard and a scion of the Anglo-Saxon Protestant hierarchy that has this country by the balls. He'd never have named a fellow conspirator in that note, because it wouldn't have been the good stuffy Yankee thing to do."

"Uh-huh. So in that case you won't object if I show the note to Sylvia."

The ice began to melt. He fidgeted uneasily. "Let's keep Sylvia's name out of this. What is it you want?"

"A name."

He was very still. I waited. Knowledge flickered at the back of his eyes but was doused at once.

"Who gave you the keys of the Willow Alley door?"

He still said nothing.

"I don't know how much he paid into that Swiss bank account for you, Terence, but I'll pay more. I'll even send you and Sylvia a wedding present from Tiffany's and give the bride away with a smile."

He didn't even bat an eyelid at the prospect of more money, and suddenly I understood what was going on. "My God!" I said. "It wasn't just a settlement! He's paying you an income!"

"Which is something you can't afford to do." He made a quick decision. "Look, Steve, I think we can work this out. You want to get even with this guy, but in fact there's no way you can touch him without blowing up the bank. I want to keep my income. Why don't we combine forces to bleed him white? Wouldn't that be a fitting revenge on a man who'd killed for money?"

I managed to keep my wits about me. I knew I had to pretend to be interested if I was ever going to prise the name out of him. "That's an idea," I said. "I like it. I can't threaten to turn him over to the law, but I could threaten to tell the other partners and force his resignation from the firm." Leaning forward, I aimed my voice straight at the microphone and said, "Let's get this straight. Was this the last man to join the conspiracy?"

"Yes, we were having a problem over raising the ten thousand Krasnov wanted. I could have managed it, but I needed all the money I had to keep me afloat and anyway I was scared the money might be traced to me. Bruce ought to have had the money, but he'd signed away all the money he'd inherited from his father because he didn't approve of inherited wealth. I was just wondering what to do next when I overheard this row. I was working late and I'd gone into your room upstairs to return a file. You'd already left for home, but you hadn't stubbed out your last cigarette properly and as the room was full of smoke I opened the windows. Directly below in this office Van Zale had the patio doors open. I think he must have been just about to leave by the back entrance when this guy had caught him and asked for a word. They were quarreling. As soon as I realized what was going on I knew our problems were solved, because a Van Zale partner can always raise ten thousand dollars, even if he happens to be broke at the time."

"Then it was either Clay or Martin," I said, my stomach churning. "They're the only ones who could come within a million dollars of being broke."

"No," said Terence. "It was one of Jason Da Costa's men."

I was gripping the arms of my chair so hard my shoulders hurt.

"Not Walter," I said. "He's so old and never quarrels with anyone."

"Right."

There was a silence while I thought of all that Lewis had concealed behind his Hollywood profile.

"You'd better talk to him," said Terence at last. "I'll signal him to come in."

"*What!*" I shot out of my chair so fast he jumped. "You mean he's here?"

"Of course!" He looked surprised. "I was in a hell of a panic when you threatened me with the suicide note, and I called him up right away. I was afraid Bruce had named us both, but this guy reassured me that Bruce would have mentioned no names." He got up, drew the drapes slightly and flicked the light switch on and off three times.

My scalp crawled. Sweat streamed down my back, and as I stood rigidly by the desk I heard the Willow Alley door swing shut across the patio.

Reluctant footsteps dragged their way across the flagstones. The drapes billowed as the doors were pulled apart.

I opened my mouth, but Lewis' name froze on my lips.

"Oh, no," said my voice. "Oh, no, no, no."

For the partner wasn't Lewis. It was everyone's friend, Charley Blair.

IV

"He would have ruined me as he ruined Jay Da Costa," said the man who had bought Paul's murder. "I saw what he did to Jay. I knew what he was capable of. It was a question of survival, Steve. My whole life was on the line."

I groped for the edge of the desk and leaned against it. O'Reilly was still at the door by the light switch. Charley was at the other end of the room with his back to the drapes. With a jolt I remembered the microphones, and clumsily I offered him my chair—his chair—behind the desk which he had been using since Paul's death. "Sit down, Charley. I don't understand—you'll have to explain. . . ." As I talked I was edging around the desk over the spot where Paul's blood had streamed from his body. The client's chair was beside me, but before I could sit down I saw the gun still glinting on the desk and realized I had my back to O'Reilly. I spun around. He hadn't moved.

"Come over here, Terence, and take the client's chair. You might as well have a seat."

All three of us were at last grouped around the hidden microphones. O'Reilly and I were separated from Charley by the desk and

I was at the fireplace. I wanted to keep on my feet so that I could be quick off the mark if I had to be, so to look comfortable I put my elbow on the mantel and lounged against it. I wanted to pick up the gun but thought Charley might interpret it as a hostile gesture and I didn't want to destroy the cozy confessional atmosphere. So the gun went on sitting on the desk and I tried to pretend it was just part of the furnishings, nothing to get worried about, just a little piece of Wild West nostalgia to remind us all that New York was a wide-open town.

I took a good hard look at both men but was prepared to bet neither of them was armed. I glanced back at Charley. His eyes were bloodshot and his full cheerful good-natured face was sunken and shadowed. His hands writhed endlessly together. I guessed he had been drinking ever since O'Reilly had called him.

"I was broke," he said to me.

I still couldn't take it in. I thought of his estates in Bar Harbor, Palm Beach and rural New Jersey, the yacht in which he traveled daily down the Hudson from Englewood to Wall Street, his private railroad cars, his fleet of Rolls-Royces, his army of children who had been educated at the best schools in America and Europe.

"How did it happen? How could it ever have happened, Charley?"

"I made a mistake back in '24," he said. "The Florida land boom. I invested heavily in real estate there, but the bottom fell out of the market, the contractor of the new town I was sponsoring discovered difficulties in draining the swampland, and the builder ran out on his contract. I kept putting more money in to save what I'd already invested and I wound up losing three million dollars."

"Three million dollars . . ."

"But I was still all right," said Charley quickly. "I raised the money, took out some mortgages. And then I saw a wonderful chance to get it all back. Do you remember Kramer?"

"The pool operator? Oh my God, Charley—"

"But he was doing wonders at the time, Steve! I was all set to pull in a fortune—I'd taken out a big loan in order to play—and then the swine pulled the plug on the pool before I'd sold out. Of course I couldn't say anything. He'd got a bad name by that time and I didn't want my reputation to be tarnished. You know my reputation on the Street, Steve. I've always been so proud of my reputation. Anyway, I gambled again on the market . . ."

It was painful to listen to him. My eyes kept watching his twisting hands.

". . . but then I really got burnt and I had to come up with more money fast, so . . . Well, I'm the treasurer of the yacht club. I got hold of some of their bonds and used those bonds to raise the money I needed."

"Did the club owe you money?"

"No."

"You mean you—"

"Yes. I embezzled the bonds. I know it was a terrible thing to do, but I was desperate, Steve, and then—oh, God, when I think of the next few months . . . The money I'd embezzled wasn't enough. I was falling behind in paying the interest on the debts I'd run up, and of course I couldn't possibly have confided in my wife and suggested we lower our standard of living. Anyway, the market was booming by that time, and I knew that if only I had two hundred thousand I could make everything come right. So I . . . I . . ."

"You went to Paul."

"Yes. I didn't expect him to ask any questions. After all, we were both gentlemen and I'd stood by him all through the Salzedo affair. But he did ask questions. Then I made a terrible mistake. I thought if I came clean he would be sympathetic, but as soon as he heard about the yacht-club bonds he refused to help me—and not only that, but he asked for my resignation." He was trembling with emotion at the memory. "He asked for my resignation," he said as if he still couldn't believe it. "He called me a criminal. My God, he was the criminal, not I! All I needed was a little money to put my affairs in order."

"But if the yacht-club business had ever come to light—if you'd gone on putting good money after bad . . . Of course Paul had to put the bank first, Charley! His first loyalty had to be to the bank!"

"No," said Charley. "His first loyalty should have been to his own kind. We all have to stick together. It's the code of our class, and Paul was breaking that code. By refusing me the money he would have ruined me, because without his help I knew I had no chance of getting back on my feet. He would have destroyed my whole life, my family, my reputation—"

"So you bought his murder."

"Yes, but you see, Steve, it all worked out. After the profits were redistributed I recouped my losses, put back the bonds and paid off my debts."

"You killed him, Charley."

"No, the others did that. They would have killed him anyway." He licked his lips. "Steve, that's past now. We really mustn't go raking it all up, and you know what an asset I am to the bank. I'm so popular, you see, and I have such a wonderful reputation."

That was when I knew for certain he had released his grasp on reality. He couldn't conceive that his precious reputation had already led him to the gutter.

"You're going to resign, Charley," I said. "I'm not working alongside Paul's killer any longer."

O'Reilly leaned forward sharply in his chair. "Steve, have you forgotten what we agreed?"

"Agreed?" said Charley, quick as a flash. His glance darted between us. "You mean you've changed sides?"

"Steve knows the truth. I've got to protect myself."

"You've double-crossed me!"

"For Christ's sake, Charley," said O'Reilly, and in his contemptuous use of the Christian name instead of his former respectful "Mr. Blair" I caught a sickening glimpse of Charley's long fall into degradation. "Use your brains. There's only one way you can stop Steve from going to the partners and forcing your resignation, and that's to pay him. Now, Steve and I have worked out this plan—"

"You fool," said Charley. "He's not interested in money. He wants revenge. He'll break you in two before he's finished with you." He swiveled back to face me. "I'll never resign," he said to me. "Never."

My nerve snapped. "You goddamned murderer!" I yelled at him. "You killed Paul! You ought to be shut up in Sing Sing and sent to the electric chair! Paul was shot to death in this very room and all you can talk about is your fucking reputation!"

"It's no good losing your temper, Steve. No one's going to believe your accusations, because everyone likes me so much. I'm one of the most popular men on the Street."

"You're insane!" My anger dissolved abruptly into horror. "You've gone mad! You've got to resign right now, this minute—"

"*Never!*" His persistent serenity was shattered so violently that I sprang back. It was as if all the fragments of his personality had burst apart. He was on his feet, his eyes glittering, his lips wet, the color rushing to his face. "I'll die before I resign!" he shouted. "And if I die I swear I'll take both you and the whole goddamned bank with me!"

I dived for the gun between us but I was too slow. He grabbed it first. Sprawling wildly I overbalanced, and the last thing I heard before I hit the floor was three shots being fired in rapid succession.

V

He shot O'Reilly first. It was lucky for me that he did. I'd lost my balance by the time he fired at me, and the bullet missed, burying itself in the bookcase. Then he turned the gun on himself.

I was still scrabbling on the floor when the boys burst in from the other room.

"My God!" I dimly recognized Sam Keller's appalled voice.

I tried to crawl up the desk onto my feet. My legs felt like wet cement.

"Did he hit you?"

I didn't know. I was in shock, unable to do anything but gasp for breath. I stared around at the carnage. O'Reilly, slumped in his chair, had been shot through the heart. His eyes bore a surprised expression. Charley had fallen forward to sprawl across the desk. He had put the gun to his head, and his brains were sprayed across the back of the chair.

"I think Steve's all right, Sam. There's no blood."

"Christ, Neil, what on earth are we going to do?"

They were twittering like frightened fledglings somewhere above my head.

"The night watchman," I said. I was still on my knees. "The guard. They'll have heard the shots. Mustn't let them see you. Nobody must know. Cover it all up."

"Take it easy, Steve," said Sam. "Shall I get you a shot of brandy?"

I found my hip flask, poured some scotch down my throat and was on my feet. "Get the hell out of here, kids."

"But—"

"Scram! Hide! Do as I say!"

They bolted back to the closet just as the night watchman's running footsteps clattered across the floor of the back lobby.

I was at the door to meet him. "Call the police, Willis!" I gasped. "There's been a terrible accident . . ."

VI

I got rid of him, slammed the door, locked it and yanked the boys out of hiding.

"Get all that recording junk stashed in the car. You've got five minutes at most, probably less."

As they clawed at the equipment I turned back to the carnage, took a deep breath and plunged in. Thanking God the gun could never be traced to me, I wiped away Charley's prints, wrapped O'Reilly's fingers around the handle and let the gun fall to the floor beside his chair. Charley had lunged across the desk to fire at point-blank range, so the powder burns with any luck might be consistent with the explanation that O'Reilly, not Charley, had been the one to turn the gun on himself. When I had finished I vomited into the grate but had recovered by the time Cornelius and Sam came rushing back to collect the last of the props.

"All right, kids," I said. "Remember you saw nothing, heard nothing. You weren't even here. I'll talk to you tomorrow. Now beat it."

They scampered away just as the police stormed down the great hall with the verve of revolutionary troops leading a charge against the British. Sinking down in an armchair, I tried to look as if I were in shock. I didn't have to try very hard.

That was when my tour de force began, and it ended a week later when the official verdict on the disaster proclaimed that Charley had been murdered by Terence O'Reilly, who had then killed himself while temporarily deranged. I lied to everyone in sight, bribed the world to the eyeballs and drank myself into a stupor each night to numb my terror. I'd never even have attempted such a suicidal gamble if I'd had the choice, but unfortunately no such choice existed. The one disaster the bank could never have survived was public knowledge of Charley's crimes.

I told the police that I had fired O'Reilly from the firm after Paul's funeral because of a conflict between our two temperaments, and said he'd been bothering me ever since. He'd claimed he was being victimized and accused me of discriminating against Catholics. When out of sheer Christian charity I had finally granted O'Reilly an audience I had asked Charley to sit in because I'd been nervous about facing a mentally disturbed man on my own.

"Although he didn't go berserk and pull the gun," I explained, "until he'd got me to confess I was a Protestant."

When questioned further I said that O'Reilly had been employed by Paul Van Zale as a general dogsbody and had always deeply resented his insignificant position.

The police swallowed the story whole and retreated with well-greased palms to oil the wheels of Jimmy Walker's wide-open town. The press boozily absorbed the details and wrote the appropriate reams of garbage. At the press conference I'd taken care to fuel the journalists with more decent liquor than they'd seen since the passing of the Eighteenth Amendment, and after I'd talked emotionally for half an hour about the mentally deranged they were all too drunk to care about asking awkward questions.

Not even my partners suspected the truth. Spinning them a variation of the yarn I'd concocted for the police, I said that when Greg Da Costa's information had led me to O'Reilly I had enlisted Charley's help in the final showdown, and not one of them dreamed Charley could also have been involved in the conspiracy. Ironically I was helped by Charley's popularity. Nobody would have believed him guilty of embezzlement, let alone murder, and so in the end his damnable "reputation" saved not only his posthumous good name but Van Zale's itself.

In fact, my partners were all so grateful to me for not only unmasking the conspiracy but neutralizing it that nobody objected when I suggested I should be joint senior partner with Lewis. For once even Clay had to swallow his jealousy in silence.

The funeral was all hell in black tails, and how I got through it I'll never know. The worst part was when Miranda Blair told me tearfully how touched she was to see me so affected by Charley's death. Afterward all I could do was go home, get drunk and pass out.

O'Reilly's estranged family claimed his body, but I didn't have to see them. Lewis coped with that particular scene, but I had to see Sylvia and afterward I almost wished Lewis and I could have swapped places.

"Did he confess?" was the only question she asked.

"Yes."

Of course it never occurred to her to question Charley's role in the affair.

That left Elizabeth Clayton. I thought I ought to see her to make sure my secrets were safe with her, but I needn't have worried. She just told me she had destroyed the suicide note and was glad all Paul's murderers had finally paid for their crime.

She did ask, "Why did Charley do it? Was it some past grudge?" But when I started to explain I saw she wasn't really listening. Motives hardly mattered to her anymore. She had lost Paul and Bruce and nothing could bring them back, not even the justice of Terence O'Reilly's murder and Charley Blair's bloody suicide.

When I left Elizabeth I paused to check that I'd left no stone uncemented in my efforts to bury the truth. There was—as always—Greg Da Costa, but I realized now that Greg had been essentially ignorant of the conspiracy in its final form. Charley had only joined at the end, long after Greg had backed away, and to explain his new wealth O'Reilly had probably told Greg he had made a fortune in the market. Greg wasn't going to go checking up on that and he was just the kind of guy who would believe that kind of fairy tale. I suspected that Charley would have increased his payments to O'Reilly to cover Greg's hush money, but they would have kept all that information from Greg. You don't tell a talented extortionist any more than he needs to know.

I did wonder if I ought to do something about Greg but finally decided I could afford to leave him well alone. With any luck he'd get himself rubbed out by his employers, but if he survived I thought he wouldn't dare try to make further capital out of the assassination. He'd be uncertain how much the police had found out as the result of the latest bloodbath at One Willow Street, and he wouldn't want to risk arrest as an accessory before the fact of Paul's murder by calling attention to his past links with O'Reilly. Greg was no genius, but he did have a certain amount of low cunning, and I was confident he'd have enough brains to lie low with his mouth shut for a change.

"Maybe Greg'll land another loaded broad!" said my brother Matt brightly, and I gloomily acknowledged this was possible. Real four-flushers like Greg Da Costa always seem to slither back onto their feet somehow.

I had no problem with my brothers. They still believed that the conspiracy had been financed by a foreign government, and so they could see no reason why another conspirator should have lain beyond O'Reilly. In fact a month after the funeral when all the dust had settled and I was daring to believe I might have survived my suicidal gamble, I realized there were only four people alive who knew the whole truth. Elizabeth and I weren't talking, but I was more than worried about Sam and Cornelius.

At the first opportunity, I had gone to the Van Zale house on Fifth Avenue to drill them in the stories I had planned to tell the press, the police and the partners, and they had sworn solemnly to keep their mouths shut and support me every inch of the way. Later I'd retrieved the tape recording from them and destroyed it. In theory I should then have been able to relax, but I kept worrying in case those boys were indiscreet. I had a recurring nightmare in which they got drunk at a party and spilled out the story to anyone who would listen. Twenty-year-old kids always think they're so smart, but as anyone my age knows there's no one quite so dumb as a kid who thinks he knows everything.

I decided I'd have to talk to them again, but for some reason—unwillingness to resurrect my memories of that night, perhaps—I kept putting the lecture off, and in the end it was not I who went to Cornelius but Cornelius who came to me.

He waited six months, and afterward when I could see how carefully he'd tippy-toed his way through the chaos I caught another glimpse of the little bastard who had talked so toughly about crucifixions. Underneath those girlish gold curls and behind those starry gray eyes was a mind like a machete with steel nerves to match.

I've often wondered why I made such mistakes with Cornelius. It's just not good enough to say he didn't look like the toughest kid in town. It's not good enough either to say I thought he was a homosexual—and my God, was *that* a mistake! Homosexuals can be tough businessmen, as Paul had advised me long ago, and I was always careful not to underrate them. I think the trouble arose because I just couldn't believe he was one of Paul's people. I had this sort of vague idea—which for some reason I found comforting—that Paul had made the boy his heir only because he had wanted to be nice to Mildred. I should have realized from the start that this was just the kind sentimental bullshit that Paul would have avoided like the plague.

It was the Friday before Christmas when Cornelius tapped on my door and asked meekly for an audience. The winter sunlight shone on his golden curls.

"Come on in!" I said cheerily. "Come to wish me a merry Christmas? I guess you're just off to get your train to Cincinnati."

"Not quite." He closed the door and glided over to my desk. "May I sit down?"

"Sure. What's the problem?"

"No problem," said Cornelius, all cherubic innocence. "But I just thought this might be an opportune moment to tell you that in the new year I'd like to be made a full partner. I think it's time that my influence in the firm bore more relation to my share of the firm's capital."

The funny little guy! It was all I could do not to laugh out loud. "Sonny," I said indulgently, "you're doing well here, but whoever heard of anyone becoming a full partner in a house like Van Zale's before the age of twenty-one?"

"With Sam's support I know I could handle more responsibility."

His persistence annoyed me. Suddenly I no longer found him amusing. "Cornelius," I said abruptly, "we're constantly dealing with middle-aged clients who would never accept a young kid as their financial adviser. I appreciate you're an able hard-working boy, but right now for the good of the firm I'm going to have to turn you down."

"I beg your pardon," said Cornelius in a voice of silk, "but I don't think you can afford to do that."

"If you're referring to your capital—"

"I'm not. This is December 1928, not July 1926, and we both know that thanks to the market you could afford to let my capital go."

I stared at him, that monster of a boy whom Paul had plucked from a sedate Midwestern suburb, and every instinct in my body told me I was in bad, bad trouble.

"Explain yourself!" I invited with my warmest smile.

"Sure. It's simple." He leaned forward confidingly. "It must surely have occurred to you after the . . . incident last July that you'd actually committed several criminal offenses? It hasn't? Well, let me give you a few examples. It appears from the recording—"

"I destroyed the recording!"

"Well, naturally," said Cornelius surprised, "we made a copy."

A blow beneath the belt couldn't have shocked me more. I went on staring. In the end he started speaking again in a friendly reasonable voice.

"It appears from the recording that you chose to join the conspiracy to conceal the truth about Paul's death. You agreed to join O'Reilly in extorting money from Charley Blair. Of course, I know you only did that to encourage O'Reilly to reveal Charley's identity, but the police might draw quite a different conclusion, mightn't they, if ever they were to listen to the recording. Then you tampered with the evidence when you made it look as if O'Reilly had done the shooting. That must constitute obstruction of justice and maybe even misprision of a felony. Or would you just be an accessory after the fact? It would be a nice point for a criminal lawyer. And then, of course, it *was* your gun. It's just possible you could have shot both men yourself. Sam and I know you didn't, but we couldn't see what went on, could we, and the police might think—"

I rocketed out of my chair, rushed round the desk and goddamned nearly ripped the lapels off his jacket as I jerked him to his feet.

"You . . ." The obscenities streamed out of me. The room swam in a hot mist of rage while Cornelius, his face pinched with fright, tried to prise himself free. Finally sanity returned. I dropped him, shoved him back in his chair and stood towering over him. "You goddamned little sonofabitch!" I shouted in fury. "Never speak to me like that again!"

"Cut the crap, Steve," snarled the boy, shooting to his feet with his chin up and his shoulders squared, "and stop acting so fucking dumb."

I gasped. So shattered was I by this rapid transformation from well-spoken schoolboy to loudmouthed maverick that it took me a moment to realize I'd backed away from him behind my desk.

"Now you listen to me," said Cornelius in a low rapid voice. "I've got the evidence to put you in jail, and if you don't give me what I want I'll use it. It's as simple as that. And don't think the evidence would rebound against Sam and me just because we've kept quiet this long. We'll say you intimidated us and we'll act the part of a couple of frightened kids and the police will just pat us on the head and send us home. But you won't have a chance. You'll be washed up, cleaned out and plowed under. All you'll need is a headstone."

"You're crazy," I said. "If you do this to me you'll finish Van Zale's."

"So what!" he spat at me. "What do I care? I'll still have fifty million bucks to fuck around with! I'll start backing talking pictures or investing in airplanes and I'll make another fifty million while you're sitting on your ass in some shitty jail!"

I reached for my hip flask. The silence lengthened.

"Think about it," said Cornelius. "Let me know when you're ready to discuss my terms." And turning abruptly he walked out of the room.

VII

I thought about it all over Christmas but could see no way out. I'd have to let him have what he wanted, but I knew that no matter how many concessions I made he would always want more. I wanted to be number-one man at Van Zale's and so did he. We were on a collision course. What I needed was to buy enough time to maneuver myself into a position where I could screw him as ably as he'd screwed me. I needed to fall back, conciliate, retrench.

But how I was going to achieve that I had no idea and meanwhile I felt as emasculated as if I'd been pistol-whipped by a woman.

I thought about it day in and day out until in January the letter came from Hal Beecher, our resident partner in London, to say he'd been wanting to return to New York for some time and perhaps he could nowadays be of more use to us at Willow and Wall than in Milk Street.

Everything fell into place with a bang. The London office had been static for some time, and shortly before Charley's death we'd discussed the possibility of recalling Hal to New York. Now, as we searched for new partners and continued our efforts to shore up the firm, it made even more sense to recall conservative elderly Hal to help guide the firm through its biennial postmurder blues, and it was no less than an inspired move to send me to London to take his place. I had the European experience and a record of taking chances that panned out well. Once I'd got the Milk Street office humming I could even start an expansion in Europe, and suddenly I could see it all, a European empire, Van Zale offices in Hamburg and Zurich, Van Zale et Cie in Paris as well as Van Zale's in London . . . And while I was piling up my successes in Europe Cornelius would be piling up mistakes in New York. After five years I could come back and kick him out. I'd have it made.

"I'm all for improving the London office," said Martin when we discussed the idea in a partners' meeting. "It's obvious the financial picture has changed there now that the foreign-government-loan business has all but ceased, and it's equally obvious we've got to make a greater effort than ever before to capture the domestic industrial and commercial markets. Paul was an expert on British industry and you spent two years with him in England, Steve. Offhand I can't think of anyone in the Street better suited to restructure our London office and evolve a really innovative new policy."

All the partners made sympathetic approving noises. I could see that Lewis was already savoring the idea of being sole senior partner in New York, while Clay was reveling at the thought of more elbow room. I permitted myself a small cynical smile. Cornelius could take care of them both and save me the bother. I now had great faith in Cornelius' ability to take care of anyone who stood in his way.

I looked at him. He was already looking at me. As we exchanged gracious smiles he said pleasantly, "You're an Anglophile, aren't you, Steve? I'm sure you'll do a great job. Do you still have a lot of friends there?"

"You bet I do," I said, smiling at him lazily across the table, and for some reason the very first person I thought of was Dinah Slade.

Chapter Five

I

It was March 1929 when I arrived in England. Caroline was to join me in June when the boys had finished school, so I was on my own. At Southampton my ship docked in the rain, but by the time I reached London the sky was pastel blue and the short grass in the parks was rippling in the spring breeze. Flinging open a window in my suite at the Ritz, I sucked in a lungful of mild air and pictured the usual winter's-end blizzard which was probably howling through New York. Next door to the park traffic was roaring down Piccadilly.

I wasted no time sighing nostalgically for Broadway but ordered up a bottle of twelve-year-old scotch, dispatched my secretary to buy the day's newspapers and had my valet unpack my best British tweeds right away.

The next hour passed very pleasantly. I browsed through the financial columns. Woolworth's was flourishing like a weed. I made a mental note to buy more shares. The financial highbrows were twittering about the effect on the working classes of "hire purchase," which I thought was a real cute English phrase, the kind you want to can and take back to the States. I cast my eyes over the big industrial names, Portland Cement, Shell Oil, Courtauld's, Austin and Morris, and remembered I had to buy a car. The Rolls-Royce would have to be black—I could remember how they despised bright colors in the City—but I thought I might buy a flashy Frazer Nash Boulogne for roaring around on weekends.

I glanced at the sports pages but found only English football, checked the list of theaters and earmarked a couple of plays. As I absent-mindedly fixed myself another tot of the best scotch that ever flowed out of Scotland I shuddered at the memory of the unaged whisky from the New Jersey stills, but America was already receding and Europe, foreign and exotic, was seeping sensuously through my mind. I felt as if I had just arrived at some splendid party. All I had to do to have the time of my life was join in.

Picking up the phone, I called Dinah Slade's office a stone's throw away in the heart of Mayfair, and asked to speak to the boss.

The line clicked. Dinah's voice said suddenly, "Steve?"

"Dinah! How are you? Did you get my letter?"

"I certainly did! Lovely to hear you again, Steve!" Something had happened to her mesmerizing English accent. The keep-your-hands-off-me-you-brute flavor had mellowed into a suggestion of maybe-you-and-I-could-get-along-after-all. "Welcome to England!"

"Thanks!" I said. "It's great to be back. How's business?"

We spent a couple of minutes telling each other how wonderful it was to be alive and well and making money. Finally I purred, "Say, Dinah, I guess your social calendar must stretch from here to Christmas, but could you take pity on a poor expatriate American and have dinner with me tonight?"

"Steve, how sweet of you to ask!" she purred right back. "I'd absolutely adore to. Come to my house first for a drink—you've got my new address, haven't you?"

This was quite a welcome. I began to feel in very high spirits. "I sure have. Thanks a lot, Dinah," I said, and after we'd fixed the time I hung up, yodeled "Yippee!" as exuberantly as any cowboy and poured myself another slug of vintage scotch in celebration.

II

I was kind of annoyed with Caroline at the time. When I had first told her of my decision to go to Europe she had been livid. "Europe! Steven, you must be out of your mind!" She had wanted a reason for my decision, but I could hardly tell her I'd just been worsted in a power struggle and that the move to Europe was a brilliant maneuver to recoup my losses.

"You enjoyed Europe when we were there with Paul and Sylvia during the War!" I said hotly.

"Yes, but when you're young you don't mind living in a foreign country for a couple of years! But now—England—all those frightful aristocrats and stuffy traditions and the terrible food and plumbing—oh, Steven, you've got to change your mind! I just won't stand for it! I refuse to go!"

We lost our tempers. Caroline locked herself in one of the guest rooms and I got so exasperated I broke down the door and hauled her out. She screamed loudly, but she was always impressed by a show of strength and although I did give her the chance to tear herself away she let me catch her in the bathroom so that we could have a steamy reconciliation beneath the shower.

"No showers in those dreadful English bathrooms," she reminded me darkly as we rolled ourselves up in a towel, but she no longer tried to persuade me to change my mind.

Still, by the time March came I could hardly wait to have a break from married life. Caroline was complaining constantly that she couldn't bear to leave her friends, charity work, birth-control organizations, home, garden, servants and all the amenities of American life. Our reconciliation under the shower had been short-lived. Caroline's interest in sex had plummeted to zero again, and the more she sulked the more annoyed I became because I was afraid her attitude would upset Scott and Tony.

Eventually I tried to engineer a truce by asking her to keep an eye on my brothers for me. This innocent request cleverly served two purposes: it placated Caroline by stimulating her vicarious interest in my career, and it made me feel less guilty about leaving Luke and Matt to manage on their own. Since they were useless correspondents, they were relieved when I told them Caroline would relay their news to me, and I made them promise to meet her once a week to tell her what was going on. How I was going to keep an eye on them when Caroline joined me in June I had no idea, but I figured that if they could keep their noses clean until she left New York I might feel more confident that they could operate without supervision.

Before I left New York I installed Luke, the respectable twin, as my watchdog at Willow and Wall. His brokerage firm continued to handle the Van Zale Participations account, but Luke took my place in running the trust. I invented a title for him, "Supervising Officer, Interdepartmental Investment Trusts," gave him a desk in the great hall and arranged for him to report to old Walter once a week, but since Walter knew next to nothing about investment trusts this meant Luke had a large amount of autonomy. Of course, Luke wasn't a banker and never would be, but he had brains of a kind, he had been watching me run the trust since 1926, and as the trust's broker he had the portfolio at his fingertips. It made sense to employ him as my deputy, and since I knew Caroline would scent trouble right away if the job proved more than he could handle I reckoned I'd taken the appropriate safeguards. Anyway, I liked the idea of receiving inside reports from One Willow Street. If Clay tried to muscle in on my territory or Cornelius suddenly decided to bone up about investment trusts, I wanted to read all about it that same day in a transatlantic cable.

That took care of Luke. As for Matt, who was enjoying himself representing Van Zale Participations at three-hour business lunches every day, I told him very plainly what kind of behavior I expected from him in my absence.

"No pool operations," I said sternly. "No bucket shops. No hustling around notorious flimflam men. No scenes in speakeasies. No gambling with gangsters. And no bumming around with those bootlegger friends of yours up in the northern hills of New Jersey. The last thing I want to hear when I'm in Europe is that Matthew Sullivan, president of Van Zale Participations, was arrested by revenue agents while transporting half a dozen jars of applejack over the state line."

Matt promised to be good as gold. Luke swore I wouldn't regret my decision to trust him. Both of them hugged me emotionally when they came down to the docks to say goodbye and I admit I had quite a lump in my throat at the thought of not seeing them for twelve months. I planned to return to New York once a year to check up on everyone, but a year is still a long time.

"Goodbye, Steven darling," said Caroline, offering me a cool cheek after my brothers had stumbled off moist-eyed down the gangway. "I guess it's useless to ask you to behave yourself, but do try not to drink too much, there's a lamb."

I would have roared like a lion, but Scott and Tony were there and Caroline and I never quarreled in front of them.

It certainly wasn't one of the brighter moments of our marriage, but even a good marriage has its sticky patches and we both felt our marriage was a good one. It was true we shared what the old fogies called "modern attitudes," but marriage is a flexible institution and just because Caroline and I had long ago hammered out our own rules our modern style didn't mean we were less successfully married than a conventional couple. I wasn't faithful to her, but Caroline knew all about that and actually encouraged me to have as many women as I wanted. "Sexual frustration," intoned Caroline with her bowdlerized version of Freud in one hand and her volume of Marie Stopes in the other, "should have no place in a modern marriage. In this dawn of a new era both men and women should be freed from the tyranny of sexual enslavement." Loosely translated, this meant that a wife should be able to say no as often as she liked and if a husband wanted more he could damn well step out and get it.

This coincided with Paul's theory that a good marriage has nothing to do with fidelity, and I must say the philosophy did have its attractions. The only aspect that bothered me was the thought that Caroline might practice what she preached as enthusiastically as I did. I wouldn't have liked it at all if she'd gone stepping out with any man who caught her fancy.

"Don't be dense, Steven!" said my wife crossly when I confessed my fears to her. "You've missed the whole point. I'm not frustrated. You satisfy me absolutely, so why should I go to bed with anyone else?"

Why indeed? I thought, much reassured, and thought how great it was to be married to a modern sexually enlightened woman. All those old dodderers who complained that true womanhood had been wrecked by the War, jazz, cosmetics and a dozen other godless disasters just didn't know what they were missing. I wouldn't have left Caroline for the world. Each time I had a fling it was a relief to go home to my smart competent wife who managed our marriage in such a splendidly understanding fashion, and I often thought how lucky I was to be married to the right woman.

Now I wasn't at all sure I wanted to sleep with Dinah Slade, but it was nice to know that if I did I didn't have to feel guilty about it. I vaguely thought I might make a play for her if she was nice enough, but I knew that nothing serious would come of it. Paul's taste in women wasn't mine and I could no more imagine myself falling heavily for Dinah than I could imagine myself going crazy over Sylvia. Dinah would be my introduction to the free-and-easy side of London social life and possibly—though by no means probably—a partner in an amusing Charleston or two between the sheets. But that was all.

When my second drink was finished I went for a walk, cutting through Green Park to the Mall, and took a closer look at the English. God, what a race! I'll never forget the shock I had when I first came to Europe and saw them at close range. I felt just the way a big bold lobster must feel when he's flung into a pot of boiling water. After all, I'd grown up on the Eastern Seaboard and my parents were society people; I know the Irish name gave people the chance to be snobbish, but my mother was descended from a Signer and we all knew that Great-Great-Grandfather Sullivan had been named in dispatches by General Washington himself. I came to England thinking I'd muscle into every old castle in sight, but all I got were glacial looks, as if I were a footman who had got so big for his breeches he'd burst his backside seam. I was never so shocked in all my life—and hurt too. I had only wanted to be friendly.

Paul took me in hand. Paul had an English personality which he could pull on like a glove and a pedigree receding to the seventeenth century, and the English, as Caroline remarked, thought he was "just darling." He taught me how to behave, how to be tolerant, how to turn the other cheek whenever the English looked at me as if I were an exotic animal who would definitely be better off running wild on the other side of the globe.

"But the English love animals!" protested Paul when I complained. "When you've proved you're tame they'll lavish affection on you!"

He was right. I became "a pretty decent sort of chap for a foreigner," which is the English equivalent of "He's a nice guy—for a Negro." Later I graduated to "He's a sporting sort of fellow—for an American," a great improvement since the English love sportsmen and think Americans are the smartest kind of foreigner because they can speak English. At the end of my two-year stay came the crowning triumph. There were no official test matches in 1919, but the Australian Imperial Forces team played England at cricket, and one day in London I met someone who asked me if I knew what the score was. Of course I had no idea, but before I could speak the guy gasped thunderstruck, "My dear chap, forgive me! I quite forgot you were an American!"

I sailed home in a cloud of glory.

However, now that I had returned to England I had no illusions about the difficulties which were waiting to depress me. If I wanted all the social doors to be flung wide open it was no good crashing around like a New York bull in a china shop. It was not enough either just to tone myself down and make sure I knew who was winning the Test Match. Someone English had to vouch for me. Someone English had to take me by the hand and tell everyone how civilized and domesticated I was. And that someone was going to be Dinah Slade.

Crossing the Mall into St. James's Park, I wandered over the lawns and paused on the bridge to watch the towers and minarets of Horseguards. Suddenly my exuberance returned with a bang. To hell with the English, I thought as I had so often thought before, England's a great country! Later, crossing Piccadilly, I savored the narrow twisting little streets of Mayfair, the sedate rows of townhouses and the old-fashioned horse carts still mingling with the tiny trucks and automobiles. It was just like a giant movie set out of Hollywood. I liked all the funny English accents too, and the English newspapers with their Old-World spelling, and the Union Jack flying everywhere instead of the Stars and Stripes. In fact, it was really a great little place and I was more convinced than ever that Americans who turn up their noses at Europe are missing a wonderful experience. Of course, America's the best country in the world, we all know that, but I don't believe it's unpatriotic to admire a country other than one's own.

Back at the Ritz, I splashed around in the bath and dressed for dinner. In an effort to look English I removed my diamond ring, wore my plainest set of cufflinks, and flattening my curly hair with water I brushed it until it gave up trying to do anything except lie down. To my relief I saw I could almost pass for an investment banker, and feeling pleased with myself I ran downstairs, grabbed a cab and sailed off along Piccadilly to Dinah's address in Belgravia.

III

She had the quaintest little mews house. The mews reminded me of Macdougal Alley in New York, but the alley was probably a couple of hundred years younger. The narrow street was cobbled. Dinah's house was painted white with black trim and there were geraniums planted in every window box. The eight other houses in the row were just as smart, and after paying off the cab driver I paused again to admire the scene before I rang the bell.

The door was opened by a small thin boy with a chocolate moustache.

"Hello, Alan!" I said to Paul's son. "Remember me?" And suddenly Paul's memory was reaching far across my mind.

"Of course I remember you!" said the little kid peevishly, speaking with a snooty English accent which would have tickled Paul pink. "I remember everything!" He offered me a sticky hand to shake and added in his high adult little voice, "Please come in, Mr. Sullivan."

I stepped directly into the living room, where a couch and armchairs were grouped around a fine fireplace. Flanking the mantel on either side were a bookcase and a dresser, both antiques, and a bowl of daffodils glowed on a highly polished table. A print of a knight hung on the wall by the staircase at the far end of the room. Having expected to find Dinah in some grand townhouse sumptuously furnished by the best decorator in London, I was greatly surprised by this cozy little *pied-à-terre*. I wondered where she gave her cocktail parties and big dinners. Perhaps she had rooms set aside above the salon on Grafton Street.

"Mummy'll be down in a minute," Alan explained. "She's late because she's been working so hard. My mother," he added, "thinks it's bourgeois for women to lead idle unproductive lives. Tell me, Mr. Sullivan, do you think the bourgeoisie are more of a threat than the aristocracy to the development of true socialism?"

I saw the smugness in his eyes and knew he was showing off. The precocious little kid! He was barely six years old, the same age as my younger son Tony who had the good sense to talk about trains, cowboys and baseball.

"Sonny," I drawled, "we don't have that kind of problem where I come from." I wandered over to take a look at the knight. "Who's this guy?" I demanded as I heard the patter of his feet behind me.

"Do you like him? I do!" His voice became eager as he forgot the bourgeoisie. "That's a brass rubbing from an old church, and the knight's called Sir Roger de Trumpington."

He was looking up at me enthusiastically with Paul's bright dark eyes. A lump formed in my throat. I could almost hear Paul say, "You're too damned sentimental, Steve!" but that only made the lump more painful. In the end I just said, "Your daddy would have been so pleased with you."

A stillness smoothed all expression from his face. He backed away. "Mummy!" he called frantically. "Where are you? Why don't you come down?" And he dashed up the stairs as if I'd turned into a monster who'd tried to gobble him up.

I sighed. I'd forgotten that the English hate any display of sentiment, and I was still staring ruefully at the stern face of Sir Roger de Trumpington when a slight sound made me look up.

Dinah was at the head of the stairs.

I sucked in my breath with a rasp. She'd lost a lot of weight, but instead of making her look flat the loss only emphasized the curves that hadn't disappeared, and those curves were now all in the right places. Her silvery dress rippled as she walked. She wore silver high-heeled slippers, a silverish circlet around her sleek dark hair and a huge diamond ring on the highly manicured fourth finger of her right hand. Her long diamond earrings swayed languidly, and smoke from her diamond-studded cigarette holder curled upward with style. Her lips were moistly scarlet, her eyes heavily shadowed, her long lashes jungle-thick. When she smiled I thought my welcome was going to be formal and cool, but when she spoke, her voice—ah, that seductive English accent!—was as warm and winning as it had been on the phone.

"Steve! Handsome as ever!"

"Miss Theda Bara? Or is it Miss Clara Bow? How's Hollywood these days?"

We laughed. As our hands clasped she said, amused, "I was determined to be the juiciest steak on the slab!"

"Pardon me?"

"Don't you still look at women as if they were meat in a butcher's shop?"

"You bet!" I said good-naturedly, realizing I was being teased, but I couldn't help being impressed by how much trouble she'd taken to look sizzling. In fact I thought it was damned nice of her to put on such a big production when we'd never exactly been the best of friends.

"You'll have a drink, of course," she said, and suddenly a white cloth was whipped off an ice bucket and there was the magnum of champagne she had promised me on the day Paul died.

"So you remembered!" I was agog with admiration.

"Of course! Do open it, Steve—men open champagne bottles so much better than women do."

"Why, sure!" It was a long time since I'd heard that kind of remark. As I broke the seal it occurred to me that European women really did have a great deal to offer.

The champagne was the prelude to a remarkable evening. We couldn't empty the magnum but we ate all the caviar before taking a cab to the Savoy, where we continued dinner in that room overlooking the river. Dinah was obviously a regular customer, because when the maître d' saw her he bowed low and we were immediately ushered to the best table by the window. We ordered Scotch salmon for the fish course and then I salivated among the clarets on the wine list before choosing a Château Latour 1920 to accompany our roast beef. I could see that Dinah was surprised I was able to discuss the wines competently with the wine waiter. American ignorance about wine is notorious—which was why Paul made me study the subject thoroughly when I was with him in England. It was all part of the plan to kid the English I was tame and civilized.

"So how's the world treating you?" I inquired when we had dealt with the preliminaries and were free to catch up on each other's news.

We chatted in a bright breezy fashion for some time. I had on my best European manners and she had on her best blasé English accent. She said she was making *rather* a lot of money—naturally I wasn't so crassly American as to ask how much—and the salon was doing *frightfully* well and they'd just bought another warehouse and the payroll kept expanding, and it was just too *exhausting*, darling, honestly, but all rather fun. Apparently her friend Harriet had the big house where all the business entertaining was done, but once a month there were house parties at Mallingham—rather divine, darling, and everyone *adored* the house—but otherwise she never saw Mallingham, she was just too busy in London making all the *filthy* money, so vulgar, darling, but what could one do? One got caught up in a materialistic treadmill and one simply *couldn't* get off. Yes, she was still a sort of socialist, but let's be honest, darling, it was rather heaven being rich, the Webbs should have tried it sometime, not to mention Lenin, Trotsky and that *horrid* man Stalin. And talking of Communists, how accidental was Bruce Clayton's accidental death, and what really did happen at One Willow Street when cool, calm, collected Terence O'Reilly suddenly decided to assassinate everyone in sight?

I had had a great deal to drink, but I still had my wits about me. I fed her the story I'd told my partners and admitted that O'Reilly was the archconspirator instead of a religious lunatic.

"And where did Greg Da Costa fit into it all?"

I explained Greg's passive role.

"But if he didn't put up the money who did?"

I put the blame squarely on the Soviet government, and was just becoming nervous when she smiled brilliantly and said in a bright voice, "Well, now that *that's* all over, Steve darling, can I have my deed back?"

"Deed?" I said, still weak with relief that she had swallowed the foreign-government theory.

"Deed, Steve. D-E-E-D. The deed conveying Mallingham to Paul."

"Oh, the conveyance. Yeah. . . . Dinah, I'm sorry but it never did turn up."

"What!" Her brittle manner cracked at the seams.

"Wait, here's what I think happened." I did feel guilty that I'd forgotten all about the damned deed, so I made a valiant attempt to explain. "Bart Mayers, who was killed shortly after Paul, was assigned to destroy all Paul's private correspondence, which was kept among the secret files in the vaults. It seems clear to me that—"

"He burned the deed to Mallingham along with my correspondence with Paul." All affectation was gone. Suddenly she was tense, direct and natural. "But, Steve, what the hell am I going to do? I must get this business straightened out. Perhaps if I wrote to Cornelius—"

"Oh, I wouldn't do that," I said.

She looked at me steadily. I forgot I was in Europe. Suddenly I was a New Yorker again, pushing for the best way to fix an awkward deal. "Look," I said. "Sit tight. You don't need that deed—you're not going to sell or lease or mortgage Mallingham. Act as if you own the place, and in fifty years' time when you kick the bucket nobody's going to know what the true story is. They'll just assume Paul conveyed the property to you and the deed got lost somewhere along the line."

"But legally—"

"Legally you've even got the statute of limitations running in your favor. What's the limit in England for real estate? Twelve years? Well, if you sit tight till 1938 the land will be yours anyway."

"I don't think so, Steve. I've been into all this. I don't think the statute of limitations would start to run until Cornelius knows he owns Mallingham. You see, I'm concealing the truth from him and that constitutes some sort of fraudulent deception. But if I gave him notice that he was the owner—if I wrote and offered to buy it from him—"

"Dinah, you were dead right about that kid back in 1926. He's poison. Take my advice, sit tight and let the Mallingham ownership ride for a few decades."

"But—"

"Look at it this way. You're not committing a criminal offense. Keeping your mouth shut may be a deception within the meaning of the statute, but it's not criminal fraud. That deed's destroyed. You've had nearly three years of uninterrupted peace at Mallingham and there's no reason why you shouldn't have at least thirty more. But if you start dealing with Cornelius, I can guarantee you're opening a can of worms. I can think of several reasons why he'd be only too happy to kick you in the teeth."

"So could Paul." She shuddered, then laughed in an effort to be debonair. "You did change your mind about him, didn't you!" she said amused. "Why? Tell me the whole story—or is it unfit for publication?"

"Honey, I could talk about that kid till dawn breaks over Green Park—which reminds me, I've got a great view of the park from my suite at the Ritz and half a bottle of the best scotch around. Why don't you come back there with me now and let me tell you everything you want to know?"

"Sweet of you," drawled Dinah, beating a double-quick retreat behind her blasé façade. "But I really do have to get home. I'm due in Birmingham tomorrow on business and I'll have to get up at some unearthly hour to catch the train."

The acuteness of my disappointment startled me. "Ah, come on, Dinah!" I exclaimed, scooping together all my charm. "I'm looking forward to telling you the inside story of my life at Willow and Wall!"

"And I'm looking forward to hearing it!" she said, matching my charm ounce for ounce. "Come up to Mallingham next weekend and we can talk to our heart's content."

I almost swallowed my glass of port. Setting it down with care, I said smoothly with as much English understatement as I could muster, "How kind of you to invite me! I accept with pleasure—thank you very much."

Maybe it was my imagination, but I was beginning to think I sounded just like Paul.

Well, I knew I was following in Paul's footsteps—of course I knew that, and she knew it too. But she was a grown woman now, not the baby she had been when Paul seduced her, and I had no doubt she could handle a fast weekend with one hand tied behind her back. I certainly knew I could. After all, I was now nearly forty-two years old, and I couldn't imagine getting my fingers burned no matter how far I fooled around with a new flame.

So I escorted Dinah home, kissed her good night affectionately and took myself back to the Ritz without bitterness. Progress had been made. The weekend loomed lasciviously ahead, and I was as happy as a puppy dog with six tails.

"Rule Britannia!" I sang as I tipped my astonished cab driver ten shillings, and taking off my top hat I flung it joyously into the air at the moon.

Chapter Six

I

The train drew into Norwich at eleven-thirty and I was leaping onto the platform even before the wheels had stopped. I was wearing my English tweeds and feeling overheated. I'd forgotten how warm March could be in England, but I had some lighter clothes in my small suitcase. My valet had wanted me to take a whole wardrobe, but as the really important business of the weekend was going to be conducted in my birthday suit I was determined to travel light.

Tossing my ticket at the collector, I plunged outside and immediately saw her sitting in a very pale Hispano-Suiza. This time her cigarette holder was scarlet, to match her lips.

"Dinah!" I darted forward, looked the wrong way crossing the road and nearly got mowed down by a bus. "I love your car!" I gasped, leaping in and giving her a kiss.

"Let's hope you love my driving!"

We roared away through the streets of Norwich. She was wearing a mustard-colored skirt and jacket, a chocolate-brown blouse submerged beneath rows of pearls, and a matching hat set at a jaunty angle.

"You look very smart!" I shouted at her as we zipped around a corner and plunged downhill. Norwich is a very hilly town.

"You too!" she shouted back.

"Do I look English?"

"What's wrong with looking like an American?"

"I want to merge with the English," I said, slipping an arm around her shoulders, "in every sense of the word."

"You'll end up buried with them if you try and seduce me while we're driving through Norwich at top speed!"

With a sigh I sank back in my seat to admire the scenery. That wasn't hard. The countryside was pretty. It took a while to get out of Norwich, because the traffic was heavy, but eventually we entered farming country and passed cute little fields fringed with hedges. I lost count of all the thatched cottages, and we passed a string of huge churches which made me realize how religious they must have been in the old days. It was boating country. At Wroxham and Horning the river was stuffed with sailboats and motor cruisers and I remembered Paul talking with enthusiasm about the miles of inland waterways between Norwich and the sea.

"We're coming into Broadland now," said Dinah. "You've heard of the Norfolk Broads, haven't you?"

I somehow managed to avoid making the obvious crack. Paul would have been proud of me.

We bowled along past little lanes and signboards painted with wonderful old English names like Potter Heigham and Hickling, and I was just thinking about lunch and glancing surreptitiously at my watch when Dinah said, "This is the road to Mallingham," and we turned off onto a rural route. Sheep were dotted in windswept fields and when I glanced up at the huge blue-and-white sky I felt the sea wind on my face and sensed the freedom of wide-open spaces. I could see little, because the road twisted secretively behind high hedgerows, and I was just thinking I could bear the suspense no longer when we arrived in the cutest little village of them all. It was like an illustration from a picture book. Openmouthed with admiration, I gazed at the village green, the gaggle of cottages, and the gigantic gray church. There were even real people walking around. A couple of old-timers were sidling into a pub called the Eel and Ham.

"It's wonderful!" I cried excited. "It's just like the movies. Jesus, if only I'd brought my camera! This is just the greatest little place!"

Dinah snuffled. I was offering her a handkerchief before I realized she wasn't about to sneeze. She was trying to keep a straight face.

"Hell!" I said annoyed. "I forgot my British understatement."

"Oh, Steve!" she said laughing. "What's wrong with a good slice of American enthusiasm? Please, please don't feel you have to pretend to be English!"

"Well, I don't want you to think I'm some untamed uncivilized wild animal."

"Darling," she drawled as we careered through a ruined gateway, "I wouldn't want to think of you in any other way. Here's Mallingham Hall."

It wasn't a bit as I'd thought it would be. I'd expected a real British stately home, but Mallingham Hall was just a little house about a quarter of the size of my home on Long Island. Yet it had character, I could see that at once. Beyond the driveway the house seemed to grow out of the soil as if it had been nurtured by some gifted gardener, and as we drew nearer I saw the honeysuckle around the front door, the ivy crawling over the flint walls and the moss clinging to the dark thatched roof. Long churchlike windows peered at me. I felt as if I were being carefully appraised by an elder statesman, and once I sensed the personality of the house I found it easy to yield to its low-keyed Old-World charm.

"How old is it?" I said respectfully.

"The foundations are pre-Conquest, but most of it's much younger than that. The great hall is over six hundred years old."

I tried to imagine six hundred years and gave up. I can visualize a million-dollar bond issue with no trouble at all, but I can't visualize huge spans of time. "Six hundred years!" I repeated, laying on the admiration too thickly to conceal that the number meant nothing to me, and when she looked quizzical I said with haste, "I like it, Dinah. I really do."

"I know." For the first time that day she ditched her blasé manner and gave me her warmest smile. "I'm glad, Steve. Come in and I'll show you around."

The big hall had a beamed ceiling. They certainly knew how to build rafters six hundred years ago. At either end of the hall was a string of little rooms, nothing grand but comfortable and cozy, like her London home. Everything was smartly painted and in tiptop shape. Beyond the living room a stone terrace stood above a lawn which sloped to a small reedy lake, and as I paused by the window I saw Alan playing near the boathouse.

It was Alan who showed me to the guest room while Dinah went to the kitchens to check some domestic details with her housekeeper. The room had a view over the lake, a sink in one corner but no sign of any other useful facility, so after I'd unpacked my suitcase I asked Alan where the bathroom was. He looked surprised but escorted me to an imposing room where a large bath stood in solitary splendor on four little legs. For one bad moment I wondered if the plumbing arrangements were as old as the great hall.

"Where's the . . ." I couldn't think of the polite English word.

"The lavatory," said Alan reprovingly, "is at the end of the corridor."

I could see I'd have to brush up my English vocabulary, to say nothing of my memories of English bathrooms.

We had lunch. Alan and his nurse joined us for steak-and-kidney pie and chocolate pudding, but afterward Dinah and I were left alone with the port.

"I thought maybe you'd like to do some sailing this afternoon," she suggested as I lit her cigarette. "The weather's improved, there's just the right amount of wind and we could sail up to Horsey Mill."

Naturally I'd have preferred to sail straight into bed with her, but I was on her home ground, she was making the rules and I had no wish to appear unsporting.

"Great idea!" I said courteously without batting an eyelid, and in fact I soon reconciled myself to postponing the bedroom romps. Dinah had a modern twenty-two-foot yacht, but that was still out of the water after the winter, so we took the dinghy and spun dizzily back and forth across Mallingham Broad. Huge white clouds billowed above us, and the wind, which had veered around, fairly blasted us east toward the sea.

I slacked off the peak halyard, shortening the sail and cutting the wobble from the mast. "You're a good sailor!" I gasped as we reached the shelter of Mallingham Dyke. "Why didn't you ever come to any of our sailing parties on the Sound?"

"I was probably too busy discussing Hegelian dialectic with the Claytons. Look out, here comes the wind again!"

She clung to the tiller while I dodged the boom, and we whipped out of the dike. Later, as we left the long channel called the New Cut and headed into another lake, the wind dropped suddenly, and in the eerie moment of calm I glanced across the water and saw the hulk of Horsey Mill.

"A windmill—a real one! My God, look at those sails! Can we go and see it? Can I—"

"Hold tight!" shouted Dinah as the wind caught us again, and I quite forgot we could have spent the afternoon indoors. We tacked back and forth, the little boat skimming over the water like a skipping pebble, and soon we were moving up the little dike which led to the mill. The wooden sails were clanking so hard I could barely hear the whistle of the wind over the levels.

We moored the dinghy at the staithe. "Let's see if the millman's there," said Dinah, but the mill was empty. However as the door was open she said I could go inside.

I stepped into the dark circular room where the shaft of the machinery rose through the ceiling, and climbed the ladder to the floor above. Since the view was obviously better at the top, I kept on climbing, fascinated by the angle of the walls, and when I reached the highest floor the boards beneath my feet were vibrating. With my back to the primitive machinery I looked beyond the outer platform. The view was continually sliced by whirling sails, but I could see far out over the broads, marshes and meadows to the clear-cut horizon. I tried to count first the other windmills and then the churches, but there were too many of them. For some time I stayed watching the lonely levels and thinking how good it was to escape from the shut-in streets of Manhattan, and when at last I retreated to the ground my first words to Dinah were: "Tell me about this neck of the woods."

We lit cigarettes in the shelter of the mill and I listened while she talked of a great inland sea long ago, of a hundred islands in the marshes, of Saxon outlaws holding out from Norman conquerors, of mists and mysticism, little monasteries hidden away in forgotten pockets of civilization, the outer reaches of an unfamiliar England.

"You mean it's always been this sleepy and rural?"

I heard about the mighty glory of the East Anglian Middle Ages. It was funny to think of their having economic booms and big-time trading deals back then. Apparently in those days Norfolk, Suffolk and Essex had been in the front line of Continental trade, and all those huge churches had been built to cater to a teeming countryside awash with prosperity.

"But what happened?" I demanded mystified.

"Some fool discovered America!" laughed Dinah. "And eastern England found it was facing the wrong way!" She told me how the tide of economic life had receded, how Henry VIII had wrecked the monasteries and how even the coastline had crumbled into disintegration. The people had gone away. Towns had disappeared beneath the sea. East Anglia had become a backwater again, with only the great churches remaining as mementos of its mighty past.

"There must be a moral in that story somewhere," I murmured, idly picturing a pastoral scene in which a bunch of archaeologists excavated a sign which read "WALL STREET."

"Yes," she said, looking across the swaying reeds of Horsey Mere. "Nothing's forever. Everything changes eventually, and it's the people who adapt who survive." She stubbed out her cigarette and carefully buried the butt. "Shall we walk to the sea? It's not far, only a mile and a half."

"Fine." I glanced at her. The wind was blowing her dark hair and she seemed relaxed. I don't know why I was so sure that we had both been thinking of Paul.

We walked down the quiet country road to a cluster of trees. A car passed us and once a cart came jogging by from the village, but otherwise we saw no one. The only sounds were the humming of the wind and the thudding of our footsteps on the road.

"Horsey Church is interesting," said Dinah. "It's just down there in the woods. Would you like to see it?"

But I wanted to get to the sea. "Forget it," I said. "Once you've seen one old church you've seen 'em all. Let's keep going."

She said nothing, but this time I actually caught the faraway look in her eyes and felt Paul's elegant hands pushing us apart. Feeling furious with myself, I made a big effort to take a civilized interest in the landscape.

"I like the stonework on those cottages over there," I said tentatively. "Would that be traditional around these parts?"

She started to talk busily about flint used as rough lumps and flint used after being dressed by flint-knappers. She talked about the technique of random flintwork with cornerstones and projecting plinths finished in brick. She talked about flints faced smooth and dressed square and how to gallet the mortar joints between them. By the time she had finished I could have built a house Norfolk style myself and even pin-tiled the roof with oak pins hooked over thin laths if I happened to have forgotten my reed-thatching technique. I wondered why the hell I had been invited to Mallingham. If she were still in love with Paul's memory she would hardly have issued the invitation on account of my beautiful blue eyes.

Dunes separated us from the sea as we followed a cart track across the last fields. It was a real scramble up those dunes. At the top I took a lungful of sea air and narrowed my eyes against the wind streaming toward us across the moody gray sea. I hadn't expected the Caribbean so I wasn't disappointed, but I was sorry the sand was so dark. However, I wasn't going to say I didn't like it and anyway I always enjoy a stretch of deserted beach, so I yodeled "Yippee!" with my usual verve and cascaded down the dunes.

She didn't follow me, and when I plowed back to her I found she had collapsed in a cozy little hollow out of the wind.

"This is a great stretch of coast!" I said, flinging myself down beside her.

"What a marvelous guest you are, Steve!" she said smiling at me. "At least I don't have to waste time wondering if you're enjoying yourself."

"You bet I'm enjoying myself!" I said, and took her in my arms.

We had a long kiss which turned into several kisses, each one longer than the last. Her mouth was supple and generous. I felt a hazy warmth, then a hot surge of power.

She shifted beneath me. "Steve . . ." Her hands pushed against my chest. When I took no notice she clenched her fists and started to fight. "Let me go, let me go, let me go!"

I muttered an obscenity, rolled away from her and crawled away into the dunes to relieve myself.

After that there was a long silence. I sat listening to the wind and the gulls until from far away I heard a succession of small jerky sounds which had to be of human origin.

"Oh, Christ!" I muttered, crawling back on all fours through the sand grass for a peep.

She was stretched out on her stomach, her face hidden in the crook of her arm as she bawled like a two-year-old. She couldn't have surprised me more if she'd thrown off all her clothes and revealed a snake tattooed on her bottom.

I put my arms around her, rubbed my cheek soothingly against hers and held her till the tears dried up.

"All right," I said. "Let's have it. I can take anything except another lecture on dressed flint."

She gulped. The mascara had smudged, and her eyes were big, dark and tragic, making her look like a heroine in an old-time melodrama. All we needed to complete the atmosphere was the honky-tonk piano in the background.

"I wanted to recapture that summer Paul and I spent together," she said, her voice high with grief. "It was the happiest summer of my life, and as the years went by afterwards I became haunted by the fear that I'd never be as happy as that again. I knew you were absolutely different from Paul, but I remembered how fond of you he was, and I . . . I . . ."

"You thought you could be fond of me too."

"Yes. I know it sounds stupid, but . . . I've been so lonely, Steve. There's been no one else since Paul died. Oh, I don't deny I tried to replace him, but each time I tried it was disastrous, and in the end I gave up trying."

"But I don't understand," I said puzzled. "What went wrong? Are you saying no man ever measured up to Paul?"

"Yes, but it was more complicated than that. The more successful I became, the less men could accept me as an individual. The less I conformed to a feminine stereotype, the more hostile and angry they became. I can't blame them either, because if I were a man I'd hate a woman who was more successful than I was. But on the other hand I couldn't help hoping that there was someone somewhere who could cope."

"Hell, Dinah!" I said good-naturedly. "All you're bitching about is that you're having a bit of trouble finding the right person. So what's new about that? The right person's never easy to find."

"That's true, but in my case I suspect it's practically impossible." She took a deep breath, and sensing she was straining to communicate with me, I wiped the smile off my face and made a serious attempt to understand what she was talking about. "I don't want a man who leans on me because I'm stronger than a lot of women," she said, "and I don't want a man who's stronger than me yet is so unsure of it that he can't accept me as an individual with a life of my own. I don't want to come home from the office and find I have to play 'the little woman' all the time—and yet I certainly don't want to come home and find I have to be one of the boys. I spend all day in a man's world and when I come home I want to be treated as a woman—but the woman I really am, not the woman some man thinks I ought to be. I'm not a serf. I'm not a clockwork doll. And I'm certainly not a pretty face. I'm a person. Nobody expects all men to be alike. Why must society demand that all women should be identical? The situation would be amusing if it weren't so hurtful."

"Are you trying to tell me in all seriousness," I said incredulously, "that any woman who's not a dumb broad makes a man feel less masculine?"

"Yes, I am. Paul was the exception which proved the rule."

"Jesus!" I said. "I wish you'd told me that ten minutes ago when I wanted to rape you and then maybe I wouldn't have busted all the buttons off my fly."

There was a split second of utter silence while our future hung in the balance and then she giggled. I smiled encouragingly. A moment later we were both laughing and the tension had vanished.

"Let's go back to the mill," I said, and as we left the dunes I took her hand and squeezed it to let her know that everything was going to be just fine.

II

When we arrived home it was six-thirty and Alan had finished his supper. Dinah told me to help myself to a drink while she read him his bedtime story, but I was missing my boys already and the opportunity to tell a bedtime story seemed too good to be passed up. After she had finished her chapter of *The Little Duke* I launched into the saga of Billy Joe "Six-Shooter" McStarrett and was relieved to see Alan behaving like a normal six-year-old instead of like a little old man who read nothing but *Das Kapital.*

"Tell it again!" he begged as Dinah shuddered, and his enthusiasm set the tone for the evening. After dinner we wandered down to the pub, and although the saloon bar was about as gay as a funeral parlor I soon found my way into the public bar, where all the local men were playing darts. I'd never played before, but when Dinah introduced me I was at once invited to join in, and time passed very happily as I hurled my darts at the board and put away tankards of dark treacly English beer. The local men became almost sociable after I'd bought the first round. The only trouble was I couldn't understand a word they said, as their Norfolk accent was so heavy, but Dinah was a talented interpreter and told me to my amazement that they couldn't understand me any better than I could understand them.

"What are they saying?" I muttered as I scored a bull's eye by accident and bought them another round of beer.

"They're saying what a wonderful sport you are!" hissed Dinah, much amused.

I knew what a compliment *that* was. I beamed around the room with pride.

It was a shock when the pub closed just when I was getting into my sportsman's stride, but when I thought of the treat in store for me I headed back very willingly to Mallingham.

"Would you like some coffee?" offered Dinah when we stepped into the hall.

"How about a quick glass of champagne?"

"After beer?" She was horrified, but she trotted off obediently and returned with a respectably cobwebbed bottle. "Your American drinking habits are unbelievably barbarous!" she said severely. "Yes, I know—don't tell me! It's Prohibition! If you ask me, Prohibition's the best excuse a nation ever had to indulge in every imaginable excess."

"You bet!" I said. "We call it making whoopee. Let's go upstairs."

"Wait—we need glasses! Unless, of course, you intend to empty the champagne into the bath and wallow in it. Knowing you Americans, nothing would surprise me."

"I'll get the glasses," I said, veering toward the kitchens. "You run the bath."

"Are you serious?"

"Don't be so goddamned British!" I prowled down the hallway and left her laughing behind me. It was so dark I wouldn't have recognized my own grandmother if we'd met eyeball to eyeball, but after I'd realized there was no electric light I got a match alight and started poking around the kitchens. A stray candle helped. By the time I'd unearthed the glasses ten minutes had ticked away and the sound of running water had stopped.

"Dinah?"

"I'm waiting, Mr. Sullivan!"

A soft wavering light was glowing in the grand bathroom which Alan had shown me earlier. I walked in and stopped dead.

"Gee whiz, lady!" I said, whistling my appreciation.

She had filled the enormous bathtub almost to the rim and had added some magic ingredient—fresh from the Diana Slade Cosmetics laboratories, no doubt—to create a billowing froth of bubbles. The light in the room came from a silver candelabra on top of the laundry hamper, and the flames from the five candles cast a sultry light on Dinah as she lounged, visible only from the chin up, in that deep old tank of a bathtub.

"'"Come into my parlor," said the spider to the fly,'" she teased, beckoning me with her toe.

"No flypaper could stop me!" I popped the cork from the bottle, filled a glass and held it just out of her reach.

"Brute!" she said, making a grab for the glass without success.

I held it a little farther away and grinned from ear to ear.

"I'm not moving another inch! Why should you see me stark naked when you're fully dressed?"

"No reason at all," I said cheerfully and stripped off my clothes. After I'd shed my shorts I filled my own glass, announced, "To my hostess!" and drained every drop before pouring myself a refill.

Her eyes were as big as saucers. She looked as though she'd never seen a man naked before.

"My God," she said in awe. "You're enormous! You look even taller without your clothes than with them!"

I roared with laughter. "Oh, are you only referring to my height? I'm disappointed!"

She laughed too, and when I offered her the glass again she stood up. The dim light reflected sensuously on her glistening flesh. Feathery moisture clung to the soft shining curves of her body.

She took a sip of champagne and looked at me. I looked back. Then I took the glass from her, tossed it over my shoulder and scrambled into the tub to ram my body hard against hers.

Chapter Seven

I

When I awoke I was sprawled diagonally across the four-poster in Dinah's room. The sheet beneath me was twisted around my left leg, the other bedclothes were strewn across the floor, and one of the pillows, which were all hanging improbably over the top of the wardrobe, had burst to ooze goosedown over the carpet. I was naked, alone and goddamned cold. Outside it appeared to be raining.

I sat up. After holding my head for a moment I staggered to the basin in the corner of the room and put my face under the cold tap. When I came up for air I heard the church bells chiming far away and remembered it was Sunday.

It was seven o'clock, time for early breakfast—or for early Communion if one was a churchgoer. Back in my own room I cleaned myself up, dressed and retrieved last night's clothes from the bathroom. I was just draping them over the back of a chair when I glanced out the window and saw Dinah below me in the garden. She was shrouded in a shapeless raincoat and huddled on the wrought-iron seat which overlooked the Broad.

I went downstairs. The kitchens were stirring, but I saw no one on my way outside to the terrace. The fresh air cleared my head. I didn't call out to Dinah, just crossed the lawn toward her, and when I reached the seat I saw she must have been there for some time, for the drizzle had soaked her hair.

"Dinah?" I stooped to kiss her cheek. "Are you all right?"

"No, I'm horribly hung over. I hate myself when I drink too much."

"Hell, I wasn't so sober myself! But we had fun," I said softly between kisses, "didn't we?"

She looked past me to the house. "Yes," she said. "We had fun." Suddenly she smiled and pulled me down beside her on the seat. Five minutes later when we'd forgotten our hangovers she removed her mouth from mine long enough to say, "Let's have some breakfast," and after another five minutes we levered ourselves to our feet.

In the dining room we drank a pot of weak coffee, but she left all the scrambled eggs, bacon, sausages and toast to me. There were kidneys too under the lid of another silver chafing dish, but I left those alone. Much as I wanted to blend with the English, I drew the line at sharing their taste for offal, and besides, a kidney isn't what you want to see first thing in the morning after an evening's heavy drinking.

"Alan should be down soon," said Dinah after telling the maid to bring another pot of coffee. "He usually wakes up at about this time."

I wanted to ask several questions about Alan but wasn't sure how to do it without raising Paul's ghost. In the end I asked safe neutral questions about his school and she told me he loved his lessons and had plenty of friends. We talked a little longer. Even allowing for maternal exaggeration I wondered if the picture she painted of this happy little kid without a care in the world was quite as accurate as she wanted it to be.

In the end I had to ask. I couldn't help myself. "He's all right, is he?" I said.

Some terrible memory burned briefly in her eyes and vanished. "Perfect," she said coolly, and added as the maid reentered the room, "More coffee?"

Now that we were up to our necks in memories of Paul I thought I might as well go on. "Do you ever talk to him about Paul?" I said when my cup was full of coffee again.

"A bit. Not much. I find it terribly difficult. Anyway, Alan never seems to want to know anything about him."

"Maybe he sees how upset you get and doesn't dare ask. No, forget I said that. It's none of my business. . Are you going to take him back to America some day?"

She looked genuinely surprised, as if I had made an extraordinary suggestion. "What for?" she said. "It's not as if he has any affectionate American relations who would make him feel welcome."

"Don't you want to show him his father's palace at One Willow Street?"

An odd expression came into her eyes. Paul was right there in the room with us now. I could almost see him reaching for an unbuttered slice of toast after pushing away the weak coffee with a shudder.

At last she said, "Cornelius will never share that bank with Alan."

"Honey," I said, "it's not Cornelius' bank."

A couple of uneventful seconds trickled away. A bird perched on the sill and sang his heart out. Beyond him the drizzle had stopped and the sun was starting to shine.

"Well, of course," she said slowly, "it *would* be nice to know there'd be no obstacles placed in Alan's way in the unlikely event of him wanting to follow in his father's footsteps."

"All he'd ever have to do is cross the Atlantic and knock on my door."

"And Cornelius?" she persisted.

"Oh, he won't be around at Willow and Wall by that time. He'll be backing talkies or investing in airplanes, and banking'll be no more than a distant memory."

She was fascinated. "Are you sure?"

"Why do you think I'm in Europe? I'm going to build up a base of power so broad that in five years' time I'll be able to reach across the Atlantic and tip him out of the nest. I've got it all mapped out."

"My God!" she said. "You do hate him, don't you! What's been going on?"

"I'll tell you the whole story," I said, but didn't. I just said Cornelius was throwing his weight around by threatening to withdraw his capital from the firm unless he got what he wanted. "The money's gone straight to his head," I explained. "He's a power-crazy punk who's got too big for his little boy's sneakers. He acts not only as if all the world's for sale but as if he ought to get a fifty percent discount. He's—"

"He's the Villain of the Piece!" she laughed, relaxing suddenly. Her eyes were sparkling, her hangover forgotten. It was good to see her in such high spirits again. "I'm almost beginning to feel sorry for him! Isn't there really anyone in the world who thinks he's sweet and adorable?"

"Well, there's his mother and sister. I guess they think he's cute. And there's Sylvia—" I saw her face and broke off. I knew it was time to kick Paul out of the room. "What are we going to do this morning?" I demanded abruptly, rising to my feet. "Can we go sailing again?"

We went sailing and took Alan with us. It was a great morning, and afterward at the Hall we had the traditional English Sunday lunch, overcooked roast beef sliced wafer thin, rock-hard roast potatoes and a slab of pulpy Yorkshire pudding. I must have been crazy with hunger because I ate everything in sight, and after the treacle tart I sagged back in my chair like a sack of gravel.

Alan and his nurse went down to the village to see a friend.

"Time to exercise!" Dinah said ruthlessly and suggested a brisk walk, but this time I overruled her and the only brisk walk we took was straight upstairs to her bedroom.

It wasn't until Alan was in bed that she got me talking about the bank again. I didn't intend to discuss my work. Investment banking isn't the most fascinating subject for a woman, and even Caroline, who took such a strong vicarious interest in my career, would yawn whenever I talked of the thrills of a giant merger. But Dinah started talking about Hal Beecher, whom she knew well, and one thing led to another until before I knew where I was I was telling her about the glories of Van Zale Participations. At first I thought that her show of attention was no more than a gesture of politeness, but then I realized she was genuinely interested in investment trusts. She was used to the business world. She read the *Financial Times* daily and had a good grasp of current economics. For the first time in my life I found I was with a woman who not only could listen intelligently when I talked about my work but could actually turn the conversation into a stimulating discussion.

"My God," I said as the truth slowly dawned on me, "you really do run that business, don't you?"

She looked at me as if I'd forgotten to lace up my straitjacket. "But of course I run it!" she exclaimed. "What did you think? Do you imagine I'm just a puppet and Hal pulls all the strings?"

"Of course not!" I protested, very hot under the collar.

My discomfort must have been entertainingly obvious, for she laughed. "Why do you think Paul took an interest in me?"

"Well, I naturally assumed . . . Well, I mean, it was kind of obvious . . . You see, we all thought . . ." I gave up.

"Even if I hadn't been his mistress I would have been his protégée. He always made that quite clear."

"Yeah." I gazed at her with new eyes, and then realizing it would be more dignified to stop gaping at her and stage a double-quick recovery, I said smoothly, "No wonder you were so special to Paul! Say, Dinah, I know it's none of my business, but while we're on the subject of how special you were to him, what exactly did Paul say in that last letter he wrote you? I've always wondered."

She gave me a puzzled look. "What last letter?"

We stared at each other.

"Didn't you get it?" I said surprised. "I always assumed Mayers found the envelope lying around and put it in the mail to you, but obviously he must have destroyed it when he destroyed all the other personal letters. Paul wrote to you the night before he died, Dinah. He took the envelope with him to the office that morning. I saw it myself."

She was greatly disturbed. "Did he give you any hint about what he'd said?"

"I got the impression it was the purplest prose that ever dripped from a romantic pen." I paused before adding abruptly, "I'll be honest with you. I told him to shelve it. He was in a bad state, not in touch with the cold hard facts of life. I didn't think it would do anyone any good if that letter ever crawled out of the envelope into the light of day."

There was a long, long silence. Then she said in a shaky voice, "Do you think he wanted to come after me to Mallingham?"

Rage shot through me. I felt angry with her for clinging to the past and furious with myself for raising the subject. Worst of all I hated Paul for staying so vividly alive long after his memory should have begun to fade.

I managed not to speak, but I clenched my fists as I turned away.

"Oh, Steve," she said. "Steve."

Her arms were around my neck. She was kissing me. "Don't let's look back," she whispered at last. "I do so hate to look back."

Sometime later I was able to say violently, "I'd like to make a bonfire of all those old memories and dance in the ashes!"

She laughed. She'd just fixed us drinks, and now she raised her glass to mine. "To the ashes!" she said boldly, challenging me to laugh with her, and the future swung round to face us as the door banged shut on the past.

II

It took me less than a month to realize I was crazy about her. Of course I wasn't in love—my craziness did have its limits—but I liked her better than any other woman I'd ever met. What I liked best about her was that she never leaned on me in any way. After all, it's a fact of life that for a man a woman is usually a bit of a burden, and no matter how much he may care for her the chances are that she'll be a dependent creature who looks to him for support. Even Caroline, who bawled loudly about women's emancipation in the course of spreading the birth-control gospel, was dependent on me for everything she needed and had never made any real effort to lead a less conventional life. I'd never objected to this state of affairs either. When a man's young it makes him feel strong and masterful to have a woman dependent on him, but I wasn't a kid anymore and I no longer needed a dependent woman to prove to me how strong and masterful I was. I had reached the stage where I could appreciate a woman who could enjoy my success without devouring it like a parasite, and Dinah filled the bill. She was no millstone round my neck. She made me feel free as air. In her independence I found my own emancipation, and I wanted to tell all those husbands who kept their wives hooked up to the kitchen sink that the taste of my freedom was very, very sweet.

So that was one advantage about Dinah: she made no demands on me because she had a busy satisfying life of her own. But there were other advantages. She was mature enough to conduct an affair without any messy scenes, she was smart enough not to kid herself that

I'd ever leave my wife, she was tremendous fun, and she was just as great in bed as I'd always suspected she would be. Well, how often does a man meet a woman like that? Not often, as we all know. I felt I was very lucky, and to my gratification she told me she felt she was lucky too.

"You're so wonderfully straightforward!" she said admiringly. "No neuroses, no complexes, no problems! I can't tell you how relaxing you are!"

I thought of Caroline, her nose in her amateur-psychology handbook as she remorselessly analyzed the effects of my father's early death. My mother, whom I'd loved, had been classified as "too narcissistic" to achieve a truly maternal response to her sons. My stepfather, whom I had liked enormously, had been called the "architect of my adolescent instability" for his friendly refusal to adopt a paternal attitude where one was sorely needed. I was told that this absence of "adequate parental authority and guidance" had contributed to my "antisocial tendencies" at educational institutions, and had resulted in Luke and Matt becoming "unnaturally dependent" on me. Their emotional development was labeled "arrested" and my concern for my brothers' welfare was called a "fixation."

When I really thought about it I realized I must have been a saint to have put up with this kind of drivel from my wife for so long.

Nuts to Caroline, I thought happily in my new mood of emancipation, but as time went on I found I could no longer dismiss Caroline from my mind just by saying "Nuts." Caroline was fast becoming my biggest headache. Scrupulously I wrote to her every week for fear that if I didn't she might leap aboard the next ship to Europe, and equally scrupulously she answered my letters by return mail to reassure me that Luke and Matt were behaving themselves, but the peace of mind I received from these regular reports only made me realize how important it was not to quarrel with her. That I was teetering on the brink of some unplumbed marital abyss was obvious even to me, coasting along as I was on the golden crest of my new affair. Caroline might encourage me to relax occasionally with other women, but I was pretty sure the boundaries of the new sexual freedom she preached would stop far short of the kind of relationship I was now enjoying with Dinah Slade.

From that deduction it was just a short step to asking myself what I was going to do when Caroline arrived in London. I analyzed my position carefully. I was crazy about Dinah, but it wouldn't last. It was true that at the moment I couldn't see our affair ever ending, but that was because I was temporarily crazy. The affair would end, I'd be left with nothing but a second divorce and limited access to my sons, and my English clients, whom I was trying so hard to cultivate, wouldn't like it at all.

I didn't want to make any bad mistakes.

The most sensible course I could see was to tone down my affair with Dinah to the point where I could make Caroline believe it was unimportant, and then involve Caroline so thoroughly in her new social duties that she wouldn't have time to keep too sharp an eye on me. It was a tricky situation, but with a little finesse I thought I could handle it.

Dinah wasn't much interested in Caroline. She just thought that as Caroline was a complaisant wife there was no problem. The ones who interested her were my brothers.

"Steve," she said one day, "just how old are these two 'boys' you keep referring to?"

"Thirty-seven." I sighed. "It's not just because I had to bring them up single-handed," I said, trying to explain why I felt so responsible for them. "It's because I've always had all the luck and I feel guilty about it. I can remember my father saying to my mother that his own life would have been quite different if *his* brother had shared his luck with him. Uncle was very successful and very rich and very mean."

"I always distrust people who make those sort of remarks," said Dinah. "My father used to say that his life would have been quite different if he'd ever found a woman who understood him, but of course the truth was that all his women understood him much too well. What went wrong with your father's life, Steve? I thought you told me he had pots of money and loads of friends and was the life and soul of every party."

"Yeah." I was silent, remembering my father.

She waited, not rushing me, but at last she said, "You don't have to tell me if you don't want to."

"Hell, it's no big deal," I said. "He drank."

"Did he? God, what a coincidence—so did *my* father! What did your mother do—leave or stay?"

"She stayed."

"Mine left." Now it was her turn to be silent.

"What happened to her, Dinah?"

"Don't pretend Paul never told you!"

It all came out. Dinah's mother had been a suffragette who had died in jail. I was just about to make some sympathetic comment when she said fiercely, "And don't you dare say 'Like mother, like daughter' because I shan't think it's at all funny."

"Jesus, Dinah," I said nettled, "where's the resemblance? You're no idealist. You wouldn't even get up on a Hyde Park Corner soapbox to crusade for your beliefs, let alone go to jail for them. You'd be too busy sweet-talking Hal Beecher into giving you a new loan to expand your million-dollar business!"

She stared at me. To my surprise I saw she was at a loss for words.

"Well, it's true, isn't it?" I said. "The one thing all Paul's people have in common is that they're plugged fairly and squarely into reality. A little sentimentality now and then is just about excusable, but idealism? Forget it! You don't get along in the world by toting around a set of romantic ideals. Paul found that out when he was just a kid, and he never forgot it."

She was still silent. I wondered what she was thinking. At last I said, "Were you afraid I'd laugh about your mother being a suffragette? What's the problem? You know how *I* feel about emancipated women!" And I kissed her with unmistakable enthusiasm.

She laughed and kissed me back. "What a sportsman you are, darling!" she teased. "All for fair play between the sexes!"

"Particularly play," I said, but I was pleased. I was kind of proud of my modern outlook on women, and in a further effort to convince Dinah that I was all for female emancipation I asked if I could visit her office to see the tycoon tigress in action.

I knew from Hal Beecher's reports that Diana Slade Cosmetics was making around four hundred thousand pounds a year, which at the going rate of exchange was well on the way to two million dollars. Twenty-four different cosmetic products were showcased in the famous Grafton Street salon and peddled by a network of salesmen in every major city in the British Isles. The salon, which preserved the firm's reputation for expensive products for the aristocracy despite a surreptitious recent trend to tout a cut-rate line for the masses, was run by Dinah's friend Harriet, an energetic spinster with a face like a greyhound. Harriet took care of the society side, the constant entertaining and socializing, while Dinah revealed herself at a party only when she wanted to give her clientele a treat. This strategy had evolved when Dinah was a new unmarried mother beyond the social pale, but now it had been revived to give Dinah an air of mystery. It not only was a neat public-relations move but also meant that Dinah could have some sort of private life. The two girls got along well. I did no more than poke my nose in the salon, since it was obviously the kind of place where no man could feel at ease for more than two seconds, but I could almost hear the purrs of the clients as they submitted themselves to God only knows what feminine rites.

In the executive offices upstairs I met the sales director, a tough little fairy with a tongue like prussic acid, and the production director who controlled the laboratory. There was another director in charge of the warehouse and inventory. The advertising department was run by a woman, a situation which would have rocked Madison Avenue, and frankly I thought the advertising could have been improved. It was too wordy, but Dinah said that English women appreciated ads which ran on and on like a three-decker novel, and she produced the sales figures to prove it, so I had to back down. There was also a lady in charge of personnel, but I approved of that because all the little typists like to run to a nice motherly figure if any randy member of staff starts pinching bottoms.

"And what do *you* do?" I asked with a grin when the tour was finished and we were drinking tea in Dinah's office. "Put your feet up on your desk and knit?"

It turned out she was just like the senior partner at Van Zale's. She spent her time being nice to people, pouring oil on troubled waters and trying to head off bloodshed in the board room. She soothed all the important clients who wanted their hands held, talked earnestly with bankers and lawyers and occasionally blew up the accountants. Memos were initialed, letters were dictated and tea was consumed. The only difference from being a Van Zale senior partner was that twice a week she popped downstairs to have her hair done.

"What about the commodities we deal with?" she said with a sigh when I told her what I was thinking. "Yours is so much more interesting than mine! I'd rather deal with money than cosmetics any day—banking's such a fascinating field."

I was so touched by this wistful enthusiasm that I suggested she come with me to Paris at the end of May. I wanted to survey the prospects which awaited a French office of Van Zale's, and since she was interested in opening a Paris salon I thought we could combine business with pleasure in the biggest possible way.

Well, we did. That was no surprise, but the revelation of the trip was how useful Dinah was to me in my reconnaissance among the *banques d'affaires* and the *banques de crédit mobilier* who specialized in the flotation of industrial undertakings in France and abroad. She did make one or two inquiries about office space for Diana Slade Cosmetics, but she was more interested in the bankers I knew and the potential clients I'd lined up. I inquired too about office space and spent time on my own while I estimated how much business I'd need to generate to make a French base a paying proposition, but mainly I was concerned with meeting people and this was where Dinah was an enormous asset, because she spoke first-class French. My French was fluent but it was Canadian, the result of handling the affairs of some Montreal clients for some years, and although I had taken courses in European French I found the Parisian accent and vocabulary very different from the French I was used to. Fortunately Dinah came to my rescue whenever I got bogged down, and I soon took her everywhere with me. The people we met were entranced by her. She was always faultlessly dressed and groomed, always so unobtrusively intelligent. Together we studied the Banque de Paris et du Pays-Bas, with its capital of three hundred million francs and its equally lush reserve fund, and plotted on the map of Europe the bank's branches in Amsterdam, Brussels and Geneva.

I like sticking pins in maps. Dinah said I ought to have been a general, and as time passed I really began to feel as if I were surveying some challenging new battlefield and pondering how to deploy my troops. I took a look at another house, the Banque de l'Union Parisienne, and studied several more. Tiring at last of sticking pins in the map, I turned to current economic conditions and gave them a thorough examination. The previous year the franc had been stabilized and the national currency restored to a gold basis. There was now an exchange rate of 25.52 francs to the dollar and 124.21 to the pound sterling, and in addition the Paris rate of discount was as low as that of any other European country except Switzerland. It seldom seemed to rise above three and a half percent.

All this was very promising, and enjoying myself hugely I dictated long memos to my New York partners, but when I was satisfied that they would be impressed by my industry I sat back to take a good hard look at the situation. Before I could think of establishing a base in France I had to perfect my French. I also needed to know a lot more about French banking procedures. I had forgotten how diverse Europe is compared with the monolith of America, and although in the States I could have got away with reviving a static office in Philadelphia while launching a new branch in Baltimore, I realized I would be wisest to conquer England completely before I attempted a French invasion. I had to cope with unfamiliar cultures, tight-knit native banking communities and an alien industrial structure. I didn't want to bite off more than I could chew. However, I remained optimistic about my prospects, and thought a European empire was still well within my grasp provided I was prepared to be patient.

"I just know I can make a success of this if I put my mind to it," I said to Dinah as we sailed back across the Channel.

"Of course you can, darling!" she said enthusiastically, and suddenly I thought how marvelous it would be to have her traveling with me every step of the way, helping me with the clients, listening so intelligently whenever I wanted to discuss business, understanding whenever I confessed to having problems. Caroline would try to help, but it wouldn't be the same. Besides, although Caroline was a successful hostess in America I couldn't help wondering how she would measure up to European standards. I sensed uneasily that the English would classify her as a strident example of American womanhood and retreat with horror behind the mask of their impeccable manners. Caroline had had only moderate success when we were in Europe before, and she had been younger and quieter then. Now that she was older and noisier I had the unpleasant feeling she was going to be more of a hindrance than a help to me at this very crucial moment of my career, and I couldn't think what the hell I was going to do about it.

Caroline was now scheduled to arrive in early July. We had decided to keep our Long Island home for use during our annual visits to the States, but she had disposed of our East Side Manhattan apartment and was shooting off letters demanding to know why I hadn't been house-hunting in England. She wanted a house in Surrey, the smart county, and a house in Mayfair.

I did get some brochures from realtors, but the truth was I couldn't face house-hunting because I couldn't face the thought that my days as a bachelor were coming to an end. I was having such a wonderful time. There were dinners and parties and weekends in the country. There were movies and theaters and nightclubs. There were Ascot and Wimbledon and even—I still yawn to think of it—the Test Match at Lords, with all my clients marveling because I knew the difference between the English cricketers and the visiting South African team. I did blot my copybook once by calling the bowler the pitcher, but Dinah gave a little laugh and said wasn't I witty, so they all thought I was making a joke.

Of course everyone quickly realized Dinah and I had more in common than the balance sheet of Diana Slade Cosmetics, but we didn't go careering around like Bright Young Things who drank and drugged while dancing the Black Bottom and then had to be fished out of the gutter the next morning and chauffeured home. I had my suite at the Ritz, she had her house in Belgravia and what happened on the weekends at Mallingham was our own business. But we were seen a lot together at the Trocadero and the "43," and everyone knew we liked Beatrice Lillie's style and cheered Mary Pickford with her shorn curls and had seen Noël Coward's operetta *Bitter Sweet* three times, so I guess the grapevine must have been humming busily.

It was a great life. When I look back I wonder how I ever found the time to go to Milk Street, but I was working hard and soon I'd yanked the office out of its dozy humdrum rut. The moment Hal left I fired the old dodderers who had accumulated, raked in some youthful brains and streamlined office procedures so that every detail was handled twice as fast. Then when the bank was ticking over with the efficiency of a Swiss watch I fixed a new blade in my invisible hatchet and set about severing clients from British issuing houses as I raked in as much new business as I could handle.

"If only Caroline wasn't coming!" I said for the hundredth time to Dinah. It was the weekend before Caroline was due to leave New

York, and I was savoring my last hours of freedom in the dunes above the beach at Waxham.

"Steve, do stop moaning about Caroline! I specially wanted you to come to Mallingham this weekend because I thought it would cheer you up, and besides . . ."—her hand slipped into mine—"I've got some important news which I've been saving as a surprise."

"Anything that takes my mind off Caroline," I said gloomily, "just has to be good news. What is it?"

She sat up and stretched herself luxuriously. For once she was wearing a minimum of makeup, and her skin was clear and fresh. Her dark eyes glowed. I was just thinking I'd never seen her look so pretty when she exclaimed in a voice vibrant with happiness, "It's the best news in the world, Steve—the best news I could ever wish for." And with a sigh she nestled against my chest, gazed out to sea and murmured dreamily, "I'm going to have another baby."

Chapter Eight

I

My first thought was, Jesus Christ, what am I going to tell Caroline? Then I thought, Oh, the hell with Caroline! And the relief of tossing Caroline aside in this fashion was so enormous that I suddenly saw the only solution to my problems. I'd been fooling myself in thinking a compromise was possible once Caroline was in London. Caroline would never tolerate my having any relationship whatsoever with Dinah. There would be rows and scenes and the children would suffer. It would be hell on earth.

Taking a deep breath, I faced the truth squarely. I loved Dinah. I didn't love Caroline. I didn't want to be with Caroline. The only person I wanted to be with was Dinah. I didn't want to stay married to Caroline. I wanted a friendly divorce and the right to see Scott and Tony as often as possible.

These thoughts all flashed through my mind in seconds and by the time Dinah turned to look at me I knew what I was going to say.

"That's wonderful!" I exclaimed. "I'm crazy about kids!" And I kissed her heartily on the lips.

Tears sprang to her eyes. "I knew you'd understand," she said. The tears streamed down her face.

"Honey, don't cry—"

"But I'm so happy!"

"—because everything's going to be fine! We'll get married just as soon as I can get a divorce."

She looked doubtful. "Oh, you don't have to do that, Steve. I know Caroline's just the sort of wife a man in your position should have, and I couldn't be that sort of wife to you."

"I don't want a wife like Caroline!" I stared at her. "Are you nuts or something? You love me, don't you?"

"Darling, of course I love you—I'm having your child! But all that matters to me is that you're pleased about the baby and that you'll be able to share him with me when the time comes. It's sweet of you to want to marry me, but I don't think it would work out very well.

You'd want me to give up my career and I'd resent losing all my independence."

"That proves it," I said. "You *are* nuts. Have I ever once suggested that you should give up your career?"

"No, but—"

"Then why should I change the moment I put a wedding band on your finger?"

"Listen, Steve darling. Don't lose your temper. It's not that I don't love you and can't appreciate the wonderful compliment you're paying me. It's just that marriage is . . ."—she fumbled for the word—"irrelevant to my way of life. You see, when all's said and done, marriage is just a bourgeois institution for people who live conventional lives."

"Crap." I was really angry. "I don't know why you're scared of marriage, but don't give me that garbage about it being a bourgeois institution. Like it or not it's an institution of the world we live in, and if you can't face up to the world we live in you're in bad trouble and so's that baby. Have you ever asked Alan how he feels about being illegitimate?"

"Well, I . . . Well, the truth is . . ."

"You've never discussed it with him? My God, Dinah, you're going to have trouble with that boy!"

"But he's still so young! How could I possibly explain—"

"Yeah, you're so damned mixed up you couldn't even explain yourself to yourself, let alone to anyone else!" I got up abruptly and walked down the dunes to the beach.

She came after me, and when I saw she'd been crying I took her in my arms.

"Forgive me, honey. I'm sorry."

"I will marry you, Steve, I will, I want to."

"Of course you do. I don't see your problem. There are all kinds of marriages—we'll just tailor one to suit us. You won't be locked up in solitary confinement with a husband who beats you every night."

She managed to laugh. We kissed.

"I hope this won't be bad for your career," she said, worried. "People don't mind so much about divorce nowadays, but it's far less acceptable here than in America."

"Honey, the one thing the British would never accept would be if I knocked up their favorite Lady of Mystery, Miss Dinah Slade, and then settled down cozily with my wife in Mayfair and tried to live happily ever after. A second divorce won't be the greatest thing that's ever happened to me, but I'll get over it and so will the British. Incidentally, how long does it take to buy a divorce over here? Are they expensive?"

This amused her, just as I'd intended, but unfortunately it turned out to be no laughing matter. The New York State divorce law is one of the narrowest in the Union, and in English law too I had no grounds for divorcing Caroline. In fact, according to the smartest divorce lawyer in London the only way my marriage could be terminated immediately would be for Caroline to divorce me for adultery.

Somehow I found it difficult to imagine Caroline meekly asking a judge to cede me to Dinah. I began to feel worried, but since the next step was obviously to delay Caroline's departure I sent her a cable which read: "REGRET BUT MUST ASK YOU TO POSTPONE DEPARTURE STOP CANCEL VOYAGE AND AWAIT FURTHER INSTRUCTIONS STOP STEVEN."

When I returned to the Ritz that evening I found with a shock that Caroline had already cabled: "REGRET BUT MUST POSTPONE DEPARTURE STOP HOSPITALIZED FOR OPERATION STOP NOTHING SERIOUS LOVE CAL."

That put me in a tough spot. Since she was ill I could hardly tell her our marriage was finished. That would be hitting a fellow when he's down, as the English say—not the sporting thing to do at all.

I was still wondering what the hell my next step should be when a letter arrived from my brother Luke. "Thought you ought to know," he scrawled, "that Caroline's operation turned out to be bigger than expected and the doctors say she must convalesce for about three months before attempting to join you in Europe. Don't ask me what the operation was because Caroline wouldn't tell me and seemed to think it was kind of crude of me to ask. It has something to do with those internal organs women have . . ."

Caroline wrote in a letter which arrived the next day,

So I said to the doctor, "If you don't tell me the truth I'll sue you. Was it benign or not?" So the doctor said no, it wasn't exactly benign but it didn't matter because they got the whole thing out. So I said: "My God, you mean I've just had cancer of the womb?" and he said: "Yes, but your recovery is progressing well and your prognosis is excellent." So there we are. Of course if I'd known beforehand that I had cancer I'd have screamed for you to come home, but now it's all over there doesn't seem much point, does there? However, darling, although I don't want to be hysterical I must admit it *would* be nice if you could come back for a visit. . . .

"I'll have to go," I said, very upset.

"She knew you'd say that," said Dinah.

"What the hell's that supposed to mean?"

"Nothing."

"Jesus, Dinah, the woman's just had cancer!"

"I know, and I think that's a very brave letter and I admire her very much and I hope she lives till she's a hundred. But look at it this way, Steve. Caroline must know about us. If she doesn't read the gossip columns herself she's bound to have half a dozen kind friends who are burning to tell her what you've been getting up to. So naturally, since Caroline isn't going to give you up without a fight, she's going to do her damnedest to lure you back to America."

I was on the brink of having a row with her but I controlled myself. Pregnancy is notorious for making women irrational and it wasn't surprising that she should be jealous of Caroline.

I fired off a cable to Caroline's doctor demanding a full confidential report by return mail, and followed it with a second cable to Luke asking him to buy up half a florist's shop and have it delivered to Caroline in the hospital. Then I tried to figure out a solution which would be fair to everyone.

Caroline's doctor reported that while the surgery appeared to have been successful the possibility of a recurrence in the future couldn't be overlooked. He recommended that Caroline stay under his supervision till Christmas.

It was August by that time. I could return to New York, have a heart-to-heart talk with Caroline, get myself divorced for adultery, whisk back to England, marry Dinah and live happily ever after. Or I could stick around in England, welcome my illegitimate child when it entered the world and negotiate a slow painful long-distance divorce from Caroline.

I chewed it over. Whichever way I looked at the situation, I had to admit I was in a mess, and finally I told myself I was in such a mess that I might as well go all the way and do the honest, decent thing.

I had to see Caroline face to face. It was no good cowering in England and sheltering behind a barrage of lawyers. I had to talk to her, explain the way things were and negotiate the end of the marriage personally with all possible tact and consideration.

I felt good after making that decision—rather as if I'd been to church after a long absence. However, then it occurred to me that I didn't want to wipe Caroline out by a surfeit of decency. If I now materialized promptly at her bedside she might look so sick that I wouldn't have the heart to tell her any bad news. I had to wait till she was fit enough to yell abuse at me in her usual style and convince me how impossible it was to stay married to her.

Scraping up all my diplomacy, I wrote to Caroline and said that I'd certainly return for a visit but that for business reasons it was vitally important for me to stay in London till mid-September. I said I had been helped to this difficult decision by a letter from her doctor saying she was heading for a full recovery. Then I wrote to Luke and asked him to deliver the other half of the florist's shop.

Dinah was relieved that I'd restrained myself from dashing to the sickbed, but she wanted me to forget all about returning to America to see Caroline face to face. Remembering her experience with Paul, I had every sympathy for her attitude, but I wasn't going to allow myself to be swayed by it.

"I've got to think of Scott and Tony as well," I said. "I've got to see them and explain to them what's going on. I'm sorry, Dinah, but you must let me work this out with my family."

She at once said she understood, but I could see she was becoming increasingly strained as my departure drew nearer. The climax came in early September when the doctor told her she was anemic and ordered her to bed for a week. She lay limply on the pillows in a wonderful Parisian negligée and looked very white and sad and brave, like a lady in one of those old-world romances who hasn't long to live.

I cracked on the third visit. "Oh hell, Dinah," I said wildly. "I can't leave you like this!" So I put off my visit home till November. By that time I really did think that Dinah needed me more than Caroline did. Luke wrote and said Caroline looked just great and was even making bridge dates again, but Dinah looked as if she could have a miscarriage at any minute and fade away afterwards on a chaise-longue.

I told myself I had to get my priorities right, and I began to think I should stay with Dinah after all until the baby was born. We could adopt the baby later to make him legitimate—maybe I could even adopt Alan too. Once we managed to marry, everything would fall into place.

"Have you told Alan about the baby?" I asked Dinah.

"No, I'm waiting for the right moment," she said, but when the right moment never seemed to come I went ahead and told him myself.

"Will you still play with me afterwards?" said Alan.

I told him I would.

"Once you and Mummy are married will we be a family?"

"You bet."

He thought for a moment. "Please tell Mummy not to let the baby out until you've married her," he said finally. "To be a real family you've got to get married first. Mummy has to wear a white dress. You'd better explain it to her."

"Sure. No problem," I said, and immediately knew I had to get to New York in double-quick time to negotiate a divorce.

I was still wondering if I dared broach the subject again to Dinah when three thousand miles away on Wall Street the market started to swing.

II

It had staggered in March. There had been a panic followed by a tide of selling, but everyone had calmed down and the setback had been described as a "technical correction." By September the market not only had recovered but was breaking all records, and everyone was laughing at bankers like Paul Warburg and my own partner Martin Cookson who continued to forecast that doom was just around the corner. I took a middle view. I didn't think there would be a huge crash, but I did think there would inevitably be some form of decline. The bond business had been suffering seriously for more than a year because the investors preferred to buy stocks, and this showed that the public was more interested in capital gains than in safety and income. This was not only bad news for investment bankers but bad news for those who hoped for a stable market.

However, I felt less worried about the financial situation after I had read the report of the Investment Bankers Association, which had been holding its annual convention in Quebec. The verdict was that the securities business would continue to prosper and stock prices would climb to new heights. The ragged behavior of the market since early September was dismissed with a flourish and the eighteenth convention of the I.B.A. duly closed on a note of buoyant optimism.

The date was the eighteenth of October, 1929.

The very next day the market started to fall. Speculative issues plunged badly, and although I cabled Luke to start building some defenses around Van Zale Participations I had no reply until after the weekend. He and his family had gone upstate to visit friends.

On Monday the twenty-first the market plunged again. My broker cabled me to ask if I wanted to sell any items in my extensive portfolio, and that evening I booked a telephone call to Lewis in New York.

Transatlantic calls are impossible. There's nearly always bad static on the line—assuming the line's open—and it's so hard to hear what the other party says that conversation is limited, to say the least. But I picked a lucky moment for my call that night and by a miracle I could hear stuffy old Lewis clearly enough to picture every pompous notch of his Hollywood profile.

"Relax, Steve! No need to worry. . . . Yes, it's been one of the busiest days in the history of the Stock Exchange and there's no doubt the market's had another bad break, but this is still just a technical correction."

I barely slept that night, and I booked another call to One Willow

Street the next morning. I had to wait hours and finally sent a cable instead. Back came a cable saying that everything was fine and that the market was holding its own. Charles Mitchell of National City Bank had arrived back that day from Europe and pronounced the situation to be "fundamentally sound." One of the great gods of Wall Street had spoken. The panic had now been officially laid to rest.

The next day six million shares changed hands, a busy day's trading by any reckoning, but when I heard that two and a half million of those shares had changed hands in the last hour before closing I knew that some nightmare event was just around the corner.

I cabled my broker and told him to sell everything he could.

I cabled Luke and told him to ditch all the speculative stock in the Van Zale Participations portfolio.

I cabled my partners and told them to cable back immediately with a prognosis.

"MORE THAN A MERE TECHNICAL CORRECTION," Lewis cabled back, "BUT THURSDAY'S FORECAST IS FOR MARKET TO STABILIZE AGAIN AS ON TUESDAY STOP RETURN TO NORMAL ANTICIPATED BY END OF MONTH."

I drank half a bottle of scotch and waited for the night to end.

I remember the dawn, the great bloodshot clouded dawn of Black Thursday, the twenty-fourth of October, 1929.

"There's going to be a crash," I said to Dinah. "I think it might be a big one."

Even then I was so busy standing on the beach watching the angry breakers that I never saw the dimensions of the tidal wave beyond.

The Crash came. People who lived through it on Wall Street said it was like the end of the world. Stone-faced crowds packed the Street from end to end, men had hysterics in front of the ticker, wailing women keened on subway cars. But I wasn't there, so I never saw the greatest gambling machine of all time crack up to strip the people of their money and the bankers of their reputation. I just saw the cables, the stark reports, the unbelievable figures of a market gone mad.

Black Thursday was followed by a lull while the market staggered around like a chicken with its head cut off, but five days later on the so-called Tragic Tuesday the market was brutally drowned beneath a tidal wave of sixteen and a half million dumped shares.

My telephone rang. It rang continuously. I sat beside it all day. I didn't eat. After a while I even forgot to drink.

The appalling cables began to stream across the Atlantic.

"STEVE WE'RE HURTING BADLY PLEASE COME HOME SITUATION DESPERATE RE VAN ZALE PARTICIPATIONS . . ."

But neither of my brothers had the nerve to cable me full details of the gory disaster which had overtaken the investment trust.

The blood streamed all the way down Willow Street into the bank on the corner of Wall.

"CRISIS OF GRAVEST PROPORTIONS," cabled Lewis. "FOR THE GOOD OF THE FIRM WE MUST ALL UNITE . . ."

"HOW SOON CAN YOU BE HOME?" cabled Martin. "IMPOSSIBLE TO OVERESTIMATE MAGNITUDE OF CRASH."

". . . SO MUST REQUEST YOUR IMMEDIATE RETURN . . ." Even Clay wanted me back.

The phone rang. New York was on the wire. Above the gasps of the static I could hear Matt sobbing.

"Please come, Steve," I heard him beg, and Luke, grabbing the receiver from him, shouted, "You've got to come, for Christ's sake come—" We were cut off.

The last cable arrived directly afterward. It said:

> SINCE YOU APPOINTED YOUR BROTHERS TO THEIR POSITIONS WE FEEL YOU SHOULD NOW ASSUME RESPONSIBILITY FOR THEIR ACTIONS STOP IT WOULD BE DIFFICULT FOR YOU TO IMAGINE THE SORDIDNESS OF THEIR SITUATION BUT I ASSURE YOU THAT IT WOULD BE IMPOSSIBLE FOR ME TO EXAGGERATE IT STOP KINDLY CABLE YOUR ARRIVAL DATE STOP MAY I SUGGEST YOU TAKE THE NEXT SHIP STOP CORNELIUS.

I tried to get hold of my brothers, but the lines were out. I booked the call, but when nothing happened I shot off a cable asking them just what the hell they'd been playing at when the Crash had caught them with their pants down. Eventually, hours later, I did manage to speak to them again on the phone and they did try to tell me what had been going on.

I thought I'd have a heart attack. Men have died from less provocation, but fortunately for my brothers I have an iron constitution.

"All right, boys," I said, cutting off the conversation as soon as I realized it was quite unsuitable for the telephone. "Keep your mouths shut, get out of sight and if you're arrested hire the best criminal lawyer in town. I'm on my way."

I finished a bottle of scotch and opened another as I thought about what the disaster meant. It wasn't just that my brothers could end up in jail. The partners would need a scapegoat, and as Cornelius had already implied, the role was tailor-made for me. I didn't just have to return to New York to bail out my brothers. I had to rush back to save my neck.

Very slowly I levered myself to my feet, abandoned the bottle of scotch and trudged off to Belgravia to talk to Dinah.

III

". . . So you see," I said heavily to her, "there's no choice. I've got to go."

I thought she'd say, "Yes, of course. I understand." But she didn't. Without a word she retreated upstairs to her room.

Following, I found her sitting on the edge of her bed and staring at the floor.

My heart went out to her. I'd never felt more miserable in my life. "Dinah . . . honey . . ." I slumped down beside her. "History's not going to repeat itself, I swear it. I'm not going to disappear into America and occasionally send you a cute letter to keep you amused. I'll come back. And I'll marry you."

She still said nothing. The silence closed in upon us.

"Come with me," I urged in desperation.

"They wouldn't let me on the ship."

"But you're only six months pregnant!"

"And big as a house. It's not just one baby, Steve. There are two."

"*What!*" For the second time in a couple of hours I felt close to heart failure. "You mean . . ."

"Twins. I've known for two months. I was saving the news as a Christmas present for you."

"Oh, my God! Jesus Christ, I can't possibly leave you!" I was distraught. I began to pace feverishly up and down the room. "Look, you've got to come with me. I'll fix the ship—we'll hire a doctor to come with us—and when we reach New York I'll find you an apartment—"

"Oh no," she said dryly. "That's one road I'm never going to travel again."

"But I'm not Paul!" I shouted. "My God, you don't think I'd sleep with Caroline while you were looking the other way, do you?"

"I underestimated Sylvia and went through hell. I've no intention of underestimating Caroline."

I was enraged by her implication that Caroline could twist me around her little finger. "Well, what the hell do you expect me to do?" I bawled at her. "God damn it, Dinah, can't you understand that I love you and want to marry you? What the hell else do you expect of me now, for God's sake?"

"Common sense." She rose to her feet and impulsively slid her arms around my neck. "Don't go back to New York, Steve."

"Christ, as if I had any choice!"

"I mean it. Don't go back. Don't get drawn into your brothers' mess. They'll drag you down with them."

"But I'm responsible!"

"Rubbish," said Dinah. "Your partners are just as responsible as you are—more so because you haven't been in New York since March—but they're hitting you as hard as they can to draw a veil over their own negligence! Let *them* cope! Let *them* clean up the mess! Good God, Steve, can't you see that someone back there at Willow and Wall is making a grab for power by using your brothers to jockey you against the rails?"

I stared at her. I felt exhausted. I was dimly aware that I didn't like her telling me what was going on. Wiping the sweat from my forehead, I tried to keep a clear head.

"My brothers—"

"Oh, fuck your brothers!" said Dinah. I was never so shocked in my life. Not even Caroline had ever used that kind of language. For one horrible moment I was reminded of the scene in my New York office when Cornelius had jettisoned his polite well-mannered Midwestern upbringing to reveal himself as the toughest kid on the block.

I backed away.

"Steve, it's so damned obvious that those brothers of yours have been sponging on you ever since they shared a cradle. Why can't you see they're just a couple of petty failures?"

My temper erupted. "Don't you call my brothers failures!" I shouted.

"Failures!" she shouted right back. "Your trouble, Steven Sullivan, is that you're too damned sentimental!"

I walked out.

"Steve!" She ran after me. "Steve, wait!"

"Go to hell." I was crossing the living room to the front door.

"Steve—" She tripped at the top of the stairs and just managed to grab the rail. She didn't scream—there wasn't time—but I saw the color drain from her face as I raced back to her.

"My God, are you all right? Here—let me carry you," I said, and lifted her to the bed.

The shock sobered us both. We started to apologize, she saying she found it hard to understand my attachment to my brothers because her brother and sister had meant so little to her, I mumbling that I didn't know how I was ever going to leave her. I forgot that chilling moment when she had reminded me of Cornelius.

But not for long. For it was unmasking time at the masquerade ball, and I was just about to find out that the Lady of Mystery, Miss Dinah Slade, was no ordinary protégée of that goddamned best friend of mine but a made-to-measure replica of Cornelius Van Zale in drag.

"I've got to go back to New York," I was saying. "My mind's

made up and there's no altering it. I'll sort out the mess, see Caroline, wangle a divorce, come back, marry you—and we'll go to Paris again in the spring!" I added, pouncing on a way to cheer her up. "Ah, honey, remember what a wonderful help you were to me there! What a way you have with the clients! Maybe I should take you into Van Zale's and train you for a partnership!"

"Steve!" She sat bolt upright on the bed, eyes shining, cheeks glowing, all our problems forgotten. "Oh, Steve, I'd like that better than anything—I've been thinking of it for such a long time! I suppose it really all began when I first saw the great hall at One Willow Street, but of course I never dreamt then that I'd never get the chance to—" She stopped. Her expression changed. "But you don't mean it, do you," she said. "You just said that as a joke. How stupid of me. I'm sorry."

"Why, don't be sorry," I said. "Tell me more." A small hard knot was forming in the pit of my stomach.

"It's nothing. You know how I enjoy my work, but you must have suspected that I was getting tired of cosmetics and wanted something more challenging. However, it's not important. Let's forget it."

"Did Paul know about this?"

"I wasn't consciously aware of it myself when he was alive, but yes, I think he always knew. If he were alive now—"

"What does his death matter?" I said. "I'm here, aren't I? Your second chance for a slice of the Van Zale pie!"

She smiled nervously. "I know it's odd of a woman to want to go into banking. But I know I could do it, Steve, I know I could! If I could only have the opportunity—"

"Forget it, Dinah," I said thickly. "Women don't become investment bankers. I'm sorry."

"But I'm intelligent, hard-working and able. I've proved I can start with nothing and build up a hugely successful business in less than seven years. Why should I be disqualified from a banking career just because I'm a woman?"

"The clients would never accept you, and neither would the partners. Sorry, honey, but there's no way you can sleep yourself into this particular saddle."

She flushed and stood up. "That was a horrible thing to say!"

"Isn't that what you've been trying to do ever since I set foot in this country last March?"

"I don't understand."

"Jesus Christ, you're so goddamned smart—don't tell me you don't understand! Why, after the very first night we spent together you got me to guarantee Alan's future at Van Zale's! I was the key that was going to open the Van Zale door for you, wasn't I, so you made a big fuss of me and gave me the time of my life—although it was kind of tedious for you, because at heart you'd rather be debating classical literature or moseying around old churches—"

"Steve, for God's sake, you're twisting everything around—"

"And no wonder you got pregnant! You got what you wanted then, didn't you—another Van Zale partner in your hip pocket and the red carpet rolled out to welcome you to investment banking!"

"I got pregnant because I wanted another child and I wanted it to be yours!"

That was more than I could take. "Ah, come, Dinah, let's not be so 'damned sentimental' about this!" I shouted. "You think I'm dumb about women, don't you? Well, I'm not! I know when I'm being taken! I know when I'm being had! You may have wrecked Paul's life, but by God you're not going to wreck mine!"

"Shut up!" she screamed. "Don't you dare fling Paul's name in my face, don't you *dare!* I loved Paul—loved him—and he was ten times the man you'll ever be, both in bed and out of it!"

"Christ!" I was on my feet. The room swam. "You goddamned bitch!"

"Do I think you're dumb about women? Yes, I do—you've no idea how to make love properly! I tried to give hints, tried to tell you what I liked, and all you cared about was rolling into bed with me when you were drunk and slamming away for a few minutes before you passed out!"

"You liked it! You always acted as if—"

"It was boring, God damn you! Boring, disappointing and unsatisfying, and if I hadn't cared for you so much—yes, I did love you—I would have told you so long ago and to hell with your precious masculine vanity! My God, if you knew all the times I've lain in bed and tried to pretend you were Paul!"

"Jesus," I said. "I could tell you a thing or two about Paul. Why, he didn't even like women all that much—he only used them to prove to himself he was no Oscar Wilde!"

"That's a filthy lie—the filthiest I've ever heard!" She flew at me. Her nails raked my cheeks. Her swollen body was torn with sobs. "Get out!" she screamed. "Get out, get out, get out! I never want to see you again!"

"Forget it—seeing you again is the one mistake I'll never make!" I yelled back at her. "Go and find some other sucker to take for a ride!"

She was still screaming abuse at me as I slammed the door.

IV

In bed two hours later I reached for the phone and called her.

"I don't want to talk to you," she said steadily.

"I wanted to tell you it wasn't true about Paul. Caroline used to say that kind of thing after she'd heard the latest cheap psychology theories being peddled at parties, but I think it's crazy, don't you? I never did believe in all that psychological garbage."

"Steve—"

"I was just jealous of Paul, I guess. It really hurt when you said you kept thinking of him when we were together. Dinah, you didn't mean that, did you, about the sex?"

She hung up on me. An hour later after I had emptied half a bottle of scotch she called back.

"I'm sorry I said those horrible things to you," she said, "but you said some horrible things to me. I wonder if you even realize how horrible they were."

"I not only realize it," I said, "but I'd say them all again." Then it was my turn to hang up.

Two hours later when all the scotch was gone I called her back. She was still awake, still by the phone, because she picked it up on the first ring.

"I want to know when the twins come," I said. "Poor wretched little kids, I'm so goddamned sorry about them. I'll take care of them if you don't want them."

"You're drunk," she said. "I'll never give them up, never, and what's more they'll be entirely mine. Fathers of illegitimate children have no rights—they can't even seek custody." And the line went dead.

I was indeed very drunk by that time, so I cried a little and let myself pass out. It was dawn and the room was getting light.

I sailed the following afternoon. I left the guys at the bank to clean up in my wake and somehow managed to arrive at Southampton on time. The ship sailed slowly west out of sight of land and I lay in my cabin with the blinds drawn.

It was a rough crossing. I drank most of the time—too much, I knew I was drinking too much, and I knew I had to stop or I'd end up like my father. Then my father's memory sobered me, just as it always did, and when the ship reached New York my mind was clear, my hands were steady and I felt ready to fight whatever battles came my way.

I went up on deck to look at the city. It was one of those brilliant fall mornings when the air is clear and the water very blue. The famous jagged skyline stared back at me sleazily, as harsh as the mouth of a gangster's gun, and suddenly I longed for London, for the solid bulk of Admiralty Arch, the honky-tonk glamour of Eros, the fairy-tale towers of Horseguards, and all the other friendly landmarks of the city I'd come to call my home.

The ship docked. It was a lengthy process, but by the time I walked down the gangway I was at least excited at the prospect of being reunited with my family.

In the customs hall I stopped to look around—and there waiting for me by the barrier I saw not Caroline, not my children, not even my damfool brothers, but my enemy, Cornelius Van Zale.

PART FIVE

Cornelius The Moralist

1929–1933

Chapter One

I

"Though the mills of God grind slowly," said the sampler which stood before the fireplace in my office, "they grind exceeding small. Though with patience He stands waiting, with exactness grinds He all."

Longfellow's lines had never been more appropriate. Throughout the Crash I had been besieged by people begging me to lock the sampler in the nearest closet, but I kept it exactly where it was. The lines had been embroidered by my father's maiden sister and formed one of a set of six samplers which had hung on the parlor wall of the farm where I had been born. My mother had given me "The Mills of God" as an Awful Warning after Paul died, and I had become so attached to it that I had had it mounted on a wooden stand. As my life became increasingly complex it soothed me to be reminded daily of a simple straightforward rural world.

The sampler was always the first thing I saw as I entered the room. It says much for my state of mind after the partners' meeting late on the afternoon of October the twenty-ninth, 1929, that I never even noticed the sampler as I reeled back into the office.

Sam had our cigarettes alight before I had finished sinking into a chair.

"What happened?"

I inhaled deeply and started to cough. I knew I had to give up smoking. I had now reached the stage of being too guilty to call a doctor whenever I had a touch of bronchitis.

"It's all right," I gasped when the worst of the wheezing was over. "Lewis got a twenty-eight-day extension on the loan by inviting the bank president to go yachting with him in the Bahamas this winter, Matt and Luke are unemployed, and I have a halo on my head and a pair of wings growing out of my shoulders."

"Wonderful!" exclaimed Sam with admiration. "And Steve? Is he coming home?"

"Yes."

"Well, now he's really got his back to the wall! Congratulations, Neil— Say, is anything wrong?"

"No," I said. "Nothing." But I was unable to repress a small shudder.

Although I would never have admitted it to a living soul, I was scared to death of Steven Sullivan.

II

Steve had just concluded a boisterous boozy English summer by knocking up Dinah Slade. We had been following his progress with interest for some time as we tried to figure out just what the hell was going on. Whatever it was I didn't like it. It was all very well for Sam to argue that Dinah Slade was doing us a favor by taking Steve off our backs, but I couldn't visualize Steve, who enjoyed power more than any other man I knew, ever being content for long to potter around the London office—or indeed ever forgiving and forgetting how he had come to be in Europe in the first place—and I certainly didn't see Dinah Slade as a nice girl devoid of ulterior motives. No woman makes a habit of sleeping with bankers and bearing them illegitimate children unless she is after something much more substantial than easy credit.

"But what can she be after?" said Sam mystified. "It can't be money, because she's got plenty of that already."

"I suspect she resents the fact that I inherited Paul's fortune while her boy didn't get a red cent."

"But that's past now! There's nothing she can do about it!"

"Wrong, Sam. She can shack up with Steven Sullivan and take us all for the biggest ride in town."

Sam just laughed, said I was ripe to play the title role in a Hollywood movie about Machiavelli and asked if I had ever considered the possibility that Miss Slade had merely jumped into bed with Steve because he was all hell with the women. I laughed too, but absent-mindedly. I was too busy remembering Paul saying to me long ago, "You and Dinah! Such ambition!" and I thought again, as I had thought so often since that conversation, that I really did not care at all for Miss Dinah Slade.

I first heard of her in the summer of '22, but I never knew her name because my mother could only bring herself to refer to her as That Woman. "Poor Sylvia has been completely abandoned," I heard her mutter to my stepfather. "Paul seems determined to stay in Europe with That Woman."

However, my great-uncle remained married to his exquisite third wife, and I had no idea that he was still in communication with

That Woman until the spring of '26, when my mother tried to tell me I could not spend a second summer at Paul's Bar Harbor cottage.

"Miss Slade is in New York!" announced my mother, much as an astronomer might announce the appearance of a new comet in the heavens. I had an impression of a rare natural phenomenon trailing clouds of doom in its wake.

"Who's she?" I said excited.

"Paul's English mistress." My mother's voice sank a full octave. The implication was that whereas an American mistress would have been wholesome, an English mistress represented the full decadence of twentieth-century Europe. "Cornelius, I cannot in all good conscience sanction your visit to Bar Harbor this year. I feel I must register some protest no matter how small against poor Sylvia's intolerable position."

I said nothing, but after considering the position I screwed up my courage and called Paul in New York. A week later I was on my way to Maine. My mother might criticize Paul till she was purple in the face, but whenever he chose to charm her she was, like every other woman, clay in his hands.

At Bar Harbor my friend Jake Reischman said to me, "What do you think of Miss Dinah Slade? All society's talking of her. Have you met your little cousin yet?"

I can remember every detail of that scene. We were lounging by the tennis court as we drank lemonade. Tennis at Bar Harbor always required unusual cunning because of the strong sea winds, and that day the wind was gusting true to form and sending fluffy little clouds scudding across the sky. My three friends, Jake, Kevin and Sam, were watching me curiously. It was typical of Jake, who prided himself on his sophistication, to bring up a chic New York society item with the air of a man who had at least three mistresses of his own and was considering annexing a fourth. We all talked endlessly about women and without actually lying tried to convince one another we had been seducing every woman in sight since the onset of puberty.

"What little cousin?" I said to Jake, and that was the end of my lack of interest in Dinah Slade. That was when she began to creep into my life inch by inch as we grasped the opportunities Paul had given us and moved inexorably on, month by month, year by year, toward that inevitable future battleground when her ambition would lock horns with mine.

III

I saw little of Paul when I was young. My parents' marriage was considered a mésalliance by my mother's family, and even after my father died we did not return East but remained in Ohio, both before and after my mother so promptly remarried. I was four when I left my father's farm and went to live in Velletria, the Cincinnati suburb where my stepfather Dr. Wade Blackett was the kingpin of the local hospital.

My stepfather was walking proof that not all surgeons are handsome, devil-may-care fellows pursued by throngs of nubile nurses. Unremarkable in looks, he had that special pedestrian manner which men acquire only when they have worked hard all their lives, prospered modestly and never taken a single risk which might have made their lives exciting. My mother had married him, as she had once confided to me in a rare burst of confidence, because she had felt it was so important for a boy to have a father.

The thought that she could have made such a mistake for my sake was horrifying to me, but I concealed my feelings, since I had no wish for her to know that her sacrifice had been in vain. My stepfather was equally conscientious. We soon found out we were conspirators in a plot to prevent my mother from guessing that he thought I was a hopeless enigma while I thought he was a dreary bore, and for years afterward we lived amicably beneath the same roof in an atmosphere of gentle but profound alienation.

People loved Velletria, Ohio. They probably still do. I thought I might like it better when my health improved sufficiently to allow me to attend a local private school, but I was wrong. I was a delicate child, small for my age, and I was regarded with such a callous mixture of curiosity and scorn that I soon carried a penknife to protect myself from the more vicious forms of hazing.

I was interested to see what happened when I was driven to use it. As it turned out I attended school for only one semester before my mother took me away, but I learned some useful lessons so the experience was not unbeneficial. I learned that it can be an advantage to be underestimated, because people become overconfident and play carelessly into your hands. I learned that one short sharp violent gesture can cow even the biggest bully. And I learned that the art of survival in adverse conditions consists of stepping on other people before they can step on you. Achilles wasn't the only warrior with a weak spot. Everyone was vulnerable somewhere. The trick was to isolate the weakness, slip it in a vise and turn the screws. True power, as I used to say to Sam, *pure* power was being able to put the invisible vise in mothballs and walk through a crowd knowing no one would dare step on you.

"Blessed are the Meek," said another of my aunt's samplers, "for they shall inherit the earth."

"Gee, I wonder how they'll manage that," I remarked puzzled after my semester at school, but my mother thought I was being blasphemous and said severely that she had had just about enough of postwar godlessness and that it was a great pity I did not care to read some stimulating intellectual work on theology instead of confining myself to the sports pages of the *Cincinnati Inquirer*.

"Yes, Mama," I said, meek enough to inherit the earth. I was terrified she would find out that my favorite hobby was gambling.

I knew perfectly well I was the black sheep of my quiet cultured intellectual family, but I made heroic efforts to hide from them the full extent of my deviation. However, pretending to be something one is not is an exhausting occupation, and as my adolescence continued I became progressively more confused and restless. I loved my mother and sister but had nothing in common with them. My stepfather was like a man from Mars. I could not remember my own father well enough to know whether or not I resembled him. Who was I, I used to ask myself, and whoever I was, what was I doing in this well-bred, elegant and stupefyingly dull suburban Eden?

I was just asking myself this question for the hundredth despairing time when my mother returned to the dining table after taking a phone call from New York and said to me in exasperation, "Your Uncle Paul seems determined to see you."

IV

Paul.

We met at weddings and funerals. My mother's marriage to Wade, Vicky's marriage to Jason Da Costa, Paul's marriage to Sylvia —I can dimly remember them all. I remember the funerals more clearly, the services commemorating my grandmother who was Paul's sister Charlotte, my ancient great-grandmother who was Paul's mother, and most tragic of all my bright pretty cousin, Paul's daughter Vicky. Throughout these family occasions Paul never spoke more than half a dozen words to me, but the abiding memory of my childhood is of Paul entering a crowded room and all heads turning to look at him in respect, admiration and awe.

Occasionally during his business trips he would visit us in Velletria and then my mother would cling to him adoringly, my stepfather's conversation would become almost interesting and my sister Emily would reach new heights of beauty and intelligence. I would watch, yearning to join in but trapped by the wretchedest feelings of inferiority, and sometimes Paul's dark eyes would flick over me curiously as if he were wondering if I could possibly be as moronic as I appeared to be.

It must have been instinct, not logic, which made him send for me, but whatever his reasons he reached out his hand, pulled me out of that world where I had never belonged and drew me east across those Allegheny Mountains to that other world where he knew I would feel at home.

I knew then who I was.

"I see myself in you, Neil," he said to me once, for he too had been the black sheep of his family, and I saw myself in him. He was the man I wanted to be, the hero I had always needed to worship, the father I had never had, and when I saw the glamour of his corruscating power I wanted to follow in his footsteps with such a passion that I could hardly help betraying my ambition to him.

"What can I do?" I was still almost inarticulate in his presence, but in my excitement I did manage to blurt out a couple of monosyllabic questions. "How can I prove myself to you?"

He told me to work hard, and then he patted me on the shoulder and left. He was not a demonstrative person and although charming he often seemed cold. Looking back, I think it was not merely my ambition but my craving for some small gesture of affection which made me toil so hard during those magic summers Jake, Kevin, Sam and I spent in Maine.

I had no special position because I was Paul's great-nephew, and if it had not been for Sylvia, who was anxious about my health, I might well have forgotten I was one of the family. By the July of 1926 I had accepted that Paul was determined to have no favorites, but I was still struggling not to be hurt by his detachment when he returned suddenly from a quick trip to New York and demanded to see me alone.

He hauled me out of the dining room in the middle of dinner and marched me into the library. Naturally I thought I had done something wrong. I was just beating back the lump in my throat with iron determination when he smiled at me, and as the expression in his eyes softened I saw all the affection he had denied me before.

"Sit down, Neil," he said. "I want to talk to you."

We sat facing each other across the small table by the window. Outside the dusk was deepening, and the twilight seemed mysterious. I could not see the expression in his eyes, but at last he leaned forward in his chair and said abruptly, "I signed my new will today. You'll get what you want."

I was struck dumb. I did try to say that what I wanted was for him to live to a ripe old age, but he cut me off.

"No platitudes," he said. "This is business. I've made a decision in regard to a large amount of money and I want to make quite sure we understand each other. In particular I want you to understand that great wealth and its corresponding power is not a blessing but a burden, and that I've chosen you to be my heir not because you're my great-nephew—I'm not sentimental about blood relationships—but because I think you'll be able to carry that burden without being ground to dust by it. Your mother has faults, but she's given you a stable family home, a civilized upbringing and a persistent grounding in Christian ethics. As an agnostic I'm sufficiently detached to admire the moral strength of Christian principles, and as a cynic I can afford to retain my innate belief in the virtues of family life. But never think yourself indestructible, Neil. Remember the philosophy of the Greeks and do nothing to excess."

"Yes, sir," I said respectfully, thinking how strange it was that words which had sounded so tedious when spoken by my mother should now sound so fraught with significance.

He told me to watch my liquor consumption and warned me how insidiously a taste for alcohol could slip out of control. ". . . And by the time you have a shot of gin in your breakfast orange juice you'll be of no use to anyone, least of all yourself. Do I hear you thinking that this can't possibly happen to you? I tell you it can. You can't imagine the pressures and tensions you'll have to live with. You'll long to do anything to relieve the strain. . . . Has that amazingly ineffectual stepfather of yours ever talked to you about sex?"

"No, sir."

"Then let me tell you this: trust no one. People will do anything for money, anything at all. Be skeptical when a woman tells you she loves you. Avoid all homosexual encounters. Yes, yes, I know you're only interested in girls, don't look so insulted! But a boy who's as handsome as you are inevitably attracts homosexual attention, and you must be on your guard against making mistakes which can result in blackmail, scandal and ruin. Always remember that in your private life one small slip can have far-reaching and disastrous consequences, and no matter how rich you are you must never forget that self-indulgent exercise of your emotions is the one luxury you'll never be able to afford. Has anyone ever told you about my disastrous entanglement with my first wife, Vicky's mother?"

He began to talk of the past. He talked for a long time while the moon rose higher in the sky and the sea shone silver far away below the pine trees. After a while I realized he was explaining himself to me with much painful honesty because he wanted me to understand his mistakes and avoid them when I picked up the life he would someday leave behind.

I listened and listened. Sometimes he would reach across the table as if by grasping my hand in his he could somehow soften that story of revenge, and once he broke off to say, "I'm sorry. You're so very young and you've seen so little of the world. This must be very difficult for you."

My hand curled trustfully in his. I was a small child again, unquestioningly loyal and obedient, willing to follow him to the ends of the earth.

"And so we come at last," he said, giving my hand a quick clasp and releasing it, "to Miss Dinah Slade."

The moonlight shone full on his face. As his dark eyes looked straight into mine he exclaimed with a laugh, "You and Dinah! Such ambition!" And he began to talk about his notorious English mistress.

I did not like what I heard.

He gave me every single detail. He spared neither me nor himself. Looking back in later life, I knew I myself would never have had the courage to talk to an ignorant eighteen-year-old boy about the marital problems which Miss Slade had so usefully resolved. He even talked about his epilepsy, and that was the hardest of all for him; I saw his fists clenching with tension, while his dark eyes seemed to burn in his white set face.

"You don't have to tell me this, sir," I blurted out at last.

"Yes, I do," he said instantly. "I must tell you everything. I must pass it on."

Finally I summoned the nerve to ask, "Are you sure you're not going to marry Miss Slade?"

He never turned a hair. "I shan't marry her," was his quick terse response. "Satisfied? Why don't you ask instead if I plan to acknowledge her son?"

I knew at once he was testing me. I kept my face impassive, but I could feel the blood already welling behind the membrane of my Achilles' heel.

"Maybe you think he's not your son," I said politely.

"He's mine. Try again."

The membrane burst. I looked at the floor and ceiling and out the window in an attempt at nonchalance, but when I looked back at him I saw that he knew. Worse still, he was amused.

"Are you sure he's yours, sir?" I said. "If Miss Slade's so enterprising perhaps she'd hedge her bets once she realized you hadn't fathered a child since before she was born."

He looked at me for a long moment. His eyes were brilliant but devoid of any expression.

My nerve cracked. I blushed. "I'm sorry . . . I didn't mean . . . Forgive me, sir, I want to take that back—"

"Be quiet. There's no need to go groveling on all fours just because you've made a perfectly valid point. Let's settle this matter once and for all. That child is mine. I know it and you'd better accept it. I'm not acknowledging him because I want to protect Sylvia and because I want to protect Alan himself from my money and position, just as your mother once tried to protect you. If you hadn't been so busy being jealous you would have recognized these very obvious reasons right away."

"I'm not jealous, sir."

"Convince me."

"Well, there's no need, sir, is there? I'm your heir and he isn't."

"Precisely!" His stern brutality vanished as if he could no longer sustain it, and standing up he patted my shoulder kindly as if I were once more a protégé who had shown promise. "In my opinion," he said as I too rose to my feet, "a great deal of nonsense is talked about the biological tie. Personally I'm a believer in adoption."

I nodded. I was no longer looking at him and he, I sensed, was no longer looking at me. Slipping his hands casually into his pockets, he moved away from me toward the door.

"You'll change your name to Van Zale, of course," he added as an afterthought.

"Yes, sir."

"Paul Cornelius Van Zale."

"Yes, sir."

He smiled. He was satisfied. "Let's rejoin the others," he said, opening the door. "We can talk again later."

Less than a week later when he was shot to death in his office I stepped forward at once to fill his shoes.

V

Everyone said I couldn't do it. I was surprised. I had already figured out that no one could stop me. The money was mine outright.

When everyone had finished telling me that I should go to Europe, to Yale, to hell—indeed to anyplace except One Willow Street—I moved into Paul's house, rolled up my sleeves and started working harder than any of them.

My friends were enrapt. I had been the quietest of the four and the shyest, yet now I was telling even my parents, "This is what Paul would have wanted," and insisting on going my own way. My confidence, mystical and absolute, ended my role of Midwestern oddity and transformed me overnight into the leader of the pack. Jake and Kevin were struck dumb with awe. Only Sam, practical as always, recovered quickly enough to beg, "Take me with you!"

Someone asked me years later, "Why did you like Sam the best of those three boys?" and the answer was that I didn't. I liked Jake Reischman best. Despite the difference in our religions we came from similar intellectual homes, and I felt I had plenty in common with him. Kevin shared my interest in sports, but he was so boisterous that I found him tiring. Sam I liked because he was so friendly, but we never seemed to have much to talk about and I found it puzzling that he seemed so uneasy with Jake. It was only later that I realized he was secretly intimidated by him. Poor Sam! Jake was such an aristocratic New Yorker, so confident in himself, his family and his place in the world. His family had been in America for over a hundred years, and in the Reischmans' sumptuous Fifth Avenue mansion conversation at dinner was conducted in German, German wines alone were admitted to the cellar and only music by German composers was played on the huge organ in the atrium. For Sam, who had frantically tried to shed his German heritage ever since his immigrant parents had been pelted with rotten eggs on the outbreak of war, Jake's pride in being German was incomprehensible.

"Well, of course it was difficult when the War was on!" said Jake astonished when one evening Paul forced the two of them to discuss what it meant to them to be German-American. "Of course it was hard, trying to do our duty as American citizens when we couldn't help but sympathize with all those German people who had never wanted war in the first place! But that war wasn't our fault. Why should I feel guilty about Prussian militarism? It had nothing to do with me!"

Sam said timidly that perhaps it was different if one was Jewish.

"What's that got to do with it?" said Jake. "I'm just as German as you are!"

"Except that your real name isn't Hans-Dieter," said poor Sam, and he told us about the cruel teasing he had suffered at school before he had rechristened himself with an all-American name.

Jake was horrified by the story. During the War he had shared a tutor with some other boys from rich German-Jewish families and he had had no idea how the less privileged German-Americans had suffered.

"You must come to stay with us!" he exclaimed spontaneously. "We'll make you proud to be German again!" And after that he took great trouble to put Sam at ease until by the end of that first summer we had all forgotten that Sam's background was different from ours.

However, although it was Paul's death which flung me together with Sam, I suspect that even if Paul had lived Sam would still have become my closest friend, good-natured, hard-working, utterly heterosexual Sam with his phonograph, his jazz records and his daring pictures of Clara Bow. In his company I could always relax. In fact my trust in him was absolute, and when I let him link his future with mine I came to realize that no two brothers could have been bound together more tightly by a blood tie than I was bound to Sam Keller by the sheer ordeal of our first two years at Van Zale's.

To say that we relied on each other heavily when we first entered the bank would be an understatement. I could not have traveled so far so fast if it had not been for Sam, and he in his turn was equally indebted to me. We were like a pair of acrobats on the highwire with nothing to save us from the long drop but our wits and the perfect coordination developed by necessity in order to survive. I saved him, he saved me, and during the two years which began with Paul's murder and ended with the annihilation of his assassins I lost count of the times Sam and I came to each other's rescue.

But we survived. We survived our ignorance and inexperience; we survived Paul's enemies; and we even survived his friends. That, on reflection, was probably our greatest triumph of all.

We worked day and night. I hired the best teachers to give us private tuition in banking, economics and law. I cultivated the oldest partner and picked his brains elaborately. We went through every major file Paul had handled and hammered the facts into a coherent summary so that we understood what the clients had wanted, how the bank had responded and what the result had been. We often worked into the early hours of the morning, but at seven o'clock we would always be up to take a swim in the pool before heading downtown to the office.

Sam lived with me at Paul's house. At first it seemed merely a useful solution to his homelessness, but we soon realized it was the only possible arrangement in view of our iron schedule of study. Our total reliance on each other made serious quarreling out of the question, but when we found we were getting on each other's nerves we decided we should take one night a week off to relax and go our separate ways. Ironically, despite this sensible decision, we still ended up together. We were secretly scared of New York and huddled together for comfort like a couple of hillbillies from the boondocks. First of all we didn't even have the courage to date; Jake and Kevin had introduced us to a few girls, but they were too upper-class for Sam and too sophisticated for me. However, Sam had already discovered he wasn't cut out for the celibate life, and eventually we fell into the habit of stopping by at a safe cozy little speakeasy in the East Eighties and pretending we were impoverished college students. It was always fun later to see the girls' faces when we took them home to Fifth Avenue.

It was a long time before I felt truly at ease in New York. Despite our Saturday nights on the town the city remained a backdrop to me, an alien setting in which I was obliged to live and work, and it was not until Steve Sullivan went to Europe in March 1929 that I felt secure enough to discover that New York really did have more to offer than Velletria, Ohio. I was twenty-one by that time, quite old enough to enjoy the pleasures of the wicked city, and more than ready to toss Paul's cautionary advice to the winds. Sam was there with me, in exactly the same position. We cast off the shackles of rigid self-discipline at exactly the same moment, and all through that doomed summer before the Great Crash when Steve was making a fool of himself in Europe, we behaved in a way which would have bleached my mother's hair snow white and prompted Paul to turn groaning in his grave.

VI

We behaved like a pair of juvenile satyrs. I guess it was a delayed reaction to Paul's death. For months we had clung to the comforting familiarity of our former life, but eventually there came a point when we had to realize that our lives had changed beyond recognition, and although we were excited by this transformation we were also frightened. It was disorienting as all the old landmarks fell by the wayside. Although we knew we had to adapt in order to survive, our confusion was so massive that we could not at first perceive the new roles we had to assume. The pressures mounted, the strain increased and when it became essential for our stability that we find a way to defuse these tensions we turned to Paul's favorite method of relaxation.

Paul might have sympathized with our desires but not with our outrageous lack of discretion and common sense. It was only a matter of time before the mills of God began to grind us exceeding small, and the grinding began in September when a girl I had seen three times in July telephoned to say she was pregnant. That same day Sam thought he had contracted some particularly revolting complaint from a recent encounter. As it turned out, both the girl and Sam were mistaken, but the incidents frightened us so much that we decided the time had come to discuss, analyze and reform our private lives.

"It was all Steve's fault," groaned Sam. "If we hadn't been so relieved to see the back of him we wouldn't have gone out and got drunk at Texas Guinan's. No wonder she said 'Hello, suckers!' Since then it's been downhill all the way."

I found a pencil and listed our new rules of conduct. "Number one," I declared, "no sex at the office. Number two: no messing around except in locked bedrooms out of sight and hearing of the servants. Number three: no picking up stray broads in speakeasies. Number four: condoms at all times. Number five: absolute respectability in dress, deportment and demeanor. Number six: church on Sunday."

"I'll leave that last one to you," said Sam, "but the next girl I like

I'm going to date for six months and I'm not going to take out anyone else during that time. And I'm going to write to my parents every week without fail."

"Maybe I'll invite my mother to visit me," I mused. "Then she can see that contrary to all her expectations I'm leading a moral Christian life."

A week later I met Vivienne Coleman. I had successfully deluded myself that I had returned to sanity in my private life, but as subsequent events proved I was merely pausing in midair while I leaped out of the frying pan into the fire.

Chapter Two

I

That summer Sam developed a passion for the old tune *Alexander's Ragtime Band* and played his favorite recording of it night and day. He had no interest in classical music but was addicted to all forms of American music from ragtime to Dixieland and from blues to bluegrass. He himself played no instrument, but when Kevin walked out of Harvard Law School, turned his back on his wealthy family and retired to Greenwich Village to write the great American novel we used to invite him and some of his new musician friends to our house for a jam session which Sam would record. My lasting memories of that summer revolve around the breakneck pace of life at the office, where we were all mesmerized by the dizzy gyrations of the ticker tape, and the breakneck pace of life at home when Kevin roared uptown with his friends, our girls streamed in to kick up their heels and we all got drunk on bathtub gin while dancing our hearts out to Charlestons like *Yes, Sir, That's My Baby*—and to Miff Mole's Molers version of *Alexander's Ragtime Band.*

That was before the mills of God prompted Sam and me to reform in September. It was also before the mills of God caught up with America in October. However, the shadow of those mills had already fallen across the investment bankers' paths, and when in early September the market faltered, staggering beneath the burden of a million dreams, the shadow became too obtrusive to ignore. Although the market recovered quickly, we held a partners' meeting to discuss future policy in the event of another such unpleasant "technical correction." There was a great deal of waffle that everything was bound to be all right, but it was obvious we were secretly uneasy in case things went all wrong. Finally the senior partner Lewis Carson, who looked like an elderly cross between Douglas Fairbanks and John Barrymore, suggested that one of the partners should have a conference with Steve's brother Luke to review our investment trust's portfolio. It was generally agreed that in the event of a decline speculative stocks would be the first to suffer, and we thought it was time to eliminate the riskiest investments.

No one wanted the job of conferring with Luke Sullivan. As Clay Linden remarked acidly, since Steve's departure Luke had become just like Mussolini without any of Mussolini's redeeming qualities.

"I'll talk to him if you like," I offered humbly. "Luke and I get on real well nowadays." That was an absolute lie, but I was always looking for ways to increase my power and I thought a toehold in Van Zale Participations could be useful to me.

The other partners all mouthed the ritual nonsense about my being too young, but once that was over they gave me the job with relief. Accordingly I wandered down to the desk which had been assigned to Luke in the great hall, but when someone told me Luke had gone to see his brother Matt I walked up Willow Street to the office of Van Zale Participations.

The trust had a showy little suite on the third floor. A bleached blonde was manicuring her scarlet nails before the typewriter in the reception room, and beyond the open door of the president's office I could see Matt Sullivan, his feet resting comfortably on his desk, a cigar in one hand and his hip flask in the other. He was talking to someone I could not see but assumed to be Luke. So angered was I by the sleazy atmosphere of the office and so enraged that the House of Van Zale could be intimately connected with such an operation, that I ignored the receptionist and walked unannounced into Matt's office.

Conversation stopped. When the other man spun round startled, I did not recognize him and yet I felt that somewhere a long time ago I had seen him before.

"Good morning," I said politely to Matt. "Forgive me for interrupting you, but since the door was open I assumed you weren't engaged in business. Is your brother here?"

"He's in the john. He'll be right back," said Matt with his usual coarseness, and stood up. He was a big man with an athlete's figure run to seed, bloodshot blue eyes and animal-like curly hair which grew low down on his forehead. "Well!" he exclaimed, his glance shifting between me and the stranger with a relish which I found incomprehensible. "Haven't you two ever met?"

The stranger seemed to find Matt's amusement as baffling as I did. We stared at each other suspiciously. He had a tough scarred fighter's face, with nasty yellowish-brown eyes and thick lips. I was just wondering if I had seen his picture in the newspaper in connection with the St. Valentine's Day Massacre when I remembered the two men who had tried to comfort Jason Da Costa long ago at Vicky's funeral.

"Say, Greg!" said Matt, really enjoying himself by this time. "Don't you remember Mildred Blackett's kid?"

Luke Sullivan chose that moment to walk back into the room. There was a short tense silence. Then:

"Nice to meet you again, sonny," said the son of the man Paul had ruined. "No hard feelings, huh?" and he held out his right hand.

"How are you, Mr. Da Costa?" I said, shaking the hand courteously. "Are you in town long? I understand you live in California nowadays."

The tension in the room slackened. What they expected me to do I have no idea; stamp my foot childishly perhaps, and flounce from the room. When I remained they no doubt assumed it was because I was too young and stupid to react with anything but friendly interest.

"I've quit on California," said Da Costa easily. "My wife and I separated and I thought I'd come back East to make a little money on the market—which is where the Sullivan boys here come in. I'm staying with my cousin Vivienne Coleman—maybe you know her?"

"Only by her reputation as a popular hostess. I didn't know she was your cousin."

"Our mothers were sisters. Say, come over and have a drink with us this evening, why don't you? We'll drink to the end of the family feud," said Da Costa, smiling at me indulgently. He had a tooth missing at the side of his mouth.

"Gee," I said, very young and dewy-eyed, "I'd like that. Thanks a lot, Mr. Da Costa. Well, if you gentlemen will excuse me . . ."

"Did you come here looking for me, Cornelius?" said Luke. He was the only one of the three who had any brains worth mentioning.

"Oh, it'll wait," I said airily, but he remained suspicious.

"I'll walk back with you to Van Zale's," he said flatly, and as soon as we were in the street he launched into an explanation. "I know you're thinking Greg's got no business to be within a hundred miles of Van Zale's, Cornelius, but you can relax. He's told me himself he's figured it's too damn dangerous for him to resurrect the assassination business in any shape or form. He just wants to forget he ever knew O'Reilly and Clayton, and anyway he doesn't need the bank to foot his bills for him now. He did well out of that hotel in California and decided to quit while he was ahead. Between you and me I think he was scared of getting on his boss's nerves once too often—he was running with a rough crowd out there. Anyway, he's just put twenty thousand dollars into Van Zale Participations. Matt and I are the only people he knows well on the Street nowadays and so it's only natural he should gravitate to us. It's all absolutely bona fide."

"Uh-huh. You never had second thoughts about taking his money?"

"Hell, why shouldn't we take it? His money's as good as anyone else's, isn't it?"

The short answer to that was no. Greg Da Costa's money was usually obtained by extortion.

"Oh, my God!" groaned Sam as soon as I confided in him. "What the hell's going on?"

"I don't know, but if Da Costa's involved it has to be a disaster."

We sat facing each other across my desk and put our brains to work. He excelled in analyzing current problems, while I had a talent for long-range planning. We really did work excellently together.

After agreeing we didn't trust the Sullivan twins farther than we could throw them, we had to admit that Luke was smart enough to keep any shady secrets well under wraps. The trust was doing well and we had no excuse for demanding to see the books before the official audit. Assuming that the Sullivan twins were currently impregnable, our only route to the truth lay through Greg Da Costa, and both of us could see right awav that this would be the rockiest route imaginable.

"God, maybe he's blackmailing the twins!" said Sam horrified.

"No, no." I had already rejected that possibility. "Matt Sullivan wasn't acting like a man in the presence of his blackmailer. Of course, that doesn't mean to say Da Costa's not setting them up for the big squeeze." I got out a cigarette and then put it away again. I had to cut down on my smoking. "There's no choice, Sam. Repulsive though it may be, I shall have to cultivate Greg Da Costa."

"Go easy, Neil. I know it's unlikely, but we could be wrong about all this."

"But supposing we're right?" Delicious vistas were opening up in front of me. "After all, Steve did appoint his brothers, and if they get into trouble . . . You're right, Sam. We've got to take this nice and easy. We mustn't go wading into the lake and frightening off all the fish. We've got to cast our lines very carefully on the water and tempt the fish to nibble at the bait. Then when they're stuffed to the gills we'll reel them in, gut them and cook them for dinner."

Sam laughed and so did I. It was certainly an attractive idea, but as it turned out it was quite the wrong decision.

II

Late that afternoon my secretary told me I had a call from a Mrs. Vivienne Coleman.

"Mr. Van Zale?" said a woman's low whispery voice when the call was put through. "We haven't met, but my cousin Greg's just told me he invited you to visit us for a drink tonight. I'm just calling to say you'll be more than welcome, but I feel I should warn you that there'll be several people present. I'm giving a cocktail party. Greg forgot that when he issued the invitation."

I assured her that I loved cocktail parties and hung up gloomily.

I arrived late at the party but not late enough to avoid the horror of being crammed into a room with sixty people in various stages of drunkenness. The pall of cigarette smoke immediately made me cough, and I had just decided I could no longer endure the incessant screech of conversation when a pretty woman with thick longish chestnut hair and a pert snub nose glided through the haze toward me. She wore a sleek black dress with a cluster of diamonds placed strategically at the bottom of her very deep décolletage.

"Mr. Van Zale?" she said as my gaze halted at a spot half an inch above the diamonds. "I'm Vivienne Coleman—how are you? So nice of you to come! Aren't cocktail parties frightful? Now, come on in and—Oh!" she gasped as someone reeled backward and spilled a tomato-colored drink all over my suit. "I *am* sorry! How clumsy people are sometimes." She glared at the offending guest, who was busy slinking out of sight. "Well, it'll be a long time before I invite *him* back to my house! Come upstairs, Mr. Van Zale, and we'll fix the disaster right away."

"Thank you, Mrs. Coleman."

"Do call me Vivienne. . . ."

I tried to guess how old she was, but she could have been any age between twenty-five and forty. Even with high-heeled shoes she was shorter than I was, and as we went upstairs I noticed that her legs were as riveting as her bosom. I had to repress the urge to lift her skirt to check if her thighs were as perfect as her ankles.

"Was that your husband I saw downstairs, Mrs. Coleman?" I inquired carefully.

"I'd be very surprised if it was. He's been dead for four years," she said, leading the way into an opulent bathroom decorated in pale mauve, and she started to sponge my suit. As she stooped to tackle the bottom of my jacket I knew I had to stop her before she reached my pants. The improved view of her bosom was already making the shirt stick to my back.

"Thanks a lot," I said, removing the washcloth from her as she paused to survey her handiwork. "I'll do the rest."

She smiled at me. She had perfect teeth and sparkling blue eyes. "Am I reminding you of your mother?" she said amused.

"Not exactly," I said, praying I wouldn't have an erection. I tried to camouflage myself by dabbing at the stain on my thigh.

"Thank God for that! All right, if there's nothing more I can do I'll go, but give me a wave when you come down again and I'll find some nice people for you to talk to."

I was so grateful to her for leaving me alone before my excitement could become embarrassingly obvious that I felt obliged to linger at the party when I returned downstairs. However, when I rejoined Vivienne she abandoned me after a couple of introductions. I felt quite irrationally disappointed.

When the guests were drifting away and I knew I could leave without appearing rude I thanked her for the party, and after repeating how glad I was that I had been invited I gave her my most innocent smile, the one women usually chose to interpret in the raciest possible way.

"I'm delighted you were able to come, Cornelius!" she responded, warm and friendly but not, so far as I could judge, hot and hopeful. "You've been the despair of every hostess in New York—I'm delighted that I've at last lured you into society!"

I never did manage to speak to Greg Da Costa.

"This is all going to work out nicely," I said glibly to Sam. "I'm going to date Vivienne Coleman and soon I'll have won Greg's confidence. Within a month I bet we'll know just where we stand with the Sullivan twins."

"Neil," said Sam apologetically, "this is so obvious that I hardly like to mention it, but you're sure, aren't you, that Greg isn't sleeping with her?"

"Oh, but he couldn't be!" I was aghast. A second later I realized I was behaving just like the twenty-one-year-old kid that I was, and I made my habitual conscientious effort to be thirty years old. "I don't think that's very likely," I said carefully. "You haven't seen either of these people, Sam, but this Vivienne Coleman's got great class. I mean, she's really exceptional. I'm not suggesting she's a nun, but I'm sure if she wanted a lover she wouldn't choose a guy like Da Costa, who looks like the back end of a stove-in streetcar."

"Uh-huh," said Sam. "Judging from his photographs Jay Da Costa too looked like the shadiest thing this side of twilight, but anyone'll tell you how he strung women along like pearls."

"Jay wasn't a gangster!"

"He didn't have to be. He was rich and privileged, and a great career fell into his lap. But who's to say how he might have turned out if he'd had to fight for survival on the Lower East Side? I know the traditional view is that the Da Costa brothers were genetic freaks, but isn't that pushing the odds a bit far? One genetic freak is possible, I guess, but two? If you want my opinion I think Greg and Stewart were more their father's sons than anyone likes to admit."

"But why don't people like to admit it?" I said, so fascinated by this analysis that I even forgot the revolting image of Da Costa crawling into bed with Vivienne.

"Because people here on the Street don't like to be reminded of how close they often come to Al Capone. Wall Street's stuffed with gangsters, Neil, and you know that as well as I do. They don't call them gangsters here, though. They call them pool operators or bank-affiliate presidents. Sometimes they even call them investment bankers."

I threw a paper clip at him, declared that everyone knew pool operators were respectable nowadays—as respectable as those decent, moral, honest gentlemen who were investment bankers—and then I drew the conversation back to our plans to cultivate Da Costa, expose the Sullivan twins and stab Steve in the back. The upshot was that within the hour three dozen red and white carnations arrived on Vivienne's doorstep and by early evening we were speaking on the phone.

"Cornelius, thank you for the flowers—that was sweet of you. By the way, are you interested in musical comedy? I have tickets for the opening night of *The Street Singer* next Tuesday, and they say it's going to be the biggest musical event of the season. Greg was going to come with me, but now he says he can't make it, so I'm in dire need of an escort. Of course if you loathe Broadway musicals . . ."

"That sounds just wonderful!" I said. "May I take you out to a late supper afterward?"

She said I could, and scampering upstairs I took a cold shower while singing the famous tenor aria from Bizet's *Fair Maid of Perth*. My sister Emily used to say that my musical taste was bizarre—"Either mathematical chamber music or hopelessly florid vocals!"—but my mother always defended me by saying it was better to have some musical taste than none at all.

Sam might have broadened my outlook to the extent that I could now enjoy listening to *Alexander's Ragtime Band*, but at heart I remained a musical snob and I thought the Broadway show was about as entertaining as toothache. However, I paid little attention to it. My glance was constantly wandering sideways to Vivienne's magnificent décolletage which began six inches from my right elbow.

After an intimate supper at Beaux Arts during which she confided to me that she had a passion for French Impressionist paintings, I asked her if she would like to come home and see my Renoirs. I was really very angry when she declined, but I kept my face impassive as I escorted her home.

"I'm so glad your money hasn't ruined you," she said smiling, when the time came for us to part. "Some rich men become so accustomed to getting what they want the instant they want it that they become just like spoiled children."

"Why hang around for a delayed delivery," I said coolly, "when you can get what you want from a door-to-door salesman?"

She laughed. "Why indeed? Good night, Cornelius."

I was livid. I hated women who teased and I resented having my serious proposition treated as no more important than the yowl of a pet poodle. Almost in tears at the thought of all that unexplored décolletage, I retired home to pour out my grievances to Sam, but when there was no sign of him I realized he was spending the night with his new girl. Moodily I flailed away six lengths of the pool to ease my restlessness. Later, sitting in my pajamas on the edge of the bed, I felt lonely. A memory of my warm understanding affectionate sister floated across my mind.

I picked up the phone.

"Hello," I said, as my stepfather answered on the first ring. "Is Emily there, please?"

"We're all in bed, Cornelius. Do you know what time it is?"

"Gee, I'm sorry," I said surprised. "I'll call again tomorrow."

"Just a minute. Your mother wants to talk to you."

I sighed. Telephone conversations with my mother were always peculiarly unrewarding.

"Cornelius? Darling, why are you calling so late? Is anything wrong?"

"No, Mama. I just wanted to talk to Emily, but it's not important."

"Heavens, this must be telepathy! Emily was going to call you tomorrow morning."

This sounded more promising than my mother's usual injunctions to eat well, get enough sleep and avail myself of New York's cultural opportunities. "She was?" I said with reluctant interest.

"Yes. Listen, darling, since we're talking I may as well tell you the *whole* story. Emily's been . . . well, there's only one word for it, I'm afraid. Emily's been . . ."—her voice sank to a whisper—"*jilted*."

"Jilted!"

"You remember that very nice West Point graduate she met last Christmas?"

"Oh, him. Yes, I didn't like him at all."

"That's quite irrelevant, Cornelius," said my mother crossly. "The point is that Emily did like him—*very much*—and we heard yesterday that he's just got engaged to that dreadfully common girl Crystal Smith . . ."

I yawned while my mother droned on about the local gossip. Finally I said, "About Emily, Mama."

"Yes, the poor girl. Of course I suggested it would be better if she got *right away* for a while to recover, and I thought it would be so *nice* for you both if she stayed with you in New York until Thanksgiving—"

"What!"

"Yes, wasn't that a bright idea!" said my mother, pleased. "You can introduce Emily to all sorts of nice young men, no doubt, and she can avail herself of all the numerous cultural opportunities. . . ."

I thought of my beautiful, chaste, intellectual sister and tried to imagine her with Sam and his new girl or with me and Vivienne Coleman. Sam and I had certainly reformed, but we were still far from being monks.

"I'd love to have Emily to stay, of course," I said carefully, "but don't you think it would be more suitable if she went to Sylvia? I hardly think it would be right if she stayed with two bachelors."

"My goodness, Cornelius!" said my mother in horror. "Are you trying to tell me your household is unfit for a young girl?"

I closed my eyes, took a deep breath and said in my sweetest mildest voice, "Of course not, Mama. I simply thought that Sylvia, as an older woman, would be a more suitable chaperone."

"Sylvia," said my mother coldly, "is visiting her cousins in San Francisco. Perhaps *I* should accompany Emily to New York."

The sweat broke out on my forehead. "That won't be necessary, Mama. And I resent your implication that I can't take care of my own sister."

"But, Cornelius, it was you who said—"

"I feel pretty insulted," I said. "Please tell Emily to come as soon as she can. Good night, Mama." And hanging up the phone, I collapsed in a heap on the pillows.

It took me at least ten minutes to recover sufficiently to wonder how I was going to arrange my personal life while I was acting as a chaperon. I sighed, then told myself not to be so selfish. A few weeks of exercising fanatical discretion would be good for me and, besides, I was really very fond indeed of my sister Emily.

III

When she arrived at the end of the week I went to the station to meet her. She wore a dark-blue coat and a little cream-colored hat with matching gloves, shoes and purse. I thought she looked lovelier than ever and not in the least like a jilted heroine.

"It's so good of you to have me, Cornelius," she exclaimed after we had hugged each other and I was escorting her outside to the Cadillac. "I simply felt I had to get away from home for a while—Mama was trying so hard to marry me off that it was becoming embarrassing. Just because I'm nearly twenty-four she thinks I'm on the shelf! Now, Cornelius dear, I want you to promise that you won't alter your way of life in order to accommodate me, because believe me, what I need most at present is a little independence! You lead your life and I'll lead mine. I'll try not to get in your way and be a nuisance."

"Emily!" My admiration for her understanding knew no bounds. I could only ask, "Why on earth are you still single? Any man who married you would be the luckiest man in the world!"

She laughed. "How nice of you to be so prejudiced! Actually there *was* someone once a long time ago whom I would have married, but . . . oh, it was hopeless! He hardly noticed me and anyway he's married to someone else. Don't let's talk about that anymore, Cornelius —it's too depressing! How's Sam?"

"Fine." I was amazed to think of Emily yearning for a married man and wondered who he could possibly have been.

Emily was saying she was looking forward to seeing Sam again. They had met only once, at Paul's funeral, for although I had annually invited him to travel home with me at Thanksgiving and Christmas he had felt obliged to go to his parents in Maine, and we had never yet had the time to snatch any other vacation from work.

"Maybe you'll marry Sam!" I said hopefully to Emily. "I'd like that."

Unfortunately it was soon obvious that I had no talent for matchmaking. Sam, awestruck by Emily's beauty and brains, was so shy in her presence that I was reminded of our early days at Bar Harbor when Jake had intimidated him, and although Emily, like Jake, put him at his ease I could see he was never going to fall in love with her. He liked bubbly, featherheaded girls who chattered incessantly about trivialities, not serious-minded young women whose favorite corner of New York was the Metropolitan Museum of Art.

Emily was delighted to be in New York but was appalled by my house. None of my family had visited my Fifth Avenue home since Paul died; that was my mother's way of registering her disapproval of my decision to follow in Paul's footsteps, and although I was welcomed and cosseted whenever I returned to Velletria I was left in no doubt that my mother would never condone my life in New York by crossing my threshold.

"I'd forgotten what an awful place this is!" exclaimed Emily as we sat up exchanging news on the night of her arrival. "How Uncle Paul, who loved Europe, could have not only built this house but lived in it I just can't imagine, but maybe he was so desperate for a European atmosphere that he was prepared to accept this horrid imitation. And I do think it's a pity when American houses are crammed with nothing but European art treasures—they always end up looking like museums, and anyway I think most European art treasures should be in Europe where they belong. It's such bad manners to denude a continent of its culture, don't you think?"

I sighed. "You're missing the whole point, Emily. This house was part of the façade which Paul presented to the public. People expected him to live in a place like this, so he did. If he had lived in a lesser house people might have thought he was less important."

She looked at me as if I were talking Greek—modern Greek, the kind that classical scholars can't understand.

I tried again. "It's a power symbol," I said. "Paul understood power. He knew that the more splash you make the less likely people are to step on you. If you're a millionaire you've got to live like a millionaire to keep the power building in momentum."

"I guess that's what Mama must have meant," said Emily, "when she used to mutter that Uncle Paul was betraying his class by living like a shoddy-rich arriviste. But Cornelius, I still don't see why this ghastly place has to be a cross between the Metropolitan Museum and some overstaffed grand hotel. Is it really necessary to have so many footmen waiting at table and at least three housemaids gossiping in every corridor?"

I heaved another sigh. Emily was still mentally back in Velletria.

"Emily, when Sam and I first came to live here we were so darn scared of the servants that we hated to come home from work, but we knew we just had to get used to it. If I tried to behave like a simple straightforward guy from an Ohio farm, no one would have any respect for me, can't you see?" With inspiration I saw an appropriate yardstick of comparison. "You wouldn't tell the British royal family to cut down on the trappings of their position, would you?"

"Cornelius!" gasped Emily, at last getting the point, "are you trying to tell me you're in the same position as the King of England?"

"No," I said in despair, seeing she was appalled. "I have more power."

"Cornelius!"

"I've had to survive, Emily!" I burst out in misery, desperate to recover her sympathetic understanding. "You don't know what I've been through at the office, the intrigues, the machinations, the power struggles and the blood baths—" I stopped. Instinct told me I was making matters worse. Finally I managed to say levelly, "There are people who don't want me at Van Zale's and because I'm so young nobody's inclined to take me seriously, but so long as I've got the money and can live here like a king they can't quite manage to ignore me."

She was silent. I got up and began to pace around the room. "So I live here," I said. "I've now reached the stage where I hardly notice the servants. I see the butler and housekeeper regularly to give them instructions and I have an aide who checks their accounts, but otherwise they're just part of the scenery too. I sold Paul's Rolls-Royces because I believe one should support American industry, so now my chauffeurs drive only Cadillacs. I have another aide who deals with the begging letters, the invitations and the general correspondence. I have a valet. I have, as you've no doubt noticed, a bodyguard. I do see that this way of life must seem unnecessarily vulgar to you, but all I want you to understand is that I had no choice but to adopt it. It's part of my inheritance from Paul."

"Well, it all sounds dreadfully exhausting to me," said Emily frankly, "but if you don't mind it I won't feel sorry for you. What happened to that nice bodyguard Uncle Paul had?"

"Peterson?" I said. "I fired him, naturally. He failed to protect Paul."

"Oh, but . . ." She bit her lip and turned away. "You've changed," she said at last.

"Yes," I said coldly, abandoning all attempts to win her approval and trying only to conceal how hurt I was. "For the better. Money gives you the freedom to be yourself. I don't have to sit around in Velletria any more while you and Mama debate whether Plutarch was a more reliable historian than Dio Cassius. I can just turn around and say who the hell cares."

"Cornelius—oh, darling, I *am* sorry!" No one could have been more contrite. Rushing over, she hugged me so hard I started to wheeze. Hastily I put out my cigarette. "I've been so beastly, criticizing you—your home, your way of life. Oh, Cornelius, how *could* I be so mean! I'm so glad to be here and so glad to see you!"

I was happy again. Hugging her in return, I promised to take her out as soon as I arrived home from the office the following day, and during the next week I spent all my spare time escorting her to concerts, art galleries and theaters. I knew I was doing it to prove to us both that I could still be the brother she had grown up with in Ohio, but we both enjoyed ourselves and I didn't grudge her one moment of the time I spent with her. Vivienne Coleman phoned several times, but I had my secretaries handle the calls. I thought it would do her no harm to think I had lost interest, but in fact I had long since recovered from my rage and daydreamed constantly of that tantalizing décolletage.

Meanwhile I was stealthily progressing with my investigation of the Sullivan twins. I had told Luke that the partners wanted a full report on the trust's portfolio, with particular emphasis on the high-risk stocks, and when he promised to work on it I said, "No hurry!" to reassure him that I wasn't breathing down his neck. While I was smoothing Luke's feathers so carefully, Sam made a discreet inquiry about the location of the trust's records and found out that the books were lodged at the office of Van Zale Participations. It could be argued that the logical place for the books was surely in the trust's own office, but the investment trust was little more than an alter ego for the bank and when Steve had managed its affairs everyone had taken for granted that the books would be kept in his office. Since Luke too now had a desk at One Willow Street, it would have been natural for him to retain the books there, and their removal from the bank confirmed our suspicions that something was wrong.

"We're on the trail," I said pleased to Sam. "What shall I do next? Maybe I'll call Vivienne again."

But Greg Da Costa called first. He asked if he could meet me in a midtown speakeasy, and when I insisted that we meet at my house, Sam and I raced home to wire the library for sound.

IV

He was ten minutes late, so I kept him waiting a quarter of an hour. These little power plays may seem petty, but they are quite essential when dealing with difficult dangerous men like Da Costa, and I had already decided to show him I had to be treated with respect.

"Good evening," I said abruptly, and without bothering with any social niceties I added, "How may I help you?"

He was disconcerted but recovered fast. "Well, it's about a business matter—"

"Then we should have set up a meeting at the office. I dislike discussing business in my leisure hours."

"Sure, but I didn't want the Sullivan boys to know I was seeing you. You wouldn't have anything to drink, by any chance, would you?"

"I never drink when I'm discussing business. What is the matter you wish to raise with me, Mr. Da Costa?"

"Maybe I should see one of the other partners," he said, responding to my coldness with a show of hostility. I guessed it would be less than two minutes before he threw all discretion to the winds. "I chose you because you seemed a nice kid and I figured we could get along."

In translation that meant he had decided I was a fool who would swallow any story he chose to feed me.

"Sure we can get along," I said. "You're here and I'm willing to do business with you. Go ahead."

"Well . . . it's about Van Zale Participations. See here, Cornelius—Jesus, does everyone really call you Cornelius?"

"Why don't you try calling me Mr. Van Zale?"

"Sorry, no offense! It's just such a quaint name. Where was I? Oh yeah. Well, see here, Cornelius, I've done a lot of things in my time, bummed around a bit, seen a lot of sights, all that kind of thing, and, hell, it's been fun, I've enjoyed it, I've had a good life. But I'm nearer forty than thirty now and I'd kind of like to settle down. I need a little stability, a steady income, a respectable job, but of course for a man of my age with my kind of, well, varied experience, it's not too easy to land the kind of job I figure I could handle. You understand?"

"No."

"Well, Cornelius, it's like this. Matt's told me all about his job as president of Van Zale Participations and I reckon it would suit me pretty well. It's not too strenuous, because Luke does all the hard work, and yet there's plenty of prestige—I like the idea of being a president, being part of the financial community, you understand? After all, I *am* my father's son. I'd like to feel that at last I had the chance to follow however modestly in his footsteps, and besides you *are* Paul's nephew, you know what I mean? You do owe me something. Now, don't get me wrong, I don't want to resurrect the family feud again, but—"

"How do you suggest I get rid of Matt Sullivan?"

"Well, Cornelius, I could tell you a thing or two about old Matt. Hell, I like Matt, he's an old, old friend of mine from way back, but he runs with a funny kind of crowd and I just don't think he's the kind of guy you want to head that investment trust. Now, I really think you and I can make a deal on this. You and Steve Sullivan aren't exactly pals, are you? Matt tells me you hate each other's guts, and frankly my sympathies are with you—I never liked Steve either. All right, here's the deal. You fire Matt and hire me to replace him, and I'll give you the evidence to light a fire under Steve."

"Forget it," I said. "I don't get rid of anyone until I've seen the evidence. Besides, I would have to consult with my partners."

He slid his tongue around his lips. The going was so much tougher than he had anticipated.

"Maybe I could put some evidence out front," he said at last.

"And maybe you couldn't. I think this is just a stunt to get a soft job."

He slid his tongue around his lips again. "Supposing I give you the combination of the safe down Willow Street where Luke keeps the books?"

"Luke will produce the books if he's asked for them."

"Not these books he won't," said Greg Da Costa. "He keeps two sets, you know what I mean?"

I knew. One set would be for the public and the partners and the other would show what was really going on at Van Zale Participations.

"I shall have to consult with my partners," I said for the benefit of my brand-new Dailygraph recording machine, a vast improvement on the old Vox we had used to record the mayhem of last year. "I cannot connive at any illegality."

"Hell, who said anything about illegality! Isn't the law so loose on Wall Street that it's almost impossible to break it? Let's just call the trouble mismanagement! And why tell your partners? They'll let Steve wriggle off the hook!"

"I still find your information hard to accept. How did you find out about the books?"

"Matt told me when we were out drinking. Once he's liquored up he couldn't keep a secret for a million bucks, and since I had my suspicions of him anyway it wasn't too difficult to winkle the truth out of him. Cornelius, I just know you and I can get together on this."

"I'll think about it," I said. "I'll call you later to arrange a further meeting. Good night, Mr. Da Costa."

I walked out of the room without giving him the chance to detain me.

"You could promise him the job in exchange for the safe combination," Sam suggested after we had listened to the recording of the conversation. "Then you could hire and fire him on the same day."

"He's obviously hoping to maneuver himself into a position where I can't fire him. He knows of the illegality and once he knows I know too he'll have me on the short end of a rope. As soon as we've covered up this mess—and for the bank's sake we'll have to cover it up—he'll turn around, accuse me of conspiring to conceal a crime and threaten to go to the police unless I let him remain president of Van Zale Participations. I know how that gangster's mind works, Sam. This is his new meal ticket. Damn him! What the hell are we going to do?"

"Be nice to him," said Sam at once. "We don't want him getting nasty and trying to peddle the facts somewhere else."

"Yes, he's got to think I might play ball with him. I'll call Vivienne," I added, trying not to sound too eager. "He'll take it as an encouraging sign if I start dating his cousin again."

But once more the telephone rang before I could call Vivienne. This time it was Emily. She had decided to spend the day visiting old acquaintances, and one of my chauffeurs had driven her out to Long Island to see Steve's wife. Emily did not know Caroline well, but it was typical that once she heard Caroline was convalescing after a cancer operation she had offered to call on her.

"Emily?" I said, glancing at my watch. "Where are you?"

She told me she was still at the Sullivans' house. The housekeeper had just walked out, the children's nurse had given notice, Caroline had had to return to the hospital for a second operation and Emily had volunteered to play the Good Samaritan.

"That's bad news about Caroline," I said, remembering our

mother reading us the story of the Good Samaritan on countless far-off Sundays. "I'm sorry. Maybe someone should cable Steve," I added, although Steve Sullivan was the last person I wanted back in New York at that time.

"Caroline said he didn't come before and he won't come now. She's very bitter about Steve—oh, it's all so sad, Cornelius! Apparently Steve's been having an absolutely blatant affair with that dreadful girl Dinah Slade. How he could! Everyone knows she almost wrecked Uncle Paul's marriage."

"Yes." I felt acutely embarrassed to be discussing marital infidelity with Emily.

"You knew about Steve and Miss Slade?" she said shocked.

"Hal Beecher told me when he got back to New York. Well, I guess I'd better go now, Emily," I said, and hung up as fast as I could.

A minute later I was still clasping the telephone, but Vivienne—at long last—was on the other end of the wire.

"Hello," I said, and although the butler had already taken my name I found myself repeating feverishly, "This is Cornelius Van Zale. How are you?"

"Ah, yes," she said, "the banker. I remember. I'm very well, thank you. How sweet of you to inquire after all this time."

I felt uncomfortable but managed to laugh. "Sorry I haven't been able to talk to you lately, but—"

"Why, that's all right! Making money must be such a time-consuming occupation!"

I seriously wondered whether to hang up, but I was very, very tired of being celibate.

"Well, my schedule's certainly crowded," I said, "but I do have a spare five minutes in three hours' time. Maybe I can call you back then in the hope of finding you in a more sociable mood. Goodbye."

"Wait! Cornelius, I'm sorry—I didn't mean you to take offense! Come and have a drink with me this evening."

"I'd rather take you out to dinner."

"Well, I—No, I guess I can cancel that. Yes, dinner would be lovely."

I began to feel I was at last making progress.

We went to Pierre's. The black marble columns in the vestibule had never seemed more erotic. Vivienne wore a midnight-blue gown with a neckline which ended within a gasp of the navel, while I wore my best nonchalant expression and tried to stop shifting around in my chair. All food seemed unbearably irrelevant.

Finally I had the opportunity to say, "I have some very fine French brandy at home which I've been saving for a rainy day. Would you—"

She said she would. I could hardly restrain myself from rushing headlong into the Cadillac. Every wasted minute seemed a tragedy.

We were waiting in the drawing room for the butler to bring the brandy when she murmured, "I guess all your girls tell you what beautiful gray eyes you have. Maybe I should admire your mouth instead." And she trailed a finger lightly across my lips.

"Forget my mouth," I said incoherently. "There are other more important parts of my anatomy."

Two minutes later I was closing the door of my bedroom, tugging off our clothes and pulling her into bed with me.

There is something fundamentally absurd about the sexual act. When I learned the facts of life during my ill-starred semester at school I simply could not believe that human beings were capable of such extraordinary posturing, and even after I had a clearer idea of the pleasure involved it still seemed obscene that two people should be driven to such desperate intimacies. My numerous short-lived affairs had blunted this judgment, but until that night I had continued to feel that my sexual encounters were divorced from the normality of my daily life. However, Vivienne changed my outlook by putting me at ease. Previously I had always feared I was laying myself open to ridicule by exhibiting such bizarre behavior, but Vivienne taught me that sex was neither ridiculous nor bizarre but as natural and logical as a mathematical progression.

I performed feats which I would have thought impossible for longer than I would have thought endurable. In between orgasms she would tell me how masculine I was until by dawn I wanted to relay her praise by bellowing it from the rooftops. At seven o'clock, an hour after I had sunk into an exhausted sleep, my valet glided into my room to wake me and promptly glided out again, but the closing door woke me and presently I prised open my eyelids, crawled out of bed and flung back the drapes. Beyond the wall the traffic was already droning on Fifth Avenue, and below me in the garden the birds were chasing each other among the trees. The sky was a pale blue, the color of peace and tranquillity, and far away downtown the great ticker of the New York Stock Exchange was silent and still.

It was Wednesday, the twenty-third of October, 1929. The vast prosperity roller-coaster of the nineteen-twenties, having crawled a month ago to the top of its highest glittering pinnacle, was pausing for one last halcyon moment before teetering over the brink into the abyss far below.

"My God," I said to Vivienne. "I'd like to stay in bed with you all day."

"Then why don't you, darling?"

"No, I've got to go to work. The market's been in bad shape this week and today's the day the bankers have to flex their muscles to restore confidence."

"How wonderful it must be to be God!" said Vivienne, pulling me on top of her as I fell back into bed. "Or do you feel more like Moses parting the Red Sea?"

Naturally neither of us dreamed that the investment bankers were soon to feel more like King Canute. I escorted Vivienne home in my favorite Cadillac, and went downtown with Sam.

We all went downtown, all the bankers of Wall Street, the famous names and the nobodies, but no bands played, no flags waved, no one cheered as they might have cheered an army marching into battle. No one even knew that a war had begun; everyone still thought in terms of unruly skirmishes, and besides there was no visible enemy, only the unregulated market soaring and plunging like quicksilver in a fragile glass, the shadowy laws of mass psychology which no one had ever bothered to understand, and the fickle crackle of paper riches which had no root in reality.

It was all so peaceful, the autumn sun falling in the dark canyons of Wall Street and shining on the spire of Trinity Church, and long afterward I thought that this eerie peace was one of the most terrifying characteristics of the Crash. People can grasp the actuality of a hurricane, an earthquake or a great fire; they can grasp the realities of war; but what they find hard to grasp is the magnitude of a disaster which arrives on a pale pretty peaceful day in a silence broken only by the sinister tip-tapping of the ticker tape.

"The market's still a little sickly, I see," said Lewis, pausing by the ticker in the great hall at noon. "I thought we were going to see a recovery today after this week's heavy selling."

"Let's just hope the market doesn't take a turn for the worse," said Martin Cookson, whom Steve had long since nicknamed Cassandra.

I was just reassuring a client that afternoon that we were seeing only another "technical correction" of the market when Sam burst into the room. As soon as I'd hung up he said, "All hell's breaking loose on the floor of the Exchange."

Rushing down to the great hall, we joined the crowd in front of the ticker and saw the prices start to plunge before the gong sounded to end trading for the day.

"It'll rally tomorrow, of course," said Lewis as we held an emergency partners' meeting. Later I told Sam I hoped Lewis arranged to have the words engraved on his tombstone.

Someone agreed with Lewis by pointing out that the day's trading had been no heavier than the previous Monday's, although Martin argued that on Monday two and a half million shares hadn't changed hands in the last hour of trading. There was much useless discussion about what we should do, but in the end we could only come to the obvious conclusion that we should present a calm soothing front to the world by uttering as many expressions of confidence as possible.

"Excuse me," I said in the humble voice I kept for partners' meetings, "but suppose no one believes us?"

Everyone looked at me as if I had uttered a blasphemy.

"Not believe us?"

"My dear boy!"

"Of course, you're very young . . ."

"I think you forget, Cornelius," said Lewis grandly, "that we're the gods of Wall Street! If we say something is so, then of course it will be so."

I wasn't the only one with doubts. With uncharacteristic emotion Martin exclaimed, "But can't you fellows see what's happening? We're already locked into a classic chain reaction downwards—the decline in prices leading to calls for more collateral from margin customers, the inability of the customers to meet the calls leading to the forced sales of their holdings, these sales leading to a further decline, the further decline leading to still more calls—"

"Bullshit!" said Clay Linden angrily. "All we're seeing now is the shaking out of the lunatic fringe which attempts to speculate on margin. Monday was a bad day, but yesterday was fine. Today was terrible, I agree, but Lewis is right—tomorrow will be better again. We've had our crash. Now for God's sake let's pull ourselves together and muster the guts to go on."

I wondered whom to believe. I was inclined to back Martin, who had a first-class brain, but brilliant people are notorious for losing touch with reality. With increasing alarm I wondered what was going to happen next.

The dawn came. The sky was gunmetal gray. Wall Street exuded a miasma of uneasiness, and everyone headed automatically for the nearest ticker.

As soon as trading opened, large blocks of shares in Kennecott and General Motors hit the floor, and almost immediately the ticker began to lag behind. By eleven the traders on the floor of the Exchange were berserk; the ticker had fallen so far behind that it no longer reflected what was happening, and only the bond ticker, hammering directly from the floor of the Exchange, told us that everyone was struggling to unload. The telephone and the telegraph screamed hysteria from one end of America to the other. People said it was the end, the day of judgment. It was as if the earth had stopped spinning on its axis.

Everything was falling. United States Steel crashed through 200, sinking like a cement block. Radio, General Electric, Westinghouse

—no meteors ever plunged to earth faster than the great stocks plummeted to disaster on the twenty-fourth of October, 1929.

The telephone lines were clogged by this time. Communications broke down, and in the resulting confusion the panic swept to new heights. Then the people began to arrive, and all roads led to Wall Street as the silent crowds streamed compulsively downtown.

When Sam and I went out we found that the people were standing neatly in rows on the steps of the Sub-Treasury Building, not talking, not moving, just waiting as if for a savior they knew would never come. They were like row after row of big black birds, subhuman, as frightening in their disorientation as the victims of some mass-executed lobotomy, and the atmosphere of fear hung over the Street as thickly as fumes over some suppurating factory.

Struggling back to the bank, we found that all work had been dislocated, and in the crowd riveted to the ticker someone said messages were flashing secretly back and forth between us and the leader of the investment banks, the great House of Morgan at Twenty-three Wall. Lamont of Morgan's was to confer with the great commercial bankers in an attempt to form a multimillion-dollar pool to shore up the market, and at half-past one Richard Whitney, the Morgan broker, strode into the Stock Exchange not to sell but to buy.

The market, still terminally ill, rallied bravely as the House of Morgan held its hand and stroked its fevered brow.

"Morgan's best bedside manner!" snorted Clay.

"Only Lamont could have described the greatest disaster in the history of Wall Street as a little distress selling!" scoffed Lewis, criticizing Lamont for employing the same tactics he himself had advocated twenty-four hours earlier.

The truth was we were all jealous of Morgan's. Naturally we were proud that the investment bankers had come to the rescue, but it had been a dreadful day, we were all exhausted and we wanted some of the Morgan limelight to cheer us up. Everyone spent much time telling everyone else that if Paul had lived he would have led the bankers' consortium and then the House of Van Zale would have been the financial savior of mankind. Everyone also expressed relief that the Crash had finally arrived. It had been terrible—disastrous, catastrophic—but it was over. It was as if we had been toiling through some arduous pregnancy, survived a hideous childbirth and produced a monster. All we now had to do was shove it out of sight in an institution and pick up the threads of normal life again.

"Whichever way you look at the situation," said Clay, "the news has to improve. We've hit rock bottom. There's nowhere else to go but up."

I noticed that Martin kept very quiet, but I supposed he was merely wrestling with the desire to say "I told you so" as often as possible to anyone who would listen.

Everyone spent the next two days insisting that everything was fine. There was a lot of selling, but prices were steady and President Hoover was booming soothing platitudes from the White House. It was not until the close of trading on Saturday that Sam and I heard that the bankers' consortium had disposed of Whitney's emergency purchases in order to recoup as much of their pool as possible.

At the close of trading on Saturday prices once more began to fall.

"But that's impossible!" I said stupefied to Sam. "If we've hit rock bottom how can we sink any lower?"

"Maybe things will pick up on Monday."

We looked at each other. That was when we both knew that the Crash wasn't over and that the worst was still to come.

The next day was Sunday. God was probably much entertained when everyone went to church. Sam and I squeezed into the back of Trinity and spent an hour wedged against a pillar, but it was so crowded we never did manage to get down on our knees to pray. When the service was over we went to the bank.

Wall Street was alive. People were working all day to catch up on the enormous volume of paperwork the Crash had produced, and we too worked till dusk. When we went home we didn't know what to do. I wanted to see Vivienne, but my head was full of figures and for once sex seemed unimportant. Sam tried to drink but couldn't finish his highball, and when he went to the phonograph I saw him look at his record of *Alexander's Ragtime Band* for a long moment before putting it away in the closet.

On Monday the brokers, bleary-eyed after working throughout the weekend to post their records and go over their customers' accounts, assembled for the next pulverizing round of trading.

The market, very sick now, began to fade, and even the House of Morgan had no more palliatives to offer. Prices plunged point after point in a steady hemorrhage of liquidation, and instead of the decorum which should attend the bedside of a dying patient there was a seizure of frenzied activity. Clerks and messengers scurried mindlessly along the Street, bankers held futile conferences, the brokers spun dizzily through their distorted routines like a colony of mad ants. Once more the ticker dropped far behind; once more Wall Street began to drown in a sea of paperwork as trading intensified and the breakneck volume of business became unendurable. No one went home from Wall Street that night. Lights burned till dawn, and those who had already been working day and night for a week moved through the great corridors of finance like automatons.

Sam and I drank coffee all night in my office and dozed for half an hour shortly after the cleaning women left.

The sun rose. It was Tuesday, the twenty-ninth of October, 1929, and just as a dying patient often embraces death with relief so we mutely waited for the final convulsions of the market which had been the envy of the world.

Ten o'clock came. The big gong boomed in the great hall of the Stock Exchange, and the apocalypse began.

Huge blocks of stock cascaded onto the market like blood streaming from a fresh-killed corpse. The ticker reeled, stuttered, gasped for breath. Selling orders gushed onto the floor, inundating the drowning brokers. In half an hour the volume of trading had passed three million and by noon it had passed eight million, with no end in sight. The carnage mesmerized us all, and in the crowd around our ticker there was no conversation, only an occasional hysterical laugh or muffled sob.

I remember going out with Sam briefly at one o'clock and finding Wall Street once more jammed from end to end. I remember the faces, the gray stark haunted faces reflecting the horrors of unimaginable disasters. I remember the silence, broken only by the shuffle of feet. I remember the stooped shoulders, the bowed heads, the battered slouch of defeated men.

When the closing gong brought the insane day to an end the volume of trading closed at a record of sixteen and a half million shares and the ruin was complete. The corpse of the market choked Wall Street, and in the foreign markets around the world the international crisis began.

"They should have closed the Exchange."

"Morgan's told them not to."

"If Paul had been alive . . ."

The hideously unimportant bickering went on and on. No one could face up to what had happened. We were in shock. Lives had been ruined, a whole world had been washed away, and we were still arguing about whether Morgan's should have forced the Stock Exchange to suspend trading.

"The public's going to make the bankers pay for this someday," said Martin. "We did nothing but tell them what fine clothes we had and now they've seen we were stark naked. They'll never forgive us and they'll never forget."

I was back in my office some unknown time later when the phone rang.

"Van Zale," I said mechanically, still thinking of Martin's prognosis of doom for investment bankers.

"Cornelius, this is Luke Sullivan."

I had a split-second premonition of utter disaster. Martin must have passed me some of his psychic powers.

"Luke," I said. "Yes." In the monumental avalanche of the Crash I had quite forgotten Van Zale Participations.

"Listen, Cornelius, I've been borrowing up to the hilt in the hope that the market would improve and put everything right, but . . . hell, I'll be honest with you. I can't get an extension on my loans, we're in a bad, bad jam and I've got to have money right away. Can you authorize a couple of million?"

The stench of danger was so strong that I nearly vomited. "No."

"Damn you, of course you can! Listen to me! This is an emergency and the bank's just got to bail us out!"

But I knew all about that trap. I knew how easy it was to be drawn into a conspiracy to conceal a crime. I had to put the greatest possible distance between myself and the Sullivan twins, and I had to do it fast.

"Ask Steve," I said.

"Jesus Christ, how can Steve sanction that kind of money from Europe? Listen to me, you stupid little kid—"

"You're fired," I said and hung up. I allowed myself one full minute to stop shaking from head to toe and then I rounded up my partners for yet another emergency meeting.

V

I was in a very awkward position. I knew I should have confided in my partners as soon as Greg Da Costa had provided evidence of the Sullivans' "mismanagement," yet in my eagerness to fashion a new weapon against Steve it had never occurred to me not to play a lone hand. Now I was hoist with my own petard. By concealing the information with such disastrous results I had provided Steve with the excuse to roar back from Europe and call me a harebrained young fool who had no business to be a Van Zale partner.

My only hope was to attack him so hard that in the resulting confusion my errors would slip by unnoticed.

"But I have to let the partners know *I* know there's all hell going on at Van Zale Participations," I said in panic to Sam. "Otherwise they won't realize how important it is not to bail Luke out with their eyes closed. What in God's name am I going to do?"

"Say Da Costa only called you just before Luke called. You had his information, but you'd had no time to act on it."

"But supposing they check with Da Costa?"

"Don't be dumb, Neil, Da Costa won't talk. He's going to deny he ever met the twins now that the Crash has busted their racket wide open, and anyway can you seriously imagine any of the partners calling Da Costa to check up on you?"

Confidence seeped back into me. I had tripped on the highwire, but my partner was catching me as I fell and jerking me back to my feet.

"God, I'm scared," I said to Sam, still shaking with fright, and then somehow I dredged up the courage to sally forth into battle.

The partners gathered in Lewis's office, the double room which had once belonged to Paul, and sat in a tense half circle around the fireplace. I said my piece. All the partners looked as if they were about to have a stroke. I never saw a brandy bottle appear so fast at a partners' meeting.

"I had a sort of instinctive feeling that there was something shady going on," I said in a hushed voice, "but of course I had no idea what was involved until Da Costa called with ideas for his new meal ticket. I mean, I never suspected, never dreamed . . . Well, they were Steve's brothers, weren't they? I guess my trust in Steve was absolute."

Everyone at once said what a fool Steve was about his brothers and how the appointments had always been eyed askance. It was remarkable how wise everyone was in retrospect. It took them less than five minutes to agree that Steve had to be hauled back from Europe to clean up the mess, and only a little more than ten to deliver a unanimous verdict that the disaster was entirely Steve's fault.

I said in a crushed voice, "I feel so guilty . . . not finding out earlier when you asked me to deal with Luke."

Someone patted me on the shoulder kindly and said I mustn't reproach myself, because if two sets of books were being kept there was no way I could have unmasked such infamy.

Luke was hauled before us for sentencing. He did try to embark on explanations, but we cut him off. Nobody wanted to hear even a tall story, let alone the truth. Martin found out the names of the banks which had given Luke the loans, Clay jotted down the horrible amounts involved and Lewis fired Luke on the spot.

Luke had hysterics. Everyone was dreadfully embarrassed, and as soon as he had been ejected from the room the brandy bottle had to be passed around again. Half an hour later, after a profusely sweating Lewis had consolidated the loans and won a twenty-eight-day extension of the time allotted for repayment, somebody remembered that Matt had to be fired too, and Lewis recovered himself sufficiently to make the necessary call.

A week later Steve arrived home from Europe.

I was at the dock to meet him. The other partners all wanted to give him the cold shoulder, and so it was natural that the most junior, least significant partner should be dispatched to the pier to represent the firm. It had been an appalling week in New York since the collapse of the market, and Emily had introduced a further grim note to the grim scene which awaited Steve when she telephoned me to say that Caroline Sullivan had died that morning in the hospital after an emergency operation.

"Poor Steve!" was all Emily could say. "Arriving home to find his wife dead and his brothers disgraced—oh, poor, *poor* Steve!"

I suddenly realized that each time she said "Steve" she made it sound as if it were the most precious word in the English language. The hackles rose on the back of my neck. "Emily!" I was so horrified I could say nothing else.

"What's the matter, Cornelius?" she said innocently.

"That married man you said you were in love with once, the one that took no notice of you—you don't mean . . . you can't mean . . . Oh God, you must be crazy!"

"I don't want to talk about it," said Emily at once.

"But Emily, he screws everything in sight! I mean—oh Christ, I'm so upset I'm saying all the wrong things. Listen, he's—he's very immoral, Emily. He's not at all the sort of man Mama would want you to marry."

"My dear, I've long since discovered that I don't care a jot for the sort of man Mama would want me to marry!"

"But he's eighteen years older than you are!" I said wildly. "He drinks too much! He—good God, Emily, he's on the brink of marrying Dinah Slade! He's already got her pregnant!"

There was a silence.

"Men don't marry girls like that," said Emily at last.

"Men like Steve Sullivan," I said, "are capable of absolutely anything."

"I think I'd better say goodbye now," said Emily. "I can hear one of the children calling. Excuse me, Cornelius."

I was tearing my hair.

"Have you gone crazy?" said Sam incredulously as I gasped out the news to him. "Forget it, Neil! You know how much I admire Emily, but she's not my type and I'm pretty sure she's not Steve's either. He'll mop up the twins' mess and disappear into Europe as fast as he damn well can. Why the big panic? You ought to be going down on your knees to thank God for Dinah Slade!"

That suggestion struck me as a trifle excessive, but I did manage to tell myself I had been worrying unnecessarily. I spent a long time wondering how quickly we would be able to shovel Steve back to Europe, and then with great reluctance I dragged myself down to the docks to meet his ship.

VI

Steven Sullivan, the most powerful of all Paul's people, well over six feet tall, with a build Goliath might have envied and a strong blunt-featured face which reduced all women to simpering submission—was it any wonder that my fear of him was mixed with my jealousy, and my hatred with a grudging admiration? He had a fast fluent charm which ensnared even the most cautious clients and a quick shrewd grasp of detail which won their confidence. Because of his florid private life the temptation to underestimate him was a weakness to which his opponents occasionally succumbed, but few people who made such a mistake survived long enough to make it again. Yet in some ways he was a simple man. He had a curious childlike devotion to his two frightful brothers, an indulgent affection for his ill-behaved offspring, and a cheerleader's mindless loyalty to Paul. I was loyal to Paul too but at least, thanks to our one intimate conversation, I was loyal to a flesh-and-blood hero, not some imaginary high-school football celebrity. Steve also had the trick of regarding himself as the only protégé Paul had ever had, and that was why, when Paul made me his heir, the decision was profoundly unpalatable to him.

To do Steve justice I have to concede that he wasn't avaricious—nor was he a fool. I doubt if he expected to inherit Paul's private fortune, but he certainly expected to inherit Paul's role at the office and as soon as Paul died Steve started behaving as if he were the senior partner at Van Zale's.

To do him justice again I have to admit that his assumption of his own superiority had a strong root in reality. The surviving partners were a mixed bunch, and although they were all, in their different ways, able men, none of them had either the brilliance or the sheer power of personality to muscle his way unchallenged into the senior partner's chair. Steve had the advantage of being Paul's favorite, but he was only thirty-nine when Paul died and his personality was too brash to conform to the public image of a leading investment banker. To do him justice a third time—God, how hard it is for me to do Steve Sullivan justice!—he was quite intelligent enough to recognize his limitations, accept them and temporarily agree to the appointment of Charley Blair as senior partner, but I knew, just as everyone else knew, that he was biding his time. When Charley died Steve's position was simplified. Charley had been so popular that he might have proved difficult to oust, but Walter was too old to be a threat, neither Lewis nor Martin had Steve's muscle, and Clay Linden, though aggressive, was not that much older than Steve and as a newcomer to the firm could hardly match Steve's twenty-year record at Van Zale's. As it happened, Sam and I outflanked Steve before he had the chance to outflank Lewis and Martin, elbow Clay aside and put Walter out to grass, but it was obvious to me as Paul's heir that the day would inevitably come when Steve and I would be fighting each other for that senior partner's chair.

I was immensely deferential to him when I first started at Van Zale's. I had to be, since I knew he would break me in half if he thought I was too ambitious, but I bitterly resented the offhand contemptuous way he treated me, and eventually I realized that if I were ever to progress an inch at Van Zale's I would have to show him I was not as weak as he thought I was. Having reached that decision, I saw all too clearly that there could be no half measures. Either I crushed him or he would pulverize me. I had a slight advantage, since I knew exactly how dangerous he was while he had no idea I had any strength at all, but a dwarf needs more than a slight advantage to win a hand-to-hand tussle with a giant. However, I had Sam, and with our combined strength we managed after a bloody, nerve-racking struggle to maneuver ourselves into a less vulnerable position.

I was on my way.

Yet I had lost my initial advantage over Steve. He no longer had any illusions about my ambition, and I knew that as fast as I scrabbled for weapons to use against him he would be planning the most foolproof way to stab me in the back. We were locked together now in an unyielding fight for supremacy, and the very thought of him interrupting his European life to return no matter how briefly to New York was enough to keep me awake night after night. I went down to the docks that morning with the dread and fear knotted solidly together in the pit of my stomach, yet when the confrontation finally came the unexpected happened and my fear evaporated. I looked at him, he looked at me, and in a flash all my fighting instincts had reasserted themselves as the adrenalin went shooting through my veins.

VII

He looked wrecked. His blue eyes were bloodshot and his face was so haggard that for a moment I thought he already knew that his wife was dead. But he was sober. The great difference between Steve and his brothers was that Steve always knew when to stop hitting the bottle.

"Hello," he said when he had no choice but to acknowledge my presence. "How are you?"

"Fine."

We shook hands limply. I had bribed my way to a spot inside the customs area, and I saw him glance beyond the barrier for some sign of his family. "Isn't Caroline here?"

"No, I'm afraid not. She—"

"My brothers?"

"Your brothers," I said, "are lying low in a cottage on the New Jersey shore, but we can discuss them later. Steve, before we go beyond the barrier and get involved with the press, there's something you should know about Caroline. I'm afraid it's bad news."

He looked blank. "She's ill again?"

"She died this morning, Steve. I'm sorry."

I saw him flinch. "Oh, God." His shoulders slumped. He bent his head and put one hand to the back of his neck as if the source of his pain were located there. "But I didn't think . . . Surely she can't be . . . I thought she was getting better." He was dazed. "She *was* getting better!" he said fiercely.

"Well, I guess you never quite know with cancer." Watching him, I saw guilt, grief, misery and shame chase one another across his heavy features until his face was impassive again.

"I'd have come home earlier," he mumbled at last, "if I'd thought she was dying."

I remained politely silent. His secretary announced that the baggage had been cleared and was waiting in the hired limousine outside, but Steve made no response and it was I who gave the man his instructions. "You and the valet ride in the limousine," I said. "Mr. Sullivan will travel with me."

We went outside. The press howled around us, and my chief aide had to bawl three times at the top of his voice: "Neither Mr. Sullivan nor Mr. Van Zale has any comment to make about the market at this time!" When my bodyguard was obliged to bare his teeth at a couple of reporters who seemed intent on making me loathe the press, I felt I had no choice but to exclaim in a scandalized voice, "Gentlemen, please! Mr. Sullivan has just lost his wife! Have you no decent Christian sympathy for a bereaved man?" And muttering to my aide to disclose the full details of Caroline's death, I pushed Steve ahead of me into the Cadillac and dived in after him. My bodyguard leaped into the front, the chauffeur touched the accelerator, and the press were left seething at the curb.

Mopping the sweat from my forehead, I noted that the furor had made little impression on Steve. His next words revealed he was still thinking of his family. "My kids," he said. "I've got to go to my kids. Where are they? Who's looking after them?"

"My sister. She's been staying at your home."

"Your *sister*? Emily?"

I explained how Emily had volunteered for the part of the Good Samaritan.

"That's very kind of her." He still sounded dazed. "Very kind."

"Now, about your brothers—"

"Give me a few minutes, would you?"

I gave him five. He found a cigarette, lit it and pulled out his silver hip flask. After he had taken several gulps of liquor and smoked his cigarette to the butt he squared his shoulders and looked me straight in the eyes. "All right. How bad is it?"

I checked the glass partition to make sure it was securely closed but still took the precaution of lowering my voice. "That's for you to decide. Luke wanted two million to set himself straight, but the loans amounted to about a million and a half—Lewis consolidated them and got a twenty-eight-day extension last week. That means you now have twenty-one days to clear up the mess. When you have a plan for fixing it, let us know. Let me stress on behalf of all the partners that we have no knowledge of any criminal activity, only of gross mismanagement."

"You realize, of course, that once one partner has guilty knowledge it can be imputed to all the others?"

"Just fix it, Steve. That's all we ask. Just fix it."

"Sure," he said wearily. "I'll work something out. What I can't understand is why Caroline didn't realize the boys were in such deep trouble. I told her to keep an eye on them for me and she was smart enough to have realized what they were up to."

"She was in it with them, Steve."

"What!" I had shaken him out of his exhaustion. He was staring at me with shocked disbelief. "That can't be true—I don't believe it!"

"Matt told me. He said Caroline wanted to pay you back for your . . . activities in London and Norfolk. It seems she was very angry that you'd developed quite such an obtrusive friendship with Miss Slade."

"Don't mention that woman's name to me!" he yelled, and attacked the liquor in his hip flask as if it were root beer.

My mouth dropped open. The car had crossed the bridge into Queens and was purring smoothly through the ugly Long Island suburbs. It was raining. I had just managed to clamp my mouth shut again when he said morosely, "That's all finished. We're through."

"But I thought . . ." I was incoherent. Surely this was the last thing Dinah Slade could have wanted. "I thought you were going to marry her," I stammered. "I'd heard—Hal Beecher heard recently from his London friends—"

"Yes, she's pregnant," he said, almost in tears as he emptied his flask. "She's having twins."

"Twins!" Somehow that was very offensive. An illegitimate child is merely unfortunate, but illegitimate twins are positively vulgar.

"Poor little bastards, and I'll never see them, never!" he muttered, wallowing in sentimentality. Then suddenly his mood changed as fury elbowed his maudlin streak aside. "Paul had a lucky escape from that woman," he said bitterly. "When I think of all the lies she told me, the way she deceived me about her true feelings . . ."

It occurred to me he was talking like a man whose pride had suffered a peculiarly painful injury. I decided that Dinah Slade must have made some bad mistake, and the thought cheered me. Maybe she wasn't as clever as I'd always feared she was.

"You mean she had some ulterior motive in seeking an affair with you?" I said guilelessly, sure that Miss Slade had been chasing a slice of Van Zale's for her son since he had been conceived. "But what could she have possibly wanted?"

He looked at me with his hurt bloodshot eyes. "The bank," he said.

I saw he was so upset that he was unable to express himself properly. "You mean she wanted the bank for her little boy," I said patiently, "and she figured the best way to get it was to be married to a partner."

"Forget the kid. Forget the marriage. She wants the bank. Period."

I seriously wondered if he were mentally unhinged. "But that's impossible!" I said with an awkward little laugh.

He gave me a scornful look. "Nothing's impossible to Dinah Slade."

I suddenly realized not only that he was serious but that he was sane. I felt as if I were in an elevator which had dropped ten floors in two seconds. "But women don't become investment bankers," I stammered. "I mean, it just doesn't happen. It can't happen. The clients . . ."

"Oh, sure," he said sarcastically, "sure. Cosmetics is for women and queens and banking's for men, we all know that. But I took that woman to Paris and she had my potential clients eating out of her hand and she's so damned smart and she's so damned charming and she makes money as easily as other women darn socks. If she ever got a toehold in Milk Street she'd have all Lombard Street in her change purse in less time than it takes to change the guard at Buckingham Palace."

I was appalled. "You mean she's just like a man!"

He gave me a pitying look. A second later his eyes shone with a dozen erotic memories before clouding with pain. "Some man!" he muttered fiercely, blinking back his tears.

It was a truly horrifying sight to see a man like Steve Sullivan reduced to pulp by a woman. Groping for words, I could only blurt out, "But how could you and Paul have found her so attractive?"

"Because she's a *woman!*" he shouted. "Because she's the sexiest woman in the whole damn world!" He had to stop to control himself before he was able to add with contempt, "You poor little kid, you'll never understand."

I really couldn't let that pass. "I understand I like my women to be women," I whipped back at him, "and not second-rate men."

He blinked. I knew he had always thought I was incapable of an erection. At last he said, "Do you have someone special in mind?"

"Vivienne Coleman. You know her?"

"Jay's niece by marriage? The brunette with the thick wavy hair and the Ziegfeld-Follies legs and the greatest tits in town?"

"Uh-huh."

There was a pause. Then: "Yeah," he said. "I know her." When he looked at me again I knew I had traveled up at least six notches in his estimation. He took another pull at his hip flask before he realized it was empty. "Well, let me tell you," he said incisively, twisting the cap back, "you're a smart boy. You just stick to that straightforward kind of woman and never get mixed up with a complicated masterpiece like Dinah Slade. And let me tell you something else. The next woman I get involved with is going to be the absolute opposite of Dinah. She's going to be pure, beautiful, quiet, sensitive—and with no ambition other than to be a perfect wife and mother at all times."

We had reached his home. The car was surging up the driveway, and as we both gazed absent-mindedly at the house the front door opened and my sister Emily walked out onto the porch to meet us.

Chapter Three

I

In fairness to myself I must stress that I did at first make great efforts to prevent the inevitable. Within minutes of our arrival I had cornered Emily and informed her firmly that I wanted to take her back to Manhattan at once.

"Cornelius, you can't be serious!" She looked astonished but, since she was no fool, embarrassed as well. "I couldn't leave the children—they've come to depend on me and I must at least wait till a new nurse is hired. Also there's still no housekeeper and the servants require supervision."

"Emily," I said, "I'm not leaving you unchaperoned beneath the same roof as Steve Sullivan."

"Oh, don't be so absurd, Cornelius! This is 1929, not 1860! Besides, I can't help feeling your attitude is insulting to me. Do you really have such a low opinion of my morals? And do you really think I'm as downright idiotic as some pusillanimous Victorian heroine? I'm more than capable of locking my bedroom door at night, I promise you!" she added, giving me a radiant smile.

I gave up. I knew it would be useless to protest further, but I spent the entire journey home wondering how I could possibly explain the situation to my mother. In the end I could only hope that since no explanation was possible my mother would never find out.

However, Steve spent few nights at home at first. He was too busy working late as he excavated the sorry history of Van Zale Participations, and instead of traveling home each night to Long Island he was obliged to catch what sleep he could in the city. His brothers were dragged up from the New Jersey shore; I could imagine him seizing them by the scruffs of their necks, shaking them till their teeth rattled and bawling obscenities at them until they broke down and wept. When he had extracted every detail of their debacle he bought them one-way tickets to Australia and personally escorted them aboard the ship which was to take them through the Panama Canal and west across the Pacific. Knowing how sentimental Steve was about his brothers, we were all impressed by this tough treatment, and Lewis even remarked that there might be some hope for the twins now that Steve had stopped spoon-feeding them and forced them to stand on their own feet. But our hearts sank at the thought that the mess was so bad at the trust that Steve felt he had no alternative but to sever the fraternal apron strings.

I was still wondering how Steve planned to sweep the mess under the rug when I received a call from Lewis asking me to attend a meeting with Steve in his office.

I knew what that meant. When I arrived promptly at two o'clock on that November afternoon Sam was a pace behind me.

"Once more onto the highwire, partner!" he murmured in my ear as I wiped the sweat from the palms of my hands and rapped smartly on the door.

Lewis and Steve were very displeased to see Sam and tried to get rid of him.

"This is purely a partners' consultation, Cornelius," said Lewis stuffily.

I doubted it. The meeting had all the marks of a power struggle from which the other partners had been carefully excluded, and I had no intention of riding out alone to do battle with Steven Sullivan.

"I'm sorry," I said, "but if this meeting concerns Van Zale Participations I want Sam to take notes so that I can review the situation thoroughly afterward."

They both knew that meant I wanted Sam to be a witness.

Lewis cleared his throat. "I assure you, my dear Cornelius—"

"Forget it, Lewis," interrupted Steve, who for all his faults had the virtue of never being pompous. "All right, boys, sit down. Cigarette, either of you?"

We declined cigarettes. We declined the offer of a drink. We sat down on the couch, I with my hands lying limply on my thighs, Sam with his pen poised above the pad of paper on his knees.

Lewis shifted uneasily in his chair and started to make a long boring elaborate speech about the honor of the firm and the illustrious name Van Zale. Sam wrote neatly on his pad, but after a while he stopped writing in English and amused himself by translating Lewis into German. Finally he scrawled, "What a lot of crap Lewis talks!" and began to write down the lyrics of *Old Man River*.

Suddenly Steve interrupted. Sam's pen skidded across the paper and scribbled busily back and forth.

"We plan on discussing Van Zale Participations at the partners' meeting tomorrow," Steve was saying abruptly, "but we wanted to talk it over with you now, Cornelius, because you're very much involved in the plan I've worked out over the last few days. Let me begin by summarizing the details so that we can all understand exactly what was going on."

Sam wrote "DETAILS" and underlined it.

"As you know, the money received from the sale of the new issue in Van Zale Participations was collected by Luke and reinvested in the market in the corporations which formed the trust's portfolio. There was necessarily a lag in time between the receipt of the money and its investment, and Luke fell into the habit of lengthening that gap until at one time there was a sum of six hundred thousand dollars held on deposit at the bank and waiting to be invested. There was nothing wrong with this; in fact, it could be argued that Luke was conscientiously taking his time about deciding where he could best put the money. Unfortunately he arrived at the wrong answer which was: into his own pocket."

"*Luke embezzles 600 G,*" wrote Sam. "*Nobody the wiser.*"

"Of course he didn't do it all at once. He started in a small way, borrowing the money, playing the market, doubling the money and putting back what he owed. Then he became more confident, and when he thought he had a foolproof racket he became overconfident. When the Crash caught him with his pants down he had all six hundred grand out in the field."

"*Luke wiped out,*" commented Sam's pen. "*Owes trust 600 G.*"

"He then panicked and started borrowing to try to win back what he'd lost, but that all went on the Monday after Black Thursday. He could only get money on twenty-four-hour loan, so he raised a new lot of loans to pay off the earlier ones and gamble again on the market—and of course the next day was Tragic Tuesday . . ."

"*Luke at the end of 2nd 24-hour loans with no loot in sight,*" wrote Sam.

". . . and that was when he finally faced reality and turned to the partners to help him out. Lewis, as you know, got the consolidated loan extended to twenty-eight days, and here we all are. Now, this is the position: the million-plus loan which is outstanding represents money borrowed on the strength of the Van Zale name in an unsuccessful attempt to recoup the six hundred grand. I propose that I borrow that amount from the bank, use it to meet Luke's debts and pay it back with interest over a period of ten years. There's nothing shady about that. Luke borrowed the money in the usual straightforward fashion and I'm paying his debts for him. But the other money, the stolen trust money, is in a different league. It has to be accounted for, and if it's not represented by stock in the Van Zale Participations portfolio then it has to turn up again on deposit at the bank. The only foolproof way to conceal the embezzlement is to wind up the trust by buying out all the shareholders so that in theory they get their money back. In practice they won't—all the investment trusts went down with a thump in the Crash. Well, that's tough on the investors, but they'll be so grateful their shares aren't entirely worthless that I think they'll be ready to cash in their chips, and once the trust is wound up and the books are closed we can breathe freely again."

There was a pause. Sam wrote: *"Bank goes into market to buy up all the shares?"* and sat looking doubtfully at it.

"I think all the partners will agree," said Steve impassively, "that the bank shouldn't be directly involved in this salvage attempt. The fewer links between the bank and the trust the better at this stage of the game. What we really want is for one of the partners, acting as a private individual, to finance the winding up of the trust."

There was another long pause while Sam wrote: *"Enter P.C.V.Z. with checkbook on shining white horse."*

"How much money would you say was needed?" I asked ingenuously.

"Now that the shares are worth very little I reckon we could wrap it up for around three million dollars."

"And of course," said Lewis, smiling benignly at me, "there's really only one partner who has that kind of money to spare."

We went over the whole story again and tried to figure out other solutions, but always we were haunted by the specter of Luke's embezzlement.

"What you're really asking me to do," I said, standing up and moving to the window, "is to sustain a loss which should be shared equally by all the other partners—or preferably unequally by Steve."

"Sonny, I've got my hands full paying back Luke's debts!"

I whirled around on him. "My name is Cornelius Van Zale and in future you'll call me by my name."

"My dear boy—" spluttered Lewis.

"You too!" I snapped at him, and as Sam's glance met mine the signal passed between us, the signal of two acrobats pirouetting to their grand finale on the highwire. As Sam started to speak I spun away from them again and stared moodily out the window.

"I think Cornelius has a right to be upset," he said in a quiet reasonable voice. It seemed odd to hear him refer to me as Cornelius when he always called me Neil. "I know you're making yourself responsible for part of the money, Steve, but those debts of Luke's are legal. It's Cornelius who's providing the money to cover up the embezzlement. No matter how foolproof your scheme is, he'll be taking a certain amount of risk. I think Cornelius has the right to be *very* upset."

I stood there looking upset. Neither Lewis nor Steve spoke. Presently Sam said, "I think there should be some give-and-take here, I really do. It's just not fair on poor Cornelius otherwise."

Poor Cornelius hunched his shoulders bitterly. The silence continued.

"Of course, it's not the actual money he minds," said Sam. "It's the principle involved. I'm sure you both understand—after all, we're all gentlemen here. We wouldn't want Cornelius to make such a sacrifice without getting any compensation, would we? It just wouldn't be right."

Lewis cleared his throat. "I'm sure Cornelius realizes that for the good of the firm we all have to make little sacrifices occasionally."

"Little sacrifices?" Sam said sorrowfully. "Three million dollars?"

We waited. Finally Lewis mumbled, "A nicer office, perhaps . . . a larger share of the profits—"

I spun round a second time. "*This* office," I said. "Paul's office. And I want as much money as you and Steve."

Lewis went a deep red, glanced wildly from Sam to me and back again, and finally turned in panic to Steve.

Steve was pale but calm. "The other partners would never stand for it," he said.

"So what?" I said insolently. "We three are the ones who count. If Clay and Martin don't like it they can move elsewhere, and if Walter doesn't like it he can retire. Tom doesn't count, because he's only been here since Charley died—he'll do what you tell him, Lewis, and so will Hal. Hal's been away too long to have any clout here at One Willow Street. That gives us a majority to dissolve the partnership and re-form it exactly as the three of us wish. The two of you can be joint senior partners"—I thought it was cunning to emphasize this attractive tidbit to Steve—"and officially I won't try to join you; I know I'm too young for the title at present. But don't forget that when the new partnership agreement's drawn up I want the same powers as you two and the same slice of the profits."

"'Joint senior partner' would be nice, Steve," said Sam winningly, picking up my cue, and he added to soothe Lewis, "Cornelius doesn't want any overt sweeping changes, just a reasonable compromise which is acceptable to everyone, and under this new arrangement all three of you benefit. Lewis has more stability as senior partner than he had before, Steve gains a title he didn't have and Cornelius has a fair share of Van Zale's at last. I think it's a wonderful idea."

"For God's sake shut up, Sam," said Steve wearily. "Lewis and I are grown men, not kids of six."

"I'm not giving up this office," said Lewis, cross as any six-year-old.

This was the concession I had been prepared to make to seal the deal. I gave Sam a barely perceptible nod, but just as Sam was opening his mouth to say, "There, there!" Steve said in his most exhausted voice: "Relax, Lewis, the office is peanuts and Cornelius knows it. You can stay here."

Lewis looked relieved.

"But I'm going to share it with you," said Steve, suddenly as strong as a two-ton pickup truck. "We'll share it, just as Jay and Paul shared it when they were joint senior partners."

Now it was my turn to panic. I looked at Sam and saw he was looking equally panic-stricken at me. I turned to Steve and saw there was a gleam in his eye. The highwire began to wobble beneath my unsteady feet.

"Pardon me, Steve," I said, stiff-lipped, "but I always understood that you'd be returning to the London office as soon as this crisis was over. After all, we mustn't forget our plans for expansion in Europe . . ." My voice trailed away.

Steve gave me a lazy indulgent smile. The lion had seen the choicest of preys and was closing in for dinner.

"We'll hire a man with first-class European experience to handle the London office," he said. "No problem. But I can see I've no choice but to stay in New York. After all, these are bad, bad times. How could I, a senior partner—incidentally, thanks for the title—run off to Europe and leave the rest of you to cope with the aftermath of the Crash? I mustn't shirk my responsibilities!" Rising to his feet, he padded over to Lewis and patted him fondly on the shoulder. " 'Now is the time for all good men!' " he quoted triumphantly. "We'll manage, won't we, Lewis?"

Lewis suddenly realized what was happening and looked relieved. He patted Steve back playfully. "We'll manage!" he said, as they both turned with a smirk to present their united front to me.

Steve had lost a battle but won the war. I moved closer to Sam in a mute appeal for help.

"Well, gentlemen," said Sam in a businesslike voice, "may I congratulate you on your agreement? Perhaps I should just outline the salient points. . . ." He read aloud from his notes. Finally he concluded, "I suggest we leave it there for today and work out the exact details tomorrow morning. I know Cornelius has an important meeting at four o'clock."

I had. With him. We got to my office and collapsed. "Oh, God!" I groaned in despair. "Why did I have to suggest he become joint senior partner?"

"He wouldn't have settled for less. You did well, Neil. You got the share of power you wanted, and your bargaining base wasn't really too strong. I know it suits them for you to wind up the trust, but in a pinch they could have the bank do it. And anyway we should have figured out that Steve would be through with Europe after his row with Dinah Slade. Bearing that in mind, the outcome of the meeting wasn't too surprising."

"But it was disastrous! What's the good of having the same powers as those two when they're sitting here like Siamese twins in New York and outvoting me on every maneuver? I can cope with that fool Lewis, but how am I going to live with Steve? It'll be all hell on earth here at Willow and Wall!"

Sam said there was bound to be some solution and told me not to worry, but I proceeded to worry myself into a frenzy. At eight o'clock I was in such a state that I called Vivienne and demanded to see her immediately. I had been sleeping with her every night since the collapse of the market, and during the aftermath of the Crash the one ray of sunshine in the bleak landscape had been my superb sex life.

"But, darling!" objected Vivienne. "I've got fifteen people to dinner and the footmen have just brought in the roast duck! Let me come over to Fifth Avenue as soon as everyone's gone."

"But I've got to see you! I'm desperate! I—I—I—" I flailed around for the winning phrase. "I love you!" I said wildly, and dashed out of the house.

Vivienne came out of the dining room to meet me as I was shown into the hall. "Darling, I'm sure you don't want to bother with these people. Wait upstairs."

"Come with me!"

"In the middle of dessert?"

"All right. We're finished." I tried to walk out, but she grabbed my arm.

"My God! Cornelius—darling—please! All right, come along—yes, I'll come with you. I can't have you rushing out into the night in such a terrible state."

I made love with a violent brevity and afterward crawled between the sheets, curled myself into a fetal position and pulled the quilt over my head. When Vivienne returned from the bathroom she wisely made no effort to disturb me but said she would return as soon as the guests had left.

When I was alone I tried in despair to analyze my behavior. I knew Steve was responsible. Every time we clashed I felt as if he had punched me in the genitals so that afterward I was driven to prove to myself that my genitals were still intact. The thought of Steve made me feel ill. Shuddering, I took a shower, pulled on my pants and sat on the edge of the bed while I smoked a cigarette.

I wondered if I could escape to the London office, but I was too young and I had no European experience. I might be ambitious but I was not foolhardy and I never sought advancement until I was sure I could handle the work. Besides, I had no desire to go to Europe. I had just spent three and a half laborious years growing accustomed to New York, and the thought of beginning again not only in a different city but in a different country was appalling to me. Also I felt no kinship with Europe, and the emotional ties which linked so many of my countrymen to the continent of their forefathers were ones which I myself had never experienced. I had no known relations there. I was truly an American, born in the heart of America, bred exclusively in American traditions and loyal only to my American heritage. Naturally there were aspects of European culture which I admired, and naturally I was interested in European history insofar as it affected the history of the United States; I was no ignoramus from a hick town. However, it remained a mystery to me why people admired European civilization so much when Europe had never been able to achieve in a millennium the united democratic federation which America had won within two centuries, and in my opinion Europe's perpetual discord compared poorly with American harmony since the Civil War. Certainly I thought it was monstrous that when the European nations had succeeded in fighting themselves to a standstill in the bloodiest war of all time they had had the nerve to ask *us* to help them out. I did see that economically America had had no choice but to put their tiresome house in order, but it made me angry to think of all the American soldiers buried in foreign graves as the result of European depravity.

I had just made up my mind that I would prefer to stay in New York with Steve than go into exile in Europe when Vivienne returned.

"My poor precious! Are you feeling better? I've managed to get rid of those frightful people," she said, sinking onto the bed beside me, "so now I'm all yours."

An hour later as I was smoking another cigarette I was still trying to work out how Steve and I could pretend to be friends without either of us losing face. Since there was at present no way I could get rid of him, it was useless to keep clashing with him, and so until the time came when I was strong enough to reach for the senior partner's chair we would have to be allies, living in peace. How I could achieve such a major miracle was certainly a challenge to my imagination, but . . .

I suddenly sat bolt upright in bed.

"Cornelius?"

"It's all right. I've just remembered something I forgot to do at work." I sank back onto the pillows. I felt sick. No, I couldn't do it. One had to draw the line somewhere. My own sister . . .

"Poor darling, you work so hard. I'm sure it's not right for a young man to be under such constant strain. . . ."

After all, Emily did love him and I had no real right to stand in her way. I could spoil her chances by drumming up such a storm of opposition from my mother that Steve would shy away, but maybe that wouldn't be in Emily's best interests. Steve wanted a woman like Emily; he would have to marry her, since Emily would hardly settle for less; and he might well come to love her very much. Fidelity was out of the question, of course, but if he were to care for Emily and make her happy perhaps the marriage would be the best for all concerned.

"Darling, are you awake?"

"Uh-huh." I sat up and switched on the light. "Guess I'd better be going," I announced, feeling quite my old self again. "There are a couple of things I want to discuss with Sam before I go to bed tonight."

"Now just a minute!" She jerked me back onto the pillows. "Not so fast! Have you any idea how badly you're behaving? You invade my house, haul me out of the dining room, rape me almost before we get to the bedroom, brood here for two hours, rape me again—yes, you were completely selfish, Cornelius!—brood some more and then without even so much as an 'excuse me' you declare 'I'm off!' and head for the door! I'm sorry, darling, but it's just not good enough. It's not good enough at all."

"I'm sorry—really sorry. I just didn't think—"

"Well, you should have! You're not in your teens anymore. If you were I'd make allowances for you, since you'd be too young to know better, but—"

I stopped her talking by kissing her, but as soon as I paused for breath she continued, "—but now you should be capable of more mature behavior. And talking of mature behavior, I recommend that you don't tell a woman you love her unless you mean it. It's a shallow trick and can only make a woman feel angry."

"But I do love you!" I said, aggrieved. I felt so grateful to her for responding promptly to my cry for help that I was more than willing to be generous.

She looked stern for three more seconds before she relented and kissed me. "I don't believe a word of it!" she said with a smile. "But I'd like to." She ran her index finger lightly over my ribs and across my stomach to my thighs. It felt delicious. As my body moved I pulled her down on top of me and smothered her with kisses.

"My God!" she said later. "I can't think why more women of thirty-six don't take a young lover!"

"Particularly a rich one," I said, watching her. The light was still on.

"Good heavens, Cornelius, you don't really think I'm after your money, do you? Let's be honest, darling—what I like about you has nothing to do with dollars and cents!"

I fidgeted with the sheet. "But you would never have bothered with me, would you," I said, "if I hadn't been Paul's heir."

"Darling, are you really that insecure?"

"Of course not. I just want to know what you really think of me, that's all. You do like me, don't you?"

"Very much! Oh, Cornelius, don't be so silly!"

"Do you . . . do you . . ." I got stuck and squeezed the hem of the sheet hard with both hands.

"Love you? I don't know," she said simply, and for a second I saw beyond the mask of her sophistication to a genuine confusion. This unexpected honesty was immensely attractive to me. I felt it was a gesture of trust which I at once wanted to reciprocate.

"I really do love you," I said shyly, and for the first time I meant it.

She was touched. I saw her eyes soften and as her hand slipped into mine I realized with shock that this small gesture was the first true communication between us.

Feeling absurdly happy, I spent the rest of the night with her and woke the next morning with my hand still clasped in hers.

Vivienne never got up till ten. Leaving her having breakfast in bed, I pattered downstairs and was just about to slip discreetly out the front door when a key turned in the lock and Greg Da Costa slipped discreetly in.

We had not met since the Crash, and although I knew he was still using Vivienne's house the two of them seemed to lead such separate lives that I had managed to avoid him completely. Our sudden confrontation took us both aback.

"'Lo, Cornelius," he said warily. "Haven't seen you in a while. Bad times, huh?"

"Yes, terrible. How are you?"

"Oh fine, just fine. Say . . . er, no hard feelings, Cornelius?"

"What about?" I said, my head crammed with thoughts of Vivienne. "Jay and Paul?"

"Hell, no! Van Zale Participations."

"Oh, that." I smiled to demonstrate how charitably disposed I was toward him. Vivienne's cousin! Suddenly Da Costa ceased to be a sinister menace and became just another fellow down on his luck. "No hard feelings, Greg," I agreed sympathetically. "Did the Crash hit you hard?"

"My head's still spinning. Say, Cornelius, we can treat that conversation as if it never happened, can't we? I've decided I don't want to get involved with Van Zale Participations after all—I never really knew what the Sullivan boys were up to anyway, everything I told you was just speculation, you know what I mean? Jesus, I wish I'd stayed in California!"

"Hm . . . well, maybe there's some way I can help you," I mused, still floating on a golden chariot across the Elysian Fields.

"Why would you want to do that?" blurted out Da Costa with pardonable astonishment.

"Because I'm going to marry your cousin Vivienne!" I announced with pride, and, leaving him transfixed in the hall, I scampered joyfully upstairs to propose.

II

"Cornelius!" said Emily in a hushed voice. "What in God's name are you going to say to Mama?"

"I shall say I've met a beautiful, charming, well-bred woman who would make me the best possible wife!" I said boldly, quailing at the prospect.

"But she's so much older than you! Are you going to have a long engagement?"

"What for?"

"Well . . . Cornelius, Mama will want to know why not. You must think of a better answer than 'What for.' Oh, Cornelius dearest, are you sure you know what you're doing?"

I was sitting in my office two hours after Vivienne had accepted my proposal. Having expected her to postpone her answer until she had made up her mind whether she loved me or not, I had been stunned by her swift acceptance, but the explanation was simple: apparently despite my repeated insistence that I loved her she hadn't dared to believe me until I had paid her the compliment of asking her to be my wife, but once the compliment had been paid all her indecision had been swept aside.

She told me she loved me, we made a date to choose a ring and then I soared home in a haze of excitement.

The excitement wilted at the office when I realized my mother had to be told of my decision before my chief aide informed the press, and in the hope that a dress rehearsal might prove helpful I called Emily at Steve's Long Island home.

"How did Emily take it?" asked Sam, entering my office as I hung up the phone.

"She thinks I'm crazy." I tried not to sound glum. "Do you think I'm crazy, Sam?"

Sam scratched his head as if I had voiced a question which had long been bothering him. "No, as a matter of fact I've decided that this is just about the smartest move you could make. You'll neutralize Da Costa once and for all—he won't dare upset Vivienne by making trouble for you—and you'll get a wife who's smart and efficient in addition to all the other assets. In fact, there's only one thing that's still bothering me. How did the Crash affect her?"

"Well, she lost a lot, of course, but she's still got a big income from her husband's holdings in South American real estate. She's told me she's not even cutting back her servants."

"Swell. So she's not after your money. Let me see. Are there any pitfalls we've missed? Oh yes, Da Costa. Did we ever establish who he was sleeping with?"

"Some high-class call girl on Park Avenue. God knows how he can afford her. Forget it, Sam! I'm the one who's sleeping with Vivienne! She hardly gets the time to sleep with anyone else."

Sam was just saying he had to look after me while I was in love and temporarily not responsible for my actions when the phone rang.

"Yes?" I said as Sam drifted out of the room.

"Mr. Van Zale, your stepfather Dr. Blackett is calling from Veltria, Ohio."

"Oh, God! All right, put him on." I ran my hand through my hair and wondered if my mother was having hysterics after receiving word of my engagement. I was just asking myself in fury how Emily could have played such a dirty trick on me when Wade said in a quiet subdued voice, "Cornelius?"

"Yes."

"Cornelius, I . . ." He stopped, cleared his throat and tried again. "I'm calling about your mother."

"Yes?"

"She . . ."

Silence.

I suddenly found I was sitting on the edge of my chair and breathing with difficulty. "What's the matter?"

"She had a stroke. Early this morning. She was rushed to hospital . . . but . . ."

I could not speak.

". . . died half an hour ago. . . . So sorry, Cornelius." The wretched man was crying. I wanted to hang up.

When I could speak I said clearly, "I'll catch the first available train. My secretary will inform you of the time of arrival. Goodbye."

After a while I realized I was still sitting on the edge of my chair and still having difficulty with my breathing. Memories of my asthmatic childhood flooded back to me, and I had to make an effort not to panic. I undid my tie, but by the time I had unbuttoned the neck of my shirt my breath was coming in gulping gasps. Praying that no one would enter the room while I was in such a humiliating condition, I tried to breathe as I had been taught years ago in the hospital, and after three sweating agonizing minutes I began to improve. I felt shaken when I had recovered. I thought I had put all asthmatic seizures behind me, and the knowledge that I was still vulnerable was unpleasant.

I thought of Paul. At least I had escaped epilepsy. I was two generations away from that disastrous family taint—three if one traced my ancestry back to my great-grandfather who, although healthy himself, had transmitted the disease to Paul. I felt convinced there wasn't an epileptic gene in my body, yet I couldn't help thinking how strange it was that I should suffer from asthma in much the same circumstances as Paul had suffered from epilepsy.

I sat at my desk for a long time and remembered his saying to me, "I see myself in you." The memory calmed me, but when eventually I had no choice but to think of my mother my breathing rapidly deteriorated again. Having no medication, I decided I must break my rule about abstaining from liquor at the office, and Sam not only brought me a bottle of scotch from Lewis' liquor cabinet but sat with me while I drank myself into a calm numb state. My breathing improved, but my mind became fuzzy. I was in bad shape.

"You'd better see a doctor before you go," said Sam concerned.

I told him about the wheezing, the struggling, the terror of suffocation. I told him about lying awake all night and fighting for breath. I told him about countless airless seconds and blacking out.

Sam gently removed the scotch from me, asked my secretary to find out about trains to Ohio and called my doctor himself to make an immediate appointment. He even volunteered to break the news to Emily, but I knew I had to speak to her myself.

We agreed to catch the evening train. Emily was so upset by the news that she fortunately never noticed the cold voice in which I conducted the conversation, but Vivienne heard my distress at once and offered to come with me to Ohio. I thanked her but said she should stay in New York. Vivienne belonged to the present and the future, and Emily was the only person who could travel back with me into the past I had left behind.

Nerving myself for the ordeal, I clutched my medication in one hand and Emily's arm in the other and dragged myself aboard the train to Cincinnati.

III

"Oh look, Cornelius!" exclaimed Emily. "Aunt Dora's samplers! Do you remember them hanging on the wall in the front parlor of the farm?"

We were in the attic of my old home in Velletria. Around us were the possessions which my mother had accumulated during the twenty-five-year span of her two marriages, and we were engaged in sorting out the clothes for the local charities, the trash for the junkman and the family memorabilia for ourselves.

"Do you remember?" said Emily, arraying the five framed texts against a dusty brass bed. "When I learned to read I used to recite them to you—poor little boy! But you loved them and learned them by heart. That's odd—surely there were six and not five? Which one's missing?"

"The mills of God," I said. "I keep it in my office, but it hasn't been very popular since the Crash." With a sigh I turned back to the trunk full of old photographs, and the next half hour passed very pleasantly as we were reminded of prewar Thanksgivings, forgotten toys and my mother's exotic selection of Easter bonnets. A glow of nostalgia cocooned us from the pain of loss.

Suddenly Emily said, "Look! Papa!"

We stared curiously at the man who had begotten us. He was standing stiffly, ramrod straight, in his black Sunday suit before the front door of the farmhouse. His fair hair was parted severely and plastered to his scalp, while his mouth, which neither of us had inherited, turned down fractionally at the corners. His light eyes were cool and watchful.

"My God!" I said startled. "What a tough customer he looks!"

"But this picture doesn't do him justice!" said Emily, who remembered him much better than I did. All I could remember was his large Western hat, which he had worn indoors and outdoors to make him look taller. "He was really rather good-looking," she added, after I had remarked how odd he looked without a hat. "And he had the sweetest smile."

We flicked through the remaining photos in the album, but in every other picture the ubiquitous hat shaded his face.

"I do wonder if Mama was happy with him," said Emily idly as she closed the album. "I always wanted to ask her but never quite had the nerve."

"But why shouldn't she have been happy with him?" I asked astonished.

"Well, it must have been dreary on the farm for a cultured, well-educated woman, and Papa couldn't exactly hold intellectual conversations with her. Don't you remember the country accent he had? It wasn't really Midwestern at all. More like Kentucky. And he used to say 'ain't' and all that sort of thing."

I digested this in silence. "Well, I'm no snob," I said, "and I have nothing against Papa, of course, but I used to think I was a genetic freak until I got to know Paul. Paul's the one I really resemble."

"Oh, I do hope not!" said Emily. "I was fond of Uncle Paul, but he was so dreadfully immoral! Cornelius, I hope when you marry you won't keep mistresses all over the place."

"Certainly not!" I exclaimed. "After all, one gets married to avoid all that kind of thing." I tried and failed to imagine myself looking twice at any woman except Vivienne. Paul's philosophy of marrying for convenience and committing adultery for satisfaction was one which had no appeal to me; it struck me as being Victorian in its hypocrisy, tiresome in its ambivalence and destructive in its bearing on the solidity of family life. I did realize that since Vicky had always lived with his mother Paul had been free to behave as he pleased, but if one had children in one's care one really had to live in a decent Christian fashion or else the children turned out to be monsters. I thought of Steve Sullivan, bucketing from bed to bed, walking out on his wife and abandoning his pregnant mistress, and shuddered. God only knew how *his* children would turn out.

"I've sown my wild oats," I said to Emily, "and now I intend to settle down and be a good husband and father." I pushed the photograph albums aside and began to pace about the attic. "I've got my entire life mapped out," I said. "For the next few years I won't have much time for anything except the bank, but when I'm—" I remembered just in time that I wanted her to marry Steve, so instead of saying, "But when I'm sole senior partner," I said, "When I'm more secure I'll be a philanthropist. I'll build an art museum to help struggling artists and I'll buy a magazine to help struggling writers. I'll promote plays. I'm going to be one of the biggest patrons of the arts in New York. Then I'll feel I've contributed to the culture of America even though I'm not artistic myself. I'd like that."

"Oh, Mama would have been so proud of you, Cornelius!"

We became sentimental again. Emily started to cry, and I shed a private tear. A death in the family is a very affecting experience.

As soon as I returned to New York I made an appointment to see a specialist about my asthma, but before I could reach his office I fell ill with bronchitis. By the time I was better my wedding day, January the fifteenth, was shimmering tantalizingly on the horizon, and when the doctor suggested postponing the wedding to allow me more time to convalesce I was horrified. I was tired of being ill; I was desperate to return to the office; and I could hardly wait to sleep with Vivienne with the blessing of God, my surviving family and the full roster of New York society.

I got my way about the convalescence, but while I was still recuperating all three of the specialists who had been attending me lined up at my bedside and told me I could never again smoke another cigarette.

I did try to argue, but this trinity of medical opinion was too much for me.

I gave up cigarettes.

I had never known that such deprivation could exist. I bought chewing gum and bags of cornchips to alleviate the craving, but post-coital relaxation was never the same. Lighting a cigarette in the dark is romantic; crunching a mouthful of cornchips borders on perversion. During our honeymoon in Florida, where Lewis Carson had loaned us his Palm Beach château, I even refused to go into town in case I should see someone smoking a cigarette, although, as Vivienne reminded me dryly, the inhabitants of Palm Beach were hardly the sort of people who trailed up and down Worth Avenue with cigarettes dangling from their lips.

We had a quiet wedding at the Little Church Around the Corner, with only sixty guests and all the photographers locked out in the street. Sam was best man, and since Vivienne's father was dead and she had no brothers Greg gave the bride away. However, both her sisters came to the wedding as well as some Philadelphia cousins, so for the first time I had the chance to meet her family. Emily arrived with Steve and his two sons, and everyone remarked afterward that the Sullivans were unrecognizable. Both boys were clean, well-behaved and smartly dressed, and Steve was sober as a Mormon. When I saw that Emily looked almost as radiant as Vivienne I decided the time had come to give her a helping hand, and at the reception afterward I closed in on Steve after my second glass of champagne.

"Don't you think you should do something about my sister?" I said politely.

He almost dropped his glass. "What do you mean?"

"Think about it," I said, and glided away.

Half an hour later he caught up with me. Champagne was still flowing as if it were piped directly from a reservoir in Central Park.

"Your sister's an honest woman," he said to me in a low voice which still managed to be aggressive. "Your sister's a perfect lady at all times."

"My sister's a fool. No self-respecting girl runs a man's house with nothing to show for it but a lost reputation."

"She does it because she's a saint."

"She does it because she's crazy about you!"

His eyes widened. He really was extraordinarily naïve sometimes. "I'm not good enough for her," he stammered with nauseating humility.

"That wouldn't bother Emily. Ask her and find out," I said before I glided away again.

He caught up with me for the last time just before Vivienne and I left on our honeymoon.

"You're a smart guy," he said. "Don't think I don't realize how smart you are. You're right too. This is the best solution for all of us. Are you really willing?"

"For God's sake!" I exclaimed exasperated. "Don't ask me—ask her!" I then escaped to Florida, but as soon as I returned to New York Emily was the first person I called.

"Cornelius! I've got some wonderful news. I do hope you won't disapprove, but . . ."

Steve had proposed to her that morning. I congratulated her wholeheartedly and said with truth that all I wanted was her happiness; if she thought she could be happy with Steve that was good enough for me.

"Cornelius dearest, how sweet of you!" My unqualified consent evidently removed a load from her mind, and she chattered on brightly about her proposal, where it had happened, what Steve had said to her, what she had said to him, what the children had said to them both and what they had said to the children. ". . . So we're going to set a wedding date soon, probably in May. Of course, I know we should wait till Caroline's been dead a year, but—"

"Quite unnecessary," I interrupted, knowing how unsuited Steve would be to long engagements. "Do you have a ring?"

The engagement was formally announced in early February, and the very next day Hal Beecher heard from his London friends that Dinah Slade had produced her twins two weeks earlier.

"A boy and a girl," groaned Hal who having known Miss Slade when she had been a penniless nobody, felt a paternal responsibility for her. "Isn't it tragic to think that such a bright girl could make such terrible mistakes?"

But I understood Dinah Slade better than Hal did. The pregnancy had been a smart move. The mistake had been her quarrel with Steve.

I often wondered how she could have made such a mistake, but I never found a satisfactory explanation. For someone playing with great calculation for high stakes, the error was incomprehensible, and I began to wonder if I had missed some vital sidelight on her character. The thought bothered me. I wanted to understand her well enough to predict her moves, and when she remained an enigma to me I found I was worrying about her future plans.

"Forget it, Neil," Sam advised. "You've outmaneuvered her. She may have future plans, but you and the bank can't possibly figure in them."

But I could only think of Paul saying, "You and Dinah! Such ambition!" and I knew very well that I hadn't heard the last of the mysterious and sinister Miss Slade.

Chapter Four

I

The Crash had shattered America, but everyone assumed the market would rise, like Lazarus, from the dead and the country would totter back onto its feet again. Every day the crowds gathered outside the Stock Exchange to await the resurrection, and if one opened one of the Wall Street windows of the bank one could hear the drone of voices, neither angry nor hysterical but merely patient and enduring. New rumors of stock swindles during the past summer were rampant, and the search for a scapegoat for the disaster became fiercer every day.

Nineteen-thirty arrived, a new decade, a new dawn. To everyone's joy the market showed signs of rising, but it got no further than its knees before sinking back into the grave.

Gradually people began to realize there would be no resurrection.

The country drifted on into uncharted economic waters and discovered that the world was not round after all but flat. The medieval sailor's nightmare became an inescapable reality, and slowly, with a grinding inevitability, we slipped over the edge of the known world and started falling into the dark monstrous void of the Depression.

"Say, Neil!" Sam would exclaim to me. "Have you heard the latest joke about the Crash?"

Everyone was laughing at Crash jokes. It was wonderful how we all laughed. Broadway blazed more brightly than ever, and motion-picture theaters were packed to overflowing. Everywhere was brilliantly gay as everyone rushed to escape from reality, and reality was the empty bottles littering the gutters, the drunken parties where no gossip was too cynical to be batted around, and the bootleggers, rich as Croesus, riding down Fifth Avenue in their limousines.

It was as if we had lost a war, the five-day war of October 1929, and were now occupied by some invisible brutalizing enemy. And again, as in the Crash, few people truly understood what was happening and no one could foresee where it could possibly end. Hoover kept burbling platitudes from the White House, John D. Rockefeller promised everyone all would be well, and the unemployment figures crept upward as the numbers slid downward on the Dow.

Sam had lost all his savings in the Crash and was bitterly depressed. I had to be careful what I said to him, and in fact I went to great lengths to avoid the subject because the embarrassing fact was that I was richer than ever. Since my accountants' primary aim had always been to provide me with tax-free income, they had never been tempted to speculate on my behalf in the lushest excesses of the great bull market, and although I had gambled on the market for fun I had sold out when I decided Martin's depressing forecasts really were the voice of prophecy. My losses had been nil.

To atone for this good fortune I guiltily increased all my charitable donations and listened patiently while everyone moaned of their disasters, but the sad truth is that when one's life is going well one doesn't care to dwell on other people's misfortunes. I did my best, but my attention often wandered.

Meanwhile my house had become as well-oiled and immaculate as a deluxe hotel. People went to enormous lengths to obtain invitations to our smart dinner parties, and later when I decided to practice my future career as a philanthropist, the invitations to my literary soirees were sought with equal enthusiasm. My friend Kevin, who had published one novel and was now trying to write the Great American Play, helped by introducing me to a wide range of literary figures, from despotic critics to struggling authors, and soon I had hired another aide to read all the important books as soon as they were published and present me with competent synopses. I was not illiterate; I like to read as much as anyone else, but my time was necessarily limited and the synopses were a necessary compromise. Hemingway was my favorite author. I read his books myself, since they weren't too long. I liked his spare tough masculine style although I thought it was a pity he so often wrote about losers.

My knowlege of current music waned as soon as Sam moved out of my house into a lavish bachelor apartment on Park Avenue, but when I returned from my honeymoon I found he had lost interest in jazz and was devoted to a far less attractive sound. He tried to make me listen to the records of Glen Gray, but frankly, as I told him on more than one occasion, I preferred listening to Miff Mole's Molers version of *Alexander's Ragtime Band.*

The third of my Bar Harbor companions, Jake Reischman, had returned from Germany, where he had been studying for three years, and was now working in his father's banking house. Sam and I would meet him for lunch sometimes, but we felt sorry for him starting at the bottom of the ladder while we were already storming the top rungs. His father had traditional ideas about training young bankers, and Jake observed glumly that he had no hope of a partnership before he was thirty.

"Work with us at Van Zale's!" I urged.

"A Jew in a Yankee house?" he said laughing.

"That's old-fashioned talk, Jake!" argued Sam. "Why, not even Kuhn, Loeb is exclusively Jewish anymore."

"Is there a Jew at Morgan's?"

We persisted, but although he said with a smile that he couldn't wish for better friends, he turned us down. I had expected it, but I was still disappointed when he said his first loyalty had to be to his father's house.

We accepted his decision as phlegmatically as we could, but soon the disparity of our positions in the banking world became awkward and we saw him less often for lunch. I would have been willing to break the tradition of New York's twin aristocracies by seeing him socially, but Vivienne told me in no uncertain terms that despite a certain blurring of social lines in the twenties, no one really wanted to encourage intermingling.

"They have their crowd," she said, "and we have ours. They prefer it that way. Think of Otto Kahn. When they finally offered him a box in the Golden Horseshoe he refused to sit in it."

"Yes," I said, "because after he'd spent years pulling the Met back on its feet he regarded that grudging delayed gesture as an insult." However, I did not argue further with Vivienne because Jake's mother was one of her deadliest enemies. Mrs. Reischman had once cut Vivienne dead at the theater and had later referred to her as a scarlet woman.

"But now I have a new respectability!" Vivienne boasted to me in the spring. "Even Mrs. Reischman will approve of me now." For after our marriage we had ceased to bother with birth control and Vivienne had wasted no time in becoming pregnant.

It surprised no one that I was delighted by the news, but everyone was astonished to discover that Vivienne was not only delighted but ecstatic. After spending her earlier years not wanting a child, she had swung to the other extreme, as if she had tired of her sophisticated society life and craved only the simplest of human pleasures. She lost interest in her dinner parties, drifted dreamily but inattentively through my soirees and spent her leisure hours reading baby books, designing her maternity clothes and hiring and firing interior decorators to produce the perfect nursery. Society would hardly have been more surprised if Mae West had announced her intention of entering a convent, but when her archenemies labeled her behavior a pose Vivienne simply smiled. "My old life was so empty," she said to Greg when he visited us, "but this is real and meaningful."

Like all her New York friends, Greg looked first polite, then disbelieving and finally amazed. He himself was doing better in life. I had shipped him to Florida, bought him a yacht and prayed he would bother me as little as possible, and so far the move had been a success. He spent his time taking wealthy tourists from Key West to the Bahamas, and actually seemed to be earning his keep. Of course I knew he smuggled rum on the side, but I figured that if he was ever caught I could buy him out of trouble without upsetting Vivienne. It seemed I had finally found the solution to the eternal problem of what to do with Greg Da Costa, and the relief was considerable to me.

The solution to my other eternal problem, what to do with Steve Sullivan, emerged in the spring when he married Emily at his local church on Long Island. A church wedding was awkward since his first wife, whom he had divorced years ago, was still alive, but ministers were becoming more flexible as they realized that the prophesied religious revival was never going to arrive, and so the problem was glossed over without too much trouble. Nevertheless Emily thought it would be better if the wedding were quiet, and so the guest list was limited to the family and close friends.

Since my stepfather was unable to attend the ceremony due to illness, I was obliged to give the bride away. Afterward I got so drunk that Sam had to help Vivienne take me home. Vivienne was livid, Sam disapproving and I felt utterly miserable. On arriving home I shut myself up in my room, burrowed under the thickest darkest blanket I could find and passed out, but when I emerged chalkily sometime later I received no sympathy from my wife.

"I just hated to think of Emily marrying that man!" I blurted out.

"You should have thought of that before you flung them together with your blessing!" said Vivienne tartly.

"It wasn't real then. It was just a game—like checkers or something. But when I walked up the aisle with Emily I suddenly realized I was sacrificing her—oh, God, poor Emily! When I think of that great coarse oaf crawling into bed with my pure beautiful sister—a virgin . . ."

"My God, Cornelius, if Emily's as titillated by the prospect as you obviously are I'd say she had nothing to worry about!"

"What a filthy thing to say!" I cried in rage. "You don't understand anything!"

"All I understand is that you're being quite ridiculous and very tiresome and I'm going to bed to rest. I have to think of the baby."

"All you ever think about nowadays is that baby!" I yelled at her. "What about me? When do I ever get any attention? I've had an unspeakable day, I'm horribly upset and what I'd like right now is—"

"Oh, all you ever want's the same thing! God, how boring men are sometimes!" exclaimed Vivienne exasperated, and flounced out of the room.

"—is a little sympathy!" I roared after her, but she had already slammed the door.

Later we apologized, and after she had graciously permitted me to make love to her—an increasingly rare event nowadays, since she had to "think of the baby"—we were friends again, but there was no doubt in my mind that this pregnancy was uphill work. I did try hard to be sensible. I thought how proud I would be when the newest Paul Cornelius Van Zale entered the world; I thought how beautiful Vivienne was even now that she was pear-shaped and how lucky I was to be her husband; I thought of my intact millions, my influential position at the office, my brilliant neutralization of both Steve and Greg, and my rosy future as a philanthropist. But the harder I reminded myself how lucky I was, the more depressed I became. I felt lonely and also cheated, as if a loved one had short-changed me behind my back. Worst and most humiliating of all, I felt sexually frustrated.

"For God's sake, Neil!" said Sam good-naturedly when I summoned the nerve to mutter to him about my most private problems. "Of course you must show Vivienne every consideration, but so what? Call up Margie and offer to bring her a bottle of hooch!"

"I couldn't possibly do such a thing!" I said frenziedly. "It would be immoral! It would be adultery! I just can't see girls like Margie now that I'm married—it's quite contrary to all my principles!"

"Then take a lot of cold showers and work harder. Jesus, Neil, what do you expect me to say?"

Everybody seemed to be peculiarly unsympathetic. My depression deepened. Certainly when Greg asked if he could stay with us for the Fourth of July holiday I had no desire to see him and was cross with Vivienne for sanctioning his request without first seeking my permission. However, not wanting to quarrel with her I resigned myself to the visit as best I could.

He arrived at the end of June, but fortunately I was busy at the office and saw little of him. I was also having trouble with a wisdom tooth and had to leave the house before he was up in order to keep a series of dental appointments. It was on the morning of the third appointment that I remembered I had left behind some important papers, and when I left my dentist's office I told my chauffeur to drive not downtown to Wall Street but crosstown to Fifth Avenue.

In the library I retrieved the papers, returned to the hall and paused. I had not slept with Vivienne the previous night and had not interrupted her sleep to say goodbye. Deciding to surprise her, I set down my papers on the hall table, removed a red rose from a nearby vase and bore it gallantly upstairs to her room.

She was talking to someone. I heard her muffled voice as I approached the door, but it was not until my hand was reaching for the knob that I heard Greg murmur a reply. I froze. Then, backing away, I tiptoed down the hallway to my room and moved noiselessly across the carpet to the communicating door. It was still ajar. If we slept apart I always left the door open so that I wouldn't feel so lonely. It had been her decision, not mine, to sleep alone in our bed when she wanted to ensure a good night's rest for the sake of the baby.

". . . so be nice to Cornelius," Vivienne was saying sternly.

I could see them through the crack between the door and the frame. Vivienne, in a frothy lace bedjacket, was sitting up in bed with her breakfast tray in front of her; she was casually opening her mail and glancing without interest at each charitable appeal. Greg, fully dressed in one of his cheap white suits, was sprawled in a nearby chair. So relieved was I to see that in private they were no more intimate than they were in my presence that it took me several seconds to concentrate on the conversation.

". . . but I hate the thought of that little bastard going to bed with you, I hate the whole idea of you being married to him—"

"Oh God, you sound just like Cornelius talking about Emily and Steve! Now listen, Greg darling, and do try not to be so stupid. Everything's fine. You have exactly the sort of life you like down there in Florida and I have exactly the sort of life I want here in New York. Believe me, I'd rather be Mrs. Cornelius Van Zale, pregnant wife of the well-known banker and resident of Millionaires' Row, than Mrs. Vivienne Coleman, the former society hostess fallen on hard times and living in obscurity in Queens! I know I didn't intend to marry Cornelius when we started on this scheme to win a little security for you by cultivating him, and maybe I wouldn't have married him if the Crash hadn't played havoc with my capital, but I did marry him and what's more I don't regret it."

"But if I'd only had a tenth of that little bastard's money I'd have married you, Viv! I know you never cared for me in that way—I know it was always Stewart you loved, but—"

"Greg . . . darling . . . please! I thought we'd buried all that!"

"I know, but when I see you living here with that little bastard—"

"Will you kindly stop referring to my husband as 'that little bastard'? Damn it, I like Cornelius! I know I married him for his money, but I'm fond of him and I'll be fonder still when our beautiful baby comes. He's a nice little boy and really quite easy to manage . . ."

I tried to back away but my legs were too stiff to move.

". . . and anyway I find him erotic in bed. A lot of women would. Oh yes, I'm sure it's impossible for a man like you to understand!

But women like powerful men, and when that power is hidden behind an angel-faced façade the erotic attraction is even stronger. You still don't believe he's tough? You should see him in bed! It's obvious then what kind of a man he is."

"Shut your goddamned mouth!" bawled Greg in agony.

"I'm sorry, darling, but I get just a little tired of your being so nasty about dear little Cornelius. . . ."

I suddenly found I was in the hallway with the door closed. It was very quiet. I felt ill.

As I went to the bathroom for my medication there was a tightness in my chest and it was becoming harder to breathe.

A long time later I was in the library, but I had no memory of getting there. My eyes ached but my breathing was steadier. I wanted desperately to talk to Paul, and when I faced the fact that he was gone and that there was no one who could help me I opened the liquor cabinet and took out a bottle of scotch.

I poured myself a drink and stood looking at it. Then I picked up the glass and poured every drop of liquor back into the bottle. Vivienne had called me tough. Now she was going to find out exactly how tough I was.

Glancing in the mirror above the fireplace, I saw my white face and stricken expression, and paused just long enough to set my mouth in its straightest line. Then I went out into the hall. I mounted the stairs. I reached the main hallway. And I walked into Vivienne's room without pausing to knock.

They were still there, still talking, Vivienne still lounging in bed, Greg still sprawled in his chair.

"Darling, what a lovely surprise!" exclaimed Vivienne. Then she saw my face.

Greg saw it too. Standing up, he said uneasily, "Something wrong?"

In a clear firm voice I said four words. To Greg I said, "Get out!" and to Vivienne I said, "We're through." I allowed myself one second to savor their shattered expressions, but before either of them could speak I walked out of the room and headed downtown to my work at Willow and Wall.

II

Nobody could accept that my decision was final. Everybody without exception thought I would crawl back to my wife for a reconciliation. No one could understand what had happened to my marriage, and the mystery was heightened when I refused to discuss it. After moving into Sam's apartment I spent sixteen hours a day at the office and the other eight in solitude in his guest room. Vivienne frantically tried to see me at the bank but was refused admittance. She then tried to call me, but since I never answered the phone myself that attempt to communicate with me was also doomed to failure. Finally she stormed Sam's apartment but was ejected by my bodyguard.

Meanwhile my chief aide had produced the report which I should have ordered before my marriage.

Vivienne's South American real estate, which she had told me reverted to her first husband's family on her remarriage, had consisted only of a small hacienda in Argentina which produced an income of less than a thousand a year. She had been wiped out by the Crash. She had been sleeping with Stewart Da Costa after her husband died, and it was common knowledge in a certain strata of society that Greg had always wanted to step into his brother's shoes. Vivienne had had a compulsive desire to go out of her way to help Greg, not merely because he was the brother of a man she had loved but because she felt guilty that she couldn't reciprocate his feelings for her. The conspiracy which linked them together was simple, straightforward and painfully easy to uncover. One professional inquiry soon confirmed all the facts I'd never wanted to know.

Emily arrived to see me, and because I was too ashamed to tell her how completely I had been fooled and humiliated, I was at first unable to defend myself when she talked about my obligations to my child. I was still longing for her to show some trace of understanding when she concluded, "And what about your marriage vows, Cornelius? What about your moral obligations?"

"They're canceled. Any contract made under false pretenses is voidable."

I thought she would at least understand that, but to my misery she simply bent her head, pulled on her gloves and said coldly, "I'm just glad Mama isn't alive to hear you."

That put my back right against the wall, and suddenly my misery was shot with anger and I recovered my talent for slicing my way out of a tight corner. I aimed for the Achilles' heel.

"Emily," I said, "do I really have to go into explicit sexual detail in order to make you understand why I can't live with Vivienne again?"

She promptly went scarlet and burst into tears. "It's just that I'm so upset about that baby," she wept. "I don't know how you could do this to your own child, Cornelius."

"You mean you think it would be better for him to be brought up in the company of two parents who never spoke to one another and made no secret of the fact that they hated each other's guts? I'm sorry, Emily, but I can't agree with that. If you can accept that

Vivienne and I are finished—and we are—then for the baby's sake you should also accept that it's in his best interests that we should live under different roofs."

I gave her a handkerchief and put my arm around her while she dried her tears. Eventually she said yes, she supposed I was right, but she still felt sad.

"There's only one other thing I want to say, Cornelius," she said as she stood up to leave, "and that's this: see Vivienne—please! It's cowardly not to face her, and she deserves at least one honest conversation with you."

"All right," I said. "I'll see her, but after that I never want to discuss this subject with anyone again. It'll be closed, finished and dead."

"You're very hard, Cornelius," was Emily's parting reproach, but she was wrong. Beneath my protective shell my emotions were no more well-ordered than pulp in a paper mill, and when Vivienne arrived to see me it was a full five minutes before I could steel myself to face her.

III

She was haggard, with dark circles beneath her eyes. She looked well past forty.

"I guess you heard that conversation I was having with Greg," she said. "I managed to figure out that much."

"Uh-huh."

"I shouldn't have discussed you sexually with him, but I only did it to show you in a good light, and Cornelius, I didn't just marry you for your money! I could never have married someone who didn't attract me, and when the baby started I realized just how much I did love you! Cornelius, please—I know we can start again. I'll be the best wife in the world to you, I swear it, and you'll never regret coming back." She broke off. She was twisting her rings round and round on her wedding finger. There was a coffee stain on the bottom of her maternity smock. "Please!" she said desperately. "Please!"

I was silent. She tried again. "I know we had a problem recently in bed, but it was only because I found it a little uncomfortable. I still wanted you just as much. After the baby comes everything'll be just as wonderful as before, I know it will."

"I can never sleep with you again," I said politely. "I'm sorry."

"But—"

"It would be impossible. I'd never even get an erection. No man could want a woman who speaks of him with such patronizing contempt behind his back."

"But I was singing your praises!"

"You called me a little boy," I said. "You said I was easy to manage. You referred to me as a dog-lover might refer to a pet poodle. You made it very, very clear what you really thought of me."

"But I—I—" She started to weep. Tears streamed down her face.

"It's finished," I said. "It's over. I have nothing else to say."

"But the baby—"

"Of course he must stay with you while he's an infant. I won't be unreasonable about custody, and I'm sure our lawyers will be able to work out a civilized divorce because I'm even willing to be generous about alimony. Since you married me for my money I'd just hate you to go away empty-handed."

I had gone too far. Her mouth hardened. She dashed away her tears.

"My God!" she said. "You cold-blooded little bastard, I'm going to sue you for every penny I can get!"

And she did. It was the messiest divorce New York had seen in years. The scandal ricocheted up and down Manhattan from the Battery to Spuyten Duyvil, and photographers made my life such a misery that I became more of a recluse than ever. I did manage to commit the adultery required by the state of New York before divorce proceedings could start, but before I began I looked under the bed to see how closely I was being observed by the press. There was no one there, but I would hardly have been surprised if I had discovered Maury Paul, known as Cholly Knickerbocker to the millions who read his society columns. Mr. Paul did not treat me kindly in his articles, and referred to me constantly as "the farm-boy from Ohio."

My partners maintained a strained silence, although once Lewis said it was a pity there was so much talk. Fortunately it was the height of summer, and since I could retreat to Bar Harbor without losing face I rented a thirty-room cottage and walled myself up with my secretary, my aides, two bodyguards and a synopsis of *War and Peace*. Sam came up later to see me, but he stayed with his parents, just as he always did when he returned to his home town. Other people tried to see me too but Sam was the only one I could face.

"There are a couple of girls I know . . ." he began helpfully, but I shook my head. I had lost interest in sex, food, drink and exercise. I was grieving as if for someone who had died, and presently I managed to confide to him that I had burned all my wedding photographs. Then I cried. Sam was appalled, and, thinking I would be ashamed of myself afterward he tried to leave in order to spare me embarrassment, but I wouldn't let him go. Clutching his sleeve, I forced him to listen to a long dreary rambling monologue about how much I had loved Vivienne and how money never brought anyone any happiness and how my life had ended at twenty-two.

"God, I need a drink," said Sam when I paused for breath. "You'd better have one, too."

"No, it'll destroy me!"

"Well, you're so destroyed already I can't imagine one drink will make much difference. What would you like? Martini, Bronx, Alexander, Sidecar, Three-Mile-Limit, Whisky Sour or a Whoopee? You look as if you could do with a Last Resort."

We had a couple of Whoopees apiece. The lemon juice and honey were soothing on the throat, and the applejack and gin were soothing on the soul. I began to feel better, and when the drinks were finished we went for a swim and lay in the sun. I started to maunder on about Vivienne again, but Sam interrupted to describe a merger he was working on between General Baby Foods and the Canadian-Atlantic Grocery Stores, and presently I was suggesting an interesting flotation which avoided any hint of common stock. Later we played tennis and I won. By this time I felt hungry, so we ate broiled Maine lobster, very fresh and succulent, followed by blueberries with ice cream.

"Now I've got a surprise for you," said Sam, glancing at the clock as we finished our coffee. It was still early in the evening. "There's a very special lady coming to see you."

I was aghast, thinking he had been fool enough to summon Vivienne, but he said this was someone who had returned to New York from overseas the day after I left for Bar Harbor.

In bewilderment I followed him to the window. A car was crawling up the drive and when I saw who my visitor was the tears filled my eyes again because Sam had produced my strongest surviving link with Paul.

I ran into the hall, elbowed my bodyguards aside and flung wide the front door. She was already walking away from the car, but when she saw me she stopped and held out her arms.

"Cornelius!"

"Sylvia?" I said, hardly daring to believe she was really there, and overcome with an enormous feeling of comfort, I stumbled toward her down the steps into the driveway.

IV

"Paul would have been so disappointed in me."

They were the first words I said to her when we were alone. Outside the sun had set, and when I glanced beyond the window I was reminded of my conversation with Paul which had also taken place at Bar Harbor at dusk.

"Cornelius, Paul's first marriage must have been very like yours. He would have understood."

"But he warned me . . ."

We talked for a long time. Her dark hair glowed red whenever she leaned forward into the last fading shaft of light, and her face, quiet in repose, was still luminous with that mysterious inner radiance whenever she smiled. To me she would always represent peace and tranquillity, an oasis of perfection in a world of false glitter and bitter back-chat, and whenever I saw her I knew why Paul had wanted her to be his wife; he might have had to work all day in the savage tundra of Lower Manhattan, but once he came home to Sylvia he could be sure of crawling out of the cold.

"If only there were no child," I burst out at last. "You can't imagine how guilty I feel, how much I hate myself for having made such a mess of everything."

"Paul felt that way about Vicky at first. Yet later he said Vicky had made sense of the whole disaster of his first marriage."

We started to talk about Paul, but stopped. We both knew our thoughts were identical.

"I don't believe I'm going to have a son," I said. "I'm going to have a daughter. Did I ever tell you that Vivienne and I often discussed names and she said how much she liked the name Vicky because it was so cute and unusual?"

"Cornelius . . ." She rose impulsively to her feet. I was already pacing around the room.

"Paul and I both had intellectual mothers and older sisters," I said. "Our fathers both died before we were grown up. We both had delicate secluded childhoods. We both had to fight for survival on Wall Street when we were very young. We both had disastrous first marriages. Sylvia, I'm beginning to think Paul passed on to me more than his money and his position. I'm beginning to think he gave me his whole life to live again."

She said that was impossible. I had never heard her speak so strongly, and as she walked right up to me I saw that her tranquillity was destroyed.

"Paul's dead," she said. "His life is finished and the door which leads to his life is closed. Don't try to open that door, Cornelius. Paul had his own special demons which died with him. Let them be."

"But the likeness—"

"It's a mirage. An illusion."

"But I want to be like him!"

"You're yourself. Be thankful." She kissed me and held me close.

We were silent for a long time, and when she spoke again it was merely to invite me to stay with her after I returned to New York.

Aware that I had trespassed too long on Sam's hospitality, I accepted her invitation with relief, but when I reached New York in September I found that all offers of hospitality were unnecessary. My house on Fifth Avenue was empty. Vivienne had moved out with the Georgian silver, the Coalport china and all the Renoirs, and was staying with friends in Tuxedo Park.

At first I was delighted, but within days I was reconsidering Sylvia's invitation to stay. I had never lived alone in my house before and I hated it. The huge rooms were lonely and the endless corridors depressing.

At the beginning of October I called Sylvia.

"Cornelius!" she exclaimed warmly, so much her old self that it was hard to believe I had seen her so agitated at Bar Harbor. "I was just about to call you! I'm having a little reception at home next Thursday for the French consul with dinner afterward. I won't ask you to the dinner, because I'm sure you'd hate it, but do stop by at the reception. It'll do you good to get out, even if you only stay ten minutes. I hate to think of you all alone in that house."

I dithered about whether to go but finally, having nothing better to do, I went. Besides, I wanted to see Sylvia again and thought that during my brief appearance I could invite myself to stay.

The reception was held in the floor-through drawing room on the second floor of Sylvia's brownstone, and a collection of immaculate footmen served some impressive champagne in addition to the inevitable cocktails. "Saint-Pierre et Miquelon!" whispered Sylvia, naming the Canadian islands where the liquor smugglers picked up the best French wines. In addition to the champagne there was a generous selection of hors d'oeuvres, a varied collection of diplomats, dowagers and dilettantes and unfortunately a small but beady-eyed bunch of debutantes. I saw them eying me as soon as I entered the room.

I was late. Sylvia introduced me to a plump contralto who talked about Wagner and to a British tea planter who talked bafflingly about South American coffee, but then she was diverted and I was on my own. Seconds later the debutantes were closing in.

"Cornelius, how are you?"

"Cornelius, remember me? Leonie from Tarrytown!"

"Why, Cornelius, I haven't seen you in ages!"

A dowager festooned with diamonds outflanked them slickly. "Mr. Van Zale, I was just devastated to hear about your recent misfortune. . . ."

The plump contralto stopped talking about *Tannhäuser* and pricked up her ears. Other people too turned to stare, but when I looked frantically for Sylvia I saw she was talking to her guest of honor, the French consul. Abandoning all hope of rescue, I began to edge away from my pursuers.

In the far corner a girl was sitting quietly, a glass of orange juice on the little table beside her. Her face was averted from me as she gazed out the window, but I did notice that she was wearing a maternity dress. The one certainty of my present situation, I thought feverishly, was that a pregnant woman would make no attempt to seduce me.

"Excuse me, please," I said to the vultures, "I've just seen someone I have to talk to." And showing them my back before they could argue with me, I wove my way through the crowd to the far side of the room.

"Good evening," I said to the girl. "I don't believe we've met. My name is Cornelius Van Zale."

She turned to look at me. Gray-green catlike eyes, cool and restless as some remote northern sea, sent a glance which flicked over me from head to toe. Pale lips parted for a second over small white even teeth as she smiled in acknowledgment. She wore no makeup and no jewelry, and her black dress was so plain it was stark. She was beautiful.

"No, we haven't met," she said. "I'm Alicia Foxworth."

"May I join you, Mrs. Foxworth?"

"Please do, Mr. Van Zale." She seemed to have no trouble with my name, but it was impossible to tell whether the name was familiar to her or whether her hearing was perfect. She spoke in one of those bloodless Eastern accents which only the most expensive education can buy, and her conversation was conducted in a low hypnotic monotone.

"Did you pick this corner because you wanted to escape from everyone?" I asked, anxious that I might have been intruding.

"No, but I can see you did. I've been watching your reflection in the glass."

Glancing at the window, I saw that by a trick of the light the room was mirrored in the pane.

"So you're a spy!" I sat down on the chair next to hers.

"No, just an observer. I was watching the debutantes and thinking there really are some compensations for being married."

"Which of these men is your husband?"

"He's not here. He was delayed in Albany as usual."

"He's in government?"

"The State Senate. He's going to try for Washington in the next elections, and since he has unrestricted access to my money I guess he'll get in." She sipped her orange juice and looked bored.

"Have you been married long?" I said tentatively.

"Three years."

"You must have been under the age of consent three years ago!"

"I was seventeen." She finished her orange juice and opened her purse for a cigarette. "It was either marriage or suicide," she said, "and I didn't have the nerve to kill myself. Do you have a light?"

I patted my pockets for several seconds before I remembered I had given up smoking. Eventually I found a bowl of matches near the fireplace.

When I had lit her cigarette she said, "You're married, aren't you? Isn't your wife here?"

"We're separated."

"Oh yes, I remember now. I'm sorry I never bother much with gossip. Where do you come from? You couldn't have lived long in New York or I would have met you before we moved to Albany. My father's Dean Blaise of Blaise, Bailey, Ludlow and Adams," she explained as an afterthought, "and he used to play tennis regularly with Paul Van Zale. How all those Yankee banking houses hang together!"

I took a moment to marvel what a small world it was and then asked her if she had always lived in New York.

"Of course. Where else is there to live?"

"Well, there's Boston—or Philadelphia—"

She gave me the New Yorker's classic response. Boston was ignored. She simply said with amazement, "*Philadelphia?*"

"Well, perhaps Europe—"

"Europe's so unsanitary," she said. "And it's so depressing not to understand what people say. I detest Europe. Where did you say you came from?"

"Cincinnati, Ohio."

"Such a pretty name! I've always wanted to go to the Midwest, but St. Louis is such a long way and my father never did approve of Chicago. Where exactly *is* Cincinnati?"

A shadow fell across our table as Sylvia paused to be a good hostess. "Alicia dear, it's really so sweet of you to come without Ralph—I do appreciate it. These politicians with their busy schedules! And how's your little Sebastian? He must be quite big now."

"Eighteen months. Yes, he's running all over the place. He's lovely." Long dark lashes swept downward to cover those gray-green catlike eyes. Her smooth opaque hair swung forward to brush against her creamy skin. She still spoke in that hypnotic monotone, but I sensed that the mention of her little son disturbed her, just as I had sensed she had nothing but contempt for her husband. When Sylvia failed to notice her distress I felt as if I had discovered an extraordinary talent in myself for interpreting a complex work of art.

". . . and I didn't know you knew Cornelius!" Sylvia was saying pleased.

"We've just met."

"How strange—you look as if you've known each other for years," Sylvia said vaguely, and swept off to attend to the British tea planter who was reclining sadly against the far wall.

I looked at Alicia. Alicia looked at me.

"Your husband married you for your money, didn't he?" I said.

"Yes."

"But you've only just found out."

"Yes."

"And you daren't leave because you're afraid he'll try and take Sebastian."

Now she was the one to be hypnotized, and as we gazed at each other I saw the missing half of my personality and felt an enormous joyous relief. The expression in her eyes changed, and suddenly my own knowledge was reflected brilliantly back at me in a blaze of emotion which lit the room. The other people seemed to fade away, the noise of conversation became a mere distant drone, and then as I reached for her hand at the exact moment that her hand groped blindly for mine, our lives touched, merged and streamed forward together in a single irreversible tide.

Chapter Five

I

When Alicia's husband arrived in New York two days later she refused to return with him to Albany and tried to remain with her parents. However, when her father flew into a rage and her stepmother refused to have a deserting wife in the house, she left them too and moved with her little boy and his nurse into my house on Fifth Avenue. She was five months pregnant at the time.

At least on this occasion I no longer had to worry about what my mother would think, although probably in view of my feelings for Alicia I would have told even my mother to mind her own business.

New York society spluttered in horror. We were shunned. Cholly Knickerbocker's column could only refer to us obliquely; our names were so drenched with sin that they would have defiled any decent newspaper. I had to hire extra secretaries to sift the fevered hate mail from fundamentalists, itinerant preachers and little old ladies in Dubuque. I had to hire two extra bodyguards to fend off the fanatics who waited at the gates of my house to pelt me with rotten eggs, and two new lawyers to cope with the legal abuse Foxworth kept slapping on me. Little Sebastian's nurse could no longer take him for walks in the park. I was called depraved, debauched and disgusting, while Alicia was described as a harlot, a hussy and a horrible disgrace to motherhood.

It never ceased to amaze me how people passed judgment on us without having any idea of the true facts. Alicia and I both believed in the sanctity of marriage and motherhood—of course we did. Our joint ambition in life was to marry, raise a family and remain faithful to each other in the conventional Christian fashion. It was all very well for my critics to scream that I had walked out on my pregnant wife and taken a pregnant woman away from her husband, but they entirely misunderstood the options that were available to me. My choice lay not between fidelity and adultery but between honesty and hypocrisy, and I'm no Victorian—I'm a twentieth-century man, and I had no intention of building my private life around a lie in order to appease the petty demagogues who dictated society's conventions. I didn't choose to meet Alicia when she was pregnant—or even when she was married—but since I had met her I saw no point in pretending we could ever have lived apart. Similarly, once my relationship with Vivienne had been destroyed I saw no point in pretending that any part of it had survived. I was honest with myself and with other people, and if that shocked everyone I was sorry but I wasn't about to jettison my honesty to accommodate them.

However, I had to admit that the uproar caused by my behavior was tiresome, and it took me some time before I became too bored with the fuss to pay it further attention. Fortunately I was busy at the office and although I missed going out for a walk in the lunch hour I was equally happy to sit at my desk with a hot dog and a bottle of Coca-Cola while I browsed through statistical reports. I had soon given up eating in the partners' dining room, as all the other partners were so priggish about my situation and I hated to see how much Steve was enjoying my discomfort. I knew that the scandal was bad for my career, but I knew too that if I continued to work hard, complete my assignments and make no mistakes my reputation as a banker would ultimately be undimmed. The worst aspect of my situation was that it seemed to confirm the opinion that I was just a twenty-two-year-old kid who was too immature to be taken seriously, but again time was on my side. I would grow older; I would eventually be able to marry Alicia; and we would sink into the most stifling respectability imaginable.

In fact we already lived quietly and my evenings were no more remarkable than my hard-working well-disciplined days. What our critics thought we did with ourselves I have no idea. Perhaps half their fun was derived from the conviction that we indulged in orgies which would have put the ancient Romans to shame, but the truth, as so often happens, was more prosaic than any fantasy. I would come home from work and we would sit on the couch in the upstairs drawing room for half an hour while we exchanged news. I would drink some tomato juice, Alicia would sip a glass of milk and we would hold hands. When our drinks were finished I would go to my rooms to shower and change for dinner before I joined Alicia in the nursery to say good night to Sebastian. Dinner would be a light meal, usually fish followed by fruit. Alicia lost interest in meat during her pregnancies and developed a craving for apples. After dinner we would listen to our favorite radio shows—we would be holding hands again by this time—but by nine-thirty Alicia would be yawning and ready for bed. She tired easily in pregnancy and needed at least ten hours sleep a night.

No middle-aged suburban couple embedded in the most respectable of middle-class suburbs could have led a more exemplary life, yet of course I have to admit there were difficulties. Unfortunately it is not in the least natural for a young couple to live like middle-aged suburban marrieds when they're in the grip of the hottest love affair in town.

Naturally I tried to make love to her. I tried several times, but the baby came between us. I could feel him. He moved a lot. He aroused all the guilt I felt as a young man brought up decently in a Christian household, and then all my brave words about being a twentieth-century man counted for nothing and I would tremble at the thought of the Ten Commandments. I didn't seriously believe God cared a jot whom I was sleeping with, but childhood beliefs often run too deep to be easily exorcized by logic, and after the third time I had failed to make love to Alicia I said, "I'm sorry, but I can't do this anymore. It'll be all right after he's born, but it's no use when he's right here in bed with us. I'm very, very sorry. Please try not to be too angry with me."

She did not answer but in the darkness I could feel her mind brushing without anger against mine. The silence continued, the tension building between us until the air seemed heavy with our frustration, until at last she rubbed against me and put her hands on my body.

Seconds later I said automatically, "You don't have to do that." I had had no idea well-brought-up young girls knew about such things. I could accept such knowledge when displayed by Vivienne, but I hated to think of Alicia behaving in a way which I had previously associated with maturer, less principled women.

Alicia took no notice of me.

"Alicia—"

"You stupid prig, don't be so goddamned provincial!" she screamed at me, and I was struck dumb with shame.

Later when she had finished and I had recovered my breath I said humbly, "Shall I . . . ?" and she said, "Yes, for God's sake do before I pass out with frustration."

Later when I took her in my arms I felt her tears wet against my cheek. "Alicia . . . darling . . ."

"No, it's all right, I'm happy. I love you. I'm sorry I screamed at you like that." She clung to me. "I wanted you so much."

"I feel terrible that I . . . I . . ." I got stuck.

"Oh, for heaven's sake, what does it matter how we make love?"

But it mattered to me. I was at heart very conventional about such matters, and as the weeks passed and we pursued what I can only describe as our very unusual sex life, I used to daydream longingly of a time when we were married, when Alicia was no longer pregnant with another man's child and when we could go to bed without guilt and indulge in good clean straightforward sexual intercourse just like any other decent married couple.

Unfortunately marriage was beginning to seem a long way off. Foxworth had not reconciled himself to the fact that Alicia was never going to return to him, and he flatly refused to discuss divorce. This meant that all his energies became focused on the custody issue, and in the battle for Sebastian he was unyielding. Alicia was an unfit mother, his lawyers argued with the full weight of public opinion behind them; no judge with any conscience could permit a child to remain with a deserting wife and her unprincipled lover; Sebastian and his nurse must return immediately to Albany.

Alicia and I fought Foxworth tooth and nail, but I knew there was no hope of winning. I was beside myself with anxiety, fearing that Alicia would become hysterical, but when the inevitable decision was handed down from the bench she accepted it quietly and I realized she had been resigned to her loss for some time. Alicia was much too clear-eyed to practice self-deception.

When the time came for her to say goodbye she kissed him calmly, told him she would see him again soon and asked him to be good. Then she gave him one last hug and walked away.

I caught up with her, but all she said was, "I have to be alone now," so I let her lock herself in her room. She stayed there without asking for me for two days. Trays were taken up to her and left outside the door, but most of the food remained untouched.

I felt sick with worry. I knew she was adjusting herself to the fact that she had lost her child because of me, and I was terrified she would be unable to endure the deprivation. I felt guilty that I was the source of her suffering, and my guilt was exacerbated by the fact that I had not cared for the child and was secretly relieved I would not have to be an active stepfather. He was dark-haired and dark-eyed like Ralph Foxworth and I could see nothing of his mother in him at all.

After Alicia had been secluded for two days I decided she would leave me, and my despair was such that I could hardly drag myself home from the office. But when I entered the drawing room I had a surprise. Alicia was waiting for me. The glass of tomato juice and the glass of milk stood on the table. Alicia wore a new dress and a different hair style and the diamond engagement ring I had bought her at Cartier's.

It was five minutes before either of us could say more than a few incoherent phrases. We just sat and held hands, but at last she said, "You've been very, very kind and patient and understanding. I'll never forget it, never. I'm sorry this has all been so difficult."

I kissed her and muttered something unintelligible.

"Cornelius, I've come to a decision."

I immediately thought she was about to announce her return to Foxworth. "Don't be silly, darling," she said quickly as she saw my petrified expression, "nothing could possibly come between us, you must know that. No, my decision is that I can't go through this experience a second time. I know I could get temporary custody of the baby till he's weaned, but I don't want it. I couldn't bear to give him up when he's six months old with a little personality all his own. I'd end up in a straitjacket at Bellevue."

"Maybe we could work out some long-term arrangement with Ralph."

"Never. He'll want custody and he'll get it. It'll be his way of paying me back for leaving him so publicly." She paused to light a cigarette with a shaking hand before adding in that same cold voice which failed to mask her grief, "I don't want to see the baby after he's born. I'll be like a mother who gives up her child for adoption. It's the only way."

"Let me go and see Ralph. I'm sure—"

"There's nothing you can do, Cornelius. I've just spent forty-eight hours thinking about this, and I've explored every possibility. I'm twenty years old and I've made the most dreadful mess of my private life and my only hope now is to face up to it and make decisions which will cause the minimum amount of pain to all concerned. In fact, my main worry is not myself but you. I don't want you becoming buried in the wreckage of my first marriage. I don't want you having to endure my nervous breakdown. I don't want you becoming involved in endless courtroom battles with Ralph. I've been bad enough for your career as it is, and yet you've never given me one single word of reproach. You deserve more from me than endless scenes and constant anxieties. I've lost Sebastian. It's dreadful, but I must accept it. I've lost the baby. That's equally dreadful, but I must accept that too. But I've gained you and you're the most important person in the world and I couldn't live without you. I've got to look to the future now and I know it'll all come right, Cornelius, when we're married and have children of our own."

Our drinks stood untasted on the table. The butler came in but withdrew halfway through announcing a telephone call.

Later when I had had my shower and Alicia was watching me as I dressed for dinner we began to plan our family.

"I want at least seven children," said Alicia. "I like being pregnant and giving birth. It gives me a feeling of power. I often feel sorry for men, never being able to experience it."

I smiled at her in the mirror as I adjusted my tie. "We'll found a dynasty!" I said, my smile broadening. "Five sons at least—"

"Six," she said. "One more than the Rockefellers."

A little color had crept into her pale skin, and her dark-ringed eyes had brightened. I saw that the thought of our future children was her way of coping with her loss, and so I encouraged her to elaborate on her dynastic dreams. Soon we had named all six sons and were planning their careers.

"I love you," she said, hugging me after we had decided that Cornelius Junior had to manage the Fine Arts Foundation if Paul was to be the leading light at the bank. Then she said wistfully, "If only our dreams weren't all so far away."

"I'll bring them nearer. I've had just about enough of Ralph acting as if 'divorce' was the dirtiest word in the English language."

"But I have no grounds for divorcing him! And how are you ever going to get him to divorce me?"

"Relax," I said. "I'll fix him."

II

Since he had married for money, I reckoned he would divorce for money.

I wasn't disappointed.

It cost me a million dollars. I never told Alicia. It wasn't that I was ashamed for myself but I was ashamed for him, selling her like that. I made a mental note to ensure that his political career never got off the ground in Washington. He really was the most contemptible character.

"I'll pay you another million for Sebastian and the new baby," I said, not bothering to hide my disgust, but to my surprise he refused.

"You can have my wife," he said. "Since she's been acting like a high-class whore there's no reason why you shouldn't pay for her. But no money on earth can ever buy my children, and you can tell her I'll never under any circumstances let them go."

Of course I never told her. She was so thrilled that he had agreed to a divorce, and I didn't want to cast a blight on her new happiness. Instead I took her to the West Coast, where I had business in Los Angeles, and the gaudy glamour of California provided a welcome relief to those long tense gray days in New York.

No one else knew Alicia as I did. Everyone thought she was so cold, never betraying emotion, and so haughty, looking down her pale perfect aristocratic nose at everyone she met. Women were jealous of her; they criticized her clothes as too austere and called her dislike of makeup an affectation, but they would never admit she was too beautiful to need either cosmetics or fussy fashions. Men admired her but were intimidated by her reserve. They found her carefully cultivated air of boredom unnerving and were repelled by her studied lack of vivacity, but it never occurred to them that this social manner was a shell protecting someone who had suffered greatly. Alicia had learned early in life that if one expected nothing one could not be disappointed, so in her eyes enthusiasm was a trap leading to disillusionment, and intelligent interest a blind alley resulting in frustration. Her father, cold and distant, had always been absorbed in his business. Her mother had died young and her stepmother had regarded her as a burden. In childhood Alicia had been either incarcerated in boarding schools or exiled to Europe with a succession of governesses, and once she was old enough for marriage her stepmother had encouraged her to marry the first man who proposed to her. Alicia's father approved of Ralph, who had already spent ten years in the banking house of Blaise, Adams, Ludlow and Bailey, and Alicia soon decided he was the savior who would rescue her from her unhappy home and carry her off to paradise on his white horse.

She married him.

Yet after the honeymoon she saw little of her savior and still less of paradise. At first she did not mind, for she became pregnant and had the baby to occupy her, but eventually it became clear that Ralph's absorbing interest was not in her but in politics. She grew lonely, marooned in Albany, and Ralph's solution of a second pregnancy only made her feel more isolated. She was sure his solution was a mere expediency to keep her quiet, but it wasn't until she arrived in New York for the annual visit to her parents and overheard a telephone conversation between Ralph and her stepmother that she discovered exactly how far she had been manipulated and used.

Alicia's father was a millionaire and she was his only child. Her mother had left her a fortune in excess of three million dollars. Ralph's political ambitions were expensive, and the stepmother's desire to be rid of Alicia had been intense. It had been a cruel and sordid conspiracy.

"You were the first person who ever loved me," Alicia said, and I thought how terrible such a confession was from someone who should have been cherished from the day she entered the world. For I saw past all her defenses, the coldness, the disdain and the ennui; I had used them so often myself when I was growing up that I could push them aside as if they were old friends. Alicia was shy, as I was; she wanted desperately to be loved for herself and not for her money; and beneath her icy composure she was intense, passionate and sensual.

"And you're the only person who's ever understood me," she added as we lay snugly in the vast circular bed of our garish hotel suite. "I feel so comfortable with you—I even feel at ease when we're silent. I love our silences."

We had been in Los Angeles only three days when Vivienne obtained her divorce from me and as if in celebration of her enormous settlement gave birth to our child. It was Christmas Eve, and when

Emily telephoned I assumed she merely wanted to offer us seasonal greetings.

We were lounging on the decadent circular bed when the phone rang. Alicia was reading *True Story* magazine, I was doing a crossword puzzle and we were sharing a bag of peanuts. We didn't answer the phone, but seconds later my secretary tapped on my door to tell me my sister was calling from New York.

"Emily?" I said, picking up the extension.

"Cornelius, lovely news! A Christmas present for you!"

"Oh? What's that?" I said, penciling in a clue. I had forgotten all about Vivienne. My first marriage seemed as remote as a tribal rite among South American Indians.

"Good heavens, can't you guess? How unintelligent men are sometimes!" exclaimed Emily, and she told me I had a daughter called Victoria Anne.

I made the appropriate noises. Emily prattled on happily about how nice it was to think there would be another Vicky in the family, and then announced she herself was expecting a baby in June. I made more appropriate noises. Eventually Emily remembered to ask about Alicia. I said Alicia was fine.

"I'm so glad," said Emily, trying and failing not to sound chilly. "Well, dearest, I won't hold you up any longer—I'm sure you'll want to rush off and drink to Vicky's health."

She said goodbye. I said goodbye. We hung up. I sat looking at the phone.

Alicia's fingers stroked the short hair at the back of my neck. "Are you sorry it's not a boy?"

"I wasn't expecting a boy." I turned to kiss her. "No, I'm glad it's a girl—I want you to give me my first son. Let me send someone out to buy some champagne."

"Lovely!" She wiggled her bare toes and adjusted her stomach so that she could sit up. When I had returned to the bedroom after dispatching an aide to the nearest illegal liquor store she said in her most neutral voice, "Darling, why are you upset?"

I told her about Paul and our parallel lives.

"And Paul's second marriage ended in divorce? Is that what's worrying you? But Cornelius, you know that couldn't happen to us! This is where your life is going to diverge from Paul's."

"Yes. Yes, I'm sure you're right." I tried to define my shadowy uneasiness. "It's not that I don't want to be like Paul," I said. "It's just that I want to feel I have some control over the likeness. I'm bothered because it's as if I'm locked into some pattern which I have no power to change. I do nothing except live my life as best as I can, yet my life mirrors Paul's at every turn."

"That's just a coincidence."

"I guess it must be, since the only alternative is demonic possession."

We laughed, and in an effort to change the subject I began to speculate about my daughter. It was only later when we had each finished a glass of champagne and consigned the rest of the bottle to my aides that I remembered to tell her Emily was pregnant.

"Cornelius, I thought you'd got over Emily's marriage?"

"I have. Maybe I'm jealous of Steve's being able to see the baby as soon as it's born instead of having to fight a legal battle for access. I don't suppose that'll mean anything to him, though. He must be so used to fathering children all over the place."

Alicia wrinkled her nose fastidiously. "Steve Sullivan's brand of apelike sex appeal leaves me colder than an ice floe from Alaska," she said, cheering me up, and opened a new bag of salted peanuts.

The Foxworth divorce flashed through the courts so fast the press barely saw it for dust, but although the speed cost me more money I reckoned it was worth it. On the twenty-ninth of January, 1931, Alicia and I were married in New York in a very private, very brief and very plain civil ceremony. For obvious reasons we decided to postpone the honeymoon, so I went back to work after the ceremony while Alicia retired for her afternoon rest. She was more than eight months pregnant by that time and had to take care not to overtax her strength.

I spent my wedding night figuring out how I could get to see my daughter, whom Vivienne had spirited away to Florida before my return from Los Angeles. I already had all my lawyers roaring at her lawyers, but as anyone who has ever footed a legal bill knows, lawyers love a stalemate, and I couldn't see them making any rapid progress. Finally I decided to hire private detectives to track Vivienne down, and to my fury I was told that she was hiding out in the little nest I had feathered for Greg Da Dosta in Key West. In addition to buying him a yacht to keep him quiet I had also given him a ranch house a mile out of town.

That was the last straw. Picking up the phone, I called the head of the Washington bureau responsible for enforcing the Eighteenth Amendment, and three days later Greg's yacht was intercepted by the revenue men. In the ensuing scuffle some zealous agent, intoxicated by the sight of so much smuggled rum, became too free with his gun and Greg was shot in the stomach. He died in the hospital after an eight-hour coma.

After debating whether to send Vivienne flowers I decided a sympathy note would be more appropriate, and I was just working on my sixth draft when she sent me a cable which read: "DON'T THINK I DON'T REALIZE WHO SPILLED THE BEANS I'LL NEVER FORGIVE YOU NEVER YOU CHEAP SONOFABITCH I NEVER WANT TO SPEAK TO YOU AGAIN."

I tore up the sympathy note and sent a cable which read: "DEEPEST SYMPATHY STOP I DISCLAIM ALL RESPONSIBILITY STOP I MAY BE A SONOFABITCH BUT AS YOU SHOULD KNOW FROM YOUR MONTHLY ALIMONY CHECK I AM NOT CHEAP STOP WHEN MAY I SEE OUR DAUGHTER STOP REGARDS CORNELIUS."

Vivienne promptly replied: "WHEN HELL FREEZES OVER," and that was the end of my attempt to communicate with her by cable.

I had not envisioned death for Greg Da Costa, only a judicious prison sentence, but when I considered the situation I saw that the mills of God had, as usual, ground suitably small. Greg had been an accessory before the fact of Paul's murder. During my infatuation with Vivienne I had turned a blind eye to this by pretending that his role in the conspiracy had been negligible, but in law accessories before the fact invariably meet the same fate as the principal participants in the crime.

Having faced this truth squarely, I shed no tears for Greg Da Costa. I even went so far as to hope he was rotting in hell, and I was still trying to beat back this highly un-Christian attitude when I arrived home from the office to discover that Alicia had gone to the hospital.

I felt ill not only with anxiety for her safety but with an agonizing frustration because there was nothing I could do. We had carefully discussed how we would behave when the baby came. She did not want me at the hospital before or after the birth. I was not to visit her there, though I could phone her, and when the time came for her to leave I was merely to send the car so that she could come home by herself. She wanted to be alone. She did not want to involve me. I was to go on leading my normal life, and eventually she would rejoin me as if nothing had happened. She had said this course of action would be the least painful for all concerned, and she had said it with such finality that I had not dared argue with her.

I could eat no dinner, and when I tried to drink I felt so sick I stopped. I kept thinking of Foxworth. My own experience of paternity, remote and unsatisfying as it was, made me feel sympathetic toward him, and at eleven I called him in Albany. He hung up on me, but sometime after midnight he called back, apologized and said he would phone the hospital to make sure he was told of the delivery.

Nobody told me. At dawn, unable to bear my tension any longer, I too phoned the hospital and was told Alicia had had a second son. I asked over and over again if they were sure she had survived, and finally they became so exasperated that they cut off the call. Afterward I held my head in my hands and stared at the floor. Then I went out. It was a Sunday, so I did not have to go to work, and on reaching the hospital I paced up and down outside it for a long time while I decided what to do. I wanted desperately to see her, but I was afraid I might upset her if I broke our agreement. Instead I called her from a pay phone.

"Everything's all right," she said in her most expressionless voice. "There's nothing for you to worry about. Thank you for calling."

"I love you," I said, but she had hung up. Everyone seemed to be hanging up on me. At home once more I had a short drink and wrote her a long letter saying how much I loved her. I would have sent flowers, but she had forbidden it. However, I thought I might give her a present later. She looked lovely in diamonds.

I called her every day. She thanked me for the letter but did not write back. We talked about the weather and whether we should go away for the weekend at Easter. I wanted to ask if she had seen the baby in spite of her decision, but that would have broken our agreement, so I only asked if she was getting on well. She said the doctor was very pleased with her.

On the tenth day after the birth she left the hospital, and when I came home from the office at six-thirty she was waiting for me in the upstairs drawing room. The glasses of milk and tomato juice sat side by side on the table. She wore a fussy cream-colored dress which I had never seen before and a neat mask of powder, rouge and lipstick. It was very odd to see her with a flat stomach.

Sitting down, we talked rapidly as if the thought of silence terrified us, and once the glasses were empty we rushed to my rooms as if we were late for some vital engagement. As usual I had a shower, but when I emerged from the bathroom I found that the bedroom was empty. I dressed quickly and went to look for her. She had disappeared. I had to accost six servants before I found a maid who remembered seeing Mrs. Van Zale wandering down the hallway leading to the east wing.

I found her in the nursery which Vivienne had designed for Vicky and which for a few weeks had belonged to Sebastian. She was sitting on a little stool in the middle of the room with her arms wound tightly around her body. I heard her dry racking sobs before I crossed the threshold.

Kneeling down beside her, I held her close for a long time. When she stopped crying all she said was, "I feel so empty."

"Where is he? I'll go and get him."

"No, you can't. He's in Albany. Ralph came down yesterday with Sebastian and Nurse. They tried to see me, but I couldn't, couldn't—It would have been unbearable. I would have died from the pain of it."

"Did you ever see him?"

"No. I was too afraid of loving him more than I already did. I've been so afraid, Cornelius, so afraid of disintegrating, not being able to go through with it, failing you—"

"You couldn't fail me. I'll do anything you want, anything at all. What can I do? Please tell me, let me help."

"Talk to me. Talk about our dreams. Just talk."

I began to talk about our six sons, one more than the Rockefellers, and our one daughter. I chose schools for them all and outlined their interests and hobbies. I had just married our daughter to a leading partner of the House of Morgan when Alicia said, "I have to wash my face. All my silly makeup's smudged," and we returned to our room. After her face was clean she took off the fussy dress and put on a plain black one.

"I'm ready for dinner now," she said, so we went to the dining room and ate broiled sole, her favorite fish, with peas and wild rice.

Later that night when she was lying in my arms I wished she was well enough for me to make love to her properly, but I knew we had to wait several weeks before the doctor could sanction such a reunion. I sighed. She sighed with me and I knew her thoughts reflected mine.

"We can have a baby right away," I said. "I mean, we can have one just as soon as you want after you feel you've recovered from this pregnancy."

"Oh no," she said clearly in the darkness. "That wouldn't be right at all, Cornelius. For the next year *you* come first. I think it's time you had a break from coping with pregnant women, and since I have approximately twenty-five child-bearing years ahead of me there's no need for us to hurry. I want your children more than anything else in the world, but for a short time I want to be alone with you without any little third person coming between us."

However, contrary to Alicia's intentions I was to have no respite from pregnant women, and just when I was preparing to launch myself into a normal sexual relationship with my wife I had a strained unhappy telephone call from my sister Emily.

III

"He's been hearing from Dinah Slade," she said.

We were drinking tea at her home on Long Island. It was a Saturday afternoon and I had driven to see her after my morning's work at the office. Steve was in Chicago on business, but on the lawn below the terrace his two sons Scott and Tony were playing baseball with a bunch of local friends. As we sat in the main sitting room with the garden doors open we could hear their distant shouts, but once Emily mentioned Dinah Slade I no longer noticed the noise. I set down my teacup carefully in its saucer and stared at my sister. She was wearing a flowing white dress and looked lovelier than ever. The baby was due in two months' time.

My voice said, "How did you find out she'd been writing to him?"

"He showed me the letter." She bent her head, and her golden hair, longer now and waved in the latest fashion, swung forward to frame her face. "She sent him photographs of her twins. He showed me those too."

I could no longer control myself. Springing to my feet, I began to pace furiously around the room. "How dare he humiliate you like that!" I shouted.

"But he was right to be honest and open, Cornelius! I was glad he felt he could discuss her with me. After all, it's just as if she'd been his wife for a short time."

"Emily, you must demand that this correspondence cease!"

"Cornelius—dearest, do calm down and be sensible, for my sake! It's sweet of you to be so upset on my behalf, but you're not being very practical. Of course I'd like to tell him never to write to her, but since he obviously wants to acknowledge the photos isn't it better that he should do so with my consent instead of behind my back? When I married Steve I decided that the one way to lose him would be to be too possessive. I reconciled myself to the fact that he'd had lots of affairs by telling myself they were all past, even his affair with Dinah Slade, but the trouble with Dinah Slade is—"

"—she's the only one shameless enough to present him with illegitimate twins!"

"And they're so cute, Cornelius!" Emily's calm façade crumbled as her eyes filled with tears. "I just know Steve's going to want to see them someday, and once he sees Dinah Slade again . . . Cornelius, I know I'm being ridiculous, but I'm terrified of her. Perhaps it would be better if we met. I keep picturing her as some irresistible *femme fatale*, whereas in reality she's probably just a nice sensible English girl with some eccentric views on marriage. Maybe I'd even like her! I have these fantasies in which Steve and I visit Mallingham and Steve plays with the children while Dinah and I discuss the Peloponnesian Wars—Steve told me she majored in classics just as I did, so we'd probably have a lot in common even though we've chosen to follow different careers."

"Exactly!" I cried, unable to tolerate her extraordinary monologue a second longer. "You have no career! You're a real woman, not a woman masquerading as a man!"

"Cornelius, what on earth are you talking about?" exclaimed Emily, so offended that she forgot her tears. "Of course I have a career! My career is raising children to be mature worthwhile people, but I quite understand that not all women can share my own particular gifts and inclinations. Do you expect all men to be bankers?

There are all kinds of women, Cornelius, and no one kind has the monopoly on femininity!"

"Uh-huh. Sure. Emily, all I was trying to say was that I like your kind best. Am I allowed no personal preferences?"

"Preferences yes. Prejudices no," said Emily, sounding more and more like my mother every minute. She was about to say more when we were interrupted. Little Tony Sullivan trailed through the garden doors, sank down next to Emily on the couch and leaned wearily against her.

"Emily, I don't feel too good."

"Don't you, darling? Hm, you do feel a bit hot. I'd better take your temperature. Excuse me, Cornelius."

She left the room. Tony and I eyed each other until in an effort to be friendly I sat down beside him. "I saw you playing baseball just now," I said. "Is that your favorite game?"

"Yep."

"I follow the Cincinnati Reds. I guess you go for the Giants, do you, or the Yankees in the American League?"

"No, the Dodgers."

We talked about the Dodgers' prospects for the coming season. He asked me if I had ever seen Babe Ruth play, and we were becoming very sociable when Emily returned with the thermometer.

"Here you are, Tony. Cornelius, help yourself to another cup of tea."

Tony Sullivan had a temperature of a hundred and one. Long afterward I remembered him as he sat on the couch with the thermometer in his mouth and watched me with Steve's bright-blue eyes.

"You'd better be in bed!" Emily said perturbed as she shook the mercury down. "Excuse me again, Cornelius."

"Of course." I said goodbye to Tony and added that I hoped he would soon feel better.

By the time Emily reappeared I was anxious to return to Alicia, so we did not linger on the subject of Dinah Slade. Emily said she felt better now that she had discussed her worst fears, and I told her to make it crystal clear to Steve that she did not approve of his conducting a nostalgic correspondence with his ex-mistress.

"An exchange of photographs and a card at Christmas is just within the limits of decency," I said strongly. "Any communication beyond that is outside the moral pale. There's a limit to what you should put up with, Emily. Remember that."

That night I talked on the phone for two hours to Sam. Emily's worries might be allayed, but mine were burgeoning with the speed of bacteria in a hot climate. Sam told me I was getting neurotic and ought to watch myself.

"Neil, this is just a broad with three kids who likes to keep in touch with her old lover! What's the big deal?"

"She wants him back."

"Trash! Knowing her, she's probably got at least three new lovers and is angling for a fourth!"

"Yeah, I guess you're right," I said without conviction and went right on worrying about Emily. Usually I saw her once a week and spoke to her regularly on the phone, but the next day I took Alicia away on our long-delayed honeymoon and once we'd set sail from Florida I forgot everyone back home in New York. I even forgot Dinah Slade. On our cruise through the West Indies our days were filled with sun and turquoise seas and silver sands and palm-fringed beaches, and our nights were no less exotic. I have idyllic memories of secluded coves and the gleaming coolness of the sand before it was covered by the warm moonlit sea. I remember the tide washing over us as we made love by the water's edge and I remember the steamy seclusion of our cabin at high noon. And always I remember Alicia, her gray-green eyes no longer as cold as some northern sea but as shining as the brilliantly colored Caribbean waters, her manner no longer chilly but as sultry as the volcano at Guadeloupe.

I hated to see Florida again and I hated to think of New York waiting for me in the north. I even hated it when Alicia's health took its usual monthly digression, because I felt we should have brought back more than just our memories of such a perfect honeymoon.

"But there'll be other honeymoons!" said Alicia, and we resolved to conceive our first child the following February during our second Caribbean cruise.

I was still wishing with a sigh that I was back on the yacht when I fell ill.

It was twenty days since I had seen Tony Sullivan and when I felt the first pains it never occurred to me to remember him. It was my first day back at the office and I had so much work to do that I wasn't even able to find the time to call Emily to ask how she was. In fact I was so busy that I decided I couldn't spare the time to be ill, so I took no notice of my symptoms.

The pains spread from my back to my neck and head. On the second afternoon of my malaise, when I nearly fainted at my desk, I reluctantly yielded to the inevitable and went home to bed.

I had a temperature of a hundred and three. Alicia called the doctor and within half an hour Dr. Wilkins was listening to my chest to find out what was wrong.

By this time I was convinced I had infantile paralysis and would never walk again. Alternatively I suspected I had brain fever and would spend the rest of my life as a vegetable, so when Wilkins seemed more puzzled than alarmed by my symptoms I felt exasperated. He was a tall, distinguished-looking man with an unflappable bedside manner which I always tried hard to dent. I never succeeded. During each one of my winter respiratory illnesses he had remained unperturbed in the face of my fractiousness, and I soon discovered that this new illness was hardly about to alter our relationship.

"Am I going to be ill for weeks?" I demanded.

"Oh, I shouldn't think that's likely, Mr. Van Zale. Whereabouts in your head is the pain located?"

"Everywhere. Particularly the right side. Is it some sort of stroke? A cerebral hemorrhage?"

"I doubt it, Mr. Van Zale, since you're in full possession of your faculties. Is your neck stiff?"

"Yes, that hurts, too."

He started feeling behind my ears and prodding below my jaw.

"Ouch!" Twisting away from him, I pressed my hand against my neck, and when my fingers touched a lump behind my ear I froze. I had read somewhere that one of the most horrible diseases known to man could begin in the form of lumps in the head and neck.

"Is it cancer?" I said wildly.

"No, Mr. Van Zale. Open your mouth, please. Wider. Wider still. . . . Ah! Yes, I thought so."

I had cried out in pain. Something had happened to my salivary glands. I pressed my tongue against them in agony and insisted that he tell me truthfully how long I had to live.

"Probably another fifty years," said Dr. Wilkins politely, folding his stethoscope and taking out his prescription pad. "You have mumps, Mr. Van Zale. I'll give you something for the pain."

"Mumps!" I was outraged. "That's a kid's disease!"

"Yes, and it can be very unpleasant for adults. You must stay in bed for at least a week, and on no account should you get up even when your fever subsides."

"But I have my work! I've got to get back to the office! Surely if I have no fever—"

"Mr. Van Zale," said Dr. Wilkins charmingly, "do you really want to run the risk of encephalitis? Of course, the brain damage in mumps cases is always reversible, but I assure you it's the most unpleasant complication."

I sank back onto my pillows.

Unfortunately my ordeal had hardly begun. My fever continued and my discomfort increased. The right side of my face became swollen until I looked like a circus freak; flesh swung pendulously from my jaw. I could no longer open my mouth, and all consumption of solid food was impossible. My most striking accomplishment lay in sucking liquid through a straw. I was just thinking in agony how fortunate it was that only one side of my face was affected when I felt the lumps swell behind my other ear and knew that the left side of my face too was doomed.

For a long time I refused to let anyone but my valet see me, but eventually Alicia forced her way in.

"*Cornelius!*" She was horrified.

I tried to open my mouth. My salivary glands screamed. Wincing, I prayed for the pain to die away, but it was several seconds before I could reach for my pad and pencil to conduct the conversation. Of course I was quite unable to talk.

"I don't know whether I should tell you this," said Alicia, "but I've been talking to Emily and she says you must have caught it from Tony. I hope you can forgive him."

I wrote: "I'll skin him alive!" but I could neither laugh nor smile. It was too painful.

Presently the swelling on my right side subsided and I was just thinking with relief that I was on the road to recovery when I awoke one night with a searing pain in the groin.

I had never been more frightened in my life. Old Wilkins was hauled out of bed and chauffeured to my door. One of the nicest things about being rich is that a doctor is always available in a crisis.

"I'm going to be impotent," I said, sweating, "aren't I?"

"No, Mr. Van Zale," said Dr. Wilkins. "I give you my word that you will not be impotent as the result of this illness."

I did not believe him. I was in despair. "Does this happen often with mumps?"

"It's not uncommon." He was writing another prescription for the pain.

"You've had other patients with this complication?"

"Several."

"And can you solemnly promise me that each one was capable of sexual intercourse afterwards?"

"They even fathered children." He took pity on me and gave a thin smile. "It could be worse, you know," he said kindly. "You do have two testicles."

I blanched as he left the room.

"This is a dreadful disease!" I cried afterward to Alicia. "I never knew it could attack the genitals! Why does no one ever tell you these things?"

"You had a sheltered upbringing, Cornelius. I did too, I guess, but I remember Ralph saying once that it could make men impotent. Isn't it nice to know he was wrong?"

I dreamed of castration. Wilkins called daily and became so annoyed at my refusal to believe his assurances that he himself offered to call in a second opinion. Realizing that I was behaving like a coward, I declined.

The next day the other testicle became affected.

"Well, you're certainly having a bad time," said Dr. Wilkins, scribbling nonchalantly on his prescription pad. "But perhaps this is better than encephalitis or damage to the pancreas. Has your wife bought a new nightgown yet to celebrate the end of your convalescence?"

I hated him. When he had gone I turned my face to the wall and didn't speak for twelve hours. It was the nadir of my illness.

Two days later I began to improve, and within a week I began to feel there might after all be hope for the future. Long dreary days of convalescence passed while I became increasingly nervous and examined myself with minute care in the bathroom (I couldn't quite summon the courage to masturbate), but at last I was pronounced fit and the moment of truth arrived. The night before I was due to return to work Alicia arrayed herself in a black satin nightgown, forced me to drink two glasses of champagne and beckoned me into bed.

"I know I'm going to be impotent," I muttered. "My balls have shrunk."

"Nonsense, Cornelius, how could they? They just seem that way because they've been swollen to twice their normal size."

"But suppose I'm little better than a eunuch?"

"Oh, do stop being so silly, darling! You're just saying that to spite Dr. Wilkins."

I laughed, and as I gazed at Alicia through the haze of champagne I thought I had never seen her look more beautiful. She had a neat exquisite body with slim legs and hips, white unblemished skin and small round firm breasts.

"God, what hell it is to be celibate!" I cried with passion, and promptly forgot the mumps.

My ordeal was over, and when I reached the office the next day I was in such high spirits that I even accepted Steve's offer of a drink when he arrived with the news that Emily had given birth to a daughter.

"To my niece!" I said, raising my glass to his with a smile, and it was only when he smiled back saying, "My daughter!" that I wondered if he was still corresponding with Dinah Slade.

Chapter Six

I

On my return from my honeymoon I had planned to tell Steve what Emily herself had felt unable to say: that he was not to humiliate her by adopting Miss Slade as a pen pal. Because of my illness this conversation never took place, and before my return to the office Emily had already informed me that she and Steve had settled the matter and that I was on no account to mention Miss Slade to him.

I might have disregarded this order, but there were so many matters demanding my attention when I returned to work that I took her words at their face value—a value which, as I later realized, was nil. I ought to have guessed that Steve, hating to see Emily upset as much as I did, had decided to keep his English correspondence to himself.

Matters might have turned out differently if only I hadn't been entombed for weeks with that disgusting disease.

The mumps had also removed me from the financial arena, and it was depressing to return to the bank and find that the economic picture was bleaker than ever. I had read the papers daily during my convalescence, but their pathetic optimism, geared to repair the broken American spirit, hardly reflected the long-term prognosis which Martin Cookson was only too willing to give me. That summer a series of banking failures swept Europe as the tidal wave of the Wall Street Crash inundated European shores, and the economic structure of the world tottered. In September another landmark was wiped out: the British pound went off the gold standard, and one look at my partners' faces told me exactly how a tribunal of the Spanish Inquisition would have greeted the news of some fearful new heresy.

America clung to the gold standard, but within six months the gold reserve was cut in half and new unthinkable national nightmares were hovering in the wings.

"My God, are we never going to hit rock bottom?" said Sam appalled.

But people were beginning to have a clearer idea of what rock bottom was. Between April and September American industry began to unravel, production falling, payrolls contracting, construction contracts cut by a third. The streets were choked with the unemployed. I used to see them waiting for a free meal, the line stretching block after block, as I rode downtown every day in my Cadillac to the bank at Willow and Wall.

"Increase the charity donations," I ordered my chief aide, and to Alicia I said, "We must do something about the poor."

We gave a charity ball and I doubled the amount raised out of my own pocket, but I was almost wondering if I too ought to tighten my belt. The investment bankers' market was drying up. It was hardly the right moment to launch new schemes for capital investment, and the number of issues was dwindling.

The one bright spot in this depressing landscape was that at long last I managed to see my daughter. My personal lawyers had been dozing during my illness and when I found no progress had been made in the custody struggle I fired them and hired a new firm. Soon I won permission to see my daughter, but Vivienne, who was still in Florida, took no notice of the New York ruling. I was on the point of heading for Key West with a full entourage of lawyers when Emily achieved a great coup by persuading Vivienne to soften her attitude.

Emily had taken care to remain on speaking terms with Vivienne; now she reaped the reward of her farsighted diplomacy. Although Vivienne declined the kind invitation to the christening of Emily's baby, she agreed that Vicky could travel north with her nurse to spend one week with her Aunt Emily on Long Island. The only condition Vivienne set to the bargain was that my child was under no circumstances to cross the threshold of my home.

Vicky was nine months old. When I walked into the nursery she glanced up from her toys and I looked into my own gray eyes. She had just enough curly blond hair to support a pink bow.

"Vicky!"

She smiled absent-mindedly, crawled to the edge of the rug to retrieve a block and returned to build a new castle.

Sitting down cross-legged on the floor, I watched her in silence, and soon she became sufficiently interested to bash her blocks aside and clamber into my lap. Nervousness overcame me. I was afraid of scaring her by a careless move, but eventually I summoned the courage to give her a hug.

She gurgled and pulled my ear hard. When I shook my head vigorously we both laughed.

"My, what a talent you have for children, Cornelius!" said Emily, impressed.

Alicia turned away without a word, and I knew she was thinking of the little boy she had never seen.

"We're going to reopen this whole custody mess," I said to her afterward. "There's no reason on earth why you shouldn't see your boys sometimes. I'll arm my new lawyers to the teeth and send them out into the field with their guns blazing."

My lawyers blazed away obediently, but it was uphill work and the opposition was still fierce. They were still wrangling when my attention became diverted by the Banking and Currency Committee of the Senate. President Hoover, convinced that the sickliness of the stock market was the deliberately engineered result of a small group of men who were selling short, had become determined to assume the role of scalp-hunter on Wall Street.

It was the end of another era, the era when Wall Street had had Washington in its hip pocket. Gone was Morgan's famous direct line to the White House. Wall Street's power was on the ebb. When the Senate formally authorized the Banking and Currency Committee to investigate Wall Street, a group of bankers including Lamont of Morgan's protested to the President, but Hoover showed them the door. In the midst of this icy struggle a rumor flew around that there was a French plot to force America off the gold standard, and the market crashed sickeningly. Unemployment was coasting smoothly toward ten million, with no ceiling in sight. Gold was rushing away like water cascading down a drain. Industrial stocks were down to a fifth of their 1929 peak and were still falling. It was said that Americans were hoarding coins under their beds.

It was 1932 and the Four Horsemen of the Apocalypse were Deflation, Demoralization, Destitution and Despair. It was also an election year, and Hoover, aware of the failure of his policy not to interfere with the economy, was scrabbling for new ways to boost his reputation.

Far away at the back of my mind I could remember Martin Cookson prophesying that someday the public would demand a scapegoat for the debacle of 1929 and decide that the ideal candidates for the role were the investment bankers.

At the start of the Wall Street investigation, when the Senate merely empowered the committee to investigate short selling, we all sighed with relief. Richard Whitney, the Morgan broker and president of the Exchange, could handle that. It was true there were certain unpleasant senators, such as Brookhart of Iowa, who threatened legislation which would put an investment banker in the penitentiary for pegging the price of a security on the Stock Exchange while unloading it on the public, but we preferred not to listen to him.

"Cheap bloodlust," said Lewis disdainfully, "is so very unattractive in politicians."

The inquiry crept on. In April and May of 1932 the nasty practices of pool operators began to come to light, and as the senators prised up stone after stone of the market graveyard everyone watched the slugs crawl into the light of day. The climax came when Walter Sachs of Goldman, Sachs, one of the leading investment banks, was cross-examined about the questionable practices of his company's investment affiliates. A shudder ran through the investment banking community, and a partners' meeting was held at Van Zale's.

"They're gunning for us," said Martin.

"They say Lee, Higginson is next on the agenda—and God knows what they'll turn up there," said Steve. "Ivar Kreuger turned Lee, Higginson inside out, and once the committee exposes his frauds they'll crucify the firm."

We all paused to consider what would happen if the committee started exhuming the affairs of Van Zale Participations. It was very quiet. Everyone looked unhealthily pale.

"At least you had the brains to send your brothers to Australia, Steve," said Clay Linden at last. "The committee can hardly haul them back to Washington to testify."

"But what about me?" said Steve. "What am I going to do when I'm hauled up before the committee? All you guys can get away with saying that you never saw the books, but once I admit I plowed through the entire disaster my knowledge is imputed to you and the bank goes up in smoke."

"Steve's right," said Martin. "It would be fatal if he were forced to give evidence. Steve, you'd better go back to Europe and the sooner the better."

"Oh my God," I said before I could stop myself, but although my partners looked at me curiously they decided I was just exhibiting a touch of youthful hysteria. Only Steve understood. His glance, wry and cynical, met mine and flicked away.

"I don't want to go to London," he said, not looking at me. "My place is here in New York and I don't want to get tied up with the London office. If I've got to go back to Europe let me base myself in Paris and work on a survey of European economic prospects. That would be a legitimate temporary assignment and would be useful to us in the future."

I gazed at him with a new respect, and for the first time in my life I almost liked him. Certainly it gave me new hope for his marriage.

There was no rush for Steve to leave, since we had had no confirmation that Van Zale's was to be investigated, but to avoid any accusation that he was fleeing the country he did begin his preparations for the move. Emily was excited about spending time in Europe and began to reminisce about the summer she had spent there after she had graduated from college. Her little girl, Rosemary

Louise, was a year old by this time and almost as pretty as Vicky; Steve's boys, according to Emily, dutifully showered their new sister with affection; and the Sullivan family's future appeared to stretch ahead endlessly into a rosy haze.

However, the writing was on the wall for the investment bankers of Wall Street, and on the twenty-fourth of January, 1933, we were all brought one step nearer to public chastisement for our past sins. The special subcommmittee of the Senate Banking and Currency Committee, which had now been pursuing its investigation for eight months, appointed a new counsel and we came face to face at last with Mr. Ferdinand Pecora, the Sicilian immigrant who intended to beat the mighty bankers of the Eastern Seaboard to their aristocratic knees.

David had met his Goliath. The fight was on.

II

Meanwhile America was swaying on the brink of anarchy, crashing from one ghastliness to the next, with twelve million now unemployed, the farmers in open revolt, banks failing daily and Roosevelt's supporters still singing *Happy Days Are Here Again.* On the day before the inauguration of our new President banks remained open in only ten states and there was not only insufficient gold left to back the currency but insufficient cash in the Treasury to meet the government payroll.

It was rock bottom at last. We were bankrupt.

Roosevelt came to power, closed all the banks against Lamont's advice and took America off the gold standard. A year before we would all have shouted that this was heresy, but since we now saw that this might well be the only cure we decided that the heresy had to be acceptable. Morgan of Morgan's was even brave enough to say he welcomed it.

Roosevelt went on, flailing around like a butcher with a meat ax, bashing everything in sight and splitting every well-worn tradition to pieces. Half the time I suspect he had no idea what he was doing, for his ignorance of economics was frightening, but he was certainly a success at demonstrating the principle that any action was better than none. In July he even started chopping up economic theory by selling gold at whatever price caught his fancy, and I believe we might all have been in hysterics at this mad behavior if we hadn't been so mesmerized by Pecora. Gradually as the investigation deepened Roosevelt faded into the background, America's convulsions were no more than an apocalyptic backdrop and all we could see was Pecora sharpening his sword.

Pecora was a crusader, a progressive, a fighter for truth, honesty and fair play. He spoke for the millions who wanted to know what had really been going on during the glittering months of the Great Bull Market, and when he saw the investment bankers cowering in their tarnished palaces he began to hammer on those closed doors of privilege and power.

"That dreadful little man Pecora!" said Lewis, looking down his nose. "I thought gangsters were the only items Sicily exported to this country!"

We all tittered but, like Lewis himself. we were all scared to death. Wall Street trembled, and in the exclusive clubs uptown, in the hallowed corridors of the Metropolitan, the University and the Knickerbocker, there was many an old Porcellian who could not bring himself to voice the upstart's name.

It soon became obvious to us that it wasn't enough just to ensure that all three Sullivan brothers were out of the country. Pecora demolished the investment banking firm of Halsey, Stuart, laid waste the National City Company and even slit open the affairs of the House of Morgan from end to end. Nothing was sacrosanct, no one was spared. Finally, when we heard that he had extorted both the articles of partnership and the banking records from Morgan's, we knew it was vital to head him away from Van Zale's. It wouldn't have taken Pecora long to make a connection between my broker's acquisition of the Van Zale Participations shares and my enhanced power in the revised articles of partnership, and once the trust's books were exposed Pecora would scalp us all.

"But how can we possibly head him off?" said Martin in despair. "He's absolutely incorruptible and he's bound to want to investigate us."

Lewis could only mutter something about buying up the senators on the subcommittee. He had been in a state of gibbering terror ever since Pecora had exposed the income tax evasions of Charles Mitchell, the president of the National City Bank.

I suddenly saw my chance. If I could save us from Pecora my power in the firm would not merely double but quadruple.

"Suppose," I said vaguely, "that Pecora receives a diversion he can't ignore. His time is limited. He knows that Congress and the public are going to lose interest in the investigation eventually, so he wants every victim he picks to provide a first-class scandal. We've covered up the trust mess pretty well. He can't know for sure that we could provide him with banner headlines. If he hears that another front-rank Yankee house offers better publicity value, don't you think it's possible that he might pass us by?"

They all spoke at once, demanding to know which house I had in mind.

"Dillon, Read," I said. "We all know what was going on there."

"For Christ's sake! You mean we could tip Pecora off?" I'd even succeeded in shocking Clay Linden.

"But Cornelius," said Lewis appalled, "it's a tradition of the Street that all the Yankee banking houses hang together. We must be loyal to Dillon, Read, just as they would be loyal to us."

"Screw tradition," I said. "It's their neck or ours."

It was theirs. Pecora passed us by, and when we realized we were safe I had Lewis almost crying on my shoulder with gratitude.

"Thank God Pecora never got the chance to interrogate me about my taxes!" he kept saying. "What an unbelievably lucky escape!"

"Tell me, Lewis," I said idly, "what exactly *did* you do on your tax returns?"

He told me. He was garrulous in the enormity of his relief. His deviousness related to a source of income other than the income from the partnership and, as I had suspected, was a variation on the scheme which had led Mitchell to his indictment for tax evasion. A fictitious sale of assets had been negotiated to establish a "loss" for income tax purposes. Whether this apparent fraud was tax evasion or merely tax avoidance was something only a court of law could decide, but even if Mitchell won an acquittal there was no doubt his career would still be in ruins.

"So for God's sake don't tell anyone," added Lewis as an afterthought, still perspiring at his narrow escape.

"Of course not!" I said soothingly.

Later Sam said, "Christ, Lewis was a fool!"

"To lie to the I.R.S.?"

"No, to tell the truth to you! What are you going to do?"

"Well, nothing right now," I said exhausted. "I want to recover from my crucifixion. But it's nice to know, isn't it, that we've got Lewis exactly where we want him?"

"Very nice," said Sam.

Chapter Seven

I

After Pecora and the Senate subcommittee went into recess for the remainder of the summer, Alicia and I retreated to the cottage I had bought the previous year at Bar Harbor, and soon the children joined us. Vivienne had finally condescended to let Vicky spend each August with me, and as my lawyers had battered a similar concession from Ralph Foxworth, Sebastian and Andrew also arrived with their nurse.

I had never been more grateful for the opportunity to lead a quiet family life. We took the children for picnics and walks, and for many happy hours I played with the model train set Alicia had bought for Sebastian. F. A. O. Schwarz must have found us good customers that year. I had ransacked their store for presents for Vicky, and although Alicia warned me not to spoil her I took no notice. Vicky was two and a half and could talk to me. We used to have long conversations after I had read her the required bedtime story, and I was continually marveling how advanced she was for her age. Naturally I had enough tact to praise Alicia's boys as well, but the truth was Sebastian was backward and Andrew was plain and neither of them bore any resemblance to their mother. For the first time in my life I understood the difficulties my own stepfather must have encountered, and as I saw again the pattern of history repeating itself I seemed to feel those mythical mills of God grinding out a belated retribution for my past insensitivity.

In September the children went away, and without them the house seemed such a morgue that we closed it at once and returned to New York.

It seemed empty too in the mansion on Fifth Avenue, and upstairs in the east wing the nursery still stood deserted, the furniture swathed in dust sheets, the blinds drawn on every window.

The mills of God were working overtime that year.

"Take what you want in life," says the old Spanish proverb, "and pay for it." My credit finally ran out on Thursday the seventh of September, 1933.

The weather was very hot, with the temperature soaring freakishly toward ninety, and the city shimmered in a humid haze. It was a gross distorted repulsive day. I thought it would never end.

Ironically I had been looking forward to it for some time because Sam was due to return that morning from Europe, where I had sent him to check up on Steve. After Pecora had concluded his summer investigations, Steve had decided to stay on in Europe until December in order to avoid the suspicion which a prompt return would have aroused, but I had at once started to worry in case Dinah Slade was beckoning him again. I still had no desire to go to Europe, but Sam had willingly volunteered to go in my place. It had seemed the ideal opportunity to combine a private mission with a business reconnaissance; I had decided that one of us should acquire at least a rudimentary knowledge of European banking, and Sam, being European-born and bilingual, was obviously better suited than I was to reconnoiter the territory.

He departed enthusiastically for Cherbourg at the end of July, and after spending two weeks in Paris with Emily and Steve he headed east across the German border into his native land.

I had one postcard from him. It was a picture of Cologne Cathedral and on the back he had scrawled one word, "*Wunderschön!*," before signing his real name, Hans-Dieter.

"Sam must be enjoying himself," I said vaguely to Alicia, and I was relieved, for Sam's feelings for Germany had always been so convoluted that I had feared he might hate the German section of his trip. Jake had given him an introduction to the Reischman office in Hamburg, and it was from Hamburg that he eventually sailed back to the States.

I went down to West Twenty-first Street to meet his ship, the *Manhattan*, and as soon as he emerged from the customs hall I sensed he had changed. It was strange that I should have sensed this, for the change was within him, but I knew him so well and no doubt there were half a dozen hints which my mind subconsciously recorded as significant. He wore a foreign suit and looked much neater than usual. His hair was shorter and styled differently, so that the bones of his face had an altered emphasis. His shoes gleamed, his cuffs were crisp and his skin glowed as if he had been scrubbing it every day with ice water.

"Hi!" he said in his familiar Maine accent. "Good to see you again! How are you doing?"

It took me a moment to realize I had expected him to speak in a foreign language. "Just fine!" I said with a smile. We shook hands. "How are you? Good trip? You look as if you've just come back from a vacation in the Promised Land!"

"That's exactly the way I feel," he said, and when I looked at him closely I saw he was serious.

My heart sank. I knew what happened to Americans who fell in love with Europe. They became restless and dissatisfied, torn between two worlds, confused, dislocated and rootless. The pleasures of Europe were like the pleasures of alcohol, acceptable in moderation and ruinous when taken to excess. In despair I tried to discover the extent of his new addiction.

"So you fell in love with Europe," I said politely. "That's nice."

"Not Europe," he said. "Germany."

"Oh." I did not know much about Germany except that I had heard they had finally found someone to put their affairs in order. "Tell me about it," I said helplessly as my chauffeur drove us to Park Avenue, and my invitation opened the floodgates to a seemingly endless torrent of information.

I listened and said "uh-huh" at intervals. Later when he had finished unpacking we went downtown, but since it was obvious he was in no mood to listen to the bank's affairs I resigned myself to the inevitable and offered to take him out to lunch. "Why don't I ask Jake to join us?" I said inspired. "You can compare notes on Hamburg."

"Great idea!" exclaimed Sam, and would have launched into another glowing travelogue if I hadn't asked him about Emily and Steve.

"Oh, Emily seemed real happy," said Sam, "and the new baby's very cute. Emily was pleased to have a second girl, because now with Steve's two boys they have even numbers."

I asked him more questions about Paris, but he was vague. He had forgotten France as soon as he had crossed the German border.

Jake met us at Lüchow's on Fourteenth Street, and while he and Sam selected German delicacies I ordered an American steak and baked potato.

". . . And I can't tell you guys how I feel," Sam was saying. He then proceeded to tell us in detail. "I was so ashamed of being German, you both know that. But once I was there, once I saw what was happening—the economic miracle, the new spirit of optimism, the thrilling spectacle of a nation surging back onto its feet after being ground into the dust—"

"What's new about that?" I said. "That's happening here now! You don't have to go to Europe to see that."

"Ah, but we have Roosevelt," said Jake ironically, "and Germany has Hitler. There's a difference."

"What does it matter who the leader is so long as he gets the country back on its feet?" cried Sam. "The end justifies the means! God, when I think of all those years of suffering and shame—"

"Well, I do agree," said Jake, "that the Allies have only themselves to blame if the Germans now follow anyone who promises to lead them out of the wilderness, but I must say I think a little rabid nationalism goes a very long way."

"I disagree," said Sam heatedly. "Nationalism, even chauvinism, is the key to German revival, and Hitler understands that."

"Oh my God, Sam," drawled Jake, very much the sophisticated New Yorker, "don't tell me that cheap demagogue's succeeded in taking you for a ride!"

"Well, of course you're just a Jew," said Sam. "You can't possibly understand the fundamental necessity of German nationalism."

I felt as if someone had walloped me between the shoulder blades. Turning dumbly from one friend to the other, I saw their friendship disintegrate before my eyes.

"I'm sorry you should say that," Jake said at last. "I wouldn't have thought the rising tide of anti-Semitism in Germany could ever have touched you, Sam." And as he spoke I remembered those days long ago at Bar Harbor when he had reached out to give Sam a helping hand.

Sam remembered too. He was scarlet, floundering in a mire of guilt and shame. "I'm not anti-Semitic," he said, his voice a shade too loud. "You're one of my best friends, as you well know. I was simply pointing out that Jews are by their very situation always on the outside of any nationalist movement taking place in the countries they inhabit. If they were more assimilated anti-Semitism couldn't exist."

"The German Jews are far more assimilated than their French or English counterparts."

"Yes, but—"

"For God's sake!" I burst out, very upset by this time. "Why the hell can't you two stop talking as if you're a couple of Europeans? We're all good Americans here. Now I know why I've always disliked Europe. It turns perfectly normal decent people against one another—and all in the name of race, nationalism and creed!"

They were silent. I looked from Jake's light hair and blue eyes to Sam's dark square familiar face.

"Racial prejudice is so goddamned ridiculous," I said violently as our food arrived.

The subject was changed quickly, but the conversation became stilted and I knew that irreversible damage had been done. At the end of the meal, after Jake had excused himself casually, Sam put his head in his hands in despair and I told him to go home to rest. It was obvious he needed more time to sort himself out.

"And don't forget," I said strongly to give him a sense of direction, "that you're an American, Sam. You were raised here and you've spent all your adult life here. You owe Germany nothing."

Without warning he turned on me. "But who *are* the Americans?" he said. "Have you never asked yourself who you really are?" And when I started to say I had no desire to identify myself with Europe he got up and walked out.

I returned to the office alone and was still struggling to forget the disastrous lunch when the telephone rang.

"Your sister is calling from Paris, Mr. Van Zale."

I felt winded again, as if I had suffered a second blow between the shoulder blades. Opening the top drawer of my desk, I extracted my medication but did not unscrew the cap. "Put her through."

The line clicked. French and American operators called to each other stridently above the atmospheric interference. Finally Emily said in a thin high voice, "Cornelius?"

"Emily—yes, I'm here. What's happened?"

"It's Steve."

I felt the first twinge of emotion, the beginning of a slow burning rage.

"He's left me, Cornelius. He's left me. I don't know what to do. Should I come home? Should I go after him? Should I wait in case he comes back? I don't know what to do, Cornelius. Please tell me what I ought to do."

"Where is he?" I said, although I already knew. I tried to open my medication bottle, but the cap was stuck. I could hardly see because I was in such a rage.

"He's gone to London," said Emily, and across the three thousand miles which separated us I heard the sad muffled sound of her weeping. "He's gone to Dinah Slade."

II

I told her to come home. Steve had suggested it in his farewell note and I saw no reason why she should remain in Paris when it was obvious he had no intention of returning to her. I couched this advice in the gentlest possible language and talked to her until she herself said she felt better. Then after promising to call her the following day I said goodbye.

Numerous emotions chased chaotically through my mind. The anger in all its different shades was easy to recognize, but it took time before I could identify my shame. I had never liked Steve Sullivan; I had always known he would make my sister a bad husband, yet for my own selfish motives I had set her on a course headed inevitably for disaster. It was useless to tell myself that I couldn't have prevented the marriage. I could easily have done so. If I had made enough noise Steve would have been sufficiently embarrassed to back away. It was useless too to tell myself it was hardly my fault that Steve had chosen to marry Emily. It was. He had thought of her merely as an angel, beautiful, perfect but sexless, and in order to view her realistically he had needed my information that she was capable of passion.

My sister was suffering, and I was just as responsible as Steve with his fool's passion for Dinah Slade. I could no longer decide whether my contempt for him was greater than my hatred. To have an affair with Miss Slade when he had thought she was no more than a good-time party girl was bad enough, but it was a mistake many other men might have made and Steve had redeemed the error by cutting himself loose from her. But to have an affair with Miss Slade when he knew she had enough ambition to castrate him had to border on certifiable insanity.

Yet I did not believe Steve was insane. The hackles rose on the back of my neck. I always knew when I was in danger, and suddenly I saw the pattern of the recent past, my emergence from the shadows of scandal, my unflagging hard work at the bank, my enhanced prestige among my partners, and I knew that it was a pattern Steve could no longer tolerate. He had decided to pursue his European base of power again, and with the knowledge that we no longer had to work harmoniously in New York, Emily had become redundant. He no longer needed someone who would pour oil on troubled waters. He needed someone who would help him beat me to pulp, and so he had turned back inevitably to my natural enemy, Miss Slade.

One could take the romantic point of view and argue that he was in the grip of a grand passion for Miss Slade, but I could not believe that Steve, who was a hardheaded down-to-earth man, could lapse into a starry-eyed fever of passion over the equally hardheaded and down-to-earth Miss Slade. I thought it more probable that they regarded each other as tough able exciting allies who as a bonus could enjoy a satisfying sexual relationship.

Meanwhile my sister, wronged and crushed, had been abandoned in Paris, and there was nothing I could do but tell her to come home. I could not call Steve and shout abuse at him; I did not know his address. I could not cable him in care of the London office and order him home; as joint senior partner he could legitimately tell me I was getting too big for my boots. I could not go whining to my partners that Steve had treated my sister abominably; they would be sympathetic but they would consider it none of their business, for it was an unwritten rule, as I had discovered myself during my affair with Alicia, that a discussion of unpleasant personal affairs had no place at One Willow Street. Nor could I demand that my partners fire Steve; he was much too valuable to the firm, and if he now chose to build up Van Zale's in Europe and leave Lewis as sole senior partner in New York, no one except me was going to argue with him.

Lewis in particular would be thrilled to have the whole of Paul's office to himself again. I was going to have to do something about Lewis. He really had become very tiresome. . . .

My secretary tapped on the door and looked in. "Mr. Van Zale, you haven't forgotten your doctor's appointment, have you?"

I had. I was tempted to cancel it, but I was afraid that might upset Alicia. "I'll leave right away," I said, and five minutes later I was traveling uptown to the specialist's office.

III

We had been trying for well over a year to have children. Alicia had gone to her gynecologist after the first four months, but he had merely told her that many couples took longer to conceive a baby, and it was not until she returned to him eight months later that he had taken her case seriously. She had undergone various tests, and when she had emerged with a clean bill of health I had volunteered to undergo an examination myself. I knew it would make her feel better if I made some demonstration of my willingness to solve the problem, but personally I suspected that the difficulty lay in her mounting anxiety. I had once read that conception is unlikely if a woman is too tense, and I had already decided that if there was still no prospect of a baby in December I would take her on another of our Caribbean cruises.

I did not consult old Dr. Wilkins. I knew he thought I was a hopeless hypochondriac and I felt uncomfortable about asking him for an examination when I had never felt healthier in my life. Instead I called Alicia's gynecologist, and it was he who recommended Dr. Glassman to me.

My Cadillac arrived at his Park Avenue office. When I was shown inside I found myself in a waiting room with flowers by the window and magazines arranged on an antique table, but although I picked up a copy of *Time* I could not read it. I was still thinking too hard about Emily.

"Would you come this way, please, Mr. Van Zale?"

I followed the receptionist obediently into the room where Dr. Glassman was waiting. He was much younger than I had anticipated. He had some light brown hair, thinning on top, dark eyes and a freckled nose. His wholesome straightforward air appealed to me.

"Mr. Van Zale? Please sit down." We shook hands and I tried to forget Emily by taking note of my surroundings. The room was large, with a high ceiling. Venetian blinds were slanted against the sunlight, which fell in broken patterns on the gold carpet. There were rows of dark books on shelves, a potted plant entwined in a wrought-iron stand and some tranquil watercolors dotted around the walls. Recognizing a picture of the Eiffel Tower, I started to think of Emily again.

". . . Mr. Van Zale?" concluded Dr. Glassman.

I recalled my thoughts with an effort. "Pardon me, what did you say?"

"I was asking you for a general statement of the problem."

"Oh, yes. Of course. Well, my wife and I have been married for some time and . . ." My voice recounted the facts effortlessly. I was trying to imagine how Emily could cope with Steve's sons as well as her own two infant daughters. Perhaps Steve had taken the boys with him. I had forgotten to ask.

"How old is your daughter now?" asked Dr. Glassman, jotting down notes.

"She was born on Christmas Eve, 1930, so she's going to be three in December."

"That's a nice age!" He smiled at me as he took a fresh sheet of paper and began to ask questions about Alicia.

". . . so when the doctor said there was nothing wrong with her I offered to make sure there was nothing wrong with me," I concluded, trying unsuccessfully to read his handwriting.

"Sure, much the smartest thing to do."

He was kind. Afterward I always remembered how kind he was. I was glad I had gone to him and not to old Wilkins.

"All right, Mr. Van Zale, I think I have a general picture of the background. Now I'd like to ask you a few routine medical questions just to eliminate certain possibilities." He took yet another fresh sheet of paper. He picked up his pen again. Then, glancing at me with his kind concerned dark eyes, he asked, "Have you ever had mumps?"

IV

I was outside in the street. The sky was a steaming hazy blue and the dust from the Park Avenue traffic swirled in the thick stifling air. My chauffeur was holding the car door wide, my bodyguards were beside me, my chief aide was waiting patiently in the front seat. I stared at them, at the trappings of my wealth and privilege and power, and was struck dumb by their irrelevance. It took me a full ten seconds to tell them to go home, and when they looked at me without understanding I had no words to explain. How could I tell them that I was no longer different? My conception of myself had changed. "Have you never asked yourself who you really are?" Sam had said to me, and now when I asked myself that same question I knew at once who I was. I was one of millions of Americans suffering in the Great Depression; I was destitute, with my most cherished dreams destroyed.

I walked away from my servants down Park Avenue, and when my senior bodyguard tried to follow me I had to tell him again to go home. He fell back. I walked on. I was alone at last, but people kept battering themselves against my solitude until I had no defenses left to protect me from the hideous seething horror of that city. There was a panhandler on every block. I walked down one of the richest streets in New York and the beggars came out to meet me with their clutching hands and crafty eyes and beaten ruined faces.

"Mister, can you spare a dime?" The voices haunted me. I had never heard them before. My bodyguards had always pushed the beggars away before they could bother me, and I had lived a life of ignorance at my palace at Willow and Wall.

I gave away all my loose change and turned east. Above me towered the shining spire of the Chrysler Building, but I did not look up. I looked ahead and saw only the fetid sweating streets and in the distance on Third Avenue the dark knotted girders of the El.

On Lexington I headed south again, and the swirling dust made me choke until I felt as if I had been disgorged in some macabre shipwreck and was being pounded to death on an asphalt beach. When the beggars accosted me once more I gave away my paper money—I had about twenty dollars—and then I gave away my watch too and my jacket and silk tie and last the gold cufflinks I had inherited from Paul.

My shirt was sticking to my back, and as I paused to roll up the sleeves I found I'd lost my bearings. Then I realized Lexington Avenue had ended and I was somewhere north of Washington Square. Blundering into Third Avenue, I walked downtown for some time, but I was still so disoriented that when I stopped to wipe the sweat from my forehead I again forgot where I was. I looked up at the street sign on the nearest corner. The notorious Dutch name, long since corrupted by English-speaking tongues, stared back at me.

I walked on into the Bowery.

Black rotted buildings full of unimaginable vermin rose on either side of me. The stench permeated the air, the stench of garbage and worse, the stench of disease and decay and despair. I had to stop again to wipe the sweat from my forehead, and suddenly the prostitutes of both sexes were accosting me and I saw the smashed bottles in the gutter and the drunks in every doorway and the shabby senseless bodies strewn on the stinking sidewalk.

Nobody believed me when I said I had no money. I saw the violence shimmering behind their eyes and I started to run, heading blindly west, but long before I reached Broadway I had to stop for breath. I leaned against a wall as I tried to control my breathing, but when my vision cleared I shrank at once into the nearest doorway. Ahead of me on the dark dingy street about forty derelicts were clustered around the barred doorway of a restaurant. Fortunately they had their backs to me, but since I had learned that it was foolish to call attention to myself I waited in my doorway in the hope that they would disperse. My heart was still thumping in my chest when I found out why they were waiting. The restaurant door was unlocked and a man emerged carrying a can of garbage. I never saw what happened to the man; I assume he beat a hasty retreat. But I saw what happened to the garbage.

The can was instantly upturned. The derelicts pawed through the bones and vegetable scraps, and in a second fighting had broken out for the choicest pieces.

A window above my head was flung open as someone leaned out to investigate the noise, but although I heard the radio playing faintly in the background I paid no attention to it. It was only when the volume of the radio was turned up to drown the noise in the street that I recognized the tune which was being played.

It was *Alexander's Ragtime Band.*

I leaned my burning forehead against the wall, and as the world grew dim before my eyes I grieved for America, for great golden glamorous America, careering through the glittering twenties as if there were no limit to its fabulous wealth and no end to the fairytale dreams which all came true. The tears streaked my cheeks. I watched the derelicts fighting over the garbage in the most spectacular city on earth, and I asked the unanswerable question of the millions who had suffered in the Depression, and the question was always why, why did this have to happen to us, what did we do, was there anything we should have done? And I felt the helplessness of people in the grip of forces beyond their control, the despair of those compelled to stand by in impotence as their lives were wrenched out of shape, and the frustration of those who believed there was no recourse, no hope and no cure.

The derelicts drifted away. I picked my way over the wreckage on the sidewalk, sidestepped two bodies and again began to run downtown.

I found Broadway at last and ahead of me was the graveyard of Trinity Church. It occurred to me that the traffic was light and I realized most people had gone home from work. I went into the church, but there was no message for me there so I left, stumbling down the Street past Morgan's to the corner of Willow and Wall.

The night watchman hardly recognized me. I pushed past, fobbing off his anxious inquiries, and hoped no one was working late. I could see no one, speak to no one. I felt mutilated.

In the sanctuary of my office I paused only until my breathing was under control and then I crept downstairs to raid Lewis' liquor cabinet.

I was crying quietly all the time, and when I entered the room and glanced at my reflection in the mirror I saw for a terrifying second a stranger I did not know. Screwing up my eyes, I pressed a hand against my forehead, and in the quiet pounding darkness which followed I felt Paul's presence in the room where he had died.

I opened my eyes, but of course there was nothing to see. I glanced back into the mirror but saw only my familiar face, dirty and tear-stained. I spun round, but I was alone.

Clenching my fists, I moved to the liquor cabinet concealed behind the bookshelves and poured myself half a tumbler of brandy.

When the brandy was gone I called Alicia.

"Cornelius, are you all right?" she said at once. "When you were late I called the office but they said you never came back after the doctor's appointment. Where are you now?"

"At the bank. I'm fine, just fine. Sorry I didn't call. I'm so sorry, Alicia," I said and started to cry soundlessly again. "So sorry."

"Shall I send a car down to you? Carter and Foster were really concerned when you sent them home. Are you sure you're all right?"

I dashed the tears from my eyes and bent forward over the phone. "I have a little work to do," I said. "Don't delay dinner. Don't send anyone. Don't worry. I'm all right. Just a little work to do. . . . So sorry, Alicia."

"All right, but don't work too hard—come home soon, darling," she said, blowing a kiss into the phone. "I'll be waiting for you."

I could not speak. I heard her hang up. Several more seconds passed before I replaced the receiver.

I was beyond tears now, but that only made me feel worse, and although I knew I had to do something to take my mind off my pain I felt incapable of action. I had squeezed my eyes shut again before I realized with a shock that I was trying to recall Paul's presence.

I poured myself some more brandy.

Paul would have understood. He had had only one daughter. That was why I had been frightened by our parallel lives, but now that the parallels had all been drawn and I had nothing else to fear perhaps I could embrace his life with relief. It would be a release, an alternative to my ruined dreams. I would become Paul. No sons. Just one daughter.

I remembered Alan Slade.

Immediately I was amazed by my previous naïveté, for of course, as I now realized, it was impossible that he could be Paul's son. It was hard to imagine Paul being deceived, but as Steve had once said, nothing was impossible to Dinah Slade. She had deceived Paul. I could probably prove it if I tried hard enough. I would try. That was the obvious thing to do. It was the project I needed to divert myself from the fact that Alicia and I—

My mind snapped shut. I stood up, knocking over my empty brandy glass, and paced around the room. I felt lightheaded, but the pain was growing duller as my mind became absorbed in this new challenge. I wondered where to begin my investigations. There was no clue in the Diana Slade Cosmetics file; I had read the correspondence there long ago and knew that the letters related only to business matters. There must once have been a file on Miss Slade, but all Paul's correspondence with various women had been destroyed after his death. Yet somewhere there had to be the evidence I wanted, and somehow I was going to find it.

Energy seized me. As I moved more quickly about the room I picked things up and put them down again as if I were a clockwork toy wound up to an unbearable pitch of tension. I did not dare stop in case I started to think about Dr. Glassman, the quiet office, the clean white bare examination room, the terrible sight of that marred seminal fluid on the slide beneath the microscope. Mumps. A kid's disease. So stupid, so unnecessary.

I burned out the memory and focused on my project. Mayers had destroyed the love-letter files in the vaults, but I must take nothing for granted. Miss Slade was no ordinary lover, and it was unlikely that Paul would have kept her correspondence in the vaults as if it were a dead file. I paused to calculate the size of the correspondence. He had left her in November 1922 and she had arrived in New York in April 1926, so one could assume they had corresponded for at least three years. If I assumed too that they had written once a month, that meant a file of about forty letters—eighty, since Paul always kept a copy of each letter he dictated. There would also be the photographs; I knew Miss Slade's technique by this time. Eighty letters and God knows how many pictures. Quite a file.

Picking up the phone, I called Sylvia. I felt better now that I had something positive to do. The phone rang, a maid answered and a minute later Sylvia was asking me how I was.

When the necessary courtesies were finished I said, "Sylvia, I have a crazy question to ask you. When you sorted out the library after Paul's death, did you ever come across any letters from Dinah Slade?"

"Heavens, no! Paul would never have kept letters like that at home, Cornelius. The letters in the library were family letters he had kept for sentimental reasons—there were some from his mother and from his sister and from your mother too, of course. But I'll tell you one odd thing which to this day is an unsolved mystery: his correspondence with Vicky was never found, and I know for a fact that he kept every single letter she ever wrote him."

"Are you sure he kept them at home?"

"He did at first, because after she died he made a sort of scrapbook of all her mementos—I found him working on it one evening, and I'm afraid I let him know that I thought he was being unnecessarily morbid. We never discussed the subject again, and later when the correspondence failed to turn up I did wonder if he had removed it to the office. I even wondered if Mayers had burned the file, but that's highly unlikely because he would never have destroyed Vicky's letters without permission from the family."

"Hm." I thought for a moment. "Did you discuss this with anyone?"

"Yes, I asked Steve to make a special search at the office and I asked Elizabeth if she knew what might have happened. I thought your mother might have liked the letters if they were still in existence, because she had been so fond of Vicky."

We dwelt on the mystery for a minute longer, and then after thanking her I hung up.

I had to find Elizabeth Clayton's number in the phone book before I lifted the receiver again to place the call.

"Cornelius?" she said doubtfully after the butler had called her to the phone. Elizabeth and I had never cared for each other; Bruce's role in the conspiracy had made it impossible for me to be more than civil to her, but even before Paul's death I had thought her cold and snobbish.

"Yes, Mrs. Clayton," I said politely. "Good evening. I wonder if you can help me. I'm trying to trace a section of Paul's private correspondence which I suspect still exists even though Mayers destroyed so many of those files after the assassination. Do you by any chance happen to know where—"

"You're not looking for Dinah Slade's file, are you?" she said at once.

I was so surprised that it took me a moment before I could say neutrally: "Why should you think that?"

"Steve was looking for it once, but he told me later he never found it. If I were you I wouldn't waste time looking for it, Cornelius. I'm sure one of the first files Mayers destroyed would have been the correspondence between Catullus and his Lesbia."

"Pardon me?"

"Oh, you didn't know? That's how they used to address each other in their private correspondence. Paul showed me some of the early letters—they were classical quizzes and really quite droll."

"Mrs. Clayton," I said, taking a deep breath, "did Paul and Vicky also have classical names for each other when they corresponded?"

There was a pause. "Why, yes," said Elizabeth, surprised. "I'd quite forgotten, but yes, you're right, they did. In his letters he always addressed her as Tullia and signed himself 'MTC.' "

" 'MTC'?"

"Marcus Tullius Cicero. Tullia was Cicero's much beloved daughter."

"Yes, of course. Thank you, Mrs. Clayton," I said, and severed the connection.

With the appropriate keys I dashed down to the vaults. I looked under Marcus, under Tullius or Tullia, under Cicero, under Catullus and under Lesbia, but found nothing. Yet I felt sure I was on the trail.

I checked the business files upstairs. Still nothing. Deciding I needed another drink to boost my flagging spirits, I trailed back to Paul's office and once more touched the spring to open the concealed bar.

The bookcase swung toward me. Paul's books, kept in memory of him and untouched since his death, stared me in the eye.

"My God!" I said. I forgot the drink. I stepped back and looked at the bookcases which stretched from floor to ceiling on either side of the fireplace.

It took me some minutes to find them, because I started at the top and they were on the bottom shelf, but eventually I saw the twin volumes standing side by side.

One supposedly contained the letters of Cicero and the other the poetry of Catullus.

I smiled, and feeling irrationally excited by my discovery, I pulled the long-lost files lovingly into my arms.

Chapter Eight

I

The files were large boxes with spines covered with red leather and labeled with gilt lettering. The width of the spines betrayed that the boxes were not books. All the volumes I had seen of the works of Cicero and Catullus had been mercifully slim.

Caressing the Catullus file, I savored the prospect of a detailed analysis of Miss Slade's machinations, but postponing the pleasure I first opened the file containing Paul's correspondence with Vicky. I had no intention of giving it more than a passing glance, but I was immediately struck by the atmosphere within. Unlike a normal file, where the most recent letter lay at the top, this file began with Vicky's first letter and proceeded steadily through the years to her last. The material was arranged with exquisite attention to detail; there were photographs mounted on thick black paper and labeled in white ink; there were press clippings, each one trimmed and mounted like the photographs; there was even the program for the ball Paul had given Vicky on her coming out. It was the record of a life, Paul's private memorial to his daughter, and when I saw the time and trouble he must have lavished on the project I was moved.

Without a second thought I started to read.

After ten minutes I realized I was deeply bewildered, so I stopped. Vicky's correspondent was a stranger to me. This man wrote sugary romantic prose laden with preposterous sentiment. This man couldn't be Paul.

Incredulously I checked the signature on his letters, but I saw only the initials "MTC" which Elizabeth Clayton had already identified. With increasing discomfort I read on. Vicky sounded very bright and gay, but Paul could only ramble on about Prince Charming, True Love, Happy Endings and how he had wanted Vicky to have them all. I could not understand why he had encouraged Vicky to hold such unreal expectations of life. I could not understand how he had allowed himself to palm off such sentimental romantic junk on his daughter.

I could not understand.

Greatly disturbed, I poured myself another brandy. Later I remembered I hadn't finished the file, so I glanced through to the end and read the notice of her death. Again I was moved. After reading her happy letters I was aware of a bereavement I had never experienced at her funeral, and I felt that at last, years after her death, I had truly come to know her.

I tried to stop myself from wondering if I had ever truly known Paul, and in an effort to block the thought from my mind I took the Catullus file and walked out of the building into Willow Street.

I made no effort to open the file in the cab. My mind was too full of memories, and when I arrived home I thought not of Miss Slade but of Alicia.

Sending my aide out to pay the cab driver, I tried to cross the hall but my nerve failed me. I slipped upstairs instead, groped my way to my room and sat numbly on the edge of my bed in the darkness.

She found me twenty minutes later. I heard the tap on the panel and saw the light from the hallway as she opened the door.

"Cornelius?"

I turned on the bedside light. The glare hurt my eyes. I was still shielding them when she sat down beside me.

We were silent, but when I summoned the courage to look at her I saw at once that she knew.

She was wearing a pale-green silk dress, and her dark hair was swept up smoothly above her ears. She wore diamond earrings but no other jewelry, and when I saw how pale she was I felt sorry for her. Poor Alicia, trying to think of the best thing to say, trying to cope with a truth too intolerable to face, mumps, just a kid's disease, so stupid, so unnecessary.

"How did you know?" I said. My voice sounded casual, almost careless, and my hands were steady as I rested them on my knees.

"I saw Dr. Wilkins a month ago." Her monotone was steady too but quiet, barely more than a whisper. "I was suspicious. I remembered that horrible complication when you had mumps, and after my doctor told me there was no reason why I shouldn't have more children I called Dr. Wilkins for an appointment. He told me that without giving you a physical examination he couldn't be sure, but he said there was a strong possibility you were—that you couldn't have more children, because both . . . because everything had been affected. He said that even so you'd been very unlucky because you might still have suffered no permanent damage if the orchitis had been less severe."

The medical term seemed as pristine and clinical as the walls of Dr. Glassman's examination room. I felt detached, as if she were talking about some unfortunate case history which had no connection with me.

"I told Dr. Wilkins I didn't understand," she said. "I said nothing seemed to be wrong, quite the reverse—imagine me saying that to Dr. Wilkins! But I didn't feel embarrassed, because he was so nice—and kind too, I never thought Dr. Wilkins could be that kind. He started talking about ducts blocked by fibrous tissue and I felt so stupid because I still didn't understand. I said there was always fluid and he said yes, but it would be empty, because nothing—or not enough of anything—could get through the ducts. It was all so difficult to understand because I've never been any good at anatomy, I'm not even sure what goes on in my own body. Isn't it strange how you live with your body year after year and never really know how it works?"

All I could say was, "You've known for a whole month?"

"No, I didn't know because Dr. Wilkins said he couldn't be sure. I did wonder if I should tell you what he'd said but you had already volunteered to have an examination and so I decided to say nothing just in case everything was all right. Besides, I didn't really believe it could have happened. I suspected, but I couldn't believe."

"I've always suspected too," I said, "but I couldn't believe it either. The physical appearance didn't bother me; I told myself it was irrelevant since we didn't have any sexual problems, but there were recurring symptoms which I never told you about—occasionally I still get that same goddamned pain. Several times I almost stopped at the Forty-second Street Library on the way home from work so that I could look up mumps in a medical dictionary, but I never did. It was so much easier to tell myself I was fit and that nothing could possibly be wrong."

It was so difficult to say what had to be said next that I stopped. We sat together on the edge of the bed, not touching each other, and the silence lengthened.

Finally I said without looking at her, "I know how much you want more children. I know how much it means to you. I want you to be happy. If you think you could be happier with someone else, of course I shall quite understand."

She never hesitated. To my dying day I shall always remember how she never even paused to draw breath.

"I wanted *your* children, Cornelius," she said. "No one else's. I could never be happy with anyone but you, and besides . . . don't you really remember those promises I made to you when we got married?"

I could not speak, but as I reached out to her blindly she reached out to me and the gesture we had first made long ago at Sylvia's party was repeated. Once more our hands clasped and interlocked, and once more our lives streamed forward together in their single irreversible tide.

II

I am not a romantic. I loved Alicia and could not imagine living without her, but I was unsentimental about marriage and knew that it was only on the silver screen that the hero and heroine walked away into the sunset to live happily ever after in a problem-free paradise. Therefore when I tried and failed to make love to Alicia I accepted the disaster stoically and waited till she was asleep before padding downstairs. On the hall table the Catullus file lay like an opiate to offer me an escape into another world, and closing the door of the library I sat down at Paul's desk.

At once I felt his presence again. I hesitated, and although there was nothing to hear or see I felt stifled. I went to the window, but the catch had jammed and as I wrestled with it in panic I felt exactly as if a prison door had slammed shut behind me.

I paused, sweating, and from the photograph frame on the desk Paul's eyes met mine. I knew then what had happened. Paul's life was mine at last. I had broken down the door into the past, but instead of finding a psychic escape into limitless freedom I had found only a dead end. I was not liberated by Paul's personality but imprisoned by it, and when I remembered Sylvia talking of the demons who had died with him I knew they were resurrected in my own body.

I thought sickeningly of Bar Harbor, of Paul talking about his impotence, feeling less of a man because of his epilepsy, turning away from his wife who knew the truth and proving himself at last with another woman.

I twisted frantically in my prison. I no longer wanted to prove that Alan Slade was no relation of mine. I wanted to prove Paul had had a son, I had to prove he was different from me after all, I had to know that there was a point when our parallel lives diverged.

I ripped open the Catullus file.

I saw the envelope at once. It was marked simply "Dinah," and the absence of an address suggested he had planned to deliver it by hand. I was about to break the seal when I saw the photographs, and putting the envelope aside I carefully followed Master Alan Slade from extreme infancy to the age of three.

He was fair-haired and his eyes were probably dark, though it was hard to be sure. He had a small pert bright face, but although I could see no resemblance to Paul I was sure, as I examined the last pictures of the two of them playing together on a beach, that he was Paul's son. Paul would hardly have been holding the child so affectionately if there had been any doubt in his mind.

Paul had always been so undemonstrative. I knew that better than anyone else.

Pushing aside the photographs clumsily, I turned to the earliest correspondence and soon found the classical quizzes which Elizabeth had described.

"What did Pythagoras and the Druids have in common?"

"Elementary, my dear Catullus. They both believed in the transmigration of souls (for Druids see Caesar's 'De Bello Gallico')."

"Who was brought to trial for stealing a Sicilian cheese?"

"Someone in one of those bawdy concoctions of Aristophanes. 'The Frogs'?"

" 'The Wasps,' my dear Lesbia, 'The Wasps.' . . ."

Flicking through the quotations and allusions, I came across more photographs and found myself in an alien land. There was a lake, rather reedy, a sloping lawn, the glimpse of a sailboat. Another picture showed a windmill standing by a narrow canal, and the sails of the mill were dark against a pale sky. I was in England, in the county of Norfolk, and when I saw the next photograph I knew I was at Mallingham.

I was staring at pebbled walls, a dark mossy thatched roof and long slim windows. Ivy grew around the front door, and the untidiness offended me. I turned back to the correspondence.

A quarter of an hour later I was still reading. It was an entertaining correspondence, witty, bright and studiously devoid of any awkward emotion. Paul had shown his usual skill at keeping her at arm's length—until he had decided he wanted to see her. His letter tempting her to America was a masterpiece of romantic nonsense, but Miss Slade had fallen for it and said yes, she would certainly visit him in New York. The next letters were concerned with details of travel arrangements, and the last, written by Miss Slade, said she was very much looking forward to seeing him again.

Evidently there had been no correspondence between them once she had arrived in America; the phone and their frequent meetings had sufficed. It occurred to me to wonder what had happened to all the photographs he had undoubtedly taken of her. I realized he might have destroyed them in an attempt to forget her at the end of 1922, but I thought it would have been only human nature for him to keep one. I was just stacking the quizzes which I had not bothered to finish when something fluttered past me to the floor.

I was face to face with her at last. It was extraordinary how commonplace she looked. Her dark hair was disheveled and her dark eyes looked surprised, as if the camera had caught her unawares. Beneath her large nose her wide mouth was smiling as if she were a schoolgirl who had escaped from some convent and was reveling in her unfamiliar freedom.

I was about to prop the photograph against the inkwell when I saw the envelope marked "DINAH" again, and this time I broke the seal.

"My darling . . ."

I stopped and checked the other letters. They all began "My dear Lesbia." I glanced at the date at the top of the page. July the twentieth, 1926. Paul had apparently planned to deliver this last message in person but for some reason the letter had been filed instead, possibly only minutes before he was killed.

My darling,

I couldn't sleep when I got home, so I decided to write this letter to give to you on board ship. But if you keep the promise I shall extract from you, you won't be reading this until your ship is steaming out to sea and then you'll know that this letter isn't a mere cheap ruse to keep you in America.

All I wish is for you to believe what I told you tonight. I love you. I'll marry you. I'll do anything you want. . . .

I stopped reading again. It took me a full minute before I could nerve myself to continue.

I do love Sylvia and I shall always be in her debt, but all I want is to spend the rest of my life with you at Mallingham. I know for years I've tried not to face the truth, but I have neither the strength nor the will to fight it any longer, and the truth is, of course, that we were meant for each other . . .

I stopped a third time. I felt sickened by the cloying clichés, physically ill. I turned the page with a trembling hand.

. . . and could make each other happy. I know you want more children, but I doubt if I have long to live and once you're a widow you'll still be young enough to increase your family with someone who can't transmit any sickness to your children. You see? Even now I can still scrape together a little cool common sense! But now I know my cynical pragmatism is useless to me and my deliberate detachment from others has led me into an emotional desert. I want my true self back again, Dinah, and only you can restore it—my youth, my faith, all my old ideals . . .

I was overcome with shame for him, horribly embarrassed. An old man sinking into his dotage, talking nonsense, crying for his lost youth. . . . It was repulsive.

. . . so I shall retire from the New York office, and whether you accept me or not I shall settle in England. I want to see Alan grow up. How nice it would be if he became an Oxford don! Now at last I can understand why my mother wanted me to enter academic life and how horrified she was when I was drawn into banking. I don't want Alan to follow in my footsteps. I want him to be happy, and I know he'd be better off without the burden of my wealth and position. Only a young man like Cornelius can shoulder a burden like that without being crushed by it, and I don't want Alan to grow up like Cornelius.

Everything stopped. Slowly the world which had revolved around Paul for as long as I could remember began to disintegrate. An era came quietly to an end and keeled forward into an open grave.

I turned the page.

I feel guilty about Cornelius [my great-uncle had written with his characteristic emotional detachment]. He works hard, he hero-worships me, he's well-behaved, civil and obedient—yet I remain lukewarm. Ironically I suspect that this unadulterated loyalty which I should find so flattering is in fact symptomatic of the fatal flaw in his personality. He would indeed be loyal to me under any circumstances—no scruple would deter him, no law would stand in his way, no social tradition would carry any weight with him whatsoever. Despite my immoralities, which I admit are considerable, I have always had a very keen sense of right and wrong and have suffered accordingly from guilt. But no such suffering will trouble Cornelius because he has no true concept of right and wrong. He's not immoral but amoral, and try as I will I can't think of him as a son.

In fact if the truth be told, he's very much the son of his father, a tough ruthless little man who despite his fanatical churchgoing habits was quite one of the most un-Christian men I've ever met. However, I have to admit he was devoted to Mildred and mild as a lamb in her presence. Strange how these mavericks who can conduct business so unscrupulously are often devoted family men—and I shall look forward to proving the validity of that observation if you'll only allow me to live with you again at Mallingham!

My darling, take your time to think about what I've said and do not, as you did tonight, reject me out of hand. I know the discovery of my illness must have been a great shock to you, but I can't believe you don't still love me when I love you so much. Remember—I'd give up the world for you.

All my love, darling, now and always,
PAUL

It was the only letter he had written by hand and the only letter he had not signed "Catullus."

I sat looking at his signature for a long time.

After a while I got up and began to walk up and down the room. My mind was confused, my thoughts disjointed. I felt as if someone had died.

A long time later—I'm not sure when it was—I realized I was looking through the photographs again. I searched and searched, not knowing what I was looking for, and then I saw *her* face and I took the picture in my hands and I got up again and began to walk up and down, up and down, and all the time I looked at her face and after a while I realized what I had at heart always known, that she was a destroyer, that she had destroyed my respect for Paul, destroyed my sister's marriage, destroyed all my hopes of coexisting amicably with Steve. She would destroy the bank too if she acquired too much power, I could see that clearly, and more clearly still I could see she wanted to destroy me because I was the one man who would always stand in her way.

Sweeping the photos into the file, I tried to close the lid, but the hasp refused to fasten. Something was jammed against the spine, and when I had pulled out the quizzes I found that a long brown envelope had wedged itself at a contorted angle to prevent the lid from lying flat.

I glanced carelessly inside and saw some kind of document. All legal papers have the same smell, but this document was different from the normal legal brief. This document had a foreign picturesque appearance.

After some time spent deciphering the archaic language I deduced that in the summer of 1922 that part and parcel of land known as Mallingham Hall in the parish of Mallingham in the county of Norfolk had been conveyed by certain people acting on behalf of Master Percy Slade to Mr. Paul Cornelius Van Zale, banker, of Number Six Milk Street in the City of London for the sum of four thousand five hundred pounds.

I checked the envelope for the inevitable papers relating to the conveyance later to Miss Slade, but the envelope was empty. I reexamined every item in the file, but there were no other legal papers and no reference to the ownership of Mallingham. Absent-mindedly I wandered to the cabinet where I kept my various private papers, extracted my copy of Paul's will and read it from end to end.

I sat thinking, idly fanning myself with the will as I reconstructed the past. He had bought the place for her when she was broke, and he had obviously planned to give it back to her, but she had skillfully used his ownership of her property to keep all his sentimental memories alive. However, since he had omitted Mallingham from his new will in 1926 he must have been on the verge of conveying the property to her at the time of his death.

That explained why Steve had been chasing the file; I could well imagine an agitated Miss Slade exhorting him to find the conveyance which betrayed that Paul was the owner of her home. What I still failed to understand was why my lawyers had treated Mallingham as if it didn't exist, but then I saw that the issue had remained submerged because all the relevant documents had been suppressed. The Van Zale lawyers in London would have the correspondence relating to the 1922 sale, but the deeds would have been handed over to Paul, and no doubt when Miss Slade had continued to live at Mallingham before and after his death the London lawyers had assumed he had conveyed the property to her through some other legal channel. Meanwhile the lawyers in New York either were ignorant of the transaction or else had wrongly believed that Paul had already divested himself of the estate through a conveyance involving the London lawyers. It would have been the obvious assumption to make when no deeds relating to Mallingham were found among Paul's papers. In fact, on further reflection I thought it was hardly surprising that the paltry little manor house, so insignificant in comparison with the rest of Paul's real estate, should have been lost in the testamentary shuffle.

There were no prizes for guessing who had the rest of the documents—and who had suppressed them. I wondered why she had never approached me, laid her cards on the table and offered to buy the place for herself. It was almost as if she had known I would have seized the chance to pay back some of Sylvia's suffering with interest, almost as if she had known we were to end up not merely rivals but enemies, but that was fanciful. Back in 1926 no one could have known that. Yet it was almost as if someone had warned her against me. I couldn't for the life of me figure out why she had avoided me like the plague, but there was no denying she had never communicated with me, and now there she was, still living at Mallingham, still acting as if she owned it, still demonstrating that possession was nine tenths of the law.

I made a mental note to get my lawyer to check the statute of limitations, though I didn't see how any such statute could run in her favor while she was deliberately concealing the true facts of the case from the legal owner. However, there was no doubt that she had decided she could well afford to play a waiting game.

And so could I.

I smiled. It was two o'clock in the morning, but my talent for long-range planning was in full flower. Mallingham had never previously been of any significance to me, but now I saw that it had become exactly the weapon I needed. I would use my ownership of Mallingham to destroy the destroyer. Nothing could be neater. And nothing could be more satisfying.

However, it was important to get my priorities right, because that was always the key to successful long-range planning. First Lewis and absolute control of the bank in New York. Then Steve. The London office was ultimately subject to the headquarters at Willow and

Wall, and once the New York office was under my thumb he would find himself outflanked. And then . . .

I picked up the photograph of Miss Slade. The dark eyes, still luminous with surprise, stared at me as if making some private challenge, and the wide smile prompted me to smile wryly in return.

"Someday, Dinah," I whispered softly to her. "Someday . . ."

PART SIX

Dinah Winning

1933–1940

Chapter One

I

Steve telephoned in the early evening. I was in the bedroom of my new house in Chesterfield Street, which I had bought following the twins' birth when we had overflowed my *pied-à-terre* in Eden Mews. I liked living in Mayfair. I could stroll to work across Berkeley Square, and the park was so convenient for Nanny. My house was only a stone's throw from the Curzon Street house which Paul had rented in the summer of '22.

I was filing my nails, listening to Reginald King and his orchestra on the wireless and wondering if I had reminded Cedric to harangue the salesmen about the special properties of the new facial mask. My memory was not as good as it had once been. I wondered whether to blame advancing age, too many cocktails or the increasing number of details which required my attention at the office, and I was just deciding that it was once more time to delegate authority to my subordinates when the telephone rang.

I did wait for Wetherby to answer it, but deciding the caller was Geoffrey, I picked up the receiver of the extension by my bed.

"Hullo?"

"Hello, Dinah," said Steve. "Guess who?"

"Oh, Lord," I said, "I can't bear parlor games before dinner. What a clear line this is! You sound as if you're just down the road."

"I am," he said. "I'm back at the Ritz."

"Good God!" Belatedly I realized that no international operator had heralded his appearance. "Why didn't you let me know when we spoke last week that you'd be coming to London? How long are you here for? Is Emily with you?"

"No, she's in Paris. I've left her."

"You've *what!* My God, you American bankers are a barbarous crowd! Haven't you any idea how to treat women beyond sleeping with them, getting them pregnant and leaving them in the lurch? It's so beastly immoral! Honestly, I think it's time someone spoke out in defense of the women you, Paul and Cornelius seduce and abandon!"

"Hell, Dinah, there are two sides to everything—"

"Yes, and I'd like to hear Emily's! I've a damned good mind to ring her up and ask her to stay!"

"Oh, for Christ's sake!"

"All right, you monster, I suppose you want me to hold your hand while you sob on my shoulder. Look, can I phone you back later? I'm just going out to dinner."

"Who with?" he said at once. "Anyone I know?"

"Yes, Geoffrey Hurst."

"Oh, old Geoffrey!" He made no effort to disguise his relief. "How's he doing these days?"

"Very badly," I said coldly. "His wife was killed last month in a car accident. I'm helping him recover from the shock."

There was a brooding silence. At last he had the decency to say, "I'm sorry to hear that. Please give Geoffrey my sympathy. Listen, Dinah—"

"I really must go now, Steve."

"But wait a minute!" he shouted. "How are the kids? Are they with you in town? Can I stop by later tonight to see them?"

"The twins," I said, "are at Mallingham. 'Bye, darling." And I slammed down the receiver.

I was shaking from head to toe. For a minute I walked up and down muttering, "Damn him! Damn him!" and then I pulled myself together, clambered into my latest silk negligée and headed downstairs for the stiffest of whisky-and-sodas.

II

I did not tell Geoffrey that Steve was back in London. I considered he had enough problems of his own, but before we had finished our dinner at Boulestin's he twice asked me to tell him what was wrong. I declined. On our return to Chesterfield Street I guiltily invited him in for a nightcap, but now it was his turn to decline. He was tired, he had had a long day, tomorrow promised to be unusually busy . . . The well-worn excuses slid courteously off his tongue, but I knew he was hurt that I had refused to confide in him.

I was just watching his Armstrong Siddeley drive away when I noticed a large black car trying to hide itself around the corner in Hay's Mews. As I hesitated on the doorstep the car crept forward, skirted a lamppost uncertainly and trickled downhill towards me. It looked like a brand-new Bentley. It probably was. Steve could never be in a country twenty-four hours without buying the first car which caught his fancy.

I walked into the house, slammed the front door but changed my mind and opened it a crack. Plunging into the dining room, I prepared to ransack the sideboard for brandy but discovered I had lost the key. I was just peering distractedly into a vase of flowers when I heard the front door close.

I froze. Various opening remarks ranging from the enraged "You bastard, how dare you batter your way back into my life again!" to the groveling "Please come back—I'll do anything you want!" all roared through my mind, but when his shadow fell across the doorway I was mute.

He was speechless too. He stood filling the doorway and blocking the light from the hall. I had forgotten how big he was, just as I had forgotten how striking he could look in his expensive American clothes. He was wearing a charcoal-gray suit with a pearl-gray tie, and his curly brown hair, silver now at the sides, was trying to spring up after being flattened with water. The lines were deeper in his face, but his eyes were that same hot electric blue and he still looked, to paraphrase Lady Caroline Lamb, rough, tough and dangerous to know.

I had to sit down. I was just wondering idiotically what on earth I had done with the sideboard key when Steve groaned with typical honesty, "Jesus, Dinah, how on earth did we get into such a mess?" and sank down opposite me at the dining-room table. The chair creaked beneath his weight and the table shuddered as he leaned forward on his elbows. The mask of raw sexuality which he so often felt compelled to wear in the presence of women dissolved, and as he smiled at me with that friendly naïveté which I remembered so well one of his huge hands slid impulsively across the table and caught my wrist in a tight affectionate clasp.

"Oh, Steve!" I gasped feebly. I was on the point of making a complete fool of myself when I spotted the sideboard key lurking on the top dish of the epergne, and I grabbed it as if it were a lifeline. "Have a drink!" I said, scrambling to my feet. "What would you like?"

"Anything but tea," he said. "I drank enough tea when I was with Emily to boost the entire economy of India. How about a quick scotch?"

Of course he had to have his wretched ice. When I gave the order to Wetherby I took the opportunity to ask why the sideboard key hadn't been in its usual place. Wetherby told me the sideboard key shouldn't be left lying around. "You should have one key, Madam, and I should have the other." "Wetherby, I'm not wearing that key around my neck day and night." "As Madam wishes." Servants were really very exhausting. Although I had abandoned my Marxist leanings I still occasionally longed for the great social leveling which Marx had promised was inevitable.

Steve and I exchanged cocktail-party questions and answers. I asked him when he had arrived, had he had a good flight, and he gave the appropriate responses. It was only after Wetherby had returned with the ice that Steve said, "I've got to stop drinking like this, but I'll be all right now I'm here with you again."

"Steve—"

"Yes, I know, don't say it, you don't want me back after the way I treated you, and I don't blame you either. How can I ever apologize or explain? God, what a mess my life's in!" he exclaimed despairingly, and having tossed back his whisky in a single gulp he poured himself another.

The nakedness of his distress made him vulnerable, and by magic I felt more composed. After drinking a little brandy I lit a cigarette with a steady hand. "You said some terrible things to me," I said, "but I said some terrible things to you. We were both to blame, Steve."

He ran his fingers through his hair. "But what happened, Dinah?" he said, baffled. "Why did we suddenly tear into each other like that? Just what the hell was going on back there in the summer of '29?"

"Ah, Steve!" I said with a sigh, and taking another sip of brandy I inhaled deeply from my cigarette and started to explain.

III

We had been hamstrung by our memories of my visit to New York in 1926. Having concluded he was nothing but a rake with a flair for finance, I had decided that he could be ensnared only if I acted the part of a fun-loving *femme fatale*. He had thought I was the hottest siren ever to emerge from England and had decided to ensnare me with a judicious mixture of copious sex and cunning British sportsmanship. Having fooled each other so successfully, we should hardly have been surprised when we found ourselves in the midst of that final violent quarrel. Our relationship, seemingly so substantial, had been a grand illusion. One can only act a part night and day for a limited time before wilting with exhaustion, and the surprise was not that our relationship had disintegrated but that it had lasted so long.

"But why did we get driven into acting these parts?" said Steve, still mystified.

"Because we wanted each other so much. I don't think we could have twisted ourselves into such contortions otherwise. I think you were fed up with Caroline, probably more fed up than you realized, and perhaps there were other reasons too that I know nothing about. Difficulties at Van Zale's with Cornelius perhaps? But whatever was going on, you came to England in dire need of a grand glamorous affair to cheer you up, and there was I, Paul's mistress—"

"That goddamned best friend of mine!"

"Yes, this was his legacy to us, Steve. I told you the truth that day in the sandhills at Waxham. I was very lonely and you were very attractive, but when all was said and done I wanted you because you were Paul's friend. I was in love not with you but with what you represented to me. I was reaching back into the past, and in order to get back into the past I had to act. I knew you'd never accept me as I really was."

"But I did!"

"No, Steve. You backed away."

I reminded him that he had pretended to be such a sportsman, so fond of fair play, so willing to be generous towards emancipated women.

"Yet what was the truth?" I said. "You tolerated Caroline's emancipation because it was no threat to you; beyond all her tough talk Caroline wasn't in the least emancipated. You tolerated my emancipation because although I was a success in the business world, my success never encroached on your territory. I was *tactfully* emancipated. But once I started talking to you in terms of money and power and the bank, I was suddenly right there batting on your wicket, a potential rival, and you responded just as you would have responded to a challenge by Cornelius—not sportingly, because you're no sportsman, Steve! Sportsmen don't survive long in the kind of world you live in. You responded by fighting back as dirtily as you knew how."

"I must have been nuts!" he groaned.

"You were certainly flattering! Most women complain that men don't take them seriously, but you took me too seriously! Later it occurred to me I should have accepted your horrified reaction as a compliment."

"You mean you didn't want the bank? But Dinah," said Steve innocently, voicing a variation on the question which Freud—significantly—had never been able to answer, "what is it you really want?"

I sighed. "Steve, it's no big mystery. I want what we all want. I want to love and be loved. I want to be secure and happy. I want a home and family and a job which allows me to use my own individual gifts. I thought I could make a success of banking and I still think I could, but if I never get the opportunity to enter a bank I've no doubt I'll live. I'm certainly not going to go jumping off Westminster Bridge in a fit of pique. What the devil did you think I was going to do if you gave me the chance to enter Van Zale's? Stab all the Milk Street men—yourself included—in the back, weight your bodies with cement blocks and throw them into the Thames? Darling, I leave such behavior thankfully to you Americans!"

"You mean you didn't sleep with me just because—"

"My dear Steve!" I couldn't help myself. I had to reach across the table and slip my hand comfortingly into his. "I'm not Madame de Maintenon or Alice Perrers. I don't seek power through the royal bedchamber. God knows I have enough power at the office, and when I stagger home to my lover the very last thing I want to do is prostitute myself in the name of more power!"

"I'm sorry." He was genuinely ashamed. "It's just that women do do that kind of thing, and—"

"So do men," I said. "Paul slept his way into his own private banking firm when he married Marietta, but everyone thought it was a clever sensible thing to do. Aren't double standards fascinating?" I was wondering whether we should adjourn to the drawing room, but I was afraid that once I'd got him upstairs I'd never get him down again. I poured myself another brandy instead. "Talking of the Van Zale family," I said, "I just couldn't believe it when I heard you'd married Emily."

That casual statement hardly reflected my past rage, jealousy and searing sense of loss, but I saw no point in becoming too emotional. I told him levelly that after I had heard of his marriage I had abandoned all hope of a reconciliation, although for the twins' sake I had felt obliged to keep in touch with him; my experience with Alan had taught me that even an absent father was better than a dead one. "And I still don't understand why you married her," I added to keep the conversation on an even keel.

He talked of the state he had been in when he had arrived home in 1929. "And suddenly in the midst of all these disasters there was Emily . . ."

I lit another cigarette and tried not to think how wonderful Emily sounded.

". . . And I felt so grateful to her that when I found out she wanted to marry me I thought, Well, why not? The kids were crazy about her. They kept dropping little hints about marriage—and so did everyone else, even Cornelius."

"But why should Cornelius—"

"That kid would sell his own mother up the river if he could make a nickel profit on the deal!"

That sounded more like the Steve I remembered, but I was disturbed to see that the subject of Cornelius still obsessed him.

"But I've finally figured out a way to railroad the little bastard all the way out of One Willow Street!" he concluded triumphantly.

I smelled New York, the glittering barbarism, the wicked steamy heat, the primitive lawlessness of a wide-open town.

"So that's why you've left Emily," I said slowly.

"Hell, no!" he protested. "I've left Emily because she was driving me to drink—but that's another story. No, the point is that now I've left her I'll have no peace till I've got rid of Cornelius, and since I've known for some months that Emily and I were headed for disaster I've done my best to plan for the future. If you want to know the truth, I've made a secret deal with Lewis Carson and we're all set to go full steam ahead. The kid doesn't stand a chance."

I thought of all I had heard about Cornelius. "Are you sure?"

"Sure I'm sure!" He was sighing in ecstasy, all his troubles forgotten, and as his blue eyes became misty with the thought of future triumphs he added dreamily, "Have you ever heard of the Glass-Steagall Banking Act?"

IV

The Glass-Steagall Banking Act, which Roosevelt had signed into law in mid-June of that year, could be compared with a flock of pigeons—the investment bankers' pigeons which had come home to roost. It was part of Roosevelt's New Deal for Wall Street, a legislative attempt to ensure that the events of October 1929 would never be repeated. Gone were the unregulated market, the despotism of the bankers and the gaudiest trappings of private enterprise. Egged on by an outraged public opinion, the federal government was moving into territory previously held by private individuals. The Securities Act, the first law aimed at Wall Street reform, contented itself by forcing corporations and investment firms to behave with greater integrity towards the people whose money they sought, but the structure of the investment banking houses had been untouched. It was left to the Glass-Steagall Banking Act to rip that structure apart. The government wanted complete separation of investment and commercial banking. No longer would the bankers be able to operate their own personal gambling machine where the odds always favored the house. Private investment banking houses such as Van Zale's had to choose between deposit and investment banking, and the divorce was so noisy that even the City of London had been deafened by the howls of outrage from Wall Street.

"Roosevelt's trouble," said Steve bitterly, "is that he doesn't understand finance. This act's going to disrupt all the established ways of underwriting and distributing securities, and reduce the amount of capital available to float new issues. If we choose to remain investment bankers we lose all our deposit business—our working capital. If we choose deposit banking we become just like a commercial bank, required to submit to government examination and supervision. Whatever we do we're castrated."

"But not for long, I'm sure," I said. "Americans are always so clever at solving problems."

"Well, it's funny you should say that. There's a rumor that Morgan's . . ."

The partners of the House of Morgan had decided that the firm should withdraw from investment banking but not, according to the gossips, for long. The theory was that once investment banking showed signs of recovery, Morgan's would return to the game under a different name. There would be two separate Morgan's, divorced by the law as required by the Glass-Steagall Banking Act but linked by the subtle ties of friendship, which not even Roosevelt could prevent by legislation.

"Don't tell me," I said. "Let me guess. You're going to follow in the House of Morgan's footsteps."

"Not quite. Lewis and I have decided that Van Zale's is going to stick with investment banking. It'll be very rough at first, but if we tighten our belts we can hold on until we set up a second Van Zale's to handle the deposit banking—a commercial bank of our own which we can borrow from whenever we like. It's the Morgan principle, but applied in reverse."

I tried to imagine what it would cost to launch a new bank. "Where are you going to get the money?" I said curiously. "Or shouldn't I ask?"

"The little bastard's going to produce the money! They say Jack Morgan's going to sell his art collection to set up his son in the second Morgan bank, so why shouldn't Cornelius sell a few Rembrandts to set himself up in the second Van Zale's?"

The light dawned. "You're going to oust Cornelius from Willow and Wall by offering him the top job at the commercial bank!"

"Exactly!" He beamed with pride. "Isn't that a great idea? Cornelius gets all the independence and power he can possibly want, and Lewis and I get him out of our hair once and for all. Then when Lewis retires—"

"Wait a minute, Steve. Doesn't there have to be very close cooperation between the two banks? Even though you have to be divorced by law didn't you just say you have to be married by gentleman's agreement?"

"But that's the glory of it!" said Steve happily. "Cornelius won't cut off his nose to spite his face. His survival will depend on ours, and vice versa. He'll just have to get along with us, and anyway once he's out of One Willow Street that won't be so difficult. We'll work out a truce."

"Steve, I hate to remind you, but you've just walked out on his sister."

"Honey, don't be naïve!" He stared at me. "Cornelius isn't the kind of guy who would ever let a personal relationship stand in the way of a successful business deal!"

"Well, I suppose that *is* just possible." I glanced at the ice in the ice bucket. The cubes were shiny, pristine and cold. "Steve, your opinion of my naïveté is going to soar to new heights, but I must just ask one last question. What makes you so sure Cornelius is going to fall in with this gorgeous scheme of yours?"

"He's got no choice!" Still fired by the glory of his plans, he gave me a sketch of the balance of power at Van Zale's. Old Walter had died, Clay Linden had moved to another house and Martin Cookson too was on the brink of resigning. Both Clay and Martin had been irked by Cornelius' rapid rise to power. The remaining partners, carefully handpicked by Steve and Lewis, would know whom they had to support in a crisis. "The fact is," said Steve, "that so long as Lewis and I hang together there's no way Cornelius can get around us. He could be difficult about the money—all right, I concede that. But if the worst comes to the worst we'll find some other way to scrape up the money for the new bank, and anyway my whole point is that Cornelius isn't going to make trouble, because he's going to be thrilled with the idea. All that power! He'll hardly be able to wait to get out from under our feet! Of course, we'll have to send a couple of the new partners along with him to keep him on the rails, but he's a bright boy and commercial banking's straightforward. He'll have a nice glamorous office and a cute secretary and his old pal Sam Keller and he's going to have the time of his life. Lucky little kid! Imagine being a bank president at his age! He ought to go down on his knees and thank me and Lewis for making it all possible!"

"Hm," I said.

"Anyhow, I'm going to be marking time in Milk Street until next June. Lewis and I agreed that it would be best if I gave Cornelius a few months to recover from the Emily business, and Roosevelt's given us bankers a few months to make up our minds which way to leap. But Lewis will do the spade work in New York, so that we can make a public announcement on the anniversary of Glass-Steagall next June, and then I'll return to New York to pick up the reins again. Meanwhile . . ." He suddenly ran down like a gramophone. "I thought . . . maybe . . . these next few months . . ." He trailed off completely.

"Hm," I said again.

"Later," he said, skipping over the awkward few months he had in mind, "we could divide our time between England and America. You could open a branch of your business in New York. It would be wonderful for the kids, wonderful for us. . . . Christ, Dinah, for God's sake say something!"

"I'm too frightened to speak. Go on."

"Well, I . . ." He groped for words. "Maybe we never did know each other the first time around, but I knew you well enough to realize now that you're the one woman I'll always want to come back to. I want to try again, Dinah. I want to accept you as you are, because I know that unlike Emily you can accept me as I am. I love you, Dinah, and I'll do anything to make things work, anything at all—Say, are you crying?"

"Steve, I'm so terrified of going down the wrong road again—I couldn't bear to be hurt like that a second time."

"Honey, there's no repeat performance scheduled, I promise you."

"But I've got to think—you've had days to think about this and I've only had minutes—"

"Sure." He stood up clumsily, edged his way around the table and enfolded me in a bear hug. "When can I see you again?"

"Saturday." That would give me forty-eight hours to sort out my most private fears.

"Here?"

"No," I said. "Norwich. I'll meet you at the station and take you to Mallingham to meet the twins."

V

I summoned all my analytical gifts. I was determined to appraise the situation with logic, yet as I lay gazing vacantly into the darkness at two o'clock in the morning I only knew that I was a plain woman with a large nose and fat hips being pursued by six foot two inches of sexy successful American manhood, and my logic floated far beyond my reach.

With a sigh I left my bed and padded downstairs to brew myself a cup of tea. As I watched the kettle boil I told myself that I really had to be sensible. I was an old warhorse of thirty-two, not a gay young filly of seventeen. This man drank too much. We had little in common beyond the world of business, and to make matters worse we had sexual problems. Also any man who walked out on a perfect wife had to be regarded with extreme caution.

But he was gorgeous.

I started gazing vacantly into space again and recalled myself only when the steam threatened to levitate the lid of the kettle to remarkable heights. As I made the tea I started making excuses to myself. I had not yet heard his side of his marriage, but it was obviously a classic disaster of marriage on the rebound. If he were happy with me he would probably be able to reduce his drinking, and although our sexual relationship would without doubt be awkward when we attempted to resume it there was no reason why we couldn't straighten out our difficulties, particularly if he was as willing as I was to be honest. It was true he shared none of my intellectual interests, but there was no law saying that two people had to have identical tastes before they could form a successful relationship. The worst problem, I thought as I made a superhuman effort to regard him dispassionately, was his inclination to regard adultery as a way of life. My experience with Paul had taught me that there was nothing which upset me so much as infidelity—possibly because I was basically an insecure person, but I wasn't concerned about my motive and I had no intention of making excuses for my old-fashioned attitude, particularly since I suspected that Steve's attitude was at heart identical to mine. I could well imagine his howls of outrage if I decided to sleep with other men. However, the plain truth of the matter was that I had no right to demand fidelity of him unless we were married, and I was almost sure that marriage with Steve would be a disaster.

I stared into my murky tea and thought about marriage. I was well aware that I could profit from psychoanalysis on the subject, but I didn't see why a psychoanalyst should get paid for doing something I myself enjoyed so much. In my teens I had wanted to get married because I had wanted to conform. In my twenties I had not wanted to get married because I had not wanted to conform. In my thirties I was so worn out by the strain of nonconformity that I was quite capable of marrying for all the wrong reasons. For example, it was likely that I might marry Steve for the sake of the children, although it was my firm conviction that children were better off in a happy home run by one parent than in an unhappy home run by two.

The trouble was that I was convinced I would be unhappily married. I had no idea why. It was not enough to cite my father's three disastrous marriages, because I wasn't my father. It was certainly not enough to burble that marriage was a bourgeois institution; that was an amusing excuse but hardly a valid one, particularly since I had abandoned my Marxist leanings. It might be argued that I was frightened of men, but Paul had long since cured me of that sort of fear, and besides, I liked men and got along well with them.

I drank two cups of tea and considered marriage from the point of view of an emancipated woman. That promise to obey was a bit offensive. The loss of one's name was vaguely obnoxious. The thought that one had given a man the legal right to commit rape was, of course, monstrous. But so what? I wasn't some poor fishwife in the East End who was chained to her husband through economic necessity. If my husband abused me I was one of the few women fortunate enough to be able to walk out and sue him into a repentant stupor. So it was nonsense to argue that I opposed marriage because I was an emancipated woman.

I gave up and returned to bed, but towards dawn I couldn't help thinking that if I really loved Steve I'd marry him without a second thought.

But I certainly found him attractive. Those electric blue eyes . . .

I fell asleep and had such pornographic dreams that I awoke blushing.

"I'm just off to my swimming lesson now, Mummy," said Alan at my bedside.

"Alan—heavens, I've overslept! Why didn't that nitwit Celeste wake me up? All right, have a nice time, darling—"

"I don't want to go."

"But Alan . . ."

The past came up to meet me. I was back with Alan in 1929 as I tried to explain to him that Steve and I had decided not to marry after all.

"But he was going to be a new daddy for me—you promised, you said you'd be a mummy and daddy, married with wedding pictures just like everyone else." His white tense little face was upturned to mine. His dark eyes were bright with anger and pain. "Why can't you be married, why not? Everyone else's mummy's married! If only you could get married, then I wouldn't have to be different anymore. . . ."

I wouldn't have thought it possible to experience such agonies of remorse. Paul had told me in 1922 that my attitude towards unmarried motherhood had been naïve, but it was not until after Steve left and Alan broke down that I had any conception of the suffering I had caused to the person I loved best. Given my peculiar circumstances, my unmarried motherhood was perhaps inevitable, but it was still unforgivably selfish. I make no excuses for myself. I had been wrong, blind, childish, stupid—and I had not only made the mistake once but was about to repeat it.

"I don't want them," Alan had said when I brought the twins home from the hospital. "Take them away." He never told any of his friends that he had a new brother and sister. Soon he stopped inviting his school friends to tea, and the headmaster of the little school he attended in Kensington told me he was worried; Alan had become withdrawn, made no effort with his lessons and took no interest in games.

I made another effort to talk to him about the twins, but he burst into tears.

"Couldn't you ask someone to adopt them? Couldn't you give

them away? Couldn't you keep them at Mallingham so I didn't have to see them so much?"

The dreadful questions went on and on.

"They're only babies, Alan!" I pleaded. "They don't mean to make you unhappy."

He remained unconvinced, and the indifferent school reports continued while I worried about him unceasingly. I wondered if he should change schools but thought it better not to disrupt him. I wondered if he would be too disturbed to go to prep school to live in the masculine atmosphere I could not provide. I wondered if he would become a homosexual. I wondered if he would develop his father's epilepsy. No possibility was too lurid to be considered by me in my anxiety, but at least I didn't have to wonder what kind of mother I was. I knew I was a complete failure.

Yet I loved my children, and in the few blissful hours I spent with them each week I knew guiltily that my own suffering had been worthwhile. It was only Alan's suffering which I found intolerable.

After Steve had left me I did not expect sympathy or approval from either my clients, the press or London society, so I cut myself off from them at once and lived like a recluse. Fortunately since Harriet had always shouldered the burden of the business entertaining, this retreat was easy for me, and soon I found that in a life devoid of social activity I could devote more time to the children. I bought my new house in London and took my time furnishing it; we visited Mallingham regularly and enjoyed long weekends in the country; I had plenty of free evenings to catch up on all the books I had wanted to read, and occasionally Cedric and I would go to the talkies together. I never went to the theater in case I should see someone I knew, but sometimes I would take Alan to an exhibition or a museum on a Saturday morning. This secluded life was certainly not without its compensations, but at the end of two years I was bored stiff and sexually frustrated. I had recovered from the brutal conclusion of my affair with Steve by that time and was willing to look elsewhere.

There was no shortage of men. I met plenty through my work, but when I found I was consistently balking at having another affair I realized that I had fallen into the old trap of comparing my new suitors unfavorably with my past lovers. Steve and Paul might have had their faults, but they had both been exceptional men.

I suppose it was about that time that I started sending Steve photos of the twins. I still thought there was no possibility of a reconciliation and I never consciously believed I wanted him back, but if I'm to be completely honest I must admit I wanted to establish contact with him again—although I told myself that I did it for the twins' sake, and for the purest possible motives. It's really remarkable how human beings can deceive themselves when they put their minds to it.

He wrote surprisingly literate letters in a big bold handwriting on the bank's very grand headed notepaper. We had two safe subjects, economics and the twins, and we stuck to them through thick and thin. He was dotingly sentimental about the twins, tough and shrewd about the economic disasters which were hitting both America and Europe. We did not talk about the past.

When he arrived in Paris in 1933 the letters continued, but eventually he gave way to the temptation no American can resist and picked up the phone. We spoke about once a week after that, just casual conversations. Sometimes he carefully mentioned Emily and their two daughters and I expressed polite interest. Occasionally we made a joke and spent much time laughing about it. Eventually in August he used that fatal phase "Do you remember . . . ," and I knew that like me he had been thinking daily of the past.

"Mummy, I don't want to go to my swimming lesson," said Alan's voice, recalling me abruptly to the present.

"Darling, we went through all this last night." I saw his mouth quiver, and all my old guilt surged through me. I did so desperately want him to be happy. "Well, you don't have to go if you don't want to," I said in a rush. "Now, darling, don't cry, because I've got a wonderful surprise for you. Someone very special's going to join us at Mallingham this weekend, someone you've always wanted to see again. It's—well, it's Steve, Alan! He's going to be working in London for a few months. Isn't that exciting?"

There was a stony silence.

"Alan?" I said in dread as his mouth ceased to quiver and turned down ominously at the corners.

"I don't want to have anything to do with him," he announced firmly and marched off to his swimming lesson without a backward glance.

I was so depressed I could hardly drag myself up to Mallingham, but eventually I left London with Alan, my maid Celeste and Miss Parsons, the governess who looked after Alan so that Nanny could devote herself exclusively to the twins. When we arrived at Mallingham Nanny informed me with suitable melancholy that the latest nursemaid had given notice. It was a fitting climax to a grisly day.

After lying awake all night I drank three cups of coffee, chain-smoked four cigarettes and drove off to Norwich looking like a fishwife. I wore an old skirt and jumper, my faded country mackintosh, a felt hat to hide the fact that my hair needed rewaving, and the wrong kind of lipstick. Since I felt as much a mess as I looked, I was convinced the renaissance of my affair with Steve was doomed to immediate collapse, but then he came bounding out of the station and exclaimed with all his old exuberance, "You look wonderful—so natural!" and I began to feel better. I did mean to warn him about Alan, but he was too busy talking about his own children; he had left his two boys temporarily with Emily but had promised them he would send for them as soon as he had established a home in London.

"Were they very upset?" I asked worried, trying to picture the little boys I had known seven years ago.

"Yes, but I told them I'd make everything come right," he said untroubled, and it occurred to me that although he was devoted to his sons he might not have the faintest idea what was passing through their minds. One of the paradoxes of his character was that although he was a clever able man he could be extraordinarily naïve about emotional relationships.

I was just wondering in despair how he could cope with Alan when he began to talk about his daughters. "I feel really bad about them," he said. "I'll just have to make it up to them later. I know Emily will be generous about custody."

"Steve, forgive me if I sound rude, but why did you and Emily ever have a second child if your marriage was going from bad to worse?"

"I thought it might put everything right," he said with typical naïveté. "Emily was happy as long as she was having babies and I figured that even if I couldn't be the kind of husband she wanted I could at least give her children. Jesus, Dinah, if you only knew the guilt I've been carrying around with me!" he exclaimed in despair, and it was there, halfway along the road from Wroxham to Potter Heigham, that he finally disclosed some details of his marriage.

Emily was without doubt a saint. She was chaste, beautiful, cultured, charming and utterly faultless as a wife and mother. When poor Steve had become bored with her chastity, tired of her beauty, exasperated by her culture, sick of her charm and exhausted by her tireless perfection he had hated himself so much that he headed straight for the nearest bottle.

"That made me feel guilty, too," he added, "because Emily hated me to drink more than one highball a night. Anyway, the more guilty I felt the more I drank, and the more I drank the more guilty I became. When I got through a bottle of scotch before lunch one day I saw the light and realized I was killing myself—I was going the same way my father went. That's when I knew I had to leave. I hated to go when she was so perfect, but I honestly felt I had no choice. It was a question of survival."

"God, some marriages do sound awful!" I said appalled. "Poor you—and poor Emily! I expect that after she's recovered from the shock she'll be glad it's finished. She couldn't have been happy either, once she realized that the man she married was quite different from the man she thought she was marrying."

"She'll be all right once she gets home to Cornelius. I'll say this for the little bastard: he's a devoted brother to that girl."

"Yes—so devoted that he married her off to his worst enemy! What's *his* wife like?"

"Alicia? Not my type. Cold fishy eyes, a marble face and a voice like stewed prunes, but the little bastard's devoted to her too, so obviously she's got something I've missed. Jesus, there's the sign to Mallingham! Wonderful! Dinah, if you only knew how often I've wanted to come back!" He scrabbled in his wallet, and as I glanced sideways I saw he had produced a picture of the twins. "Cute little things!" he said with that baroque sentimentality in which so many Americans excel. Many English people think such sloppiness is inexcusable, but I've always thought how pleasant it must be to give way to such gaudy emotion without a trace of embarrassment. "They look just like my brothers did when they were little."

Oh, *Lord*, I thought, remembering my fortunately brief meeting with Luke and Matt years before at Steve's party, but I knew that Steve meant to be complimentary.

I had called the twins Edred and Elfrida, after the hero and heroine of one of my favorite children's books, *The House of Arden*, by E. Nesbit. Having discovered the secret of traveling backwards in time, the fictitious Edred and Elfrida had journeyed into the past to meet their dead father and bring him back alive to the present. It had taken me several months to connect my revival of interest in this story with my intense longing to return to the past to be with Paul.

The car passed through the ruined gateway of my home and roared up the drive to the front door. "Prepare for the onslaught," I managed to say to Steve before the front door flew open and the twins hurtled out.

"Mummy, Mummy, Mummy!" They had shrill voices and strong lungs. Edred grabbed my arm and swung from it while Elfrida flung her arms around my knees in an attempt to stop the circulation in my legs.

"What a welcome!" laughed Steve as I staggered backwards against the car.

They slewed around to look at him. I saw three curly-haired heads and three pairs of electric blue eyes and felt weaker than ever, but fortunately Steve wasn't in the least disconcerted. He hugged them with uninhibited pleasure and mentioned the magic word "presents." Bedlam followed as the twins howled with anticipation, and I was still leaning weakly against the car when I saw Alan standing in the doorway.

"Steve," I began in an agony of anxiety, but Steve had seen him too.

"All right, kids!" he said cheerfully, swinging Elfrida down from his shoulder and pulling his suitcase from the car. "Open this up and find your packages."

The twins at once turned the suitcase upside down so that all the contents spilled on the ground, but Steve never looked back. In six long strides he was standing in the doorway. I could no longer see Alan's face, but I heard the gentleness in Steve's voice, and suddenly I saw that Steve's emotional simplicity was exactly what Alan needed after my tortuous, guilt-ridden demonstrations of affection.

As the twins shrieked with glee over their presents Alan flung his arms around Steve while Steve patted his shoulder and held him close.

That was when I knew I would marry Steve. As the tough talk and tougher poses fell magically away I saw only the strength of his generous compassionate nature, and I moved towards him as compulsively as a salmon swimming upstream from the sea.

Chapter Two

I

That night when the children were in bed we went for a walk but it rained, forcing us to turn back. As we returned to the house I suggested we retire to my upstairs sitting room, in the hope that the intimate atmosphere there would help us, but on our arrival he took a chair after I had sat down on the sofa. The specter of our sexual estrangement haunted us. The only difference between us was that I had foreseen the difficulty while he had not, and I suspected he was baffled that he was unable to give me more than a series of fraternal hugs.

"We've got to face this, Steve," I said as he lit my cigarette.

"What?" he said, but he knew. He shifted uncomfortably in his chair.

"Us. It. Bed." I helped myself to some whisky and scraped up all my courage. "I know I compared you unfavorably with Paul. That was a stupid thing to do, pointless and unfair, but I did it because I was angry not with you but with myself. I was frustrated because . . . oh, God, how hard it is to talk about these things! I wish I had Caroline's talent for discussing sex as if it were the weather!"

"That didn't do Caroline much good. I don't think she liked sex too well." He clasped his glass tightly. "She just pretended she did when she wanted to be nice to me."

"Yes, well, I . . . I can't do that, Steve. At least not for any length of time. Maybe I could if I'd never had a good sexual relationship, but as it is I can't help feeling I don't want to settle for less. Yet the truth is that no man except Paul has ever been able to—well, call it what you like. I'm too embarrassed to call it anything. I must be more Victorian than I realize." I guzzled my whisky. "I've got to care," I gasped in a rush. "I know theoretically one should be able to enjoy sex for sex's sake, but I'm not made that way. Unless I care it's useless, and that's why our affair was such a baffling disappointment to me. I did care, but nothing happened. Of course, now I know the fault was mine because I was too busy acting a part to trust you, but when we had our terrible quarrel I hadn't grasped that unpleasant home truth and it was so much easier to put all the blame on you by saying you weren't as good as Paul. If we can be honest with each other now—if I can trust you—I know it would be very different. Do you understand what I'm trying to say?"

"Sure. I'm not dumb. You're trying to convince me it was your fault I was lousy in bed. You don't have to do that, Dinah." He stood up and prowled aimlessly to the window. Outside it was dark, and I could hear the rain tapping against the pane.

"I'm not saying it's your fault, and I'm beyond debasing myself to wrap your self-esteem in cotton wool. I'm trying to be truthful, Steve, because I don't believe there's any hope for a joint future unless we exorcize all those specters which ruined our old affair. I do care about you very much and I want desperately to make this work, but—"

"Will you marry me?"

I understood at once. I had so often craved reassurance myself that I had no trouble recognizing that same craving in someone else. Having already made up my mind that I could make no commitment until our sexual problems had been resolved, I now saw that no resolution was possible until the commitment had been made. Only my unconditional promise to marry him would restore the self-confidence I had destroyed when I compared him unfavorably with Paul.

I thought in panic, I can't do this! But then back came the inevitable reply which had carried me through every past crisis: Oh yes I can.

Moving swiftly to him, I slipped my arms around his neck. "Yes," I said. "I love you, Steve, and I want to marry you more than anything else in the world."

That was all I needed to say. He kissed me on the mouth, and without another word we withdrew to my bedroom, undressed with speed and slid silently between the sheets into each other's arms.

II

Neither of us was mad enough to believe we would immediately be transported into rapturous bliss, but we achieved our reunion without difficulty and were happy. The ice had been successfully broken. Now all we had to do was heat the water, and heaving sighs of relief, we fell asleep with his body still half entwined with mine.

When we returned to London we began to look for a house where we could live after we were married. I was loath to leave my house in Chesterfield Street, but it was hardly big enough to accommodate Steve, his valet, his secretary and his two boys in addition to me and my ménage. It was already hardly big enough to accommodate the twins now that their fourth birthday was approaching. During the summer they often spent the week at Mallingham so that they could have more scope to run wild, but their winters were always spent with me in London.

Steve raised no objection to my wish to remain in Mayfair, and eventually we decided to buy a large house just around the corner in Charles Street. We signed the contract during the week before Christmas.

It was 1933. Ramsay MacDonald led the National Government, but neither the Labour nor the Conservative party seemed to have any message for me. On the extreme right Churchill breathed fire like an archaic dragon, and on the extreme left Lansbury burbled unrealistic idealism. The middle was a big yawn, characterized by Baldwin loafing around doing nothing. Intellectually I was attracted to the concept of pacifism, but I thought the successful motion of the Oxford Union, "This House will in no circumstances fight for its king and country," smacked of adolescent instability. I was too old to support the adolescents, too cynical to rally around Lansbury and too much of a successful capitalist to align myself with leftist thought no matter how much it attracted me as an intellectual doctrine. I vaguely liked the idea of the League of Nations and thought its decisions could probably be upheld by resolute international collaboration. Churchill's theory of the importance of military power to back the League struck me as typical of a man who had spent his childhood playing with toy soldiers.

In England Westminster dozed.

In America Roosevelt had little fireside chats.

In Germany Hitler was practicing his goose step, but he was so unsavory I couldn't believe he'd last long. Japan had invaded China, but nobody cared about that, because it was so far away. The War was long ago now, the economy showed signs of picking up, the masses were better catered to than ever before, and more of those masses were buying cosmetics. The year 1933 might not have been utopia for the poor miners in the depressed areas of South Wales, but my sales in suburbia were booming, pacifism was a cozy comforting doctrine to flirt with, and I was rich, still moderately young and quite definitely in love. The only cloud which floated across my idyllic horizon was Scott and Tony Sullivan's announcement that they planned to return to the States with Emily.

Steve was so upset that his first impulse was to rush across the Channel to talk to them, but when his guilt made it impossible for him to confront Emily he turned instead to the telephone. There were long tortuous conversations which I refused to listen to. A lot of whisky disappeared. Finally the boys flew to Croydon Aerodrome to spend a long weekend with us, but although I tried hard to give them a friendly welcome I soon saw I was wasting my time. I was competing against Emily, and Emily was obviously God's gift to motherless children.

"Emily says . . . Emily does this. . . . Emily does that. . . ." Emily, Emily, Emily. Their sharp hostile voices lingered lovingly over her name; their eyes regarded me with implacable enmity. At the close of the weekend they cornered their father, locked the door of the room to keep me out and begged him to return with them to Paris.

Steve talked to them for three hours and emerged haggard. More whisky disappeared. We took the boys to Croydon, kissed them goodbye and said we hoped they would change their minds when we had our new big house.

"I doubt it," said Scott coldly. "Anyway, by that time we'll be back in America with Emily."

Scott was dark like Caroline, tall for thirteen years old, and pugnaciously self-confident. Tony was equally tough but not so sure of himself. I liked him the better of the two.

"Maybe we could come for a visit next summer," he began, willing to be generous, but he quailed when Scott glared at him.

"What can I do?" Steve said afterwards in despair. "Of course any court would insist they return to me—Emily's not even their legal guardian. But if I force them to live with me they'll end up hating my guts and making us all miserable. My only hope is to give them time to calm down, and when they finally accept that I'm never going to live with Emily again they'll become more reasonable."

"I suppose Emily doesn't mind looking after them?" I said curiously, trying to imagine how I would feel if I were saddled with my stepchildren by a defecting husband.

"Dinah, looking after children is Emily's mission in life. All her charity work back home is tied up with children's welfare."

"The very mention of her name makes me feel hopelessly inferior," I said depressed.

"Let's go home and get stewed."

We did our best to laugh off our gloom, but it was a dismal evening, and the next morning we both turned to our work with relief. In Milk Street the resident partner greeted Steve with the news that he was moving to another house, so although Steve had not intended to assume sole control of the London office he still found he had the familiar reins thrust back into his hands. Privately I hoped he would fall in love again with his earlier dream of a European empire, but I had reconciled myself to his inevitable return to New York. I liked the idea of opening an American salon. I felt it was exactly the challenge I needed now that my business was ten years old, but I did not want to emigrate permanently to America, and I suspected that dividing our time between two continents might prove difficult in practice. However, I was determined to give the scheme a try. I liked New York, and perhaps if I returned I might succeed in laying Paul's ghost to rest.

I wondered what I would think of Cornelius when we met.

Cornelius never wrote to Steve. I found this total silence unnerving, but Steve was unperturbed. "What's the little bastard going to say?" he said with a shrug. "With his past marital history he can hardly start preaching to me!" And when he laughed at the memory I saw he no longer took Cornelius seriously. Cornelius was almost ousted from the Willow Street nest. Cornelius was past history.

I often thought of Cornelius. Once upon a time everyone but Paul had regarded him as an effeminate nonentity, but that opinion had long since fallen by the wayside. The newspapers and magazines now watched him with bated breath, and I watched, too; I had followed him every step of the way through his ruthless divorce and his cold-blooded seduction of another man's pregnant wife, which had been so luridly chronicled in the international gossip columns. Cornelius was twenty-five years old, rich, handsome and notorious, and from a distance of over three thousand miles I could feel the mysterious force of his brutal sinister faceless personality. I thought of him as faceless because in all the photographs I had seen of him his face had been devoid of expression. I did realize that this was probably a device he used to shield himself from the intrusions of the press, but nonetheless it made his personality the more repugnant to me and I knew, whenever I saw his picture, that I was afraid of him.

The thought that he was the legal owner of Mallingham still gave me the most appalling nightmares, and I would often dream that I returned to Mallingham to find him lying in wait for me in the empty house. Usually I would wake up as he walked towards me, but once I stayed asleep long enough to see the knife in his hand.

The second time I awoke screaming Steve demanded an explanation, but when I confided in him he roared with laughter.

"Honey, this kid doesn't run around waving stilettos!"

"The knife," I said coldly, "is, of course, symbolic."

He tried to take me seriously. "Dinah, you'll take Mallingham's secret to your grave. We've been through all that."

"Yes. Yes, I know I'm being silly."

He tried again. "Hell, Dinah, this is just a little guy who orders hamburgers in high-class restaurants and spends a wild party holding hands with his wife on the nearest love seat!"

"Yes. Not Jack the Ripper. Yes, I do understand. I just wish we didn't always end up on opposite sides, that's all. Steve, what *do* you think Cornelius felt when he heard you'd left Emily for that recurring menace Dinah Slade?"

"Well, I'll bet he was livid. Sure he was. But what can he do about it except help Emily with the divorce?"

"I think he'll want revenge."

He sighed patiently. "Honey, you've just had a nightmare and you're in a melodramatic frame of mind. This isn't grand opera, this isn't Chicago, and New York is Fiorello La Guardia's town now, not Jimmy Walker's. Cornelius isn't going to go running around with a hatchet, symbolic or otherwise. For the good of his career he's got to stay on good terms with me. Even if he does want revenge he's going to have to forgo it, and anyway Emily won't want any bitterness which will upset the children. She'll calm Cornelius down, just you wait and see."

I waited. Emily arrived back in New York and sensibly, with the minimum of fuss, instituted divorce proceedings. When she wrote to Steve to give him news of the children Cornelius' unbroken silence seemed louder than ever, but I said nothing and began instead to organize a spring wedding. I decided it would be foolish for me to become neurotic over Cornelius and besides, I had too many other matters to attend to.

Nanny loomed large on the horizon. She had threatened to give notice when Steve had reentered my life and had been appeased only when I told her of the wedding plans.

"It won't be in church, I suppose?" was her gloomy reaction when I mentioned we were waiting for Steve's divorce.

Nanny was a religious fanatic who radiated gloom in the presence of every person over twelve. After Mary Oakes had retired to get married I had had great difficulty replacing her, first because of my notoriety and second because the twins had always been "a handful." I could never keep a nursemaid longer than six months, and I had employed two nannies in rapid succession before I found the nanny who had enough fortitude to endure the scandal, the hard work and the chaos of disappearing nursemaids. I kept her because she somehow managed to retain the twins' respect as well as their affection, but I found her very tiring.

"When are you going to tell the children, madam?" she inquired, looking at me as if I were preparing for a clandestine marriage.

I had been so afraid that some disaster might prevent the marriage that I had wanted to keep our engagement a secret until the divorce was granted, but when Nanny said sternly, "I think Alan should be told," I promised to break the news to him. Alan had never asked either Steve or me if we intended to marry, and we were so conscious of our broken promise of four years ago that we now had a superstitious reluctance to raise the subject with him.

However, Nanny had laid down the law, so that evening I summoned all my courage, followed Alan into the dining room when he retired to do his homework, and once more began to talk of wedding plans.

"A real wedding?" said Alan suspiciously. "With photographs?"

"Yes, darling. Absolutely real with photographs galore."

"I won't have to be there, will I?"

"Oh, but—" I checked myself, clamped down on an emotional response and tried to be reasonable. "Why don't you want to come?"

Alan started taking books out of his satchel. "It would be embarrassing. I don't want to go to a wedding where everyone will stare at me and tell each other I never had a father."

"But you did have a father!"

"Not a proper one who married you in church."

"But he wanted to marry me just before he died!"

"Why didn't he marry you before I was born?"

"Well, he was married to someone else, and—"

"Why didn't he divorce her?"

"Well, I . . . Well, you see . . ."

"Why did he leave us alone all those years?"

"He wasn't sure whether he wanted to marry me."

"Why not? Why did he make you have a baby if he wasn't sure? Why did he go away? And why didn't he leave me anything in his will? Why did he leave everything to that Cornelius person as if I didn't exist?"

"But Alan, I've told you before—he was going to make a special provision for you!"

"Well, he didn't, did he?" said Alan. "And I know why. He was embarrassed about me. Cornelius is embarrassed, too—that's why he's never written to me even though I'm his cousin. Tony told me Emily said she'd like to meet me, but of course she won't want to now that you've taken Steve away from her. I'm cut off from my relations," said Alan, working himself up to an enraged peroration, "and it's all your fault and I don't care whether you and Steve get married and why don't you just leave me alone?"

I slunk away. "What am I to do?" I said in tears to Steve.

"Talk back to him! Stand up for yourself! Don't let him get away with that kind of nonsense—can't you see he doesn't want to get away with it? For God's sake!" exclaimed Steve, exasperated. "Here, let me talk to him."

An hour later Alan marched into the drawing room where I was pretending to read a newspaper. "I'm sorry, Mummy," he said in a small high voice, and burrowed his way into my arms.

Steve, who had been watching from the doorway, disappeared noiselessly towards the stairs.

"It's all right, Alan," I said. "I do understand if you don't want to come to the wedding."

"Steve said I might like to come to the wedding because the registry office will be small and the only people there will be people I know. But he said I needn't come to the reception afterwards."

"That's sensible of him. Wedding receptions are usually very boring."

Alan sat up, pushed back his pale hair and examined a bruise on his knee. "Mummy afterwards I want to go to a new school and be called Alan Sullivan. I want Steve to be my father. I'm going to call him Daddy. He said I could if you didn't mind."

I thought of Paul playing with Alan on that Long Island beach.

"Please, Mummy!"

"All right, darling. Yes. If that's what you really want."

He smiled. His dark eyes shone. He was happy.

After Alan had skipped back to his homework Steve entered the drawing room and sat down beside me.

"You did the right thing, Dinah."

"Yes." I made a great effort. "Thank you, Steve—for being so kind to him and so generous." There was a pause while I tried to say something else but could not.

His hand slid over mine. "Dinah, Alan will come back to Paul. It's just that right now Paul's no use to him, but be patient. It'll be different later."

"Do you really think so? Then I feel better," I said, and tried to close my mind against the past.

I failed. We went to the suite he still retained at the Ritz, and in the humiliation of my failure I started acting again, putting the clock back to 1929. At first I thought he had been deceived, but when he said casually afterwards, "I thought we were going to have an honest relationship, Dinah?" I started to cry.

He immediately held me so close I thought my ribs would crack. "I could strangle him!" he growled.

I had to laugh, but my tears refused to stop. "No, I won't talk of him, Steve, I refuse to, talking keeps him alive and he's been dead more than seven years."

"Trust Paul to achieve true immortality!" He sighed, released me and lit us both cigarettes. "It's the only kind of immortality that exists—I don't believe all that nonsense about life after death. Who the hell wants to go wandering through eternity with no booze, no sex and no entertainment of any kind? Real immortality isn't up there in the heavens—it's right here on earth. It's living on in people's memories and influencing their lives. But God damn it, I'm going to have the last laugh on Paul Van Zale! He may have struck every note on your whole damned keyboard, but he never managed to marry you!"

I laughed again and suddenly loved him so much that I slipped beyond Paul's reach. Extinguishing our cigarettes, I switched off the light and pulled him back impulsively into my arms.

His divorce was granted in March. We promptly set our wedding date, and on the twenty-fifth of April, 1934, eight years after our first meeting in front of a Greenwich Village nightclub, we were married at Caxton Hall.

III

I wore a bright-green silk dress designed by Schiaparelli. Since I could not by the remotest stretch of the imagination be described as a virgin bride, I saw no point in decking myself out in pastels or even in a discreet navy blue. Fashion suited me at that time. The squared shoulders and leg-o'-mutton sleeves had the magical effect of making my hips look slim, and since skirts were once more flapping within inches of the ankles this long look gave me a sleek streamlined appearance. I spent two hours over my makeup and used at least fifteen of my own products, from the Orange-Blossom-of-Rhodes body lotion to the brand-new Circe-the-Seductress perfume, a cunning blend of scents which included jasmine, tuberose, oil of geranium and ionone. When I finally emerged from the salon my employees gave me a royal farewell and Steve reeled so far with admiration that his top hat fell off.

I was so nervous I could hardly crawl into our new Rolls-Royce.

"I'm terrified," I said to Steve.

"Honey, I haven't been so scared since England went off the gold standard."

Only the children and our closest friends were at the civil ceremony, which took place in a sunny room dominated by an elaborate flower arrangement. Mrs. Oakes assumed the role of mother of the bride and wept happily into her best lace handkerchief as she played her role to the hilt. Harriet was there, but although I had invited Geoffrey he had made an excuse not to be present. I was sorry for Geoffrey was one of my closest friends, but since I had made a similar excuse to avoid his wedding three years before I felt I could hardly be angry with him. I was very fond of Geoffrey and might well have married him in the dark months after Steve's departure, but when he took me out to dinner it was not to propose to me but to declare his intention of marrying someone else. That served me right. I had rejected him too often before, and one cannot expect a healthy good-looking man to remain in love indefinitely with a woman who keeps getting pregnant by other men. Facing the facts stoically, I had made a special effort to be nice to his wife, who was shy, pretty and the exact opposite of me in every way, but I minded Geoffrey being married and I minded it particularly when my fortunes were at their lowest ebb and I needed a sympathetic friend to convince me life would improve.

His wife was just as nice to me as I was to her, and knitted little jackets for the twins. When she was killed in the car accident I was able to commiserate with Geoffrey without insincerity, and after he had told me every gory detail of the accident I told him every gory detail of Paul's assassination. This exchange of tragedies brought us closer together again, and we remained close even after Steve had blazed back into my life.

"Curious how you're so partial to Americans," commented Geoffrey, facing my fate with the same stoicism I had summoned to help me accept his marriage, but he was friendly to Steve and even went so far as to tell me he preferred Steve to Paul. Considering he had loathed Paul, I hardly found this a compliment, but at least it encouraged me to send him a wedding invitation.

I was sorry not to see him at Caxton Hall.

Alan wore his best gray flannel suit with his new school tie, Edred wore a sailor suit and Elfrida wore her favorite blue party dress with the pink smocking and sash. Nanny was dressed in black and carried a prayer book. Amidst a hushed dignified atmosphere which reduced even the round-eyed twins to silence, I ceased to be Miss Dinah Slade and became the fourth Mrs. Steven Sullivan.

"I did it!" I said dazed to Steve afterwards as he kissed me. "I actually did it!" The gold ring on my wedding finger was almost hidden by the enormous diamond he had given me to celebrate our engagement. "I'm really married . . . with a husband . . ." I looked up at him to make sure he was there.

"You see how easy it was?" he said, laughing.

Speechless with happiness, I clutched his arm and smiled foolishly at the photographers who were waiting for us outside. The story of a notorious romance which had blossomed into respectability was obviously destined for attention in the popular dailies, and I looked forward to rising from the pages of the *News of the World* to a paragraph in the *Daily Mail.* Perhaps by the time I died I might even qualify for an obituary in the *Times.*

The next hurdle was our reception for three hundred at Claridge's. Originally we had planned a small party, but once we started inviting our clients the list had burgeoned with great speed. I worried about whether such a celebration of our quiet wedding was in the best of taste, but Steve swept my doubts aside by insisting that we'd earned the right to throw a party. I supposed we had, but when we entered Claridge's I quailed at the ordeal awaiting me and wished we had retreated immediately for the honeymoon.

Two glasses of champagne later I was enjoying myself so much that I even forgot to worry about the children. Alan had departed with his governess for the British Museum, and since Nanny had had one of her "turns" after the ceremony, the nursemaid Clara was left to struggle ineffectually with the twins. They had a wonderful time stuffing themselves with sausage rolls, shoving caviar down each other's necks and shamelessly preening themselves in front of anyone who made the mistake of saying how adorable they were, but after my third glass of champagne I could regard even the twins with tranquillity.

The party roared on, but eventually a small sticky hand clutched my sleeve. "Mummy," said Elfrida, "Edred's been sick behind a curtain."

We rescued Edred and mopped him up.

"Mummy, I want to go home now."

"Yes, I do too, Mummy."

"All right, darlings. Let's find Clara and put you all in a taxi."

We dispatched the twins and looked at each other.

"Time to go!" said Steve, and I nodded thankfully.

For our wedding night we withdrew no further than the most luxurious suite of the Savoy, but at eleven o'clock the next morning we were boarding the Golden Arrow en route to the French Riviera.

IV

"So I finally succeeded in kicking Paul out of bed!"

"All the way across the Mediterranean to North Africa!"

We laughed. I was stupefied by my happiness. The sun shone brilliantly on the splendors of Monte Carlo, and the world floated past me in a sensuous haze.

"Time to extend the dynasty?"

But I had lost my desire to emulate Queen Victoria. I was no longer obsessed with the idea that numerous children would guarantee me affection, and all that concerned me was that I should have enough affection for however many children I chose to have. "Maybe I should be content with what I've got," I said to Steve. "I seem to have made such a mess of bringing up Alan, and the twins never listen to anyone except Nanny. But I would like another little girl," I added impulsively, unable to resist the prospect of married motherhood.

"And why not? Don't forget you'll have me to help you with the kids now," said Steve encouragingly, so I threw away my Dutch cap with relief and we did our best to bring home a permanent souvenir of our honeymoon.

Nothing happened. It was maddening. However, I was in such a state of bliss that nothing could depress me, and when I eventually returned to the office I found that my attention kept wandering from my work.

"I want to retire to Mallingham and do nothing but knit, give birth and lactate," I said dreamily to Harriet.

"Darling, are you feeling quite well?" said Harriet concerned. "You don't sound yourself at all."

"Where's all that famous ambition which won Paul's heart?" Geoffrey asked me later when he came to dinner.

"Resting," I said serenely. "I feel like England—I've won the War, survived the aftermath and now I'm in my pacific stage. All I want to do at present is to lead a quiet, tranquil life and turn my back on all the blood and thunder."

But unfortunately tranquillity had no part to play in the future that Cornelius Van Zale had planned for me, and the very next day he achieved the bloodiest coup of his singularly bloodthirsty career.

Chapter Three

I

I was just filing a nail and wondering if I were pregnant when the phone rang. I was in my office above Grafton Street. We had bought the house next door to our original house two years ago, and my office was no longer above the salon, which had now expanded to the upper floors. I had the large front room on the first floor of our new acquisition, and although I had at first found the high Georgian ceiling chilly I had softened the severity of the room's proportions with a judicious mixture of antiques. In a desperate attempt to escape from the rococo atmosphere of the salon I had acquired a Georgian mahogany pedestal library table which I used as a desk, some Queen Anne hoop-back chairs and a matching pair of walnut bureau bookcases attributed to Coxed and Woster. Cedric said I should have "gone modern," but I couldn't abide the new functional designs of the Bauhaus School.

After I had finished signing the letters I had dictated that morning I glanced at the sales figures. I still had my upper-class clientele, but now my products had percolated through to the middle classes and I had just negotiated a distribution agreement with one of the better chains of chemists which covered the suburban market in the south. My current campaign was to launch a line of multicolored lipsticks. Lipsticks had done so well in the three traditional shades of dark, medium and light that I thought the time had come to give the customers more choice, and when my male salesmen argued against the idea at the sales conference I pointed out that of the three types of customer, blond, redhead and brunette, each favored a wardrobe consisting on average of two or three "becoming" colors. Lipstick, I reasoned, should no longer be bought simply to match one's complexion. It should be considered as an essential part of a woman's costume. Seven new lipsticks were now in production, and Cedric and I were engaged in a fierce battle to name them. Cedric favored naming them after film stars, but I said this was too vulgar and suggested lush Italian names like Francesca and Venetia. Cedric snorted and the battle continued, with everyone from Harriet to Steve offering names ranging from the exotic to the banal.

I jotted down a note to ask Cedric if the sales representative for the northeast could be falsifying his figures, rearranged one of the roses which Steve had delivered to me daily, and was just toying absent-mindedly with my nail file when the phone jangled, making me jump.

"Your husband, Miss Slade," said my secretary.

Nobody at the office seemed capable of calling me Mrs. Sullivan. "All right. Hullo?" I said. "Steve?"

"Dinah, how busy are you?" There was a hard tense edge to his voice. "Can you come over to Milk Street right away? There's something goddamned odd going on at Willow and Wall."

I was flattered that he had chosen to involve me in his work, but I was also astonished. Although I privately hoped that when he was sole senior partner I might have the opportunity to learn about banking at last, I had told Steve in all sincerity that I was willing to shelve my plans indefinitely. I knew he had to be thoroughly secure before he could accept me working alongside him, and I had also faced the possibility that such a degree of security might never come. The sudden invitation to Milk Street not only took me aback but frightened me with its hint of disrupted plans, disorganized defenses and a brutal bolt from the blue.

Telling him I would leave Grafton Street immediately, I hurried over to the City.

They were expecting me at Van Zale's. I was shown immediately through the dark Dickensian interior past the clerks to the back room where Steve worked. He had thrown out the heavy Victorian furniture, but the modern cocktail cabinet and functional sofa made me pine for the nineteenth century. On his desk stood photographs of me and the children.

He kissed me and offered me a drink. I knew he had been drinking heavily, because his face was flushed.

"No, I won't have anything," I said. I never drank during business hours. "What's all this about?"

He had telephoned America at four o'clock. It was not one of the days when he had his regular call booked, but that day was the anniversary of the Glass-Steagall Banking Act and Lewis had planned to make a public announcement about the bank's future and the formation of the new bank, the Van Zale Manhattan Trust. Lewis and Steve had been in detailed correspondence for some months. Everything had been organized and settled.

"So I call One Willow Street," said Steve. He was drinking his whisky neat. "I want to find out how the press conference went, but all I find out is that Lewis is taking a long vacation in Florida and that no partner is available to speak to me. No one goes to Florida in June. All the partners don't rush out to lunch or go into purdah at high noon. I raise the roof. I get cut off." He dumped an empty whisky bottle into the wastepaper basket, pulled another bottle from the cocktail cabinet and refilled his glass. "I place another call. I'm still waiting."

There was a silence. "But what could possibly have happened?" I said nervously. His extreme tension had affected me and I was sitting on the edge of my chair. I had never seen him in such a state. He resembled the favorite in a boxing match who bounces confidently into the ring only to find his opponent already poised to knock him cold.

Before he could answer my question the phone rang, and he gestured to the extension which he had had installed when he and Hal Beecher had worked together in that room in 1929.

"Pick that up."

We both reached for our receivers. Since Steve's private line was being used, the call did not come through the switchboard, and I heard the murmur of great distance beyond the erratic waves of static.

"Mr. Sam Keller in New York is calling Mr. Steven Sullivan in London."

"My God," said Steve to me, "they've actually called me back. That means Sam's been briefed. Sullivan speaking," he added sharply to the operator.

"Go ahead, Mr. Keller."

For once the transatlantic telephone reception was clear. I heard a stranger's voice, deep and charming, saying leisurely, "Hi, Steve! Sorry no one was around to take your call earlier, but—"

"All right, Sam. Cut the crap and give it to me straight. I want the whole story in twenty seconds flat."

"Sure, Steve, sure. Well, first of all let me say that there's absolutely no cause for alarm, but there's been a little rearrangement here. Lewis has decided to take an early retirement. Now, Steve, I can't go into detail on the phone about Lewis' problems, but they were kind of substantial, if you follow me, and in the end he was the first to suggest that for the good of the firm he should retire."

Steve was sweating. I saw his knuckles gleam white as he gripped the phone. "Sam," he said, "who's in charge now at One Willow Street?"

"Well, that's just it, Steve. The Lewis disaster put us all in a difficult spot, and—"

"God damn it, Sam, answer me! Who—"

"Cornelius. He's decided to stay here, Steve. In the circumstances he felt it was his moral duty."

There was an absolute silence before Steve said, "Get him. I want to talk to him. Put him on the line."

"Gee, he's not here right now, Steve, but he sent you his compliments and—"

"Who's going to head the new bank?"

"Martin. As a matter of fact it's all worked out wonderfully well. Cornelius and Martin always got along, and Martin has the stature to head a new commercial bank. He's taking with him the two partners you and Lewis planned to send with Cornelius, and the other partners are staying here, just as you arranged. Of course, Cornelius will have to appoint some more partners, but—"

"Cornelius can't do one damn thing without my approval. He's violating the articles of partnership."

"Well, of course he wants to work with you, Steve! Of course he does! But actually I think you've forgotten the written agreement in which you authorized the hiring in your absence of replacements for the three partners who were to go to the Van Zale Manhattan Trust."

"That agreement was with Lewis!"

"Lewis assigned his powers under that agreement to Cornelius."

"That's illegal!"

"No, Steve. Pardon me, but we checked with Dick Fenton. Because of the wording of the agreement and the scope of the articles of partnership—"

Steve said what the Van Zale lawyer could do with himself. The flush had faded from his face, and he was white. Wiping the sweat from his forehead, he emptied the whisky in his glass before he spoke again. "You can tell your pal I'm getting the first ship to New York."

"That would be great, Steve. We'd sure like to see you. But don't get too mad just because Cornelius wants to follow in his great-uncle's footsteps—you know what a mystical feeling he's always had for Paul. And anyway Cornelius really wants to be friendly with you about all this. In fact, he was saying to me only this morning: 'Gee, Sam,' he said, 'isn't it wonderful that we've got Steve pulling the Milk Street office to its feet again?' And he's right, Steve. We're so lucky to have you there, and now the European economy's improving maybe we can open a German office at last."

"If Cornelius wants a German office he can damn well come over here and open one himself. I'll see you next week, Sam."

"Wait! Steve, are you still there? Thank God, I thought you'd gone. Uh . . . Steve . . ." He stopped.

Steve and I looked at each other. We both knew then that Cornelius had been listening to the entire conversation.

"Steve, I've just remembered that Cornelius asked me to tell you that he's having a big dinner party next weekend for the Morgan partners and their wives. He says he's not sure how to entertain them after dinner, but he thought that once the ladies had withdrawn the men might like to listen to certain old recordings from the twenties. There was one in particular he had in mind. It was recorded on July the seventeenth, 1928. He said to be sure to mention it to you because he felt it would bring back so many interesting memories."

Steve was ashen. He did not reply. The whisky stood untasted in his glass.

"Well," said the friendly voice in New York, "we'll give you a great welcome, Steve, whenever you choose to come back on a visit, but meanwhile I can tell Cornelius, can't I, that you'll be staying on to take care of our European interests?"

"You can tell Cornelius that next time I hope he has the guts to talk to me instead of sitting on an extension and letting you do all his dirty work."

Steve severed the connection. The whisky slopped in the glass as his hand shook.

"My God," he said. "My God." He seemed incapable of further speech, and I was so shocked to see him so shattered that I too could think of nothing to say. At last, realizing that one of us at least had to remain calm, I said carefully, "I think I understood all that. Cornelius knew that you and Lewis together could always overpower him, so he smashes your coalition by forcing Lewis into retirement. Then he tames the discontented Martin by offering him the new bank. With that stroke he succeeds in getting rid of every single partner—except Hal, and you've always told me he was too tame to count—who was at the bank when Paul was assassinated. Charley and Walter are dead, Clay's resigned, Lewis has retired, Martin's been dispatched elsewhere and you're in London. That leaves Cornelius with a bunch of new partners—"

"Window dressing," said Steve. "Solid, mature yes-men, paragons of respectability. Now that Lewis is gone and Martin and I aren't there they'll simply follow Cornelius like a bunch of sheep. Then he'll pack the vacant partnerships with his own men and maneuver himself into a position where he can cut my throat."

"But how can he possibly do that when you have complete autonomy here?"

"Because Van Zale's in London isn't in fact a separate entity from Van Zale's, New York. It's true I'm allowed a free rein, but ultimately I'm always answerable to One Willow Street. And I'm vulnerable. All Cornelius has to do is set me up on the brink of a precipice and then kick me over the edge. He's got me by the balls."

"But I still don't understand—" I broke off as I saw he was reaching for the whisky again. "Let's go home, Steve, and get out of this office. You'll feel better once you're away from the scene of the crime."

On our way home in the car he explained to me how Cornelius could ruin him. He gave only one example but said he could think of others.

"Supposing someone comes to me for a loan to expand their business. Since I'm a banker in London instead of a banker in New York, the situation goes like this. . . ."

I listened, struggling to concentrate. In England a period of two weeks elapsed between the time the issuing house, such as Van Zale's, put an issue on the market and the time at which it was required to make payment to the borrowing company. Thus Van Zale's would normally have between ten and fifteen days during which it could receive money from subscribers to buy stock in the issue. In this period a large part if not all of the money due the borrowers would be collected. This was where British practice differed from the American, for in America the company wouldn't deliver its securities to the banker until it had received payment for them in full. This was why the American investment banks had to form syndicates and borrow from commercial banks; they had to pay for the securities before they could sell them to the public.

However, in England the borrowing company was more lenient to the issuing house, and Van Zale's would be allowed not only two weeks to pay for the stock but the use of the incoming subscribers' money during that time. The one danger was that if the issue didn't sell, the issuing house had to come up with the balance at the end of the two-week period, and to safeguard themselves against this potentially awkward situation the issuing house would insure the issue so that if it failed to sell within the two weeks the insurance company would provide the money to tide them over until the sale of the issue was completed. Usually there was no problem in getting an issue underwritten, but difficulties could arise.

"For instance," said Steve, "supposing I agreed to market a South American issue which I thought was safe but which the underwriters distrusted—South American issues have an uncertain reputation. Supposing I found myself unable to insure the sale of the issue and unable to dispose of it in two weeks. It's not very likely, but it could happen. What would I do? I've got to produce this money on the nail and no one here will help me. Well, there's only one thing I can do. I cable New York for backing, and naturally they give it to me. Except that if Cornelius was in the saddle waiting to stab me in the back, they might not. That would be my final curtain. I wouldn't be able to produce the money on time and word would get around that my parent house wasn't backing me up. My reputation would be deader than a dodo in no time flat. I'd be finished."

The car drew up outside our house, but neither of us made any effort to get out. As the chauffeur opened the door for us Steve said, "Dinah, I'm sorry, but I can't face the children—can't face anyone—until I've talked this out. Can we go down the road to the Ritz?"

We ended up drinking champagne. "So cheering in times of crisis!" I said firmly, but I wanted to stop him drinking whisky.

"I don't know what to do," he was saying, not listening to me. "My best bet is probably to move to another house before he outflanks me, but I hate the thought of quitting Van Zale's, I hate the thought of being beaten by that snot-nosed little kid and I'm damned if I'm going to let him get away with this."

"Could you move to another American house in London—Morgan Grenfell, for example?" I was thinking what a relief it would be if he were to settle permanently in England and we were no longer faced with the challenge of dividing our time between two continents. Much as I had been looking forward to opening a salon in New York, I had become increasingly disturbed by the thought of being away from Mallingham for six months of the year, and besides I was by no means certain we wouldn't spend most of the year in America in order to accommodate Steve. Having by this time foreseen numerous crises arising, I now realized more clearly than ever that it would be better for our marriage if Steve could resign himself to working in Europe, and I even wondered if Cornelius' midsummer mayhem might not turn out to be a blessing in disguise.

"Not Morgan's," said Steve. "I'm too unconventional for them." His eyes darkened as the name of Morgan was repeated, and I remembered Sam Keller's velvet-voiced threat on the phone.

"Steve," I said very, very carefully, as if he were a piece of pottery five thousand years old, "what exactly is this hold which Cornelius has over you?" And it was then that I first heard what had happened in 1928 when Charley Blair and Terence O'Reilly had died in Paul's office and Cornelius had set out in his waders along the bloody road to power.

II

No story could have shocked me more. It wasn't simply that Charley Blair had financed Paul's death, though that was shocking enough. It wasn't even the lawlessness of New York, where respected men took the law into their own hands and bribed the police not to interfere. What shocked me most was the thought of Cornelius, little more than a baby, effortlessly manipulating the corruption to his best advantage.

"But Steve," I said at last when I could speak, "how could you ever have believed there would be any lasting future for you at Van Zale's after you found out what kind of a man Cornelius was?"

"Hell, Dinah, he was just a kid!"

"All the more reason why you should have been scared out of your wits. If he was like that at twenty, what in God's name is he going to be like when he's forty? And what can he possibly be like now he's twenty-six? How valid do you think his present threat is? Would he ever dare play that recording to the Morgan partners?"

"No. He wouldn't. But what he's really saying is that he could use his own version of the past to discredit me without damaging himself. My style's never been popular in the most respectable corners of the Street, and Cornelius knows that. He also knows that if he started a whisper campaign by dropping a few hints to any of the Wall Street insiders my name would be mud in all the front-rank houses within six months. Then I'd be in Jay Da Costa's shoes. An investment banker depends on his reputation, and once that's shot he might as well blow his brains out. God damn it, Dinah, what *am* I going to do?"

I drank some more champagne and lit a cigarette. Then I crossed my legs, blew smoke at the ceiling and assumed my calmest expression. "Why should Cornelius be the only one to follow in Paul's footsteps?" I inquired. "You can follow in them too. What did Paul do when he was kicked out of Reischman's?"

"He founded his own house— My God!" He was thunderstruck by the possibility, but I saw his excitement die. "Well, there's no way I can do that," he said. "I don't have the capital."

"Would you be prepared to stay in England if you could raise the capital here?"

"You bet I would. Cornelius could whisper along Wall Street till he's blue in the face, but he'd have to shout out loud to get the message across the Atlantic and he's not going to go broadcasting the events of July the seventeenth through a megaphone. I'd be safe here."

"Then your worries are over, darling. I'll sell my business. Lord Malchin offered me two million pounds for it back in 1930, and it's worth much more now."

"*Christ Almighty!*" shouted Steve in a voice which must almost have reached Willow Street, and as everyone else in the room jumped with fright he joyously called to the barman, "Give us another bottle of champagne!"

I had to laugh because everyone was looking at him as if he had escaped from the zoo, but I did manage to say, "Steve, we must keep sober so that we can think this out."

"You're right," he said and amended the order to half a bottle. "Honey, would you really do that for me?"

"I want you to be successful and happy, Steve. I want to live in England. And I really would like to learn a little about banking. Would it be possible for me to—"

"Well, of course you must be a partner in the firm!" he said hugging me. "We'll be unbeatable! And we'll knock the hell out of those bastards at Willow and Wall!"

"Yes," I said, "but we must take great care and make no mistakes." I was already wondering what Cornelius would think when he discovered it was *I* who was turning the tables on him by backing Steve with my money, and I wondered too if he would realize that for Steve's sake I was prepared to fight him all the way to the very end of the line.

That was the day I ceased to be a pacifist. Most people did not start to drift away from pacifism until a year later, when Mussolini walked into Abyssinia in defiance of the League, but my change of heart took place on that June day in 1934 when I realized Steve had to fight Cornelius to survive. At first I thought my decision to fight was merely a personal one which had no broad application to the world beyond Van Zale's, but unknown to me I was on the road to the wilderness where Churchill was already exiled, shouting advice to which no one would listen, thundering prophecies which no one would believe.

III

It takes time to sell a business for the best possible price, and I was reluctant to rush matters. Steve was also anxious to increase his roster of clients before he launched his own issuing house, since the more clients he had the more were likely to follow him when he left Van Zale's.

We discussed our plans carefully. Steve calculated that he had at least one year and probably two before Cornelius moved against him, for after the upheavals in New York that summer Cornelius would be anxious to let the firm settle down before he risked further disruptions. Eventually we decided that Steve would work for a further year at Van Zale's without betraying a hint of his future plans, but in the summer of 1935 I would complete the sale of my business and Steve would begin secret negotiations to establish a link with a strong secondary, or second-rank, house on the other side of the Atlantic. Since Steve was himself an American with first-class transatlantic connections and considerable European experience, it seemed foolish to ignore these assets in seeking to establish a new house, and he told me there were plenty of American firms who would welcome the chance of a reputable link with London. Only the front-rank houses could afford the luxury of having their own men in associated houses in Europe; the other firms were usually obliged to come to arrangements with independent foreign banks to help them with their European business.

When the American link had been established and the new issuing house was ready to be launched Steve would resign from Van Zale's and open his house as near to his old firm as possible, preferably in Milk Street itself. It would be less effort for the clients if they merely had to follow him a couple of doors down the road.

"There's only one thing that worries me," said Steve, "and that's this: I'll probably have my hands so full at first that I won't be able to offer you more than a . . . a . . ."

"Sleeping partnership," I said amused. "Quite. No pun intended, of course."

He laughed, but he was still embarrassed. "You mustn't think I don't want you to help me," he said. "You mustn't think I'm keeping you out in the cold."

"I know. Don't worry, Steve. The most important thing is that you should be free to establish the new house without distractions. Anyway I'm in no hurry because I want to rest between my two careers and enjoy the new baby."

After the doctor had confirmed that I was at last a candidate for married motherhood, I had decided that this, my third and final pregnancy, was going to be the one I had the leisure to enjoy. Accordingly I delegated all my work to Harriet and went to the office only twice a week to make sure my friends weren't murdering one another in my absence.

As I spent more time with the twins I was interested to discover how different they had grown from each other. Elfrida's passion was animals; no story was worth reading unless it had an animal in it, pictures of horses festooned the walls of her room and her white rabbit which lived at Mallingham was worshiped with all the ardor that the ancient Egyptians had reserved for their animal deities. Edred, on the other hand, cared for little except the grand piano. While his goldfish remained unfed and unloved in their bowl he would thump the keyboard with a concentration which amazed me, and with anxiety I wondered if this leaning towards music could indicate a resemblance to my father. Meanwhile Alan was showing more resemblance to Paul; his new school was a success, and suddenly as if by a wave of some magic wand he was coming top of his form in every subject and winning a place in his prep school's first eleven. Presently he gave up reading books for schoolboys and embarked at the edge of eleven on Dickens, Scott and Thackeray. By the time he was twelve he was reading Homer in the original and his headmaster was telling me with pride that a Winchester scholarship was a certainty.

I could hardly believe the transformation wrought by Alan's change of identity, but the best part of the new Alan was his new attitude to the twins. He was no longer hostile but indulgent, and once I even found him helping them with their reading books.

All three children were encouragingly enthusiastic about the prospect of a new baby in the family.

"I hope it's a girl," said Elfrida, who had just had a row with Edred about the latest corpse in the goldfish bowl.

"I don't care what it is," said Edred, "but if it has a good ear I'll teach it to play the piano."

"It'll be nice to have someone else to run errands for me," said Alan. "I hope it's a girl, because girls are easier to train."

It was a boy. I was secretly disappointed, but the baby was so good-natured that I soon forgot my regrets. He was the only one of my children who resembled me physically, for the twins were little replicas of Steve, and Alan was looking more like Paul as he grew older, but George had wisps of dark straight hair and eyes that soon turned brown and a large flappy mouth which seemed to take up half his face. He was also much fatter than my previous babies, but that only made him more cuddly.

It was Steve who decided that our son should be named after no less a hero that the patron saint of England, and he was so much enjoying being an Anglophile that I hadn't the heart to tell him that Saint George had been a Cappadocian adventurer of dubious reputation. However, any warrior who can ride to sainthood on the myth of a slain dragon can at least claim to have been resourceful, and I raised no objection when the baby was christened George Steven at Mallingham Church.

It was soon after the christening that Steve went to the Continent to woo a potential client who had interests not only in England but in France, Germany and Switzerland. He had been a client of Reischman's, but in March 1935 when Italy invaded Abyssinia and Hitler adopted conscription in Germany in defiance of the Treaty of Versailles, the great House of Reischman closed its doors for the last time in Hamburg and Hitler moved to annex the Reischman fortune. However the head of the house was too clever for him; Franz Reischman had already filtered the fortune into Switzerland, and still keeping one step ahead of his enemies, he and his family slipped out of Germany on their long journey west to their cousins in New York.

Sam Keller, who was now Steve's main contact at the New York office, was enthusiastic about Steve's decision to go to Germany and thought he could profitably explore the vacuum left by the Reischman closing.

I thought of Hitler employing men like the notorious "Judenfresser" who had once said that the head of a prominent Jew should be stuck on every telegraph pole from Munich to Berlin. I thought of Göring reviving the medieval chopping block and ax for capital punishment and declaring that the headsman must always wear impeccable evening dress. I thought of Goebbels declaring after the burning of books that Jewish intellectualism had finally been extinguished.

"Well, business is business, honey," said Steve, "and you can't judge all Germans by the antics of those goons around Hitler."

"People get the government they deserve," I said, but I said nothing else because I was a novice at banking and no one was denying that the German economy had improved.

Steve was gone for two weeks, and although we spoke on the telephone he divulged no details of his business negotiations until he arrived home.

I met him at the Aerodrome. He looked very tired and I realized he had been drinking.

"What happened?" I said upset.

He slumped in the car beside me, and when the chauffeur drove away I closed the glass partition.

"The deal fell through with the Reischman client. He wanted money for a steel foundry and was hoping I could arrange for a flotation in America via Van Zale's, New York. It was a straightforward deal, but . . . Dinah, I can't do business in that country. I talked to some of the Reischman men in Switzerland and they told me stories which made even the *Time* magazine paragraphs look pale."

I was about to speak, but he gave me no time. He was saying hurriedly as if he thought I would be disappointed instead of relieved, "Don't get me wrong. It's wonderful how Germany's pulling itself to its feet at last, and all the Germans I met were very friendly to me. I'm not a preacher. I don't go around passing moral judgments and I hope I'm not the kind of foreigner who walks into a country and tells it how to behave, but Dinah, Paul trained me and Paul was trained by Reischman's. They picked him up when he was down and out, and he never forgot what he owed them. Of all the Yankee houses in the Street ours was the most pro-Jewish, and when I think of our unwritten partnership with Reischman's, enduring year after year and surviving even Paul's death, I know I just can't go raising capital for Nazi Germany. Paul would turn in his grave. It would be a betrayal of all that Van Zale's stands for, but how in God's name am I going to explain that to Sam Keller?"

I remembered that sociable charming voice and thought I could imagine the young man who owned it. "Sam would understand, wouldn't he?"

"Not a chance. He's a Nazi sympathizer."

"Surely not!" I was genuinely shocked.

"Oh, they know all about Sam Keller at Reischman's. Apparently when he came back from a visit to Germany in '33 he was saying 'Heil Hitler' all over New York." He reached for his hip flask, the legacy of Prohibition, and unscrewed the cap. "But I don't want to get into a fight with Sam before I'm ready to quit Van Zale's," he said after a mouthful of whisky, "so I'm going to pretend that although the deal fell through the visit was a success in establishing promising German contacts. That'll give us time to push ahead with our plans before Sam realizes I've been lying."

"I'll talk to Lord Malchin," I said. "I really do think he might be interested in making another offer for the business. Harriet said Lady Malchin had invited her to dinner again."

The next three months were nerveracking. Lord Malchin's Pharmaceutical and Cosmetics Products nibbled tentatively at the prospect of acquiring the business but made an offer I refused to consider. I was determined not only to get the best price but to get the best possible deal for my friends who worked with me. I started to woo Sir Aaron Shields of Shields Chemicals, who manufactured everything from cosmetics to dynamite, but Sir Aaron looked bored. However, Lord Malchin thought he had a rival and made a better offer. After that there was a pause; Sir Aaron still yawned, Lord Malchin rested serenely on his laurels and I became rapidly more distraught.

"Oh, for God's sake let me fix this!" exclaimed Steve exasperated, and to my astonishment extracted a large bid from a cosmetics firm in New York. Lord Malchin dropped his monocle, Sir Aaron looked winded and the two of them plunged into an orgy of competitive bidding.

The New York firm retired. They had made the bid only because they had owed Steve a favor, but Lord Malchin and Sir Aaron battled on until Lord Malchin, who was not only richer but more benign towards my colleagues, won.

Three and a quarter million pounds changed hands gracefully, and Steve began negotiations with the American investment banking house of his choice, a firm called Miller, Simon. It was a young house, founded in the twenties by men who had trained with Kidder, Peabody in Boston and Halsey, Stuart in Chicago, and it was one of the few aggressive young firms which had survived to see the dawn of the New Deal.

Our plans were progressing smoothly again, and it was not until Mr. William Le Clair of Miller, Simon arrived in London for his annual European holiday that we realized we were being watched with growing suspicion from One Willow Street.

For the first time in two years Steve received a direct communication from Cornelius.

Chapter Four

I

Cornelius sent a letter. It was an extraordinary work, Victorian to the point of artificiality and calculated down to the dot of the *i* in his signature to drive Steve into a towering rage. The letter was typed on thick white paper embossed with a Fifth Avenue address, and I was with Steve at the breakfast table when he ripped open the envelope.

Cornelius had dictated primly,

Dear Steve,

I have now waited two years in the hope that you might feel constrained to offer me some explanation of your conduct when you abandoned my sister in order to pursue your obsession with Miss Slade. Unfortunately I have waited in vain. However, the purpose of this letter is neither to tell you how profoundly upset I was by the injury to my sister nor to censure you on your choice of sexual partner; the past, though iniquitous, is unalterable. On the contrary, my purpose in writing this letter is because I wish you to know that I am deeply concerned for our future professional relationship.

Your reports to Sam about your triumphant progress through Germany were, as we now realize, grossly inflated and as far as we can judge your expedition there served no useful purpose. I concede you have acquired an impressive roster of clients in London, but I am now informed by the same source which earlier reported to me the news of Miss Slade's sixteen-million-dollar coup d'état that you have been flirting mysteriously with the senior partner of Miller, Simon. If you have a valid explanation of why you should bother to spend so much money cultivating this sound but second-rank house I should very much like to hear it.

Perhaps you should consider returning to New York to review the future of our partnership. I cannot say you should consider returning to my sister, since I am convinced she is better off without you, but she is loyal to you even to this day, and has won the unstinted admiration of all New York by her devotion to you and your children. Her heroism is not diminished simply because it is misguided. In fact the hardship of recent years has revived again in America a respect for decent moral values and other Christian concepts of which you appear to be totally ignorant. Perhaps it is time you ceased to be an expatriate in an environment of decadence and returned for a visit to the time-honored traditions of our native land.

I remain with respect and sincerity, your partner,

CORNELIUS

"Jesus Christ!" yelled Steve, and rushed headlong from the breakfast table.

Alan was away at Winchester by that time, but I hastily told the astonished twins to finish their breakfast while I went to inquire what was wrong. In the library I found Steve already in the middle of an incensed reply, and when I asked if I could read the letter he merely grunted his assent.

Seconds later I burst out laughing. "Honestly!" I exclaimed in delight. "I haven't read anything so entertaining since Lady Bracknell's dialogue in *The Importance of Being Earnest!* You're not taking it seriously, I hope?"

He looked at me with suspicion, his pen motionless.

"Well, it's obvious, isn't it?" I said carelessly. "He wants to quarrel with you so that you resign immediately. Then once you're no longer a Van Zale partner he'll be free to launch all kinds of nasty rumors about you before you launch our new house. It's clear he's found out exactly what's going on."

There was a silence. When he did not look at me I realized he was not only angry that he had failed to see the trap but mortified that I had recognized it on sight.

"Steve . . ." I was deeply embarrassed, wishing I had had the sense to point out the truth in such a way that he could have pretended he had discovered it himself, but before I could say anything else he had cut off my apologies with an impatient movement of his hand.

"Hell," he said, "you're right. Damn the little bastard. I won't reply at all." And he tore up his unfinished letter.

"Steve," I said with tact, "wouldn't it be better if—" I ran out of tact and stopped awkwardly.

"Go on," he said dryly. "I'll listen. God knows, where Cornelius is concerned I need all the help I can get."

It was an admission a lesser man could never have made. Kissing the top of his head, I smiled at him in admiration and said squarely, "Act as though you're much too good-natured to quarrel seriously with him. Sound annoyed but above all tolerant and even vaguely amused."

There was another pause. "Sure," he said. He took a fresh sheet of paper and sat looking at it.

"I'll do a draft if you like," I said, "and then you can alter it as much as you like, just as you would alter a letter submitted by your secretary."

He offered me his chair and pen without a word and watched over my shoulder as I wrote with gusto:

MY DEAR CORNELIUS,

Why all the fuss? My "triumphant progress through Germany," as you so kindly phrased it, resulted in excellent publicity for Van Zale's, and if I have my doubts about doing business with the Nazis it's only because I hate to think of people like our friends the Reischmans treated as if they were cattle—or worse. In short I'd recommend you to concentrate a little less on my caution in Germany and a little more on my English successes. Why you should complain about my taking an old friend like Bill Le Clair out to dinner I have no idea, but may I inform you that we expatriate Americans like to see someone from home occasionally. If you'd ever been out of the States you'd know that!

And what's all this prune-mouthed description of Dinah as my "sexual partner"? She's my wife! How would you like it if I said "How's your sexual partner?" when I inquired after Alicia's health? And what's all this earnest condemnation of promiscuity? I agree I've been no saint in the past, but neither have you! In fact since you wrote me this extraordinary letter you've probably been to bed with at least six other women besides Alicia—and don't tell me that you, with your obsession for aping Paul, practice the marital fidelity you preach! Anyway as far as cold-blooded sexual exercise is concerned, what does it matter where and with whom you perform the sexual act? I'll bet it matters precious little to you, despite the amusingly pious tone of your letter. I'm sorry about your sister, who's a good woman, but at least I'm not hypocritical enough to pretend that such a dead relationship is still alive. I'll leave that final hypocrisy to you, Cornelius.

Regards,
STEVE

"He'll never believe I wrote that," said Steve. "It's much too cool and British and debonair, and he knows I'd just wade in waving a meat ax."

"You can make it more obscene!" I suggested, making him laugh, but he refused.

"It's the right reply to the little bastard," he said. "I'll have my secretary transcribe it just the way it is." It was only after he had reread the draft that he asked curiously, "How did you know Cornelius is obsessed with Paul?"

"Everything points to it. The way he took Paul's full name after Paul's death. The way he went to live at Paul's house and work at Paul's bank. The way he called his daughter Vicky. The way Sam Keller talked about a 'mystical' feeling Cornelius had towards Paul."

"I think he's a lot more faithful to his wife than Paul ever was." He folded the draft carefully and tucked it away in his pocket. "He's just crazy about that funny little fish-eyed girl."

"She obviously represents the Eastern-Seaboard aristocracy to him. He probably feels inadequate because his father was merely an Ohio farmer." I was still holding his pen. Idly I drew a picture of a mermaid on the note pad as I considered the unknown Alicia with her piscine eyes. "What I can't understand," I remarked as an afterthought, "is why they're not hard at work reproducing themselves. Why is there no little Cornelius sitting beside them on the love seat? Cornelius is just the sort of power-hungry despot who would equate a horde of sons with virility and virility with power."

Steve laughed. "Well, the happy couple on the love seat aren't talking, but my own theory is that he came out of an attack of mumps the worse for wear. Do you know what can happen to an adult male who gets mumps?"

I shuddered. "I detest medical horror stories!" Curiosity overcame me. "Good God, do you mean he's impotent?"

"Apparently it needn't affect performance. But you can forget the hordes of sons." He shrugged, glanced at his watch and turned to the door. "But so what? They have children from their previous marriages—there are plenty of other couples in the world who are worse off than they are."

"But not many frustrated fathers like Cornelius. That's just the sort of disaster which could have a very unstabilizing effect on him, Steve. A whole avenue of power would be closed to him, and all his aggression would have to be channeled elsewhere. My God, look what Henry the Eighth did when he started crashing around trying to reproduce himself!"

"Was that the guy with six wives? I always kind of liked him. Honey, I've got to get going now or I'll be late for my first appointment."

We kissed and parted, but for a long while I remained thinking about Cornelius, rearranging the puzzle of his personality and studying each shadowy feature as carefully as I would have studied an opponent's pieces on a chessboard.

Cornelius never replied to Steve's letter, but gradually the telephone calls between Steve and Sam ceased and Steve bent all his energy towards establishing our new issuing house. It was an anxious time for us both, but at last the house was ready to be launched and on the twelfth of February, 1936, Steve cabled his resignation to his partners in New York and later announced that the new London issuing house of S. & D. Sullivan and Company had opened its doors at Number Twelve and a Half, Milk Street.

II

Having made our historic coup, we held our breath, pricked up our ears and surveyed the landscape.

In America at One Willow Street an icy silence greeted our announcement.

In England the National Government had been reelected to power and Baldwin was busy puffing his pipe. The government dithered vaguely over foreign policy, one moment supporting the League but the next moment giving way to Italian aggression, and the Peace Ballot revealed massive support among the people for the League of Nations, for disarmament, for the belief that the fascist dictators would submit to nonmilitary coercion.

But in Germany that March Hitler reoccupied the demilitarized zone of the Rhineland and no one tried to stop him.

"Well, we won't think of Hitler," I said brightly to Steve. "Boring little man!" And in fact I was so busy helping to arrange our huge celebration party to promote our new house that I didn't have the time to pay attention to international affairs. In May we gave our famous masquerade ball at the Savoy, and five hundred guests came to celebrate with us.

"It'll cost the earth!" I said when Steve first suggested the idea, but he simply laughed and told me we could well afford to pay. This was true, but I remembered my penniless days too clearly to embrace extravagance with ease, and also my riches were still mostly on paper. After the taxes had been paid and our new house established we were hardly the richest couple in England, and as a precaution I set up a trust for the children and established a fund for my old age. I did not tell Steve. I was afraid he might interpret my insecurity as a lack of confidence in him, although in fact he would most probably have approved of my foresight; he was no fool. However, his attitude to his money was very different from my attitude to mine, and I thought it was extraordinary as well as ironic that he seemed to have little interest in his income after it was earned. Making money was the game which enthralled him, and once the commission had been safely salted away he forgot about it and plunged back into the chase. He had only the sketchiest notion what his brokers were doing, and the idea that he could make himself immensely rich by imaginative management of the money he already had bored him. So long as he had enough money to live exactly as he pleased he was satisfied, and fortunately for him he always did have the money he needed; but he was haphazard about his private financial affairs, and I often thought how odd it was that although he usually had no idea of the balance in his checkbook he could and did calculate his clients' affairs down to the last farthing. He reminded me of a doctor who tirelessly saved people's lives while his own family staggered unnoticed beneath the burden of a dozen minor ailments.

Another anomaly of his position was that although he had made fabulous amounts during his years at Van Zale's he had surprisingly little to show for it. He had lost money in the Crash, he was now paying generous alimony not only to Emily but to his first wife in California, he was overwhelmingly generous to me and all seven of his children, and he liked to live well. In his eyes a ball at the Savoy was not an extravagance but a necessary business expense, and when I pointed out that we could promote our new house successfully on a less lavish scale he was incapable of seeing my point of view.

"If we're going to make a splash let's whip up a tidal wave!" he exclaimed exuberantly, and there was no doubt later that the ball's huge success more than vindicated his policy of extravagance. The event was reported in all the international magazines and described with breathless detail in the popular press. However, England is not America, where size and spectacle are all-important, and I knew that a certain segment of society considered our celebrations vulgar.

My friends, who were pleased by the degree of autonomy I had won for them from Lord Malchin, wished me well with good grace. Harriet came dressed as Lady Macbeth, Cedric masqueraded as a Tottenham Hotspur football player and both did their best to pretend that my decision to sell had not upset them.

My own feelings were ambivalent. I regretted the sale yet embraced it. It was indeed the end of an era, but it was also the beginning of another. I had had thirteen extraordinary, exciting, arduous years of Diana Slade Cosmetics, but it was time to move on, and on the horizon was the new issuing house, intricate and mysterious, its doors leading into a mouth-watering new world of challenge and adventure. I went to the ball to celebrate the future, and although I was nostalgic about the past I had no regrets.

It took me a long time to decide what I should wear, but after fobbing off the double-edged suggestions that I should dress as the Virgin Queen or Catherine the Great, I decided to go as Cinderella. I went to Norman Hartnell, who dressed Gertrude Lawrence and Evelyn Laye, and he designed a gorgeous creamy-yellow gown in the style of the late eighteenth century and shoes encrusted with metallic discs to give the illusion of glass slippers. Steve's costume was originally intended to recall the eighteenth century too, but he soon decided that the necessary wig would be tiresome and that George Washington's identity wasn't the most tactful to assume in the circumstances. It was I who suggested he masquerade as the Duke of Wellington, and he eventually made a dazzling entrance in skin-tight white trousers and a cutaway coat which made me realize how sexy men's fashions were in 1815. He complained he couldn't sit down, but I told him that everyone occasionally had to make sacrifices in order to be beautiful.

All the children came to the ball, even Alan who had obtained a special exeat from Winchester. He was dressed as a turbaned Indian page, and the twins came as a Dresden shepherd and shepherdess. They were an absolute menace with their crooks, but Nanny somehow managed to prevent them from doing too much damage.

Nanny was dressed inevitably as Nanny and looked as Queen Victoria might have looked if she had been taken by magic carpet to the cities of Sodom and Gomorrah. Since she had her hands full watching the twins, the latest nursemaid was in charge of George, who was now fourteen months old and could stagger along in drunken fashion on his fat little legs. George came as a cherub. We popped him into a little white tunic and attached a pair of silver wings to his back, but fancy dress bored him and after pulling off the wings he fell asleep beside a tray of petits fours.

We hired the best band in London, ordered eight hundred bottles of 1928 champagne at twelve pounds a case and flung open the ballroom doors.

"Some party!" gasped Steve as we snatched a dance with each other sometime after two.

I thought of his party ten years before on Long Island when I had listened to the band blaze into the Charleston. The twenties seemed far away now, almost as far away as that remote epoch before 1914. I looked around at the luxury from which all brashness had been ruthlessly excluded. The band was playing an old-fashioned waltz.

The dancing lasted till dawn, when a party of us drove to Mallingham for breakfast. It must have been a long night for the chauffeurs, but we slept on the journey and awoke ready to begin the party all over again. At noon I was suddenly smitten not only by exhaustion but by a desperate desire to be alone, and abandoning my guests, I rowed out over the Broad and found a quiet spot in the reeds. Steve arrived an hour later. He rowed the dinghy around the Broad until he found my hiding place, and after climbing into the rowing-boat so clumsily that he nearly capsized it he fell asleep with his head on my breast. It was a quiet ending to such a flamboyant occasion, and kissing him with relief I lay back to watch the clouds floating over the wide Norfolk sky.

All but the oldest and most conservative of his clients followed Steve up the road to the new house, and across the Atlantic a new man was dispatched without comment to pick up the pieces at Six Milk Street.

A month later I read that Mrs. Cornelius Van Zale had held a dazzling fashion show in her beautiful Fifth Avenue home and that all the proceeds of this charitable gathering had been donated to medical research. For the benefit of European readers the article noted that Mrs. Van Zale was the wife of the well-known philanthropist who had just launched a new foundation to assist struggling writers and artists, and there was also a picture of Alicia looking devastating in a little black dress which had probably cost at least fifty guineas. I thought Steve had been unkind to her in his descriptions. Mrs. Van Zale said when interviewed that she and her husband had simple tastes and liked nothing better than a quiet evening alone together while they listened to their favorite radio shows; they were looking forward to their usual quiet summer holiday at Bar Harbor with their three children; they did not care to travel abroad. Mrs. Van Zale was a regular client at Miss Elizabeth Arden's salon and was dressed by Chanel, whose designs she liked because they were "simple" and "quiet." She had no views on politics but understood that her husband was in favor of international peace.

In Europe the British and French governments, also much in favor of international peace, rushed to arrange for nonintervention in the Spanish Civil War, and all the major European powers, including Germany and Italy, signed this agreement at the end of August. But in the autumn Germany and Italy swung into the Rome-Berlin Axis and agreed in future to hunt as a pair.

It was such a relief when the papers purged themselves of all foreign news to concentrate on the Abdication.

"This shows the British at their worst," said Steve, who was having to tolerate a large amount of anti-American sentiment. "All this talk about divorce and the Church is just an excuse. They don't want Mrs. Simpson to get the King because she's a foreigner."

"Darling, it's much more complicated than that!" I protested, but I did not argue long with him, because I had spent many years admiring the King when he was Prince of Wales, and although I did not care for Mrs. Simpson I thought some sort of compromise should be found to accommodate them.

I was very much immersed in current events at that time because I had so little to do. Steve was totally absorbed by his work, which he would willingly discuss with me whenever he had a spare moment, but I was becoming more and more uncomfortably unemployed. At first I had enjoyed my leisure. I had met all my friends for lunch, gone to matinees, tried—unsuccessfully—to understand modern art, and joined the Left Book Club. But after a while these occupations had palled. I missed the cut-and-thrust of the business world, and the round of trivial social activity seemed shallow. I loved seeing more of George, but one cannot and should not expect intellectual stimulation from a child less than two years old no matter how adorable, entrancing and unique that child may be. The twins were at school all day. Alan was away. My servants ran the house with splendid efficiency.

I was bored to tears.

Finally, after the Abdication, when I felt I couldn't face reading one more article on the ideological significance of the Spanish Civil War, I plucked up my courage and asked Steve if I might accompany him to the office each day and begin my apprenticeship as unobtrusively as possible.

"Well, look, honey," he said. "Give me a little more time, could you? I haven't forgotten my promise, but while the house is so new I don't want to do anything which might disturb the clients—and you know how old-fashioned the English are."

I left the room without a word. I could not argue with him, because I knew that what he said was true and I had no wish to handicap our joint enterprise. I decided I had to wait until the house was a year old, but when the first anniversary came and Steve made the same excuse I couldn't help saying, "Steve, how would *you* feel if you'd been out of work for a year and your wife wouldn't lift a finger to get you an interesting job?"

I spoke in a mild voice, but he immediately lost his temper. That was when I realized how guilty he felt about my exclusion. "I can't help the clients' attitudes!" he shouted. "Jesus, Dinah, I have enough trouble being a foreigner! How the hell do you think they'd react if I brought in a woman to help me run the show?"

"Well, at least I'm not a foreigner!" I said, trying to make a joke of it.

"Dinah," he said, "face facts. There'd be tremendous prejudice against you, and that prejudice would rebound on me. And I'll be honest with you. I can't afford it. I've had too many setbacks lately."

That was when I first learned that some of his major clients had returned to Van Zale's.

"All the more reason why you should take on extra help," I said calmly.

"You're not even trained."

"I can learn."

"I know, but—"

"You don't want me there."

"Dinah, it's the clients."

"No, Steve, it's you."

"Well, honey, I've been thinking a lot about this and I figure it would really be better for our marriage if—"

I walked out.

I walked through the streets into St. James's Park and down Whitehall to Downing Street. I did not know why I went there except that when I saw the railings I remembered the suffragettes and thought how lucky I had always been, cushioned by Paul's money and influence from the intractable facts of life. Pausing only to marvel at my past hypocrisy, I walked back into Whitehall and found a taxi to take me home.

Steve was waiting up for me. The empty bottle of whisky was the first thing I noticed when I entered the library.

"Dinah—"

"Steve darling, I'm so sorry." I kissed him. "I shouldn't have got so upset. I think I've been very stupid for a very long time. Of course it's quite impossible for me to work at Milk Street, and it's not your fault either. I think when we originally agreed to go into it together we weren't being at all realistic."

He was stunned by my concessions. "It's not that I don't want you there," he stammered. "I promised you and I hate to break a promise. But the clients—the situation—"

"I understand. Don't worry about the promise. I release you from it."

"But I know you must be bitterly regretting giving up your business—"

"Never." I lit a cigarette with composure. "One must get one's priorities right. I sold my business for several reasons, not least of which was that I was tired of it and wanted a change. I also sold it to help you outwit Cornelius, who's obviously quite one of the most dangerous men I've never met. My mistake was not in selling the business. I'd do that all over again if I had to. But I do think it was a mistake to think we could work together at our issuing house."

There was a pause. At last he said awkwardly, "I'd really like to. If it weren't for the clients—"

"Let's forget the clients, Steve."

He reddened in an agony of embarrassment and drank some whisky. "Some husbands and wives can work together, I guess."

"Yes. But we can't. It's much better to face up to this, Steve, and accept it. It would be a disaster if we tried to work together."

"There's no need to go into reasons!" he said, as if terrified I intended to broadcast from the rooftops that he could not work with a wife who was cleverer than he was, but all I said was a tranquil "There's no need to go into reasons. It's simply a fact of life."

"But it's so baffling," he said with the naïveté which had always touched me. "I don't get it. I know it's a fact of life, but I can't understand why."

"Simple biology. You've got to feel you're a winner. Coming second is the biggest genital-chiller known to man."

"But that's not biology! That's all in the mind!"

"Maybe the mind of a twenty-first-century man will be different.

And maybe I wouldn't want to go to bed with him, anyway. You're the one I want to go to bed with, Steve, and you're right here and now in 1937."

"But you must resent me so much—"

"Rubbish. Oh, darling, can't you understand? As I said earlier, it's all a question of priorities. In the very beginning when I didn't love you I didn't want to marry you because I knew instinctively I'd never be able to cope with a situation like this. My ambition had to come before everything, and the marriage would inevitably be doomed. That's why I was always so frightened of marriage—I saw it as an infringement on my right to put my ambition first, a right which I equated with the right to survive. But I define survival differently now, Steve. I've at last got what I've always wanted, love and security, and I'm not jeopardizing that for all the issuing houses in London! Of course I shall eventually go out to work again—and the sooner the better before I go completely round the bend—but I no longer equate survival with making a million pounds. I'm not in blinkers any more. I've got wider horizons."

Three quarters of an hour later in bed he said worried, "But what will you do, Dinah?"

"Do?" I said vaguely. "Oh, do. Yes, I see. I'm going to follow in my mother's footsteps. Thank goodness that in this day and age I won't end up in prison being forcibly fed."

He was so astounded that he sat up in bed and switched on the light. "Just say that again, honey. I think I must be going crazy."

I obligingly said it again.

"But why? I thought you said you were so angry with your mother! I thought—"

"Oh, it was all a misunderstanding," I said equably. "I realized that this evening. You see, I thought she was campaigning for stupid things like the right to smoke in public and drive a bus—all the sort of thing that the War made possible without any help from the suffragettes. I thought her cause was a pathetic embarrassing antiquated piece of history which had no possible relevance to me. I was wrong." I sighed. "I've been wrong about so many things, Steve. Isn't it amazing to think that when I first met Paul I thought I knew absolutely everything there was to know?"

"I guess we all think that at twenty-one. About your mother . . ."

"Oh, yes. Well, of course she was campaigning basically against accepting cynicism and hypocrisy as a way of life. She must have been an idealist and she must have reached the stage where she felt that no further compromise with cynicism and hypocrisy was possible. So she took a stand. She stood up for what she believed in. She said, 'This is wrong and must be stopped.'" I paused, thinking of the headlines in the newspapers. "That's what we'll all have to say one day," I said. "All of us."

He asked me how I was going to follow in my mother's footsteps, but I didn't know. "One could get up on a soapbox at Hyde Park Corner and prattle about equality for women," I said, "but what good would that do? Obviously it would be better to prattle from the back benches at Westminster, but the political parties are so dreary at the moment and anyway I'm no longer sure where I stand politically. I'll have to think about it."

I was still thinking about it after the Coronation in May when Steve told me another important client had defected to Van Zale's. He had his explanations ready. There had been trouble with Miller, Simon; they suffered from a fundamental ignorance about Europe which made communication difficult. The new man at the Van Zale office was a two-faced sharpshooter who would stop at nothing to get the clients to return to Six Milk Street. The defecting client was just a stuffy Englishman who wanted to play safe by returning to a long-established house. The market was difficult, Germany was a menace. . . . The explanations went on and on.

The truth, which I had suspected at the masquerade ball, was that Steve's personality was fundamentally alien to the English. When he had been representing an established house with the whole weight of the Van Zale reputation behind him this defect had not mattered, but now that he was on his own he stood out in the Lombard Street community like a samurai at Sandhurst. He was too flamboyant to appeal to the financial men of the City with their shadowed faces, quiet demeanor and rigid codes of conduct. Steve may have been successful in his profession, but the feeling lingered that he was not a gentleman, and even six months after the debacle of the Abdication any American was automatically viewed with suspicion.

How far Steve was aware that he had been judged by the English and found wanting I had no idea. He was such a curious mixture of the shrewd and the naïve that it was hard to guess how sensitive he was to the feelings which lurked behind his defecting clients' polite façades. He must have known something was wrong, yet he might easily have refused to believe that his personality was responsible for his troubles, and I had no intention of impairing his already shaky self-confidence by pointing out a few home truths. Besides, this would have been pointless. One cannot expect a man to alter his entire personality to suit his clients, and so Steve and I went on, he making excuses and I listening to them without argument, until I gradually realized he was drinking far, far too much.

He had always been a heavy drinker. I had accepted that and made no effort to change him, but I was conscious as middle age overtook him that the ravages of alcohol were finally taking their toll on his appearance. He had a splendid physique and superb health, but now he was fifty years old and not only looked it but often looked older. His curly hair was gray, his face was heavily lined, his striking eyes were often dull and bloodshot. He had put on weight, too, and as I noticed this steady decline in his looks I realized that any decline in his career could hardly have struck him at a more vulnerable time in his life.

My anxiety about him increased that summer when Emily the Saint decided to bring all Steve's American children to England to see him again. Naturally he was grateful to her, because the pressures of his business made it impossible for him to leave England for a visit to America, but I became nervous when Emily announced that she had rented a house by the sea at Bognor Regis for two months. I did not seriously suppose Emily would attempt to seduce him, but I was terrified she would as usual arouse all his guiltiest memories.

"Shall I come with you to Southampton to meet the ship?" I offered tentatively, although Emily was the very last person I wanted to meet. I felt sure she would have reduced me to despair in no time at all.

"No, no," he said. "That would be hell. I always think there's nothing worse than a wife and an ex-wife trying to be nice to each other while the husband looks on."

I agreed, but I still hated to see him go off alone. He met the ship, installed Emily and the children in their Bognor house and staggered back to London.

"How did it go?" I said, hardly daring to ask.

"Fine," he said, pouring himself a triple whisky. "The little girls were very cute and I hardly recognized Scott and Tony because they'd grown so much. They all seemed well and happy and pleased to see me, so I thought I'd go back to Bognor tomorrow with the twins and George."

"Good. How's Emily?"

"Lovelier and sweeter than ever. I wish to God she'd remarry. It makes me feel so guilty to think of her living alone, bringing up my children single-handed, and all without a single word of reproach."

How I managed not to scream I have no idea. I clenched my fists, counted to five and said in a mild voice, "Steve, don't let the children spend the whole summer at Bognor—let's have them to stay as often as possible. It'll be fun, and since Emily has the children all the time she'll be glad to relax by herself for a change. Why don't you suggest it?"

To my relief he did, and soon I had the chance to see my stepsons again and meet my stepdaughters. The little girls were four and six years old, both pretty and both painfully shy. They clung to their nanny and asked hourly when they could go home to "Mama." Scott was seventeen, tall as Steve and handsome in a dark sultry way which was most attractive, but although Emily had improved his manners I still found him hostile. However, fortunately Tony was so charming that he made up for Scott's shortcomings. He and Alan picked up their friendship with ease once Alan had returned from Winchester, and Steve thought that the next year Tony might cross the Atlantic on his own to spend the summer with us.

My own children with the exception of Alan regarded the American invasion without enthusiasm. The twins considered Rosemary and Lorraine hopelessly babyish and Scott and Tony awesomely adult. When George complained that the little girls kept getting in his way I became harassed enough to wonder how Emily coped when they all descended on Bognor, but of course from the moment my children first crossed her rented threshold Emily made sure everyone had a wonderful time.

"There was this lovely, lovely lady," said George after the first visit. "Like a queen. I paddled in the sea and she held my hand when a big wave came. Then we had jam sandwiches for tea and chocolate cake and pink ices."

"We all played French cricket," said Edred. "It was absolutely ripping. Everyone played, even Emily and *even Scott*. We laughed and laughed and afterwards had lots of lemonade which Emily had made herself."

"Emily has real gold hair," said Elfrida. "I asked her if it was dyed and Nanny was livid with me, but Emily just laughed and said it was real. She had a jolly nice bathing costume and she told me how pretty my dress was and asked if you had my clothes specially made for me, so I said no and told her about Marshall and Snelgrove. She was nice. We talked for ages."

"I'm so glad, darling," I said in a cocktail-party voice.

"You can come down to Bognor with us next time if you like, Alan," said Steve. Alan had been at Winchester during the first visit to Emily. "I know Emily wants to meet you."

"Thank you," said Alan, who had long since rejected his Van Zale relations as thoroughly as he had rejected Paul, "but no."

"Why?" demanded Edred. "Emily's your cousin. She explained it to us. Your father was her mother's brother—"

"Grandmother's brother," corrected Elfrida.

"I'm not interested in distant relatives."

"How rude!" said Elfrida. "And Emily's so nice!"

"Elfrida," I said gently, "leave Alan alone. He may have all sorts of reasons which you know nothing about."

"Oh, you always take Alan's side!" stormed Elfrida, and she rushed from the room.

"I need a drink," I said to Steve.

"God, so do I!"

We drank and went on drinking. Eventually in early September Emily went back to America. I was never more relieved to know that the *Queen Mary* had left Southampton, and my consumption of alcohol went into an abrupt decline.

Unfortunately Steve's did not.

It was early in 1938 when I first heard the rumors which Cornelius was disseminating about him. I had been in Norfolk inspecting the flood damage, for that February the sea broke through Horsey Gap to make Mallingham an island again and the waves had even reached the walls of the Hall. By the time I returned to London I was exhausted by the effort of cleaning up the mess, but I was determined not to cancel an important lunch I had arranged to further my new career. I had decided to interest myself in women's education. It seemed to me that the more women were well-educated the more likely they would be to object strongly when they later found themselves underpaid, underprivileged and underestimated by their co-workers, and my vision of the future encompassed a world where so many women were sufficiently well-educated to hold well-paid jobs that the government was forced to legislate against discrimination by sex. I was prepared to admit that this was a somewhat radical vision, but I was surprised when so many people found it shocking.

I was just expressing these sentiments over lunch at the Savoy to my three guests, all of whom had important posts in the world of women's education, when I heard an American say at the next table, ". . . and so I went to Van Zale's in New York."

"Did you see Van Zale himself?" asked his English companion.

"Yes, he was very competent, just a young guy, but it was clear he knew what he was doing. Later I told him how surprised I was that Sullivan quit. Have you ever met Sullivan?"

"No, but we've all heard of him, of course. He'll come a cropper before long. He drinks, you know."

"So Van Zale said. In fact, Van Zale said that Sullivan's 'resignation' wasn't voluntary—they had to get rid of him and were nice enough to let him leave with his reputation intact."

"Well, I'm not surprised," said the Englishman. "But they've got a good man at Van Zale's in Milk Street now, an American but educated in England, really a very civilized sort of chap." And he began to talk about the benefits of an English education.

My guests were still talking enthusiastically about founding a new organization to promote grammar-school education for girls, but I could no longer concentrate and as soon as I decently could I went home.

I decided to tell Steve about the conversation because I saw it as a chance to bring up the subject of his drinking without fear of triggering an unpleasant scene. I knew what happened when one attempted to criticize a heavy drinker for his habits, but I thought that if I merely repeated the story Steve's anger would be directed not at me but at Cornelius.

I succeeded almost too well. He immediately wanted to sue Cornelius for slander, but he calmed down, became more rational and promised me solemnly that he would cut down on his drinking.

I had heard that story before, but I nevertheless encouraged him to try while I carefully pruned our social calendar so that we led a quieter, more relaxed life. I also shelved my ideas of carving out a career as a fund raiser for various educational schemes. I had no idea whether I would have been a success in this field, but it seemed obvious that the last thing Steve needed at that time was a wife who was pursuing her own career with success while his was foundering. Instead I thought it might be wise to discover how much talent I did have for fund raising, so I selected a charity connected with bettering the lot of the poor in the East End and put myself to work. It was good experience for me, it passed the time and Steve could hardly regard it as a threat, particularly since I was exhibiting conventional behavior for a woman of my class by dabbling with charity work. I was also able to help the poor, a fact which I often forgot but which was undeniably true. The women in the East End certainly gave me food for thought. They had countless children, lived in one room without running water, shared a lavatory with thirty other families and died of malnutrition and exhaustion when they were about my age.

I often thought how lucky I was, even as my problems with Steve increased, and to divert myself from both the dreaded shadow of alcoholism and the sordid facts of the East End I turned back once more to the newspapers and magazines.

In the new magazine *Picture Post* there was a photograph of the well-known millionaire Mr. Cornelius Van Zale at a New York ball given to launch his new art museum and celebrate his thirtieth birthday. Mr. Van Zale expressed a genuine admiration for certain types of modern painting; he thought Picasso was probably a good investment, and he was hoping to acquire some pictures by Modigliani. When interviewed later by *Time* magazine about his first thirty years, Mr. Van Zale said he was quite pleased with them and hoped the next thirty years would be as interesting. When asked about his philosophy of life Mr. Van Zale said he believed in the old-fashioned American virtues of thrift, hard work and loyalty to one's family and the flag.

Meanwhile in Europe the swastika was rampant. We used to see the newsreels whenever we went to the pictures, and as we heard the hysteria of the Nazi gatherings I would close my eyes and see not modern Germany on the screen but the tortured art of Dürer and Bosch. The old metaphysical concept of evil took root in my mind; for the first time I felt truly close to the medieval intellects who could so clearly visualize the fires of hell and the screams of the souls in purgatory, and the fires seemed to roar again before me in a nightmare which not even Bosch could have foreseen.

Emily was going to bring the children to England that summer, but hesitated at the last minute because the international situation was so grave. Tony came on his own but left well before the end of August.

In September the British Navy was mobilized, Hitler shouted that Czechoslovakia was the last territorial demand he would make and Chamberlain flew to Munich to make peace.

When he came back with his piece of paper I said wonderingly to Steve, "Doesn't he know? Can't he see? There *is* no compromise with these people. Duff Cooper sees that, Eden sees it, Churchill sees it . . ."

But the country, swooning with relief, didn't want to see it, couldn't bear to look at the fires which were raging ahead of us in our doomed corridor of time. Even I had to look away, and when Steve's final collapse came it was a relief to exclude the outside world and turn instead to our severe and all-consuming personal problems.

At the end of the year he lost two more important clients. Business was bad anyway for bankers, and for Steve it was disastrous. While he was in bed for a week after a bout of suicidal drinking I went to our house, used my power as a partner and demanded to know the exact financial position.

It was bad, worse than I had anticipated, and I knew the house was doomed. The correct decision was obviously to cut our losses, salvage the remains of our capital and retreat to Mallingham for a while, and as soon as I considered the prospect I realized how tired I had become of my London life. London would be unsuitable for the children anyway when war came, and Steve would need a quiet place to recuperate. We would still have enough money to live a comfortable country life; Steve could take his time to decide what to do next, and if he could only give up the drinking I was sure he would have no trouble finding a first-class job. It would probably be better if he made no attempt to reenter banking, but he could perhaps act as a financial consultant for one of the big American companies in England. I wondered what I would do if he wanted to return permanently to America, but in fact, as I soon realized, Steve had no desire to return a failure to New York and give Cornelius the satisfaction of watching him find a job. He also had no desire to concede defeat at Milk Street—and no desire whatsoever to give up drinking.

I tried to reason with him, but as anyone who has ever lived with an alcoholic knows, they can be very unreasonable people. Finally he flew into a rage, said it was all my fault he was in such a mess and told me to get the hell out of his business affairs. This also was fairly typical behavior for an alcoholic. I didn't argue with him, but I didn't stay with him either. I could still hear the doctor telling my father's third wife that once the alcoholic picks a victim that victim has to escape in order to preserve his own sanity. Accordingly I packed two suitcases, collected Elfrida from her day school and caught the train to Norwich. Nanny was already at Mallingham with George, Edred was now away at prep school and Alan as usual was at Winchester.

I left a note for Steve which read:

I'm very sorry, but I've already lived with someone who drank himself to death and it's an experience I can't go through again. I love you and I want you to get well more than anything else in the world, but I can no longer help you. Only you yourself can do that now.

DINAH

He arrived at Mallingham at dawn the next day. After leaving the train at North Walsham he had walked the eight miles east to Mallingham. He was worn out, disheveled but sober.

"Dinah."

I awoke with a start and in the dawn light saw his face. Leaping out of bed, I ran to him.

"Steve—darling—"

"I'll give it up," he said. "I'd give up anything for you." He kept asking me if I loved him and I kept telling him that it was because I loved him that I had left.

"I had to take some positive action—it was terribly important—I had to make you realize—"

"I was afraid you didn't love me," he said. "I was afraid that if I was a failure you wouldn't love me anymore." And he said the words Paul had always denied me, told me he could never look at another woman and wouldn't want to live in a world where I didn't exist.

I kissed him, slid my arms around his neck and stroked his untidy hair. Then I said, "There's a place in Hampstead. It's very exclusive and very, very private. Harriet told me about it. Several of her clients from the salon have been there to have a nervous breakdown or stop drinking or both. There's a resident doctor. It isn't run by quacks."

"But if everyone in the City knows I'm at some place for crazy people—"

"It won't be difficult to keep it quiet. We'll simply say you've gone back to America to attend to some private family matters. Luke and Matt have just returned to the States—you can say you went out to California to help them settle down." I did not argue with him about his future in the City. I was bending all my will towards getting him to the nursing home.

After a long silence he said, "How do I get into this place?"

"I'll ring them up and find out."

"God," he said, "I've got to have a drink. I'm sorry, but I can't think clearly anymore unless I have something. Forgive me—I can't help it. I love you, but . . ." He opened a drawer of the tallboy, rummaged among his pullovers and produced a bottle of vodka.

"Steve," I said, "we won't bother about phoning Hampstead. Let's just drive there straightaway."

"Whatever you say," he said. "Whatever you want."

I drove him all the way to Hampstead. It took four hours and he was unconscious when we arrived. The doctor was very understanding and even lent me his handkerchief when I broke down. I cried for some time, but afterwards I felt calmer and more optimistic. The critical first step towards recovery had been taken and I could at least allow myself to believe he might recover.

Two weeks later in early February when Hitler was already eying Poland and Chamberlain was finally realizing that no further compromise was possible, I had a telephone call from Cornelius' right-hand man, Sam Keller.

Chapter Five

I

I was in London when he telephoned. I had to be there during the week with Elfrida, who attended a day school in Hammersmith, and although Steve was allowed no visitors I wanted to be near the nursing home in case the worst happened and he walked out. After a light supper I had just escaped into the romantic fantasy of Tennyson's poetry when the telephone rang. The head parlormaid answered it. When she entered the room I told her to say I was not at home, but curiosity overcame me and I asked who the caller was.

"A Mr. Keller, madam. He sounded like an American gentleman."

My volume of Tennyson thudded to the floor as I rushed out into the hall.

By the telephone I paused until I was calmer and then said casually into the receiver, "Mr. Keller?"

"Yes, good evening, Mrs. Sullivan—how are you?" he said, and suddenly I was back at Milk Street five years ago in 1934 when that same voice had told Steve that Cornelius had outwitted him. Yet this was not an overseas call. From the quality of the sound I knew that Sam Keller was in London. "Excuse me for calling when we've never met," he was saying with the leisurely charm I remembered so well, "but I was wondering if by any chance you'd be free to have lunch with me tomorrow. I arrived in London yesterday and I'm staying at the Savoy."

I was terrified he had discovered what had happened.

"How nice of you!" I said graciously, knowing I had to find out how much he knew. "Thank you."

"Shall we say one o'clock at the Savoy? I'll be waiting in the lobby."

"Lovely!" I said with a meticulous display of warmth, and after ringing off I stared for a long time at the silent phone.

II

I dressed with great care in a pale-beige long-sleeved dress which looked well with my fox furs, and wore a dark-brown broad-brimmed hat with matching handbag, gloves and shoes. I took a full hour over my makeup and when I looked in the glass I was satisfied. My skin, my strongest point even though I was thirty-eight, was clear and glowing; with makeup I could still hide the tiresome minor wrinkles. I had chosen a muted shade of lipstick to tone down my wide mouth, my nose was subdued by careful shadowing and my eyes looked softly knowing. Deciding I looked exactly as Sam Keller would want me to look, I gave my reflection one last smile and swept outside to my chauffeur.

The pigeons in Trafalgar Square were pinched with cold but the sun was shining on Nelson, and as we passed the National Gallery I glanced down Whitehall to Big Ben shining against the pale winter sky.

I thought of Hitler gobbling up Bohemia and Moravia to complete Chamberlain's humiliation, and was just picturing a blond handsome Sam Keller, the perfect specimen of the master race, when the car drew up at the Savoy.

I was on time, which meant five minutes late. As the commissionaire opened the door for me I strolled into the foyer and glanced nonchalantly around for my smart, sleek, heel-clicking Nazi.

A tall dark man with a square honest face and broad workmanlike shoulders whipped off his horn-rimmed spectacles and ambled towards me with a warm friendly hopeful grin.

"Mrs. Sullivan? Sam Keller. How are you?" He offered me a large firm hand to shake while his admiring eyes made me feel as if I were the only woman in London who could possibly interest him.

"How do you do, Mr. Keller." Shaking hands weakly, I found myself being spirited into the Savoy Grill. Naturally he had the best table booked for us, and naturally the waiters fell over themselves to pay us attention.

He asked me if I wanted a cocktail before we ordered, but when I merely suggested a glass of wine with the meal he held out a hand for the wine list, which immediately appeared between his fingers. Meanwhile I was scrabbling for a cigarette, but he had discarded the list and struck a match even before the cigarette touched my lips. Under cover of this mundane social ritual I took a closer look at him. He had the trick of making his immaculately cut suit look as comfortable as a pair of dungarees, and so strong was his aura of casual charm that I had the absurd longing to unhook my corsets, sag in my chair and pour out to him the story of my life.

"Is your wife here with you?" I asked politely, finding it impossible to believe he had reached the age of thirty-one without some woman steering him to the altar.

"Oh, I'm not married yet," he said, lighting his own cigarette. "I leave the marriages to my friend Cornelius." And through the smoke of our cigarettes I looked into the soft dark friendly eyes of Cornelius Van Zale's hatchet man.

The nervousness sank like a dead weight to the pit of my stomach.

When our menus arrived we spent some time discussing the food and comparing the Savoy with New York's Plaza Hotel, but eventually the food was ordered and the headwaiter was hovering over the wine list.

"We'll take a bottle of the Piesporter Goldtröpfchen '24," said Sam Keller.

He had an American accent with the usual slack consonants and an unusual way of mauling the English long *a* so that it was neither long nor short but a strangled mixture of the two. He also, unlike most Americans, did not roll the *r*'s which the English leave silent, and this made his speech seem even more casually articulated. So when he pronounced the words "Piesporter Goldtröpfchen" with every consonant vibrating and every un-English vowel sound ringing faultlessly true I was so startled that I nearly knocked over my glass of water.

He looked alarmed. "I'm sorry. Aren't people drinking German wines anymore in London? If you'd care for something else . . ."

"Good heavens, no! I like German wine very much."

"Well, I wouldn't want to give offense," he said, "and I know Americans are sometimes insensitive in Europe. Having been born on this side of the Atlantic, I sometimes like to pretend I'm a European, but that's just wishful thinking, I'm afraid, because the truth is I'm one hundred percent American and my ties are exclusively with the United States. And talking of America . . ."

He was very smooth. It was impossible not to be impressed. ". . . is it really true Steve's gone back there on a private visit? That's the story they handed me at Milk Street, but I thought I'd check it with you before I passed the word to Emily and the children to expect a visit from him."

I referred with just the right amount of worried reticence to Steve's brothers and hinted nebulously at some new family crisis. I had already cabled Luke and Matt to ask them to confirm this story to anyone who inquired, and I thought the lie could certainly be sustained for the length of Sam Keller's visit to London.

"Gee, that's too bad," said my host, gazing at me with great sympathy. "That must be worrying for Steve."

The waiter arrived with the wine, displayed it and uncorked the bottle while we watched. I was twisting my napkin under the table as I tried to guess how far Sam believed me.

"What brings you to London, Mr. Keller?" I asked, changing the subject as soon as it was decently possible.

He told me to call him Sam. "Well, it's real sad," he said with a sigh, "but I've come to wind up the Milk Street office and close our doors."

I had heard of Americans pulling their capital out of London, but I was still shocked. Biting back the obvious remark about rats and sinking ships, I said dryly, "So Cornelius is hauling up the drawbridge over the Atlantic moat!"

"Now, don't get us wrong!" he said easily. "If America later wants to float a war loan we'll be at the front of the syndicate. This is purely a routine precaution to avoid any risk of capital confiscation."

"By a German government at Westminster!"

He laughed as if complimenting me on my sense of humor. "Sounds crazy, doesn't it!" he agreed good-humoredly. "But of course Neil has to think of every eventuality. Hell, we don't want to talk about politics, do we? It's enough to read about it in the press every darned day!" He raised his glass with a smile. "To England!" he said willingly as he drank his German wine.

"To all those Americans," I said, "who understand that no man is an island and no moat is ever unbridgeable."

I might not have spoken. Not a muscle of his face betrayed any emotion. Instead he said as he put down his glass, "You must tell me about your children. Do you by any chance have a photograph of Alan? Is he like Paul?" And later when he had marveled at the likeness he said with a sincerity I could never have questioned, "Paul was a great man. I owe him everything. Someday I'd like to meet your son to tell him what a great man his father was."

I was touched. A second afterwards I realized that he had intended me to be. He had diagnosed my hostility and had played his trump card to neutralize it. As the fear closed in on me again I noted his skill with the detached respect of one grandmaster for another and tried to read the pattern his moves were forming on the complex chessboard of our lives.

"I'm sure your friend Cornelius shares your opinion of Paul," I said. "He thinks of Paul as a father, doesn't he?"

"Why, no," said Sam, "I wouldn't say that. Neil has actually become very interested in his own father in recent years. He's just bought the Ohio farmhouse which his father used to own."

I wondered if this surprising observation was supposed to reassure me that Cornelius had no cause to be jealous of Alan.

"I thought Cornelius had a mystical feeling about Paul?" I said, quoting his own phrase to him.

He failed to recognize it. "Well, he hero-worshiped him originally—we all did. And there was a time when he thought his life was mirroring Paul's. But the two of them were pretty different, you know, and Neil's mature enough now to accept the difference and welcome it."

"Welcome it? You mean he thinks he's better than Paul?"

"I didn't say that. But Paul, great man though he was, had his weaknesses, didn't he, and they happen to be weaknesses Neil doesn't share. For example, he's a devoted family man, faithful to his wife, loyal to his sister, wonderful with the children . . ."

A syrupy paean followed. By the time our first course was finished and the second had arrived I was so bored that I said, "Tell me about his halo. How big is it? And does he wash his wings every night or only on Sundays?"

Sam laughed. "Am I overselling him? I just wanted to give you the other side of the coin because I can well imagine the kind of opinions you've been getting from Steve."

So we had returned to Steve at last. I watched the waiter refill our glasses and wondered what was coming next. "Why should it matter to you what I think of Cornelius?" I said lightly to Sam.

"It doesn't matter to me," he said, "but Neil is kind of anxious that you should think well of him. As a matter of fact, that's the other reason why I'm in London. I didn't just come to close the doors at Six Milk Street. I came on Neil's behalf to offer you the olive branch of peace."

"Sweet of Cornelius!" I said. I could no longer eat, but I continued to prod the grilled sole and poke the boiled potato. "I adore olive branches. What form does this particular olive branch take?"

"I'm serious, Dinah," said Sam, looking serious. "Neil's well-intentioned towards you. Of course, when he was just a kid he got all hot under the collar because you made life tricky for Sylvia, but he was too young then to understand what life was really all about. And of course he was kind of ambivalent about Alan for a while, but not after Paul made him the heir. And then there was all that business about Emily, but hell, he now realizes what you and I knew from the word 'go'—that Emily and Steve should never have married and that Emily's happier without Steve than she ever was with him. And as for Steve using your money to set himself up to smash us in the teeth—we might as well call a spade a spade, mightn't we!—Neil understands that you loved your husband and just wanted to do your best for him. Why, Neil even said he hoped Alicia would have done the same for him in such a situation! In fact, Neil was very much impressed by that display of courage, Dinah. He said it made him realize that you were one of Paul's people, just like us. And he couldn't help wondering if, like all Paul's people, you invariably knew when to cut your losses."

He stopped. The headwaiter hovered but flitted on towards the next table. "Gee," sighed Sam, regarding his plate with innocent pleasure, "this Dover sole's just the greatest fish. . . . Well, anyway, here's the deal. If you care to bring your children to America to escape the war Neil will set you up in a new cosmetics business. I've got the written proposal with me—all you'd have to do is sign your name. He says he has great confidence in your business ability and the utmost faith that you and he could work successfully together."

"How kind. Will you think me unbearably naïve if I ask what happens to Steve?"

Sam cleared his throat. This was the difficult part requiring all his charm and skill. With appalled fascination I waited, my food abandoned and my wine untouched in my glass.

"Listen, Dinah," he said, looking at me sympathetically with his honest brown eyes, "we don't know each other well and your personal life is none of my business, but I can see you're a very attractive woman who could easily win the admiration of the very best men around. Why should you settle for less than the best? Or, to phrase it another way, why should you put up with all this nonsense Steve's been handing you lately? We're not blind and deaf at Willow and Wall, and we realize you must have had your problems. Believe me, Neil's been thinking a great deal about this, Dinah. He's had your situation in mind for a long time."

"I bet he has," I said. "He's been thinking of the best way to destroy Steve and he's devised a scheme which looks as if it ought to be foolproof. But you tell your friend this: I'm going to stand by Steve. And you tell your friend this too: that even if I changed my mind the last place I'd ever run off to would be the lion's den at Willow and Wall."

There was a pause. A stillness smoothed Sam's features, and as his warm manner receded so did his overpowering sincerity and charm.

"Won't you at least think it over?" he said at last.

"Never. I'm sorry, Sam."

He ate in silence, finished his wine and motioned the waiter. "Coffee, Dinah? Dessert?"

"No, thank you."

After he had signed the bill he escorted me to the foyer in silence.

"Thank you for the lunch," I said to him as evenly as I could. The strain of the conversation was at last affecting me and I felt so exhausted I could hardly stand. "I'm sorry it had to end so abruptly."

"I'm sorry, too," he said neutrally, and then suddenly he was neutral no longer. Putting a hand on my arm, he said in a low urgent voice, "Dinah, be reasonable. Take the offer. Otherwise there's no way you can win this hand, no way at all. It's impossible."

"Never tell me," I said, "that something's impossible! Run back and tell your boss that I refuse to play Chamberlain to his Hitler and if he offers me a bit of paper to sign I shall tear it up and scatter it to the winds!"

"That's not a very reassuring analogy, is it?" he said casually. "After all, no well-informed person seriously believes England can hold out for long against Hitler once war starts."

I stepped back from him, my exhaustion forgotten and the rage streaming through me in a dark dizzy tide.

"You bloody Nazi!" I cried. "You just watch me beat Cornelius! And you tell him he'll go to his grave knowing he never got the better of me!"

And leaving him stunned and speechless in the middle of the foyer, I walked out of the Savoy with my head held high and the rage still roaring through my veins.

III

By the time I arrived home I felt I had been patriotic but unintelligent. I should have lingered with Sam to discover what Cornelius planned to do if I refused his proposal, although instinct told me that Sam would have given nothing away even if I had ultimately invited him to bed. He had given his loyalty to his own particular Führer long ago at Bar Harbor, and I knew that his loyalty would be both unswerving and incorruptible.

I studied my imaginary chessboard. Cornelius' plans for Steve were easy to read: he wanted revenge not only for Emily's humiliation but for the destruction Steve had wrought in Milk Street when he left Van Zale's. Cornelius' plans for me were less easy to decipher, but I was sure that despite all Sam Keller's protestations those plans were hostile. As Sam himself had admitted, it had been my money which had backed Steve, and I doubted that Cornelius would find that fact easy to forgive. Yet I could not imagine what he had in mind for me. His offer to set me up in business was obviously part of his revenge on Steve, but once he had had his revenge it was hard to predict his next move.

I studied Cornelius' character again, but when I began to feel as if I were alone and blindfolded in a dark house with an armed robber bent on rape, I mixed myself a stiff gin-and-French and phoned the nursing home to find out if Steve was capable of receiving visitors.

The doctor was sympathetic, and after telling me Steve was making good progress he said I could call at the nursing home the next morning for half an hour.

I had another drink, looked at my dinner, tried listening to the wireless and ended up reading Tennyson again. It was the anthology Paul had given me long ago. Usually I kept the book at Mallingham, but since I had rediscovered Tennyson's poetry I had brought the book to London. For a long time I looked at Paul's inscription on the flyleaf, and then I thumbed through the pages until I came to the poem he had quoted.

"I detest poems glorifying war!"

"Ah, but *The Revenge* isn't really about war at all. . . ."

I could hear our voices as if it were yesterday.

At Flores in the Azores Sir Richard Grenville lay . . .

How comforting it must have been to live in Victorian times when all wars were little wars and England was impregnable! I had already heaved a sigh of nostalgia before I remembered that *The Revenge* had recalled a time when one small English ship had faced a fleet of the huge galleons of Spain.

For some were sunk and many were scattered and some could fight no more,
Oh God of battles, was there ever a battle like this in the world before?

I fumbled for a cigarette and lit it. It was quiet in the house. Presently I began to read again.

And he said "Fight on!" though his ship was all but a wreck . . .

I stopped. I could no longer see. Closing the book, I moved restlessly through the house, but when I went to bed I slept badly, and I was already drinking coffee when the dawn broke over London.

At nine o'clock I telephoned Geoffrey in Norwich and asked if he could recommend a private-detective agency, and by ten I was drawing out a cash advance. After I had instructed the detective to keep a twenty-four-hour watch on Sam Keller I stopped at Fortnum's to buy Steve a tin of his favorite biscuits and then set off for Hampstead.

Halfway up the Edgeware Road my chauffeur said to me, "Madam, I have no wish to alarm you, but we're being followed."

I somehow managed to stop myself pressing my nose to the back window. "What kind of a car is it?"

"One of those little Fords, madam. A 1935 model, I think."

I wondered which detective agency Sam Keller was using. "Has he been following us for long?"

"He was there when I was waiting for you in the City, madam."

My own private detectives were in Fetter Lane. "All right," I said. "Lose him, would you, Johnson? I detest invasions of privacy."

Johnson lovingly caressed the Daimler's wheel, and we swept into the side streets south of Maida Vale.

The Ford was lost in three minutes but I was shaken by how little I had fooled Sam Keller, and when we reached Hampstead I made Johnson leave me some way from the nursing home.

A nurse showed me to the doctor's consulting room. Again I was assured that Steve was making excellent progress, but although the worst physical distress was over he was still heavily sedated.

"When can he leave?" I said.

"I would recommend he stay at least another two weeks, Mrs. Sullivan, and preferably longer. It's a great mistake in these cases to leave too early."

"Yes, I do understand that. Doctor, have you by any chance received inquiries from people who wanted to know if my husband was here?"

"Not to my knowledge, and you can rest assured that if we did we would divulge no information of any kind. A large part of our success can be attributed to the fact that our patients have total privacy."

I felt reassured and he took me upstairs himself to Steve's room.

"Half an hour, Mrs. Sullivan," he said as he opened the door. "But no longer, please."

"Dinah!" shouted Steve exuberantly. He threw his magazine at the ceiling, bounced out of bed, swept me off my feet and kicked the door shut.

"Darling, I thought you were supposed to be heavily sedated!"

"I've just had the most almighty stimulant!"

I laughed, clutched him greedily and forgot my fears about Sam Keller. I even forgot Cornelius.

"Heavens, Steve, are we supposed to do this?"

"Well, if I die trying," said Steve, "what a wonderful way to go."

We laughed and kissed again. Later after he had survived with flying colors I told him how much better he looked, but when I saw the lines of strain in his face I knew he had suffered greatly. I sat down on the edge of the bed. At once he grabbed my hand as if it were a lifeline, and his hot tight trusting clasp was unbearably poignant. Tears filled my eyes, but I blinked them away and lit a cigarette.

"Darling, we've only got a few minutes and there's so much to tell you." My voice became crisp and businesslike. I gave him the latest news of Elfrida and George and showed him Alan's and Edred's latest letters from school. I told him I had telephoned the office in Milk Street and had been assured that no disaster had happened in his absence. "Now tell me everything," I invited, still keeping a sharp eye on the time. "Has it been hell?"

"Well, I've had better vacations. Oh Christ, Dinah, I don't want to conduct a self-pitying monologue on how goddamned awful it is not to have a drink! Why do you keep looking at your watch? Who's the lucky lover and when's the assignation?"

"The assignation's come and gone, darling. I lunched at the Savoy yesterday with Sam Keller."

I told him every detail of Cornelius' offer. I thought it would be good for his self-confidence to hear my response, but his fighting spirit was so roused by the story that it was all I could do to stop him rushing headlong to the Savoy.

"I'll crucify that kid Sam Keller!" he yelled.

I opened the tin of Fortnum's best Scottish shortbread and offered it to him. "Have some of this, darling, and calm down. Sam Keller's not a kid anymore and neither's Cornelius. They're two dangerous and determined men who would be only too delighted if you made a very public appearance in London after we had told everyone you had gone to America. Don't give them the satisfaction of watching you play straight into their hands."

He took a stick of shortbread and rammed it into his mouth. I mixed us each a glass of barley water.

"Cornelius obviously has a list of old scores to settle," I said. "It's all frightfully Old Testament and tiresome of him, but the fact remains that if we stay together, and we shall, and if you get well, which you will, all his plans are going to misfire. He's pulling out of London. We'll be in different continents. If we sit tight and leave him well alone there's not one thing he can do to touch us. Or is there? I keep wondering if there's something I've missed."

Steve drank his barley water in one gulp, grabbed the box of shortbread and launched into a long muddled tirade about what he would like to do to Cornelius. I listened absent-mindedly.

"Yes, darling," I said when he paused for breath. "But what would Cornelius like to do to me?"

Steve gave a short cynical laugh. "What most men would like to do, I guess. Then he could pat himself on the back and tell himself he'd followed in Paul's footsteps all the way down the line."

"According to Sam, Cornelius isn't much interested in Paul anymore."

Steve gave another short cynical laugh and an even shorter more cynical expletive.

"Steve," I said. "Do humor me for a moment, because this could be very important. We've underestimated Cornelius before and it's absolutely essential, especially now we're vulnerable, that we don't underestimate him again. Now think. You know this man well and in fact you probably know him even better than you realize. Put yourself in his shoes. There I am in New York, prospering in a cosmetics business which you yourself have so kindly sponsored. You have a list of old scores to settle with me. What would you do next? Are you really so sure you'd just jump straight into bed with me in order to follow in Paul's footsteps?"

"Dinah, I don't care what Sam said to you yesterday. Cornelius worships Paul like a savage worships a totem pole."

"Then why should Sam give this impression of indifference—almost of a turning away from Paul? It made me wonder if Cornelius had been disillusioned in some way. You see, Steve, the interesting part is that Cornelius could hardly have known Paul. If he did hero-worship him I suspect he worshiped not Paul himself but the power Paul represented to him."

"Paul was certainly powerful," agreed Steve, "and he certainly liked to make everyone think he was tough as steel, but Jesus, he was soft as butter underneath, wasn't he? Of course, he kept it well hidden, but if Cornelius could have seen him on the morning of the assassination—"

A nurse looked into the room. "It's time, Mrs. Sullivan," she said pleasantly.

"Five more minutes!" wheedled Steve, and she smiled at him as she left the room.

"Steve—"

"Yes, that morning when he was weak as water, talking about giving everything up and running after you to England, a middle-aged man chasing a girl half his age—sorry, honey, but that was the way it seemed to me at the time! And when I think of the struggle I had to persuade him to file that last letter he wrote you—"

As the jigsaw of Cornelius' personality revolved before my eyes, the missing pieces came sailing softly towards me out of obscurity.

"That letter was never found, was it," I said.

"Well, we worked that out years ago. We know Paul must have filed it before he died and Mayers burned the file."

"Steve, that's just what we don't know. Supposing Cornelius read that letter and found out his totem pole was a fraud."

"It would certainly explain the inconsistency between my memory of him and the picture Sam gave you, but Dinah, there's no way Cornelius could ever have seen that letter. He didn't even start to work at Van Zale's until after Bart Mayers was killed, so he would never have had access to your file."

"Unless the file survived." I started to tremble. "The file with the deed, Steve, the Mallingham conveyance—"

He bounced out of bed again, enfolded me in his arms and held me close. "Now, honey, calm down. I know you've always had nightmares about that goddamned deed, but just listen to me. If that file survived I would have found it, but if I did slip up somehow and Cornelius found it instead, he couldn't have stumbled across that deed. We never did know for sure that it was in the file, and this proves it couldn't have been there. Just think for a minute. Can you seriously imagine Cornelius finding a weapon like that and then keeping it in a closet like a pervert with a collection of feminine underwear? He'd have been hitting us over the head with it long before now."

There was a long silence before I said slowly, "Yes, I suppose that's unanswerable. You must be right."

"Of course I'm right. If you'd ditched me and gone to New York, Cornelius would have figured out a dozen different ways to screw you —in every sense of the word—but there's no way he could ever have snatched your home."

I began to feel better. When the nurse reappeared to send me on my way I was able to say goodbye calmly. I offered to visit Steve again as soon as it was permitted, but he himself suggested I stay away.

"Sam's more than capable of having you shadowed," he said, although I had taken care not to worry him with the story of the Ford. "Let's leave nothing to chance, Dinah."

I promised to write to him every day instead. Then I went home, and with me went the thought of Cornelius, his shadow floating on the surface of my mind like oil on water. I felt like someone who had developed a mortal illness. For short spells I would forget about him, but then I would feel that subtle pressure on my memory, and my knowledge would swing back sickeningly into my mind. I began to wish we had met. Reality could hardly have been more oppressive than the compulsive flights of my imagination.

I thought often too of Sam Keller and read my detective's reports with interest. Sam was having a busy time. Every day of the working week he went to Milk Street, on weekends he had invitations to the country to visit clients, and in the evenings he spent much time wining and dining a certain American actress whom I was told he had met in New York. He never got drunk or made a fool of himself. His private life was discreet, his business life immaculate, and various reports of his charm and good manners reached me as Van Zale's in London was wound up with a swift, efficient, ruthless precision.

"A model Van Zale protégé," I commented dryly in one of my daily letters to Steve.

I saw the little Ford several times, but since I never went near Hampstead the driver wasted his petrol. Johnson the chauffeur became very interested in the situation and I had to tell him sharply on more than one occasion that he was not to raise the subject with me again.

At the end of March Steve was permitted to leave the nursing home, but I still avoided Hampstead and we traveled separately to Mallingham. With the beginning of the spring holidays Edred and Alan arrived home from school. Steve looked better, but he was very subdued, and although he tried to conceal his depression I sensed that his mood was bleak. The doctor had told him to convalesce at Mallingham for a month before he attempted to return to work, but I knew he was aching to get back to the office, just as I knew he was aching for a drink. I was still wondering with anxiety how he was going to cope with the grave business problems which awaited him in London when Sam Keller dealt him a blow below the belt.

A photograph appeared in the popular papers.

It was a fake. An old photograph of Steve and me had been transposed upon a photograph of the Hampstead nursing home, and the caption made it clear Steve had been receiving treatment there. The word "alcoholism" was never mentioned, but since we had told the world that Steve was in America and since his drinking habits had already been the subject of gossip, anyone but a moron could have guessed the truth. I knew at once as soon as I saw the photograph that there would be disastrous repercussions.

I confronted Johnson the chauffeur, who broke down and confessed: the driver of the Ford had paid him a hundred pounds to divulge the address to which he had taken me on my sole visit to Steve. I dismissed Johnson on the spot, but that hardly helped. The damage he had done was irreversible and Steve was already in a towering rage.

"I'll sue!" he roared and refused to listen when I pointed out not only that truth was a defense to libel but that the more noise he made the worse the situation would become. The English, hating scenes, would immediately deduce he had taken to drink again.

He still refused to listen. "I've got to do something—I'll be ruined unless I get a full retraction and a public apology!"

He was quite out of touch with reality. I did try to reason with him, but he told me to leave him alone. The agony continued. Finally I went out into the garden to calm down, but once I stepped outside I heard the car start, and racing to the stables I found him at the wheel of the Daimler with a half-empty bottle of whisky on the seat beside him.

"Steve, *please!*" I was in tears. "Please be sensible—please don't go anywhere!"

But he was implacable. He was going to the Savoy to force Sam Keller to issue a statement acknowledging that the photograph was a fake.

I tried to wrench the keys from the ignition, but he heaved me aside, shot the car out of the stables and roared off down the drive.

I could not follow him, because we had no other car at Mallingham. After running frantically across the lawn I sank to the ground in despair, and I was still crying when Alan knelt quietly by my side.

"What am I to do?" I wept. I was ashamed of crying in front of him, but I couldn't help myself. "What in God's name am I going to do?"

"There's nothing you can do—you've done everything," he said abruptly, and giving me his handkerchief, he put his arm around my shoulders.

He was sixteen. Although I often thought of him as grown up he was still only a schoolboy, and horrified by the thought of being a burden to him, I did my best to pull myself together. "I've got to be sensible," I said evenly at last. "I must be realistic. This is the end of my hopes that Steve will recover sufficiently to salvage his reputation, but we'll still cope somehow. A quiet retirement at Mallingham, a peaceful country life—"

"God, I'm so angry with him," said Alan.

"Oh, Alan—darling—"

"I'm sorry, Mother, but I'm absolutely livid and when he comes back I'll jolly well tell him so. All this is very bad for you—and very bad for the children," added Alan severely.

"But, Alan, he's ill—he can't help himself—"

"The whole trouble began," said Alan, not listening, "when he got ideas above his station and thought he could be king of the City. He should never have left Van Zale's."

"Darling, you mustn't make such sweeping criticisms when you know nothing about banking!"

"Nor do I wish to know anything!" cried Alan, very heated by this time. "Personally I think the pursuit of money for money's sake is morally indefensible and ideologically obscene!"

"Yes, darling," I said helplessly. "Yes."

"What matters is beauty and art and peace and— Oh, damn!" exclaimed Alan in despair. "This is the hell of a time in the history of the world to yearn for beauty and art and peace." And springing to his feet he shoved his fists furiously into his pockets and blundered away across the lawn.

When I followed him into the library I found him listening to the little wireless I had given him for his birthday.

"What's happening?"

"Nothing. The usual talk about Hitler." He switched off the wireless. "I'm sorry—I shouldn't have walked out on you like that."

"I came to say thank you for coming to comfort me." I kissed him before adding levelly, "I'm sorry this is so upsetting for you."

"It's just that I can't bear seeing you unhappy."

"I understand." I kissed him again and returned to the hall where we had recently had a telephone installed. I thought I would warn Sam in an attempt to abort the inevitable scene, but when I telephoned the Savoy I was told that Mr. Keller had left that morning to board his ship at Southampton.

I spent a long time wondering what would happen when Steve found that the bird had flown, but I worried needlessly. Steve never reached the Savoy. He drank his way as far south as Newmarket, and then on an empty stretch of road he lost control of the car and careered headlong into a tree.

Chapter Six

I

He was still alive when I reached the hospital. He had four broken ribs, a ruptured spleen and other massive internal injuries. His head was bandaged and part of his face was hidden by thick dressings, but he was conscious. He tried to smile when he saw me, but it was too difficult.

I kissed him and held his hand. Finally I was able to say, "Get well soon so that I can take you to Mallingham and look after you properly."

"That's what I want," he said, and whispered, "Sorry, Dinah."

I went on holding his hand. Sometime later he said, "I've had a wonderful life here in England. You . . . the children . . . nothing else matters. But so stupid to throw it all away."

"It's still there, Steve, at Mallingham."

"Mallingham," he said, and the word seemed to lead him in another direction, so that the conversation veered into a darker, more obscure channel. "Ah, but Mallingham's like the bank, Dinah. Not real, not flesh and blood . . ." He coughed and started choking. Minute spots of blood spattered the sheet. The nurse motioned me to move, but I could not, for he was still clutching my hand, and my fingers refused to release his. I hardly thought he would speak again, but when the choking stopped he whispered, "I was better, wasn't I?"

"Better—"

"I loved you better than he did."

"Yes," I said, "and I loved you better than I ever loved him. You won, Steve! You're winning!"

A film seemed to cover his eyes as his vision diminished. His hand relaxed in mine. He was at peace at last, quiet and serene, all ghosts exorcized, all cares smoothed away.

The nurse slipped forward to feel his pulse. A doctor entered the room. More nurses arrived.

Eventually someone said to me with professional kindness, "Mrs. Sullivan . . . I'm so very sorry . . ."

Someone else led me away. I sat somewhere for a long time until the hospital almoner asked if there was anyone who might take me home.

I asked for Geoffrey Hurst.

II

He came at once, paid and dismissed the taxi which had brought me from Mallingham, discussed the hospital formalities with the almoner, took me to the nearest pub and bought me a double brandy. Since his wife had been killed in a car crash, he knew the country through which I was struggling, each monstrous feature of the distorted landscape, and he led me steadily on until the landscape was once more familiar and I rejoined the road I thought I would never see again.

I brought Steve back to Mallingham, but I did not bury him with the Slades but by himself in my favorite corner of the churchyard. I did not set up a plain English stone in memory of him either, but a large black marble monument which was the extravagant memorial he would have wanted. Then I planted flowers to bloom in coming years and a cherry tree which would flower every spring in memory of him, and I was satisfied.

The children cried a great deal, but their grief was good for me because I had to pull myself together to comfort them. I could not afford the self-indulgence of a Victorian decline complete with chaise-longue, lavender-scented handkerchiefs and untouched trays of food, and eventually I felt my strength returning. I paid some important bills, put the London house up for sale and began to reply to the numerous letters of sympathy which I had received.

I had had one from Willow Street but had not had the nerve to open the envelope. I had also received a letter from Long Island, but I had not read that either. However, when the other letters had been answered I turned to those two letters from America and steeled myself to read them word for word.

Emily had written:

DEAR DINAH:

Just a word of sympathy for you in your bereavement. The children are grieving very much for Steve and want to send their love to you and everyone at Mallingham. Tony says he would still like to visit you this summer if it's convenient, but will quite understand if at the moment you feel you can't have an extra person to stay.

With best wishes for the future,

Sincerely,
EMILY

I smoothed the letter carefully with my fingers before putting it aside.

From One Willow Street I had received not a formal typed communication from Cornelius but a handwritten note from Sam Keller.

DEAR DINAH:

In writing to express my deepest sympathy I want you to know that neither Cornelius nor I would ever have wished such a tragic accident on Steve. Your first impulse will naturally be to blame us for his death, but perhaps later you will be able to acknowledge that a car smash is something neither of us could have ordained. I'm sorry about Steve; it was a sad end to a brilliant career. I'm sorrier for you because I discovered for myself when we met how devoted you were to him. And I'm sorriest of all that there's nothing I can do to help you except tell you how sorry I am.

Sincerely,
SAM

That was easy to answer. I simply wrote:

DEAR MR. KELLER,

Some people are like Jason Da Costa: they put a pistol to their heads and pull the trigger. And some people are like Steven Sullivan: they drive off an empty road into a tree. Tell Cornelius I shall neither forget nor forgive.

DINAH SULLIVAN

Emily's letter was more difficult to answer because my feelings for her were so ambivalent, but I wrote:

DEAR EMILY,

Thank you for your letter. It was extremely nice of you to write and I hope you'll forgive me for not replying earlier. I'm sure the news was a great shock to you and the children.

Tony can certainly come to stay this summer, but the international situation is so precarious that I hesitate to encourage his visit. However, I'm sure you're sufficiently well-informed to give Tony a realistic idea of what might happen, and once he's in possession of the facts perhaps he can reconsider his decision and alter or confirm it as the case may be. We would be very pleased to see him if he wants to come.

Yours sincerely,
DINAH

I felt better once the letters were answered. I made arrangements for Elfrida to attend a day school in Norwich in the autumn, and then we returned to London so that she could complete the summer term at her old school. George and Nanny came with us. George was four and more than ready for kindergarten, so I arranged for him to go to a school in Belgravia three mornings a week. Edred and Alan were away again at their boarding schools. Life went on.

Nobody wanted to buy the house, because nobody was sure what was going to happen in London, but I continued to bully the estate agents. Our house in Milk Street was wound up, its doors closed. I was comfortably off, but since I thought it would do me good to have a job I toyed with the idea of returning to my long-postponed career in education. However, the atmosphere of the times was running against me, and now all I wanted was to withdraw to Mallingham and gather strength from the past as Hitler prepared to set Europe to the torch.

I thought of Mallingham's past, of those hundreds of years which stretched back to the days when Godfrey Slade had rebuilt the hall of Alan of Richmond's manor. My ancestors had heard Napoleon knock on England's door, and Philip of Spain, and countless unknown French who had waged the Hundred Years' War. My world was very old and well-accustomed to conquerors who thought themselves invincible. At Mallingham I could think of Hitler without fear. I could listen with amusement to J. B. Priestly poking fun at him on the wireless, I could face whatever new madness billowed out of the newspapers and I could meet the stench of the swastikas which came reeking across the sea.

Appeasement was dead at last. On the first of September Hitler moved into Poland, and two days later, little more than twenty-five years after the lamps had gone out all over Europe, we set off once more into the dark.

III

I was gardening when war was declared. It was a hobby I had undertaken with enthusiasm now that I had more leisure, and I was planting bulbs for next year. As I weeded the ground carefully I wondered where we would all be in twelve months' time, but my mind refused to dwell long on the future. It was more comforting to think of the past centuries, and when I did think of the present I merely considered how my flowers should be arranged and how difficult life would be with petrol rationing and whether George would have to go to the village school. I worried too about my stepson Tony. He had come to England in July, he was still with us and he wanted to stay.

"But Tony," I said after I had decided I must have a serious talk with him, "wouldn't it be better now that war's broken out for you to be in your own country? When the Germans invade—" I stopped. It would never do for me to sound like Sam Keller. "If the Germans invade France it's going to be increasingly difficult in Europe, and I'm sure Emily would feel you should return to America. I'm only surprised you haven't already had a letter from Cornelius ordering you home."

He looked at me mutinously with Steve's bright-blue eyes. "Cornelius is no friend of mine," he said.

It all came out. Despite Emily's kindness he had been unhappy at home. Cornelius, who had assumed the role of surrogate father both to Emily's daughters and to Caroline's sons, did not like him, and Alicia barely ever glanced in his direction.

"It's because I look like Dad," said poor Tony, and he asked me directly for the first time if I held Cornelius responsible for his father's death.

"Yes," I said.

"Scott won't believe it. He thinks Dad brought the whole mess on himself. Scott's very mixed up about the whole thing."

"How does he get on with Cornelius?"

"Real well. Scott likes Cornelius. Everyone likes Cornelius, everyone thinks he's wonderful, especially Emily, which is why I can't talk to her about any of this," said Tony, speaking very fast, "but I can't live there anymore, I wish we'd come to live with you after Dad left Emily, that was a terrible thing Scott and I did to Dad—"

"Tony, you mustn't feel guilty about that. You were so young and it was such a difficult situation and Steve realized what you were going through. You mustn't think he didn't understand."

"I wish Dad were alive so that I could explain."

"He would have been very glad that you wanted to live here, and I'm very glad, too. Would you like me to write to Emily for you?"

But he said he didn't mind writing to Emily; he just didn't want to have anything more to do with Cornelius.

For some time I tried not to think about Cornelius, but as the war dragged inactively into the early days of 1940 I found I was at last able to revive my memories of the recent past. In February when I had lunch with Geoffrey in Norwich I even found I could reminisce about Steve without wanting to cry.

"I'm not going to tell you you'll remarry one day," said Geoffrey sensibly, "because that sort of remark used to make me so angry after Jill died. But I'm glad things are going better for you, Dinah."

"I keep thinking I ought to do some war work." We began to speculate about the future. Geoffrey was past forty, and although he had volunteered for service the army had taken little notice of him. He thought it likely that he would be consigned to a desk in the army's legal department, but meanwhile he was still working in Norwich, where he was now the senior partner of his firm.

"I'd much rather be in uniform," he said, "because then I might have the illusion that something was going on. This is a damned odd sort of war with nothing happening."

Yet when the pace quickened and the disasters began to overtake the British army on the Continent my nervous anticipation increased. I felt that some unimaginable fate was gliding towards me, and to stifle my fear of the future I once more shrank back into the past. I played all my old Noël Coward records, read ream after ream of poetry, and one evening in an orgy of nostalgia I sorted out my photographs of Paul and Steve and selected the best to decorate my upstairs sitting room. I already kept my favorite pictures of the children there for the room had long been my personal retreat, and now I crammed it with souvenirs so that whenever I crossed the threshold I was plunged back into my best memories of the past.

Alan noticed the change as soon as he returned from Winchester for the Easter holidays. Tony had joined him there, and they were both planning to go up to Oxford later, Alan on a scholarship and Tony using the money he had inherited from Steve. Both of them talked of enlisting on their eighteenth birthdays, but Alan was not eighteen until the March of 1941, and I insisted that he should begin his career at Oxford even if he did not intend to finish it. I felt sick with worry whenever I thought of his future, and was thankful Edred was only ten. He was still at prep school in Sussex, and reluctantly I had arranged for Elfrida to be a weekly boarder at her school in Norwich. Transport was becoming increasingly difficult, and Mallingham was too far from Norwich to make daily journeys practical. George was already at the village school. He was happy there, and his Norfolk accent, which he had immediately acquired, amused us, but I kept wishing he too could have gone to school in Norwich. However, I told myself it was good for George to mix with working-class children, while prep school would eventually iron out the accent.

"Aren't you being rather snobbish, Mother?" inquired Alan as he glanced curiously at my redecorated sitting room and listened to me sighing over the problems of educating George.

"Yes, darling, I'm a dreadful snob. I think I always was, but now I'm not ashamed to admit it."

"Victorian too," said Alan. "Nobody decks out a room like this nowadays."

"Yes, hopelessly Victorian. I'm all the things I've always tried not to be—with one exception. I'm no longer a hypocrite."

Alan smiled guardedly but did not comment. I was glad when all the children were home for Easter because it took my mind off my nebulous uneasiness, but eventually the twins left and it was time for Alan and Tony to return to Winchester.

The night before they were due to leave I awoke abruptly. One moment I was lying inert in bed and the next I was sitting bolt upright in the dark. There was nothing to hear, but again I was conscious of some indefinable force looming larger on the horizon, and on an impulse I slipped out of bed, pulled on my dressing gown and tiptoed downstairs. I thought I would head for the kitchens to make myself some tea, but at the bottom of the stairs I paused. I was in the hall. I had not switched on any lights. Insomnia had troubled me intermittently since Steve's death, and I had grown accustomed to using a torch for my nocturnal prowls. It saved fuel, avoided disturbing people and did not endanger the blackout.

Suddenly I felt convinced I was not alone. I was aware of a presence at the far end of the hall, but I wasn't frightened, only excited. Mallingham was part of me and if there were ghosts I doubted that they would be hostile. Swinging my torch's beam swiftly across the hall, I saw movement and stepped forward. The shadow moved again. I had a glimpse of pale skin, brilliant dark eyes and a graceful turn of the body as he looked back at me.

"Paul?" I said.

He was transfixed.

There was a silence. We were some way apart, perhaps twenty feet. What unnerved me most of all was how much I wanted him to come back from the dead.

I laughed. "Sorry, Alan!" I called ruefully. "Did I startle you?"

"You did a bit. Are you all right, Mother?"

"Yes, I was going to make some tea. Do you want some?"

"All right—thanks. I'll just unplug my wireless," he added unexpectedly. "It needs a new flex and it gets overheated if it's left on too long. When I woke up I thought for an awful moment I hadn't turned it off properly earlier, so I came creeping down with my torch. Of course I switched the torch off when I heard you. I thought you were an enemy agent. What a relief to find it was just you playing Lady Macbeth!"

I laughed again, and presently he joined me in the kitchens as I made the tea.

"I keep feeling most unpleasantly nervous," I said when I sat down opposite him at the table. "That's why when I saw you tonight and thought—don't laugh—that you were Paul's ghost, I was enormously relieved. It was as if the disaster I'd been expecting wasn't gruesome after all but magical and exciting. Maybe Steve's death has finally unhinged me—or perhaps my eccentric inheritance is catching up with me at last!"

"My dear mother," said Alan, "you're the sanest person I know. It's the world that's mad. Milk?"

"Thanks."

We sipped our tea. Suddenly he said, "What was he really like?

And don't for God's sake just say he was wonderful, because that's not what I want to hear."

"Paul?" I said. "Paul was a romantic and an idealist who compromised every romantic ideal he possessed in order to pursue his ambition and his revenge."

"Curious," said Alan. "I pictured him as many things but never as Faust. Did you really love him? Now, be truthful, Mother—"

"I loved him as much as I was capable of loving anyone at that particular time, but probably I would have loved him better if I'd been older. Our ages were all wrong, you know. He always used to say that we'd missed each other in time."

We went on sipping our tea. Finally Alan said, "Tell me everything—all of it," and I talked till dawn.

Somewhere in the middle of our umpteenth cup of tea Alan said, "But what makes you so jolly sure that Cornelius hasn't had the wretched Mallingham conveyance all the time?"

We looked at each other steadily across the table.

"Because I can't believe," I said, "that Cornelius would have found that deed and not taken immediate action."

There was a silence. At last Alan said in a mild cautious voice, "Mother, do you remember that nice little kitten Chalky I had when I was small? And do you remember what a nasty cat he became when he grew up? He liked to catch birds and play with them for a long time before he finally administered the *coup de grâce*."

There was another silence, heavier than the one before, and I slowly began to feel sick. Pushing away my cup, I left the table and moved rapidly into the scullery to the sink.

"Mother, I'm sorry."

"It's all right, Alan." The nausea was already passing. "Quite all right. I'm glad you reminded me of Chalky." I stopped gripping the edge of the sink and turned to face him. "Darling, I think we'd better try to snatch a little sleep now before breakfast. You've got such a long journey ahead of you today and I don't want you to arrive at Winchester in a state of exhaustion."

He went to bed. I returned to my room but did not sleep. Later that morning I took the boys to catch their train.

"Don't forget to ask Mr. Grimsby to replace the flex on my wireless," said Alan, kissing me at the station, and I promised to bring the mended wireless with me when I visited Winchester at half term.

I kissed Tony, wished both of them a safe journey and stepped back as the guard blew his whistle.

"Look after yourself, Mother!" Alan called as the train drew out of the station.

I went home and for a while could think only of Chalky, but gradually the Germans ousted even my fear of Cornelius from my mind. The British army was collapsing in France, and in a mighty pincer movement the Germans swung around to drive the British into the sea.

I listened to Churchill. We all listened to Churchill, and Churchill's voice was the voice of nine hundred unconquered years stretching behind us into infinity in our tortured corridor of time.

On Saturday the twenty-fifth of May I scraped up the remains of my petrol ration and drove into Norwich to meet Geoffrey for lunch; I could no longer bear to wait at Mallingham. When I returned home I still felt restless. George had gone out to tea with a friend. The house was empty and should have been peaceful, but soon all my familiar uneasiness had returned and I went outside again to sail the dinghy across Mallingham Broad. It was a fine afternoon, perfect for sailing, the wind steady but not too strong, the sun sparkling on the clear water, the birds skimming over the reeds. I tacked all the way to the dike and even wondered whether to go on toward Horsey Mere, but some instinct made me turn the tiller and head for home.

I saw him when I was halfway across the Broad.

He was sitting on the terrace. He was waiting for me, just as I had long been waiting for him, and suddenly all I knew was not fear but relief that our waiting should at last be at an end.

He was dressed immaculately in black.

The wind was whipping at my hair and I felt so exhilarated that I tacked more daringly than ever across the water and cut my corners so fine that the little dinghy seemed to dance in triumph across the shining surface of the Broad.

Reaching the jetty, I tied up the dinghy and paused to watch a gull soar across the sky. I was wearing a pair of shabby slacks, a Fair Isle jersey and no makeup, but I needed no armor, for I was on my own ground and ahead of me across the lawn was Mallingham, the source of all my triumphs and tragedies, over six hundred years of times past, unspoiled, untouched, shimmering in the brilliance of that late-spring afternoon.

I tossed back my hair, straightened my back and faced the terrace.

For a long moment we were both motionless, and then I began to walk across the lawn towards him.

He stood up politely and took off his hat. The sun shone on his fair hair and burnished it to a gleaming gold.

I never hesitated, and as I went on walking uphill across the lawn I continued to look past him to the walls my ancestors had built when America had been a wilderness. At the corner of the terrace I mounted the six steps and was level with him. We were exactly the same height, and this bizarre likeness seemed to symbolize not only our equality but our shared inheritance from Paul, who had brought us face to face at last fourteen years after his death.

I was still. Now it was he who moved, and as he stepped forward I saw the lost innocence in his romantic, poet's face, the shadow of a corruption which only the most frightening power can buy.

"Miss Slade," he said. It was not a slip but a deliberate error, and I knew that he had always thought of me as Miss Slade just as I had always thought of him by his first name.

We had known each other for such a long, long time.

"Welcome to Mallingham, Cornelius!" I exclaimed in my most sociable voice. "Do come in. May I offer you some tea?"

He gave me an enchantingly boyish smile. "Why, thank you!" he said in a voice rendered attractive by the purest of American accents. "That would be very nice."

The preliminary skirmishes ended abruptly. We went indoors and our last battle began.

Chapter Seven

I

We were fascinated with each other. After years of speculation the desire to compare the fruits of our imagination with reality was irresistible and we both succumbed to the temptation.

Finally Cornelius laughed. "Perhaps we should spend the first five minutes putting each other under a microscope!" he commented, and even that remark illustrated the gulf between my mental picture of him and the man he really was. No one had ever told me Cornelius possessed any quality remotely resembling a sense of humor.

None of his stone-faced photographs had done him justice. They had caught the perfection of his exquisitely molded cheekbones, the unbelievable shade of his hair and the splendor of his black-lashed gray eyes, but not the spark of his wry intelligence and his utter masculinity. Men might once have thought Cornelius effeminate, but I was sure no woman had ever made such a mistake. It was true he was short, but he was perfectly proportioned. If he had been a Hollywood actor they would simply have given him a petite leading lady, and every woman in the audience would have sworn he was at least six feet tall.

Most unnerving of all, there was a slight but unmistakable family likeness between him and his great-uncle. I recognized not only Paul's straight handsome mouth but the mysterious air of confidence in his movements, the grace which hinted at an athlete's muscular coordination. Like his friend Sam Keller he was the most attractive man.

I suddenly remembered I was wearing slacks and a dirty pullover and probably reminded him of the Wreck of the Hesperus.

"We'll have tea upstairs in my sitting room," I said. "Excuse me while I speak to my housekeeper." And I left him in the hall while I went to the kitchens in search of Mrs. Oakes.

Later when I showed him into the sitting room I said, "Excuse me again, but I never receive visitors while I'm wearing trousers, so I shall now go and change. I won't be more than five minutes. Do sit down."

I left him with my photographs of Paul, Steve and the children, just as I'd planned, and after escaping to my room I leaned back against the door panels until I was breathing more evenly. I felt frightened for the first time since I had seen him, but I steadied myself and began to change. I used only the minimum of makeup, but I brushed my hair up into a knot to make me look efficient and put on the traditional businesswoman's uniform, my classic smooth black tailor-made coat and skirt with the white silk blouse and the row of pearls. Without thinking I stepped into a pair of high-heeled shoes, but fortunately I remembered his height and took them off. There was no point in annoying him unnecessarily. I was just searching in my wardrobe for a pair of flat shoes when I heard Mrs. Oakes enter the sitting room next door with the tea tray.

Emerging two minutes later, I found that Mrs. Oakes had gone, the silver teapot was standing stoutly on the table and Cornelius was looking at my best photograph of Elfrida.

"Your daughter's pretty," he said. "I guess she must be about the same age as my little girl."

"Elfrida is a little older than Vicky, I think." I sat down to pour the tea and was aware of his glance flickering without expression over the pictures of my sons. He already had his back to the photographs of Paul and Steve.

"Did you come to see Tony?" I asked as he sat down opposite me on the sofa.

"No, I came to see you," he said with a smile. "I must apologize for not calling first, but I felt I knew you well enough to stop by unannounced. How's Tony getting along?"

"Very well. I thought Emily might have asked you to persuade him to return to America."

"She did, but I have no intention of doing anything of the kind. I'm delighted if Tony's happy here. He certainly wasn't happy in the States, and to be honest I found him a great trial. It was a pity. I did my best, but nothing worked."

"Rather ironic, isn't it," I said, handing him his cup, "that you should find yourself looking after Steve's children."

"Well, Scott's no problem. And as for the little girls . . ." He shrugged to indicate not indifference but equanimity. "Since I was responsible for Emily's marriage to Steve it's only right that I should now assume responsibility for the results. 'Though the mills of God grind slowly,'" added Cornelius surprisingly, "'they grind exceeding small. Though with patience He stands waiting, with exactness grinds He all.'"

"Ah yes," I said, "the *Sinngedichte* of Friedrich von Logau. Such a heavy-handed translation by Longfellow, I've always thought. How long have you been in England?"

"Twenty-four hours. I arrived yesterday after a long, uncomfortable and devious passage from Germany, where I had to go to sever some connections which Sam had unwisely made when he was in Europe last year." He sighed. "I knew I'd hate it and I did. I can't speak German, no one wanted to speak English and I was terrified everyone would think I was a spy and march me off to a concentration camp. It was all very tiring—and I couldn't even get fresh orange juice for breakfast," he added crossly as an afterthought.

"Why didn't you send Sam to correct his own mistakes?"

"I thought he ought to stay at home and practice being neutral." Cornelius looked glum. "My worst dread is that as soon as America enters the war he'll be interned. God knows what I'd do without Sam at Willow and Wall. I don't even like to think about it."

"So you foresee America entering the war?"

"Well, that's what we usually do, isn't it? We'll come in eventually, straighten you all out and pick up the sordid bits and pieces. The only difference between this war and the last is that after this one the Pax Britannica will be as dead as a dodo and we'll see the dawn of the Pax Americana." He sipped his tea meditatively. "Europe will be a museum piece," he said, "but perhaps still a field for American economic expansion. I think I'll eventually invest in the tourist industry. You have such nice old buildings here, really very quaint. I can understand why you spend so much time looking backward into the past instead of concentrating on the present and preparing for the future."

"We are tomorrow's past," I said, reaching for a cigarette, "and the future is only a continuation of what has gone before. Do you have a light?"

"I don't smoke." But he sprang up, reached for the box of matches above the fireplace and lit my cigarette for me.

We looked at each other across the flame.

"Why are you here?" I said quietly as the flame died.

When he replaced the matches he paused by the fireplace. "Well, you won't believe this," he said ruefully, "but I come waving the olive branch of peace again."

"Same olive branch?"

"Right down to the last identical olive. Look, Dinah, this feud is quite unnecessary, and now that Steve's dead I consider the whole unfortunate matter closed. Forgive me—perhaps I should have offered my condolences, but in the circumstances I really felt they would have been inappropriate. I despise hypocrisy," said Cornelius, giving me a straight honest look with his black-lashed gray eyes, "and I wouldn't have wanted to insult your intelligence by telling you how sorry I was about Steve."

"Quite."

"I'm sorry you equate his accidental death with the suicide of

Jason Da Costa, but I honestly don't feel they're comparable. However . . ."—he cleared his throat—"I accept that you have a right to be angry with me, and I'd like to do what I can to make amends. You must be worried about your children and the imminent invasion. Maybe you're also worried financially. Well, all I'm saying is that there's no need for you to worry anymore—just say the word and I'll arrange for you to leave the country and work in America until the war's over. I know we could make a lot of money if we did business together, so I suggest we meet in London this week to work out a suitable agreement with our lawyers. Let me assure you again that my offer to set you up in a new business in New York is completely bona fide."

I stood up to face him. He stopped leaning lightly against the chimneypiece and straightened his back.

"Do I have a choice?" I said.

"Why, of course you do! You can say yes. Or you can say no. Only," said Cornelius, with a sigh as he moved to the window and gazed over Mallingham Broad, "I really wouldn't advise you to say no."

He stroked the wall of my home with his index finger and sighed again. "This is such a lovely, lovely house," he said. "I'd just hate anything to happen to this house, Dinah, I really would. I hope it survives the war."

It was absolutely quiet. He turned dreamily to face me, his movements languid, his beautiful eyes glowing. He was intoxicated with his triumph, exhilarated by his power.

At last I said, "How can I be sure it survives the war?"

"I can arrange for it to be handled with care during the occupation."

"Oh, but the Germans won't be coming," I said. "Didn't you know?"

"Tell that to the British army in France! But you don't really have to worry about the Germans, Dinah," he said, reaching into the inside pocket of his jacket and pulling out a long brown envelope. "The only person you have to worry about is me."

He opened the envelope. He drew out the Mallingham conveyance. And he fanned his face with it leisurely as he watched me.

"May I pour you another cup of tea?" he inquired kindly as I sank down in my chair.

I did not answer. He poured more tea for us both, tucked the deed carefully away in his pocket again and once more sat down opposite me on the sofa.

"If I accept your offer to come to America," I said steadily at last, "does that guarantee Mallingham's safety?"

"Well, naturally it does, Dinah! And if things go well I'll even convey the property to you. But that, of course"—he smiled at me—"would depend on how . . . agreeable you are in New York."

I saw the expression in his eyes and read his mind as effortlessly as if it were a slogan on a poster fifteen feet high. This was no naïve hankering to follow in Paul's footsteps; this was the exercise of sexual power in the pursuit of revenge. He would humiliate me in New York, shame me before my children and still have Mallingham reduced to rubble. There was no promise he could ever make which would guarantee to me the safety of my home.

I had always thought I would be overcome with terror when I received incontrovertible evidence of his final plan, but now I found to my surprise that my knowledge at once gave me new courage. I had always been resolved to outwit Cornelius; now I was fanatical in my determination not to be defeated by him. Men like Cornelius Van Zale deserved to be beaten to their knees. I could never let him win. It would be an outrage.

I thought of *The Revenge*, of Sir Richard Grenville exhorting his men to fight on, and I smiled.

"My dear Cornelius!" I exclaimed. "Is that a proposition? What a compliment! I've never been propositioned before by a handsome millionaire seven years my junior! I feel positively rejuvenated!"

He was watching me closely, his hard dry narrow mind calculating the chance of success with great shrewdness and minute attention to detail. He would not be an easy man to fool. With a pounding heart I forced myself to look guilelessly at the stark bones beneath his pale skin, the brutal line of his mouth and the bleakness of his stone-cold gray eyes.

"But why should I be surprised?" I added pleasantly. "You've always followed closely in Paul's footsteps, haven't you?"

"Paul's dead," he said, and for a split second I looked straight through the windows of his eyes into the full dark complexity of his bereavement.

I felt as if I had seen some horrible mutilation. In an effort to conceal how shaken I was I made a great business of stubbing out my cigarette, smoothing my skirt over my knees and taking a sip of tea.

"When can we meet in London to draw up this agreement?" I said abruptly.

He was reassured by the businesslike tone of my voice. "Monday?" he suggested, crossing one leg casually over the other.

"I'm afraid it may be difficult for me to leave here before Tuesday. Would you mind waiting until then?"

"I'm sure the occasion will be worth waiting for!" he said gallantly with his best boyish smile. "Will you have dinner with me afterward? I'm staying with the American ambassador, but maybe I can take a suite at Claridge's for the evening. I feel a new partnership deserves a little celebration."

"Delightful!" I said. "But may I recommend a suite at the Savoy? It's so beautiful in the early morning to look down the river and see the dawn break beyond St. Paul's."

I'd hooked him. I saw the fascination creep into his eyes, the prurient interest, the barely suppressed shimmer of eroticism.

"I'd like that," he said.

I let my smile linger and rose to my feet. "I'll come downstairs to see you off," I volunteered. "You have a long drive back to London."

He gave me the card of the Van Zale solicitors in Lincoln's Inn. "Shall we say two-thirty on Tuesday at that address? I'll be there unless I hear from you to the contrary."

"All right. Yes, that's fine." Clasping the card tightly, I showed him downstairs and across the hall to the front door.

His chauffeur-driven limousine was waiting in the drive.

"On loan from the embassy," explained Cornelius, pausing to say goodbye. "The ambassador's been very hospitable to me."

He held out his hand. I shook it without hesitation. As my flesh crawled I reminded myself it was the first and last contact I would ever have with him.

"So long, Dinah. It was fun meeting you at last. I'm glad we were able to do business together."

"See you on Tuesday, Cornelius!" I watched him drive away, and when the car had disappeared I swung very slowly to face the house.

I looked at it until my eyes ached in the hot glare of the sun, and as my vision blurred I could see only the quotation from *The Revenge* which Paul had inscribed long ago in my treasured volume of Tennyson. Blindly I moved indoors, but long before I reached the library I heard Paul's voice ringing in my ears:

"'Sink me the ship, Master Gunner! Sink her—split her in twain!
Fall into the hands of God, not into the hands of Spain!'"

II

I thought about it for a long time, and later, much later, when the hall clock had chimed midnight and I was still moving restlessly around the house, my mind closed upon the decision and I knew there was no turning back. I had stopped weeping hours ago and was calm. I felt I could see everything so clearly, past, present and future, and as they fused within me I saw truths which I had once thought were dead but which I now knew could live again and give my decision meaning.

I thought first of Mallingham. Even if I could somehow save it from Cornelius what would happen to it in the brave new world of the Pax Americana which Cornelius had forecast with such relish? War always brought huge social upheavals; I could remember the postwar world of the early twenties too well not to know what kind of future awaited a Europe which was once more in ruins. There would be poverty, unemployment and a widespread desire to share whatever wealth remained from the war. The socialists if not the communists would then surely come into their own and we would see the leveling, the crusade against inherited wealth, the rejection of the aristocracy, the indifference if not outright hostility towards the large country houses which survived. The conservative I had become found this prospect deeply disturbing, but the socialist I had been long ago accepted the prospect with resignation. England's grandeur had been built in the previous centuries by the sweated labor of millions to be enjoyed by a fortunate few, but in the twentieth century those millions would inevitably demand their equality. And what would happen to Mallingham then? Would it be requisitioned by the state, torn down and replaced with new bungalows for the proletariat? Or perhaps converted into flats? Or a hotel? I saw clearly that if neither Cornelius nor the Germans destroyed Mallingham the English of the future almost certainly would. Everything changed; nothing was forever. Mallingham had come to the end of its long and splendid life, and it was my task, as the last Slade who would ever care for the house, to see that it died not ingloriously but with dignity and honor.

Having thought of Mallingham, I thought of myself. I knew there could be no compromise with Cornelius. But even if Cornelius had never existed, could I have returned to the all-consuming task of earning a second fortune in order to keep Mallingham safe from the ravages of a changed social order? I could make the money; I had proved that to myself long ago. But I had proved too that in sacrificing my time and talents to the pursuit of money I had seen little of my children, still less of Mallingham and nothing whatsoever of the ideals which I had come to believe in with all my mother's passion. I had been so terrified of the circumstances of my mother's death that I had spent years backing away from her idealism, but, as I had told Steve, I now saw her struggle differently. When her cause was stripped of its rhetoric and wiped clean of its emotional sexual divisiveness I saw she had been fighting not just for the right to vote but for justice, for equality before the law, for the concepts which Pericles had championed twenty-five hundred years ago and which applied to neither one sex nor the other but to all mankind. I wanted not to worship at the altar of Mammon for the rest of my life but to work for those ideals of democracy; I wanted not to sacrifice myself endlessly for Mallingham but to fulfill myself by leading a life which would benefit others; and last I wanted my children not to grow up regarding me as a money-hungry stranger who would sell her soul for a house but as a comfortingly familiar figure who possessed ideals which knew no compromise and a romance which no cynicism could destroy.

I thought of Steve's dying words: "Mallingham's like the bank, Dinah. Not real, not flesh and blood."

Steve had known the truth at the end.

I heard Alan's voice—Paul's voice—saying decisively, "The pursuit of money for money's sake is morally indefensible and ideologically obscene."

Paul might once have said those words, but when I had known him he had been too deeply enmeshed in his moral quicksands to struggle free. He had lost his struggle with corruption and that was why he had left me at Mallingham before Alan was born. But I was not lost, not yet. I had been as deeply enmeshed as he had ever been in the pursuit of wealth and power, but I was being given the chance to pull myself free of those quicksands, just as he had been given the chance when he had met me. He had let the chance pass by and in the end his decision had destroyed him. But I could still take my chance and I was going to take it. I would take it and survive.

Let Cornelius keep his wealth and power! Let him live with the gods he had chosen for himself! But I was going to show him before our paths parted forever that he was powerless against me, and that no wealth on earth could buy him the revenge he sought.

I was going to win. I knew that now. I was on the road to victory and nothing could turn me back.

My knowledge transformed me, and as I watched the dawn break over Mallingham Broad I began to plan with exhilaration how my great victory over Cornelius would be waged and won.

III

The fire would have to look like an accident, of course. I did not want to risk a possible charge of arson by destroying a house that wasn't legally mine. However, Cornelius would know the fire was no accident; that was the glory of the scheme. He would know it but he would never be able to prove it, and for the rest of his life he would live with the knowledge that although he owned some charred acres in Norfolk, he had never owned and would never own any part of me.

I am unsure when I remembered Alan's wireless with its dangerous flex. It must have been at some point during breakfast, because when

I had finished my coffee—I could still eat nothing—I went to his room and found the wireless on the table. Tucked in the coiled flex was a note which read: "Mother—don't forget, please!"

Yet I had forgotten. It was almost as if I had known I was going to need the wireless, but of course I couldn't have known.

I plugged in the flex and waited. After ten minutes I could smell the burning as the flex began to smolder. Turning off the wireless immediately, I unplugged it again, destroyed Alan's note and took the wireless to my upstairs sitting room.

Then I went downstairs to talk to Nanny and Mrs. Oakes.

"I think it would be better if you took George away to the West Country now that the Germans are almost at the French coast," I said briskly to Nanny. "Lady Harriet has already offered to lend me her cottage at Croyde Bay, and I'll telephone her now to make sure it's still available. Can you be ready by two, do you think? I can drive you to Norwich to get the London train."

And to Mrs. Oakes I said gently, "I've decided to close Mallingham for a while and send George and Nanny to Devon. Would you and Mr. Oakes mind terribly if you went to Mary a little earlier than usual this year? I can see you onto the Yarmouth train this afternoon."

Fortunately the parlormaid and the housemaids were all local women, so I simply paid them a month's wages and said I would continue to pay them while the house was closed. I was between cooks at the time, so I had no other staff to worry about.

Then I spoke to George.

"Georgie, you're going to have a lovely holiday by the sea. I won't be able to come with you at first, but I'll join you and Nanny later."

"Can I take my jabberwocky?"

"Yes, of course, darling."

"And a lollipop for the train?"

"Definitely a lollipop."

He was satisfied. I kissed the top of his dark head, and finally waved him goodbye as his train drew out of Norwich station soon after noon.

I was alone at Mallingham by the end of the afternoon.

I started to pack the things I would need for my visit to London. I thought it would be best if I went through the motions of going to meet Cornelius even though I had no intention of presenting myself at Lincoln's Inn; it would look better afterwards if there was an inquiry. I decided I would stay at Harriet's house, plead illness and at the last moment cancel the appointment. Later when Cornelius was declaring that his patience was exhausted I would write him a note to say I was still considering his offer, and he would storm off to Mallingham to find nothing but ashes. The hall was secluded and some way from the village. Someone would eventually be certain to see the house burning, but with luck no one would know when the fire had started and I would have an alibi of sorts.

I wanted to pack every one of my photographs, but I knew that would be unwise, for if investigators found I had salvaged my most precious possessions they would naturally be suspicious. But I took my favorite photographs of Paul and Steve and put them into my suitcase.

It was a long night. I slept a little, but most of the time I was wandering around from room to room. Sometimes I wondered if I were sleepwalking, because my dreams seemed to blend with reality until I was no longer sure what was truth and what was fantasy. The walls of time seemed to have disappeared. I was with Paul and Steve —how odd it was to see them together at Mallingham!—but other people were there too, my father and his father and strangers whom I did not recognize. But they all knew me and they were so proud of me, I could see their smiles, and when the dawn came, the last dawn Mallingham would ever see, I was in the courtyard by the medieval walls of the hall, and Godfrey Slade was riding off to the Crusade to fight for his beliefs against the vast power of the Saracen. I tried to talk to him but he spoke a language I did not understand, and although I knew I could communicate with him in Latin the Latin words were beyond my grasp. And then Paul was there again, quoting the love poetry of Catullus, and above us the sky was so brilliantly blue that I could only marvel, What a wonderful summer!

But as I stared at the sky I heard the drone of a German plane and knew it was the summer of destruction, the sun-drenched days of 1940 when we stood in the dark on the very edge of the world.

The past fell away. I was at Mallingham on Monday, the twenty-seventh of May, 1940, and the hour of my victory was at hand.

I backed my car out of the stables and put my suitcase into the boot. I had just enough petrol left to get me to the nearest station.

As I walked back into the house the phone rang.

"Dinah?" I heard the tension in his voice at once.

"Geoffrey! What is it?"

"Haven't you heard the news?"

"I haven't had the wireless on for hours. What's happened?"

"Just before seven o'clock last night they sent out word that Operation Dynamo was to commence. I've only just found out myself. It must mean that they're evacuating the British army from the French coast."

Earlier in the year the government had foreseen that private boats might be needed to supplement the navy in certain circumstances, and on May the fourteenth during the BBC's nine-o'clock news the owners of vessels of thirty feet and upwards were requested to provide details of their craft. My yacht was smaller than thirty feet, so I had not registered it with the Small Vessel Pool, but Geoffrey and I had discussed the possibility of using it just the same. We both had friends who had registered their boats.

"Word's going around that they now want anything that can float," Geoffrey was saying. "I've just spoken to a client in Dover and he says the whole southeast's humming. Apparently Ramsgate's the port to make for. That's where the small boats are being assembled, fueled and dispatched."

"Where's the army?"

"God knows. Of course there's nothing in the papers or on the wireless—everything's top secret."

"If the boats are assembling at Ramsgate, the target must be somewhere between Calais and Dunkirk." I tried to think. "I can get the yacht ready in an hour, I think. How soon can you be here?"

"I can leave straightaway, but Dinah, go over your supplies now so that I can bring anything we need from Norwich. Have you got a pencil and paper? All right, let's make a list."

We talked for ten minutes until we were sure we had forgotten nothing, and after I had replaced the receiver I paused to amend my plans. Little amendment was necessary. What pleased me most was that I now had a cast-iron excuse for canceling my appointment with Cornelius without arousing his suspicions, and an even better story if I was later summoned to give evidence at an inquiry. I could say that in my haste to rush off to France I had forgotten to turn off the wireless. Nothing could have been more plausible.

Before I began to prepare the boat I telephoned Harriet again. We had spoken the previous day to arrange for George and Nanny to stay the night with her before they set off for her Devon cottage, and now I asked if she would telephone Cornelius' solicitors at two o'clock to inform them I had unexpectedly been drawn into a top-secret war maneuver.

"Operation Dynamo!" Harriet was appalled but calm. "For God's sake take care of yourself, Di. Good luck. I'll pray for you," she added—most unexpectedly, for she was an atheist.

"Well, I wouldn't say no to a prayer or two," I said. "Thanks."

I rang off and glanced at my watch. I had little time and there was still plenty to do. Moving through the house, I opened all the doors to allow the fire to travel quickly and up in the sitting room I pulled the sofa close to the wireless so that the flex would brush the upholstery. Then I laid a casual trail of newspapers from the sofa to the tall wicker wastepaper basket which I placed beneath the curtains. I had decided it was best to start the fire upstairs because the thatch would catch fire sooner.

Geoffrey arrived at noon. I was dressed in my sailing clothes, my trousers and a heavy jersey.

"What's your car doing outside?" he demanded. "Were you going anywhere?"

"To London, but I've canceled my plans." I wondered whether to put the car away again. What would be the natural thing to do? Yes, I would definitely put it away. I wondered if the stables would catch fire and thought they probably would, for the roof was also thatched and sparks would be carried on the wind. After I had put the car away I quickly opened my suitcase, whipped out the two photographs and shoved them inside my jersey.

Geoffrey was loading the boat, but he paused to kiss me when I arrived breathlessly at the jetty. Neither of us spoke. For a moment I thought of the Dunkirk beaches which lay waiting for us, but before I could feel frightened my thoughts turned back to Cornelius. I saw then that my earlier passiveness towards him had mirrored England's pacifism, that his mounting aggression had echoed Hitler's goose step, that my determination to stand against him was a bizarre reflection of post-Munich England. It was unfortunate that the parallels now had to cease. With the British army in retreat I found it difficult to picture England beating Hitler, but I could already see my victory over Cornelius Van Zale.

The moment came half an hour later, when we had finished loading and were ready to leave. Pretending I had forgotten something, I left Geoffrey by the boat and entered the house for the last time.

The silence, deep, intense and moving, enveloped me. I started to cry but dashed the tears away. This was triumph, not tragedy. This was my finest hour.

I hesitated only once more and that was when I reached the top of the stairs and looked back at the medieval hall. I felt as if I were looking back into the past, towards Steve and beyond him to Paul, and I thought how odd it was that an obscure manor house in the remotest part of Norfolk should have played such a large part in their wealthy, sophisticated, cosmopolitan lives. A second later I saw I was misinterpreting the past. It wasn't the house which had played the leading role. I had automatically assumed it was because I had always identified Mallingham with myself; I had been too young, as Paul had once said, to cut the umbilical cord which had tied me to Mallingham, and for years I had been too insecure to see my own identity. But I was insecure no longer. The journey to maturity which had begun when Geoffrey had wheeled the hamper into Paul's office had ended at last, and now Geoffrey was with me again as I set out into a new life and a different world.

It was time to sever the umbilical cord.

The rafters of the hall soared above me. I stared, feasting on the sight for the last time as my heart blazed with the most passionate love, and then I walked with pride into the room where I had outwitted Cornelius Van Zale, and calmly turned the knob on Alan's little wireless.